To Spit
Against
The Wind

To Spit Against The Wind

A NOVEL

By Benjamin H. Levin

THE CITADEL PRESS
New York

To
MADELINE
*for her unalterable faith
and limitless patience*

THE MAIN characters in this work are
real, the events are historical,
and the letters and excerpts from
Paine's writings have been
carefully quoted. The author has
included a few imagined minor
characters and unimportant
incidents. For this, he asks
forgiveness.

1

IN 1750, the little village of Thetford in England was as unchanging as the arc of a swinging pendulum. The seasons varied its weather, but nothing altered the tempo of its dull, unruffled life. One cold October morning a spindling boy of thirteen walked through its main street, treading carefully, for the surfaces of the puddles were frozen. He carried a leather-bound book in one hand and in the other a pouch that was pulled shut with a drawstring. It contained the boy's lunch—a large biscuit, a turnip, and a cold boiled potato. His breeches were patched at one knee with an oval of red velvet. The boy felt that his mother had chosen the piece of velvet in order to annoy his Quaker father and he had rubbed a clod of earth into the patch's bright color on the very first day.

When the boy reached the village tavern, he caught up with the lamplighter on his rounds. The man turned his weary body at the sound of the approaching steps. Relieved to see only the boy, he permitted the encrusted lids of his bleary eyes to droop half shut again.

"Late! Late!" he whispered, as though the boy were a confidant. "Late as cold-pokered rum. Aye. . . . They'll be after me 'ide fer the mornin' waste o' wick an' tallow."

The windows of the Bell Inn reminded the boy of what he had heard there and he asked, 'Have they cut him down yet?"

"Who? That poor basta'd on the gibbet? Na. . . . Ya knows bett'r 'n that. 'E'll 'ang there till the rope rots. All o' Thetford ain't seen 'im jig yet."

"But he's naked!" protested the boy. "There's not a stitch

[1]

of clothes on him. And a stranger. No one knows him in Thetford."

"Aye! An' that's why they'll let 'is bones swing in the wind. Fer all o' Nor'olk ta see 'im. An' Su'olk too. As example ta vagrants that steal."

The lamplighter gave a laugh that sounded like an old horse snorting and glanced up and down the narrow street. "Late!" he cried and raised an arm against the boy. "Wot in 'ell d'ya stop me fer?"

It was late for the boy, too, for he suddenly heard the sound of the school bell. He rushed to the end of the street and turned into Cage Lane. The instant he turned into the cobbled lane he saw the gallows at the crossroad. He had promised himelf that he would not look. With his eyes half shut, he hurried past the almshouse, which seemed as stooped as the people within it, and past the humble Friends' meeting house, only to find that, despite his resolution, he was irresistibly drawn to the crossroad. There, high above his head, just as he had seen it yesterday, the nude corpse swung and gyrated at the end of a matted rope. The man's head hung forward from a broken neck. The face was covered by long, wind-twisted black hair, through which a sharp nose thrust itself. The stranger had been accused of picking a pocket in the Bell Inn and, though the three silver shillings had not been found in his possession, "justice" had been swift. That had been on Friday. And during the night thieves had stripped the corpse bare.

Still staring at the naked corpse, the boy backed away, toward the school. When he reached the abutments of the prison, the "cage" from which the lane got its name, he glanced at the stocks that stood before the prison wall. The village idiot sat within the frame. The stocks were splashed with dried mud, and the young idiot's head and hands, which protruded through the stock holes, were encursted with dirt. A twinge of compassion compressed the boy's lips. He

[2]

stepped toward the stock and suddenly a frozen clod of earth flew past him and struck the thick stockboard with a thud. The boy turned and saw a classmate grinning. He was Nip Tanner, the turnkey's son.

"Leave him be!" ordered the boy.

For an answer, young Tanner tore up a clod of dirt rooted with grass. As he aimed it at the idiot, the boy rushed forward and struck the swinging arm with his book. The clod flew wide of its mark and the thrower turned in anger.

"An' 'ow would ya like ta 'ave yer own 'ead bashed in, ya stinkin' shaker!" He was younger, shorter, and thinner than the boy, but there was a viciousness in his bone-thin face and an animal look in his eyes that were frightening.

"His punishment is the stocks," defended the boy. "Only the stocks."

Without warning, the Tanner urchin rushed wildly at him. They fell to the road in a fierce flailing of arms and legs. The turnkey's son fought with swift movements of his feet and with clawing hands. The boy tried to defend himself without lashing out. He struggled to imprison his assailant's arms and to avoid the kicking shoes. Nip Tanner was breathing heavily; his runny nose was snuffling; he gasped for air. As they tumbled over each other, his wet mouth found the boy's ear and he sank his teeth into it. With a suppressed scream, the boy grabbed at Tanner's shock of hair and tore at it with all his strength. His bleeding ear was free now and, as he rose to his feet, the hair still in his fist, Tanner's hands clawed at his arm. He let go of the hair, lashed out a forearm, and caught Tanner in the face. It bowled the youth over and, as he scrambled to his feet and ran up Cage Lane, he turned and shouted: "Tom Paine, widout a brain! Shakes an' shakes, the dirty fakes!"

Young Tom Paine knew that the invectives were not Tanner's own. He had heard them before. He straightened up and took stock of himself. His coat was torn at the sleeve and one

[3]

pocket was completely ripped away. He touched his ear gingerly, and his fingers came away sticky with blood. He pulled his shirttail from his breeches, tore off a piece of the cloth, and dabbed at his hurt ear. The idiot in the stocks had not moved. His head hung in the same arc of hopeless resignation. Young Paine wondered what the poor fool had done now. One could not make him understand the meaning of poaching—that one must not look for birds' eggs on private property or trespass just to watch quail nesting in a meadow. He gathered up his book and his bag of lunch and stepped to the stocks. He opened the pouch, took out the potato, and offered it to the imprisoned simpleton.

"Hungry?" he asked. "Here. Eat it!"

He touched the potato to the idiot's mouth, but there was no response. He was about to brush back the filthy matted hair when he noticed a swarm of head lice crawling over the tresses. He put his hand under the chin, lifted the head, and knew that the idiot was dead.

The boy had lost all desire to attend school now. If he should enter the classroom late, the usher's bony hand would be upon the scruff of his neck. He would march him to the window from which one could see the pillories. ". . . An' that, Tom Paine, is where you shouldst be," he would declaim. "An' if you were on a privateer, you'd go without rum an' rations. Stragglin' in as you please!"

Reverend William Knowles, the school usher, compared all things with his experiences as a chaplain aboard a man-of-war. On the days when the shrieks of a condemned man being dragged to the gallows would hush the classroom, Knowles would attempt to dispel the students' soundless unrest by whispering, "He has been judged. He has been judged!" He would raise his minister's hands, his palms would draw slowly together, his fingertips would touch, and he would say solemnly, "When I was a young man on board ship, he would have been lashed and keelhauled. It is much gentler to be

[4]

hanged. Keelhauled! Do you know what it is like to be keel-hauled?" He would purse his lips and his eyes would seek a corner of the classroom's dark-raftered ceiling, as though to remind him of a ship's beams and aid his memory. "When I was on the *Reliance,* in the service of both His Royal Majesty and God ..." There was no pupil who had not heard his description of being keelhauled, but he told it each time with new embellishments.

The boy retraced his steps and turned into Bridge Street. Beyond the neglected town well, which was encircled by worn cobblestones, he reached a grey flintstone church. His aunt, a member of the Church of England, took him here occasionally to hear a Sunday sermon. It was in this church-yard that his sister, Elizabeth, who had died in infancy, lay buried. And it was in the belfry of this church that the boy had found a secret sanctuary.

The vestry door was unlocked this morning and he tiptoed through a room that smelled of musty, ancient leatherbound books and the ashes of an untended hearth. He reached a spiral staircase and stepped warily upon its creaking treads, his hands gripping a banister of smooth, dark-stained oak. At the top of the stairway, he climbed a ladder to the belfry itself. Here, beneath a steeple that rose sharply skyward, a single bell hung. The square belfry had narrow embrasures from which one could view the entire countryside.

He placed his book and pouch on the wide-planked floor and stepped to one of the embrasures. From the belfry's height, the little village of Thetford looked drab indeed. The streets were unswept and the grey stone homes nestled against each other as though for mutual support. The sight disturbed him and he looked away. He stepped to the southern embra-sure and from there, past the farrier's, past the Elizabethan Bell Inn, past the brook at the end of Bridge Street, he could see the easy-sloping hills of Suffolk County. His heart tripped at the sight of the heather whose green bracts defied the late autumn. And yet, not even a dog could stray into those meadows without punishment!

From the northern opening, he could see the circular, grass-covered earthwork of Castle Hill and the ivy-covered, grey stone abbey of the Cluniac monks. Sometimes, from this secret vantage point, he would watch the monks on the circular parapet, walking two and two, like tower-clock figures. Their sandaled feet would move with unhurried stride and their long-chained crucifixes would swing, pendulum-like, against their rope-belted tunics.

The boy turned from the embrasure and saw two mice sniffing at his pouch. They scampered away as he moved toward them and took the biscuit from his pouch. He broke it and placed a piece upon the belfry flooring. With an outstretched foot, he pushed it slowly toward the mice. They sat on their haunches and watched him distrustfully, so he took his book to the eastern embrasure, through which the sunlight shone, and seated himself with his back against the wood studding.

The book was *A Natural History of Virginia,* which Reverend Knowles had lent him. Young Paine was fascinated by its descriptions of what lay on the far side of the Atlantic: a land where the forests swarmed with game, the lakes and rivers were thick with fish, and there were no fences and no poaching. A land where a boy could grow into a free man and call his destiny his own!

For a moment the boy looked up from his reading to watch the church mice. They were eating the broken biscuit like squirrels nibbling on a nut. Their grey fur, thick against the coming frost, matched the shadows in the belfry. Suddenly there was a whir of wings, a shrill, piercing shriek, and a wild scampering of tiny feet. Startled, the boy saw a large owl beating the flooring with its wings. As the bird rose, a mouse dropped from it. The owl plummeted down, sank its talons once more into the quivering grey fur, and spiraled upward

[6]

into the hollow pyramid of the steeple. Up in its dark peak there was a scuffle of wings, a rasping sound, and then all was still.

The boy craned his neck and looked up into the dark. Suddenly a few drops fell toward him—two on his coat, three on the flooring—drops of blood, red, even in the shadowed belfry. He stepped back to avoid more. His shoulder jarred the bell and swung it upon its yoke. The belfry vibrated with a clang that seemed to rush outward through all the embrasures. He hurriedly placed his hands upon the bell to end its arc but its heavy clapper, swinging back, struck it once again.

His sanctuary lost, he grasped the pouch, tucked the book into his coat, and rushed to the ladder. By the time he reached the courtyard, the village was alive with people. Windows were raised, shopkeepers were in the doorways, and men were hurrying toward the church. Beside the white-dusted miller's wagon in front of the Bell Inn a group were gesticulating and pointing skyward. The boy turned into an alley that led to the backs of the houses. He hurried across narrow vegetable plots. As he reached the back of his own home, he noticed his mother in her garden. She was gathering the tatter-tied sticks that she used against the sparrows and the robins. He was about to turn back when she straightened up and saw him.

"What's the bell ringin' for, Thomas?" she asked. "What's it ringin' for?" she repeated.

"It's a mistake. It got rung by accident."

The boy walked forward, hoping to sidle past her. Suddenly she noticed his torn sleeve, his ripped pocket, and the dried mud on his breeches and coat. She dropped the sticks and shouted for his father.

"Joseph! Joseph!" she shrieked. She grasped his injured ear and he clenched his teeth against the pain as she marched him into the house, through a kitchen, through a small sitting room, and to the doorway of a staymaker's shop.

[7]

The boy's father was fitting a corset on a plumpish woman, the bootmaker's wife, in her best trappings for the pleasant occasion. Her black boots were laced with bright red thongs. Her clean white stockings were stretched upward over her stout knees until her beribboned garters lost themselves beneath her lace-ruffled, linen pants. At her back, the boy's father was tugging at the corset tapes; in front, the woman was pushing against the stay that thrust up her uncovered bosom into two large melons of pink flesh.

"Later," said the boy's father without looking up. "I shall be with thee in just a trice."

The boy's mother stared in anger at the bootmaker's wife. "Now!" she cried. "Can't I see ye now?"

She would have stepped into the shop, but her husband had forbidden her entry except to clean it. It was there that he had struck her once, his strong fingers leaving their outline upon her cheek together with a trickle of blood from her nose. He had not argued with her. He had simply struck her and looked at his hand, as though it had defied his will. "Thy nose is bleeding," he had said. "There is fresh well water in the bucket. All of the house is thine, but come no longer into the shop."

The boy's father finished tying the corset laces and asked, "Thou art pleased, madam?"

The bootmaker's wife turned so that she could look directly at the boy's mother in the doorway. Her lips widened into a smirk. "Only wi' the stay, Joseph. Y're no' like my Clifford. "The top o' a woman's boot is only the beginnin' o' 'is 'eart's work. Now effen 'e made stays . . ."

Joseph Paine undid the tapes and motioned to the screen, over whose top petticoats and a green satin gown had been hung. Not waiting to see if his client went there, he walked to the doorway, thrust his wife before him, and entered the sitting room.

"What is't now, Frances?"

[8]

Her thoughts still on the bootmaker's wife, the mother was reluctantly recalled to the boy's torn and mud-stained clothes. "Look at 'im!" she cried. "An' ye insistin' schoolin' makes a gentleman outa a brat! Look at 'is coat! 'E should work, I tell ye. Or is't t' Oxford ye think ye'll send 'im. 'Eathen as 'e is."

The father noticed the boy's ear that had begun to bleed again. He brushed the boy's dark hair from about it with tender concern.

"I have told thee. I shall see to his apprenticeship."

"An' wot's wrong wi' 'im workin' 'ere? In the shop where ye c'n keep an eye on 'im?"

"A staymaker?" protested the father.

" 'Tis as good a craft as any. Better 'n some."

The corsetmaker looked at his son. He knew his wife's reason for wanting the boy apprenticed in the shop. She had been after him to do this for almost two years. She had been thirty-seven years old when they had married. He had only been twenty-seven then. She had accused him of infidelities from the very beginning. The villagers had recognized her jealousy and had cruelly made the most of it. Women, coming for their fittings, had brought their vulgar jests into the corset shop—witticisms based on her maiden name of Frances Cocke. Bolstered by his Quaker orthodoxy, her husband had never appeared to hear them. It had been different with Frances.

"How dost thee feel about it, Thomas?"

The boy looked up at his father. He abhorred the idea and hoped that his silence would express more than an ineffectual protest. The father placed a hand upon the boy's shoulder and squeezed it affectionately.

"I shall make a pact with thee, Frances. I shall take the boy into the shop. But from now on, see that thee mention no more of his indoctrination into the Anglican Church. And thy sister is not to meddle. He is a Friend, as I am. And neither thee nor thy sister shouldst consider him otherwise."

[9]

There was a glint of anger in the mother's eyes. The hesitant movements of her thin lips strangely distorted her mouth and, finally, she compromised unwillingly. "Very well. Take the Grace of the Lord from 'im if ye want. God knows as I've tried."

"It is settled, then, Thomas," said the father. "I take thee into the shop. Tomorrow thee will go to the school and say thy good-bys."

"I have no friends there. Except the miller's son. I shall go to the mill and see him there." The boy turned a defiant eye upon his mother as she hugged a shawl about her bony frame. "Twas me rang the church bell," he challenged. "I tolled it for the death of a mouse."

Young Tom Paine had never thought that the making of stays could interest him. Now, for the first time, he glanced about his father's shop with an evaluating eye. Sunlight, shining in through the hand-blown glass window, touched the fabrics on the counter with patches of limpid gold. His father lifted their ends and named them: "Silk . . . linen . . . satin . . . cotton. Touch them. Feel their texture. Learn to know them even in the dark." He hesitated and added, "There are times when thine eyes must not see what thy hands are doing. It is a strange craft for a Friend. Thou hast been baptized into the Church, thine aunt has taught thee the catechisms, and thy mother has dragged thee all the way to the Bishop of Norwich for thy confirmation; but still thou art my son. Thou art a Friend. Now tell me, what were thee doing in the belfry?"

The boy looked up into his father's solemn face. Unlike his mother's sunken cheeks and furrowed brow, his father's countenance was tranquil and unwrinkled. He told his father of his sanctuary and the predatory owl. His father smiled and permitted his hand to rest gently upon his son's shoulder. He led him to a heavy table made of smooth oak planks. It was piled high with huge strips of whalebone. "From the skeleton of the whale," he explained. "The bone has different textures. Some of it is brittle, some of it is friable. The strips should be cut so that they should bend and yet not break. Touch the bone. Run thy hand along its surface. Not seen by an unpracticed eye, it has a structure—like the grain in stone that a good mason seeks before he touches it with a chisel."

The boy ran his hand over the surface of a tremendous bone. He disturbed the heavy air that hovered over it and a strange, aromatic scent arose from the table. He looked up at his father.

"These bones were touched somewhere by ambergris," the father said. "Had they known of it in the time of the Temple, they would not have used frankincense and myrrh."

The boy ran his hand again across the bone. "'Tis like polished wood," he said.

"Not wood," said the father. "Ivory. The ivory of the sea."

The boy looked about the shop with a new eye. Sheets of brown paper were hung on the plastered wall. They had been rubbed with whale oil to keep them from crumpling. They were cut in hourglass shapes and were covered with markings —left side, right side, front, back. On a low table lay shears, tape measures, cuttings of pattern paper, and pieces of bright cloth. The cloth was as different from the drab grey his mother wore as was bright sunlight from deep shadow.

"Will it take me long to learn?" he asked.

"Thou'lt serve thy apprenticeship as thee wouldst in any other staymaker's. In the home, we are father and son. In the shop, I am thy mentor. And now, if thee will take the broom, thee will start the day."

In the afternoon, the boy had his first look at his father at work. The butcher's young wife was being fitted, while his father stood behind her, smoothing the oiled paper against her back and tracing her outline with a heavy crayon. Suddenly he heard her whisper, "Ye are ugly, Joseph, and stupid."

It was not true, thought the boy. His father was a handsome man. He was straight as a birch tree. And tall. His eyes were

[11]

as blue as the stripes on their saucers, and his hair, where it was too short to be pulled back, curled into ringlets like a girl's. It was true that his face was solemn but, when there was cause, his smile was pleasing.

"Ye have a heart like a miller's grindstone and the blood in thy veins is as sour as Tucker's farthing cider," the boy heard her whisper.

"The stay will not fit thee if thou standst not upright."

She turned so that the pattern paper crumpled in the father's hand. "Ye never made one t' fit me. Do ye think I be soft wax that'll turn shapeless where ye squeeze? Damn yer Quaker soul!"

The boy busied himself at his task. He heard her rush across the floor. There was an angry rustle of silk and an impatient shuffle of feet behind the screen. When she stepped into view, fully dressed, there was an aroused flush in her cheeks. She held a length of crimson ribbon in one hand. She tossed it to the boy's father and cried, "Take it t' bed with ye, Quaker Paine! Perchance ye c'n dye it black an' tie it about yer member that must be in mournin'." She hurried to the street door. An unsupported stocking drooped halfway to her ankle.

The boy studied the unfinished pattern that his father dropped upon the table. "It be not a good form," said the father. "Madam Hipple lacks the patience for being fitted." As though what had happened were days ago, he gathered a half-finished corset onto his lap and proceeded to sew narrow whalebone ribs into its linen backing. The boy went to the patterns that hung on the wall and studied the outermost one critically. He lifted it from its hook and brought it to his father. The elder Paine continued his sewing as though he were alone in the shop. The boy stood before him and waited. Finally the father said, without lifting his head, "Thee art an apprentice, Thomas. The patterns are not yet a portion of thy duty."

"The form is made wrong, Father."

Joseph Paine interrupted his needlework and looked up at his son. "Not just this one," said the boy, "but the others . . . and the one thou wert fitting." Encouraged by his father's silence, he continued, "I watched thee. Thee marked one side, and then the other. But the two sides do not match."

"Madam Hipple moved about."

"This one, too," insisted the boy. "If thee look closely, both sides of the pattern are not the same. They are not . . . not . . ."

"Symmetrical," said the father. "Evenly matched."

"Symmetrical," said the boy.

"Most people are not symmetrical, Thomas. We are fashioned in the image of God, but not symmetrically."

"Then we can make them look that way. May I, Father?" He picked up the crumpled pattern. Joseph Paine nodded. The boy folded the pattern in the center. Taking the shears, he carefully cut around his father's crayon markings. "See," he said. "It saves half the time. One marks only one side, both sides come out even, and the stay is . . . symmetrical." He unfolded the pattern and held up a perfectly uniform shape.

Joseph Paine spread the pattern upon the table and studied it closely. He ran a forefinger, calloused by needlework, down the center crease. His red lips puckered themselves into a soundless whistling. Finally, he turned and said, "Thou art a precocious boy, Thomas. Perhaps I should not have taken thee from thy schooling."

2

TOM PAINE stood on the crest of a hill and looked into a valley. A brook trickled downward over a rock-strewn bed. It was dammed into an artificial cataract where its water spilled over a large mill wheel and turned it upon a creaking axle. The miller's home was in back of the mill, adjacent to a wooden shed. Four years before, when he had begun his apprenticeship, Paine had come here to visit his one friend, and had spent the entire afternoon. He was drawn to the Colberts' home for, unlike his own, it was filled with laughter, rich food, and chilled wine. In the winter there was a crackling fire of oak logs in the tremendous stone fireplace. And, of course, there were always Peter and Annette. Sabbath mornings he would spend at the Quaker meeting house with his father. Returning home, he would wait for his mother, who attended services at the Anglican church. They would have a meager breakfast and then he would rush off to the miller's. His mother had disapproved of such visits from the very first. "The Colberts be Cath-o-lics," she had protested, as though the very name of the religion carried with it an aura of anathema. "Papists!"

She had not been able to win her husband's support. He had looked at her calmly and had said, "If I may quote to thee from thine own Bible, Frances, in St. John it is written, 'In my Father's house are many mansions.' One cannot judge what one hath never seen. I shall not say to Thomas, 'Thou shalt not go!' "

Now, after four years of Sundays, Paine stood on the hill and smelled the fragrance of the early June grass. Suddenly the Colberts' dog came tearing up the road. As he neared Tom Paine, he burst into a wild, joyous baying. One could hear shouts now, from the bottom of the hill. The dog tore away and raced back to a girl and a crippled boy who were struggling upward. As the dog reached them, he turned and rushed back to Paine, his tongue lolling from his mouth. When he reached Paine, he skidded to a stop, turned, and tore back again to the oncoming two until the shortened gap allowed the young friends to embrace.

The cripple relinquished his sister's hand and flung an arm

[14]

about Paine's shoulder. A midwife's haste had twisted his back and deformed one leg, but it had not robbed him of a pleasant face framed by a shock of black hair, like a stallion's mane. As if to compensate for his twisted back, his chest and arms were massive.

The girl slipped a bare arm through Paine's and clung to him tightly. Her skin was as brown as a hazelnut from long hours in the sun. Her hair was as straight and black as her brother's and her dark eyes were filled with challenge. Unlike the English, who insisted on speaking from between clenched teeth, her red mouth was always open in either simulated surprise or warm laughter. She turned to her brother and laughed. "Do you think 'e will let me today, Pierre?" It was a standing wager between them.

The brother's name was Peter, but their grandparents insisted on calling him Pierre and she preferred the name. Paine knew what she meant. She asked her brother the same question every Sunday. And it was always answered by young Paine presenting his cheek. Now, to their amazement, Paine put his free arm about her and kissed her on the mouth. She drew back, flushed and startled. She sucked in her lips, as though to taste them. She turned and raced down the hill. Paine could see patches of white on the soles of her feet. The big-chested dog tore at her heels as she ran.

After dinner, Paine sat with Peter at the edge of the dammed-up brook. They watched the water splashing on the paddle buckets of the mill wheel. They sat in silence for a while and then Paine said, "In the flats of Holland they use the wind to turn the millstones. And in the dry, windless regions of Asia they use bullocks, tethered to horizontal spokes. Here we use the gravity of the water."

"I want none of your knowledge, Tom. I want to know why you kissed Annette." Paine stared at the water that continued to spill over the paddles. "She's in love with you, you know."

[15]

Paine looked up at his friend, startled. "Yes! Do you think her still a child?"

"I . . . I meant nothing by it. It was a farewell. I find it difficult to leave; and yet I cannot stay in Thetford. I feel my days spilling away like the water in the brook. At least it turns a mill wheel. I do nothing. I must go away."

"Away? Where?" asked Peter. *"Vous avez courage!"*

Paine did not understand. He had come to the Colbert home nearly every Sunday for four years, yet had learned almost no French from them. "I'm going to sea," he confessed.

"To sea?"

"There's a privateer in Harwich, signing on hands. I met the second mate at the Bell Inn."

"You go to the pub at the Inn?"

"Occasionally. On Saturday nights. I'm seventeen, Peter. I can't live forever in my father's stay shop. There's a big world outside. I want to see it!"

Peter's thoughts drifted back to their grammar school and Reverend Knowles's telling of his own days at sea. He would have liked to burst out, "I'll come with you!" But he knew that he could not. At the patter of Annette's bare feet upon the rocks he rose, with the aid of his powerful arms, and hobbled away.

"Pierre!" Annette called after him. "Pierre! Don't go!"

Paine watched her as she called after her brother. She was dressed in a homemade smock, and his staymaker's eye could perceive how narrow her waist must be beneath the loose folds of the coarse cloth, how firm and high her young breasts must rise under the tight tunic.

"What have you said to him, Thomas?"

"I'm sorry, Annette. It seems I am robbing him of a friend for a while."

"Et moi?"

"And thou, too, Annette. I'm going away. I must!"

She stared at him and cried, 'I will not let you, Thomas. I have no one here but you . . . and Pierre. I will go with you. Do you not love me?''

Paine was bewildered. He had not thought of love. His eyes were like his father's, with a blue so deep that, when his pupils were dilated, they seemed black. "I . . . I will return," he stammered.

She reverted to the French inflection of her home. "Ye-es, you may return. And I may be the Queen of France! But what makes you think I will be here when you return. Look at me, Thomas! I am a grown woman! You English hate us. For three generations we have lived here. And you have not accepted us! We are Catholic! Who would marry a Catholic, eh? Except maybe someone like you?''

"But your father married an Englishwoman."

"*Oui.* A woman give' up many things to marry. A man refuse to give up none." She embraced him and asked, "How long will you be gone?''

Paine shrugged. "I don't know. A year . . . two.''

"*Elle est une démence!* When do you go?''

"Tonight.''

For a long moment she clung to him without speaking and then she said, "You make love to me *ce soir,* Thomas?''

Paine could feel his heart begin to race, but he forced himself to shake his head.

He pushed her gently from him. "I cannot," he said. "I cannot, Annette.''

A burst of anger fashioned itself in her throat, but she saw the misery in his face and swallowed the invective. "*Très bien.* I will not have you leave in anger. But you must say *au revoir* to the family. Come.''

She left him and hurried to the shed where her brother would sit when saddened. After a moment they came out. Peter's arm was about his sister. Paine joined them and they walked, without words, to the Colbert cottage.

[17]

The low dwelling was built in the French style. The casement windows, fashioned by hand, opened outward from the center. The thatched roof added an English note. Rumor had it that Grandfather Colbert had slain a French aristocrat in a field near Rouen. The reasons were as varied as the telling. He had run away and settled here in an unfriendly England. The English had sold him a worthless wooded hill and were astonished to see him build a mill. Milling was the only craft he knew. He was not aware that amidst the meadows, reserved for the nobility's hunting, there were only crops of potatoes and turnips. Yet he and his mill had survived.

When they entered the cottage, the Colbert grandparents were seated close to the gigantic hearth as though now, in June, the memory of its winter's warmth was still a comfort. Age had thinned their noses, recessed their eyes, and hollowed their cheeks. Even their loud voices, for they were hard of hearing, seemed to be a product of the past. The father, *Père* Colbert, was a broad-shouldered man whose thick neck and large round head made him seem shorter than he was. But for his black hair, dark eyes, and the persistent smile upon his large mouth, he seemed more Flemish than French. His wife was like an English sparrow—petite and twittering. Her sharp features were untouched by a single bit of fat. They loved each other, these two, and it was like the mating of a sparrow and a quail.

"Tom is leaving us," said Peter bitterly. "He's going to sea!"

The grandfather sat, leaning forward, his massive bony hands resting on his knees. As he grew aware of Peter's speaking, he cupped his large-jointed fingers behind an ear whose center had grown dark with bristly hair.

"The sea?" he repeated in disbelief.

"On a privateer."

"And your Quaker father? He consents?" He watched Tom Paine flush. "The English give these pirates the legal

[18]

right to plunder and kill," he said. "And the French do the same. But you cannot watch brutality with . . . with passivity, *mon fils.* You are against it or you become a part of it."

Paine watched their faces in silence.

Père Colbert, seeing that Paine did not intend to speak, lifted his shoulders and dropped them in a gesture of defeat. He put an arm about his wife and remarked, "We have lost a son. *Ainsi soit-il.* Perhaps for just a while. The leaf would like to be a twig, the twig a branch, the branch a tree, the tree a forest. And in the end there is only the hearth. Go, woman. Get the bread."

She pattered to the oven that was fashioned like a low pottery kiln and took three slender loaves of bread from its dark cavern. Annette spread a piece of washed sacking upon a split-rail table and wrapped the loaves, a weekly gift to the Paines.

Peter had hobbled to the open casement window and looked to see what was left of the setting sun. His father joined him. *Père* Colbert put an arm about his son. "Do not be angry, Pierre. Not with Thomas nor with God. We would like to go too. I, if I were younger. You, if your legs were straight. This we must admit. It is a curse of humanity that such things should stir the blood. Do not walk to the clearing with them. It could be that your sister would like to say *adieu privé.*"

It was almost dark when Paine returned home. Once in his room, he lighted a candle and gathered the things he would take with him. He dared not leave a farewell note. He would send one from Harwich. The second mate had said that even the cabin boys of the privateer *Terrible* came back wealthy from their raids. But it was not the money. He hungered for a sight of the world that lay outside Thetford.

Paine reached the small port of Harwich at sunset. He had walked thirty miles in fourteen hours. The town's frame homes were encrusted with gull droppings, the chandlers' shops were limed with desiccated salt, and the alleys and narrow streets were filled with refuse and bird-shunned garbage. The slack-tide water was black with mire when he reached the wharf, yet he was fascinated by the ships tied to it by their hawsers.

The cobblestone street along the wharf was congested with coaches, drays, and farmers' wagons. Uncouth women, shapeless in tattered sackcloth smocks, sauntered among the hogsheads and tarred trunks.

Paine walked along the water's edge and studied the anchored hulls with their masts, their furled sails, and the ratlines that ran to their crow's-nests. He found the *Terrible,* her name painted upon her prow in flaking lettering. Her keel, settled upon the low-tide, muddy bottom, exposed a below-the-waterline portion of her hull. The black barnacles, drying seaweed, and decaying vegetation that clung to her timbers added their stench to the smells that hung like a pall in the humid evening air. A gangplank rose steeply to a badly mended rail.

On the vessel itself, crates of chickens were tied on the deck. Alongside an open hatch, a dozen pigs were in a pen. They were squealing and pushing to get at the slops that had been spilled under their trotters.

A half hour after he had stowed his possessions, Paine had his first meal aboard the *Terrible*—sea bread that the men called biscuits and a stew made of boiled potatoes, diced hogs' intestines, and bacon rind. The spoon left a nauseating taste of rancid grease in his mouth. The crew watched him with curiosity. They seemed neither English nor French nor anything but a scum of derelict humanity.

" 'E ain't 'ungry," commented one.

"C'n ye na see 'e's still breast-fed? A plum puddin' might whet 'is appetite."

There was a guffaw of laughter and, as though disturbed by

it, rats squealed and clawed behind the timbers. Paine heard a tread of feet behind him and suddenly a brutal hand shook his shoulder. He turned and looked up into a face that startled him. A livid scar ran from an empty eye socket, down an unshaven cheek, and lost itself in the shapelessness of a smashed chin.

"Cap'n wants ye!"

He followed the man to the captain's quarters and was amazed to see his father there. There was neither anger nor recognition on his face.

The captain himself had the appearance of a gentleman. There were silver buckles on his shoes, white stockings below his satin breeches, and ruffled lace on the cuffs of his shirt. A pistol butt extended above a wide satin sash.

"This is your son?"

Paine's father nodded. Tom watched him take a pound note from a purse and extend it to the captain.

"'Tis not enough. The price is five quid."

"Thou didst say one."

"Aye. Twas before I saw 'im. The price is now five quid."

Paine's father hesitated. He walked to Tom and embraced him. "Do the best thee can, Thomas. And when thy time is up, come home. Thy mother and I shall be waiting for thee."

"'Old on. Ye c'n 'ave 'im fer three. I know ye've got three quid in yer sow's ear. An' it's worth at least that ta 'ave a genteel lad back 'ome again unspoiled."

"That and more," said Joseph Paine. "But our bargain was one pound. And I would not give thee one and tuppence to have thee break thy word."

A touch of anger flashed into the captain's face and as quickly left it. "A quid it is. I wouldna' 'ave a Shaker's brat e'en if ye left 'im."

Tom followed his father from the ship. At the edge of the wharf, a horse was tethered to a pile. It was the miller's dappled mare. Tom looked up into his father's face, but the elder Paine said nothing. During the entire trip back to Thetford, neither father nor son spoke.

3

AFTER PAINE'S abortive trip to Harwich, the little village of Thetford seemed almost a prison without walls. He knew that his father had been right, yet something intangible was lost between them. And his pride kept him from the Colberts. It was they, he thought, who had sent his father after him. He was no longer a child now, dreaming of Virginia's meadows, but he still thought of the ships upon which Reverend Knowles had served as chaplain. He worked in his father's shop by day and began to spend his evenings in the village tavern. The pub room of the Bell Inn was always filled with the smell of warm beer, sweating bodies, and unwashed clothes. The wainscoting was stained by smoke and the rafters were coated with soot from the fireplace.

Once inside, Paine would sidle his way to a table in an alcove and sip at a mug of ale. Harry Snook, the village hostler, would join him. Still begrimed from his work at the farrier's, he would bring half hoops of metal that looked as though they had been cut from tiny wagon wheels. Undisturbed by the loud voices, the raucous laughter, or the swish of skirts and the tinkle of belled garters beneath them, Snook would place the metal arcs upon the drink-stained table and he and Tom Paine would study them. They tried to determine why a strip of metal, fashioned into half a hoop, should bear more weight at its center without bending than a straight piece of metal supported at each end.

"It's the hammerin' wot does it."

"Nonsense," said Paine. "The flat pieces are hammered. The stress is carried away from the center by the arch and exerts a portion of the force at its ends."

It was difficult to make Snook understand the meaning of "stress." It did not deter him from bringing strips of metal, which Paine considered using as a substitute for whalebone. And Snook brought whatever books or pamphlets he could beg or receive in lieu of gratuities from passengers on the stage. It was Snook who brought Paine his first copy of Sir Isaac Newton's *Mathematical Principles of Natural Philosophy* and a pamphlet that contained David Hume's *Essays Moral and Political.* Snook could not read, but he enjoyed listening to Paine, who did. There was nowhere else to go in Thetford but Tucker's Bell Inn. For Paine, it was an escape from his father's Quaker decorum and his mother's shrewish tongue. At fifty-five, she still harangued him on how she, a solicitor's daughter, had belittled herself by marrying a staymaker, a needleman, and he a Quaker besides!

In time, Paine gathered a following at his table in the Bell Inn. Heavy chairs were scraped along the ashen floor planks so their occupants could be within listening distance of his voice. Latecomers stood, mug in hand, and forgot to sip or, having drunk, neglected to wipe the foamed beer from their lips. Paine attracted the older men most. They were fascinated by his logic and the succinct phrases with which he pointed out their political wrongs and grievances. The young drank their boisterous fill and retired to the Inn's rooms above the pub; but the older men, beached by time, without accomplishment or security, listened to Paine's reasons for their destitution. He spoke of Arkwright's spinning frame, of Crompton's spinning mule, of Hargreaves' carding machine—strange names to those in Tucker's pub. He told of estates that, although he admittedly had never seen them, had hundreds of rooms to be kept in order and heated and a multitude of servants to be clothed and fed. His eyes glowed in the candle-

[23]

light as he insisted, "They have only two hands as we do, only twenty-four hours in each day; from whence, then, doth this wealth come?"

He spoke in a soft voice that carried no further than the alcove, but one night Tandy Mason, an excise officer, sleeping over on his rounds, stopped to listen to Paine's inflammatory phrases. Disturbed, he marched to the bar, drained mug in hand, and waited until he caught fat Tucker's eye. "Tis sedition," he whispered, an index finger beneath a hairy nostril. "Tis a Guy Fawkes whelp in that corner, an' mark m' words, it's the Bell Inn will suffer fer 'is talk."

Tucker waddled to Paine's table, where his own son had joined the listeners. Without attending to Paine's words, Tucker studied his flushed cheeks, his gesticulating hands, and the fire in his eyes. He wondered at this slender youth whom he had known since a child, at this Quaker-sired stripling who had not once gone to an upstairs room or acquiesced to any female overture. He waddled back to the bar and, leaning his moon-faced head toward the tax collector, confided, " 'E's the Quaker's boy, Tom Paine. There's no more 'arm in 'im than a cricket on the 'earth."

One morning, Joseph Paine shoved aside a slab of uncut whalebone and seated himself on the heavy table in the corset shop. He held a miniature corset in his hands. It looked as though it had been fashioned for a doll. He turned it this way and that as he studied it. There was an innovation in the center of its outward rise that puzzled him. He could hear his wife calling up the stairs. Her voice had grown more shrill with each passing year. She could perform no household triviality without invective.

She opened the door to the shop and protested, "Y're son is not sleepin' . . . 'e is drunk. If ye would not give 'im money, 'e would not drink. It would'a been better if ye 'ad not gone after 'im three years ago. Chasin' in the night all the way t'

'Arwich. By now 'e would appreciate a clean sheet an' a mended shirt, 'stead o' spendin' 'alf the night wi' the bitches in Tucker's pub." The sight of her husband's unconcerned back goaded her. "Well!" she shrieked. "Ist goin' t' sit there on thy thee-an'-thou ass or ist goin' up an' leg-pull 'im from 'is bed?"

Joseph Paine set down the corset model and turned to his wife. "Tom is not drunk, Frances. He is a late riser. He hath always been one; but thee wilt not reconcile to his habits."

"An' if 'e does not drink, why does 'is room smell like wine mash?"

"He goes to the pub for company."

"Bitches!"

There was a sound of footsteps and young Paine was in the doorway, listening. All his life his mother had presented a cold and unsympathetic front and now, at twenty, when he could guess what might lie beneath her sharp-tongued exterior, he could not force himself to put an affectionate arm about her spindly frame. "Madam Tucker sends her regards to thee," he said. "She spoke with Aunt Agatha in Norwich."

His mother was unimpressed. "Dinna' talk t' me o' Madam Tucker. 'Er as wot gets 'er finery from ... from ...." She retreated into the sitting room as a proof of her disapproval.

Tom stepped into the shop. He noticed the corset model in his father's hands and asked, "What dost thee think, Father?"

"I cannot see the purpose of the curved middle stays."

"They are a support and a divider. They support the bosom upward, without pressing against it. And they divide the breasts into a wide cleft."

"To what purpose? An added vanity?"

"No. It creates a comfort. The space between permits an area of air, to reduce the sweating and the inflammation of the tender skin."

The father placed the doll's stay on the table. "Thee speakest of women as though thou knowest them well. From here or from the Bell Inn?" And when Tom did not answer, "Thy apprenticeship is over Thomas. Thee art a master staymaker. There is neither work nor income enough for two craftsmen in the shop."

"The money doth not matter."

"Nay. I cannot pay a master an apprentice's wage."

"But father . . ."

"Where will thee go?"

Tom knew that it was neither the lack of work nor the money. He wondered how long his father had known what was in his heart. "I shall go to London," he said.

"Then it hath been settled and I shall tell thy mother. I think she hath resigned herself to thy leaving." He hesitated and confided, "It was she that sent me after thee, to Harwich."

Two mornings later, while Paine waited in front of the Bell Inn for the early stage, the Colbert wagon approached. April sunshine touched its shafts and its white, flour-dusted sides. Peter Colbert sat, statue-like, with the reins in his large hands. With the shaftboard of the box in front of him, one would never guess his deformity. Annette sat beside him. She held a bundle on her lap. Her dark hair had been combed up to where a narrow ribbon imprisoned it, but from there it fell free and its strands touched her flushed cheeks. Her dark eyes glistened as though the morning dew had settled in them. When they reached the Bell Inn, Peter reigned in the mare. With one powerful arm, he lifted his sister and set her down from the box in an effortless arc. He looked down without comment as Annette offered the bundle to Paine. Paine recognized the sacking. It was the kind with which she had always wrapped the loaves of bread on Sunday.

"For your trip to London. It is not my mother's baking, but my own." She hesitated as he accepted it and said, "It was not my doing, Thomas. Nor Pierre's. It was Papa's. He thought it only right that your father should be told about Harwich. Pierre and I did not know."

"I'm sorry. It was wrong of me to stay away. And *Grand-mére,* and *Grand-pére* . . . how are they?"

"They are well." Suddenly she started to weep. First her lips quivered and then her eyes brimmed over. She rushed into his arms. It was a poor embrace; the bundle of baking was between them. He could feel the wet of her tears as she kissed him and suddenly she turned to the wagon and reached up an arm. Peter lifted her as one would a child. He leaned across and extended a farewell hand.

"You will write from London? I have no one in Thetford. No one."

"I'll write," promised Paine. "I'll write." But Peter was already turning the mare about. The iron rims of the wagon wheels grated over the cobblestones.

London was not the city young Paine had imagined. There were lamp-lit squares, but there were also dark alleys, where ragged men and uncouth women tottered into and out of gin mills. There were dank courtyards with slimy walls, which were filled with hoarse, drunken voices. In the sunless shop district, it was a city that was never quiet. An endless stream of humanity jostled by and horses and coaches clattered incessantly in the streets.

Tired, hungry, his few possessions wrapped in a bedsheet, Paine trod the city's inhospitable streets. At almost every step, he fought to ward off the petty thieves and beggars who besieged him. They sensed from his sober clothes, his bundle, and his ruddy cheeks that he was not a Londoner. Finally, in an alehouse, he was directed to a shop on Hanover Street, Longacre, where he might find employment as a journeyman staymaker.

When Paine reached the shop, he was surprised to find a large establishment. Tables and benches ran along one wall.

Behind them hung a profusion of patterns and measuring tapes. Two shelves were crammed with spooled ribbons and trimming lace. Four staymakers busied themselves with needlework. In a far corner, an apprentice hacked at whalebone that was piled upon heavy planks.

Paine followed the owner into a separate room and was amazed at its elegance. Carpeting, as red as a cardinal's wing, was spread upon the floor. Two crystal chandeliers hung from a high ceiling. On the walls, between candles that were set into gilded sconces, fabrics were stretched on display. He had only seen swatches of such fabrics in Thetford. Exhibited silks were dyed vermillion, the delicate green of spring grass, and the blue of a robin's egg. Sketches of beautifully proportioned women, in elegant stays, were tacked on the wall beneath the sconces. Like the Venus de Milo, the heads and arms of the models were missing; but the gifted artist, despite the stiffness of the tinted corsets, had painted their bodies and their legs in provocative postures.

Paine glanced away from the posters and saw the owner watching him. He had seated himself at a carved desk, crossing one well-shaped leg over the other, as a woman might, and his green, doeskin breeches clung tightly to his well-developed thighs. He motioned Paine to a gilded chair and proceeded to write quickly upon a sheet of foolscap.

"Your name? Your age? Your place of birth? And where did you serve your apprenticeship?"

Paine watched the owner. He dipped the quill into an inkpot and shook off a clinging drop with a graceful flick of his belaced wrist. A powdered wig made him seem older, but the taut skin of his clean-shaven cheek and the firm neck above his white stock made Paine judge him as a man in his early thirties. He pushed the foolscap toward Paine and handed him the inked quill. "Make your 'X' here."

Paine signed his name in a fine script. Surprised at the penmanship, the owner took Paine's hand in his and examined it. The fingers were tapered, almost like a woman's. Except where Paine's needlework had calloused the tip of an index finger, the skin was soft to the touch.

"Have you fitted stays?"

Paine thought of his father and the sheet-partitioned section of the shop. He shook his head. "I can follow a pattern well. I have devised a number of innovations."

The owner showed no interest. "This is my fitting room," he said and nodded to a low, velvet-covered dais in front of a full-length Florentine mirror. Getting up, he walked with simulated elegance, just short of a woman's swaying, to a far wall. He opened a door and disclosed a candle-lighted dressing room. "I have the finest clientele in London. Both the wives and the mistresses of the nobility come here for their stays." He pursed his pale lips after each sentence as though he expected some unseen cherub to kiss them. "I do not promise it, but after a period ... if all things go well ... perhaps I shall teach you the art of fitting." His long-lashed eyes studied Paine's fresh young face. "I promise you, you will like working for Perry Craigstone."

"Thank you," said Paine.

Paine was late for his first day at work. He had walked the streets to find a lodging and had spent a restless night. No one paid any attention to him as he entered the shop. Seeing an unoccupied bench, he presumed that it was his. There was a little pile of ribs, a pattern, and a bolt of muslin on the table. He seated himself and an apprentice approached him, holding out an unwashed hand. Paine sorted the whalebone strips as though he did not see the boy.

"For the beer," the boy said. "I needs a ha'pence for the beer."

"For whose beer? Thine or mine?"

"It doesna' matter. We all puts in a ha'pence."

The staymakers looked up from their work. One of them

[29]

rose and shuffled toward Paine. He took a pot from the boy, rubbed a bony finger against his fleshless nose, and explained, "We 'as a copper o' beer fer mornin', an' we 'as one fer noon. Syme as ever'where else. If tha dost no' drink, tis yerself as is dry. Tha payest syme as all." He took the coins from the boy's hand and dropped them, with spaced clinks, into the pot. "Na, put in that ha'pence. Tis the rule."

Paine looked about him. He put his hand into a pocket, hesitated, and changed his mind. "It's an unfair rule. I think it should be changed."

"An' is it tha as will change it?"

Suddenly Paine remembered his father in the cabin of the *Terrible.* "I do not keep thee from drinking," he said, "And I shall not be forced to drink with thee, or pay for what I do not drink."

The man looked toward his co-workers. They left their benches and joined him. They glared at Paine and clenched their fists. The door to the fitting room opened and Perry Craigstone entered the shop. He held a bright halfpenny coin between his forefinger and his thumb. He walked to the gathered needlemen, in his mincing stride, and let the coin drop into the pot. Turning to the apprentice, he ordered, "Now go get the beer!" He took Paine by the arm, led him into the fitting room and turned upon him in vexation.

"Country bumpkin! Do not preach to 'em! They would rather drink than eat. One does not dispute with 'em. One buys 'em."

"Giving them the ha'pence doth not make it right. There will be tomorrow and the day after that. And the day after that. I have no liking for beer in the morning."

"And would a broken head make it right? You will learn London in due time, Master Paine. I think I shall teach you. Here!" He extended a small box that was partly filled with halfpence. "Take a few coins; for they will ask you again at noon, and again in the evening."

Paine shook his head. "Thank thee. I shall try to compromise."

During the next few days, Paine made a miniature corset model from discarded cuttings and pieces of whalebone. It was a doll's stay, with a triangular divider and two soft, padded pouches as a support for the breasts. At the end of a week, he took the doll corset into the shopowner's fitting room. The owner studied the model carefully. He glanced at Paine again and again, as Paine explained it.

"The divider will permit a pocket of air between the . . ."

The owner interrupted Paine with a flutter of his hand. He took a much-used pattern from a heap and held it up. "You will make such a stay to fit this pattern. You will work on naught but this." Paine glanced at the pattern and noticed "Lady Hampton" marked upon an edge.

"Stand up straight, Master Paine. Let me look at you. And now turn around. Yes, around." He made a pirouette in the air with a raised finger. "And where are you lodging? Leicester Court?" He made a disparaging clicking noise between his teeth. "I shall give you an address where you can lodge more comfortably. The place is close by. The sheets are clean. The food is . . . edible. And I do not think the girls will trouble you if they know I sent you. Madame Simpson's." He pursed his lips and added, "You must remember to read my note to her. She will stand upon her dignity, but read it anyway. She is illiterate. And do not hesitate to tell her more than once that you are working for Perry Craigstone. She is forgetful."

"My lodging is paid until Saturday night."

A smile tugged at the corners of Craigstone's lips. He was about to reach into a pocket but thought better of it. "No, no. Do not leave. You shall dine with me tonight. Would you like that, Master Paine?" He stepped to Paine's side and picked a piece of lint from his sleeve. "Your waistcoat has an odd color. Quaker gray? Of course. And your breeches. They must be harsh to the touch." He brushed his fingers across the homespun cloth.

Paine could not believe his good fortune. The shopowner must have been impressed by the corset model, he decided as they drove to Piccadilly. Evidently, too, his employer had not only bathed but scented himself, for within the coach, there was an essence that was sweeter than the heather on the meadows outside of Thetford. Outside the coach window, shops, homes, courtyards, and alleys passed in an endless line to the continuous clop-clop of the horse's hoofs. Everywhere, a milling humanity seemed bent upon endless, unaccomplished missions. The April sun had begun to set. A vaporish mist drifted between the grey buildings and settled in the streets.

The coach turned into a rectangular courtyard and drew up in front of a large inn where a wooden sign *The Golden Peacock Inn* was nailed above a square doorway. A hunchback stood outside the doorway, as though on guard. He was dressed in a dirty leather jerkin, red breeches, and someone's high boots, which reached to his crotch. He held a crop in one hand and a short trumpet in the other. The beggars and wretched idlers who stood in apathy or sat hunched on the courtyard's flagstones, roused themselves as the coach drew up. A tattered beggar tried to knock the trumpet from him with a sudden rush, but the hunchback was too quick for him. Turning his back, he blew a hoarse blast and, in an instant, two stout men armed with cudgels rushed from the inn. They came none too soon, for all the beggars now encircled the coach, stretched gnarled hands from tattered sleeves, and cried, as though with one voice, "A crust of bread! A crust! A coin! A coin! For the sake of God and King, a coin!"

Paine looked out upon the sea of unwashed, starving faces. Like starving dogs the cudgels did not seem to frighten them. Instead, they pressed upon the coach with wild cries and Craigstone, judging well the exact moment, opened the further door and tossed out a handful of copper coins upon the flagstones. The tavern guards opened the near coach door and helped Paine and Craigstone alight, while beggars, on hands and knees, searched for the coppers that were but half visible in the failing light. Unintelligible cries arose from them as Craigstone took Paine's arm and marched him to the door.

Paine did not think he could eat. He felt as though a huge fist had grasped his entrails and twisted them. They passed through a corridor and there was a smell of roasting meat and baking and the sound of sizzling fat. "You are now walking into the land of gout," said Craigstone as he placed an arm about Paine. "And this is the only place where the nobility and the commoner meet upon an equal ground—the ability to pay. Here there is no dignity and no finesse. Here there are pigs both at the table and upon it. Where did you say you are from? Heterford?"

"Thetford. In Suffolk."

"Ah, yes. Thetford."

They entered an immense room filled with the smell of wines and hot food, the clatter of dishes and glassware, and a hundred voices raised in talk and laughter. Craigstone was evidently no stranger to it. He inspected the room, lifted his walking stick, and pointed to the table of his preference.

After two glasses of wine, Paine forgot the starving rabble outside. His face grew flushed and his eyes, wide with excitement, shone like black gems. Craigstone, picking daintily at his food, watched him enjoy the dishes that he ordered: turtle soup, lobster, shoulder of venison covered with mushroom gravy and sided with breast of quail.

"A little more wine?"

Paine held the glass to his lips and looked about him. Gallants, their ring-studded fingers holding the stems of their glasses with feminine daintiness, toasted their mistresses. Young women, powdered and rouged, their wigs drooping long curls, shook their heads in mock protest or arch laughter. Their slender necks rose swan-like from their partly revealed bosoms. In the smoke-filled half-light of the room, their profiles were like ivory cameos.

Here and there, Paine noticed older men. Their stocks were undone beneath their heavy chins and their wet lips were like red gashes in their sweating jowls. Their women struggled to seat themselves upon such meager laps as had not yet been encroached upon by protruding paunches. Everywhere women hugged men, lifted their skirts and petticoats above their knees, and unlaced their stays to let their breasts slip from within their lace-edged shelter.

"More wine?"

Paine shook his head. The glass he held was still half filled. And what he watched sobered him, for he was suddenly conscience stricken. He could eat no more. He glanced about the hall. On every table, food lay wasted. Even the floor had droppings of edibles that were trod upon by waiters, hosts, and departing guests. In the midst of his thoughts, stirred by Quaker frugality, Paine felt the touch of Craigstone's silver-headed walking stick upon his shoulder.

"Shall we go, Master Paine?"

Paine rose, a bit unsteadily, and followed Craigstone through the labyrinth of aisles between the tables. As they reached the corridor, he could not resist looking back into the hall. It was still filled with a sea of laughing faces, revealing the intimacies of the diners and the coarseness of their public embraces. Above the hubbub were the sounds of broken glassware and overturned chairs.

In the courtyard, where Paine had forgotten them, the human derelicts still milled about. He did not know if these were the same ones he had seen before or some new company of beggars that had taken their turn to besiege *The Golden Peacock Inn.* The hunchback was still there, however, and he blew his trumpet to summon a coach from the patrolled street outside the courtyard.

In the swaying coach Paine slept until it stopped. The nap

and the night air revived him, and Craigstone opened the door and led him down a dark alley to a heavy door that was set into a wall without a single window. In answer to Craigstone's knock, a small shutter in the door was pulled open and a portion of a face thrust itself into the aperture and studied them. There was the rasping sound of a bolt sliding along ungreased metal, the door swung back, and they were permitted to enter.

Craigstone seemed to know the way down a narrow stone stairway to a large basement room filled with noise, epithets, shouts, curses, the smell of unwashed bodies, the sharp odor of urine, the stink of excrement, and the taint of moldy earth. Blended with all these was a subtle scent of perfume, and an irritating vapor of snuff.

As Paine's eyes grew accustomed to the dim light, he saw that the benches that ringed the basement were mostly filled with young gallants, dressed with elegance, as Craigstone was. Many had swords at their sides. In the midst of a group of swagerers sat a young woman with a traveling cloak about her shoulders. The hood was thrown back to reveal an elegantly coiffured wig. A delicate hand held a mask to her face. Below the benches, behind a rail that circled a shallow pit, was a melting pot of London's humanity. Thieves rubbed shoulders with gifted artisans; servants of the nobility, their pilferings not yet come to light, jostled shopkeepers, draymen, journeymen, and pimps. Uncaught highwaymen stood aloof, pistols tucked beneath their bulging waistcoats. And sitting on the dank, earth floor, at the edge of the pit itself, were a few lean and hungry derelicts, come to turn a stolen linen-knot of shillings into a fleeting smile of fortune. In the pit itself the cocks were still held by their handlers, their wings pinioned to their sides by fingers that were half lost in ruffled feathers. Light from the torches touched the red of their combs and their wattles, and glinted from the sharp metal that was strapped upon their spurs.

[35]

Paine watched the bet-takers as they made their rounds, while the rabble at the rail cried out hoarsely, impatient at the delay. He felt the touch of Craigstone's walking stick upon his shoulder. "Wouldst wager, Master Paine?"

Paine shook his head.

Craigstone raised his stick. "A full pound note!" he cried. "A pound!"

A bet-taker rushed to his side. Craigstone held the bill away from him. "Which is the favorite?"

"The speckled one, sir. The champion o' Cheapside, Gov'-nor. Brought 'ere from the Bahamas."

A pound on the other. Half a pound for me and half for my young friend."

"It's a lost quid, Gov'nor. It's the Bahama cock as wot's the fav'rite."

"I would rather not wager," insisted Paine.

There was a trumpet's blast and the bet-taker grasped the note. Within the pit, the handlers placed the gamecocks beak to beak and released them. There was a whir of wings and the cocks collided in mid-air, their feet rending at each other in demoniac frenzy. The tip of a silver spur caught the Bahama gamecock's breast. A red gash crimsoned the speckled feathers and he fell on his side, his wings fluttering. A wild, mad shout tore from the throats of the watchers, as though a single animal with 100 mouths had bellowed it. Paine sat, transfixed. The seemingly victorious gamecock sprang, falcon-like, upon his victim and the wounded, speckled cock rolled on his back and shielded his body with a wild raking of spurred feet. The seeming victor could neither stem nor alter his descent and stretching his wings, in a useless effort, fell straddle-legged, with exposed breast, into a clawing of metal spurs. A shower of brown feathers and a spurt of blood were in the air to-gether. Animal cries and epithets, goadings, shouts, and curses filled the earthen room as the cocks rolled over and tore away from each other.

[36]

Paine glanced about and it seemed to him as though he had been lowered into a segment of Dante's inferno. He had not imagined that there was so much violence in man. Even the young woman with the cloak had sprung from her seat, had torn the mask from her face, and was waving it wildly above her head and shrieking ... shrieking ... shrieking. ... Only Perry Craigstone sat unperturbed, tapping his walking stick against the wooden bench.

Suddenly the speckled bird sprung at his antagonist as though a great hand had lashed him forward. The brown cock rose to meet him, rose higher than the Bahama bird's forward spring and raked the speckled neck with a downward thrust of spurs that instantly dripped red. Both gamecocks locked together, falling, tumbling, feet clawing, beaks ripping, wings beating. The speckled cock's throat became a gored distortion of feathers and blood. He struggled to rise and faltered. One wing flapped crazily as his legs gave way. The victor sprang forward for the kill and in an instant the Bahama cock's owner sprang into the pit and cried, *"Il est fini! Il détruire mon coq! Au secours!"*

A thunderous roar rose from the watchers as they sprang to their feet. Three men rushed into the pit to prevent the owner from touching the cocks. The first man sent the owner sprawling. He rose and shrieked again, *"C'est fini! Miséricorde ... pitié! C'est fini!* The other two reached him. Suddenly he fell to the earthen floor with a gasp and lay, staring at the shored ceiling that was lost in darkness.

In a corner of the pit, the brown cock proceeded to rip the speckled bird to gory shreds. Nor would it desist until its handler sprang into the pit with an open wicker cage and a portion of a balanket.

The fallen owner still lay sprawled on the ground. A caretaker sprinkled fresh earth upon the bloodstains in the pit. He prodded the owner with a muddied boot and turned him over. The hilt of a knife extended from his back. "He's dead!"

cried Paine, half rising from his seat. "Murdered!"

Perry Craigstone pursed his lips at him. He laid the head of his walking stick upon Paine's shoulder and pressed him to his seat. "Your winnings, Master Paine."

Paine looked at the notes in Craigstone's hand. "I did not wager. I said I would not wager." In the pit they were removing the body as though it were a sack of meal. "And do not press me with thy cane. I do not like the feel of it."

"Well then, shall we leave?"

"It would please me well."

Back in his lodging, Paine could not sleep. He stumbled across the dark room and groped for the pitcher and the bowl on his dresser. He poured water over his head and let the cool wetness run down his face. The room, furnished with only the necessities, was almost like his own at home; only here a single window looked out upon no growing thing or visible patch of sky. There was only the rust-brown brick of a dark and narrow alley.

He sat on the bed and saw, in his mind's eye, once again, the fighting gamecocks. The remembrance of the mad, hoarse cries from the scene filled his ears and caused his temples to throb. The cocks tore at each other, obsessed by a lust for utter extinction. They rolled over and over in a timeless raking and flapping until the knifed owner fell to his knees, tumbling over upon his back. How much of London was like this? How much?

Despite misgivings, Paine changed his lodging at the end of the week. When he knocked at the door of the house Craigstone had recommended, a youngster of about ten, dressed in an embroidered waistcoat, red satin breeches, yellow stockings, and silver-buckled shoes that were much too big for him hesitated to let him enter.

"I have a note for Madam Simpson."

The boy extended his hand and Paine, remembering Craigstone's admonition that the woman could not read, insisted, "The note is for Madam Simpson."

He was allowed to enter and knew immediately that he could not afford the new lodging. The vestibule was carpeted and led into a drawing room that was filled with hassocks, cushioned sofas, and a tremendous ottoman. Heavy damask draperies had been pulled shut across arched windows. The room was filled with the subdued glow of candlelight. As the boy left, Paine glanced after him and could see, through a doorway, a portion of a dining room. A tremendous sideboard stood upon heavy, carved legs. Decanters and glasses, in tiered rows, were reflected in a polished mirror.

The boy returned in a few moments, a dishevelled woman shuffling in his wake. The woman's stout figure was tented in a red velvet wrapper. Strands of her brown hair fell, unconcerned, to her shoulders. Her naked feet were in doeskin sandals. She waved the boy away and watched Paine as he read Craigstone's note aloud. A smell of fragrant powder, like scented miller's dust, clung about her.

"What is the charge for the lodging?" questioned Paine, still holding his possessions wrapped in a sheet in his arms.

" 'Ow much? Well now, an' didna' Perry tell ya?" She gave a laugh that rippled the red wrapper. "Me an' Perry ... we 'ave agreements." She reached for Paine's bundle. " 'E won't let ya down. An' now 'ow 'bout a drink t' Perry's 'ealth, eh? An' t' 'is friends."

In the morning, Paine went immediately to the fitting room to determine the cost of his new lodging. Madame Simpson had been evasive and he feared getting into debt. But Perry Craigstone too was unconcerned. Mrs. Simpson, it seemed, was under obligation to him.

"Point is, how is your lodging? Did you like the girls?"

Rather than complain, Paine did not tell his employer that he had not seen any girls, although he had heard them, and that he had not had any dinner but had been served a platter of cold beef and pudding in the kitchen. Actually, even his sleep had been disturbed by revelry. From the late hours of the night until early morning there had been the sounds of girls' voices—gay and shrill and uninhibited. There had been teasing protests, the hoarse voices of men, drunken laughter, and someone's racking cough.

In the dawn, hushed like a meadow after the rolling thunder of a summer squall, he had turned in bed, half asleep, and had suddenly remembered his day's work. He had dressed hurriedly and rushed down the stairs. His lodgings was to include breakfast but there had been no one in the dining room and no one in the kitchen—only a disarray of unwashed glasses, empty wine bottles, and a vitiated air that was touched by a scent of cologne and made heavy by a smell of snuff.

That night, at a late dinner, he met the girls. There were six of them. Madam Simpson ran through their names like a litany, calling them her chickadees, and introduced Tom Paine as Perry Craigstone's young man. A blush touched Paine's cheeks as he nodded to them across the dinner table. None had dressed for dinner but were in colorful wrappers. Every gesture of their supple bodies gave credence to the lack of any other garment. The boy who had admitted Paine, proud in his ruffles and his satin breeches, made the rounds with a decanter of wine. The girls fondled Paine's protesting shoulder and attempted to kiss his averted face. Madam Simpson served the courses, waddling back and forth between the dining room and the kitchen and then, losing her temper at the giggling and unaccustomed uncooperativeness of the girls, shrieked, "What in 'ell's the matter? Is't the first time Perry's sent a booby 'ere?"

Paine ate as quickly as he could and rose to leave. He started to make his excuses until the smiling faces impressed on him that any social amenity was ridiculous. In his room, he lighted a candle and started to pack. He would have to seek some other lodging. He would go back to his first one in

Leicester Court. London ws a far cry from Thetford and his Quaker upbringing, even far from the Colberts with their plain talk and their earthiness. He had not thought of the Colberts in a long time. Yes, London was a far cry from even the Bell Inn.

He blew out the candle flame and lay on the bed, fully dressed, and listened to the sounds in the house. He drowsed, tranquil with the pervading warmth of the wine that Madam Simpson had insisted that he drink. When he stirred, thinking that he should have left, his senses awakened to the sounds of revelry such as he had heard the night before. Below, drunken voices were raised in the chorus of a bawdy song—deep bass voices, hoarse from shouting.

He could hear footsteps coming up the stairs, and suddenly he heard his own door being thrust open. He had forgotten to bolt it. He sat upright and saw Perry Craigstone in the doorway, holding a lighted candle. Paine could tell by the flushed face and the wavering candle that Craigstone was far from sober. "Well now," Craigstone whispered, opening his eyes wide with an evident effort. "And how is my country lad?" He tried to purse his lips but his tongue remained between the wet lips as though it had forgotten its purpose. His body kept leaning forward as though to defy its center of gravity and straightened itself only upon reaching the supporting chest of drawers. He held the candle horizontally, above the chest, until its flame almost flickered out. He set the candle's base onto the melted drops of tallow and turned to Paine who had jumped out of bed.

Paine tried to avoid Craigstone's arms. "No, no!" cried Craigstone drunkenly. "Be nice t' Perry. Come m' pet. We've a game to play." He tried to wink a drunken eye. As Paine tried to leave, he barred the narrow passageway between the bed and the chest. Paine tried to maneuver past and Craigstone wrapped both arms about him. As he felt Paine struggling free, he shouted, "Fan-ny! Come up, you bitch!"

[41]

Paine felt that Craigstone could be calling no one else but Madam Simpson. He clapped his hand over Craigstone's mouth and Craigstone promptly bit one of his fingers. Blind anger overwhelmed Paine and he lashed out with a fist. The blow caught Craigstone full in the face and sent him sprawling across the bed. A trickle of blood ran from Craigstone's nose and Paine wiped it with the edge of the bed sheet. Gathering his packed possessions, he blew out the candle and left.

4

MANY MONTHS later, in the little town of Sandwich, in Kent, Tom Paine looked out from the doorway of his own shop. A mist had begun to settle in the narrow street and an overcast September sky threatened rain. He wondered if rain would keep Mary Lambert's mistress from coming for her fitting. It should not. It was such a short distance to the shop. He could see the gables of Madam Neuberry's mansion from where he stood. A small wooden sign that he had lettered, hung above the shop's doorway:

THOMAS PAINE
Staymaker

He had been touched by pride when he had opened the shop. Now, his pride, unfed by any accomplishment, had died. He had come to the little town because he had heard that there was no staymaker. Soon he had learned that there was also nothing else. There was not even a news stall where he could purchase a London gazette. Alone, he cleaned the shop and the rooms, albeit haphazardly. Alone, he prepared his own meals. And in the evening, when he went to the tavern, he could find no townsmen or travelers with whom he could discourse on the events of the times.

He had made a mistake in leaving London. He should have defended himself against Perry Craigstone's false charge of debt. When he had left Craigstone, he had found employment in the shop of a Mr. Morris. The months that he had spent with Morris had been happy ones. His employer was a contented, middle-aged man who had had a good education and was interested in the sciences. Under Morris' direction, Paine had begun a serious study of Newtonian science and astronomy. Together they had attended the philosophical lectures of Ferguson and Martin. Through Morris, Paine had made the acquaintance of Dr. Bers, the astronomer, and attended several lectures at the Royal Society. Nor had his interest been confined to science. After shop hours he had sat with Mr. Morris and debated controversial political and religious views until the older man would raise his hands in resignation and protest: "I have not your youth, Master Paine. And a wife who does not like to slip into a cold bed alone."

Nevertheless, he had brought Paine Denis Diderot's *Pensées Philosophiques,* as well as translations of Voltaire and Montesquieu. It had been a stimulating time until Craigstone had found him and accused him of debt. He should not have run away, he knew now. He could have paid the charge. He had saved that much. But to pay a debt one did not owe . . .

He had found work in Dover. He remembered the shop well. Such meager light as there was from the befogged and shadowed street had to thrust itself in through unwashed and mud-spattered panes of glass. Most of the fine stitching had to be done constantly by candlelight. It was not like home, where his mother had cleaned the shop after hours and arranged the markers, patterns, shears, and needle cushions in their customary places.

Dover, too, had been a place where Paine had found no

companionship. The narrow, crooked town was a string of shops and homes that had hidden itself between the channel at its breast and the chalk cliffs at its back. The beach was a heap of tumbled stones over which the incoming tides dashed themselves futily. Small boats, fishing sloops, and schooners were tied to every wharf. Lights bobbed at night on the channel, seemingly all the way to the very coast of France; but no single lamplight was permitted on any street that faced the sea. The tradesmen spoke only of the avilability of French wine and French goods. The poor spoke only of the price of fish. And the entire town stank of fish! Paine seemed to smell it, even in his clothes. He had stayed six months in Dover—the cold, bitter months of a grey winter. When he had learned of the opportunity in Sandwich, he had rushed to open his own shop.

Paine returned to his workbench and examined the corset that he had completed for Mary Lambert's mistress. It was through Mary's recommendation that Madam Neuberry had ordered the stay. But it had started to rain now. He could hear the patter of the first drops on the window. Now, Madam Neuberry might not come and he would not see Mary Lambert.

Qutside, wind whipped through the street in angry gusts, and he remembered a political pamphlet he had bought on a trip to Dover for whalebone and linen. He began to look for it on a shelf that was cluttered with gazettes and books, but his search was interrupted by a rattling noise at the shop door. It was unlocked, yet someone, in a frantic hurry, was having difficulty in opening it. He went to it and threw it open. Mary Lambert rushed in, followed by a swirl of rain. Her hooded cape dripped a circle of water upon the floor. Her young face, flushed by the wind, was wet. Paine helped her undo the cape and took it from her. Her stockings were splashed with mud and from her shoes puddles spread upon the floor.

"Mary," he protested. "In such a rain!"

Her wet mouth smiled at him and little pearls of water clung to the long lashes of her eyes. Paine tossed the cape onto a workbench and hurried her into the combined sitting room and kitchen behind the shop. He pulled a joint stool up to the cold fireplace and started to build a fire.

"I could not stay away. Madam Neuberry would not come, 'cause o' the rain."

Paine was paying little attention. He was blowing upon the shavings that he had finally coaxed into a flame.

"I'm supposed t' be in the sewing room. Lettin' out the seams o' one o' Madam Neuberry's gowns. She gets fatter every year. I won't be missed. An' I could say I came 'ere t' borrow some green thread."

Satisfied with the fire, Paine turned to where she had seated herself on the stool. "I have no green thread."

"An' 'ow could I know unless I came," she laughed, her clothes still dripping water.

"Thou'lt catch a death of cold," said Paine. "I shall lock the shop and get thee some dry clothes."

She looked at him in surprise. I have no others."

"I'll get some of mine."

When he returned, she had already undressed. She had moved closer to the crackling fire. With her back to him, she had a half-wet shift about her shoulders. He turned away as she threw it aside and put on the shirt he had brought, and then watched as she thrust his shirt into the breeches that reached down almost to her ankles. She was petite. The sturdiest part of her was her shock of long, brown hair that she was now parting and rubbing between her palms, in front of the fire. She looked like a child, dressed for a frolic, in her father's clothes. She flung back her hair, with a toss of her head, and laughed at him. "Thou'rt a modest man, Tom Paine."

"We'll have to hang up thy clothes and dry them. I'll fill the kettle for tea."

"No! No! Those are my duties. An' let me find wot we needs. I love strange cupboards."

She had turned aside and suddenly turned back again. "Art angry with me, Tom Paine?" He shook his head. "Wilt kiss me, Tom? Please?"

He took her in his arms and, bending over her, kissed her tenderly. Her lips seemed still wet with rain. She raised herself upon her bare toes and clung to him. A pulsing throbbed within his temples and a flush of warmth inflamed his cheeks. She rested her head against his chest. "Thou'rt a gentle man, Tom Paine," she said and left him to set the table for the tea.

"Thou needst a wife, Tom Paine," she pointed out as she busied herself with the few dishes. "No single thing is in a proper place. Thy cupboards are a disgrace. An' all needs a proper cleanin'." She saw him looking at her, startled. "An', if not a wife, than a 'ousekeeper," she compromised.

"I cannot afford one."

"There is one who would work for naught."

He laughed at her. She looked comical as she pattered about the room. She had rolled the shirt sleeves to her slender elbows. One hand held up the breeches to keep them from dropping to the floor.

"Thee would not like it," he dissuaded. "My work doth not make for a happy marriage. Fitting stays!" He thought of his mother's constant suspicions and bitter anger. "I do not even like it myself. It should not be a man's craft."

" 'Tis better than the excise."

"What dost thee know of excise?"

"My father was an exciseman."

"And there thou art wrong. I would like the excise."

She came to him and seated herself possessively upon his lap. "Thou must not wish it, Tom. When my father was a customs officer at Dolphin Key, it wa'nt bad. But then 'e was transferred t' the excise in the field. Collectin' taxes in the ports. I'd see m' mother waitin' the long winter nights. Waitin'. M' father's rounds would take 'im away fer months at a time. " 'E was like a sailor on land."

Paine's eyes, bright with excitement, stared at something she could not see. "People," he thought, "all kinds of places and all kinds of people—talking to them, listening to them, learning what is in their hearts, finding what it is that touches their very souls beneath the crust of their poverty."

She felt his withdrawal and tried to coax him back. "Thou'st a craft already, Tom. The excise may be a man's callin', but the people 'ave no respect fer a gauger. An' tis dangerous at the waterfronts. They said father 'ad an accident. But we felt 'e 'ad been murdered. An' the pay is a pittance. A pittance! With father gone, wot we 'ad in the 'ouse at Dolphin Key was sold fer the debts. We were left adrift. Tis a 'ard thing t' beg. . . . I didna' weep too much when mother died soon after."

Paine brushed back a lock of hair that had fallen down across her forehead and placed a finger upon her lips. "Sh! Enough now! No sad thoughts or I'll not tolerate thy housekeeping." It was the first time she had spoken of her past. She had seemed lonely when she had first come up to the shop with her mistress. Paine had been drawn to her by a need for companionship. He had no thought of marriage. He had no intention now. He shook her playfully. "Come now, what kind of husbandry hast thou? The kettle is protesting with its steaming throat and thee takes no notice of it!" She left his lap and pattered to the fireplace. It was as though the warmth of a kitten had left him. She was still in the room and already he missed her touch.

When they finished their tea, Paine brought the quilt from his bed and spread it before the fireplace. She changed into her dried clothes. He brought her cape from the shop and hung it before the fire. They sat on the floor, tailor fashion. The two small logs had lost their crackling flicker and glowed

[47]

warmly. Most of the room was now in deep shadow.

"I think tis still raining," she said. "But I must get back. I'll be missed." She moved closer and nestled in his arms. Paine's cheeks were ruddy with the firelight; they were as smooth as a child's. The dark lashes of his eyes were as thick and as long as a woman's. "Thou'rt the gentlest o' men, Tom Paine. I love thee."

He bent over her and kissed her. "I'll go see if the rain hath ceased."

He returned from the shop, took her cape, and held it for her.

"Hast stopped rainin'?"

"No, but it's late. Thee shouldst go back."

When they reached the Neuberry estate, they found the front gate locked. Behind its wrought iron, Paine could see a massive lock. Its curved bar was thrust commandingly through two contiguous rings. Mary Lambert saw Paine evaluating the height of the gate and the stone wall on either side. "No! No!" she protested. "I'll knock. Someone'll 'ear me." She grasped the iron swivel bar and clanged it against the metal breastplate; timidly at first, then loudly.

A light appeared in an upstairs window. "Tis Madam Neuberry," she said with a sigh of relief. "Go home, Tom. Thou'rt gettin' soaked."

He waited at her side but no one came to open the gate. The window where the light had shone went dark. Behind the trees and the shrubbery, the Neuberry mansion was a shadowed outline against the grey rain. Paine grasped the knocker and clanged it loudly. A light appeared to one side; low, indefinite, as though it shone from a hut where the stables were.

"Tis Miggin, the grounds keeper," said Mary. " 'E's 'eard us. 'E'll be 'ere directly."

They could see a lantern now, swinging toward them. A light shone again in an upstairs window, a sash was raised, and a voice screamed: "Mig-g-gin ... don't you dast open that gate!"

The grounds keeper walked to within sight of them and raised his lantern, while Mary Lambert waved to him. He turned to the window and called, "Tis Mary Lambert, M'am."

"I know who tis, you stupid ass. An' I'll 'ave no bitches in my 'ome. Go back to your dirty bed. You 'ear me? Go back to it!"

"M'am ... please, M'am." Paine clapped a wet hand over Mary Lambert's mouth. As the window turned dark and the lantern retreated, he could feel a warm wet upon his fingers that he knew was not rain. "Never ask for forgiveness where there is no wrong. Come."

She was sobbing as he led her back to the shop. "Thou'rt a proud man, Tom."

He laughed as though he were untouched by her predicament. "Thee hast discovered my Achilles' heel," he said. "I have no humility."

Tom Paine married Mary Lambert on September 27, but the town of Sandwich did not accept them. They did not remain much longer. "I 'ave an aunt in Margate," his wife suggested. She was touched by a sense of guilt for Paine's complete loss of trade. "We could move to Margate."

Nine months after he had hung his sign in Sandwich, Paine moved to Margate. He had no difficulty in finding work, but a great unrest possessed him. In the evenings, he was torn between a sense of duty to Mary and an overwhelming desire to seek the company of thinking men. His mind thirsted for news and philosophies. He read Locke's *Essay Concerning Human Understanding* and all but committed to memory his *Two Treatises on Government.* He read translations of Rousseau and sought companions in the mold of staymaker Morris for whom he had worked in London. He would return from a tavern, disheartened by his inability to convey to others the things he felt. Men would sit at his table, listen to his talk of physical laws rather than a malevolent providence that governed the world, and neither accept nor dispute his opinions.

He would return to his lodging and find his wife in bed for the sake of warmth. He would slip beneath the covers and take her in his arms. The warmed bed would accent the ephemeral scent of her young skin. Her hair had the fragrance of a meadow's virgin grass in May. He would run his hand over her nightgown and caress the twin hills of her breasts, widened at their base from lying upon her back. He would let his hand wander down upon her belly. It was no longer sunken in upon itself. She had not said it, but he knew she was with child. She turned to him and kissed him and he knew she had been crying. "Ye do not love me, Tom. Ye married me because . . . because . . ."

He placed his hand upon her mouth and would let her say no more. "There is no one else, Mary. I go to the tavern more to talk than to drink. New ideas are taking shape in the minds of men. I want to know what they are. The world is at the beginning of a new destiny. I want to be a part of it. When our son grows up, I want him to live in a world where he can earn more than just bread for his belly and clothes for his back. I want him to afford pride. To look his fellow man in the eye and not have to say 'Sir' and 'm' Lord.' "

"Ye look men in the face now, Tom."

"Yes. And it puts no coppers in my purse."

"An' if tis not a son, but a daughter?"

He was silent for a moment and then, vehemently, as though he were in hot dispute with someone instead of in bed with her, he cried, "It shall be the same! Yes, why not? Why should she not have the same right to work . . . to fulfill an ambition, if so she wishes! Doth one pay less homage to a queen, minimize her talents and abilities, question her command?"

[50]

"I shall give ye both, Tom Paine. Girls t' delight yer 'eart an' boys t' preach yer philosophies to. I shall give ye so many little Paines, they shall overrun the countryside. I shall give ye one each year. Wilt love me an' love me, Tom Paine?"

He thought of his childhood in which he had been raised alone. "Yes!" he said emphatically. "Yes! I would like a large brood."

"Then love me, Tom. Love me. Only me."

Beneath the covers, her body was like a child's who had eaten too much for dinner. He took her in his arms and kissed her.

In the morning Mary Lambert had been well. In the evening she took to bed with a chill. The physician studied her pallid face. "I would suggest cupping," he said and, in the midst of his preparations, a convulsion trembled her body and stretched it into a rigid spasm. Blood gushed from her mouth where her tongue was caught between clenched teeth. In his hurried efforts to pry open her mouth, the doctor broke two teeth. A wrench of anguish tore at Paine's heart. He clapped his hands upon the physician's back and sent him crashing across the room.

"Mary," he whispered. "Mary! Tis thy Tom." He smoothed the moist hair from her forehead. He wiped away the blood that trickled down her chin. He stared in distress at her swollen tongue that still bled through the red gap made by the missing teeth. Gradually, the spasm left, her body relaxed, and her chest heaved a deep sigh. Her eyelids fluttered open and, as her eyes focused upon him, she forced a wan smile.

"Stay wi' me, Tom," she pleaded. "Stay wi' me. I feel so cold." Her body was wet with perspiration. He pulled the covers up about her neck and stroked her cheek.

"Thou'rt a gentle man, Tom. A gentle man. I'm so tired.

So tired. Stay wi' me, Tom. I'll nap fer just a little while. Stay wi' me."

Paine sat by her side and listened to her shallow breathing. He was grieved by her labored respiration. She had yet another seizure, which lasted longer than the first. Mary Lambert died in the night, and the unborn child died with her.

5

PAINE RETURNED to Thetford in June. He had been away for three years, but it did not seem so long. The village had not changed. The gallows still stood at the crossroad and the stocks in front of the prison on Cage Lane. The Anglican church was still on Bridge Street and, next to the smith's, the Bell Inn still thrived. The early grasses were bright green in the fields and the heather was like a purple mist on the hills.

In his father's shop, the whalebone still had its old smell. Untainted by sweated hands, lying on oak planks that were scrubbed by his mother's husbandry, it still had about it a taint of blubber and a faint, aromatic scent of ambergris.

His mother had not changed; she still had a lean and irascible look. It was like the other side of a coin to his father's complacent countenance. On the third day, at breakfast, Paine said, "I think I shall study for the excise, Father."

"Tax-collecting is not commendable to Friends."

" 'E is not a true Quaker, Joseph. Wouldst rather 'e spend the rest of 'is days with 'is 'ands on a biddy's shift?"

"It will take him away from home again."

"As what would not? Tis a steady pay. An' no worry 'bout pleasin' the gouged. There's no work like gove'ment work, I say. Now when m' father was in practice, God bless 'is soul . . ."

"I think I'll go to the mill this morning," said Tom Paine in an effort to end their bickering. "I haven't seen the Colberts since . . . since . . . ."

They looked at him strangely and then his father said, "The mill is shut. The Colberts have gone back to France."

"Why dost thee say gone back? Only the grandparents were French. *Père* Colbert married here. Peter and Annette were born here."

"The grandfather wished to be buried in French soil. Among his own people. And so they all went back."

"Do not say 'back,' " Tom insisted. "After two generations they were as much English as French!"

" 'Ear 'im. 'Ear wot 'e says. They was Cath-o-lics. Papists! Sent 'ere by the Pope t' spy on us. But they couldna' do naught wi' their poison mill. An' there's talk in the grocer's as what they was French spies!"

"Thee ate their bread!" cried Tom, rising from the table in anger. "Was their bread more digestible than they? Why? Because it was for naught?"

The father rose and restrained him. "Woman's gossip, Thomas. Let it not disturb thee. There is no more truth in it than a unicorn's horn."

That noon, Tom Paine walked to the old mill. When he reached the crest of the hill, he saw what was left of the buildings. Someone had set fire to them. The roofs were burned away. Only the sturdy stone walls still stood.

In three weeks Paine mastered a brief course of study and petitioned for an appointment as an exciseman. But the summer went by and no word came. He spent his days in his father's shop and his nights in Tucker's Bell Inn. The drinking of gin had become popular, even in Thetford. It was cheaper than beer or ale and induced a greater spirit of gaiety. But Tucker's Inn was no longer the same to Paine. Snook had left and old friends would not drink with him or listen to his talk. It was as though his going to London had stamped him with

[53]

an ambition they did not approve and his return had marked him as a failure for whom there was only ridicule. At home there was his old room, overlooking the vegetable patch. It was a portion of privacy in his father's house, but it held no comfort for him. He grieved for Mary and was lonely in the night.

Sabbaths, despite his mother's protests, he went to the meeting house with his father. They would walk down Bridge Street, side by side, in their slow gait, and the townspeople would whisper, "There go the Paines, as like as two peas in a pod." And yet father and son differed in many ways, not only because the elder was taller and had broader shoulders, but because the father was a complacent man while the son's inquisitive eyes contained a strange defiance.

In September, Paine called upon Frederick Falkland, the recorder of Thetford. Falkland's parlor was his office. He conducted his business, such as it was, from behind a cluttered desk. He rose from behind it and greeted Paine warmly, as he did everyone. Never seen in a public place, except at Sunday service, he was pleased to have anyone come and interrupt his work. "The Excise Boards," he commented when Paine told him why he had come, "why, they are riddled with corruption and nepotism. Will writes me from London . . . he is a solicitor now, and young for a solicitor . . . have you run across him in London? Will writes me that stamping has become a condoned practice."

"Stamping?"

"Approving consignments of merchandise without inspecting 'em." He looked at Paine slyly. "For a gratuity. And passing on a portion o' that gratuity."

"It cannot all be corrupt."

"Tis a poorly paid profession, Tom. And the public entertains antipathy and not respect for a gauger. He is a most unpopular person. And what if you are sent to the ports? Smugglers do not hesitate to use the knife."

"I'll not stay in Thetford to vegetate."

[54]

"I can get you admitted to the service as an unattached officer. And with Will's help, in London . . ."

"I would be beholden."

Falkland held up a thin hand. "An unattached officer has to wait for a vacancy." He studied Paine's face. "An appointment could be arranged. But there's always a gratuity. In the proper place."

"The position pays but fifty pounds a year!"

Falkland raised defenseless hands. "I can do no more without a gratuity. Tis not for me, Tom."

Rather than pay a bribe, Paine waited for four long years and then, on August 6, 1764, he was appointed an excise officer to the Alford Outride, Grantham Collection. It was a country station that required a horse and Paine borrowed the money from his father.

At daybreak, Paine embraced his father affectionately, kissed his mother, and left them. His mother remained in the doorway but his father, as though touched by a premonition, was loath to see him go. He caught up and walked beside the horse. The village was still asleep. A red sun rose above the trees, dispersed the night's mist, and forecast a hot day. Little halos of dust were kicked up by the horse's hoofs. When they reached the wooden bridge, the father let his hand drop from the bridle.

"Always remember, thee art a Friend, Thomas. And now go with God."

As though there were nothing more to say, the elder Paine turned and retraced his steps. His wife still waited in the doorway.

The country lanes that led Paine to his first excise collection were different from the highways to London. They were bordered by estates that were enclosed by stone walls, green hedges, or railed fences. Above the trees, he could see the stone turrets of castles or the brick chimneys and gabled roofs of immense houses. The meadows shimmered in the sun and the forbidden, cool shade of fenced-in woods was filled with the cry of birds and the discernible rustle of feeding fawns. All seemed at peace and yet, at nearly every crossroad, Paine came across a rotted body that had been left upon a gallows to stink in the sun. The sight of each decaying corpse filled him with bitter anger. Their crimes could never have been as vile as their punishment!

Halfway to his destination, the lane widened into a dusty road that had been rutted by heavy wagon wheels. A wide stretch of farmland lay on one side. In the center of the cleared land there was a long, low, almost windowless building. Its sloping roof was patched with brown straw. Its grey stone walls looked cold, even in the summer sun. Paine noticed the field hands at the far edge of the farm and, as he approached them, he realized that the building was a workhouse. He curbed his horse and watched the homeless as they worked in the field. He was touched to see the many small children. Their thin, unwashed faces were bitter and grim. Aged people, in rags, worked side by side—starved old women, with shreds of dirty cloth tied indifferently about their shrunken breasts; bent old men, their stick-thin arms stretched earthward like broken scarecrows in the windless heat. Paine's horse tossed his head and whinnied at the smell of fresh clover. Not a single forlorn head lifted from its labor to look Paine's way.

In the distance Paine heard the baying of hounds. The sound came from a stretch of woods to his right, and suddenly he heard the hunters' horns and saw the dogs, the horses, and the men as they broke into an open field beyond a long, stone fence. At first he did not see the fox. His eyes were intent upon the riders' red coats and the flash of the horses' shod hoofs. Then suddenly he saw the russet fox skimming across the stone wall. Stretched out, for a long instant, between the top of the wall and the sky, he was on the ground tearing across the road and into the workhouse field. Over the wall came the dogs, in a dispersed pack, their baying suddenly hushed, as though the effort of springing over the stones had cut the sound from their throats.

As though to lose his scent among the field hands, the fox tore right through them. After him came the hounds and after them the hunters. Not a single worker straightened a back or lifted a head and suddenly dogs, horses, and riders smashed through them as though they were bushes in the ground. Paine sprang from his horse and rushed into the field. An old man lay where he had been bowled over by a horse. His fleshless hand clutched a broken and bleeding shoulder. Through the tatters of his filthy shirt, the pale scars of an old lashing were visible.

"Let me carry thee to the workhouse. Thy shoulder is terrible." Paine offered his arms, but for answer the old man drew back, fashioned a bit of spittle in his mouth, and spat at him.

Paine stood in indecision, appalled. Then he regained his horse and rode on.

By evening, he reached the village of Micklin, his first station. He stabled his horse at the edge of the village and walked the short distance to his first assigned call, the Micklin Drum Tavern. There, a wind-torn and sun-bleached drum hung precariously from a huge, rusted angle iron, above a timbered facade of imitation Gothic arches. On the ground floor, a large window was draped with dirty, brown sacking, and a wide door hung upon stable hinges. It had been shut against the heat of the day and, now that the sun was setting, it had not yet been opened. A notice had long ago been painted directly beside it. Paine read the faded lettering:

YOU CAN GET DRUNK HERE FOR A PENNY,
DEAD DRUNK FOR TWOPENCE.
STRAW PROVIDED FREE.

Paine pushed open the tavern door and stepped inside. It was as though he had stepped into a heavy fog of stale beer, spilled gin, sweating unwashed bodies, and foul air. He waited for his eyes to adjust to the dim room and walked with careful tread to the bar. At first the owner of the Drum Tavern did not appear to recognize him as a gauger. Tax collectors wore, almost as an insignia, bottles of ink that were tied with string to the buttonholes of their greatcoats. Quills thrust themselves past their pocket flaps and they carried marked sticks for measuring. Paine had only a drawstring bag such as he had once used for school. Within it, he carried his quills, his ink, and his ledger. He opened it and placed his credentials upon the bar.

The owner, an unshaven, wide-jowled man, scowled immediately.

Paine sensed a need for compromise. "I shall want a warm meal," he said, "something to drink, and a place to sleep. The charge will offset a portion of the tax. It'll not be a hardship."

"I dina' 'ave much as is not stamped," said the owner.

"Then so much the less work for me," smiled Paine.

The owner rubbed a clenched fist against the stubble on his face. He should dislike this young gauger. "Gin-n-y!" he shouted and a slender girl of about fourteen sidled through a doorway and hurried to the bar. "Tend t' it. Call me if needst."

The tavern owner led Paine into a kitchen behind the barroom. "Thou'lt eat 'ere. Martha's a' exc'llent cook. 'Ere, let m' take the coat. An' waisc't. 'Ot as tis."

"I should stamp thy stock now."

The owner's underlip thrust out wetly and then he grinned. "Nonsense. Yer day's work's done. The sun 'as set. Twill keep till morn I says. 'Ere, 'ave a drink wi' me. Burgundy. Straight from the coast o' France. Not mine, mind ye. Wallington's. The last gauger as wot 'ad 'is rounds 'ere. I kep' it fer 'im." He seated himself across from Paine.

"Just outside the village," remarked Paine, "past the crossroads, I saw courtyards and a settlement of homes . . ."

"Aye! Tinneville Courts. Fine places, years ago. Townfolk

[58]

lived 'ere as ran the farmers' marts. At the Surrey crossroads. 'Ere's no more marts. No more small farmers. Enclosure system they calls it. Drum Tavern was filled wi' yeomen an' shopkeepers when I was a lad. 'Em as drank fine wines an' brandy. M' father was proud o' the Drum Tavern, 'e was."

"No. . . . What I meant to ask . . . In the courts, I saw all the windows bricked over as though to keep out the cold. But sealing them also keeps out the light and the air. And keeps in the heat of summer. It seems foolish."

The tavern owner let out a guffaw that was half belch and half laughter. "Wot! Dost think the landlords give a fat monk's fart 'bout light an' 'eat. 'Ere's been a tax put on windows in the shire. An' so the landlords brick 'em up. An' when the poor basta'ds used more candles they up an' taxed the bloody tapers! An' now the filthy beggars sit in the dark like sick cats. Me, I'd go t' London or Manch'ster, could I sell the Drum Tavern. The stinkin 'ole wot its become! I c'n read an' 'rite an' figure."

The tavern owner grew friendly during the course of the meal. When Paine expressed a desire to retire early, he hesitated and informed him, "I 'ave only two bedrooms . . . mine an' m' daughter's." He looked at Paine sharply.

Paine glanced across the breadth of the kitchen with its immense hearth. It was, after all, a two-story building.

The owner shrugged his heavy shoulders and apologized, "The upstairs is wi'out beds. Jus' straw on the floor. Fer those as wants to sleep over. I'll talk t' Ginny."

"I do not mind a straw pallet," said Paine. "I assure thee."

A smile touched the owner's wide face. He hesitated and called, "Gin-n-y!" And when she appeared in the kitchen doorway, "Light 'im t' the dorm, Ginny. 'E's not finnicky. So 'e says. Well, go on. Go on, dast ya! Seeing as wot y've grown so choosey."

The girl lighted a candle and led Paine through the tavern and up a flight of stairs he had not noticed. At the top of a landing she pushed open a door and held the candle high. The charred ceiling showed that the vast room had once been partitioned into separate quarters. Its floor was covered with straw. It looked like an immense loft. When Paine reached out for the candle, the girl held it away at arm's length. "I canno', sir. I mus' return it. Father's strict. We 'ad a fire once't."

"For just a moment. I assure thee I shall give it back."

Grudgingly, she let Paine take the candle. He held it closer to the floor and tossed the straw about with his foot. Vermin and bugs scurried away from his disturbing shoe. A fetid smell rose from the rotting straw. Paine looked into the girl's eyes. Her irises were black in the candlelight. "Father did not insist!" she protested. " 'E's not sure of your stamping!"

"I am thinking only of the kitchen bench. Twould be better than this."

She reclaimed the candle and led him down the stairs. At its bottom she turned and offered, "I dina' mind. Come."

Instead, Paine left the tavern and walked to where his horse was stabled. The wicket was unlocked. He found his horse's stall and bedded down for the night. The air was tainted with a sharp, ammoniacal odor, but the scent of the hay was fresh.

For a year, Paine rode the countryside and collected taxes, only to be unexpectedly dismissed. It came as a shock. He was in a village of but half a dozen shops, at the Grantham border, when a young outrider brought him a copy of the minutes of the board. He tore open the notice:

August 29, 1765

Thomas Paine, Officer of Alford Out-Ride, Grantham Collection, having on July 11, STAMPT HIS WHOLE RIDE as appears by the specimens thereof—

He read no further. It was true that he had sometimes approved consignments of merchandise without inspecting them. It was done on the basis of the invoice and the good name of the tradesman. But he was not alone; it was a condoned practice. There had been no bribery involved.

He held the official notice and was filled with mixed emotions.

"Mr. Paine," said the young outrider who had brought the advisement. "Forgive me, an' if I may say so, sir, but I think as wot you 'ave been singled out as a troublemaker. Malcolm Simms says as wot you all but 'it 'im."

"Did he say I struck him?"

"All but, 'e says. Was 'e not so fast on 'is feet."

Paine recalled a discussion with a fellow exciseman; a man who claimed kinship to a member of the board in London, a stupid fool whose sum total of intelligence was the knowledge of such figures as made him suitable for his excise work. The fellow had insisted that it was misfortune and not England's laws that was reducing the workers to serfs. Paine had sat quietly, without reply. But when the fellow had labeled the indigent as being merely stupid, fornicating beasts, he had been unable to control himself. Smashing his glass to the floor, he had cried, "You have just stamped thyself with that same badge of poverty, Simms; for from others I have learned that thou fornicates and, from my own observations, I can attest to thy stupidity."

Paine had not thought that the words would lead to his dismissal. He looked at the young outrider. He had never seen him before. "Dost thou have a round, or dost thou now replace me?"

The young man shrugged. "I am unattached, sir. I still wait for a vacancy."

On an impulse Paine asked, "Dost thou know that there is a tax of a full pound on a gallon of spirits? That mathematically, the tax per quart, only the tax alone, is equal to the weekly wage of the poor?"

The outrider stared at Paine. High light-blue eyes were

unperturbed and his young face was untouched by concern. The statement meant nothing to him.

"What is thy name?" asked Paine.

"Nandor Reeves, sir."

"Between here and Micklin, Nandor, in two weeks' time, in just two weeks, I have seen three hungry children hanged for stealing food and two men end their lives upon a gibbet for snaring rabbits."

Nandor Reeves was without comment. Paine took the pouch that contained his bottle of ink, quills, ledger, and a rolled wine-stained measuring tape. He had weighted an end so that it would drop quickly to the bottom of a cask. "I make thee a gift of these," he said. "Return my ledger to the board and keep the rest. And may thou work for the British Government with a lighter heart than I. Neither their parliament nor their church hath a single dram of humanity in it."

The year that Paine had spent in the saddle had arched his back and braced his shoulders. His dealings with people had broadened his views, and his studies had touched his face with dignity. Rather than go back to Thetford, he offered his services, once more, as a journeyman staymaker. For a while he worked for a Mr. Gudgeon in the little town of Diss, in Norfolk County. But Gudgeon was no Morris with an interest in the sciences. He had no single thought outside the four walls of his shop that constituted his little world. So, at the end of three patient months, Paine left him.

Breaking away from the confining needlework of staymaking, he accepted a position as an usher in a Mr. Noble's academy in Goodman's Fields, a little suburb of London. Here he taught English grammar and syntax. Desiring to be closer to the heart of London, he soon transferred to a school in Kensington, but this did not satisfy him either. He rebelled against the endless explanation of simple phrases or clauses to a group of youngsters whose interests, like his own, were beyond the windows of the school where the hedges were bursting into green.

On July 3, 1766, almost a year after his dismissal, he wrote to the Board of Excise:

Honorable Sirs:
    The time I enjoyed my former commission was short and unfortunate—an officer only a single year. No complaint of the least dishonesty or intemperance ever appeared against me; and if I am to succeed in this my humble petition . . .

A year and a half went by, but Paine received no new appointment. It seemed that attending political gatherings, expressing sentiments against unfair taxation, and raising one's voice in defense of the common man were frowned-upon activities and, since Paine himself was only a commoner, a journeyman needleman, . . . unpardonable.

Paine finally called on an old classmate and enlisted his aid. William Falkland was married now and looked forward to being a barrister. His wife's dowry had not cured his lisp, but it had given him an air of overweening self-confidence. His thin face was more pallid than ever, as though it never saw the sun. His eyebrows were arched above faded brown eyes, like bits of shredded straw. Nevertheless, Falkland accomplished in a few weeks what Paine had been unable to achieve in eighteen months. Grudgingly, Paine learned that all things were possible with proper influence and on February 29, 1768, he was reappointed to the excise and assigned to the district of Lewes, in Sussex.

In that town, lodgings above a tobacconist's shop had been recommended to him, and he sought out the shop owned by a Samuel Ollive. A light snow had fallen and the mid-winter sun offered no warmth with which to buffer a cold wind. He found the tobacco shop on Bull Lane, on the ground floor of an ancient, half-timbered house that adjoined a nonconformist chapel. The structure had been an inn during the reign of

Queen Elizabeth and had been known as Bull House. A heavy, wooden door and a corner entrance lent it a commercial atmosphere. Above the shop was a wood-frame dwelling with a pitched tile roof and a stone chimney.

Paine hesitated before the structure's dreary face and then, urged by economy, thrust open the door. The scent of tobacco pervaded the shop. What sun there was shone through clean windows and touched upon the counter, the bins, and the shelves. They had seen younger days, but were neatly kept. The wood floor was scrubbed and a small, worn rug lay at the door's threshold. A slender, unassuming man stood behind the counter. He was dressed in tan-colored cloth, and beneath his waistcoat a plain, grey shirt was buttoned to his neck. Paine introduced himself, stating that a Steven Pudgeon, a fellow exciseman, had sent him.

"Pudgeon, . . . Pudgeon. . . . Ah, yes. I had expected an older man." He glanced at Paine sharply and then lowered his eyes, as though he felt that it were discourteous to judge him. "Excuse me," he said and, stepping to a doorway, he called, "Sarah! Sarah! Please. Wilt come a moment?"

Paine heard the quick patter of feet and a woman came into the shop. Her grey dress created a false impression of stoutness. To Paine's practiced eye, three or four petticoats hung beneath the voluminous, unruffled cloth. Her stay created an artificial rotundity that her sparse bosom did not fill. "He is the new boarder that Steven Pudgeon hath sent. My wife, Sarah Ollive."

Sarah Ollive studied Paine and then, as though to discourage him, she said, "We do not permit spirits in the house. And no visitors, except an occasional gentleman friend. And he must not stay late. We retire early. We cannot object to tobacco, since we sell it."

"We are Friends," Samuel Ollive pointed out, as though to impress upon Paine that there was no personal objection in what his wife was saying.

Paine nodded. "My father and I are members of the Society of Friends, in Thetford."

"Dost thee hear, Sarah?"

She smiled and looked at Paine in a new light. "Come," she said. "I shall show thee the room. It is the large, front one that overlooks the lane."

Paine followed Sarah Ollive up a flight of stairs. At the end of a short corridor, she opened a door and led him into a tidy bedroom. A brick fireplace was set into one wall. The hearth looked freshly scrubbed. She noticed him glance at it. "We have no objection to thy use of it. The draught is good. But thee wilt have to provide thine own kindling and thine own coals."

Paine was delighted with the room. The bed was large and a heavy quilt was turned down to show a stout pillow. A locker stood at the foot of the bed and in front of the window was a chair, a sturdy table, and a pair of candlesticks. "This is fine," said Paine. "Fine. It remindeth me of home."

"Then if thou wilt come, I will present thee to the rest of the family." She led Paine through a parlor behind the shop and into a warm kitchen. A slender girl was busy in front of a stone hearth. At a large table, two youngsters were intent upon a single reader. Sarah Ollive introduced the boys. They looked up at Paine with unsmiling faces. Their skin was pallid; their water-blue eyes showed neither interest nor concern. It seemed to Paine that they had never known the hot sun on a meadow or enjoyed the cool shade of a tree. With a start, he realized that he was being spoken to.

"My daughter, Elizabeth," Sarah Ollive repeated. Paine turned and caught the girl watching him. He was startled by her beauty. Bent over, in front of the hearth, she had not appeared very tall. Her dark hair was parted in the middle and combed modestly to each side. The lashes of her eyes were like thick velvet shadows. A slightly tilted nose gave emphasis to the fullness of her mouth.

[65]

"Thy humble servant, Miss Ollive," had been Paine's intented greeting, but he was late with his phrase. Before he could speak the words, she was back at her work. He turned to the father and asked, "If thou wouldst direct me to a stable, for my horse, I'll get my belongings and return."

One of the boys sprang from his chair so that he almost overturned it. "Thou hast a horse? May I ride him?"

"Thomas Ollive!" the mother reprimanded. "Thee hast no manners? Samuel! Dost thee stand there and speak no word?"

"Samuel will direct thee to the smith," said Sarah Ollive, as though even the telling of its location were a man's portion, and then added, "No, I think thou shouldst be shown the way."

The boys bowed their heads and she addressed the quieter brother. "Get thy muffler and thy cap, Joseph. Go thou with Mr. Paine. And see that thee informs Elisha Watson that I have sent thee."

The city of Lewes appealed to Paine. It was not free from slum courtyards, gin rows, and beggars, but it possessed a sense of bustle. The factories and shops were numerous and the twisting streets were filled with carriages, coaches, and well-dressed, complacent townspeople.

It was not long before Paine was offered and accepted an evening cup of tea in the Ollive kitchen. In exchange for the warmth of the hearth, he tutored the Ollive boys. They began to call him Uncle Thomas, and neither Sarah Ollive nor her husband dissuaded them. Given to speaking little themselves, the Ollives enjoyed Paine's presence and his endless conversation. His talk was filled with interesting incidents that happened on his tax-collecting rounds. Now and then, he would glance at Elizabeth, as he related some humorous occurrence. Though he detected a play of laughter about her lips, she kept her dark-lashed eyes fixed steadfastly upon her weaving.

On Sabbath mornings, when he did not oversleep, Paine

accompanied the Ollives to the nearby meeting house. Joseph and Sarah Ollive would walk quietly ahead, careful to avoid the mud-filled holes in the narrow paving; then the boys, surreptitiously jostling each other; and lastly Elizabeth and Paine. He would extend the crook of his arm with somber etiquette and she would lightly touch her wrist upon it. She was ten years younger than Paine, for he was now thirty-one, but her quiet demeanor, her primness, and her slender height made her seem older than she was.

When spring came, his fellow exciseman, Steven Pudgeon, introduced Paine to a friend named Thomas Rickman. Pudgeon had been away on port rounds all winter and was surprised that the two did not know each other. "Why, Clio lives but up Bull Lane. You mean you 'ave not met? We call 'im 'Clio.' Meanin' as wot the White 'Art Club 'as monikered 'im. For 'is songs."

"Mediocre verse, I assure you," smiled Rickman. "And the musical compositions are not of the best."

The three went immediately to the White Hart Tavern where, in a large room wainscoted and with high rafters, a well-polished bar ran along one side beneath a painting of a white hart in the clearing of a forest. From an open doorway, there was the smell of a roast being turned upon a spit and, at one end of the room, where benches ran along a tremendous length of table a group sat engaged in heated discussion.

Pudgeon led them to the group and introduced Paine to his friends: a Mr. George Lee, who rose and offered a dry, bony hand; John Horne, who seemed rather reserved; Stephen Albernathy, who nodded a well-shaped head that was covered by a curled wig; Midge Crothers, who seemed as affluent as Albernathy; and three rather shabby men. Though Paine did not catch the names of the last three, he learned that they worked in the Grantham excise.

The group, Pudgeon explained, were members of a small society called the White Hart Club and were interested in poetry and reform politics. Singing, it appeared, was as much a part of their evening as drinking and talking. To prove it, they joined their voices in a burst of gaiety, their arms draped over each other's shoulders as though to give their singing a greater resonance. As the song ended, one of the excisemen lifted a thin arm, from whose wrist a frayed cuff hung loosely. He pointed a bony finger at Pudgeon and cried, "By God! Thou hast brought us a bird who cannot sing!"

Paine's cheeks flushed red as all turned to look at him. Smiling, he defended, "Neither can a grouse, nor a squab, and yet they are preferred to the meadowlark at table."

A burst of laughter greeted Paine's answer.

"True!" cried John Horne. "True!"

They seemed to accept his excuse, so Paine joined in the next song. He had a fair voice and carried a tune well. From then on he strove to remedy the songless past of his Quaker upbringing.

As spring wore on, Paine began to spend less and less time with the Ollive family. By summer, he spent most of his evenings with the jovial group at the White Hart Tavern. Those few evenings when he was not at the tavern he would spend in his room, writing humorous verses. He would read the verses to his new friends, over their ale, or as a prelude to political debates, in which they found him both witty and obstinate.

The club members would bring guest speakers and, upon one occasion, Midge Crothers, a barrister, brought John Wilkes, the publisher of the *North Briton*. Paine was greatly impressed. The *North Briton* was the only outspokenly democratic newspaper in the country. He had expected the publisher to be middle-aged and was surprised to find him a tall and rather homely young man, with a disturbing squint, so that one could not look him in the face long without embarrassment.

Paine wrote a patriotic ballad for the club, based on the

death of General Wolfe during the taking of Quebec. He felt that it was the best thing he had yet done, and he rushed into the Ollive kitchen with the finished stanzas and suggested that they be the first to hear them. The neglected Ollive boys smiled expectantly. It had been a long time since Paine had tutored them. A sea-coal fire glowed in the hearth against the chill of the oncoming autumn. Elizabeth sat in front of it, engaged in her interminable weaving. Bubbling over with enthusiasm, Paine read from his fine script:

THE DEATH OF GENERAL WOLFE

In a mouldering cave, where the wretched retreat,
    Britannia sat wasted with care;
She mourn'd for her Wolfe, and exclaim'd against fate
    And gave herself up to despair.
The walls of her cell she had sculptured around
    With the feats of her favorite son;
And even the dust, as it lay on the ground,
    Was engraved with the deeds he had done.

Suddenly Sarah Ollive rose from her chair and urged the Ollive boys to bed. "There are three more stanzas," said Paine.

"And if there were twenty more . . . wouldst thou have them sit up and listen to such ungodly rhymes?"

"Sarah!" protested Samuel Ollive. "Thee hast no right . . ."

"No right!" cried Sarah Ollive. "Spending his nights with drink and heretics! When thee hast offered him the comforts of a home."

"There is no heresy in the White Hart Club. John Horne is an ordained minister. Albernathy's father is a member of the House of Commons. Clio Rickman . . ." Paine cut short his defense and glanced at Elizabeth. She sat as though she heard no single word. "If thou wouldst have me seek other lodgings, if my personal habits are so objectionable . . . I meant to offend no one."

Sarrah Ollive hesitated and then said before she turned to the boys, "I did not say thou wert not welcome here. I only wished thee would mend thy ways. And it hath been a long Sabbath since thou hast come to meeting. It is not a good example that thou showest. Come, Thomas . . . Joseph . . . get thee to bed."

When spring came, however, Paine had not changed his ways. His ballad had been a great success. It had been published in the *Gentleman's Magazine* and Rickman had set it to music. By the time summer arrived, Paine had been offered memberships in three literary clubs and was on his way to gaining a reputation.

None of this, unfortunately, had lessened his uncompromising attitude, as was proved one July night when he left the White Hart Tavern later than usual. A lively debate had taken place and, as always, Paine had been most obstinate. He had been angered that a club member should have defended a comment, made in the House of Lords, that starvation wages were an economic necessity.

"What!" Paine had cried. "Are the workers men or beasts?"

"There is a growing tendency for the workingman and his family to use tea, sugar, and white bread," said George Lee.

"Then I have a point for Parliament to consider. A country's wealth is dependent upon the purchasing power of its labor."

"Ah, there you are wrong, Tom Paine," said Albernathy. "The economists claim otherwise. Give luxuries to the laboring class and they will become shiftless, unmanageable, and foment the economic ruin of England."

"Economists! And what dim-witted, bird-brained economists say that? Economists such as Arthur Young, who insists that the staple diet of farm laborers should be potatoes and rice?"

"The country's economic advisers, Tom. The advisers to the King himself."

"The King. Now, there you have it! The very King himself. Do you gentlemen realize, have you given it any thought, that the very existence of a king, in any country, is a relic of barbarism?"

There had been a hush at the table. It had been as though Paine had knocked over a decanter of wine and everyone had waited for him to right it.

Stephen Albernathy had forced a wry smile. He was related, though not directly, to royalty. He was interested in social reform; but Paine's remark was clearly tainted by sedition . . . were it not so utterly ridiculous. "Who would you have rule, Tom?" he had laughed. "The nobility? You would then have 500 coffers to fill instead of just one."

"Could Englishmen not rule themselves, instead of paying to be governed?"

"Rule themselves? Why a man cannot even curb his own passions."

At that remark, anger had so possessed Paine that he stormed out of the tavern and had gone far down the street before realizing that his emotions were carrying him past the tobacco shop. He retraced his steps ruefully and let himself in with the key that the Ollives had finally permitted him.

The July night was hot. The small shop was filled with the heavy smell of tobacco. And then, in the dark, he was aware of the sound of weeping. He walked behind the counter and pushed open the door. A light shone in the Ollive kitchen and he could hear voices lamenting. He went to the kitchen and found the Ollive family gathered about the table—all but Samuel Ollive. The two boys looked up at him with tear-streaked faces. Mrs. Ollive's head was cradled in her arms. She was sobbing bitterly. Elizabeth was trying to comfort her. Paine looked at Elizabeth questioningly and she whispered, "Father is dead."

Paine was shocked. He knew that Samuel Ollive had complained of the summer heat . . . of shortness of breath . . . but *dead!* He took a candlestick and climbed the stairs to the Ollive bedroom. Samuel Ollive lay on a large four-poster. Paine pulled back the coverlet. In the candlelight, the thin features of the motionless face were rigid and waxen.

Paine returned to the kitchen and insisted that the boys go to bed. Sarah Ollive raised her wet eyes to Paine. "What shall I do? Now, what shall I do?"

Paine looked from her to Elizabeth's sad face. "Run the shop," he said. "I shall help thee."

Sarah Ollive shook her head and sobbed.

"My excise work doth not take up all my time. I shall help thee."

She was but half convinced. "Dost know how to turn the snuff mill? Blend the tobacco?"

"What we don't know, we shall learn. And thou shouldst get a line of groceries. The sale of such items would be more to a woman's taste. I shall help thee with the accounts. And with the purchases."

"Poor Samuel, poor Samuel, poor Samuel," Sarah Ollive wept.

Once returned from the funeral, Paine decided to examine the cellar and snuff mill. He studied the worn millstones and his ingenious mind was instantly stirred into thinking of a way to improve their turning. He ran his fingers through the pungent snuff in the bins and wondered about their blends. Along one wall were casks of American tobacco. Strings of tobacco leaves hung from the beams, evidently for aging. This was better than making stays, he thought. But he would not trade it for the excise, poorly paid as it was.

Paine went up to the kitchen when he felt certain that the few relatives had left. Elizabeth was clearing the table. Sarah Ollive, her eyes red from weeping, her black bonnet still on her head as though she had forgotten it was there, extended her hand to Paine. "Thou art a good friend," she said. "And we are beholden for thy offer to help us with the shop. With thee, I think we shall manage." She hesitated, glanced at her daughter, and then turned back again to Paine. "But thou wilt have to find new lodgings. Thee understands, of course. Two women in the house . . . and I now have no husband. Thee knows tis not right. There would be talk."

Paine was about to protest; he was more than comfortable in his large well-kept room. But he forced a smile. "I shall find other lodgings."

In the next few weeks, he tried to make the tobacco shop show a profit for the Ollives. He gave up his evenings at the White Hart Tavern and devoted what time he could to the making of snuff. Elizabeth and the boys helped him. Though he experimented with different blends and sifters, the trade complained that the snuff was poor. "Twas not like Samuel's mixture."

"Think," he would urge Elizabeth. "Was there something your father added, something he did?"

"I was not down here often. Father did not want me to smell of tobacco and snuff."

Her dark eyes would look at Paine somberly, as though with challenge. He would step close to her and sniff at her clothes. "Canst sniff it in my wrappers when the whole cellar smells of it? Hast thou then a separate nose for scents?"

The boys would snicker, but she would not chide them, for, when they would leave, Sarah Ollive would hurry down the cellar stairs. . . .

The summer turned to autumn, the autumn blended into winter, and the new stock of grocery and household items added rather to the Ollive's debts than to their income. Paine found he could not stay away from his circle of friends at the White Hart Tavern and gradually he was drawn back to them.

One Sunday, when Paine called at the tobacco shop, Sarah

Ollive insisted on seeing him in privacy behind a closed kitchen door. "I miss thy lodging money," she said, coming straight to the point. "And thee rooms elsewhere, while thy old room is not occupied."

"I am not afraid of public censure. If thou wishest . . ."

"No!" she interrupted him. I cannot have thee back a single man. Canst thou not see it?"

Paine looked at her, startled.

"Thee shouldst be married. Thee shouldst have a family of thine own."

Paine smiled and shook his head.

"I speak for Elizabeth. She is a comely girl."

Paine felt his ears flush red. "She hath hardly looked at me. I am ten years older . . ."

"As it should be. Samuel was older than I."

Paine thought of Steven Pudgeon, who had recommended him to the Ollives. He had gone home with Pudgeon on one occasion and had been aghast at what he had seen. Pudgeon's wife had been dressed in rags, cleanly washed but tattered. A brood of barefooted children had pattered about in the airless kitchen, their thin little bodies covered only by frayed undershirts.

"Sure an' I canna' keep my position without appearances," Pudgeon had defended. "Would they not give the boot to a government man in a ragged shirt, now? An' a piddlin' little is left for them. The poor little basta'ds."

It was true, thought Paine. An exciseman dressed as well as a tradesman; when not at home, he ate and drank as well as an artisan, yet was paid as little as a common laborer. But it would be different with the Ollives. Mrs. Ollive owned the Bull Lane property. Living with them again, he would devote more time to the shop. And, as a mother-in-law, Sarah Ollive might want no more than the rent he had formerly paid for his room.

"May I speak with Elizabeth?" Paine asked.

Sarah Ollive left the kitchen and returned with her daughter. Paine had meant alone, but the mother seated herself and rested her arms in her lap as though she had no intention of leaving. Elizabeth stood quietly at the table's edge. Her hands hung at her sides; her gray dress fell primly to her ankles. She held her head down and Paine could see the part in her black hair. It ran upward in a little white path. He waited until she lifted her eyes and looked at him. "I have asked for thy hand in marriage, Elizabeth," he said.

She cast her mother a fleeting glance and, stepping to Paine, she kissed him fully on the mouth. He was taken by surprise. Her lips had a moist freshness that startled him. He hesitated, raised a hand toward her, and, in the midst of his hesitation, she turned from him. She rushed to her mother and kissed her fondly on the cheek. Then, as though abashed, she left the kitchen.

On March 26, 1771, Thomas Paine married Elizabeth Ollive at St. Michael's Church, in Lewes. Paine had left the wedding arrangements to his future mother-in-law and was surprised at her choice of the church. "We have relatives who are not Friends, Thomas," she said. "And 'twill give a greater validity to the service." Paine refrained from objecting.

The wedding was a quiet ceremony; only a few relatives came; Clio Rickman was best man. As the small wedding group left the church, three coaches drew abreast of its grey stone steps. Tumultuously, a dozen White Hart friends tumbled from the coaches. They had mistaken the time and were late. Wrapped in greatcoats with long wool scarfs flung about their necks, they rushed to congratulate the surprised Paine. It was evident that, despite the early hour of the day, they had all been drinking. There were cries of, "The bride! The bride!" and in an instant a tight circle formed about Elizabeth. Sarah Ollive tried to wedge herself into it, but could not. The Ollive relatives stood on the flagstones and stared at Sarah Ollive, aghast. She started to weep. Clio and Paine looked at each other and together, by sheer force, broke into the circle.

Elizabeth was being hugged and kissed as though Paine's friends had known her all their lives. Rickman tore a final embracer from her and the freed Elizabeth turned to Paine. He expected to find her furious with indignation. Instead, her face was flushed with gaiety and her mittened hands tried to hold back her exuberant laughter.

The friends encircled Paine and insisted that he go back with them to the White Hart for a drink and a toast to his wedding day. When he begged off, they lifted him bodily, despite his protests, and carried him to one of the waiting coaches. "Clio! Clio!" Paine shouted above their cries of "You gay dog! You still water that runneth deep." "Clio . . . please see them home. Please . . . I shall break free as soon as I can. Clio . . ." The rest of his words were lost as they stuffed him into one of the coaches and tumbled in after him.

It was long past midnight by the time Paine left the White Hart. Only a few of the revelers staggered with him to the tavern door to wish him Godspeed. The rest sprawled on the benches, unable to rise, or snored with their heads on the wet table. Only John Horne accompanied him. Together they staggered through the narrow lanes. The early March winds were gone and the air was crisp and unusually clear. Paine looked up at the sky above the housetops and insisted that Horne stop and listen to him.

"Tell me, Reverend Horne. Look up at the sky and tell me, doth God watch even the little sparrow fall and shed no tear?"

"You are befuddled, Tom Paine."

" 'S not true!" insisted Paine, straightening his back. "I quote from Pope's *Essay on Man* . . . as thou well knowest:

Who sees with equal eye, as God of all,
A hero perish or a sparrow fall!

And now look up at the sky and tell me. How many sparrows in how many worlds? And how many worlds in how many constellations?"

The smallish Horne struggled to lower Paine's arm that was raised aloft, pointing to the dark sky.

"I am not befuddled, Reverend Horne. I just want to make clear my point . . . my point . . . that a man's destiny is not in the stars . . . that every man fashions his own destiny, or permits others to fashion it! There are more stars in the heavens than there are destinies in our world, John Horne!"

"Art sober?" asked John Horne, shaking him. "Art sober, Tom? You have a destiny of your own tonight. At home."

"Aye. There's the rub! I shouldn't have done it, Reverend Horne. I shouldn't have done it. I had not the courage to say 'no.' "

Horne urged Paine to quicken his lagging steps. "You talk nonsense, Tom. Elizabeth will make a fine wife. With her Quaker upbringing, you have a lot in common. More than most."

They reached the tobacco shop and Paine noticed a light in a second-floor window. It was in his old room; the one into which he had already moved his belongings. He stood and stared up at the window. "That's my room!" he cried. "I feel badly, John. Filled with guilt. She's been waiting for me and the night's half gone."

Horne patted Paine's shoulder. The light at the window wavered, grew brighter, and then grew dim. "Tis Elizabeth! Tis my wife! John, my friend, wilt thou forgive me?"

"My blessings go with you, Tom. Good night. Good night." He watched Paine cross the narrow lane and fish in a pocket for his doorkey.

Paine found the way to his room through the dark. He expected to find his door slightly ajar or at least a bar of light above the doorsill. There was neither. He tiptoed across the landing and pushed open the door. Except for a glow in the fireplace, the room was in darkness. And yet . . . and yet it was from this room that John Horne and he had seen the light. In the fireplace, red and silver embers showed where a fire had burned itself out. He reached for a taper on the mantel and lighted a candle. The bed was freshly made and a clean sheet was tucked beneath two pillows where there had always been only one. He walked to the window where, from the street, he thought he had seen Elizabeth's shadow. A faint scent of cologne seemed to hover about the drapes. It could not be! Elizabeth had never used it.

He tiptoed into the narrow hallway, past the boys' room where they slept together, past Sarah Ollive's room, and reached the bedroom that had always been Elizabeth's. He stood for a moment and listened intently. There was no sound. He tried the door and found it unlocked. He thrust it open and tiptoed into the room. There was no one there. Where was Elizabeth? With her mother? He returned to his own room, undressed in the dark, and went to bed.

In the morning, it was as though nothing had happened the day before. No one spoke of the wedding. When Paine caught Elizabeth's eye, she looked abashed and turned her head aside.

From then on, although Sarah Ollive retained ownership of the property, the business was carried on in Paine's name. The women ran the shop and Paine continued to work as an exciseman. He spent the weekends going over accounts, grinding and mixing snuff, and tutoring the growing boys. On the Sabbath, they attended the Friends' meeting house as a family group. Sarah Ollive now walked between the boys and Paine beside his demure wife. He still extended his arm to her, but she rested only an elbow upon it, for her hands were in a fur muff that was a wedding gift. If it had been planned as a marriage of convenience, then the Ollives had managed it well.

After the first night, Paine was too proud to go to Elizabeth's room, and she never came to his. At first, he waited for her. He kindled a blaze in the fireplace to take the chill from the room; he assembled the scattered gazettes and papers on his table and arranged the books on the mantel. She never came. When he ate his meals at home, she served him pleasantly but without comment. The boys called him Uncle Thomas, as they always had, though he was now their brother-in-law. Elizabeth never addressed him by name. Slowly, once again, he began to spend an occasional evening at the White Hart Tavern, and drifted from the Ollives.

One summer night, at the White Hart Tavern, he found his friends gloomily assembled on the narrow paving that fronted the tavern window.

"Steve Pudgeon's wife has died," said John Horne without overture. "We wait but for you to go extend our regrets." Without further explanation the little group set off for Pudgeon's home.

What Albernathy, Rickman, and John Horne expected to see, Paine did not know. They had never seen aught but the acceptable facade of Steven Pudgeon: the manners and the clothes that he wore for the benefit of the outside world. They had heard him speak of money in the terms of a government official, money that, though not his, yet by merely passing through his fingers, lent him an air of being free from need. Now Paine knew they would see the reality. In the damp rooms at the edge of Lewes, three half-naked children were huddled in a shadowed corner of the Pudgeon kitchen. The walls showed ugly, damp grey craters where the plaster had fallen from them. Though it was late October, the sooted hearth was cold.

Paine glanced into the bedroom. Two women, poorly clad, black shawls draped about their unkempt heads, sat on stools beside an unpainted wood coffin that rested upon trestles that had been pushed against an old bed. Within one end of the coffin, Paine could see an emaciated face. Despite its shut lids, the fleshless head had been raised, as though to give it one last look at the bare, grey walls.

[79]

A hurt as deep as a knife thrust seared Paine's heart. He felt himself stifling. He edged his way outside and stood in the courtyard. The refuse with which it was littered was discernable in the deepening October twilight. Without apparent reason, his mind drifted back to petite Mary Lambert whom he had married in Sandwich. If she had lived, would this have been her life . . . and finally her death . . . now that he was an excise officer? And Elizabeth Ollive . . . Elizabeth Paine . . . how would things be for her if they left her mother?

It was the death of Pudgeon's wife, bringing into sharp focus the abject poverty of an exciseman's family, that urged Paine to write his *The Case of the Officers of Excise.* After all, few tax collectors were stupid illiterates. With the exception of such as Simms, they were sensitive, intelligent men.

With the help of Rickman and Albernathy, Paine circulated a petition and urged the officers of excise to each subscribe three shillings to further their cause. It was his intention to petition for an increase in their pay. The contributions would offset the cost of printing the petition, its distribution, and its presentation to Parliament.

Paine had expected a reply from half the excisemen in the kingdom. He was touched and inspired to find that almost all of them answered him. The three-shilling donations came to a total of over £500. The sum would more than pay for the care of his horse and his lodging in London, while he petitioned the members of Parliament. Greatly encouraged, he began the draft of a protest against the insufficient pay of excise officers.

One night, as he worked on his draft, he was startled by a knock on his door. He was surprised to see Sarah Ollive. She was in a night kerchief and wrapper. She looked younger in the candlelight. Without her many petticoats, her body was as slender as a girl's.

"I hear thou art going to London," she said without preliminary conversation.

"When I have finished my memorial."

"And thou hast five hundred pounds, expense money. Art thou taking Elizabeth?"

He had not thought of taking her. In these many months, he had not thought of Elizabeth as his wife.

"She hath never been to London. She would like to go. It would draw her and thee together. I feel thee wouldst return a husband and not . . . not . . ."

"And she doth not care enough to be a wife at home?"

The remark angered Sarah Ollive and she retaliated, "And dost thou stay at home instead of gallivanting with thy rum-drinking friends? And she so ashamed of the look of thy room, with thy books and papers scattered about. It is I and not she as tidieth thy quarters!"

"I give thee a portion of my earnings for my keep and my obligation. I refuse to purchase affection."

"Affection! And dost thou speak to her, or anyone, of aught but thy John Wilkes journals and the country's injustices?"

Paine paced the room as though Sarah Ollive were not there. He turned and faced her. "'Twill be no different in London. All my time will be devoted to the excise memorial." His voice softened and he asked, "Doth she truly have affection for me? Thou hast not persuaded her into this matrimony?"

"She is thy wife."

"I cannot take her with me! I cannot divert money entrusted to me, for her expense. But I shall return with recognition. Grant me but a month and when I return . . ."

Sarah Ollive was unconvinced. "Then go alone! I insist thou art a wastrel and a profligate!"

Paine resumed his work but could not shut Sarah Ollive's visit from his mind. Perhaps he should take Elizabeth with him. But the problem was leaving her alone at a lodging, day

after day, while he petitioned. And the additional cost! No—
he would spend no more of the £500 entrusted to him than
was absolutely essential. He dipped the quill into the inkpot
and resumed his draft:

> The most effectual method to keep men honest is to enable
> them to live so. ... There is a striking difference between
> dishonesty arising from want of food, and want of principles.
> The first is worthy of compassion, the other of punishment.
> Nature never produced a man who would starve in a well-
> stored larder, because the provisions were not his own. ...

The candles burnt low and dripped tallow over the candlesticks. The short wicks made the yellow flames sputter. Paine's eyes tired. When one of the Ollive boys came in the
morning to call him, he was fast asleep at the table. His arms
and head rested on scattered sheets of paper.

6

ONCE ARMED with his finished pamphlets from the printer,
Paine rushed to London to see Will Falkland. He was surprised to find him changed. Falkland was a barrister now and
could practice in the courts as an advocate. His wig was costly
and his dress meticulous. He greeted Paine cordially and,
upon Paine's excited insistence, put on a pair of silver-rimmed
spectacles and read *The Case of the Officers of Excise.* Now and
then, he looked over the top of the pamphlet, lifted his spectacles, and studied Paine from between half-shut lids. When
he finished, he placed the memorial carefully upon his desk
and shook his head. "A plea to the British Government? For
money?"

"And what is wrong with it?"

"Oh, it is lucid . . . forceful . . . I have always maintained that you have a genius for expression, Tom. But to petition for money! No offense, Tom . . . but a nobleman is attended to more, in Parliament, than a noble cause. May I suggest that you do not involve yourself? There is already a record of a past dismissal. . . ."

"Involve myself! Am I not one of them, Will? The excisemen are overworked. And underpaid. Dishonesty is all but forced upon them. As is their poverty."

Falkland pushed the memorial across the desk. "I can accomplish nothing. Nor would I venture. I would be stigmatized." Suddenly his pallid face broke into a wide smile. "Wouldst like to meet the ablest petitioner in all of England, Tom? He has a fistful of petitions in every pocket. To the King, to Parliament, to the East India Company. He has a friend in every government bureau. You must have heard of him. Charles Fox has written of him. As has Edmund Burke. His name is Dr. Franklin."

The name was somehow familiar, but Paine could not place it.

"He is often seen at the Excise Coffeehouse on Broad Street. Shall we go there and meet him?"

The Excise Coffeehouse, Paine saw at once, was not the White Hart Tavern. The large, wainscoted room was like the drawing room of a wealthy home, with chandeliers hanging from the ceiling and candle sconces set into each wall panel. The men, few of whom were young, were expensively and modishly attired. Their voices were restrained, their discussions not heated.

"We're in luck," said Falkland, and led Paine to the extreme end of the room. A decanter of sherry and a flask of yellow brandy had been placed upon a large, round table. Five men sat about it and held their glasses with unaffected nonchalance. No one could deny their appearances of either position or wealth. Their shirts were ruffled, their waistcoats

[83]

were adorned with gold or silver buttons, and gathered lace hung at their wrists. In their midst, seemingly at home, sat a rather stout man in simple country cloth. His long, honey-brown hair, combed without affectation, hung down over his ears to a strong, short neck. His lips seemed to wear a constant smile, as though he were in continuous agreement with those about him, and yet his dark-lashed eyes looked as though they were committing to memory every word that was spoken.

There were nods of recognition between Falkland and the group as he introduced Paine. "Gentlemen, gentlemen . . . may I offer you London's newest petitioner. Single-handed, armed with but a pocketful of pamphlets, he intends an attack upon our Houses of Parliament." Pointing with open palms toward each seated man, he named them: "Sydney Travers; James Baldwin; Clyde Keats; Sir Joshua Harvey; and our colonial friend, Dr. Benjamin Franklin. And this, gentlemen, is Thomas Paine. A townsman. We grew up together, in Thetford. He is an officer in excise who is petitioning for an increase in pay for underpaid excisemen." He had hesitated at the word "underpaid" and ended his introduction with a disarming smile.

Paine nodded politely to each man. To his surprise, the youngish James Baldwin said, "I have already read the memorial. It is extremely well expressed." He called for extra chairs and extra glasses to be brought.

"Thank thee," said Paine. "And if I may?" He drew a handful of pamphlets from a pocket and distributed them.

Sir Joshua Harvey drew a reading glass from a pocket of his flowered waistcoat, glanced at the heading on the pamphlet, replaced the glass, and dropped the printed memorial on the table. He looked directly at Paine, evaluated his common clothes, and challenged. "Everyone in public office is under-paid. And having thus and so quickly agreed with your memorial, now what?"

There was a flicker of anger in Paine's eyes. "I do not ask

for agreement, sir. Every thinking man, having read it, will agree with it. I am asking for an expression of that agreement." There were cries of "Hear! Hear!" and Sir Harvey inclined his head.

Sydney Travers raised his glass to his lips. Candlelight glinted from a large ruby on his little finger. He studied Paine, sipped his brandy, and then, setting down his glass, he asked, "Paine? Thomas Paine?" And when Paine nodded, "Mr. Paine, as a constituent of government, in my small way, may I point out that government is based upon precedent? I am a member of Commons, and I am also a commissioner on the Board of Excise. Years ago . . . no, no, let me finish . . ." as he saw that Paine was about to interrupt him. "You have brought us an impulsive young man, Falkland."

He turned back to Paine and waved the petition in his hand. "I was about to say . . . the magistrates in Quarter Sessions have fixed local wages since the sixteenth century. The salaries of excisemen were fixed by law almost 100 years ago. Were Parliament to change them now, they would not only shatter an old precedent but set up a new one. And this new one would be used as a steppingstone for petitions for salary raises in all other government offices."

Paine was irritated that a member of the excise should take such a stand. "Sir," he replied, keeping down his voice with difficulty, "May I say that the very meaning of the word 'precedent' makes it apparent that we cannot use the stick of a century ago with which to measure today's needs? These are changing times, sir. And we must change with them."

Dr. Franklin toyed with his wineglass. Apparently impressed by Paine and evaluating the short temper of the memorial's author, he said in a quiet voice that carried well, "If we are to speak of the meaning of words, Mr. Paine, may I define 'petition?' I think Sam Johnson's *Dictionary of the English Language* would concur with me when I say that a 'petition' is a formal, written request. Especially a request

[85]

addressed to a political group for a particular grace or grant. A formal request, written with finesse and grace and wisdom, . . . but still, Mr. Paine, written begging."

Paine turned a flushed face to Franklin. "Justice doth not beg, sir. Justice insists!"

Franklin puckered his lips. "I have seen a touch of benevolence tip the scales of justice, Mr. Paine. But the sharp edge of a sword . . ."

Falkland regretted that he had brought Paine. He rose from his chair, recalled an almost forgotten appointment, tendered his excuses, and drew Paine away from the irritated group. To his surprise, Franklin followed them and asked for a few words with Paine. He led Paine to a corner table and ordered a bottle of Madeira. Paine realized that he had spoken rashly. He felt like a schoolboy in front of Franklin.

"You are an impulsive young man. That is wonderful. But you need harnessing. The most willing horse can pull no wagon without shafts and traces." He motioned to the glasses when the wine came and began to read Paine's petition. He reached:

> To the wealthy and humane, it is a matter worthy of concern, that their affluence should become the misfortune of others.

He reread the paragraph and then continued. When he came to:

> It hath always been the wisdom of Government to consider the situation and circumstances of persons in trust. . . .

he looked across the top of the pamphlet and studied Paine. He saw a man in his middle thirties, an inexpensive wig indicating either poor circumstances or a lack of vanity, a sharp nose in a rather thin face, and deep blue eyes in which a fire of some kind seemed to have been kindled.

The eyes looked back at Franklin, unabashed. "Art

[86]

thou impressed enough to offer thy help, sir?"

Franklin smiled and shook his head. "I cannot. I came to England as agent for the province of Pennsylvania. Now I also serve New Jersey, Georgia, and Massachusetts. I carry more grievances than a beggar has boils. You have not heard of our Sons of Liberty and their Boston Tea Party? Or the Quebec Act? Or the East India Company's monopoly?"

Paine shook his head. "Only vaguely. Besides the excise, my business is not in tea but tobacco."

Franklin loosened the plain stock beneath his plump chin. "Ah, tobacco!" he whispered as though Paine were an old confidant. "That is a tender commodity indeed. Our largest purchasers of tobacco are the Dutch. And now the British Navigation Act forbids us to ship our tobacco leaf directly to Holland. Hear you!" he said, shaking a stout finger at Paine. "The leaf must be sold first to an English merchant, shipped here to your country, unloaded, resold to a Dutch distributor, and then put on board ship again and sent to Holland. And even before the act, Turkish tobacco sold throughout Europe at a lower price. And what tobacco do you deal in, Mr. Paine? Turkish or American?"

Paine was greatly impressed by the quiet dignity of this largish man. He was evidently a man of means and yet he dressed without ostentation. Paine judged him to be in his late sixties, yet still in excellent health.

Paine thought back to the question of tobacco. In the shop, they were still using a portion of the late Samuel Ollive's stock. He sought in his pocket for the snuffbox that he had begun to carry. He pressed it open and offered it to Franklin. Franklin sniffed, looked at Paine, and smiled. He rolled a pinch of the snuff between his thumb and forefinger. "Virginia leaf," he said. "Unblended, 'tis too mild for snuff. I have been told that in the Indies they add a pinch of piper nigrum. You have a sale for this?"

Paine flushed and admitted, "I have little gift for the trade."

"And a rash petitioner. But I like thy spirit and thy phrases. I am, among other things, a printer and am impressed by the memorial. I would say that it shows talent. Would you consider going to the Colonies, Tom Paine? We have a need for such men as you." He lifted his glass and chuckled, "In the Colonies, we have no precedents."

Already drawn to this American who called him Tom Paine so quickly, Paine remembered *A Natural History of Virginia* that Reverend Knowles had once loaned him. He had dreamed about America then, but now he had other fish to fry.

"Do you hesitate to leave England?" questioned Franklin. There was a note of tenderness in his voice. "I have spent the last ten years here. I am acquainted with your opulent gentlemen . . . your society of landlords. But I have also seen those of your people who live in the most sordid wretchedness, clothed only in rags."

Paine shook his head. "Thou tempteth me, Dr. Franklin, but just now I am dedicated to the plight of the excisemen. I shall stir up so much public opinion that even the King will be cognizant of it."

"And of its petitioner," smiled Franklin. "A word of advice. Never present a petition if you can get another to do it for you. Draft it, enroll as many sympathizers as thou canst, and then engage a most popular man to present it. Like a Midas touch, the fame of a popular endorser ensures its support."

"Thou?" suggested Paine.

"No, not I," laughed Franklin, getting up heavily.

"Dr. Samuel Johnson?" guessed Paine, since Franklin had mentioned him.

Franklin shook his head. "An excellent choice, my young friend. You learn quickly. But Henry Thrale and his wife, Hester, have spirited Sam Johnson to France. You will come up with someone. And now I must get back to my friends."

Paine watched Franklin leave. There was something magnetic about the man. He must find out more about him.

Paine took Franklin's advice to heart. He sat in his lodging and penned a letter to Oliver Goldsmith. He had inquired about Dr. Franklin and the American was better known than Paine had thought. It seemed that many prominent Englishmen had become his friends: the scientist, Joseph Priestley; the philosopher, David Hume; the economist, Adam Smith. He had received honorary degrees from Oxford University and from the University of St. Andrews in Scotland. He was a fellow of the Royal Society and had been awarded its Copeland Medal. Paine recalled him to mind as he had seen him in the Excise Coffeehouse. He wondered at his quiet, unassuming dignity.

Paine's thoughts drifted back to his letter to Goldsmith. He had gotten as far as "Honored Sir:" and no further. He realized that he should invite the author to some public place. He could not receive him in this room, with its single chair and unswept floor. This man of wealth and reputation would be affronted if, by some remote chance, he should come. For there was no doubt but that *The Vicar of Wakefield* and *The Deserted Village* had stamped him as one of the most famous men in England. Even a simple endorsement by so celebrated an author must help the petition. But would Goldsmith answer a complete stranger? Concern himself with an exciseman's poor wage? He returned to his letter writing:

Honored Sir:
    I present you with the case of the Officers of Excise. I act, myself, in the humble station of an Officer of Excise, though somewhat differently circumstanced to what many of them are, and have been the principal promoter of a plan for applying to Parliament for an increase in salary. . . .

Oliver Goldsmith answered Paine's letter and offered an appointment for a meeting. Paine went at once to Falkland and showed him the reply. "I must impress him!" cried Paine. "I must impress him! But what can one offer a wealthy celebrity?"

"Wealthy?" laughed Falkland. "He has no wealth. Why the man's an eccentric. He spends to the point of extravagance on the most ridiculous things. He's munificent to friends and causes without reason. Only six years ago he would have ended in a debtor's prison were it not for Samuel Johnson, Joshua Reynolds, and Burke. And his play, *The Good Natur'd Man,* was a failure."

"I had no intention of asking him for money," protested Paine.

"A prescription for your memorial?" And when Paine seemed puzzled, "Oh yes, he's a physician, didn't you know? He studied medicine, but without receiving a degree, mind you, at Edinburgh. Let me tell you about this Goldsmith. I had a client who sued him. This Goldsmith wandered throughout Europe, where he supported himself by playing the flute and by begging. By begging! Later, here in England, he worked for publishers as a hired writer. A hack!"

Paine folded Goldsmith's letter of reply and placed it carefully in a pocket. Suddenly he felt a deep aversion for Will Falkland. Like father, like son, he thought, remembering the older Falkland's love of money and regard for prestige; the talk of his dipping into the tithe funds. . . .

Two evenings later, at the Excise Coffeehouse, Paine waited for Oliver Goldsmith. It had grown late. He had just begun to doubt that the author would come, when he saw a man being directed to his table. Paine had learned that Goldsmith was forty-four, but this man seemed older. He was on the tall side, thin, and had sloping shoulders. As he reached the table, Paine saw a receding chin, a short nose, and timid eyes above which a preponderance of wrinkled brow seemed to occupy almost half a face badly scarred by smallpox. He gave Paine a shy half-smile and removed a brown beaver fur hat. Most of his lank hair had deserted him and he combed what was left sideward, across the back portion of his head.

Paine sprang to his feet and welcomed him. "Dr. Goldsmith?" The author extended a bony hand that ended in heavily-veined fingers. "Here, let me help thee with thy cape." The man seemed so quiet and unassuming that, to look at him, one would never think him a success.

Paine called for brandy and then, realizing that Goldsmith might have a preference, asked, "Dr. Goldsmith, thy pleasure, sir?"

Goldsmith smiled a shy half-smile and brushed a slender hand into the air. "I drink wi' thee, an' t' tha' petition. I 'ave found it extremely well written." He leaned to one side and whispered a change in the drinks.

"My humble thanks, Dr. Goldsmith. And I would not have troubled thee except that I find a closed door at every knock and a deaf ear to every plea."

"An' do ye not 'ave faith in the goovernment and tha' representation it extoonds?"

Paine was surprised to find Goldsmith's hesitating speech marked by an Irish brogue. For a half moment he wondered if it were assumed as a jest.

"My enthusiasm hath not faltered, Dr. Goldsmith, but I have learned that the names of considerably more than half the Commons are in the books of the peerage and baronetage. And the rest are almost all of gentry origin."

"An' the excise gatherers, are they truly penurious?"

Paine noticed the wide eyes. It was the only change of expression in Goldsmith's pale, melancholy face.

"They do not starve, Dr. Goldsmith. When on their rounds, the Excise Officers are warm, well fed, and in pleasant company. But after they clothe and feed themselves, there is nothing left for their families. I have been in their homes and they are not pastoral scenes. Their hungry children are in rags, their sucklings are turned from dried-out breasts to watered tea, and their wives are resigned to a drab and emotionless existence." Paine suddenly recalled what Falkland had said regarding Goldsmith's endorsement of causes and quickly added, "Charity will not help them. Dr. Goldsmith. Only government recognition and justice."

"An' ye want froom me . . . ?"

"What influence thou couldst bring to bear."

Goldsmith caressed his warm mug. To Paine, it was a new drink. It tasted like hot, spiced ale mixed with the pulp of roasted apples. "I 'ave a friend," said Goldsmith, "General Oglethorpe. Dost know James? 'E 'as estooblished a refuge for debtors an' paupers. A colony called Georgia."

"The excisemen are not beggars," said Paine, keeping anger from his voice with difficulty. "I am an excise officer myself, Dr. Goldsmith."

"Twas a thought. An' if the way froom England were by road 'stead o' salted wat'r, I would suggest it still. I assure ye, I shall do w'a I can. I'm engaged in a new play. It takes oop most o' m' day."

"I shall look forward to seeing it." Paine had passed the theatre in Drury Lane and the one in Covent Garden a number of times. He had not as yet attended any performance. But if it were Dr. Goldsmith's play! Someone he had met!

"*She Stoops T' Conquer.* Sam Johnson doesna' think mooch o' the title; boot I dina' care to change it."

"I like it!" cried Paine.

"Then let us drink a toost! A first toost t' *She Stoops T' Conquer* an' t' tha' petition!"

"To their immediate success!" toasted Paine.

"I like tha'," confided Goldsmith. "I think we shall be friends."

Much to his surprise, Tom Paine and Oliver Goldsmith did

become friends, but the petition failed to prosper. Paine spent the entire winter in London, endeavoring to interest members of Parliament, but he could gain neither attention nor support. Frequenters of the Excise Coffeehouse and the Tankard Tavern had more interesting subjects to discuss than underpaid gaugers. Even at Child's, despite Goldsmith's endorsement, Paine's obstinate petitioning gradually wore out his welcome. The first one to notice him enter the warm, spicescented room would whisper, "Pssst! Here comes Goldsmith's Paine in the ass!" The members who were in the ministry would immediately turn up their collars or wrap their mufflers about their ears.

Finally, on April 2, 1774, Paine's memorial was presented as a motion in the House of Commons. He arose early, wandered along the Thames, and stared at the Parliament buildings.

Armed with a pass that Dr. Franklin had procured for him, he entered the House of Commons, seated himself in the gallery, and waited for his motion to be presented. The morning drifted into noon before a House clerk rose and offered:

THE CASE OF THE OFFICERS OF EXCISE.
With Remarks on the Qualifications of Officers, and on the Numerous Evils Arising to the Revenue, from the Insufficiency of the Present Salary—

The clerk had a lisp that was worse than Will Falkland's. In a disinterested monotone, he ran together the protesting phrases that Paine had so carefully written and reworked; while the members of the House sat with disinterest on their faces and boredom in their every attitude. As the clerk droned on, they sniffed at pinches of snuff or nibbled at their fingernails in open disrespect.

Sydney Travers, who had defended the precedent that had determined wages since the sixteenth century, was nudging a fellow member and pointing up to Paine. The friend was a big-bodied man with a full round face, a large prominent nose, and wide grey eyes that were shadowed by heavy black brows. His ears were delicately small for so large a head. Paine did not know that he was Charles James Fox. Nor did he know that the two men were looking at him with interest and not with derision. He simply felt that the excise case was lost. He did not wait for the entire reading of the twenty-page memorial but rose from his seat and left.

Finally convinced a week later, that his memorial would bear no fruit, he packed his belongings and set out for Lewes. Trees were in blossom along the road. The meadows were bright with green, but they did not lighten his heart. The £500 were spent and he had accomplished nothing. He had imagined a different homecoming. He had imagined a fulfilled mission and the consummation of his marriage. Talk of the "marriage of convenience" had drifted outside the Ollive household. There were rumors, among his friends, that he was impotent.

He slowed his horse to a walk when he reached Bull Lane. He hesitated in front of the tobacco shop. Summoning his courage, he dismounted, thrust the door open, and entered as the clapper bell tinkled a half-hearted summons. Pine stared aghast at the shelves. They were all but empty. The groceries were gone. The tobacco bins were bare, and here and there a single household utensil was but a reminder of what had once been stocked. Joseph came into the shop and, seeing Paine, rushed to him. "Uncle Thomas!" he cried. "Uncle Thomas!" and embraced him happily. His grey shirt was patched at the elbows. The sleeves seemed to have grown too short for him. His smile did not mask his lean cheeks.

That night, after the boys had gone to bed, Paine sat with Elizabeth and Sarah Ollive. They went over such records as had been kept. Trade at the shop had almost entirely ceased. They had taken whatever they had needed, from the shelves, and unpaid debts had accumulated.

"I shall be back to work again on Monday," comforted Paine. "The largest portion of my salary will go to paying the debts. And we shall start again. I have friends in London now who will help me. And I have found out what is amiss with our snuff. Hast thou missed me, Bess?"

"Confine thyself to her Christian name, Mr. Paine. Yes, we all missed thee, when we were hungry."

"I admit to the fault in leaving. I shall make amends." He glanced at Elizabeth, but she rose and left the room.

The next day he spent in taking inventory of what was left in the shop and checking the neglected tobacco in the cellar. Most of Friday he spent in writing numerous letters and then, on Saturday morning, he received a letter from the Board of Excise. He unfolded the paper and read with bitterness:

> Friday, April 8, 1774
> Thomas Paine, Officer of Lewes Out-Ride, Sussex Collection, having quit his business, without obtaining the board's leave for so doing, and being gone off on account of the debts which he hath contracted, the said Paine, having been once before discharged, it is ordered that he be again discharged.

The wording, "being gone off on account of the debts which he hath contracted," startled Paine. He had not gone off without advising the board. He had asked for a leave of absence. Now he was being accused of having left Lewes in order to elude creditors. He could be arrested upon sight for the debts of the tobacco shop. He decided to go back to London and borrow what money he could. Sarah Ollive said nothing except, "Thou wert born under a star of misfortune, Tom Paine." Only Elizabeth walked with him to the threshold of the shop, took his hand, and wished him Godspeed.

When Paine returned to Lewes, he found the shop closed and a notice posted on the door:

To be sold by auction, on Thursday the 14th of April, all the household furniture, stock in trade, and other effects of Thomas Paine, grocer and tobacconist. Also a horse, tobacco, snuff mill, with all the utensils for cutting tobacco and grinding snuff; and two unopened crates of cream-colored stoneware.

When Paine let himself into the shop, an angry Sarah Ollive barred his way. Paine thrust a hand into his pocket and took out the notes he had borrowed. "There will be no auction," he promised. "Give me the list of creditors. They will all be paid."

"We do not want thee back, Tom Paine. Thou hast everyone's care in heart but thine own. We are better off without thee than with thee."

Elizabeth must have been listening, for suddenly she stepped into the shop and protested. It was the first time she had spoken a single word in Paine's defense. "'Tis not right! To turn him out without a lodging!"

"Wouldst go with him? Wouldst leave thy mother in her gray years? And thy brothers? Wouldst go begging in the streets for Tom Paine whilst he spends his nights in taverns . . . planning how to change a world whose sufferings even the Almighty cannot help. Bring down his packings!"

Paine glanced from mother to daughter. Two tears fashioned themselves in Elizabeth's eyes and brimmed over her dark lids. "I shall get my own belongings," said Paine and brushed past them.

Paine sold his horse, together with almost all of his books, and paid every creditor. He gave to the Ollives the greater portion of what money was left and, on June 4, 1774, accepted a separation from Elizabeth. He made no comment as a solicitor drew up the necessary papers. The solicitor glanced at Paine strangely as Sarah Ollive testified that Elizabeth had lived separately from her husband and had never had any issue. A local clergyman, who acted as a legal witness, regarded Paine with hostile unbelief.

When Paine left, he waited outside the solicitor's office. The day had turned warm. The men who walked by had their waistcoats unbuttoned. The women lifted their skirts as though to cool their ankles. He looked up at the solicitor's window and saw Elizabeth watching him. She raised a hand and waved a hesitant good-by. Sarah Ollive turned her from the window. It seemed that they were waiting for him to go. Sarah Ollive wanted no leave-taking in the street.

Paine himself went to the White Hart Tavern. The large room, shielded from the sun, was shadowed and cool. He had hoped to find some friends to whom to say farewell, but the tavern was almost deserted. Here, he had spent many a night in heated debate; criticized England's corruption and the laws that kept her masses in servile poverty. Here, in good fellowship, with his arms flung about Rickman's stout shoulders or John Horne's spindly back, he had lifted his voice in many a ballad's tune. Now, in the early noon, the chairs and the worn benches were empty.

The porter shuffled toward him to make certain that it was indeed Tom Paine—Tom Paine whom he had never seen by daylight. Paine clasped his bony hand and cried, "Good-by, Tim Nolan. Good-by. And good-by to all the Irish kings thou claims for ancestors." He waved a hand to the empty benches and insisted, "Wish all my friends good-by for me. Dost thou hear, Nolan? Tell them Tom Paine hath gone back to London with a millstone round his neck."

The porter's head bobbed up and down. He twisted it upon his scrawny neck and looked at Paine sideward, like a wingless bird. He could not determine what Paine was doing there so early in the day.

Stepping once more into the bright sunshine, Paine went in search of the noon coach to London. He had borrowed a large sum from a new friend, George Lewis Scott, a London member of the Board of Excise, and now he had to repay him.

7

IT TOOK Paine almost two years to repay his debt to George Scott, two years in which he continued to educate himself as well as those he taught. He was first a preceptor in a school in Kensington, conducted by a Mr. Gardiner. Later, he taught in a school for boys in Chelsea.

Influenced by Oliver Goldsmith, he tried his hand at writing, only to find that no magazine would publish his essays or articles. To write that a man should earn his nobility, and not merely inherit it, was in bad taste! To insist that dumb brutes were entitled to humane treatment and to suggest that regulations be passed forbidding the starving or abuse of domestic animals was ridiculous! His essay on England's traffic in slaves was looked upon as meddling with a private venture. The English themselves owned no slaves. They merely dealt in them as a commodity, just as they did in copra or ivory. A London editor returned one of Paine's articles with the comment that he had never seen "a marriage of such gilded phrases with such distorted views."

One night, seeking Scott at the Excise Coffeehouse, Paine found him in earnest conversation with Dr. Franklin. They were speaking as though they were old friends. A young man sat with them at the table. "You know each other," cried Scott as Franklin greeted Paine. "Admirable! Admirable! And do you know Dr. Franklin's grandson?"

Paine shook the young man's hand and Scott introduced him as William Temple Franklin. There was an unmistakable resemblance between grandfather and grandson. Though his eyes were brown, instead of blue like the elder Franklin's, he had the same round face. Above a wide, intelligent brow, a whisp of sandy brown hair showed from beneath a powdered wig. The grandson, although not foppishly attired, had little of the grandfather's simplicity. The stock beneath his strong chin was adorned with frills, his waistcoat was made of flowered brocade, and a gathering of lace ruffles encircled his wrists.

"I know not whether to call young Will an American or an Englishman," said Scott. "You have been here eight years, Will, or nine?"

"Ten," said young Franklin.

"Accepting such education as we English have to offer. And an English perspective on the world. Is't not true?"

The young man nodded. Scott put an arm about Paine's shoulder and confided, "My dear Dr. Franklin, did you know that this young man has a penchant for agitation?"

"I know your friend well," said Franklin. "I have read a number of his unpublished essays."

Paine looked from Scott to Franklin and said quietly, "I have decided to go to the Colonies, Dr. Franklin."

Scott did not take Paine seriously. "What will you agitate for there? Just treatment of colonists as English men? King George has a long arm, my friend. Has he not secured Charles Fox's dismissal from Parliament . . . simply for expressing his sympathy for the American colonists? And you neither have Burke's tongue nor Fox's influence. Did you know that he inquired about you? He saw you when your memorial was read in Commons. And then you dropped from sight."

"I have given up politics," said Paine. "It hath cost me much and gained me little. I would like to establish an academy in one of the American towns. With that I am well acquainted. And I have a recommendation from David Williams, the principal of a boys' school in Chelsea."

"David Williams," commented Franklin. "I know him well."

"A Deist!" said Scott.

"And an advocate of political liberty," retorted Paine.

Franklin chuckled. He shook a stout finger at Paine. "There, do you see? The fires of political attachment are untended, but the embers insist upon glowing. No matter. Permit me to give you my personal letter of recommendation. Go to Philadelphia. There you can present it to my son-in-law, Richard Bache." He glanced at Paine's mustard-colored coat and grey breeches, which had grown threadbare in their two winters' hard service. "And go as a cabin passenger. Put always thy best foot forward."

"Thank thee, Dr. Franklin. And if Pennsylvania is aught like Virginia—the Virginia that I read about as a boy . . ."

Franklin rose heavily to his feet and lifted his glass to them. "Scott, Paine—I give you my word. Each colony is like a bride that will give you warmth and affection, sustenance and children. The Colonies are a new world and if there is aught of evil there, it is because men have brought it with them. My grandson remembers not enough of the life there. As for myself, if the next packet brings me no better news of my wife, I shall not stay long in England."

Scott remained with Paine after Franklin and his grandson left. He stared into his empty glass and sighed, "Now there is a man with many talents. What a pity to waste them at the Court of St. James's. There must be a need for good schools in the Colonies. Else why would Dr. Franklin have brought young William to our corrupt England? Let us drink to your new school, Tom. To Tom Paine, who goes to seek his fortune in a savage land and write his essays among a belligerent and illiterate people. No, no! Forgive me. I truly wish you well. And if there is aught you need, . . ."

In September, 1774, Paine booked passage to Philadelphia on the *London Packet,* under a Captain Cooke. He had written to his parents and to his friends in Lewes and had said his good-bys in London. He went aboard the ship and placed his belongings in the cabin. He had been advised that, except for homespun clothes and fur hats, apparel and shoes ran high in the Colonies. He had filled a secondhand chest with clothes and, on top of them, had crammed the manuscripts of his unpublished essays and articles. He had been told that there would be three fellow passengers, but he had not met them.

He went on deck to get a last view of England. A tremendous group of indentured servants was walking up the gangplank. Some of them seemed gentle, others as brutal as beasts. Some had indentured themselves in preference to a debtor's prison term. Others had bound themselves as a means of paying for a passage to the Colonies.

Paine stood at the rail and looked to see if a familiar face had come to the wharf to wish him Godspeed. The captain joined him. He was a clean-shaven man with a ruddy face that made him seem younger than he was. His cold grey eyes marked him with a domination that his gentleman's manners did not mask.

"Thy fellow passengers are toastin' their fare-thee-wells in the *Crow's Nest.*" He pointed a thick finger in the direction of a waterfront tavern whose sign was embellished with faded blue anchors. "Wilst join me in the cabin till full tide?" As though Paine's answer was of no importance, he turned and marched to his quarters.

Paine would rather have stayed on deck. He had looked forward to the ship's leaving, the anchor being hoisted, and the hawsers being cast loose from the pilings. He had wanted to watch the maintop men raise the mainsails, the mizzentop men guide the mizzen sails, and the foretop men stand in readiness at the cleats. It was something he had wanted to experience ever since he had been fascinated by Reverend Knowles's stories of the sea.

He followed Captain Cooke into his cabin and was surprised at the furnishings. It was like a small sitting room in a

London house. The walls were paneled in rubbed walnut and the doors of the cabinets were decorated with beaded, stained glass. An open bookcase was recessed into a wall and yet seemed to stand upon the backs of two carved gargoyles.

Paine studied the books' titles while the captain fetched a decanter and glasses from a cabinet. To Paine's surprise, there was an English translation of Voltaire's *Candide,* a copy of Adam Smith's *Theory of Moral Sentiments,* John Locke's *Reasonableness of Christianity,* and a worn leatherbound Bible.

"The sea is the mother o' contemplation," said Captain Cooke as though, without turning around, he knew exactly what Paine was doing. He filled the glasses with red burgundy. "To an uneventful passage. 'Tis a pleasant time o' year."

Paine could not speak of the sea. He knew little of ships and oceans and charts and courses. He had studied astronomy, but the stars and the heavens had always seemed an arc that touched upon land in every direction. "Contemplation is not confined to the sea, Captain Cooke," he said. "We also contemplate upon land."

"A-a-ah!" cried Captain Cooke derisively. He seated himself heavily upon a massive chair. "Upon land one contemplates only people—scurryin' about like ants as though their births, their destinies, an' their deaths were important. But at sea, one begins to ruminate upon God. There is no beginning an' no end to the tides, the heavens, an' the winds. Man is like a bit o' spray that is gone at the first touch o' sun."

There was a knock on the door, it was pushed back a bit, and the boatswain thrust in his head. "Fog settlin' fast, sir. Rollin' in all about."

Captain Cooke rose from his chair with agility despite his large frame. Paine followed him out on deck. He was amazed how quickly a dense fog had .)ved in upon them. The wharf and the edges of the buildings were lost to sight. A deck hand hurried with a torch to light the ship's lanterns. In a few minutes, Paine heard the sound of footsteps on the gangplank, the creaking of boards, and a nearby voice call, "All 'board, Mr. Sanders!" The fog drifted like a thick grey smoke about the boat. He could hear the creaking of stays. There was a patter of feet, the rasp of pulleys, and suddenly the slap of a rising sail that had caught the wind. He looked upward, but the masts were lost in a grey mist. He could feel the ship being rocked by the wind. A foghorn sounded in the distance. Another answered close by. Unseen, at the bowsprit, the ship's own horn gave answer. Dead ahead Paine could now see the cabin lights and the stern lanterns of an anchored brig. The ship was underway. The fog had settled so thickly over the banks of the Thames that nothing could be seen. England was slipping fast away. He had not even waved farewell to his native land.

When they were three weeks out at sea, a "putrid" fever broke out among the indentured servants. Three died—two young women and a man. The captain ordered their bodies cast over the side of the vessel during the night.

One of the passengers, unable to sleep, had gone out on deck and witnessed the hasty burial. He was horrified by what he saw. He rushed back to the cabin and awakened the others. "I insist that we go to the captain's quarters and voice a protest. No prayer!" he cried. "Not a single word of God spoken! I tell you I watched them! They dragged those poor wretches out of the hold and tossed them into the sea like sacks of meal. I don't know how many there were. I saw three!"

Paine held on to the posters, against the rolling ship. Since there were only four in the cabin and it could accommodate twelve, they all occupied lower berths. They now sat with their legs hanging over the sides of their bunks. They had been roused from a sound sleep and at first did not quite realize the reason for their fellow passenger's anger.

[103]

Finally, Paine suggested, "Since we can do no good for those who are already gone and since, no doubt, there will be no one else cast into the sea this night, I suggest that we wait until morning to call on Captain Cooke. After a sound night's sleep he will be more amenable to Mr. Dandrich's protest. And to ours, gentlemen." Dandrich was not quite convinced, but the other passengers assented.

In the morning the passengers called upon Captain Cooke. He listened quietly to Dandrich's tale. "I have no alternative, gentlemen. Until I am assured that 'tis not the putrid fever, I want no one near the sick nor the dead."

"They are Christian people," protested Dandrich. "If they must be buried at sea, they should have at least a Christian prayer said for them."

"Can you pray, Mr. Dandrich?"

"I do not know the prayers by rote."

One of the passengers stepped to the bookcase and extended his hand toward the leatherbound Testament. But the captain sprang forward and spun him about. "Nothing leaves these quarters!" he cried. "An' I do not want ye comin' here! From now on, if there's any matter to be taken up, speak to Mr. Sanders."

Out on deck, the passengers looked at each other, defeated. "I am of the sect of Friends," offered Paine. "We are not given much to Bible praying, but I have an Anglican aunt who had me commit to memory many of the psalms. If it shall make us feel better, I shall conduct the services for the dead ... if others there be."

Four days later, six more of the indentured servants died, and the first mate sought out Paine. "Captain's orders, sir, but there is t' be no congregatin' 'bout the dead. 'Tis the putrid fever, sir. But y're t' go aft an' say 'em from the stern."

That night, Dandrich shook Paine awake. "Now!" he whispered. "They're bringing them out now!" Paine rubbed the sleep from his eyes and went up the hatchway. Outside, the moon had cast a yellow ribbon across the sea and splashed its gold upon every sail. The sky was netted with stars. Two sailors, trailing a length of noosed rope behind them, were hurrying to the forward hatch. They were naked but for a patch of white cloth about their faces. They lowered the end of the rope into the hatchway and, after a moment, hauled out a body. They did not touch it but dragged it across the deck, loosened the rope from under the armpits, and tossed it over the rail. Paine went to the ship's side and watched the body bob up and down in the dim yellow light. But it was not until he heard another splash and saw a second corpse that he realized his purpose in coming out. Rushing to the stern, he began to chant:

> The Lord is my shepherd; I shall not want.
> He maketh me to lie down in green pastures;
> He leadeth me beside the still waters. . . .

After the first three lines, the words cleaved to the roof of his mouth. They refused to be spoken. The psalm did not seem right. What kind of shepherd was the Lord . . . looking down on those bobbing bodies that were now drifting into the ship's moon-gilded wake? There was another splash, the patter of feet, and then another. . . . He was again in the belfry of the Anglican church, watching the Cluniac monks, their tonsured heads uncovered in the chill morning, their metal crucifixes swinging, their soft fingers telling their beads . . . and there were again the squeals and the flutter of wings in the steeple.

He was brought back to an awareness of the ship by the sound of splashing water. The two sailors were dipping buckets into the sea and splashing each other. Little cries would escape them as the cold water struck them. They stood on the deck, shivering and rubbing themselves with wet hands. In a moment, they were gone.

On every night that followed, the noosed rope lifted more

dead from the hold. Their names were not asked for. They were no longer checked on the manifest. The bodies were dragged across the deck and tossed into the cold sea.

At the end of the second week, members of the crew began to fall ill and, by the third week, a passenger was stricken. The mate quarantined the cabin and the captain no longer left his quarters. Halfway across the Atlantic, Paine himself fell sick. He lay in his bunk, racked with fever, and tormented by the thought of being tossed into the sea. He had left for the Colonies with such high hopes . . . such high hopes.

Not until the ship reached the mouth of the Delaware did Captain Cooke leave his quarters. By then the sickness seemed to have burned itself out. There had been no new victims for more than two weeks. Almost half the crew was gone. Of the 120 indentured servants, only five had escaped the disease and two of the passengers had died.

On November 30, 1774, nine weeks after leaving England, the *London Packet* docked in Philadelphia. The door of the passenger cabin was thrown open to a fresh wind and the mate and a sailor entered. Paine was too delirious to be questioned and the mate searched in the chest for the name of a friend or relation who could care for him. Besides a bundle of writings, there were many letters of recommendation. One was addressed to a Richard Bache. The name was vaguely familiar.

Captain Cooke, still loath to enter the passenger cabin, had the letter brought to him on the wind-swept deck. He read it in the clear sunlight:

September 10, 1774

The bearer, Mr. Thomas Paine, is an ingenious, worthy young man. He goes to Pennsylvania with the view of settling there. I request you give him your best advice and countenance, as he is quite a stranger there. If you can put him in the way of obtaining employment . . . till he can make acquaintance and obtain a knowledge of the country, you will do well, and much oblige your affectionate father. . . .

BENJAMIN FRANKLIN

8

PAINE DID NOT become aware of his surroundings until after Christmas. When he finally looked about, he realized that the room was a place in which he had never been before. He waited for the soft bed to roll with the movement of the ship, braced himself for the motion, but it did not come. The walls did not slant but stayed true as a plummet's line. Across the small room, a frugal fire burned in a brick fireplace. A clean white pitcher and bowl stood impressively upon a polished maple dresser. Beside them, still tied with a yellow ribbon, lay his bundle of essays. Sunlight filtered through a curtained window and beyond it he could hear voices, footsteps, the turning of wagon wheels, and the clop-clop of horses' hoofs.

There was a bold knock on the door and it was pushed quickly inward. He saw a short young woman, plump as a well-fed partridge. Beneath her voluminous skirts, one could only imagine the mincing steps that carried her forward. She had a cherub's bright round face and thick brown curls that hung down to the nape of her neck. She set a tray on the edge of the bed and smiled at Paine. "Well, now. Thou'rt sittin' up, finally. Twill give m' arm a rest. Breakin' as it does ta 'old up yer 'ead an' force the gruel into ya."

Was he back in England, wondered Paine. Had the ship turned about and gone back to London?

"An' now maybe we c'n send fer the barber," she chattered. She lifted a spindle-back chair and set it beside the bed. "Me cuttin' tha beard wi' a scissors all these weeks."

[107]

Paine raised a hesitant hand to his face. He was more startled by his sunken cheeks than by his growth of beard.

"Where am I?"

She lifted a bowl and spoon from the tray and permitted herself a mock curtsy. "The widow 'Iggins, sir. I takes in boarders. When they is well recommended, 'at is."

"But where?" cried Paine impatiently.

To his consternation, she thrust a spoonful of warm gruel into his mouth. "On Bread Street, sir. When Captain Cooke 'eard as tha 'ad letters from Dr. Franklin, 'e sent fer Dr. Kearsley. 'E recommended tha 'ere. Dr. John Kearsley, 'at is. A fine doctor. An' a gentleman." She thrust another spoonful of gruel into Paine's mouth as he was about to form a question. " 'E 'ad ya taken off the packet, sir. Carried all the way by two sailors. Nothin' but skin an' bones ya was. There's talk yer ship 'ad the plague."

Paine tried to raise himself higher on the bed. The effort made his head spin. He shut his eyes in pain. When he opened them, the widow Higgins was looking at him strangely. "M' late 'usband, Artemus, closed 'is eyes the same way when 'is 'ead 'urt. Only 'is eyes was brown . . . not like you'rn."

Paine shut his lips against the spoon and to his amazement the widow Higgins grasped his ear and tugged at it mightily. He opened his mouth and it was immediately filled with warm gruel. " 'At's fine," she said. "An' when ye finish tha'll take a nap. "Tha'll na' get up until Dr. Kearsley says so. 'Cept fer the pot. 'At's under the bed."

Two weeks went by before Paine was permitted outdoors. He spent a great deal of time looking out the frosted windows of Mrs. Higgins' two-story, red brick house. There was little to be seen on Bread Street. A few houses such as he was in and a few shops near the corners of the street. He could make out a bootmaker's and a gunsmith's. While still in bed, he had heard carriage wheels and heavy drays in the street. Now its narrow middle was piled high with snow and neither horse nor wagon could push through it.

January was half gone when he finally stepped forth to see the city. Mrs. Higgins called to him from the doorway: "If tha but recalls 'at Bread Street is ha'way 'tween Second an' Third, tha'll na' get lost!"

Paine turned east on Mulberry Street and walked toward the river. At Third Street he passed the St. George and the Dragon Inn. Swinging before the wind was a gilt-bordered sign with an expiring dragon painted on it. The creature dripped a trickle of blood where St. George's sword had pierced him. The colonials seemed to be fascinated by bright colors. All about him the storefronts and the hanging carved signs were bright with yellow, red, and blue pigments.

At Front Street, Paine was amazed to find a fire company. He looked through a frosted pane of glass and saw horses in their stalls and an open wagon. Its sides were hung with buckets. At the bank of the river, at Appletree Street, there was a ferry slip. He read the signboard: AUSTIN'S FERRY. Despite the afternoon sun, the wind was cold and piercing. Large cakes of ice bobbed up and down on the white-capped water of the Delaware. He walked south alongside the river. As he reached High Street, he saw a schooner. Its sails were furled and its hawsers were looped about the pilings of a dock. Heavy carts were on the wharf. The air was thick with the smell of linseed oil, tar, cording, and fresh canvas.

He turned up High Street and passed a fish market. Its stalls were deserted, closed against the bleak winter months. Ahead of him, he saw the tall steeple of a church. It would be Christ Church, of which Mrs. Higgins had spoken. As he walked toward it, past the homes and the shops, he began to evaluate the city of Philadelphia. It had not the provincial atmosphere that he had expected to find. The wide, straight streets were more impressive than the lanes of the English towns or the dirty courts and winding alleys of London.

He reached the church, stood before the red brick building,

and studied it. It was a far cry from the gothic grey stone churches of England. Its many white-framed windows were tall and arched. A wooden balustrade, ornamented with urns, enclosed the flat roof of its lower wings. At its back was a brick tower and rising from it a wooden belfry that ended in a sharp steeple.

He entered an impressive doorway and found himself in a structure filled with light. A high ceiling was supported by tall, fluted columns, and a painted white balcony ran along the rear. The pulpit was directly in front, and behind it Paine noticed the tall pipes of an organ. There was no one about and, through a side door, he found the steps that led to the steeple. To his amazement, they were made of stone; the risers were very high and the treads were very rough.

When he reached the belfry, he stood in awe at the impressive sight. The city, congested with shops, houses, and taverns, lay between two rivers—the broad Delaware, up which the boat had come, and the winding tree-lined Schuylkill. He looked toward the wharves and docks of the Delaware. Now he could see not only the schooner, anchored at High Street, but a brig and two packets. Westward, toward the Schuylkill, the small houses gave way to large ones with fenced-in lawns and shade trees. To the north, he seemed to discern large estates. He was not certain. The snow had drifted across the fields. He was tired. The climb to the belfry had indeed been arduous. He had walked enough for his first day out . . . and seen enough. He was glad that he had come to the Colonies.

Paine's walks grew longer each subsequent day and, as he learned the city, he was fascinated by it. The principal streets were lighted by well-spaced lamps, and were paved in the middle for carriages, with narrow brick sidewalks. Shade trees grew in front of the houses and, unlike England's uncovered wells, water pumps with long handles were spaced along the streets. The city had no slums, no destitution, and no gallows at every crossroad! This was a land he could love. His heart went out to it. It seemed to possess a freedom. Freedom! He loved the very ring of the word.

By the end of the week, when Paine climbed to the belfry of Christ Church, the city had become full of landmarks. Near the river, he recognized the tall, English-looking London Coffeehouse. In the center of town, the tower of the State-house. Closer by was the newly finished red brick Carpenters' Hall. He could see the Friends' Meeting House and to the south was the unmistakable Gloria Dei, the Swedes' Church, its spire rising needle sharp against the sky.

Only one thing bothered him. He had hoped to found a "much-needed" school in the city of Philadelphia. Like George Scott, he had thought the provincials to be poorly-educated, unreligious men who lived in a half-savage land. He had learned, instead, that the city had little need for a new school. Christ Church gave charity instruction to Anglicans, the Lutheran and German reformed churches jointly supported a primary school, the Moravians ran an elementary school on Sassafras Street, and even the so-called ignorant Baptists had founded a Latin grammar school. Nor were schools confined to the churches. There was a successful boarding school in Vidal's Alley, and a Quakers' nonsectarian Friends' School had long been in operation. It seemed that here, as in England, schoolmasters fell from every tree.

At the end of January, 1775, Paine presented himself and his treasured letter of introduction to Dr. Franklin's son-in-law. He had not given much thought to the status of Richard Bache, but a discreet inquiry had disclosed him to be at the head of an extensive importing and exporting business—a man of means and excellent reputation.

His wife, Franklin's daughter, Sarah Bache, at once insisted that Paine stay for dinner. They were starved for personal news of her father and their nephew in England. "We have

[111]

not seen little Will for nine years . . . or is it ten, Richard? We shall hardly know him when he's back."

On Richard Bache's recommendation, Paine was soon engaged by several gentlemen as a private tutor to their sons, and it did not take him long to set up a schedule that would allow him the greatest amount of free time. With an earned dollar once more in his pocket, he could now set out in search of such company as he enjoyed—the company of thinking men.

With his inquisitive bent, he soon learned that there were over 130 licensed taverns and coffeehouses to suit every purse and taste—from the sailors' groggeries along the Delaware wharves to Daniel Smith's City Tavern, which was furnished after the London mode, at great expense, and paid for by a voluntary subscription by the more affluent gentlemen of the city. The smaller coffeehouses served inexpensive yet savory dishes: a fried fish from the Delaware called a porgie, a chowder made from clams, a tasty pepper-pot soup, and oysters that he was told were carted from the Chesapeake Bay.

In the more expensive taverns, even the plain Friends ate like gourmands. They stuffed themselves with enormous portions of duck, chicken, beef, and pig. They tempted their appetites with tarts, creams, custards, jellies, and floating islands; and they were not adverse to tankards of beer, porter, punch, and wine.

Paine singled out a large inn as the most interesting spot in the city. It was a hotel with three stories and an attic on High and Fourth streets. Its wide front made it appear as though it had elbowed its way between two shops. Heavy shutters defended small sash windows and above a wide doorway hung an enormous painted wood sign: HOTEL—INDIAN QUEEN. Two large shrubs, potted in half-barrel tubs, were on a wood platform on each side of the entrance. Against a frame wall was a hand-hewn bench for the benefit of those who waited, on sunny days, for the stagecoach or for the opening of the offices of the *Pennsylvania Chronicle,* published but two doors away.

Sitting in the Indian Queen one evening, listening to the conversation about him, Paine noticed that the talk was growing heated, for everyone about him was speaking openly of a taxation and rebellion. As he sipped his brandy, two men approached his table. He recognized one of them instantly, Reverend John Muhlenberg, who had engaged him as a tutor for his two young sons and had invited him to dinner upon two succeeding Sundays.

Paine rose and shook Reverend Muhlenberg's hand. "Be seated," Muhlenberg smiled. "I have brought a friend to meet you. Mr. Paine, may I introduce Mr. Robert Aitken? He has a bookstore and print shop on High Street, near Second. Opposite the Jersey Market."

"I have passed it," said Paine.

"As who hasn't! His shop was the first in the Colonies to print the Bible in English . . . and to accept some of my comments. Eh, Robert? And this is Thomas Paine."

Paine saw a smallish man who seemed withdrawn by timidity. While Muhlenberg ordered brandy for his guests and a tankard of ale for himself, Robert Aitken stared at Paine. "Reverend Muhlenberg 'as told me aboot the essays ya 'ave permitted 'im ta read." His speech was heavy with a Scottish brogue. " 'E says ya were a frien' o' Oliv'r Goldsmi'."

Paine nodded.

"An' Sam'l Johnson, an' Bur-rke. Meanin' the Edmund Bur-rke, sir," Aitken continued.

Paine lifted an eyebrow at the exaggeration. Not knowing to what Robert Aitken was leading, he hastened to correct him, "I have only been introduced to Dr. Johnson and have spoken to Edmund Burke but twice."

Aitken hurried on as though Paine had not spoken. "I 'ave started a magazine, Mr. Paine," he explained. "I call it the *American Museum.* Ma wife thinks the name odd, noo, an' I think as I shall change it ta the *Pennsylvania Magazine.* Tis a fact, noo, as I am 'avin' trouble wi' the second number. I . . . I need a' editor. A good editor woul' brace the magazine, noo."

Paine looked at Muhlenberg and the big man pointed a stubby finger at him. "You," he whispered. "Mr. Aitken means you."

"Twill no' pay much," Aitken hurried to inform Paine. "Seein' as it 'as only six 'undred soobscribers, noo. But twill leave ya time fer other woork."

Paine sat as though he had been struck dumb. To be paid for expressing his thoughts and convictions—a thing he would gladly do for nothing! He realized that his mouth was open. He shut it, swallowed, and cried, "Mr. Aitken, you have an editor!" His eyes were bright. "Your *Pennsylvania Magazine* will be read in all the Colonies, Mr. Aitken," he promised. "And copies shall go to England . . . to France. . . ."

Robert Aitken wondered if he had not been too hasty in accepting Muhlenberg's recommendation. The minister tapped him on the shoulder and leaned toward him. "You think he is *verrückt,* eh?" he whispered. "I say no! I have read his essays. He is touched with genius, Robert. Let him edit your magazine and in a few short months he will make it famous. Mark my words, Robert . . . famous!"

9

THE NEXT weeks were cheerful ones for Paine. Devoted now to furthering the fortunes of the *Pennsylvania Magazine,* he made the rounds of the coffeehouses, the inns, and the taverns in search of local news. He himself wrote at least one piece for each issue and, so that its readers would think the magazine had many contributors, signed his articles and essays with pseudonyms such as *Vox Populi, Aesop,* and *Atlanticus.*

In them, however, he did not discuss politics nor give any hint that he was for or against the growing escalation of rebellion and near-treason now spreading from Boston to South Carolina and splitting conservative Philadelphia in half. The magazine itself was purely of a literary cast and he himself felt hampered by his lack of knowledge of what was going on outside Pennsylvania, or what had happened immediately before his arrival.

When he had sailed on Captain Cooke's ship, news from Virginia had not yet reached London of Patrick Henry's and George Washington's defiance of the British Ministry in closing the port of Boston. He was on the seas when in September the First Continental Congress had assembled in Philadelphia and, at the insistence of John Dickinson, had sent a series of petitions to the King before putting into effect an embargo on all British goods. Nevertheless, with his unerring eye for the underdog, one thing had already become plain to him: what kind of Englishmen were these colonists who could prate passionately of freedom and liberty yet fail to recognize the mote in their own eye?

Join the fight to break the chains of slavery? Lead 1,000 men to rescue the beleagered Bostonians?

Yes! But what of the slavery of nearly 500,000 Negroes, brought from Africa by New England slavers to be sold to Southern plantation owners to hoe their fields of tobacco or cotton?

The spectacle aroused in him the same feelings he had experienced at the sight of the village idiot in the stocks, the workhouse inmates at work in the fields, the poor of London crowding around Craigstone's coach. In an instant he knew he had stumbled upon the Colonies' Achilles' heel and decided to write an essay exposing it, quite unaware that there was

[115]

already in Philadelphia a small group deeply interested in forming an antislavery society in the city.

All through February he labored on "African Slavery in America" by "Justice and Humanity" only to find, upon completion, that writing a polemic was one thing but getting it published in Philadelphia was another. Rejected by Aitken out of hand as "too controversial" for the *Pennsylvania Magazine,* the manuscript lay lifeless in his room until it occurred to him to seek advice from a certain Dr. Benjamin Rush, whom he had met casually in a bookshop and had found already deeply interested in the subject. Rush's advice was to submit the essay to Aitken's rival, William Bradford, the publisher of the *Pennsylvania Journal and Weekly Advertiser,* using his name as an introduction. Thus armed, Paine called upon Bradford and, as Rush had predicted, found an ally at once.

On March 8, 1775, the essay appeared as a postscript in the journal and caused a sensation. Full of curiosity to see how it was being received, Paine himself walked down Front Street at noon and stopped to look through a window of Widow Robert's Coffeehouse. Here and there, inside, men seated at tables already had a copy of the journal. They were neglecting their food in order to read the postscript.

Across an open field that sloped toward the river, Paine could see the London Coffeehouse, so he turned his steps in that direction to see what the essay's reception might be there. Once inside, he ordered a bowl of clam chowder and looked about him. There was a *Pennsylvania Journal and Weekly Advertiser* in almost everyone's hand. Near the bar, one man was reading aloud from it to a group about a table. He watched the listening faces. They seemed intent. More than one was flushed by anger. In a further part of the large room, someone struck a table and crashed a glass against the floor. A belligerent voice cried: " 'N I sees Will Bradford, I asks 'im to 'is face, 'oo is this black-lovin' evangelist what signs 'is name Justice an' 'Umanity? Justice! Bradford's gettin' soft in the 'ead!''

Paine stared at him and wondered how far the arc of the protest would carry. He took his own copy of the journal, turned to the postscript, and read the essay once more. What he had written in England had been a mild protest against the slave trade. Here, he had expressed an insistence upon its abolition. Let the townspeople read it, he thought. Let them argue it pro and con. Let the circles of their talk widen like the ripples made by dropped pebbles in a pool. "I have written only what I sincerely believe and I will defend it!" he assured himself.

Ten days later, he met with the group of men already interested in forming an antislavery society. He had no sooner entered the doors of the Indian Queen than he was embraced by Dr. Rush who had been keeping watch for him. He led Paine to two tables that had been pushed together and introduced him to a seated group: "The Reverend Jonathan Boucher; Mr. Bradford, with whom you are already acquainted"—Dr. Rush gave Paine a wink—"Mr. David Rittenhouse; Mr. Oliver Gerry, a relative of Mr. Rittenhouse; Mr. James Wilson; and of course your friend and patron, Reverend Muhlenberg."

Dr. Rush turned to a young man who had risen from his chair and stood as though at attention. He seemed in his early twenties. He was short and slender, with unsmiling lips above a narrow chin and dark restless eyes that filled his face with melancholy. Dr. Rush introduced him as Monsieur Brissot and then, as though risking an inaccuracy, he enlarged upon the introduction: "Jacques Pierre Brissot de Warville. He is here on a visit from France. He is much impressed by your essay and has asked to meet you." Brissot thrust an arm behind his back and offered Paine a courtly bow.

"And this, gentlemen, if I may present him now, is Thomas Paine, the author of 'African Slavery in America.' "

The men who hitherto had not met Paine had possibly pictured him as a well-dressed, aristocratic intellectual. They

[117]

saw, instead, a bright-eyed slender man, dressed in Quaker snuff-colored homespun, with a powdered bobtail wig that was much the worse for wear.

"I am a publisher, gentlemen," said Bradford, "as you well know. And though a competitor presently engages his services, may I offer a toast to Mr. Paine for his article on slavery. People are discussing the essay in every home and public place. I am glad to have had the courage to print it. You would not sign your name, Tom Paine, but I drink to you nonetheless."

Paine smiled and nodded his head to the men who lifted their glasses. All of them were well attired and gave every indication of living quiet, comfortable lives. "If I left the essay unsigned, gentlemen, it was not for lack of courage to defend it, but because my name, unknown as yet, could have added nothing to it. Could I have signed it Dr. Franklin, or yours, Reverend Muhlenberg . . ."

"My friend is a firebrand," said Muhlenberg. "I have discussed many things with him at my home. He will debate the shape of a wax candle, the number of spokes on a wheel, or the most direct road to God."

The man who had been introduced as James Wilson cleared his throat. So as not to be misunderstood, he prefaced, "I am here because, like you gentlemen, I think slavery and the traffic in it an evil. But slaves are private property, Mr. Paine. Have you ever known men to voluntarily relinquish private property?"

Anger touched Paine's eyes. He noticed that there was a little roll of fat above the bunch of lace at Wilson's throat. His eyesight evidently poor, he wore a pair of unbecoming spectacles whose ends he thrust into his powdered wig instead of about hs ears. He seemed a reserved, unfriendly man.

"A thief steals my horse and sells him to you, Mr. Wilson. Would you protest my claim to have him back?" Paine raised a detaining hand as Wilson was about to answer. "I know . . .

you will defend that you paid for him in good faith. But there is no good faith if you bought him with the knowledge that he was stolen. And if there are rights to a stolen horse, then what about a stolen man? Reverend Muhlenberg, does not a black man have a right to his freedom? And you, Reverend Boucher, does not a dark-skinned man have a soul, a right to salvation, and a right to live without chains?"

A flush crept into Wilson's stout cheeks. Speaking in a brogue that he had not yet fully mastered, he answered, "I am a lawyer, Mr. Paine. And I do not need you to teach me the points of law. Did I condone slavery, I would not be here. But my profession insists that I see both sides of the coin. I was born and raised in Scotland and I know the English. England will never give up her slave trade. Rather than relinquish a profit she will have thirteen Governor Tryons and as many Earl Percys. England may twist the law to her own purpose, but, on the statute books, it is still the law."

Suddenly Oliver Gerry, the young man who had been introduced as Rittenhouse's relative, sprang to his feet and smashed his fist on the table. "I say no!" he cried. "England shall not have her way. Fashioning laws for a people 3,000 miles away! I am a Bostonian, gentlemen. I am here with my family, as a guest of my cousin, David. My warehouse in Boston Harbor has been ransacked and burned. And if any think that we shall submit to English profit, then they do not know Sam Adams or John Hancock, or 100 others in Boston. And do you gentlemen think me the only man who has left Boston to find sustenance for his family? I say damn the English laws!"

Rittenhouse rose and calmed his cousin. Young Brissot was leaning forward, his dark eyes ablaze with interest. "Gentlemen, gentlemen," Bradford placated. "We are gathered only to toast Mr. Paine's essay on slavery." He looked at Wilson and added, "And to discuss it calmly. The question of slavery and politics are not allied."

"But they are," said Paine quickly. "They are. And if I may quote John Donne, 'No man is an island, entire of itself; every man is a piece of the continent, a part of the maine.' "

Brissot spoke, his English words sounding nasal and apologetic in the hubbub of the Indian Queen's large room. "Messieurs . . . messieurs. . . . *C'est vrai.* It is true! The whole is the sum of its parts. An' France . . . no, messieurs, all of Europe watches to see what the parts will do."

As though considering Brissot's words, they sat about the table, for a moment, with their drinks untouched. Paine said, "I have an appendage to my essay on slavery. Would you gentlemen care to hear it?"

There were nods of assent and Paine took a sheaf of papers from his pocket. They expected him to read from them but, as though he had committed to memory each phrase and every word, he recited in a clear unhesitating voice, glancing from one to the other:

> When I reflect on the horrid cruelties exercised by Britain in the East Indies, . . . When I read of wretched natives being blown away (blown away, gentlemen, by being tied to the mouths of cannon), . . .
>
> When I reflect on these and 1,000 instances of similar barbarity, I firmly believe that the Almighty, in compassion to mankind, will curtail the power of Britain. . . .
>
> Ever since the discovery of America she hath yearly (without provocation and in cold blood) ravaged the helpless shores of Africa, robbing it of its inhabitants to cultivate her stolen dominions in the West. . . .
>
> When I reflect on these, I hesitate not for a moment to believe that the Almighty will finally separate America from Britain. Call it independence or what you will, if it is the cause of God and humanity, it will go on.
>
> And when the Almighty shall have blest us, and made us a free people, may our first gratitude be shown by an act which shall put a stop to the importation of negroes for sale, soften the hard fate of those already here, and in time procure their freedom!

There was a long moment of silence when Paine finished. Bradford broke it by stating quietly, "Your appendage is tainted with sedition. No publisher in the Colonies will print it. Not even I."

Muhlenberg looked about. "Gentlemen," he said quietly. "Perhaps there is a point to what Mr. Paine would hope for. His words may be seditious . . . but why could they not be the seeds of our own freedom? Could we not separate ourselves from England?"

"You are not English!" cried Wilson. "You are German! Having severed your ties with your own country, it would mean little to sever them with ours."

"Gentlemen. . . . Please!" cried Paine.

"And Hancock and Adams!" stormed Muhlenberg. "Are they not English?"

Reverend Boucher raised both his hands and, in deference to his calling, they hushed their voices. Jonathan Boucher was not an abolitionist but had come at Muhlenberg's persuasion. He looked from one to the other. "I spoke to Washington in May," he said. "He said to me: 'All we ask is justice from Britain and a fair share in the Parliament that makes our laws.' Gentlemen, I, too, am loyal to the Crown!"

"And so, too, is Dr. Franklin," said Rittenhouse, looking away from his cousin. "I received a letter from him but a month ago."

"I am acquainted with Dr. Franklin," said Paine. "I have the greatest respect and admiration for him. But you do not know England, gentlemen. England, with her nobility and her corrupt wealth! To her we are a colony—a possession—such as the West Indies or India. You deceive yourselves because you speak the same tongue. You dream of representation. But to England colonization means but one thing—exploitation! I have observed that we have an opportunity for freedom, for equality, and for self-government . . . government in which all will have a voice. But it will not be offered, gentlemen. It must be insisted upon!"

They sat, silent, as though his impassioned words had cast a spell upon them. They had met to speak of slavery and Paine spoke, instead, of their own freedom. The quiet was broken by Wilson's derisive laughter. "Government in which all will have a voice? The common man? Come now, Mr. Paine. Dost not know that if the common man can but sign his name and count to ten, he considers himself literate?"

"But he has common sense! A common sense that makes him aware of his natural rights. A common sense that insists upon his dignity and stirs his heart against oppression!"

There was a ripple of laughter about the table and Paine's face grew flushed. It seemed that he had taken Wilson's remark too seriously. To their surprise he rose and lifted his glass in a toast. "To you Mr. Gerry and to whatever friends you may have in Boston Harbor, I dedicate my pen. My common pen! I have heard of your Sam Adams and your John Hancock. If you would see me at any time, I shall be at Robert Aitken's, when I'm not here." He turned to David Rittenhouse and informed him, "Your news of Dr. Franklin is no longer fresh. I assure you, he is no longer in England. Within a few weeks, with fair weather and God's grace, he should be here. And it would give me great pleasure to see your orrery. I have the greatest interest in such things."

"It is now on exhibit at Nassau Hall, at the College of New Jersey. It would be my pleasure to accompany you at some time."

Paine turned to the French visitor. "Mr. Brissot, I hope that upon some other occasion we will be able to speak only of slavery. Dr. Rush," he apologized, "I did not mean to be bad company." He bowed good-night to each of them, a courtly gesture that was not quite in tune with his rather shabby wig and his plain, snuff-colored coat. Astonishment showed upon all their faces as the guest of honor abruptly left them.

He was still agitated as he approached his lodgings, but even so he was surprised to see a light in the lower window.

Curious, he thrust open the door, but the mischievous wind immediately blew out the candle. There was just enough glow from the fireplace to discern the room's furnishings and suddenly he noticed the widow Higgins, asleep in the rocker, like a child. The laces of her bonnet were undone and trailed past her plump cheeks. Her clasped hands were nestled within the folds of her aproned lap and the rocker, tilted backward, held her shoes inches above the wood floor.

He did not know whether or not to awaken her. She had never waited up for him before. He took a taper from the mantelpiece and relighted the candles. Suddenly he noticed that the musket and horn were gone. Mrs. Higgins had kept her late husband's musket and powder horn above the fireplace. Paine had never seen them moved and now they were gone. The wooden pegs upon which the musket's polished stock and its barrel had rested were still there. So was the peg from which the powder horn had hung.

The rocker creaked and Mrs. Higgins said calmly, "I 'ad ta take 'em down, Tom Paine. 'E will not permit the display o' firearms in 'is 'ouse. 'E is a Quaker, like thaself."

"Who?"

She hesitated for a moment and said, "William Tucker. Dost know 'im?"

Paine shook his head and she chided him: "Sure an' 'ow canst tha. Wi' tha traipsin' off as soon as thou'rt in tha breeches, an' not comin' back till late night."

Paine realized that the lighted taper was still in his hand. "A spot of tea?" he asked. Now he was bribing her. He felt that she was angered by something and he wished to cajole her. Whenever he was home early, or on the Sabbath, she offered him tea and her company. He was usually too busy to accept either, and now, for the first time, he asked her, "A spot of tea?"

"Tea! Dost tha not e'en pay attention ta what I'm tryin' ta tell tha? Will Tucker an' I are gettin' married. Dost think a

[123]

woman c'n live by 'erself like a . . . like a Cath-o-lic nun! Dost
think me ninety years old, Tom Paine?"

He had never given any thoughts to her age. Or even to her.
He had taken her for granted. He had accepted his clean bed,
his warm room, and a breakfast without giving them a second
thought. He had paid for his weekly lodging by counting out
the coins and leaving them upon the kitchen table.

"Married?"

"Aye," she said, taking a deep breath. She lifted her hands
from her lap and folded her arms under a bosom that was
more than ample for so short a woman. "An' tha canst not 'ave
tha room 'more. I 'ave looked about an' found new lodging
for tha on Second Street, near Elfreth's Alley. If thou'lt 'ave
it. I'll not 'ave tha think as I've turned tha out in the street."

He did not know whether to congratulate her or not; she
did not look especially happy.

"Well, dina' stan' there!" she ordered. "I'll na' 'ave tha say
as I kept tha from tha scribblin'!"

Before he reached the stairs she cried, "An' will tha not
e'en wish me luck! An' I as wot nursed tha back ta 'ealth.
Shame on tha, Tom Paine!"

He turned back and noticed, in consternation, that she was
weeping. He knelt beside the rocker and folded an arm about
her to comfort her. Gently, he brushed an accusing tear from
each eyelid. In the candlelight, her eyes seemed dark and
widely round, like a child's. She took off his beaver hat, his
wig with a dust of powder on it, and ran her fingers through
his hair. "Wouldst kiss me, Tom? Fer luck?"

He did not know how to refuse. Her lips were as soft and
moist as a willow bud in a spring rain. It had been a long time
since he had kissed a woman. Suddenly she sprang from the
rocker and turned her back to him.

"Tis done. Now go! Dost think tis the widow 'Iggins tha
kneels beside? The banns 'ave been made an' tis Mrs. Will
Tucker tha hast kissed!"

He could understand politics, philosophy, astronomy, mathematics. But women . . . He picked up his wig and his hat and climbed the stairs.

10

PAINE'S NEW lodging on Second Street was a single room above a cordwainer's shop and was reached by a narrow flight of stairs. Grudgingly, he admitted to himself that he would miss Mrs. Higgins. She had attended to all his needs. Now he must make his own bed, tidy the room, ask after a washer-woman for his linens, and do a dozen chores that he had accepted from Mrs. Higgins without giving her a thought.

Not far from his new lodging, however, Paine found a tavern that served meals quite inexpensively. It was on a bank of Dock Creek and had a strange name "A Man Full of Trouble," yet supplied him with brandy and a table where he could sit and think.

Editing the *Pennsylvania Magazine,* he realized, would still take much of his time, but his new interest in politics now called for satisfaction at once. What James Wilson had said about the common man had irked him. Was he, Tom Paine, not a common man? Did he not believe in the dignity of all men and their equality before God? Here, in this new land, the common man had at last an opportunity for freedom and self-government. And if not now . . . when? He would appeal to the common man. He would write a pamphlet for the masses. Yes, in the teeth of criticism by pessimistic Wilsons and royalist Bouchers he would call his pamphlet *Common Sense!* The name was good. He savored the sound of it. But he must not be adroit. He must come to the point without mincing words.

His mind began to form a tentative outline for his *Common Sense.* Thoughts and phrases were stored for future use:

Each man should reap the fruits of his own abilities and the harvest of his own labor!

There should be no privileged orders . . . enjoying the pleasures of life because of inherited office or land.

A man should not be told that he has been fashioned in the image of God and yet abused and discriminated against and spat upon because of his "unaccepted" heritage!

It is true, thought Paine. The common man fights a nation's wars, tills its land, labors in its workshops, offers up his tithes, pays the taxes, and, when he is old and useless, he is permitted to die . . . neglected, unwanted, and disgraced. I shall write of that common man, thought Paine. I shall write of him in my *Common Sense.* I shall not be as subtle as Voltaire nor as political as Wilkes, but as common as earth and man! The pamphlet will advocate separation from Britain and present arguments for independence! They may take me back to England and hang me in Thetford, upon the very gallows that I passed each day as a boy, . . . but not before I have had my say!

At the end of April, while Paine worked nights accumulating facts for his pamphlet, news of what had happened at Lexington and Concord began to drift into the quiet decorum of Philadelphia. Soon the coffeehouses, the hotels, and the taverns were filled with speculation and debate, with gesticulating arms and raised voices. Though Aitken would permit no political sentiment to be expressed in his magazine, he could not forbid its editor from making the rounds of public places and listening to the conflicting talk.

As a result, Paine began to frequent the Royal Standard Inn

on Market Street. Their prices were higher than he could afford and their sentiment was loyalty to the Crown, but it was frequented by influential men and he felt that he should sup there upon occasion. It was here that he had already met wealthy George Clymer and Thomas Mifflin. And it was here that he now became acquainted with men he had never heard of: Nathaniel Greene, of Rhode Island; his aide, Colonel Kirkbride; and Daniel Roberdeau, of the Pennsylvania Militia. Greene, who took to him immediately, perhaps because of their common Quaker faith, appeared to be a brigadier general of the Rhode Island Militia. Roberdeau, whom some still called "that educated West Indian," since he was not an Englishman, had long since become a prosperous merchant in Philadelphia.

Paine glanced about as he entered the inn one particular evening and noticed Robert Morris, Rittenhouse, Clymer, and Mifflin seated together and engaged in earnest conversation. Rittenhouse made room for him as Paine approached, but the others were so heatedly engaged in their talk that they merely took time to nod their heads.

"Tis no secret," Clymer insisted as Paine seated himself. "The British plan was as simple as a child's primer. They first marched from Boston to Lexington and then to Concord simply to destroy the military stores."

"Adams and Hancock were fools to stop them," protested Morris. "Government is no different than business, and in business the weaker makes what compromise he can with the stronger."

Paine studied Robert Morris as Rittenhouse called for another glass. He was a tall man given to stoutness. Aloud he said, "Compromise, Mr. Morris, yes. But complete capitulation! I assure you, gentlemen, England knows not the meaning of the word compromise."

"Our friend is a humorist," said Morris, "and yet he speaks with an authoritative voice on politics."

Paine knew that Morris was referring to a fable, titled "Cupid and Hymen," that he had published that week in the *Pennsylvania Magazine.*

"Forgive me. I have not yet read the piece," said Clymer.

"You know not what you missed. Believe me, I have the greatest respect for Mr. Paine's humor and wit."

When Paine had appeared in the Royal Standard Inn before, he had been toasted amidst a center of good friends. But now . . . now he could sense an undercurrent of antipathy. Was it only Morris and his wealth? Was it Mifflin, too? It was said that he was tainted by ambition. It could not be George Clymer . . . he liked the man . . . but he was Morris' good friend.

Paine looked about. Had he been shrewdly led away from the talk of politics? Well, he would bring it back. He was not working on *Common Sense* for naught. "Gentlemen, gentlemen," he urged. "Let us get back to the talk of Lexington and compromise. Shall we take the business of hats, gentlemen? Beaver hats are as popular in Europe as they are here. Hatmaking was once an American industry. Instead of raw furs, the Colonials sent hats to England. But this aroused a protest from English hatters. They appealed to Parliament and that august body forbade the Colonials to make hats in the future . . . but not without a compromise, gentlemen. They permit us to make hats for our own use, at home. Can one call the strangling of a growing industry a compromise?"

"We still sell them the pelts," said Morris.

"And so do the Dutch and the French! You came here almost thirty years ago, Mr. Morris. Are you still English? Do you have so little regard for the Colonies where you made your fortune?"

Morris rose from his chair as quickly as his ponderous frame would permit him. Clymer and Mifflin stared angrily at Paine.

"Forgive me," said Paine. "I meant no personal affront. I

spoke in generalities." He turned his eyes from Morris' flushed face. "You, Mr. Rittenhouse, will bear me out that the owners of smelting furnaces are required to send the raw iron to England. There it is worked up and sent back to us in a finished form. Can anyone deny that a growing metalworking industry has been destroyed? Are we so lacking in courage that we cannot insist on what is right? If we are English, we should be permitted to live and work as Englishmen. If we are not, then we have a right to our own destiny!"

They sat in silence. They did not protest, but Paine could see that they did not agree. Was it the public place that made them mute? "Shall I tell you more, gentlemen?" he asked. "Shall I, a newcomer from England, tell you more of what you must already know? I came to the Colonies thinking it a land of freedom and opportunity and I find, instead, that it is no more than King George's personal cash box. We supply England with a wealth of raw materials and we give her profits by buying her finished products. What we buy from France or Italy or Spain, we must not buy directly, but through an English merchant, paying him his usurious profit! There is no free market for us, gentlemen. And we cannot protest—for King George has said that, let the consequences be what they may, it is his unalterable determination to compel us to absolute obedience! And if I may cite an instance, it is almost a year since General Cage has sealed Boston's harbor from the rest of the world. I do not know how many of his Britannic Majesty's men-of-war are anchored near the wharves of King Street, but it does not seem that they could be there for the single purpose of compromise."

"Boston's Port Act can be repealed!" cried Morris. "A payment of £15,000, for the tea that was wantonly destroyed, would lift it."

"Ransom?"

"Reimbursement for the waste of private property."

"And I say it is ransom for a town! What say you, Mr.

Rittenhouse? Has not your cousin told you of ships tied at the docks for a year; of warehouses burned and businessmen ruined; of idled sailors, clerks, and artisans walking the streets; of famine in their homes?"

"And I say that a compromise would restore Boston's prosperity," insisted Morris.

"But not its freedom, gentlemen. Not its freedom! I understand the Carolinas have sent rice and considerable sums of money to Boston. BUT NOT TO PAY FOR THE TEA! Delaware has sent money and promised more. All the Colonies have sent contributions of food . . . even our neighbors in Canada."

Rittenhouse nodded. "Oliver advised me that at the time he left Boston, Quebec sent more than 1,000 bushels of wheat."

"But not for ransom, eh, David? I know England well, gentlemen, and I promise you that there would be no end to other acts were she to lift the Port Act. Did you not have a Sugar Act! Followed by a Stamp Act? The needs of England's profligate and idle nobility are boundless."

Morris looked about the table and his glance came back to Paine. He was angered by the turn of the conversation and had not touched his glass. This newcomer might be a wit, but he was also an irritant. "There are taxes wherever there is government," he said quietly. "And he who wishes to avoid them may always live in the woods."

Paine smiled. "Mr. Morris is mistaken," he said. "To a man who seeks freedom, even the woods are lost. A proclamation of the British Government has forbidden any settlement west of the Alleghenies."

Morris pushed back his chair. "Excuse me, gentlemen. I go to New York in the morning and have an early stage to board. And John Butler's irascible coachman waits for no one."

No one protested Morris' leaving. It was an opening wedge for their own good-nights. They left, one by one, and Paine remained and finished his brandy. Talk drifted to him from nearby tables, but it was lost upon his ears as he stared into his glass. Apparently there were separationist gatherings in all the other colonies, but not here, in complacent Philadelphia. To listen to voices that spoke as he thought, he would have to go north to Massachusetts or south to Patrick Henry's Virginia. Here, in the city that Dr. Franklin had recommended to him, there were only deaf ears, fat paunches, and timid Friends who hid their profits and their sentiments beneath the dignity of their religion.

This land to which he had come was beautiful . . . its opportunities could be boundless . . . but England's domination had begun to stifle its trade, destroy its industry, and curtail the freedom and ambitions of its men. In one more generation, three at the most, the American Colonies would be but another exploited satellite of England. Its countrysides would be blackened by workhouses, its towns filled with ragged beggars, and the Anglican Church its religion of state. For this, he could have stayed in England!

It was no early coach that had urged Morris from the table. Nor the late hour that had hastened the departure of Rittenhouse, Clymer, and Mifflin. It was their loyalty to the British King or their misgivings of a separation from England that shut their ears to his talk. When they spoke of Concord, they spoke of it as though it were in some other country. When they mentioned Lexington, it was as though what happened there were the actions of rebellious children against an irate parent. Did self-government mean so little to them?

During the first days of May, 1775, delegates to the Second Continental Congress began to drift into Philadelphia, and Paine watched the hubbub that their arrival created. Bells were rung while excited men, women, and children assembled in doorways and watched from windows and stoops. So many spilled out into the streets that the horses could barely press through.

It was an exciting two weeks. The coffeehouses, the taverns, and the hotels did a thriving business. Delegates visited each other in their lodgings and met in inns, where they renewed old friendships with the drinking of toasts, the tasting of dried smoked sprats, and the exchange of news.

Paine, a nonparticipating bystander, rushed from meeting place to meeting place to get a view of the delegates. At the Cross Keys, those who had been invited to Dickinson's mansion praised his food and his burgundy. At the Royal Standard Inn, those who had dined at Mifflin's Fort Hill, just above the Schuylkill Falls, toasted the elegance of his home. At the Indian Queen, those who had enjoyed the hospitality of Joseph Galloway did not hesitate to comment upon their host's austere and haughty attitude. The names and the faces of delegates were strange to Paine; he wondered when he would get to know them.

Fortunately, on May 5, Franklin returned to Philadelphia and immediately took Paine under his wing. Appointed a delegate to the Second Continental Congress and welcomed back as a member of the Pennsylvania Assembly, he did not attend the coffeehouses very frequently but, as an exception, he took Paine to the City Tavern, where the most influential delegates met.

Here, in a large raftered and wainscoted room, with an immense stone fireplace, leaded windows, and gilt-framed paintings of the hunt, Paine felt as though he were in the drawingroom of an English mansion. Franklin introduced him to all who were present. Many had read a few of Paine's essays, and the fact that Franklin sponsored him made him more acceptable to their company. Of them all, Colonel Washington impressed him most. Powerfully made, elegantly dressed, almost majestic in his attitude, he seemed to stand out from the rest even though the Virginia delegates seated around his table included Peyton Randolph, Benjamin Harrison, the three Lees—Henry, Francis Lightfoot, and Richard Henry—and, last but not least, tall unassuming Thomas Jefferson. His reddish hair was like a woman's, Paine noted, with bangs in front and the sides combed down over his ears. But his grey eyes and his resolute chin made him seem a man who would not be easily swayed by someone else's counsel.

Standing before the table, slightly aloof, yet listening, was Patrick Henry. Tall, lean, and handsome—as though a sculptor had chiseled the Grecian features of his face with delicate care—one could not avoid the blue eyes beneath the straight dark brows. He was dressed in a plain suit of parson's grey. His brown wig was unpowdered and carelessly arranged. He was like a poor country cousin of the aristocratic Virginians and, when Franklin introduced him, he said in a slow drawl that was new to Paine: "Mah plaisure, suh. Ah have raid yo writin's. Yo comments on the natural resources of ouah yearth are most intrestin' . . . most intrestin'." So two nights later, at the Indian Queen, Paine was delighted to have Samuel Adams himself approach his table and sit down. Many of the delegates had found the informality of the Indian Queen more comfortable. When Samuel Adams noticed Paine staring at John Hancock at the other end of the room, he asked, "Hast not met our wily friend, John?"

"Not yet."

"Then do not stare like Dick Whittington's cat at the king. He is no different than I. Except that my father left me a broken-down brewery and his a substantial fortune. But I will say this for him—he will not relinquish a finger though you insist upon a full hand. A few years ago, when the customs officials seized his sloop, *Liberty,* for unloading a cargo of Madeira without paying the import duties, he fought tooth and nail for his rights. His defense, in the law suits that followed, was a delight. Come, I shall introduce you. Take my word for it, twill not be long before the British tag a price upon his head."

"And yours."

"Aye and mine. They would have had our heads in Lexington, were it not for Paul Revere."

They wound their way between tables and stopped where Hancock was in heated conversation with John Dickinson, again a Pennsylvania delgate. Paine was suddenly disappointed. He saw a slender man, neither dashing nor handsome in appearance. He created an impression that he had inherited his wealth rather than earned it, which, though true in part, belied his abilities, his courage, and his determination. If not aristocratic in bearing, he yet reflected an aura of affluence, with embroidered overcoat, gold buttons, brocade waistcoat, and well cared-for wig. His face, though not strong, was placid. Paine was soon to change his first impression and learn that there was a deep, self-made stream within him whose course refused to be altered.

When Sam Adams introduced him, Hancock glanced quickly at Paine and then back again at Adams. "I've heard of him," he said. "An abolitionist. Bring me no more Quaker Tories, friend Sam. My craw is already filled with Dickinson, here. He wants to draft yet one more petition to the King. An 'Olive Branch' petition! Well, you have my word for it. King George will eat the olive and spit the pit back into our face!"

"Mr. Paine is a separationist," explained Adams.

Hancock turned an examining eye upon Paine.

"He's an agitator for personal reasons," said Dickinson. "An Englishman, but lately come to the Colonies. I've heard him insist that we are at war. That we refuse to accept the fact, but that we are at war."

Paine glanced at Dickinson. He seemed a docile man, with a thin, rather long nose set in the full oval of a woman's face. Yet one could not deny that he was handsome. Paine heard Hancock ask, "And what say you, John? That we are not at war?"

"I say that Mr. Paine is a fool and a rebel. What happened

at Lexington was a rebellion against the quartering of British troops, against the closing of Boston's port, against excessive taxation—a rebellion against acts of Parliament but not against the King!"

Hancock's shrewd brown eyes turned once again to Paine. "And you, Mr. Paine," he questioned, one small hand straightening the folds of lace that hung from beneath a braided cuff.

"I am not a delegate to Congress, Mr. Hancock," Paine parried. "But you are. And you were at Lexington. What say you?"

"I say that there are some who are not delegates, like New York's Gouverneur Morris and Franklin's bastard son, William, who influence Congress as much as, or perhaps more than, we who were elected."

"Do not feel offended on Franklin's behalf," soothed Sam Adams. "I assure you that the illegitimacy of his son is as well known as his Tory sentiments."

As Paine was about to speak, Hancock suddenly cried, "Hold, Sam, hold! Here comes your elegant kinsman. Call to him. I would speak with him."

To Paine's surprise, Sam Adams whispered to him, shielding his lips with his hand, "You've not met cousin John. Three hundred miles from home and he needs write his wife, Abigail, his every thought. And hangs on her reply before his every act. Like a schoolboy, not yet fled his mother's apron strings."

Paine watched as John Adams approached them. He was a little stout, but aristocratic in his bearing. A finely chiseled nose was set with dignity on a full face to which his thin lips gave a touch of uncompromising harshness. His wig was elegantly curled at the sides, powdered grey, and tied in the back with a wide silk ribbon. Despite the warmth of the night, he was dressed in tight-fitting black velvet breeches and overcoat.

[135]

"We are speaking of Lexington," explained Sam as John Adams reached the table.

"Our Englishman, Mr. Paine, asks if we are not already at war," said Hancock. "Would you not say, John, that it depended upon a technicality . . . as to who fired the first shot? It is what we have been debating in Congress."

John Adams' brown eyes gave Hancock a reproachful look. "Debates in Congress, as you well know, Mr. Hancock, are not to be the subject of table talk."

Hancock resented the reprimand. "We have reached no conclusion as to who fired the first shot," he insisted.

"Then I should have stayed in Lexington and removed all doubt," laughed Sam Adams. A wisp of brown hair showed where he had pushed his wig up on his forehead against the heat of the room. He seemed either unaware of, or unconcerned by, a large wine stain on his waistcoat.

Paine knew that the Second Continental Congress was preparing a memorial for London, proving that the British and not the Americans had fired the first shot at Lexington. So he waited until he caught Hancock's attention and said, "We are at war, gentlemen. Whether we wish it or not, we are at war. Not because of Lexington but because of Concord! England gives not a tinker's damn who fired the first shot. Nor doth she care about the sentiments of Congress. Those she can change by the confiscation of property and the destruction of trade. But the sentiments of the common man, so far from England, she will not bend so easily to her will. It is thirty-two miles from Concord to Boston, gentlemen, and I have learned that, as the British retreated along those miles, they were harrassed and shot down by our farmers and militiamen from behind trees, hedges, fences, and stone walls. The British have been humiliated! Boston is filled with their wounded. I have learned that, before they reached its safety, they suffered 273 casualties. The English do not like to be humiliated. I know them well. I have but lately come from them. And now we are at war—whether we wish it or not. War or enslavement!"

Hancock turned an evaluating eye upon Paine. "You have come to the wrong port. You should have come to Boston."

John Adams seemed touched by anger. "I hope to God that you are wrong, Mr. Paine. War is a beginning for which I can see no proper end. And even if we won, whereof I have my doubts, how would we govern? I know of no civilized country that does not have a monarchical form of government, and here we have no colonist of royal blood. Whom would we crown king, Mr. Paine? Or would you suggest a king for every colony? Where would one get so many kings? Not wanting England's, would you send to France . . . Spain . . . the Austrian court?"

"I have heard," said Sam Adams, "that along the road from Concord to Boston, as the British retreated, there were many cries of 'Long live King Hancock!' "

Hancock smiled.

Dickinson rose and swept his glass from the table. Anger paled his girlishly thin face. "Sedition and treason!" he cried. "I will not remain in its company!"

11

LATE IN May, 1775, Paine came out with a kind of ironic, semiserious by-product of his continuous work on *Common Sense.* Entitled "Reflections on Titles," it pointed out the basic absurdity of all such distinctions based solely on inheritance. He had thought of it simply as one more of his essays and was surprised, therefore, upon entering the Black Horse Inn the day after its publication, to find himself hailed with ironic cheers. Fortified with copies of the *Pennsylvania Magazine,* the storekeepers and merchants who crowded the tables looked up and greeted him with: " 'Ere comes 'is Royal 'Ighness! Make way for the Prince of the Quill!''

Amused but dubious, he was relieved to see Sam Adams, seated alone at a far table, also waving his hat at him in mock courtesy and motioning him to his table. "It surprises you to see me here? I am not affluent," he confided to Paine. "I cannot afford the Royal Standard or even Yohe's, next door. Nor can I abide their Tory sentiments. And the food is more to my liking here. Have you tasted the smoked tongue? The cherry pie? Or their fish house punch? Wait . . . wait. . . . I must have you taste it." He watched as Paine sipped a proffered sample. "And now," he asked, "the reason for the jesting?"

"You have not read the latest issue of the *Pennsylvania Magazine?*"

When Adams shook his head, Paine pulled a copy from a coat pocket. "They were stirred by an article on the absurdity of titles, Mr. Adams." He leaned forward and winked, "Aimed, perhaps, at His Majesty, the Honorable Plunderer of His Country. I have called the article 'Reflections on Titles.' It begins: When I reflect on the pompous titles bestowed on unworthy men, I feel an indignity that instructs me to despise the absurdity. . . ."

"Enough! Enough!" laughed Adams, reaching across the table for his magazine. "I must have a copy for myself. He glanced at the end of the article and asked, "It is signed *Vox Populi.* How did they know it was yours?"

Paine shrugged a shoulder in amusement.

Sam Adams' face grew sober. "And how come you with your *Common Sense?*" he asked.

It was no secret that, although the *Pennsylvania Magazine* offered no political comment, its editor was writing a separationist pamphlet. "It is slow work," confessed Paine. "I try to tread a middle ground . . . to give offense to no one, yet encouragement to all. Before summer ends, perhaps, it will be done."

"You have chosen a lonely path," said Adams. "And I admire you for it. But I would not be a friend if I did not warn you that last fall, on the eve of the First Congress' adjournment, Washington sought Richard Henry Lee and my cousin John at their lodgings, to ask their assurances that their policy did not have independence as its aim."

"And you?"

"By then I had already been dropped from the evening levees of the Pennsylvania aristocrats. I had been classed, with Paul Revere, as one of the 'vulgar' men. Yet Washington came to me, too, and asked for my pledge."

Paine looked Adams full in the face. "I do what I think is right and neither censure nor threat shall deter me. I cannot devote all my time to the pamphlet, but I assure you, I shall finish my *Common Sense* in due time." He smiled and added, "Just now, I am engaged on a new article that I shall entitle 'Reflections on Unhappy Marriages.' Art married, Mr. Adams?"

Sam Adams touched his lips with the fingers of a small hand that denied participation in any physical activity. He was ten years older than his kinsman, John, and his face had lost the leanness of youth. There was a slight dimple in a rather stout chin. "I have a second wife," he said. "Elizabeth. She may not be as gifted a letter writer as John's Abigail, but she has made me a most excellent spouse. Despite my meager income, she is a most efficient manageress of my two children (by my first wife), a black slave girl, and my Newfoundland dog. I am content when I am home. But to get back to your *Common Sense* and independence. It is rumored that Parker acted under my orders at Lexington . . . that I am eager to see even bloodshed for the sake of separation."

"And are you?"

Sam Adams hesitated. For a long moment he did not speak

and then he said, "Finish your *Common Sense,* Mr. Paine. Finish it!"

In the three weeks that ensued, Paine strove mightily to follow Sam Adams' advice. For to him the debates in the Second Continental Congress had suddenly begun to seem absurd, as well as unrealistic. They were arguing, Sam Adams informed him, on whether or not to send one last "Olive Branch" petition to the King and, if so, what language it should contain; on whether or not they were at war with Great Britain and, if not, what should be done to help the New England militia gathering about Boston. Independence was not being considered, and on the floor of the Congress even the word was not being whispered.

To Paine, at work on the last pages of *Common Sense,* it seemed a travesty so preposterous that not even John Adams' success in persuading the delegates to send Virginian and Pennsylvanian riflemen to the New Englanders outside Boston, to name the whole group the "Continental Army," and to choose George Washington as its commander-in-chief—not even this—went to the root of the matter. For close on its heels had come the news of the bloody battle of Bunker Hill.

So strongly did he feel that, even on the day of Washington's departure from Philadelphia with the riflemen, he swallowed his pride and, standing on the street with John Adams, waiting for the parade, appealed to the New Englander to come to his dingy room and at least read his completed manuscript. Before them militiamen were already clearing the way, pressing the onlookers back on the commons, past the hitching posts and the whortleberry bushes. Delegates to the Congress were standing on the Statehouse steps or leaning from its raised windows, while an enthusiastic group crowded the roof of the Coach and Horses Inn, waving their hats from the balustraded catwalk.

Before Paine could complete a sentence, however, there

[140]

was a sudden roll of drums and the sound of fifes and the first riders of the approaching cavalcade swung into view. George Washington rode at its head, Mifflin and Reed at his side. Dressed again in his blue and buff Virginia uniform, Washington sat gracefully on his horse, the stirrups strapped low to accommodate his long, black-booted legs. A number of delegates followed in carriages. Philip Schuyler and Charles Lee kept each other company. The wealthy Dickinson, Galloway, and Harrison sat together, as though they had a common interest. The Virginians were accompanied by liveried servants.

Music broke out and a troop of Philadelphia light-horsemen came into view. They seemed superb in their short, brown jackets, their white breeches, and their smart high-topped boots. Their brown saddlecloths were trimmed with silver braid and their flat round hats were bound with silver thread. The many officers of the militia came abreast and were followed by the musicians in their red coats, blue waistcoats, and breeches. The drummers seemed but boys. A wild cheer broke from the watching crowd. Light infantry followed, then the grenadiers, then the riflemen—there seemed 2,000 of them.

Paine turned to John Adams and, lifting his voice so that it would be heard above the beat of the drums, the shrill fifes, and the cheering watchers, almost shouted, "I expected to see you in a carriage too, Mr. Adams."

John Adams shook his head. "This day belongs to the Virginians and the Pennsylvanians. To the rescuers and not the besieged Bostonians. And were I to ride with Hancock, I think he would turn his back on me."

Paine raised a curious eyebrow.

"He is angry with my cousin Sam, but he is furious with me. Some say that he had not wanted the army's command but wished only the refusal of it. But I know John Hancock better. There's no end to the man's vanity. I could not see him as a military man, with his comforts and his gout—and no service in the field. When Sam supported the nomination of Washington, our Mr. Hancock looked put out; but when I, too, endorsed the choice, one could not but see his anger. He is deeply offended and no longer speaks to me."

Paine watched the last of the troops pass by. As the sound of the military music grew faint, Adams turned to him and said whimsicallly, "I wish that I could go. if it were not for Abigail and all the duties that still remain at home, . . ."

It seemed a strange wish to be coming from John Adams.

Paine watched the onlookers disperse. It had been a strange display—a display of newly appointed officers and men marching off to what would, in any other circumstance, be called *war,* and yet all insisted that no such thing existed. The greatest number professed a loyalty to a king they did not know and a country they had never seen. It was ludicrous.

"Mr. Adams," he said, as John Adams turned to leave, "could I impose upon you to come to my lodging? It is not far. I have a manuscript I would show you."

"A manuscript, Mr. Paine?" He pointed to the departing troops with his hickory cane. "There goes action, and you talk of manuscripts! I do not know how it is with you, but I am worn out with mere scribbling."

"It will take you but two hours," suggested Paine.

"Very well," said Adams reluctantly and went with him.

"What is it?" he asked, once he had seated himself in the only chair in the room.

"I call it *Common Sense.*"

"Oh?" Adams raised a questioning eyebrow. "Sam has mentioned it."

"It contains some thoughts on independence. Read it, Mr. Adams."

Adams read the first two pages politely, and then suddenly his attention was fixed fast. He read without raising his eyes, stopping only to lift the pages, one by one:

[142]

And that the *elected* might never form to themselves an interest separate from the *electors,* prudence will point out the propriety of having elections often.

On this and not on the unmeaning name of King, depends the *strength of government and the happiness of the governed.* . . .

Paine watched as Adams read on and on. Little beads of sweat collected on the New Englander's forehead, but he seemed unaware of them. Paine thought of offering him a drink . . . asking him to remove his coat . . . but he did not want to interrupt him. Adams read quietly for more than an hour. Now and then he raised his head. His brown eyes looked ahead, yet seemed to see nothing, as though his mind were debating, within itself, the right or wrong of what he had just read. At such times his stubby hands would rest upon the sheets of paper. He would cross his legs and his knee-length breeches would creep up to show where his stockings were tied with black ribbons above his plump knees.

When he finished reading the manuscript, he lifted his head and looked at Paine without speaking. Finally he said, "You have no great liking for titles, nor for kings, Mr. Paine."

"The disregard has been forced upon me. I have seen a copy of 'The Olive Branch Petition' and its very address affronts my sense of freedom and my dignity as a man. It is not addressed to a government but

> To the KING'S most excellent Majesty
> Most Gracious Sovereign,
> We, your Majesty's faithful subjects . . ."

"But this is no petition, Mr. Paine. It is a tirade. It is an insistence upon complete separation from England . . . for complete independence!"

"That is what I mean it to be. I can see no other reason for a Continental Army marching north to Cambridge and Boston. To what other end is an army formed but to wrest what it can by force?"

"You mean open war?" cried Adams. He rose to his feet and tossed the manuscript pages upon the bed.

"Mr. Adams," said Paine quietly, "with Washington sent by Congress to Boston with six paltry regiments, the new Continental Army intends with force of arms to get revenge for Bunker Hill, the acts of Parliament, and the proclamations of the King. If that is not war, if Bunker Hill is not war, then the meaning of the word is foreign to my understanding of it. And if it is war, then one cannot keep its motive secret and at the same time beg for its support. Is it not incongruous, Mr. Adams, that I who am but lately come from England should consider myself an American, while so many of you who were born here should consider yourselves English?"

John Adams' face grew flushed. "You do not understand. It is incumbent upon us that we talk softly, Mr. Paine. We, from Massachusetts, can do little by ourselves. It is my fear that the Virginians will aid us only to a point. Titles to their lands depend upon royal grants. And New York is vociferous in denouncing all talk of separation." He removed a sheet of folded foolscrap from a pocket. "This is what the Assembly of Delaware instructed her delegates. And I urge you, Mr. Paine, to make no mention of it."

> In every act to be done in Congress studiously avoid as you have heretofore done, everything disrespectful or offensive to our most gracious Sovereign, or in any way invasive of his rights and prerogatives. . . .

"Disrespectful to a gracious Sovereign? Mr. Adams, I knew his mentor, in England. Disrespectful to a seducer of mistresses would be more . . ."

They were interrupted by a knock at the door. It was Dr. Rush who entered. His eyes widened with surprise at seeing John Adams. "A heated dispute in a heated room, gentlemen," he laughed. He walked to a window and opened it wider. He glanced at the scattered sheets on the bed, looked

[144]

at Adams, hesitated, and said to Paine, "Dr. Franklin would like to read your finished *Common Sense.*"

Paine shook his head. "I do not wish to offend him, but I cannot let him see it. He is not in accord with it. I showed him portions of my first draft and there were many observations that he would have me delete. He would emasculate my similes and reduce my arguments to a child's prattle." He searched through the sheets and, finding one that contained an example, he cried, "Hear ... hear ... this among others he would have me strike out completely." A touch of anger hastened his words as he read:

> A greater absurdity cannot be conceived of than three million people running to their seacoast every time a ship arrives from London, to know what portion of Liberty they should enjoy.

"That paragraph touched no thought of censorship in me," said Adams. "But there were many others."

"It will be printed as you have just read it," promised Paine. "And Congress and the Colonies will accept its irrefutable arguments."

John Adams shook his head. He searched in his voluminous pocket for more papers. Finding what he wanted, he observed, "You are too impulsive, Mr. Paine. Out of a regard for your sentiments, I shall corrupt a privilege and advise you of one more decision. Congress will not consider King George a 'Royal Brute' merely because you call him one in your pamphlet. Congress is drafting a new resolution, setting forth the grievances of the Colonies. You have my word for it, and perhaps Dr. Rush will bear me out, that it will be adopted. Wouldst hear a portion of it, Mr. Paine?" Without waiting for a yea or nay, Adams read in a firm voice:

> Lest this declaration should disquiet the minds of our friends and fellow subjects in any part of the Empire, we assure them that we mean not to dissolve that union which has so long and

so happily subsisted between us, and which we sincerely wish to see restored.

Paine was aghast. "And Washington is riding off to take command of a Continental Army . . . for what? For the restoration of servility and taxation?" He turned to Dr. Rush.

The physician shrugged a calm shoulder. "I did not come to participate in your debate, gentlemen." He hesitated and said, "I have found a printer for your *Common Sense,* Tom."

"Where?" cried Paine. "By heavens! Where?"

"A Robert Bell, on Third Street. Between Willing's Alley and Pear Street." And when Paine seemed not to grasp the location, "Almost adjacent to the Friends' Almshouse."

"Will you come there with me, Dr. Rush?"

There was an instant's hesitation while Dr. Rush's face grew flushed. "I cannot. My work at the Medical College . . . I am here, at this moment, between sick calls." Suddenly he confessed, "I'm sorry, Tom. I am in complete accord with that portion of your *Common Sense* that I have read, but I cannot go with you to the printer's. You have nothing to fear from the popular odium to which such a publication might expose you, for you can live anywhere. But my profession and my connections tie me to Philadelphia, where, as Mr. Adams will bear me out, most of my friends and even my family are hostile to a separation of our country from Great Britain. I have done what I could in asking after a printer."

Even as Dr. Rush spoke, the anger in Paine's eyes dwindled and died. He could not be wrathful with this man to whom there was more than just the elegance of his dress and his confident poise.

"Do not feel badly. I shall see Bell myself."

Adams looked from Paine to Dr. Rush and then back again. "I fear you are making a mistake, Mr. Paine," he said slowly. "This Robert Bell is a rogue. He is a man of doubtful religion,

[146]

openly keeps a mistress, and is not to be trusted. He is forever but a chalk line beyond the law."

Dr. Rush smiled. "And yet he published the first American edition of *Blackstone's Commentaries.*"

"Would he but publish my *Common Sense,* I would not care what else he did," said Paine.

"This will lead to no good end," warned John Adams. Yet it seemed that he could not force his eyes from the papers that lay scattered upon the unmade bed. "I warn you," he repeated, "it will lead to no good end."

It was late afternoon by the time Paine reached Robert Bell's. He was surprised that he had not noticed the shop before. A bookstore fronted the printing section and above a narrow doorway hung a sign that read, JEWELS AND DIAMONDS FOR SENTIMENTALISTS. This Robert Bell evidently considered himself a wit. The store window displayed an offering of secondhand books at reduced prices. There were copies of Johnson's *Rasselas,* James's *History of Man* and *The Letters of Montaigne.*

Inside the store, to Paine's further surprise, a counter was stacked with Bell's reprints from works by Gray, Locke, Defoe, Goldsmith, Young, and Priestley. A young woman, in her late twenties, bade Paine welcome, inquired after his need, eyed the ribbonbound sheets under his arm, and informed him, "Mr. Bell pays for no copyrights and buys naught as wot is an owned manuscript."

"If you will forgive me . . . the nature of my business is with Mr. Bell."

The woman hesitated, walked through a doorway and was back in a moment. " 'E's busy. But 'e'll spare ya five i' the shop."

Paine walked into the printing shop and looked about him. It seemed no different than Aitken's except that, where Aitken's shop was neat, this one seemed to have been struck by a storm that had left everything in disarray. The airless room was filled with the clatter of a press, the scent of printer's ink, and the heavy stink of fresh glue. To one side, an apprentice was engaged in binding books, almost like a staymaker, with a needle and stout waxed thread. At a scarred desk that was cluttered with papers, printed sheets, and fonts of type sat a most unimpressive and busy-looking man.

Paine undid the ribbons and placed his manuscript upon the desk. Bell ran through the first few pages, giving no thought to their contents, riffled through the sheets, and read a paragraph here and there. Then, to Paine's indignation he gathered up the pages of the manuscript, thrust them aside, and returned to his work. He had asked no question and made no comment.

"Read it!" urged Paine. "Read it, Mr. Bell! Dr. Rush has recommended you."

"Aye," he said, pursing his thin lips. " 'E boot said 'twa an int'restin' poomphlet o' independoonce. An' can ya no' get yer Boobie Aitken ta print it noo? An' dina' tell ma as Will Bradford doesna' lak a few extra poonds."

"You have not read it!"

"Coom' na, laddie. D'ya 'ave ta drink the last droop from the tanka'd ta ken it's sweet 'r soor?"

"I predict it would earn you a considerable profit."

"Profit is't? Tis treason, mon. Would ya 'ave m' shoop staved in lak a cooper's bar'l, m' press bashed ta smithereens an' meself dragged back ta England ta be 'anged? Fer wot? Fer the sake o' a few pieces o' eight in m' pocket? Take it, mon," he cried, thrusting the sheets back into Paine's hands. "D'ya no' ken the noomber o' printers in the toon? Foorty-two, mon. An' ye 'ave ta coom' ringin' m' bell?"

All through the rest of the summer Paine tried in vain to persuade one of the more than forty printers to print and publish his *Common Sense,* and only by a fluke did it ever see the light. Ironically, the fluke was of Paine's own making.

In September, 1775, heartened by the success of Benedict Arnold and Ethan Allen in seizing Ticonderoga and its valuable guns, the Second Continental Congress authorized an invasion of Canada. Paine was astounded when he heard of it. It did not make sense. The Congress refrained from declaring American independence from Great Britain yet ordered an army to march into an adjacent English colony. And for what? To vanquish them? To win them their independence when they would not insist upon it themselves? Not knowing if it would be printed or, like *Common Sense,* gather dust in his room, he sat down at once and wrote a dissertation that he called "A Serious Thought."

Aitken, as usual, refused to publish it. So Paine again made the rounds of the Printers: Keimer, on Second Street; Andrew Bradford's *American Weekly Mercury;* Burton, the magazine publisher in Logan's Alley. But only at last did William Bradford, touched perhaps by a sense of guilt for having refused *Common Sense,* print his "A Serious Thought" in the *Pennsylvania Journal and Weekly Advertiser.* The immediate result was astounding.

Men gathered in taverns, oyster houses, and coffeeshops and discussed and debated the new disseration. Farmers who brought their harvested crops to the Jersey Market bought or borrowed a copy of the journal. The arguments for independence that "A Serious Thought" contained stirred them all. It was signed *Humanus* and there was much speculation as to its author.

The eventual result was even more gratifying. One night, Paine met Robert Bell in A Man Full of Trouble Tavern. The Scot's face was ruddy with drink. One could not tell if he were celebrating or drinking to forget. The absence of convivial friends at his table suggested the latter. "Moost'r Paine!" he called. "Moost'r Paine! Coom' tha 'ere an' 'ave a wee nip wi' ma. So no one would print tha *Common Sense?* But yer Bradford has doon this?"

Paine smiled and laid a piece of eight upon the table.

"Tha'rt a marked mon, laddie," Bell advised him. "Tha mought sign it *Humanus*, boot . . ." He touched a knowing finger to his child's nose. "The English Goov'rment wi' no' take it lightly, noo."

Paine tugged a few copies of the *Pennsylvania Journal and Weekly Advertiser* from a pocket and riffled them at Bell. "The English government? There need be no English Government for us. This is but a single shot. *Common Sense* is a broadside —a broadside that will alert the Colonies from Massachusetts to Georgia. Its reading will satisfy the farmers to leave their ploughs, the weavers their looms, and the tanners their hides. If someone would print it."

Bell leaned across the wet, stained table and challenged, "An' the Quakers? Wi' make 'em ta carra a moosket lak a good Presb'terian?"

"The Friends will raise no dissenting voice. The pamphlet will wipe out both slavery and foreign government."

"We-el noo. Ah lak tha Paine, boot Ah dina' care fer the white hoorse tha rides."

"Nor the fortune it could earn you."

"Foortune ya say?"

"A fortune and more. Do you know how many extra copies of the *Pennsylvania Journal* Bradford printed because of this dissertation? And they are now as scarce as King George's amnesties. My *Common Sense* will be bought in all the Colonies. Post coaches will drop them at every crossroad and hamlet. Copies will be shipped abroad. And to the man who but prints it . . . You worry about the smashing of a press, Mr. Bell. Why you will be so affluent, you will no longer need a shop!"

Bell placed his hands upon the table. Paine did not know whether it was to steady himself or to help him think. His fingernails were black with printer's ink. Little tufts of red hair contrasted with the pale skin of his knuckles. "Ah'll do't," he said, staring straight at Paine. "Ah wi' print tha doomn poomphlet. An' tha Calv'nist fishery poorts canna' say as oonly 'ey defy the King!"

"I shall guarantee you against any possible loss," promised Paine. "And no harm will come to you. Art drunk or sober, Mr. Bell?"

When Bell voiced a protest against the insinuation that a Scot could become befuddled on such piddling brew as Colonial beer, Paine said, "Then let us draw up an agreement, though it be a verbal one, that if any loss will arise, I shall pay it . . . and I shall give half the profits, if it should produce any." It was a pessimistic phrase in which to couch profits and Paine hurried to explain. "I, myself, intend no benefit by it. I shall give Colonel Joseph Dean and Captain Thomas Prior the other half of the profits, to lay out for the troops that are going to Quebec."

"Tha hast m' woord on it," promised Bell at last. "Tha hast the woord o' Roobert Bell. Sound as a resolootion in a confession'l."

12

ON JANUARY 10, 1776, *Common Sense* was published. For months before it appeared, many of Paine's friends had urged him to let them read parts of it, but Paine had insisted that no one could see it until all of it was in print. He had permitted John Adams to read it in manuscript and Adams had not refrained from voicing his derogatory sentiments in public:

> The injudicious pamphlet offers a troublesome and danger-
> ous new doctrine . . . a leveling spirit . . . insisting that one man
> is as good as another. . . . I hope it will not be printed.

Nevertheless, Bell had kept his word, although with maddening procrastination, and now Paine had his pamphlet, with its title page inscribed: Written by an Englishman.

Waiting impatiently until evening, when his friends might gather at the Indian Queen, he stuffed twenty of the pamphlets into his pockets and rushed first to the hotel. He had hoped to find John Adams, but he was not there. It was rumored that he had found a second home at the lodging of Mrs. Yards. Nor was Dr. Rush at the Indian Queen. The physician had become an infrequent visitor. Paine noticed Robert Morris and then Sam Adams, who waved a welcoming hand. He was surprised to see Thomas Jefferson. He had thought him at home for the holidays. David Rittenhouse was there, sketching the scrollwork of some new ornamentation upon a sheet of paper. George Clymer, now treasurer of the Continental Congress, was at his side, as was William Rawle. Paine never knew what to expect from lawyer Rawle. The man was forever vacillating between patriotic leanings and a regard for legal precedent, between rebellion and his Quaker upbringing.

Paine unwrapped the wool muffler from about his throat, took the bound pamphlets from his pockets, and waved them in the air. *"Common Sense, gentlemen,"* he cried. *"At long last, my Common Sense."*

There was an immediate scraping of chairs as they gathered about him. Paine's eyes were wide with anticipation as he distributed the pamphlets that still smelled of freshly dried glue. Tables were pulled together. Clymer brought extra candelabra and set them at each end. Paine removed his overcoat and his hat but refused to sit down. Tense with emotion, he stood quietly at first and then circled the seated men, watching them, studying their varied expressions, his eyes traveling from face to face as they read the pamphlets. *Common Sense* was prefaced by an introduction and he eyed his friends keenly as they read:

The cause of America is, in a great measure, the cause of all mankind. The laying of a country desolate with fire and sword ... is the concern of every man to whom nature hath given the power of feeling; of which class, regardless of censure, is THE AUTHOR

Jefferson stopped reading and covered his pamphlet with his hands. Paine noted the action. Could it be that he would read no more? He watched him cross the room and engage the Indian Queen's host in earnest conversation.

A tall, rather young man approached the group. Despite a rolling gait, he walked with a belligerent assurance. One could not tell if he were moved by mirth or derision. Clymer welcomed him and rose to introduce him. "John Paul Jones," he presented; and with an extended hand he designated those about the tables: "David Rittenhouse and Samuel Adams, whom you have met, William Rawle ..." When he came to Paine, Clymer hesitated and introduced him as "Thomas Paine, editor of the *Pennsylvania Magazine.*"

The young man inclined his head to each of them. To Paine he said, in a dialect that was a mixture of Scottish brogue and southern drawl, "Ah've raid your denoonciations, Mr. Paine. Ah 'ope as you've a' eye ta the future an' noo' the poost."

Paine leaned over Sam Adams' chair and whispered, "Who is he, Sam?"

"Sh-sh ... Do not offend him. He has a fine sense of humor and yet a violent temper that knows neither compromise nor abatement. He has learned that Congress is adopting a resolution for a Continental Navy and wishes to be a part of it."

Paine offered Jones a pamphlet and he accepted it. His eyes were not unfriendly but coldly aloof. Jefferson was back and advised, "Gentlemen, I do not think a public place suitable for what we have at hand." Suddenly he noticed Jones and placed an affectionate arm about him. "You still cannot stay home, I see."

"Fred'ricksboorg? Tis a toon fer fat Will."

"But better than the West Indies, John?" Jefferson turned toward the tables and apologized. "Forgive me, I have known John since he was twelve. It was Willie Jones and not God who reformed you, eh John?"

The Scot smiled his harlequin's smile.

"Gentlemen," said Jefferson, "our host has graciously permitted us the use of his private sitting room. I suggest we retire to its seclusion with ... with Mr. Paine's *Common Sense.*"

Paine turned to Jefferson. "By noon tomorrow, 500 copies will be bought, passed from hand to hand, and read by 1,000 pairs of eyes."

"I do not doubt it," said the unruffled Jefferson. "But tonight, I think we should read it in private. Come along, John."

There was a scraping of chairs and, taking their pamphlets with them, they left the tables and made themselves comfortable in a small room off the main saloon. Candles had been lighted, as had a fresh fire. A serving maid came in and inquired about their drinks. Paine did not seat himself but walked to a window that fronted on Fourth Street. A flurry of snow had begun to drift down from a grey-black sky. He turned from the window and saw that his friends were once more engrossed in the pamphlets. There was a deep silence in the room. It seemed to Paine that he could tell which portions they were reading:

... Society is produced by our wants, and government by our wickedness; the former promotes our happiness *positively,* by uniting our affections; the latter *negatively,* by restraining our vices. The first is a patron, the last a punisher.

Society in every state is a blessing, but government, even in its best state, is but a necessary evil; in its worst state, an intolerable one.

... *Wherefore,* security being the true design and end of government, it unanswerably follows, that whatever *form* thereof appears most likely to ensure it to us, with the least expense and greatest benefit, is preferable to all other. . . .

Paine walked to the fireplace and stirred the logs. The flames licked hungrily where the bark had not caught fire. There was a crackle, and a burst of sparks was sucked into the chimney's draft. He could tell that his friends were now reading his basis for the design of government, his pointing out that *"nothing but heaven is impregnable to vice,"* his tracing the growth of regulations to laws, and his principles of *elections and electors.*

There was a knock on the door. Paine opened it, hesitated, and admitted Reverend Muhlenberg and Reverend Boucher. "Well, well," cried Muhlenberg, looking about and shaking the melting snow from his hat. "We were told that you were here. Isn't this cozy! Are we intruding, gentlemen?"

Paine felt that Muhlenberg was welcome, but Jonathan Boucher . . . He had not seen the clergyman since the "toasting" of the antislavery essay, but he had heard reports of his Royalist activities. Popular protests had forced his resignation and it was rumored that he was returning to England. Had he come to Philadelphia to secure a passage?

Jefferson drew up chairs for them and, reluctantly, Paine handed a pamphlet to Boucher, as he did to Muhlenberg. He resumed his vigil by the fireplace. After a moment, Boucher glanced up from his pamphlet. "Mr. Paine," he admonished. "I have read the first pages of your *Common Sense,* but I see no invocation to divine providence."

Paine's face was flushed by the firelight. Addressing the group, he said, "Gentlemen, it is true that my pamphlet is not prefaced by an invocation to the Supreme Being, but you must forbear the lack of it since a King, who is closer to God than I, since he governs by *divine right,* is just as neglectful in his proclamations—and is never called to answer for it by the clergy."

"Do you then admit to sacrilege!" cried Boucher, rising to his feet.

Suddenly a voice filled the room. It was John Paul Jones. The words seemed to come effortlessly from his mouth and yet they carried to the walls and the beams. "Sit doon, Englishman! D'ya hush yer tongue or laive!"

Boucher glanced at Jones. It did not seem credible that this ruddy-faced young man would lay hands upon him. But Jones's round, unflinching eyes suggested the possibility. Boucher seated himself in silence.

Paine glanced at Muhlenberg for guidance. He saw an eye wink in the big man's placid face. "I'll go for a decanter and more glasses," said Paine, as they continued to read:

... Absolute governments (though the disgrace of human nature), have this advantage with them, that they are simple; if the people suffer, they know the head from which their suffering springs, they know likewise the remedy, and are not bewildered by a variety of causes and cures. ...

When Paine returned, he walked among them and filled their glasses. Rittenhouse covered his with the palm of his hand. The act prompted Paine to suggest, "Come, gentlemen, shall we drink to the birth of a new freedom?"

Boucher, lifting his glass, said, "I drink, gentlemen; but hearken, I drink because I am dry, and not to sedition."

"Sedition my quill!" cried Paine. "I have written no single thing you would not think yourselves, and admit, did you but give the matter time for thought. You are history, gentlemen! The fate of unborn millions ... their miseries or their contented freedom depends upon your timidities or your acceptance of TRUTH! Drain your glasses, gentlemen, and read on."

He left them and busied himself at the fireplace, poking the crackling logs into flame. Again and again he turned, one arm resting on the mantelpiece, and observed them as they read:

Mankind, being originally equals in the order of creation, the equality could only be destroyed by some subsequent circumstances. The distinction of rich and poor may in a great measure be accounted for. . . .

But there is another and greater distinction for which no truly natural or religious reason can be assigned, and that is the distinction of men into kings and subjects. Male and female are the distinctions of nature; good and bad the distinctions of heaven; but how a race of men came into the world so exalted above the rest, and distinguished like some new species, is worth enquiring into, and whether they are the means of happiness or of misery to mankind. . . .

Suddenly, in the hush of the room, where even the crackle of the fire seemed self-contained, there was the scraping sound of a chair being pushed back. Reverend Boucher rose, tore his copy of *Common Sense* in half, and turned to Paine. "If this pamphlet be not treason to the Crown, then I know not its name!" He walked to the fireplace and cast the ripped pamphlet into it. "Art coming with me, Reverend Muhlenberg?"

Paine watched the pages of the pamphlet curl and catch flame. Charred ends were sucked into the chimney's draft. He listened for the scraping of a chair, but it did not come. He turned and studied the faces that were looking from Boucher to Muhlenberg.

"I have as yet read no sentiment with which I can honestly disagree," said Muhlenberg.

"And I say, the pamphlet's seditious phrases point a path that can lead only to the gallows. I shall have no part in it! Gentlemen, I bid you good night."

Paine offered him a fresh pamphlet as he stormed out. "For your leisure moments." Reverend Boucher refused to touch it. It seemed, for a moment, that if he had held a cane, he would have used it on Paine.

In the quiet that ensued, Jefferson glanced at the remaining

[157]

pages of the pamphlet while Sam Adams reached for a decanter and poured a tall drink for himself. "Gentlemen," said the Virginian, "I would prefer to read the rest of this alone. Not for Reverend Boucher's reasons, but because I would like to digest it. It seems too heavy a meal for quick gobbling."

They assented and drank to Jefferson's suggestion. Paine watched as they left, one by one. He waited for John Paul Jones to leave, but the young man sat and poured yet another drink.

"Do you know Mr. Jefferson well, Mr. Jones?"

There was no answer for a moment and then Jones laughed. "Forgive me," he said. "Ah am noo' yet accoostoomed ta ma noom. I' dina' ring quickly enough upon ma ears."

To Paine's questioning look he explained, "John Paul is ma noom. Ah were befriended by Willie Jones. Hast 'eard o' 'im? A No'th Ca'olina planter."

Paine shook his head.

"Hast ever needed a fraind, Paine? Weel, Willie is such a fraind. An' two y'ars ago, out o' regard fer 'im, ah adopted the surnoom o' Jones." He winked a round eye and lifted his glass to Paine. "Aye, that amongst other raisons."

Paine glanced at Jones over his wineglass. "When we were introduced," he asked, "what did you mean by my denunciations?"

Jones hesitated and then confessed, "A've woorked in the slave trade, Paine. Dost think the less o' me? Ah were chief mate o' the slaver *Brigantine* fer two y'ars." When he saw the look of disapproval on Paine's face, he added, "Boot that were mor'n seven y'ars ago! An' noo ah wants an American shoop. Ah needs as many frainds in Congress as ah cain mooster."

"I am not a delegate, Mr. Jones."

"Aye, boot ya 'ave influence. Ah raid yer scribblin' in Fred'ricksboorg, an' in Richmond, an' in Charleston."

[158]

"I'll do what I can," Paine promised. "I do not have Mr. John Adams' influence. Nor Mr. Hancock's. Mr. Hancock is the naval man."

Jones sprang from the chair and laughed. He extended a hand in friendship and clapped Paine on the shoulder. "D'ya no' ken an opportunity when tha sees one?" He pointed to a *Common Sense* pamphlet. "Thar's yer influence, mon. As full o' devastation as a broodside from a mon-o-war. By full tide tamorra thou'lt be asked opinions o' the weather an' the wind. Coom' wi' me ta the river froont an' we'll celebrate. Ta the Albatross Inn at Austin's Ferry. Ah promise tha a night ta remoomb'r. Willie Jones lairned me the Albatross. Twere there tha foorst called me John Paul Jones." Paine hesitated and then succumbed to the young man's enthusiasm.

As John Paul Jones and Paine turned into the lobby of the Indian Queen, they were met by a wild hubbub of voices and a group of gesticulating men. Dickinson was there, as was Rittenhouse, who had not gone home. Rittenhouse rushed to Paine and thrust a large sheet into his hands. "Distributed this night!" he cried. "A manifesto by King George. Mr. Dickinson claims there are copies everywhere. Posted in all the inns and coffeehouses. Copies have been tacked on the very doors of the Statehouse!"

Dickinson thrust his way to Paine's side. "What say you now, Mr. Paine?"

Paine was startled that a manifesto by the King should be posted on the same day that his pamphlet was finally published. It seemed that England was more aware of him than he thought.

"I say read my *Common Sense,* Mr. Dickinson. I have none left, but you can obtain a copy at Robert Bell's for two shillings."

"And the King's proclamation?"

Paine glanced with seeming unconcern at the printed sheet in his hand. His eye caught the words:

His Majesty's government has the right not only to tax but to bind the colonists in all cases whatsoever!

He tore it in half and then into quarters and let it drop to the floor as a group gathered about him. "A waste of paper and printer's ink. And now, gentlemen, if you will excuse me, . . ."

Jones was happy to thrust a wedge for Paine through the still-gathering crowd. As they reached outdoors, Paine turned to him and apologized, "Mr. Jones, would you mind if I accompanied you on another night? My thoughts are upon other things."

"The King's basta'd prooclamation?"

"Perhaps, Mr. Jones. Perhaps. . . ."

On the way to his lodging, Paine realized that he had been too hasty in tearing up Dickinson's copy of the King's manifesto. His pride would not let him seek a fresh copy and yet it was important that he knew what it said. It would have to wait until morning. What was done was done. And yet, no matter what the proclamation threatened or cajoled, it had no validity, for its very seal assumed that monarchy was divine, while his *Common Sense* showed it to be a stupid folly. The phrases of his pamphlet ran through his mind like the beat of a drum whose cadence he had invoked and now could not hush:

> To the evil of monarchy [his pamphlet cried], we have added that of hereditary succession; an insult and imposition on posterity. . . . One of the strongest *natural* proofs of the folly of hereditary right of kings is that nature disapproves it; otherwise she would not so frequently turn it into ridicule by giving mankind an *Ass for a Lion.*

He realized that he had written a pamphlet not so much against the King of England as against kings everywhere; not as an American but as a cosmopolitan; not as an instigator for freedom in the Colonies but for freedom in the world! For he had written:

> ... The sun never shone on a cause of greater worth. Tis not the affair of a city, a county, a province, or a kingdom, but of a continent! Tis not the concern of a day, a year, or an age; posterity are virtually involved in the contest, and will be more or less affected, even to the end of time, by the proceedings now.

He reached his lodging. The snowfall had ended. It had been no more than a succession of flurries, yet little drifts lay everywhere in white patches. He went to bed but could not sleep. Getting up, he wrapped a blanket about him, in the cold room, and lighted the candles. He reread the copy of *Common Sense* that he had perversely denied to Dickinson. He sought for words that could be deleted or made more emphatic. The candles smoked in the airless room; a grey vapor rose from above the yellow flames. He thought a fresher air would give more light, and then his keen mind imagined an aperture from base to candle flame ... permitting a duct of air to rise. ... The flame would be brighter, without flickering. ...

He tore his mind away from thoughts of candles and concentrated on the pamphlet. It was not too late for changes. He ran a dry quill under the printed lines:

> I have heard it asserted by some that, as America hath flourished under her former connection with Great Britain, the same connection is necessary toward her future happiness. Nothing can be more fallacious than this kind of argument. We may as well assert that, because a child hath thriven upon milk, it is never to have meat. ... America would have flourished as much, and probably more, had no European power had anything to do with her.
> ... But she hath protected us, say some. That she hath defended the continent is admitted; and she would have defended Turkey from the same motives, viz., for the sake of trade and dominion.

... We have boasted the protection of Great Britain without considering that her motive was *interest,* not *attachment;* that she did not protect us from our *Enemies* on *our account,* but from her *Enemies* on *her account!*

But Britain is the parent country, say some. Then the more shame upon her conduct! Even brutes do not devour their young, nor savages make war upon their families. . . . Europe and not England is the parent country of America. This new world hath been the asylum for the persecuted lovers of civil and religious liberty from *every part* of Europe.

Small islands, not capable of protecting themselves, are the proper objects for kingdoms to take under their care; but there is something very absurd in supposing a continent to be perpetually governed by an island. In no instance hath nature made the satellite larger than its primary planet!

A government of our own is our natural right!

O ye that love mankind! Ye that dare oppose not only tyranny, but the tyrant, stand forth! Every spot of the world is overrun with oppression. Let us receive the fugitive, and prepare, in time, an asylum for mankind.

Paine's tired eyes blinked in the candlelight. He began to riffle through the remaining pages of the pamphlet. Suddenly there was within him the thought: *We must have a declaration of independence!* He turned to the pamphlet's last page and read:

Were a manifesto to be published and dispatched to foreign courts, setting forth the miseries we have endured, and the peaceful methods which we have ineffectually used for redress; declaring at the same time, that not being able, any longer, to live happily or safely under the cruel disposition of the British court, we have been driven to the necessity of breaking off all connection with her; at the same time, assuring all such courts of our peaceable disposition toward them . . .

There was as yet no such manifesto. He, Thomas Paine, would write one. He would call it a . . . *A Declaration of*

Independence! As in *Common Sense,* he would point out the grievances of the Colonies, the cruel disposition of the British court, the necessity for independence, and a peaceable disposition to all governments. A declaration of independence!

13

IN THE next four months, *Common Sense* swept through the Colonies like wildfire. The pamphlets spread to the farms and outlying settlements like a fever, while stagecoaches rushed copies to Trenton, New York, and New England. Copies were carried in saddlebags to Baltimore, south to Virginia, and down to Georgia. Everywhere, foes and friends alike read it, and the cleavage between loyalist and patriot grew deeper and sharper.

In Cambridge, Washington compared its impact on public opinion with that of the British fleet's destruction of Norfolk and its attack on Falmouth. "A few more such flaming arguments," he said, "added to the arguments of *Common Sense* would secure a majority in favor of a separation between England and her Colonies." Said King George III, "America must be a colony of England or treated as an enemy." In Philadelphia, Benjamin Harrison admitted that because of it he had changed his mind. Sam Adams gave it to everyone he could find, while its hostile critics ranged from Franklin's son William to the already aroused John Adams.

To Paine, however, it appeared now as simply a prologue to a genuine declaration of independence. Up north, Washington won his fight to drive Howe and Burgoyne from Boston. The British had departed in seventy-eight ships, taking with them 1,100 Tories. Yet already the heterogenous volunteer Continental Army was beginning to melt away, while in Halifax and London the British prepared for a seizure of New York by an even greater armada. In Canada, the gallant Arnold had been wounded and failed at Quebec, Montgomery had been killed at Montreal, and the Canadian venture of the Continental Congress had ended in disaster. If ever there was needed a clear, ringing statement of the Colonies' resolve to fight to the end and become an independent nation, now was the time.

Already, too, the delegates to the next session of the Congress were beginning to drift back to Philadelphia. No novelty now, they were beginning to arrive quietly and the townspeople formed no welcoming committees to greet them. Paine himself welcomed them back, however. He sought them out in their lodgings, in coffeehouses, and in inns, in order to speak with them and air his views on separation. Yet in almost every instance he found simply a feeling of indecision. Few seemed willing to be the first to put his head in the hangman's noose. Paine reported this problem almost daily to Sam Adams, and it was the wiry New Englander who finally suggested a solution: a "caucus."

"What is a caucus?"

"It's a name the Algonquin Indians used for a meeting of their chiefs," Sam grinned. "Believe me, it is in such informal gatherings, by commitments to vote for them, that resolutions get adopted." Adams' brown eyes were like a squirrel's. They studied one shrewdly one moment and looked at one with unconcern the next, as though digesting what they had seen. "Let them divide the work between us," he offered. "Let us write to those not yet here and, after a caucus, if a resolution calling for a declaration of independence is offered in Congress, it will come neither as a surprise nor without support. But make no overture to 'King Hancock.' He has grown cool of late."

It was true. Perhaps because Washington had at last driven

[164]

the British from Boston, and now there was little chance anyone could take his place. John Hancock had lost his initial enthusiasm. He had brought his young bride, Mistress Dorothy Quincy, to Philadelphia and had taken up elegant lodgings at Mrs. Yards's, where John Adams also stayed. Whether to impress his bride or the populace with his presidency of the Continental Congress, Hancock now always appeared in public in a carriage attended by four liveried servants, mounted on richly caparisoned horses, and escorted by fifty horsemen with drawn sabers. The entourage had become the dread of tavern owners. It was not unusual for the President of the Congress, as well as his cavalry, to prance off without paying their bills.

In answer to one of Paine's letters, a few days later, Jefferson arrived and Paine was delighted to see him. The tall man brushed a gloved hand down his horse's withers and across its flank. He seemed more concerned by the caking dust on the large bay than that on his own clothes.

"I am not late this time, eh?" he laughed as he slipped off a glove and extended an effeminate hand. When Paine did not answer, he explained: "Last year I was ten days upon the road. I journeyed in a phaeton, with two spare horses. I lost my bearings between Fredericksburg and the Potomac. And again between Wilmington and here. But now, with just one horse, I am early. And I have entrusted the reply to your letter to no courier but myself. The answer is yes. Set a time and place for the caucus and I shall bring the Virginians with me."

Paine smiled. He had written to a number of delegates, but they had shied away from letters that contained sentiments of sedition. Apparently the Virginians were a dauntless lot. "The Masonic Lodge has offered its hall. On Lodge Street, in back of Pemberton's. Do you think there are some who would raise an objection to the choice?"

"No more than to the resolution that will be proposed."

"In about a week then," promised Paine. "Sam Adams is

[165]

busier than I and has promised to bring even Hopkinson and Clark from New Jersey."

Jefferson glanced up at the Statehouse. Atop its steeple a weather vane, wrought like a fleshless fish, was motionless in the humid air. "I shall look forward to seeing them," Jefferson said. "And now I must see to my horse."

Three weeks later, Paine stood in the Masonic Lodge and watched the selected delegates drift in. It had not been easy to persuade them to come. Without the help of Sam Adams and Richard Henry Lee, it could not have been accomplished. Twice, the meeting had been postponed and now, finally, on June 6, 1776, after numerous messengers and personal pleas, the caucus that Sam Adams had suggested was being held.

As the delegates entered the hall, Paine noticed that they did not mingle but formed separate groups: New Englanders, Southerners, and Loyalists. Franklin had not come, but perhaps it was just as well, thought Paine. He had only recently quarreled with his son and discarded his loyalty to England, where he had many friends and with whom his son-in-law did much business. Paine walked to the door and looked out into the warm night. John Dickinson, slightly out of breath, was hurrying to the steps. Paine extended a hand to the latecomer. "You said you would not attend, but you are welcome."

The drafter of "The Olive Branch Petition" searched in a pocket for a letter. "I have recently received it from my mother, Mr. Paine."

Paine interrupted Dickinson's search for the envelope. "I know," he said. "I have been told of it." And so he had. For Dickinson had made a point of showing it everywhere, pointing with a trembling finger to the words:

Johnny, you will be hanged; your estate will be forfeited; you will leave your wife a widow and your children orphans, beggars, and infamous.

[166]

"I do not like it, Mr. Paine," he said now. "I do not like it." But Paine had left his side.

Paine glanced about the room and studied the delegates who had come. He recalled that, when he had left England, he had thought of starting a "much-needed" school in the Colonies. How wrong he had been! Here, in this gathering, there were aristocrats who had been educated in Scotland and in England; men who had been taught French and Spanish by private tutors . . . graduates of William and Mary in the south; of Harvard, Yale, and Dartmouth in the north; of the College of New Jersey and the Philadelphia College in the middle Colonies. For a moment, he was touched by a feeling of inadequacy, but he shook it from him, as he saw that John Adams was sitting next to his cousin Sam. They were engaged in earnest conversation; that was a good sign. John Adams had written: "In the course of this winter appeared a phenomenon in Philadelphia, a disastrous meteor, I mean Thomas Paine." But after the tremendous acclaim *Common Sense* had received, he had become reconciled to the booklet's sentiments.

Paine hardly recognized Sam Adams. He was spick-and-span as he had never seen him, from his powdered wig to his new shoes. He seemed to have been converted from his untidy self into a mirrored image of his cousin John.

At one end of the room, Richard Henry Lee was whispering to Thomas Jefferson, and Benjamin Harrison had joined them. Paine did not like the Virginians sitting together, for there was a growing antipathy between the rival colonies of Massachusetts and Virginia.

John Hancock seated himself beside John Adams. He had not been invited but had heard of the caucus and had come. Suddenly Roger Sherman rose, changed his seat, and joined John and Sam Adams and John Hancock. They were doing here exactly what they would do in the Congress, on the morrow, thought Paine. Suspicious of each other, the southern delegates would look to the Virginians for leadership and the northern colonies would seek their cue from Massachusetts.

Sam Adams looked to Paine and nodded, as if now was the time to call the delegates to order. To his relief, Richard Henry Lee rose and did so. Tall and imposing, despite a thin oval boyish face, he had but to rise in any gathering in order to draw immediate attention.

When the room grew hushed, instead of addressing them, Lee relinquished the floor to Paine. Paine looked about. "Gentlemen," he said without preamble, "Gentlemen . . . it has come to my attention that tomorrow there will be placed before the Continental Congress a resolution calling for a declaration of independence and a confederation of the Colonies. The resolution will be offered by Mr. Richard Henry Lee of Virginia."

Dickinson sprang from his seat, glanced from delegate to delegate, and cried, "I, for one, shall have no part in it. I have been tricked into coming here!"

Benjamin Harrison rose ponderously from his chair. His usually jovial face was touched by anger. His large head turned slowly as he stared from Virginian to Virginian—from Richard Henry Lee to Jefferson, from Jefferson to Carter Braxton, from Braxton to Francis Lightfoot Lee. He turned, faced the Connecticut and Massachusetts delegates who had grouped themselves together, and addressed the delegates: "Sirs, if most of you have been advised of this resolution, then may I say that I, like Mr. Dickinson, have been kept in the dark. And so that it may not be said that I vacillate in my determinations, may I state here and now, independence— yes! As my illustrious friends from Virginia well know, I have accepted their aspirations for separation. But a *confederation of the Colonies . . .* NO!" Turning to face Hancock and Sam Adams, he cried in a voice that grew suddenly high-pitched, "My sentiments as regards the northern Colonies can best be summed up by what my good colleague, Mr. Carter Braxton, expressed in the Virginia Convention not too long ago; *'I abhor their manners—I abhor their laws—I abhor their religion— I abhor their governments!'* "

John Hancock sprang from his chair and cried, "Such a nest of abhorrence could only be fashioned from a jealousy of our ports, our shipping, and our commerce. The South cannot dominate both the waters and the land. And by God, she never shall!"

Paine wished that Franklin had come. Franklin was the catalyst of compromise. But better here than in the Congress tomorrow. "Gentlemen, gentlemen," he pleaded. And when he finally gained their attention, "Am I wrong in believing that Virginia proclaimed a public fast, as an expression of sympathy, when the port of Boston was closed? Is it not true that the Battle of Lexington so shocked Virginia that Washington sprang up and cried, 'I will raise a thousand men, enlist them at my own expense, and march at their head for the relief of Boston?' And who among you believes that New Englanders would refuse to march south to protect your own personal property from destruction?"

There was a moment's hush and in the midst of it Sam Adams rose and faced the Virginians. He raised his short height upon his toes, in the absence of a platform. "Since the Virginians have fasted and prayed for our welfare, I shall recommend—no, I shall insist—that an Episcopal clergyman open Congress tomorrow."

The group was taken by surprise. Samuel Adams was a member of the strictest sect of New England Calvinists. So bitter an enmity existed between them and the Episcopal Church that it extended deep into politics.

Richard Henry Lee rose and accepted the proposal. "I know not what will come of it, gentlemen, but tomorrow I shall offer the resolution for independence to the assembled Congress." There were no loud protesting voices, but a murmur filled the hall. With an orator's gift for timing, he waited

[169]

and added, "A resolution for independence *and a confederation of the Colonies!* One is useless without the other, as a hand without fingers or defense without arms."

John Adams, as though refusing to rise when forced into compromise, spoke from his seat. "My political straw in the wind, gentlemen, tells me that Mr. Paine has worked long and arduously upon the drafting of this resolution that he brings now to light for our belated edification."

Richard Henry Lee rose and said emphatically, "The resolution is not Mr. Paine's, but mine. In all deference to his sentiments, with which, indeed, I agree, it is I who drafted it."

"A manifesto declaring collective independence," continued John Adams, "I say now, as I shall in Congress tomorrow, is a grievous error. And yet it may, by a majority vote, be adopted. If it is, I shall abide by it and support it. But this plan of Mr. Paine's for a representative government, as outlined in his *Common Sense* and his other wishful dissertations, . . ."

Suddenly, he could contain himself no longer. He rose to his feet and gesticulating with flailing arms, cried, "A government for the people and by the people . . . this Paine-envisioned democratic republic . . . I say it will not, it cannot, succeed! Though it be dubbed by the visionary name of United States of America, it is a scribbler's soap bubble, a bubble that will burst with the first ray of trial that will touch it. If Mr. Lee's resolution is approved tomorrow, and I hope to almighty God that it will not be . . . if a new government is to be formed, then let us not be swayed by visionaries. A constitutional monarchy, fashioned after England's, is our only hope!"

"Hear! Hear!" cried Dickinson.

"First things first," said Richard Henry Lee. "Let us first adopt our independence. And may I suggest, gentlemen— with due respect for Mr. Adams—may I suggest that we permit Mr. Paine to draft a declaration for that independence.

[170]

Common Sense has shown that he is well-fitted for it."

No word was spoken but Lee could see disagreement upon almost every face. Only Sam Adams and Thomas Jefferson seemed impressed by the suggestion.

"May I add, gentlemen, that there is no doubt but that one-half million booklets of *Common Sense* will be sold by midsummer ... a dispersion without precedent. The sentiments have even spread to the countries of Europe. And though Mr. Paine will not call attention to it, I shall. He has turned over all of his financial interest in the pamphlet to the cause of independence!"

The delegates turned their eyes upon Paine's shabbiness. He did not know if they were impressed by his largess or thought him a fool.

Rober Sherman rose awkwardly to his feet. As though his linen stock, his cuffs without a frill, and his hand-knitted black stockings were not enough, his very mien laid emphasis upon his Puritan upbringing. A plain man, keeping much to himself, he was said to have been a shoemaker before he had become a lawyer, a judge, and a successful merchant. Laconic when he spoke, he said simply, "Gentlemen, if we are not gathered here for liberty, then we are gathered here for naught. For myself, I have freedom. If not freedom from taxation, then freedom from much else. But as a delegate to Congress, I represent those whose liberties are curtailed and whose freedoms are oppressed. If a resolution for independence will be offered tomorrow, I shall cast my vote for it. My staying here longer will not alter my intention nor do I think that debate among us here will influence the decisions of those who intend otherwise. As a member of the legal profession, I consider discussions upon a prospective resolution within the scope of a convened Congress and nowhere else. My apologies, Mr. Paine, Mr. Lee. May I say goodnight, gentlemen?"

The delegates watched Roger Sherman turn and leave. As

[171]

though the Connecticut delegate had dismissed them, the rest rose, one by one, and left. Sam Adams lingered at Paine's side as the caucus abruptly ended. "There's an oyster house on Water Street," he confided. "Fresh-caught Delaware porgies and imported beer. And a red-haired serving maid with an Irish brogue. Wouldst join me?"

"I know the place," said Paine as they walked out arm in arm. "And her name's Maggie Maguire."

"And I thought I was going to corrupt you," Sam Adams laughed. "Thou art the original chameleon. Before your sun has set, you will be painted all the colors from rascal to saint. Surely you must know that for all your fame and instigation, they will not choose you to draft the declaration?"

Paine looked up at the summer sky and smiled. "If I do, it will be as anonymous as my *Common Sense* first was. I have no intention of affronting any man."

"Then stay away from the Statehouse tomorrow. The conservatives will be goaded by the sight of you. You are not the touchstone of compromise, Tom, but the instigator of dispute. You rankle the well-bred and the men of substance. Even my cousin, John, looks down his nose at you. Your articles in the magazines are more rabble-rousing than erudite. They have affronted everyone. You have been here but a couple of years and you have angered the gaming men by promoting a tenderness for dumb brutes; you have blamed the clergy for condoning slavery; you have censured the wealthy for their childish defense of honor; and you have encroached upon domestic tranquility by insisting upon equal rights for women. And there . . . and there you have it. You're a common man, Tom, bearing the banner of the common man!"

Paine tried to stay away from the Statehouse the next day, while he worked on still another separationist article, but his heart was not in it. When noon came, he rushed to the Statehouse only to find that the Continental Congress had adjourned for the weekend. He knew where many delegates

[172]

would be between this Saturday noon and Monday morning. They would be spending the weekend at the country estates of friends; estates to which he had not yet been invited; affluent estates that ran along the banks of the Schuylkill and stretched as far as Paoli.

In the City Tavern, however, he found Jefferson sharing a table with a fellow delegate from Virginia. Jefferson introduced him as George Wythe. "My former law professor . . . and still my adviser. You've heard me speak of him."

The older man smiled quietly and informed, "Spelled W-Y-T-H-E, but pronounced like 'Smith.' I have endorsed your *Common Sense* and your answers to Cato's letters."

Jefferson smiled and glanced at Wythe, as though for permission to speak of the debate in the Congress. "The adoption of Mr. Lee's resolution appears to be like prematurely weaning a calf. This morning, when Richard presented it, delegates from most colonies and even from your own Pennsylvania rose immediately to protest it."

"Who?" cried Paine. "Who?"

"Be not bitter against them. They were instructed to protest a declaration for independence. Mr. Dickinson led the opposition and in his wake were Mr. Wilson, Robert Livingston, and Mr. Rutledge."

"And the resolution's defenders? Was there none who spoke out for it?"

Jefferson nodded. "Mr. Samuel Adams. Our friend here, Mr. Wythe. I would have. Forgive me, I am not an eloquent speaker. But, Mr. John Adams . . ."

"John Adams?"

"You are surprised? Then may I say that one could not ask for more brilliant arguments. He insisted that the debate was closed when General Washington took to the field. When American blood was shed. 'We have stamped ourselves with either independence or treason,' he said, 'and if I am to choose, I choose the former.'"

"It was Mr. Sherman," George Wythe said quietly, "who first voiced a considered opinion. 'How can we break with England without first having the assurance of a single friend ... of France, of Holland?'"

"No country, Mr. Wythe—neither France, nor Spain, neither Holland, nor any other—will form an alliance with a people who lack the courage to declare their own independence," Paine countered. "Time leads to disinterest, gentlemen, in nations as well as in people. Everything waxes or wanes. Even the tides are of no interest when they are slack."

When Monday came, Paine could not stay away from the Statehouse. He walked into its deserted courtyard. Here, the windows were opened slightly and he could hear voices raised in debate. He could not catch the words, but he could recognize the speakers—the pleading voice of Dickinson, Sherman's slightly nasal tone, the loud and boisterous Sam Adams, the orator's voice of Richard Henry Lee, and the almost imperceptible sound of Franklin speaking, preceded by a hush and followed by silence. What he would not give to be within that Assembly Room!

When the delegates finally left, he watched their faces and could see no happy ones. He wondered to whom to attach himself in order to gain the information he sought. Samuel Adams joined him and drew him away.

"What happened? What happened today?"

"All I can tell you is that, though Rutledge has hysterically summoned John Jay back from New York, to help him hold the Tory line, and though Dickinson urges the delegates to stand fast by their instructions, the tide now runs strongly toward independence. We have recessed for three weeks. Until the first of July."

"Three weeks!" cried Paine as he watched the other delegates leave the Statehouse. "Three weeks!"

"Do not look so hurt. A cooling-off period. The delegates

from New York and New Hampshire are asking for new instructions. We must give them time to receive them. Wait, . . . wait. . . . I forgot to tell you. It was agreed that a declaration of independence be drafted, so that we would have it at hand in the event of a successful issue upon our next meeting. We have voted upon a committee to prepare it." Adams could see the expectancy in Paine's face and hastened to add, "No, Tom. You must remember that you are not a delegate, though I wish you were."

"Richard Lee?"

Adams shook his head. "No, not Lee. One would think that the author of the resolution would be chosen to help draft its declaration. But no. Some say that it is because he has been called home by family illness, but I maintain that there was an intrigue against him. They did not take kindly to our caucus, Tom. Nor to Lee's close association with me and the Massachusetts hotheads." He waited a moment and said, "The committee elected to draft the declaration consists of my cousin John, Franklin, Roger Sherman, Rob Livingston, and Tom Jefferson." He smiled and added, "I think cousin John was tricked into it. He has no truck for the drafting of such a declaration—for either its sentiments or its danger. And it serves him right. When he was nominated to head the committee, instead of declining with grace and honesty, he insisted that the honor be bestowed upon Jefferson. 'He is a Virginian,' he insisted. 'A Virginian ought to appear at the head of this business.' Hancock and Paine didn't know what to make of it. Are you related to our delegate, Robert Treat Paine? No? I have been meaning to ask you. Then, when Jefferson agreed to head the committee, he insisted that John serve on it. So now he may be hanged for a sheep instead of a lion. Wait now, here they come."

He had been facing the Statehouse doors and noticed a group of delegates leaving in a body. Paine turned and watched Jefferson, Franklin, and John Adams descend the steps. They caught sight of him and Sam Adams and walked toward them.

"Congratulations," said Jefferson and extended a hand. Paine was perplexed.

Sam Adams placed an arm about Paine's shoulder. "I meant to tell you, Tom. You were nominated Secretary to the Committee on Foreign Affairs."

"You mean they have chosen a horse when they have as yet no carriage?"

"There will be one," said Jefferson. "Right now, I should be pleased to see what John Adams claims to be your own ill-advised version of the kind of declaration we should make."

14

IF, UNTIL THEN, Jefferson had considered Paine a man of means, he must have been disillusioned when he entered Paine's lodging. A dingy room with grey curtains, it was cluttered with hatters' boxes that were stuffed with old gazettes and magazines. Dusty reference books lay in an untidy pile on the bare floor. The bed was unmade and only the one chair offered a visitor a place to sit.

"There is not enough time, Mr. Jefferson," Paine explained, as he stepped to the dresser he had turned upon its side and took from it a manuscript from among the clutter of quills, candles, inkpots, and half-finished articles piled upon it. "There simply is not enough time."

Jefferson said nothing but seated himself upon the only chair in the room and read the manuscript's title, "A Declaration by the Representatives of the United States of America, in General Congress Assembled."

Tall and slender, each gesture touched by grace, he held himself erect even when reading in a chair. Soon, he looked up and said, "You realize, Mr. Paine, that until now, I have not written a single pamphlet in favor of independence. Unlike Washington, and others, I have not even uttered a single word in defense of your *Common Sense.*"

Paine smiled. "If you will forgive my saying it, Mr. Jefferson, the public expects opinions, like weathercocks, to turn with the wind. Read on, Mr. Jefferson. Read on."

Jefferson read another paragraph, rose, walked to the window, and pulled aside a greying curtain. Thinking that he had heard some disturbing sound, Paine joined him. Jefferson pointed across the street to where a drayman's team was hitched in front of a grocer's shop. On the narrow brick pavement, indentured servants, laden with bundles, followed their mistresses. "Mr. Paine, how can you write into a declaration that all men are created *equal* and *independent,* when a child can see that they are not."

"Created so by God. The inequality is forced upon them by man. When I wrote in my *Common Sense,* 'Mankind, being originally equals in the order of creation,' no one protested it. There were dissenting voices against some principles but not against the principle that all men are created equal."

"We have not yet a Utopia that will accept it."

"Then let it stand for now. Let it be a dream within the concept of this declaration—so that posterity will not be a stranger to its thought."

Jefferson remained at the window and read the declaration's many grievances against Great Britain. He hesitated at the end of one of the paragraphs, turned to Paine, and reread it aloud in a voice that was filled with emphasis and slow-sounding vowels:

[177]

> He (the Christian King of Great Britain) hath prostituted
> his Negative for Suppressing every legislative Attempt. . . .

He fixed his mild grey eyes upon Paine. "I think you use
the word 'prostitute' too loosely, Mr. Paine. Does the word
fascinate you?"

"Forgive me," smiled Paine. "Perhaps I do use the word
too loosely. I abhor the sale of a commodity that should be
offered only for love. Shall we say a past scar?"

Jefferson resumed his reading:

> He (the Christian King of Great Britain) hath waged cruel
> War against human Nature itself, violating its most sacred
> Right of Life and Liberty in the Persons of a distant People
> who never offended him; captivating and carrying them into
> Slavery in another Hemisphere, or to incur miserable Death
> in their transportation hither. This piratical Warfare, the op-
> probrium of infidel powers, is the Welfare of the Christian
> King of Great Britain, determined to keep open a Market
> where Men should be bought and sold . . . and that this Assem-
> blage of Horrors . . .

Jefferson looked up and Paine knew that it was the clause
on slavery that touched him with concern. "It is not a new
sentiment," Paine defended. "It but reiterates and gives emphasis to what I have expressed in my essay on slavery more
than a year ago."

"I own slaves myself, Mr. Paine."

It was true. Paine, with his passion for ferreting out facts,
had learned that four years ago, when Jefferson had married
the wealthy young widow Mrs. Martha Skelton, she had not
only brought to him the munificent dowry of 40,000 acres of
land, but 135 slaves. And yet, he had not actually bought
them . . . they were a marriage gift. So Paine asked, "Are
you averse to giving them their freedom, Mr. Jefferson?"
And when Jefferson seemed to hesitate, "Then let us pass
some resolution for restitution. Or let us, at least, until

a more propitious day, end the traffic in them."

Jefferson curled the pages of the manuscript in his hands. "First things first, Mr. Paine. You strain like a hound on a leash at the scent of game. This is to be a Declaration of Independence. Independence for the Colonies. How they govern themselves or what laws they pass is not for this Declaration to outline."

Paine rushed to his improvised desk, grasped a quill and thrust it into Jefferson's hand. "Then castrate it, Mr. Jefferson! Strike out the phrase, '. . . that from that equal Creation men derive Rights inherent and unalienable . . .' Strike it out!"

"You know not the meaning of compromise, Mr. Paine. You talk as though this draft has already been presented to Congress and adopted. Whereas I have not even commented upon it. I say that even the committee will reject it. If not completely, then at least the slavery clauses."

"Sherman and Adams are New Englanders. They have no need for slaves. And Dr. Franklin's sentiments are as my own."

Jefferson stared out of the window. Finally he said, "Nothing is more certainly written in the book of fate than that these people are to be free, Mr. Paine. Nor is it less certain that the two races, equally free, cannot live in the same government. Nature, habit, and opinion have drawn indelible lines of distinction between them."

"Habits change," Paine objected. "Opinions not only differ but alter. No line of distinction is indelible if man wills it otherwise."

"And I advance it, as a suspicion only, that the blacks, whether originally a distinct race or made so by time and circumstances, are inferior to the whites in the endowment of mind and body."

"And your wife's half sister, Mr. Jefferson?"

Suddenly Jefferson's lips were touched by anger and compressed into silence. The instant that he had asked it, Paine knew that he had erred. "Forgive me," he said. "I did not mean ..."

Jefferson waved a forgiving hand and resumed his reading of the draft. When he finished, he said, "I shall offer it to the committee without comment. I predict that Mr. Adams will not like your referring to King George as a tyrant. And you have harangued Great Britain too much."

"I have another copy of the draft. I would like to offer it to Mr. Adams. You would not mind?"

"No. I think it would encourage compromise."

Paine reached for a decanter and glasses that stood upon the dresser's side. He hesitated for an instant, rinsed the glasses with a little wine, filled them, and offered one to Jefferson. "To few changes by thy committee, Mr. Jefferson, and a speedy adoption."

"I drink to it," said Jefferson. He hesitated and placed the not-too-clean glass to his lips.

During the next two weeks, Paine was filled with a despondency that deepened almost into despair—a pit of despair that was filled with rumors of what was happening to the Declaration of Independence. Each time he met Sam Adams, he was told of deletions and changes that tore at his heart. Sam was not on the committee. How did he know these things? The committee was supposed to be working behind the closed doors of Jefferson's rooms. When Paine was with Franklin or Sherman or Livingston, they never spoke of the Declaration. Yet Sam Adams seemed to possess a full knowledge of the committee's progress.

By the end of June, Paine felt that he must see Jefferson again. He must know how much of Sam's news was rumor and how much was truth. Jefferson had moved from the hospitality of the Randolph House. He now had quarters in the home of a young German bricklayer named Graaf ... a new house on the south side of Market Street, between Seventh

Street and Eighth Street. Paine was admitted to Jefferson's quarters on the second floor; two rooms—a parlor, which also served as a study, and a bedroom. Their tidiness was a far cry from Paine's unkempt lodging.

Jefferson seemed to welcome the interruption. He had evidently been engaged in answering letters. He seemed tired. In answer to Paine's questions, he handed him the finished draft of the Declaration. He lounged in a comfortable chair while Paine audibly read the script. Paine looked up into Jefferson's face. He had noticed that "to advance from that subordination in which they have hitherto remained" had been changed to read "dissolve the political bands which have connected them with another."

Jefferson said quietly, "If you must find fault, find it with me. Livingston and Sherman commended every phrase. Mr. Adams offered no change. Though he does not relish King George being called a tyrant, he has promised not to oppose it. Dr. Franklin suggested a few alterations. The word 'subordination' was not to his liking."

Paine read on and noted with a pang that "have been endowed by their creator" had been substituted for the phrase "from that equal creation." So be it, he consoled himself; the "equal creation" idea was still expressed, and Jefferson was a better master of rhetoric.

As he read on, Paine noted more and more alterations. "Undisguised tyranny of the King" had been entirely omitted. "Deluge us in blood" had been modified to "destroy us." There were so many changes that the draft had lost the mask of Thomas Paine and now wore the façade of sensitive Jefferson. But it was a Declaration of Independence ... independence! And Jefferson had retained the antislavery clauses.

"Dickinson and Robert Morris have asked to see the draft, too. They know it is finished."

"Then permit them, Mr. Jefferson. Quaker Dickinson will

not object to freedom for slaves and Mr. Morris may not object to freedom for us all.''

On Monday, July 1, Paine dressed himself with meticulous care and set out for the Statehouse. As he walked west on Chestnut Street, the sun forecast a hot day.

Many delegates to the Continental Congress had already arrived at the Statehouse and milled about in front of its locked doors. Paine nodded to Roger Sherman, the large, ungainly Connecticut delegate who had served on the Declaration's committee. He wondered if Sherman knew which portions of the draft had originally been his. He nodded to Maryland's Thomas Stone and William Paca. Their fellow delegate, Sam Chase, had remained at Annapolis.

Paine noticed John Adams, hurrying as though he were late, and then John Hancock came into view. As though his dignity would suffer if he walked alone, two liveried servants walked in front and two behind him. Other delegates followed him past the west wing, past the frame sheds, around the walled-in courtyard, and through its gateway on the Walnut Street side. The stout gates were never closed, and people were permitted to pass in and out of the courtyard at all times.

Paine himself entered the courtyard hesitantly, like an uninvited guest. Jefferson, Sam Adams, Livingston, and Franklin were already gathered in a group. To one side, Robert Morris, George Clymer, and Dickinson stood together. Dickinson's face was not a happy one. Dr. Rush, absent from many sessions, was present now. He was talking with Benjamin Harrison, who seemed already perspiring despite the morning hour. He was touching a lace-edged handkerchief to his forehead and his chin.

The Statehouse door opened and the keeper rang a hand bell. It was five minutes to nine as he watched the last delegate enter and saw the keeper shut the door. He was alone in the courtyard. He felt left out. This session of the Congress would debate Richard Henry Lee's resolution, and he would hear no single word. Perhaps, within hours, they would vote upon the Declaration of Independence, and he would hear no single yea or nay. What he would not give to burst through that door and insist, "I have a right to be here! I have earned it!" Had not Jefferson shown him a letter from John Adams in which, in anticipation of this day, he had written: "History is to ascribe the American Revolution to Thomas Paine!"

Paine left the courtyard and retraced his steps to Chestnut Street. He felt shackled to an enforced passivity. In his lodging room he stood at the window and stared out at the teeming rain. The day already seemed interminably long. Once the rain was over, he dashed from his lodging determined to see Sam Adams. Sam lodged close by, at Miss Jane Port's, on Mulberry Street, and he would be able to tell him what had happened.

Miss Port, in side curls and a starched cap with plum-colored ribbons, opened the door. She had a most fetching smile. "Mr. Adams? He is gone. He came home but a short while since, wet as a cat in a tub, changed his clothes, and left again." No, she did not know where. "Wait! He did say something about a Maggie Maguire; wringing out the wet heart of a drowned man!"

Paine found Sam Adams in the oyster house on Water Street. He was seated alone, before a tankard of beer and a plate heaped with lobster. He was happily engaged in cracking pink claws with the handle of a heavy knife. He shook his head at Paine's insistent questioning. Unhurried, he refused to start anywhere but at the beginning. Taking time to eat and drink, he suggested that Paine do the same.

"We could risk no vote today, Tom," he said finally. "The ranks of our independence men were too thin ... with George Wythe at Williamsburg, Gadsden in South Carolina, Rodney in Delaware."

"Then Lee's resolution was not adopted!" cried Paine.

[183]

"You sit there, calmly picking at that . . . that dead crustacean and . . ."

Sam Adams fluttered his grease-stained fingers at Paine. "We have had to put off the decision. Allen and Biddle rather than vote yes, have resigned. Good riddance. Morris and his partner, Tom Willing, are still opposed to independence, but they are not men who raise their voices on the floor. Tomorrow will be different. Maryland's delegates have been instructed to vote *yes*. And New Jersey has sent fresh delegates who are pledged to independence. They arrived today, in all that downpour of rain."

"And Delaware . . . what of Delaware?"

"McKean has sent for Caesar Rodney to break the deadlock."

"Rodney? Rodney is with the militia, in Dover. Eighty miles from here. McKean's a fool!"

Sam Adams twisted a succulent bit of lobster meat from the tendon that held it. "Rest easy concerning Delaware. McKean says Rodney will be here tomorrow if he has to travel to Dover himself tonight and bring him back by moonlight."

Paine's mind had been counting the delegates and the colonies. "Then we have the nine states needed to adopt the resolution?"

"It is what I told you with my first breath. Sit down, damn you. And let me enjoy this . . . this crustacean, as you call it. See now how the little monster has taken vengeance upon me by staining my waistcoat."

The morning of July 2 began with a blazing sun that soon filled the brick dwellings with a stifling heat. Paine awakened none too early. He hurried to the Statehouse to corroborate Sam Adams's optimism. As he reached Fifth Street, he saw Jefferson hurrying toward the Statehouse from Sixth Street. Jefferson waved a hand and, instead of turning toward the courtyard, continued over Chestnut Street and met him in

[184]

front of the Statehouse steps. He had on a light summer suit and carried a collapsible knee desk. His smooth face wore a confident smile.

"I fear we are a bit late, Mr. Paine. Just a bit." The front door was open, perhaps because of the growing heat, and he hurried up the steps. As he entered the hall, he realized that Paine had not followed him and he turned back.

"I am not a member of Congress, Mr. Jefferson."

"You may be within the hour. Come."

"The doorkeeper?"

"Come!"

Paine entered a wide center hall. At one end a spiral stairway led to an upper floor. On each side of the hall three arches rested upon tall, fluted columns that rose in Hellenic stateliness to support a twenty-five–foot ceiling.

The Pennsylvania Assembly had moved upstairs and lent their East Room, on the ground floor, to the Continental Congress. The doorkeeper nodded to Jefferson. He stood in front of double doors that were set into a wide frame. Above the frame, molded into the plaster, was a carved ornamental face.

Paine followed Jefferson into the large, paneled chamber. It was a beautiful room, lined on two sides with tall arched windows. A handsome glass-prism chandelier hung from its center. Twin fireplaces, painted white, were set into the far wall. President Hancock sat in front of them and faced the room.

"You can sit near me, in Richard Lee's chair, since he has not returned."

Paine glanced at the gathered delegates. Suddenly he remembered Sam Adams' admonition: "You are not the touchstone of compromise, Tom, but the instigator of dispute." He shook his head. "Forgive me, Mr. Jefferson. Until the resolution is adopted, I would rather sit quietly in back."

Paine seated himself and looked about him. There should

[185]

be sixty-eight delegates, but there were many empty chairs. Dr. Franklin was seated in front, next to Jefferson. His chair, at the end of a row, was pulled out a little from the rest. He had on a fresh, Quaker-brown suit. He seemed tranquil and composed.

To one side of him was a Dr. Hall, sitting quietly alone. Paine had met him at the Indian Queen. He was from the parish of St. John's, and he had ridden nearly 800 miles—six weeks on horseback—to represent Georgia as a delegate.

John Adams was already seated close to a window that opened on the courtyard. He had laid his drawstring lawyer's bag on the window sill, had taken papers from it, and was settling himself. To the right, behind the president's chair, a door opened and Sam Adams came in. He caught sight of his cousin and joined him. It seemed that he had not changed last night's stained waistcoat.

At nine o'clock Paine heard the doors behind him being closed and locked. He continued to look about him. Robert Morris was not present. Nor was John Dickinson. Sam Adams had said that they might not attend.

Lewis Morris had turned about at the sound of the doors being closed. He noticed Paine and his face assumed a surprised expression. But three days ago he had confessed to Paine that, although, as a New York delegate, he was committed to vote against it, his sympathies were for independence . . . because of *Common Sense.* He had offered Paine the hospitality of Morrisania, if ever he were in New York. Paine nodded to Morris and smiled.

To Paine's surprise and impatience, the morning began with trivial matters. Charles Thompson, the clerk of the court, a portly and scholarly gentleman, arose from his desk, a little to the left of President Hancock's table, and began to read letters aloud. He read in a monotone and his voice was dry and rasping, as he disposed of his pile of requests, conjectures, complaints. . . . The delegates listened indifferently. Outside, it had again begun to rain. Water ran down the window panes in little jagged rivulets. The doorkeeper entered and began to shut the windows at their tops. In the midst of his rounds, clerk Thompson finally began the reading of Richard Henry Lee's resolution:

> That these United Colonies are, and of a right ought to be, free and independent States; that they are absolved from all allegiance to the British Crown, and that all political connection between them and . . .

No time was lost in voting upon the resolution. New Hampshire was called first and voted. *"FOR."*

"Massachusetts: *FOR."*

"New York." The delegates rose and suddenly McKean sprang to his feet. He glared at the New York delegates—at Robert Livingston, Lewis Morris, and William Floyd—as though he dared them to cast their votes against independence. His hawk's nose seemed to dominate his thin face. Livingston started to speak when suddenly, despite the downpour of rain, there was the unmistakeable sound of a horse and rider dashing into the courtyard. McKean rushed to the Assembly Room doors and pummeled upon them crying; "Open up! Open up! It's Rodney!"

The delegates rose as one man to watch for Caesar Rodney who must have galloped all the way from Dover. In a moment, McKean brought him to the doorway. Rodney was splattered with mud from head to spurred boots. He swayed with exhaustion. But for McKean, who supported him, it seemed he must drop to the floor. Paine had met Rodney but three months ago, at Robert Bell's. He had come to purchase 500 copies of *Common Sense,* for distribution among his militia. Now he stood, sopping wet, dripping a puddle on the floor, waiting to catch his breath.

He was an odd-looking man—tall, as slender as a reed, with a small head, as though it had stopped growing when he was still a child. A green silk handkerchief was tied over the left side of his face, where it was eaten away by a cancer. Emaciated, he looked like a man who was dying . . . and so he was. Affluent and a bachelor, he had been advised to go to England for surgical attention, or at least the ease of his pain. Instead, he was here to vote for independence and forfeit the benefit of England's medical attention.

The quiet of the Assembly Room changed to a murmur of voices as the delegates resumed their seats. The clerk called for a continuation of the vote, while the New York delegates whispered among themselves. Lewis Morris watched McKean lead Rodney to a chair and finally said. "The delegates from New York are personally in favor of Mr. Lee's resolution. As soon as our instructions are modified, we will vote 'for' with the others."

"Rhode Island." William Ellery rose and voted. *"FOR."* Mild-mannered Stephen Hopkins, his fellow delegate, shook his head but did not contest the vote.

"Connecticut: *FOR.*"

"Pennsylvania." There was a moment's delay, for Colonel Humphries and Thomas Willing were still against a vote for independence. Red-faced and stubborn, they finally gave ground. They admitted that, with Robert Morris and Dickinson absent, the votes of Franklin, Morton, and Wilson carried the Colony. John Morton raised a hand, "Pennsylvania votes *For.*"

"New Jersey: *FOR.*"

"Delaware." McKean rose, stared defiantly at its single dissenting delegate, and voted. *"FOR."*

"Virginia: *FOR.*"

"North Carolina: *FOR.*"

"South Carolina." Yesterday the Colony had been opposed. Now Edward Rutledge rose pompously from his chair. He was proud to be the youngest delegate to the Continental Congress. He had pointed out to Paine, when he first met him, that he had studied law in London. He would not be averse to giving advice ... if called upon. He glanced about and announced, in a nasal drawl, "South Ca'olina, FOR."

"Georgia: FOR."

"Resolution adopted," said the clerk,

Instinctively, Paine glanced at Jefferson. The Virginian had placed his portable desk across his knees. Paine had seen it before. It was a narrow, box-like affair that the ingenious Jefferson had designed. It had a single drawer and a hinged top that could unfold to twice its length and lift to any angle by a folding support. The papers upon it were most likely a draft of the independence declaration. There would be a copy on the clerk's desk, ready for the debate. Paine settled back while the clerk brought up another matter.

"Resolved: That the Marine Committee be empowered to contract with shipwrights to go to Lake Champlain and build a fleet there ... designed to keep the British in Canada. These marine carpenters are to be given one month's pay in advance, etc., etc. ... Each should be allowed a ration and a half plus one-half pint of rum a day. Etc., etc. ..."

At last the clerk picked up the sheets of the Declaration of Independence and announced in his dry, unconcerned voice: "... drafted by a committee of five, appointed for the task on June 10, 1776. Said committee consisting of Mr. Thomas Jefferson, of Virginia; Dr. Benjamin Franklin, of Pennsylvania; Mr. Robert Livingston, the delegate from New York; Mr. John Adams, the delegate from Massachusetts; and Mr. Roger Sherman, the delegate from Connecticut."

Paine could see that John Adams, still seated near the window, was studying a collection of papers on his lap. Sam Adams was whispering to him. Suddenly Paine was aware that the clerk had begun to read the Declaration:

When in the course of human events it becomes necessary for a people to dissolve the political bands which have connected them with another, and to advance from that subordination in which they have hitherto remained, and to assume among the powers of the earth, the equal and independent station . . .

The clerk's voice continued and suddenly Roger Sherman raised a hand and interrupted him by rising awkwardly from his chair. "If I may make so bold as to comment upon the line 'equal and independent station,' I believe that, in view of our now pressing need of foreign allies, the term 'independent station' would seem a flaunting one. I beg the indulgence of the Congress, since I served on the drafting committee, and should not have waited until now for comment upon the matter, but it did not come to my attention until at this reading by Mr. Thompson. I would suggest that it read 'to assume among the powers of the earth the equal station.' "

"Why not 'separate' for 'independent?' " suggested Sam Huntingdon.

"Both 'separate' an' 'equal.' " Paine recognized young Rutledge's drawl. "Ah would suggest the phraise raid, 'assume among the powers of the earth, the separate an' equal station.' "

"Separate" and "equal" was adopted to take the place of "equal" and "independent." Paine could see Jefferson carefully making the change upon his draft.

The clerk continued the reading and then, as though Roger Sherman's suggestion had been an opening wedge for criticism, there came a multitude of comment upon every phrase; the original defended, the change protested, the protest challenged.

John Adams rose and pounded the floor with his hickory walking stick. He was accustomed to rising on his toes for emphasis, but now, his temper worn thin, he waved his arms. He turned about like a weathercock in a changing wind and glared at the delegates. "There are rankling words and caustic

[190]

phrases in that Declaration that I do not personally condone,"
he cried, shaking his stick in the direction of the sheets in the
clerk's hand. "I did not like them in committee and I do not
like them here! But I did not then and I do not now protest
them! If we cannot compromise on expressions, then we shall
never agree on the actions that they will necessitate. But you,
gentlemen, you," he shook a lifted stick at them, "must you
judge a barrel of apples by the first specked member that you
pick from it? Let Mr. Thompson read the whole draft. Let him
read it! All of it!"

Adams seated himself. Paine watched the faces of the delegates as the clerk resumed his reading. Many seemed restrained and sullen. Paine heard Thompson read: "We hold
these truths to be self-evident . . ."

No truth is self-evident, thought Paine. It has to be
searched for and arrived at. In the first draft the words had
been "we hold these truths to be sacred and undeniable."

Thinking of the change, he almost missed the next portion
of the draft. The clerk was enumerating the many grievances,
reading from a second sheet:

> For cutting off our trade with all parts of the world.
> For imposing taxes on us without our consent.
> For depriving us, in many cases, of the benefits of trial by
> jury.
> For transporting us beyond the seas to be tried for pre-
> tended offenses.
> He has plundered our seas, ravaged our coasts, burnt our
> towns, and destroyed the lives of our people.

A protesting murmur filled the Assembly Room. Thompson waited for silence to be restored and began to read the
antislavery clauses:

> He (the Christian King of Great Britain) hath waged cruel
> war against human nature itself, violating its most sacred rights
> of life and liberty in the persons of a distant people who never

offended him ... determined to keep open a market where MEN should be bought and sold ...

There was a deep murmur in the room. As it grew, the clerk raised his voice to be heard, but the muttering turned to loud protestations. It was a half hour before silence was restored and Mr. Thompson was able to conclude the reading of the Declaration. Immediately, there were loud cries that the antislavery clauses and its indictments against the King be stricken from it. Not only the Georgia delegates, but delegates from Maryland, North Carolina, New Hampshire, and South Carolina rose to their feet and protested. Only the Virginians sat undisturbed, as though they, themselves, owned no slaves.

Rutledge rose and raised both arms as an intermediary. The rain had stopped, but the windows were still shut. The room was like an oven and the flies still tormented the delegates. "Ah offer a resolution that the session be adjourned until tomorrow."

It was the middle of the afternoon, but the resolution was carried.

When Congress adjourned, the delegates went, almost in a body, to the Long Room of the City tavern. Paine went with them and, seating himself beside Roger Sherman, whispered, "You were the first to insist upon a change in the Declaration. For the sake of humanity, you must not let the antislavery clauses be expunged!"

Sherman sat unperturbed. His big hands, which had once cobbled shoes, rested upon his brown velvet breeches. With unruffled calm he said, "My primary interest is in liberty, Mr. Paine. A frog that clambers up a foot and slips back two will never reach the top of the well. Mr. Livingston and Mr. Adams share my opinion. Though not completely satisfied with the draft in committee, we offered no change and accepted such criticism as Dr. Franklin submitted. The adoption of the Declaration was our only concern."

Paine led Jefferson aside and pleaded, "The delegates look to you. Could you, as a slaveowner, but set the example and defend the antislavery clauses . . . ."

"My sentiments are with you, Mr. Paine, but it is impracticable." He seemed tired . . . vexed.

"You have many southern friends whom you can persuade. And it will not matter to the New England colonies."

"Do not goad me!" Jefferson cried, suddenly losing his consistent calm. "Have you no eyes that you cannot see the faces of the New Englanders! Our northern brethren feel quite tender under the censure of that clause; for, though their people have few slaves themselves, yet they have been considerable carriers of them to others. I presented the antislavery clauses in the Declaration. More I cannot do."

Paine turned away, disheartened. Seeing John Adams, he hurried to him as a last hope. "John," he entreated, "John . . . this is a Declaration of Independence. Not alone independence of government but independence for man . . . based upon the equal rights of man. Could such liberty permit any fashion of slavery?"

"I give you my word," said Adams. "I did not protest the clauses on Negro slavery in committee. You were in Congress today and saw that I did not oppose them. At the cost of disfavor, I intend to defend them; but I do not want the King called a *tyrant* in the Declaration. It is too personal an affront. And do not press me, for if you look about you, you will see that most of us are not too happy with this Declaration. The delegates do not look forward to a single government for all the colonies. Every state is concerned for its own sovereignty." He noticed Paine looking toward Franklin and advised, "And foster no dependence upon Dr. Franklin. The Declaration's criticism of the English people rankles him. Statesman-like, he has offered little comment, and yet I know that soon, if no one else will censure it, he will strive to have those phrases deleted. He has too many strong friends in

England. He is more interested in having expunged 'these were effected at the expense of our own blood and treasure, unassisted by the wealth or the strength of Great Britain' than he is in your slaves."

Disheartened, Paine left the City Tavern.

Wednesday, he watched all day as the delegates wrangled over the text of the Declaration. Phrases were shortened. Clauses were changed. Abuses were deleted. The sharp edges of caustic terms were tempered. Even "to advance from that subordination" was expunged from the very first sentence. True to his word, John Adams gave an able defense of the antislavery clauses. His oratory fell upon deaf ears. Jefferson was occupied with quill and ink upon his collapsible knee desk. Paine saw him scratch out sentences, change words, and alter meanings. When would it all end?

Thursday morning was brilliant with sunshine. Because of the rains, the Delaware had inundated Dock Creek and an east wind carried a disturbing scent from Howell's tan yards in Hudson's Alley. Other than that, it was a glorious day.

Paine sat in the Congress, in his now accustomed seat, a black, painted hickory armchair, commodious even for a Harrison, and listened unattentively to the first resolution:

Resolved: that an application be submitted to the Committee of Safety of Pennsylvania, for a supply of flints and cartouches for the troops at New York ... etc., etc. ...

He noticed that Robert Morris had returned. There were two more resolutions and then clerk Thompson read the amended Declaration of Independence. As though no single alteration had as yet been made, the debate upon the Declaration's connotations was immediately resumed.

"By a self-assumed power" was protested; "were likely to" was changed to "would inevitably; McKean insisted that "to send over Scottish and foreign mercenaries to invade and destroy us" must be expunged! "There are too many Scottish descendants among us."

Jefferson noted each change on his draft, which threatened to become all but illegible. As the day wore on, the delegates began to insist on eliminating not merely phrases but whole sentences. They accused Jefferson, to whose authorship the entire draft was now attributed, of being too verbose. John Adams, waving his own copy of the draft in a stubby hand, objected to almost every proposed change.

Finally the clerk read the much-altered draft once more, and a hush descended upon the Assembly Room as Hancock rose and asked the delegates if they were ready to cast their votes for the adoption of the Declaration of Independence in its amended form.

Paine looked toward Franklin and Jefferson where they sat side by side. Jefferson, weary, was studying his mutilated draft. Franklin was smiling. He had stretched forward the one leg that was troubled by gout. He was whispering to Jefferson in a seemingly endless confidence.

Sam Adams rose and moved that they cast their votes. "A change of political attachment has evolved itself," he said. "It was first a question of whether or not. Then a choice of expression. And now it seems that only a record of the voting is needed."

The New Hampshire delegation was called upon first. The senior member, Josiah Bartlett, tall, somewhat careless of his appearance, was the first to accept the Declaration of Independence.

"New Hampshire: *FOR.*"

"Massachusetts: *FOR.*"

"Rhode Island." Mild-mannered Stephen Hopkins rose to cast his vote. On Tuesday, at the first reading, he had declared, "Expunge all else, gentlemen, and leave the antislavery clauses, and I shall accept and defend this Declaration to the utmost of my abilities." Now the antislavery clauses were gone. He stood solemnly, his hands clasped behind his Quaker-brown muslin coat, and looked about. Finally he said, "Gentlemen, I will not be shown the door by any man, and so I publicly withdraw from the Society of Friends and vote *yea* with Rhode Island's delegates."

A murmur filled the room. Quaker Joseph Hughes, the North Carolina delegate who had opposed Lee's resolution, rose to his feet and stared aghast at Hopkins.

"Rhode Island: *FOR.*" The clerk's voice was dry and rasping.

"Connecticut: *FOR.*"

"New York." Lewis Morris rose. "New York asks the indulgence of Congress . . . to be permitted to cast its vote on a later date . . . since its delegates are still forbidden to vote for independence."

"Pennsylvania." Robert Morris looked about him. Dickinson had not returned. Dr. Benjamin Rush was absent. The votes of Franklin, Morton, and Wilson, would be enough to carry the Colony. He rose, thrust out a thick underlip, like a pouting child, stared at Hancock, and declared, "I think that a good subject will follow if he cannot lead. I vote *yea.*" If others were impressed, the clerk was not. His voice droned on: "Pennsylvania: *FOR.*"

"New Jersey: *FOR.*"

"Maryland: *FOR.*"

"Delaware: *FOR.*"

"Virginia: *FOR.*"

"North Carolina: *FOR.*"

"South Carolina: *FOR.*"

"Georgia." George Walton, small yet smartly dressed, a self-made lawyer from Augusta, got up from his chair. Hot-tempered Button Gwinnett rose behind him. Before either could speak, Dr. Lyman Hall got to his feet. He looked unhurriedly about the Assembly Room. He was tall, greying at the temples, and most impressive in appearance. He nodded

[196]

to Paine, who had supplied him with 100 copies of *Common Sense* to take back with him to Georgia. He turned and smiled to Franklin, to Jefferson, to Hancock. Finally he said dramatically, "I am the senior member of the Georgia delegation. It is done, gentlemen; mathematically and providentially. The votes have been cast, from the north to the south. as straight as a plummet line. And it is prophetic that I, the last delegate to the Congress, should cast the last vote for this Declaration of Independence and in doing so, adopt it. Georgia votes *yea.*"

Clerk Thompson echoed, "Georgia votes *for.* The Declaration is carried."

Hancock stepped to the clerk's desk. There was a minute of whispering and the clerk announced: "It is ordered that the Declaration be printed and copies sent out."

No one cheered. The delegates sat as though no Declaration of Independence had been adopted at all.

15

THE DAY after the city's wild celebration over the adoption of the Declaration, Paine went to Aitken's shop with an article on conscription. He found Aitken's sign being repainted and the words PENNSYLVANIA MAGAZINE being expunged.

"The *Pennsylvania Magazine* is na moore, Mr. Paine," said Aitken. And when Paine lifted a questioning eyebrow, "Ah'll no' 'ave a paper filled wi' tha seditious writin'. Tha'rt a marked mon, Tom Paine! Ah'll 'ave nou' ta do wi' wot is controoversial. Tha lov'st Booby Bell so much, 'e c'n proont wot tha writes from noo, as 'e 'as tha *Common Sense.*"

"If it's Bell's success that rankles you," said Paine, "may I remind you that I first offered you the publication of *Common*

Sense?'' There was no answer as Paine watched PENNSYL-
VANIA MAGAZ still disappearing under a layer of fresh paint.
"Listen," said Aitken at last. "Tha thinks Congress c'n gi'
us independence ba vootin' it. An' ah tells tha if 'twere
tongues coul' ma' it so, then Scootlan' woul' na 'ave a English
King. Woul' she noo? Ah'll na 'ave a magazine, boot ah'll 'ave
ma press, an' ma foonts. An' ma life, Tom Paine. Didst think
ah coom' ta the Colonies ta be 'anged?"

Paine attended the final sessions of the Continental Congress, but there was nothing for him to do. He had been
appointed Secretary to the Committee on Foreign Affairs.
The States had no foreign affairs—no representatives abroad
and no foreign ambassadors at home. New York relieved her
delegates of their restrictions and they cast their votes for
independence. The title was changed to "The Unanimous
Declaration of the Thirteen United States of America" and
the Congress, in order to spread the "blame" for the Declaration, resolved that it be "engrossed on parchment and signed
by every member of Congress."

To Paine, the days that followed seemed to lack a vital
interest, as though the mainspring of their hours had run
down. He caught up with his mail. His room was filled with
unanswered letters and even unopened ones. The packets
from Europe, the stagecoaches from the New England colonies, and the postriders from Virginia and Maryland had
brought a continuous stream of them.

He opened a letter from France. It was from a Jeanne
Manon Phlipon and bore the address of an engraver in Paris.
It was written in French. It was a long letter and evidently
complimented him upon his *Common Sense.* He laid it aside to
be translated.

There was a letter from a Maximilien Robespierre—a law
student of eighteen who had read *Common Sense.* He had been
greatly impressed by it and was evidently a devotee of Rousseau. There were letters from England, too, where *Common*

Sense had been surreptitiously distributed. There was a letter from Guy Falk and one from Edmund Burke. There was mail from his old friends, John Horne and Clio Rickman. He settled down to write delinquent replies.

A letter from Joseph Paine disclosed that his father had read a copy of *Common Sense.* The letter neither praised nor censured the opinions that the booklet expressed. He must send some money to his parents, thought Paine, before the mails to England were barred. After deliberation, touched by nostalgia, he decided to send what he could to the Ollives. Elizabeth was no longer his wife, no letter from England ever made mention of her, but he still wondered about her. It was not possible that the four walls of a single lodging room should be his destiny. Perhaps, someday. . . .

In the evenings, Paine would go to the Statehouse courtyard and watch Colonel Nixon drill the Philadelphia Associators. The volunteers had no uniforms, but they had bucktails on their hats.

On Saturday mornings, Paine would walk to John Cadwalader's garden and watch the Silk Stocking Company practice. They were a colorful group, with green jersey caps and light green uniforms whose breasts were crossed by white leather belts. The word LIBERTY was painted on their cartouche boxes.

Again, Paine felt left out. There was no *Pennsylvania Magazine* to edit and day by day the attendance at the Continental Congress thinned. Pain-racked Caesar Rodney had returned to his militia post in Dover. Lewis Morris had left to join General Washington. Even Colonel Dickinson, with his womanly, oval face and his timid attachment to the British Crown, had left for war now that independence had been unanimously adopted. Paine decided to go too. He would offer his services, such as they might be, to Daniel Roberdeau, who had been elected a brigadier general and was now at Perth Amboy. A battalion had left, but a few days ago, to join him.

Paine had no affairs to settle and he was sure that the Congress could spare him.

He did not reach General Roberdeau's "Flying Camp" until the end of July. Perth Amboy, he found, was a large stretch of wooded flatland, in the center of which General Roberdeau had ordered a section of timber cut down for his camp. When Paine arrived, Roberdeau welcomed him warmly and introduced him to his aides—a Lieutenant Stephen Lincoln, who had come with the Maryland Militia, and a Captain Horace Braintree, of Boston, a man in his late forties, who had served under Israel Putnam in the French and Indian wars.

"You have come to the wrong camp," said Roberdeau, striding back and forth. "We are confined here with nothing to do, as though the very woods have imprisoned us. The men grow listless with waiting and every day that passes brings them closer to the termination of their enlistments. Exactly what have you come for, Mr. Paine? To write a commentary on my victories?"

"I have come to join the Pennsylvania Volunteers. As a common soldier."

Roberdeau did not believe him.

Paine turned to Braintree and offered, "At least things are better now in Boston."

"Better!" cried the Captain. Anger flushed his face and showed a livid scar across all of one cheek. "I was back in Boston but two months ago. I tell you, Charlestown looked like it was razed. The British basta'ds tore down every wooden building and used them for firewood. In Boston proper, I could not believe my eyes. The steeple of the West Church, of the Old North Church, wharves, and even ships were smashed, and the wood used to keep the damned British at toasting fires . . . while the townsmen who had not left froze in their homes!"

[200]

"Let me tell you what the basta'ds did," continued the Captain. "Not the stupid mercenaries, nor the besotted regulars, but the officers. The British officers, mind you!" He grasped Paine by the arm and insisted in a trembling voice, "They ripped out the pulpit and the pews of the Old South Church where I attended services as a boy, with my parents. The church library was fed into the fires. Its floor was covered with tanbark. The church was turned into a riding school and its gallery into a tavern room. When I went into it, my townsmen had cleaned up the largest portion of it, but the church still stank of stale beer, foul excrement, urine, and manure. Write that in your periodicals, Mr. Paine! Advise that to an unsuspecting world!"

In the moment of silence that followed, Captain Braintree turned and left. "Lieutenant Lincoln," said Roberdeau, "would you see to quarters for Mr. Paine?"

Paine shook his head. "I meant what I said," he insisted. "I wish to become one of the militia. Give me a musket and point out to me the encampment of the Pennsylvanians. I ask for no more."

Paine slept that night in the open, among the enlisted men. The next day he ate breakfast with the militia.

He had arrived as the sun was setting and had seen little of the camp. Now, having eaten, he walked about and studied it. Some of the accommodations were made of boards, some were tents that had been constructed from sailcloth. A few were made of fieldstone and turf, but most were shelters of brush and birch bark. Here and there, like a snobbish aristocrat, slightly aloof, there would rise a proper tent or a colorful marquee. The shelters ran across the cleared land, in a wide circle, as far as the eye could see.

Despite the rising heat of the day, the men were building innumerable campfires. They squatted about them amid their powder horns and cartouche boxes, bullet molds and pouches of extra flints—and here and there, haversacks, rolled blankets, and a few bayonets. They were a far cry from the British regulars that Paine had seen in Dover.

On the outer perimeter of the camp a number of backwoods volunteers were gathered. They seemed remarkably stout, hardy men garbed in round wool hats, leather leggings, Indian-style moccasins, and loose hunting shirts the color of faded leaves. Paine was fascinated by them. These men seemed never to have needed a Declaration of Independence. They must have insisted upon it the instant they stepped on American soil!

Roberdeau's clearing nestled between the Raritan River and Arthur Kill. During the night, a cool breeze swept into it from Raritan Bay. One such night, Paine awoke to find himself covered by a warm hunting shirt. A tall, rawboned young man smiled at him. "You was a-chatt'rin' like a chipmunk. An' it not yet fall. Now, up in the mountains, where I comes from . . . This here a valley, aint it?"

"Where do you come from?"

" 'Toona. Up past the Blacklog Mountains."

"And it's colder there?"

"Nights," the boy grinned.

"What urged you . . . what made your mind so set on volunteering?" asked Paine.

The boy looked reflective. "Waal," he said, "they was talk about the British stirrin' up the Injins agin. An' they was talk 'bout not lettin' us drift past the Alleghenies. An' I hear now that Gen'l Washington in New York has told the boys we're all independent, so I'll go along with that."

Paine received a delayed letter from Colonel Kirkbride, containing the news that the delegates had signed the Declaration of Independence on August 20. Paul Revere, the silversmith, had sent a pair of silver inkwells for the occasion. Yet, Kirkbride wrote, many were not ready to accept independence and feared it. The letter contained a clipping from the *New England Portfolio* that called the Declaration

> . . . an incoherent accumulation of indigestible and impractical
> political dogmas, dangerous to the peace of the world and
> seditious in its local tendency.

Bored with the "Flying Camp," Paine decided to try to reach General Greene and, a week later, marched northward, across the flatlands of New Jersey, toward Fort Lee on the Hudson. On the evening of the fourth day, he reached a crossroads tavern near the banks of the Passaic River. It was a single-story structure with narrow windows and a sloping roof. A hanging sign informed the traveler: "Cock and Bull Inn. Eat well. Sleep fyne."

Weary and footsore, Paine decided to spend the night. He had brushed the road dust from his clothes and was about to enter when he heard the whinnying of horses and the clink of braces. He stopped in front of the tavern's cross-beamed door and lifted a hand against the rays of the setting sun. Three sideless wagons, pulled by tired plow horses, came into view. As they came closer, he was aghast by what he saw. They were filled with wounded men who clung to each other to keep the turning wheels from scraping against them. Ragged strips of red-stained cloth, evidently torn from varied garments, had been tied clumsily about their heads and arms and legs. Mud-stained muskets, bayonets, and powder horns lay on the wagons in discarded heaps. Paine was filled with compassion as he ran toward them. On the first wagon, a man with a bitter, weather-beaten face stared sullenly from beneath a filthy wig. "Whose men?" cried Paine.

"Stirling's Brigade," said the wagoner. "From New York." He pointed a mud-encrusted finger at the Cock and Bull Inn. "Tory or Whig?" he demanded.

Paine lifted an uninformed shoulder. "I've but come myself. A Philadelphian."

The man grasped the reins from the wagon driver, held up his arm as a signal to the others, pulled up the tired horses, and began to unload the wounded.

Puzzled, Paine helped him make the men comfortable in the straw of the nearby barn and, once they were fed, watered the horses and sat down amidst the hubbub of the now crowded inn, where the wagoner soon joined him.

Now that he had washed and cleaned his wig, he looked more like a landowner of some substance than the small farmer Paine had at first thought him. "Jason Witherspoon," he introduced himself and extended a friendly hand. His voice was throaty. "May I join you?"

Paine nodded and said quietly, "Paine is my name. At your service, sir."

A shaggy eyebrow arched itself above a keen brown eye. "Not Thomas Paine? Mr. *Common Sense?*"

Paine took a sip of brandy and nodded.

The man's red face broke into a wide grin. "Well, now . . . let me look at you. I always wanted to see the man who scattered *Common Sense* over the countryside. Do you know that there are those in New York and Harlem Heights as would skewer you and toss you into the North River with an anchor fluke tied to your feet? Aye, even in White Plains there are some."

It was the first time Paine had heard of the existence of such animosity. "Why?" he asked. "Why?"

"For what you have incited the Colonies to do, Mr. Paine. I'm a provisioner. I hear what is said in Howard's Tavern at Jamaica Pass, in Red Lion Inn on Gowanus Bay, at a dozen hostelries and New York hotels. My God! Mr. Paine, where have you been? I watched the British begin to mass a fleet in the North River as long ago as the end of June. With a spyglass and these eyes, Mr. Paine—these very eyes—I stood on the catwalk of the Porpoise Inn, on Dock Street, and watched the British warships drift into the bay and bring

General Howe from Halifax. Didn't your General Washington know you can't hold New York against a fleet that can sail round it? One hundred and thirty transports and ships of war. And 30,000 men." Witherspoon laughed bitterly. "I was in New York City, Mr. Paine, when the Declaration was publicly read. Your jubilant patriots pulled down the mounted figure of King George. And two months later, when General Howe landed an army on Long Island, there were no patriots. My God! Haven't you heard of Washington's retreat from New York? Pell-mell to White Plains and Peekskill, with Fort Washington left behind."

"I do not believe it!"

Witherspoon sprang from his chair so that it fell backward with a clatter. Regaining his composure, he righted it and seated himself. "Forgive me, I think I have spoiled your appetite for food. May I call for another flask of wine? Or is it brandy?"

Paine shook his head. "My apologies. I've been away from Congress too long. And from the news. You have startled me by it, but, I assure you, neither strategy nor numbers shall prevail for the British. Not so long as every American defends his own freedom."

"Mr. Paine, I am not a Tory but a Whig. Else you would not find me transporting the wounded. But I see no freedom. I make it my point to know, Mr. Paine; and I know that in the British army in New York there are close to thirty regiments of the line. Battalions of light infantry, battalions of grenadiers, battalions of guards, brigades of artillery, light dragoons, and over 8,000 Hessians, perhaps as many as 10,-000. My God! Mr. Paine, an army of 35,000 professional soldiers, fully equipped and abundantly supplied. I could weep when I think of Putnam's men, and Washington's and Lee's trying to hold them off. I was with Old Put fifteen years ago. Do you think I do not love my land and my own freedom? I have been told that this is the greatest expeditionary

[205]

force that Great Britain has ever sent out from its shores. At a cost . . . at the staggering cost of close to a million pounds!"

Paine's eyes blinked at Witherspoon. "They could never afford it!"

"The British will see to that, Mr. Paine. Aye! With interest. There will be so much confiscated goods that it will take years for all of their ships to carry it back to England."

Alone in his room, Paine stared out of the window. It had begun to rain. It was a rain that was whipped by a cold autumn wind. The sky was as dark as the future seemed. Beyond a staggered line of young trees, he could see the outline of the barn, a black shadow against the dark grey sky. He had counted close to fifty wounded men. They were not all Smallwood's Marylanders. Some were from Haslet's Delaware Continental Regiment. As he thought of what they had told him and pieced their information together, he realized that Witherspoon was not in error. The British must have not only General Howe and General Clinton in New York, but Von Heister's Hessians and possibly even Cornwallis' men.

Washington's army was made up of men no different than the militiamen and volunteers in the "Flying Camp." They were valiant men—eager for independence—but untrained and meagerly equipped. Soberly, Paine had to admit to himself that the Continental Army was led by an amateur commander-in-chief and that he was supported by amateur officers. It was not David and Goliath—it was a tired hare set upon by a pack of fresh hounds. Had he aroused the country to an impossible achievement? Was America's freedom so unobtainable? Was the "rebellion" over?

He spent a restless night, arose at sunrise, and did not take time to eat breakfast. He purchased some provisions and set out, despite a cold, driving rain, toward Fort Lee.

16

PAINE REACHED Fort Lee on September 19, to learn that
Washington's forces had been badly defeated on Long Island
and driven from New York. Greene confirmed the fact, re-
gretfully, that as a result they were badly split now into three
parts: one north of White Plains under Lee, one at Fort Washington across the river, the third under Washington retreating
toward Peekskill. At Fort Lee, he himself was wholly on the
defensive.

"I fear me," he said, "I was no help at all. I was so ill of
a fever that I had to take to my bed in New York before the
action really began. Didst hear that the command of my
troops was turned over to Old Put?" He gave a deep sigh.
"From the youngest general to the oldest! Twas a most ill-
timed fever."

"You do not think General Putnam was competent?" asked
Paine, prodded by journalistic inquisitiveness.

"Of course. Of course! We were outnumbered on every
side." And then, as though to change the subject, "Thou art
staying, Tom?" And when Paine nodded, "Then thou shalt be
my aide-de-camp. Thou art a godsend. I am weighted down
with unanswered letters. I shall get thee a brigade major's
commission. We have few uniforms as yet . . . only distin-
guishing ribands." Paine noticed Greene's—a wide pink ribbon, worn across his waistcoat. "Come, I'll get thee a pair of
boots and some decent clothes."

Settled in Fort Lee, aide-de-camp Paine spent most of his
morning hours on Greene's correspondence. At night, he
wrote articles and stories of what was happening at Fort Lee.

These he dispatched to the *Pennsylvania Journal and Weekly Advertiser.*

As the days went by, more and more stragglers drifted into Greene's camp. They brought eyewitness accounts of the Long Island battle and the Manhattan retreat. Paine questioned them endlessly. It seemed that the newcomers did not speak to Paine alone. The entire camp soon knew of Howe's claim that the Continentals had suffered over 3,000 casualties and that the New York Tories thought the war finished. The news dispirited the troops and filled their minds with apprehension. Great numbers of them straggled away and deserted. To cheer his countrymen, Paine wrote only of Washington's genius in having saved the army by a masterful retreat. One evening, General Greene and Colonel Snarl entered the log cabin that served as the fort's headquarters. Greene looked over Paine's shoulder and watched him write:

> Washington has snatched a beaten army from the very jaws of a victorious force and under the nose of the greatest armada ever seen in American waters. . . .

Paine looked up from his writing and turned his bright, searching eyes upon Greene. "You know Washington well. Tell me, Nathan, is the war in good hands?"

Greene could not believe what he heard. Was he being asked to judge his commanding general's actions? He seated himself on a balnketed cot, looked at Colonel Snarl and then back again at Paine. Finally he said, "He is like a wild stallion, Tom. There is no stopping him. At Kip's Bay, when the troops fled, he tried by sheer threat to halt them and rally them. When they disregarded his orders to make a stand in a cornfield, he dashed his hat on the ground and cried, 'Are you the men with whom I'm to defend America!' He threatened them with a pistol and, when that failed, he dashed in among them and lashed at them with his riding crop."

A smile tugged at Paine's lips. His eyes glowed in the

candlelight. "'Tis true," said Colonel Snarl. "I saw him sit his horse in a deserted field, blind with rage, as the Hessians advanced. He would have been shot or captured had not an aide reached him before I could, seized the bridle, and hurried him away."

"I see you have both become most attached to him," said Paine.

A week later, accompanied by Greene, Paine walked along the river's shore, beyond the outposts of the fort. The day was clear, with late October freshness. He could see Fort Washington across the Hudson. Its outposts were built upon a great height—an outcropping of gigantic rocks that dropped, in a sheer cliff, to the water's edge. There, on the island of Manhattan, part of the Continental Army was still encamped in a fortified position.

"Congress still wants New York held," said Greene, "but look at it, Tom! Look at the fort. God knows why Howe delays. The North River is in front of it, the Harlem River in back of it, and to the south is the British fleet ready to lift sail at any hour. What manner of men have we in Congress, Tom, that they consider neither the cost nor the feasibility of their desires? They consider the holding of New York necessary, and yet, what benefit can arise to us from its preservation? It is a piece of ground no bigger than a square mile! Two-thirds of the town belongeth to the Tories. I said burn it! And they refused!"

Paine looked at Greene in disbelief. "You would have burned New York?" he cried. "Has war changed you so much, Nathan?"

Greene hesitated for an instant and then said bitterly, "War hath not changed me, Thomas. But I find that I cannot change war. And do not debate it with me. General Washington himself sent my memorandum to Congress. No town can be held in the face of an enemy who can land on both sides of an island, in its middle, and cut the defender's forces in two."

[209]

He struck down his arm and cried, "The men who sit in Congress are either Tories or fools! They would call the tune but will not pay the piper. Come, let us go back. I have more letters to write."

On November 12, General Washington crossed the Hudson at Peekskill and rode to Greene's camp at Fort Lee. He was accompanied by General Putnam and a group of aides-de-camp. The gathered officers almost filled Greene's cabin. Paine had been eating breakfast with General Greene, and the table was not yet cleared. There were not enough chairs and Paine rose from his to make it available.

Paine had never met Israel Putnam. He saw a round, open face that was weather-beaten, yet stamped with the lines of a jovial disposition. His head was crowned by an unruly shock of slate-grey hair and he had a tremendous breadth of shoulders—like a bear. It was said that he was sixty-seven, but he seemed far from an old man.

Washington did not seem in the best of spirits. Little lines of bitterness had settled about his wide mouth. He refused to be seated as Greene introduced Paine, but waited until the orderly had cleared the breakfast dishes and left. An aide shut the door and stationed himself in front of it.

"I have come to consult you about the defense of our fort," said Washington. "Yesterday, three British ships sailed around our obstructions and the chains and passed up the North River."

Paine looked at Greene but, before his friend could speak, Putnam offered, "Colonel Magaw has assured me of the fort's impregnability." His voice was deep and insistent.

Washington stared at the cabin floor, seemingly deep in thought. Little shafts of sunlight shone through the warped boarding of the pitched roof and dappled the trodden earth with scattered yellow coins. A spear of light fell full on Washington's face and, until he moved, was reflected by the blue-grey eyes beneath his heavy brow.

As though just aware of the introduction to Greene's new aide-de-camp, he turned to Paine and smiled. He glanced at the ribbon across Paine's breast, as though to assure himself of Paine's proper rank and said, "Major Thomas Paine? The author of *Common Sense?*" He extended his hand as Paine nodded. "It is my pleasure, Major Paine. Did we not meet before?"

"In Philadelphia," said Paine. "More than a year ago. Dr. Franklin introduced us."

Washington's eyes grew retrospective and then, as though recalled to the purpose of his visit, he turned to General Greene and said, "Fort Washington gives no credit to my name. It has no casemates, no barracks, no decent officers' quarters, no fuel, and no water."

As though to influence Greene, Putnam interjected, "I have the utmost confidence in its commanding officer!"

General Washington seated himself and stretched his long legs. Paine was surprised to see a hole worn in one of the polished boots. As though he had not been interrupted by Putnam, Washington commented, "When I said there was not water at the Fort, I meant that, in case of a siege, water could be gotten only from the river, 230 feet below. And now that our blockade of the river has been proven ineffective, and all of Howe's army ..." He turned to an aide and questioned, "How many did we estimate in his force?"

"Twenty thousand men, sir. Completely equipped."

"An army of twenty thousand British can now operate freely both by land and by sea." He looked up at Greene and said quietly, "We maintained both forts or we abandon both ... the one on the cliff and this." There was no challenge in his voice. It was a statement of fact.

Paine could see a twinge of indecision sober Greene's face. "Sir," he said, "if Colonel Magaw wishes to hold Fort Washington, then I can most assuredly hold Fort Lee. And if needed, I shall send him as reinforcement a regiment of Maryland and Virginia riflemen, and Colonel Baxter with his Bucks County militiamen."

Washington rose from his chair without a word. He inclined his head, motioned to General Putnam and to his aides, and turned to leave. Suddenly, as though remembering, he turned back to Paine and asked, "Do you have a mount, Major? I give you permission to select one from my stable. And if General Greene can spare you, . . . I can use another aide-de-camp." He smiled widely at Greene and Paine was surprised to see two badly decayed teeth.

On the third morning after Washington's visit, Paine was awakened sharply from his sleep. One of the two young officers with whom he shared a cabin was shaking his shoulder.

"We are abandoning camp, sir. I let you sleep as long as I could."

Abandoning Fort Lee? Paine rushed to the door and looked out. The entire camp was in confusion. It had rained all night —a cold November rain. Though some men were forming ranks, others would not leave the warmth of their fires, and there were some who dashed about as though directionless.

"What time is it?" asked Paine. "What is the hour?"

The young officer rushed away and left the question of time unanswered. Paine hurried to General Greene's quarters. He found him stuffing personal possessions into a hide bag and casting sheets of correspondence into a makeshift fireplace. He glanced at Paine but once and continued his packing. "Cornwallis and his men have landed on the Jersey side. We must join Washington at Hackensack or we are lost."

Paine rushed back to his cabin. Confused militiamen and groups of stragglers were milling aimlessly about. An orderly led a saddled horse to Paine's quarters and emphasized General Greene's solicitous insistence that he join him. Paine could not get himself to leave the enclosure grounds. His arithmetical mind insisted upon counting the number of tents left standing . . . upward of 300! And the men were leaving their very blankets strewn about. They were marching away and leaving the breakfast camp kettles still boiling over the fires! He led his horse past the wooden shelters and looked within them. No less than 1,000 barrels of flour were being abandoned! There were no wagons. No wagons! He felt sick at heart. The fort looked as though a storm of great violence had swept through it. Reluctantly, he mounted and turned the horse toward the fort's open gate.

It felt good to be in a saddle. It was two and a half years since he had sold his own horse, in Lewes. It seemed a lifetime ago. Under other circumstances, he would have been exhilirated by the riding. He soon reached Greene at the head of the column. All semblance of mirth had deserted his cherubic face. His eyes were spiritless and the corners of his mouth were tugged downward. They rode for a while in silence and, when they halted to wait for the lagging foot column, Paine said, "The men seem in good spirits. They cannot wait to join General Washington."

Greene looked up at the grey sky that threatened more rain. He spoke into the wind. "The very word 'Washington' hath become as a beacon to them. They think that there will be warm food and shelter for them at Hackensack. Clothes to take the place of what they left behind in their haste. We shall find nothing at Hackensack!"

"But you said . . ."

"I know. But the country is flat and I have learned that Washington hath not a pick or shovel with which to entrench. If he stays, he will be cooped up in the narrow space between the Hackensack River and the Passaic. He will be gone before we arrive."

The column was catching up. A cold wind whipped across an open field and Paine saw the men bend their heads and their shoulders into it as they marched. General Greene lifted an arm and urged them forward.

General Greene was right. Washington had stopped at

Hackensack only long enough to regroup, rest his men, and count his losses. Filled with impatience, Paine left Greene's column and urged his horse southward. Halfway to Newark, he overtook Washington's men. He was filled with anguish by what he learned: 200 American officers and more than 2,000 private Continentals had fallen into the hands of the British when Colonel Magaw had surrendered Fort Washington. The amount of supplies that had been abandoned was staggering. Between the surrendered Fort Washington and the abandoned Fort Lee, the Americans had lost 150 iron and brass guns, 12,000 shot and shells, close to 3,000 muskets, tents, blankets, clothing, camp kettles . . . it was a disaster. A disaster! The Tories would make the most of it. The British would publicize it.

But what did the enlisted men think? It was important to know what they thought. Paine watched them—dispirited, wearied with marching, cold, hungry, straggling across the wet rutted dirt road that was beginning to freeze. Washington's force seemed truly the wretched remains of a broken and defeated army. But no one must know. No one! He would refute what the British would claim. At the first resting place, wolfing down an issue of biscuits and smoked dried beef, he began a news article for the *Pennsylvania Journal and Weekly Advertiser*:

> Fort Washington being obliged to surrender, by a violent attack made by the whole British army on Saturday, the 16th of November, the Generals determined to evacuate Fort Lee.

When November 30 came, 2,000 men whose term of enlistment was completed, Maryland and New Jersey brigades, grouped themselves into columns and marched away. Three days later, though their enlistments were not up until January 1, the Pennsylvanians deserted in great numbers. No effort was made to stop them. To Paine, the hurt of their leaving was magnified by the thought that they would cross the Delaware and carry home with them the proof of a lost rebellion. What would happen to his dreams of independence for America? He was sending articles of encouragement to the *Pennsylvania Journal* but he did not know if they were being printed, ... if they were being read. He decided to write a pamphlet. A pamphlet had persuaded the country to declare its independence ... it could be that a pamphlet would encourage the support and the defense of that independence!

Paine had no sooner started to write in Newark, then the order came to retreat again. To retreat to New Brunswick— the British were too close. He laid aside the work on his pamphlet and wrote to the *Pennsylvania Journal and Weekly Advertiser:*

> From Hackensack bridge and town, our troops went to Newark. The enemy approached slowly and seemed desirous that we should fight for it. From Newark (in inclement weather) our retreat was to New Brunswick. ...

Paine rode behind a column of marching men and stragglers. The days among the brambles and the corn husks had wreaked their havoc upon them. Their garments were in rags. They were shod like tramps. When they marched, there was no sound of fife or drum. They shuffled in detached groups, their hands in their pockets, their muskets thrust carelessly under their arms. When they stopped to rest or regroup, many walked off into the bordering fields to search for fruit that a farmer might have neglected to harvest. At night, they scattered from the rutted road where the mud froze into sharp, jagged ridges and encamped in the woods. Paine watched them as they made clearings for themselves and lay down to get what sleep they could under a gray comfortless sky that soon turned a murky black.

At New Brunswick, Paine learned that Greene's men had finally joined them, so he turned back into the road and went in search of Greene. He found him in a fieldstone farmhouse that General Washington had selected as his headquarters for the night. Beside Washington and his aides there were Colonel Grayson, Colonel Joseph Reed—now the adjutant general of the army—and General Ewing, whose brigade had deserted in great numbers.

A crackling fire seemed the only warmth in the room. The officers sat with long, cold faces. They were discussing their desperate plight. Should they continue their retreat to Philadelphia or stand at Trenton and fight? Even so, did they have any chance of staving off the pursuing British and Hessians?

Washington summed it up. "My neck does not feel as though it were made for a halter. What if we lose? If needs be, we can retire into Augusta County in Virginia. Numbers will be obliged to repair to us for safety while we carry on a predatory war. If overpowered, we can cross the Allegheny Mountains. But first, we must fight and give our men one chance to taste victory."

He looked around grimly.

"Congress has fled and left all decisions in my hands. My decision is that we stand at the Delaware, entrench and await the enemy, and fight."

The iron determination in his voice was spellbinding. Defeated in New York, unsupported by the Continental Congress, deserted by half his men, refused all reinforcement by the New Jersey Militia, Washington was, to Paine a man he could follow anywhere and to whatever end.

Already he himself had nearly finished his pamphlet calling on all Americans to rally to this man in the hour of trial, and now he redoubled his efforts to finish it before being forced to leave New Brunswick. Nevertheless, for the safety of his army, Washington had already decided to continue his retreat to Princeton, fifteen miles to the south, so once again Paine watched the hungry men group themselves into units while, his finished draft stowed tightly within his coat, he urged his horse through the column of slow-marching men.

He would head south to Trenton, he decided, turn west for Philadelphia, and get his pamphlet printed before there could be any battle at the Delaware.

He would call it *The Crisis*.

As he neared Philadelphia, he found the road filled with coaches, chaises, creaking wagons, and saddle horses. Men, women, and children, on foot, with large packs upon their backs, plodded against a bitter north wind. It seemed that the city was being evacuated. When he finally reined in his horse in front of Robert Bell's printing shop, he found the Scot packing.

Bell shook his head vigorously at Paine's draft of *The Crisis*. "Y're daft, mon. Where 'ave ya bin? The British 'ave marched inta Trenton Toon as aisy an' comfortable as ya plaise, noo. An' wot's ta stoop 'em froom marchin' 'ere? Sure an' Washington 'as sent us Major General Israel Pootnam ta defend us. An' wi' wot? 'Defend the city at all costs,' 'e says. Boot wi' wot mon?"

Trenton in the hands of the British? News had traveled faster than he had. He must not seem disconcerted. "I assure you, Mr. Bell, Congress will recognize the danger and . . ."

"Coongress? 'Ere is no Coongress, mon! They decreed a day o' fastin'—as though the roomblin' o' an empty stoomach woul' frighten a redcoat's moosket—an' packed their belongin's an' rooshed ta Baltimore."

"All of them?"

The Scot's round face cracked into a pumpkin's grin. "Noo! No' all o' 'em, mon. The affluent an' big-respected Allens noo—they 'ave rooshed ta join up wi' 'Owe in Trenton Toon. Better a warm British coot than a Continental rag fer a shirt. Can ya blame 'em, noo?"

"I do not believe it!"

"Belaive wot ya will, noo."

Paine thrust the manuscript of *The Crisis* into Bell's hand. "Print the pamphlets, Bell! Please. . . ."

[217]

"A waste o' goo' paper an' expoonsive ink."

"I guarantee you a profit!"

"Proofit? Y're daft, mon. Didna' Ah tell ya 'ere is no Coongress ta show it ta. An' the city can no' keep the British oot."

Paine pushed past the Scot and into the untidy shop. He glanced at the still unpacked type. "May I print the pamphlets myself?" he challenged as he heard Bell's footsteps follow him. "You made a small fortune from *Common Sense.* Why deny yourself another? Print *The Crisis,* Bell. Print it!"

Robert Bell extended a hesitant and unconvinced hand. "Tis boot a mere 'andful o' pages. Should Ah risk the shoop fer it? An' m' neck?"

"*Common Sense* has already marked you. This will mark you no more. Except for posterity. The finger of history has just touched you, Robert Bell! I, Thomas Paine, have said it. And now, print the pamphlets!"

As Robert Bell had informed him, Paine found no friends in Philadelphia. Congress had moved to Baltimore. Some of the delegates had traveled there; others had gone home.

Paine stayed in patriot-abandoned Philadelphia only long enough to pack his saddlebags with the freshly printed pamphlets. As he rode back to rejoin the Continental Army, deserters did not hesitate to inform him that Washington had abandoned New Jersey. He had crossed the Delaware and placed the river between himself and the British.

As Paine hurried northward, on the Pennsylvania side of the river, he was told the same story by all. If he would find Washington's men—they were in the woods, strung along the banks of the Delaware, all the way from Killbrides' Ferry across from Bordentown to McKonkey's Ferry across from Maidenhead. By late afternoon, he came across the troops. They were in the fields and in the woods on both sides of the road. They milled about or sat on the hard, frosted ground with their feet stretched toward wood fires. Some had thrust their ramrods through pieces of meat and were holding them into the flames.

A few miles south of New Hope, at the foot of Bowman's Hill, Paine found a dozen officers quartered in a stone house. They directed him to Washington's headquarters, at the farmhouse of a William Keith, just south of a hill, near Pidcock Creek. As Paine approached it, he could see lilac bushes that December had robbed of their last bit of color. Tall, red-cedar trees shielded the stone house from the wind. To one side was a barn and a little further a grist mill. He entered a door at the west end of the farmhouse and found himself in a corridor-like room that had been converted into a sickroom. Ailing militiamen lay on blanket-covered straw pallets. Their eyes regarded him without interest. He walked through a doorway and into a large adjoining room. It was well heated by a massive fieldstone fireplace. A half-dozen young aides-de-camp sat about a long table. They looked up as he entered and Paine nodded to the two whom he knew—Edward Jennings Randolph, a young Virginian, and John Laurens, whose father was a good friend.

General Washington sat at a heavy, round table that he was using as a desk. Another young aide-de-camp and General Sullivan, who had been captured on Long Island and exchanged, sat with him. The table was cluttered with rolled maps, letters, and books. Washington was engaged in writing and, as each letter was finished, the aide placed it into an envelope. As Washington addressed it, the aide held a bar of sealing wax into a candle flame.

Washington must have been aware that Paine had stepped to his side, but he did not look up. When he finished still another letter, Paine placed a copy of *The Crisis* on the table, hesitated, and stepped away. Washington took the pamphlet and began to read it. Paine walked quietly to the long table where the aides-de-camp were seated.

Young Laurens rose, shook Paine's hand, and introduced him to the others. "Captain Alexander Hamilton," he said. "Lieutenant Randolph, with whom I believe you are acquainted. Lieutenant Tilghman." He seemed to hesitate for an instant—"Lieutenant Isaac Franks. Gentlemen, I give you my father's friend and mine. Mr. . . . Major Thomas Paine, the author of *Common Sense.*" He gave Paine a broad smile.

As Paine shook their hands, his eyes were drawn to young Isaac Franks. He seemed no more than nineteen. His dark expressive eyes suddenly reminded Paine of the Jews he had seen in Jonathan's Coffeehouse, in London.

Paine's eyes left the lieutenant's face only to find that he, himself, was being observed closely by the young captain. Hamilton flicked a finger in the direction of Paine's green ribbon and asked, "Major Paine? And in what field, Major?" And when Paine hesitated, "I, myself, am a captain in the artillery."

"A most interesting field of endeavor, Captain Hamilton," said Paine. "In war, next to engineering—the quick construction of a temporary bridge or the immediate erection of a fort —I should think artillery most fascinating."

The young captain gave Paine a condescending smile. "It does take some knowledge of gravity and force, Major Paine. . . ." He hesitated as he saw Paine was irritated.

"I studied Newton's law of motion in England," said Paine. "Perhaps before you were born, Captain Hamilton."

"Forgive me, I only meant to point out that the necessary arc of a forty-pounder shortens considerably the distance to its vulnerable target and, yet, I believe that the effect, within its short range, is more decisive than a pamphlet, such as *Common Sense,* spread over a countryside."

Paine did not wish to argue. He was still chilled and tired from his long ride. He had been in the saddle since sunrise. He glanced at Washington. The general was absorbed in reading *The Crisis.*

[220]

Suddenly Paine heard himself defended by Lieutenant Franks. "Are you averse to liberty, Captain Hamilton?" the young officer asked. "It was the sentiments expressed in Major Paine's *Common Sense,* as much as any one thing, that burst into flame the desire for an independent America."

Captain Hamilton turned his grey eyes upon Lieutenant Franks with studied rudeness. He flicked an imaginary thread of lint from his immaculate coat and said, "Liberty? I assure you, gentlemen, I have as staunch a desire for it as Major Paine, but I cannot conceive of a collection of states as he can. A confederation of governments is fit for neither war nor peace. When I am with my artillery, I say when to fire and where. No one disputes my decisions, and it is the target only that suffers."

Paine could stay silent no longer. "Liberty for the few, Captain Hamilton?"

Hamilton studied Paine's borrowed boots that were caked with mud. "Liberty for all, Major Paine. But government by those who can govern. By the propertied and the educated."

For a moment the officers were constrained to silence and then Hamilton said, "I bow to you Major Paine as an essayist. I have been following your articles in the magazines. But I would like to question your article on dueling. Now, gentlemen, I ask you. In what civilized country and in what time has a man of honor had any other redress against an insult than by a challenge to a duel? No court's decision, no redress of money or estate, can scrub away the spoken words of slander or affront!"

Paine looked about the table. So now it was out. This young man—this Captain Hamilton whom he had never seen before—had been angered by his essay on dueling. "Have you read my article on dueling, gentlemen?" asked Paine. Lieutenant Tilghman shook his head. Laurens and Franks nodded.

"Gentlemen, if I may defend an essay with which one of

you is unfamiliar, I affirm that the custom of dueling is absurd and settles nothing but a greater dexterity. Those who advocate it, as Captain Hamilton seems to do, insist that the laws have not provided proper or adequate redress in certain species of injuries."

"Nor can they!" cried Hamilton. "Satisfaction for extrajudicial offenses necessitates the duel. And until some other mode of redress will be devised and established by gentlemen . . . by gentlemen, mind you . . ."

"Captain Hamilton. . . . Captain Hamilton! If I may remind you, in my article in the *Pennsylvania Magazine,* I pointed out that the practice of dueling sprang from monkish superstition. It obtained on a conclusion that innocence would be pointed out by victory, and guilt punished by defeat. But experience has taught us not to expect a miraculous interposition whenever superior strength, superior skill, . . ."

Paine had been watching Washington from a corner of his eye. The general had been underscoring passages in the pamphlet's text. He rose and turned to the debating officers. "Lieutenant Franks, would you be so kind as to get my orderly to bring my last bottle of Madeira. I have saved it for an occasion. I believe the occasion is now. The wine was a gift from General Greene. Major Paine has brought us a most inspiring pamphlet that he has aptly called *The Crisis.*" He held out the pamphlet. "Would you be so kind, Major?" Sensing the excitement in Washington's face, Paine deferred the reading of the pamphlet to the General.

Washington looked about him—at the young officers who all but worshiped him and whom he treated as his own sons. "I give you *The Crisis,* gentlemen:"

These are the times that try men's souls. The summer soldier and the sunshine patriot will, in this crisis, shrink from the service of his country; but he that stands it NOW deserves the love and thanks of man and woman. Tyranny, like hell, is not easily conquered; yet we have this consolation with us, that the harder the conflict the more glorious the triumph. What we obtain too cheap, we esteem too lightly; tis dearness only that gives every thing its value. Heaven knows how to put a proper price upon its goods; and it would be strange indeed, if so celestial an article as *freedom* should not be highly rated. Britain, with an army to enforce her tyranny, hath declared that she has a right (not only to tax) but to *"bind us in all classes whatsoever,"* and if being *bound in that manner* is not slavery, then there is not such a thing as slavery upon earth. Even the expression is impious, for so unlimited a power can belong only to God.

"Must I read more, gentlemen?" He stepped to Paine and flung an arm about him. "The pamphlet is signed *Common Sense,* gentlemen. Hast more of these pamphlets, Major Paine?"

"Two full saddlebags."

"Lieutenant Laurens, will you distribute them? See that every brigade commander is given copies. Advise them that *The Crisis* must be read at the head of every regiment. Captain Hamilton, arrange a council with Generals Greene, Mercer, Stirling, and Roche de Fermoy." He waved away General Sullivan as he rose from the round table and stepped to Washington's side. "Do not deter me, John. I have made up my mind. The hour to strike is here. What better ammunition for a soldier than this? If our spy's information is correct, then Christmas Day is our appointment in Trenton."

Captain Hamilton rose to his feet. He seemed elated. "What of the artillery, sir?"

"Colonel Knox will take it with us."

"The ice?"

"Damn the ice! When we wanted to abandon New York, Congress insisted that we hold it, fortify it, defend it! To what purpose? Now we are our own men. With the help of Providence, we shall have a taste of victory. Well, why do we wait?"

Hamilton turned to go. As though on second thought, he hesitated and offered Paine his hand. "My apologies. I did not mean to be rude. I hope we can be friends?"

"Of course. Reform withers and dies when it meets with no opposition."

Hamilton grinned. "Thank you, Major Paine. Then I still maintain my stand on dueling." Paine watched the young officer turn smartly on his polished boot heel.

"The copies of your pamphlet . . . ," reminded Lieutenant Laurens. He and Paine left the room together.

17

BY THREE o'clock in the afternoon on Christmas Day, Paine found himself on the march toward the river where Glover's fisherman had assembled their boats. There were to be three crossings over the Delaware. One near Bristol, one at Trenton Ferry, and a main one—commanded by Washington and divided into two corps, under Greene and Sullivan—at McKonkey's Ferry, nine miles above Trenton itself.

Paine stood with a small group of officers, at Washington's side, and watched Glover's men pole the boats to the shore. The men called them Durham boats. They were tremendously long; Paine estimated about fifty feet. They were at least eight feet wide, yet seemed but two feet deep. Furnished with heavy steering sweeps that could fit either pointed end, they could evidently travel in either direction.

The men themselves had gathered behind a hill, at McKonkey's Ferry, out of sight of the opposite shore. Each man had been given a blanket, cooked rations, and forty rounds of ammunition. The officers had no need to slow their march. They were a draggling lot. Paine watched the advance party, the Virginia Continentals of Stephen's Brigade, wade out to the boats and clamber into them. Mercer's was the second section. As dark began to fall, the embarkation was hurried.

When a Pennsylvania rifle regiment began to fill the boats, Paine waded out to one of them. He had not known that his worn boots leaked. The icy water about his ankles was an excruciating shock. Once in the boat, there was no way to dry his feet. Even as he contemplated removing his boots, the boat had filled so that there was no room to sit. The crewmen were pushing the boat into deeper water by leaning against their setting poles and walking on running boards that were built along each side. Looking back, he could hear the splash of water and vaguely see the forms of horses being led to other boats. Even as he watched, the sky was shrouded by dense clouds and darkness covered everything.

The crossing itself proved difficult and hazardous. The river was filled with cakes of ice, some so large that they would not budge. A Marblehead fisherman, stationed in the bow of the boat, thrust at the ice with a boat hook. A militiaman added his weight against the pole. The moon broke through the clouds and Paine saw a line of boats scattered across the river, like dead whales. They seemed almost without movement, as though they had been frozen into the ice-caked water. Then the moon was obscured and it was dark again.

Paine calculated the time and felt that the entire division that he had joined would not cross until midnight. They would need time to assemble them, and it was a nine-mile march to Trenton. He wondered if they would reach the town by daybreak. Would the crossing at Bristol go well? The crossing at Trenton Ferry? He must take off his boots and warm his feet. Somehow, he must dry them! This was the end of Christmas Day, but no one had talked about it—neither officers nor men. Suddenly, out of the dark sky, hail and sleet, driven by a high wind, broke upon them like a malicious squall. There was no room to huddle in the boat. The men raised their blankets and spread them over themselves and their comrades. Their ends flapped crazily in the wind. They were soon covered by hailstones and freezing rain. Now and then, an unexpected gust tore a blanket completely away from the frozen hands that held it. It was swept away like a huge wounded bird and was lost in the wet dark.

When they reached the New Jersey shore, Paine had to summon his will to step into the freezing water. He watched the men march away and was amazed to see the sleet frozen solidly upon their hair and their clothes—until he realized that his were no different. He noticed a group of officers and hurried toward them. The riflemen who stood on guard had ripped their blankets and tied sections about their feet and over their heads. Their arms were raised to shield their faces from the northeast wind that beat into them. Paine espied Washington in the midst of a group of officers, superintending the landing of the troops. He had never seen the general so determined. He was wrapped in a dark cloak that flapped madly in the wind. Between his raised collar and his hat, his face was thrust unsheltered into the driving sleet that cut like a knife.

Paine searched along the riverbank for his horse. His wool stockings squished in his boots as he walked. He stopped for a moment and watched a fieldpiece being lifted from a beached boat. Bootless, the men sank knee-deep in the freezing mud as they struggled with it in the dark.

A quarter mile up River Road, Paine found his mount in the midst of a small troop of Philadelphia light-horsemen. Almost immediately, the entire division, under General Greene, started off. They marched slowly behind four field guns, which creaked heavily across the frozen, rutted road. At Birmingham, four miles from the landing, the column halted for a meal of prepared rations. It was still sleeting. Eastward, toward Trenton, one could see day breaking through a grey mist.

Paine rode to a rise in the road and from there he could see the town. He knew Trenton well. He had been there often with Colonel Kirkbride. Bordentown was only five miles away. Trenton was cut in two by a shallow but rapid creek, the Assunpink. It had but one bridge, made of stone with a single arch. To the northeast of the creek, there were about seventy or eighty houses; to the south, no more than fifty. There were two parallel main streets—King and Queen—and, as in Philadelphia, they were crossed near the river by Front, Second, and Third Streets. Paine knew that most of the residents had left. The houses, the jail, the taverns, and the churches had been turned into quarters for the British officers and troops.

The order to march had been given while Paine still studied the town. He watched Mercer's corps pass by. He saw that Washington had joined Greene's division. He rode along with them and in a little while they could hear a brief exchange of musket fire. Greene and Washington reined in their mounts as they reached the edge of the town. Immediately there was a tremendous commotion as men, fieldpieces, and light-horse-men spread out to encircle the town.

Paine wheeled his horse in the direction of King Street and, coming to its edge, found two fieldpieces, under Captain Hamilton, already pointed down it. A regiment of Hessian regulars was advancing up the street. Hamilton gave the order to fire and the shot tore into its ranks. Paine was in the act of dismounting when his horse reared at the close and unexpected boom of the guns. He was thrown from the stirrup and tumbled almost at Hamilton's feet. He could see the young captain grinning at him as he rose.

"Will you admit this is more effective than pamphlets?" Hamilton shouted at him.

The Hessians fired a volley and then fell back in disorder

as scattered Continental riflemen fired back at them. As Hamilton's artillerymen primed the fieldpieces, the Hessians rushed two guns into the street and fired them. In their haste, the shots went wild. Paine spied his horse across the street and, just as he went to retrieve him, Stirling's troops charged down King Street. Paine was swept along with them.

The Hessians were frantically reloading their fieldpieces as two more were wheeled into the street. Suddenly Weedon's Virginians, with fixed bayonets, rushed past Stirling's troops. Led by a young lieutenant and Captain William Washington, a kinsman of the general, they fell upon the Hessian guns and captured them. The lieutenant stumbled as he reached the Hessian battery. Paine saw him fall to his knees, rushed to his side, and encircled an arm about him. Between his glove and his sleeve, he felt the warm blood.

Helping the officer to his feet and half dragging him, Paine managed to get him through an open doorway and into the shelter of a house. The place seemed but recently deserted. Blankets and pillows were tossed upon couches and chairs in a large drawing room. Pallets were scattered over the floor and the remains of a fire glowed among the ashes in a fireplace. What was left of a smashed chair lay in front of the firescreen. It had evidently been used for firewood.

Paine let the officer sink slowly to a pallet in front of the fireplace. He seemed no more than a boy . . . eighteen, perhaps. He suppressed a cry of pain as Paine unbuttoned his waistcoat. "I think I took a ball in the shoulder. It has cut an artery . . . perhaps."

Paine removed the officer's stock and stuffed it gently against the wound. "I am indebted to you, sir. My compliments and my thanks. I am Lieutenant James Monroe, of General Weedon's 3d Virginia Regiment." A movement of his arm twisted his lips with pain. Outside, there was a fresh sound of artillery fire and musketry. "We took the brass pounders, didn't we?"

"You must not talk. I shall try to find a surgeon for you. I am Thomas Paine, attached to General Greene's ..."

"*Common Sense* Paine? Your humble servant, sir. I am an admirer and ..."

Paine touched his fingers to young Monroe's lips. As he did, they heard heavy footsteps on the floor above. Monroe looked at Paine, startled. Paine cautioned silence and tiptoed to a wide circular stairway. He climbed upward, supporting a portion of his weight on a wide mahogany banister. Past the landing and through an open doorway, he saw four Continental riflemen in a back bedroom. Despite their frozen faces and their ragged, sopping uniforms that dripped puddles on the floor, they were laughing. They had torn bedsheets into strips and were drying the touchholes of their muskets and wiping their flints and priming pans. As Paine entered the room, a band struck up a tune outside—a British marching tune, with fifes and drums. It was incredible!

Paine and the riflemen rushed to the windows. The house was set in a clearing and they could see into Queen Street from the back bedroom. Colonel Rall had reformed his ranks. Flanked by a dozen light-dragoons and a band playing, he was marching the Hessians, with fixed bayonets, back up Queen Street. They looked steadfast and determined in their fresh red coats and white cartridge belts, except that most, surprised in bed, had not had time to button their spatterdashes, others were without hats, and some were barefoot.

"Now there's a bloody Hessian basta'd wot earns 'is pay!" cried one of the riflemen. Even as he spoke, shots spattered from every doorway that bordered Queen Street. From the upper end, Forrest's battery blazed away at the advancing Hessians. With his officers and men falling on every side, Rall ordered a charge. Stirling's riflemen rushed into the street, shoulder to shoulder, and opened a deadly fire. The Hessian grenadiers faltered, broke, and ran. Jägers, from the Lossberg Regiment, swept past the retreating grenadiers and charged

[229]

up Queen Street. Thirty of them fell before they could reach Stirling's riflemen. Rall, turning about on his horse to order a withdrawal, was suddenly struck by bullets and fell from his horse. A Hessian officer and two men rushed to him and half dragged him, half carried him, into a nearby house, while the Hessian footmen retreated toward an orchard, where gunfire drove them back. They threw down their muskets and raised their hands.

Back in the drawing room, Paine examined Monroe's wound. A red stain had spread down half the waistcoat. Monroe's fingers were encrusted with blood where he had pressed tightly against the red stock. "I think the bleeding has ceased. There is not too much pain. Would you ask after Captain Washington? Would you bring me news of him?" Paine promised and rushed outdoors.

On King Street, the Americans were tossing their hats in the air and shouting themselves hoarse. Their joyous cries were as loud and frightening as Indian war whoops. With their ragged clothes and their unshaven faces they looked as fierce as they sounded. The Hessians, with lowered colors, filled the street. Their officers raised their hats on the points of their swords as tokens of surrender. Camp followers milled about, awestruck and terrified. A mixture of sleet and snow was falling. A fog of acrid gunpowder hung over the town. Now and then there was the boom of a single fieldpiece. It was nine o'clock and the battle was over.

The prisoners were marched into King Street. Paine counted ten brass fieldpieces, half a dozen wagons, forty horses, and well over 1,000 muskets, rifles, and bayonets. He estimated 1,000 prisoners. He could see at least thirty commissioned officers.

Back in camp, on the west side of the Delaware, Paine could not find his horse. He had to thrust his way thorugh hundreds of infantrymen, who milled about the seemingly unconcerned prisoners. Many of the militia disregarded the warmth of hastily built campfires in order to satisfy their curiosity concerning the captured Hessians who could speak no English.

With a realization of the victory's importance growing on them, there was a jubilant celebration among the officers in the Keith farmhouse. Hamilton, his face flushed with excitement, even his sharp English nose no longer pale, rushed to Paine as he entered and pumped his hand. His blue military coat was soiled with mud and gunpowder. A large tear ran from a shoulder to the coat's red facing. He had evidently changed his boots and his yellow breeches but wore his coat proudly, as a decoration of battle.

"You are an intrepid infantryman, Major Paine. I saw you charge down King Street with Stirling's troops."

Paine did not know if Hamilton were serious or not. Surely he must know the truth. "Let's say that I was carried off by . . . by the fervor and the courage all about me."

He left Hamilton and threaded his way through the excited officers. He must get to Philadelphia, he felt. He must report to the Continental Congress and write a news article for the *Pennsylvania Journal and Weekly Advertiser.* He must not let the British minimize this victory. But first he needed a horse. He could see Washington now, leaving the circle of happy officers and returning with a drink. Paine removed the ribbon that designated his commission, folded it, and gave it to the General as he approached. Not a loquacious man, Washington permitted himself an inquiring smile. "My most competent weapon is my pen, sir, and not a musket, as both *Common Sense* and *The Crisis* have shown. I must return to Philadelphia, and to Baltimore if need be. Great Britain will say that tonight was no more than a piddling skirmish. I intend to show the battle in a different light, sir. If I may borrow a mount. I seem to have lost my horse."

"A gift! You may take one from my stables as a gift." He

looked around at his officers. "And now, gentlemen, on to Princeton!"

News of the Trenton victory traveled faster than Paine. When he got to Philadelphia, he found that the city had roused itself from despair. Townspeople had begun to drift back. Shops had reopened. And in the taverns and inns, patriots spoke again with confident voices.

He found his old lodging cluttered with accumulated packets of mail. There was a letter from his parents. They were well. They thanked him for his gift. He tore through the bundles of letters. He hoped that Elizabeth might have sent some small note. Had she remarried? His father had made no mention of her. But then, why would he? He realized that his parents had never met Elizabeth. They had not attended the wedding service in Lewes, and he had not taken her to see them in Thetford. If it had not been for Sarah Ollive, . . . perhaps things would have been different. He would send a little more money to his parents. And to Elizabeth. The boys must be quite grown by now. He wondered if they would remember him. They had always called him Uncle Thomas.

Several mornings later, after the news of Washington's Princeton victory had arrived, Paine was awakened by the sound of drums. He hurried outdoors. People were lined along the full length of Market Street. Men stood in front of tavern doors and shops. Despite the cold, women and children looked out from raised windows. The Hessian prisoners were being marched through Philadelphia. There were more than 1,000. They seemed handsome in their well-kept uniforms—the Lossbergs in scarlet, the artillerymen in dark blue coats with crimson lapels. Rall's regiment in solid blue, Knyphausen's in black. Well-fed, hearty-looking men, they marched with black knapsacks on their backs and white tight-fitting spatterdashes on their legs. It seemed incredible that the haggard, frostbitten Continentals, most of them out of step, were their guards.

Gossip reported that they were being taken to Lancaster and the western counties. Some might be sent to Virginia, to work as field hands. When they had finally marched by, the cold winter sunshine upon their backs, Paine returned to his lodging. He had finished the draft of a new pamphlet but had taken it to a printing shop on Second Street, owned by Styner and Cist. He would have no more to do with Robert Bell, he decided. Bell continued to print and sell *The Crisis,* for which there seemed to be an unending demand, but insisted that he had made no royalty arrangement with the author. He was printing them on his own!

Paine wondered what the Tories would think of his new pamphlet for in it he had written:

> Universal empire is the prerogative of a writer. His concerns are with all mankind, and, though he cannot command their obedience, he can assign them their duty. . . .
>
> If ever a nation was mad and foolish, blind to its own interest and bent on its own destruction, it is Britain. . . . Blessed with all the commerce she could wish for, and furnished by a vast extension of dominion, with the means of civilizing both the eastern and western world, she hath made no other use of both than proudly to idolize her own "thunder," and rip up the bowels of whole countries for what she could get. The blood of India is not yet repaid, nor the wretchedness of Africa yet requited. . . .
>
> If I have anywhere expressed myself overwarmly, tis from a fixed, immovable hatred I have, and ever had, to cruel men and cruel measures. I have likewise an aversion to monarchy, as being too debasing to the dignity of man. . . .

The Continental Congress returned to Phiadelphia by the end of spring. Inspired by the arrival of two French ships, laden with war supplies, it raised forty-three new Continental regiments and sent them to General Washington at Morristown. Grown to over 8,000 men, the American army was no longer retreating. Contingents captured Hackensack and Elizabeth Town. As General Washington marched his main body of troops to New Brunswick, Sir William Howe withdrew first to Perth Amboy and then to Staten Island. By summer, the entire province of New Jersey was entirely evacuated by the King's troops!

Paine watched the optimistic delegates return to the Continental Congress. There were many new faces to take the place of old members. Dr. Franklin was now in France. Patrick Henry was serving as governor of Virginia. John Hancock had accepted a commission as a major general, at the head of a New England militia, perhaps to prove that he could have done as well or better than could Washington. Thomas Jefferson was not only absent from the Congress but had declined to serve with Dr. Franklin as a commissioner to the court of France.

One morning, while attending a session of the Congress, as its Secretary to the Committee on Foreign Affairs, Paine became aware of a militia guardsman who was hurrying through the Assembly Room. He would whisper to Henry Laurens, who was now the elected president of the Continental Congress, leave, and then return greatly agitated. His rushing back and forth had not gone unnoticed, for even as Paine stepped to President Laurens' side, the staid and ungainly Roger Sherman joined them.

"It is a Marquis de Lafayette," explained Laurens. "He is on our doorstep, asking for admittance. I received a letter from a Major Benjamin Huger, of South Caroline, advising me of his coming. It seems that his ship, unfamiliar with our waters, reached an island off the South Carolina coast. Major Huger informs me that Mr. Deane has promised the marquis a major general's commission for a fellow officer by the name of de Kalb and commissions for others in his party."

Delegates gathered about Laurens' table. James Wilson shook a remonstrative finger at Laurens. "Henry, we have been overwhelmed by adventurers seeking positions in our army. I do not think the duties of Mr. Deane, as American agent in France, include the reckless promises of commissions to unqualified men. I see no reason to honor Mr. Deane's commitment."

Gouverneur Morris, who had reached Wilson's side, spoke up. "Gentlemen," he said, "we are endeavoring to gain the favor of France. A rebuff to the young Marquis de Lafayette would be taken as an affront to its court. Silas has written to me to expect him. He is the scion of an ancient and aristocratic family, the Noells of France!"

Paine returned to his desk and searched among his voluminous notes and correspondence. "Did Mr. Deane give a reason for his coming?" he asked Morris. "Does he express a sympathy for our cause or . . ."

Gouverneur Morris interrupted him. He had a habit of rearing back his leonine head and staring when he was angered. "If a desire for youthful glory were his only reason, Mr. Paine, his connections with the French court would necessitate our welcoming him!"

Paine found what he had been searching for. "A letter regarding the marquis, gentlemen," he said. "Received by me but a week ago. I had thought, at the time, that it was chitchat and not of political interest." He scanned the sheets in his hand and read: "All of Paris is discussing the gallant idea of a romantic boy going to help the Colonists. He has made no secret of his project—his name is le Marquis de Lafayette. I do not know if he is prompted by a love of liberty, a hate for Britain, or a desire for adventure and glory. Be the reason what it may, the publicity does our cause no harm. With the help of Silas Deane and his own money, the marquis has purchased a ship and outfitted it. I write you this so that you may know of him; for it does not seem that so intrepid a young man will be kept long from your shores. He has named his ship the *Victoire.* . . ."

Paine ended his reading and glanced about him.

[235]

"Mr. Morris," suggested Laurens, "could I ask you to step outside and ask this French gentleman for his credentials and, lest we raise his hopes prematurely, explain to him that we already have a full complement of officers?"

Morris thrust out his broad chin. "You do me an injustice, Henry! Do you take me for a rustic that you think I would submit a French aristocrat to the indignity of discoursing on the public steps of a Statehouse?"

Laurens was not intimidated. He glanced about the Assembly Room for a delegate who could speak French. "Mr. Lovell," he asked, "would you be so kind?"

James Lovell, a delegate from Massachusetts, rose. Paine, stirred by curiosity, followed him from the room.

A crowd had gathered outside the Statehouse. They were attracted to a solidly built coach that was equipped like a gypsy wagon. Tents, trucks, valises, and pots and pans were strapped on its top. Tired horses and mud-stained wheels gave evidence of a long journey. Four French officers sat inside and stared back at the curious, who circled about them.

Behind the coach, five tired men sat on horseback. Despite the expensive saddles and trappings, two rode coach horses and another a dispirited pack animal, while a valet, dressed in a French hussar's uniform that was too large for him, sat in a dogcart. On the Statehouse steps, two men were brushing the dust from their uniforms. They were evidently the Marquis de Lafayette and the Baron de Kalb.

The baron was a tall man with a breadth of shoulders that suggested extraordinary endurance. Ten years ago, Paine's letter had said, he had called himself simply Jean de Kalb and had been secretly sent to America by the Duc de Choisel to inquire into the intentions of the Colonies and to report on their resources.

Paine turned from him and studied the young marquis. He seemed a stripling of no more than twenty. Paine had expected a powerfully built, impulsive young man. He saw, instead, a thin youth with an undistinguished face: a high and receding forehead; a nose that was turned up; lips that were thin and tense, as though they withheld a conjecture that might be in error; a chin that seemed without strength and skin whose pallor did not suggest a soldier's life. It was evident that, unlike Baron de Kalb, he knew only a few English words, for he handed a note to de Kalb and the baron passed it on to Lovell.

"Le Marquis de Lafayette desire that you take thees note to your Congress." The baron's voice was deep and guttural.

As Paine followed Lovell back into the Statehouse, he pointd to the note in Lovell's hand. "I will see it sooner or later. All foreign papers end up on my desk."

Lovell unfolded the note. He glanced at the crest, hesitated, and translated:

> After the sacrifices I have made, I have the right to expect two favors; one is to serve at my own expense, the other is to serve, at first, as a volunteer . . .

"Without pay and without command," repeated Paine. "I wager you, James, Congress will immediately tender them both honorary commissions. A drayman would be a fool to refuse a willing horse the chance to pull a mired wagon."

18

THE OPTIMISM of the Continental Congress did not last long. A report that Howe's fleet was making ready to sail from Sandy Hook had come to Paine's attention some weeks ago. Scouts of Caesar Rodney, who had watched the embarkment, had spoken of the fleet as an armada containing more than 250 warships and transports across whose gangplanks innumerable horses had been guided, countless fieldpieces had been tugged and pushed, and at least 18,000 armed men had marched. It had taken more than a week to fill the holds with provisions. Now came the news that on July 24 it had sailed.

The delegates talked of little else than the probability that Philadelphia was its destination. Watchers with spyglasses were stationed on the roofs of riverside homes and warehouses. Small craft, manned by both sail and oar, were sent scouting down the Delaware as far south as Wilmington.

When it was learned that the fleet had been sighted sailing up Chesapeake Bay, General Washington—who had long since started south from his camp on the Neshaminy—spent the night near Germantown and in the morning grouped his troops for a march through Philadelphia.

It was noon when they came into view, to the sound of fifes and drums, and, from where Paine was standing, he could see Washington riding at the head, the Marquis de Lafayette at his side, while the staff officers followed, preceding a troop of light-horsemen, who clattered over the cobblestones. A wild cheer rose from the spectators as Washington and the marquis reached the Commons in front of the Statehouse. Lafayette looked taller in the saddle. His military coat lent an air of sturdiness to his thin body and the golden epaulets widened his shoulders. He appeared to be an excellent horseman; his polished boots touched the stirrups lightly. He had been appointed a major general, without command.

Paine had already been formally introduced to Lafayette, at a lavish reception to which members of the Continental Congress, army officers, and affluent townsmen had been invited. Washington had attended and invited the young aristocrat to join his staff. The reception had been given in honor of the young marquis, but it was said that it was the blond youth's money that had paid for it.

Paine had watched as the guests had formed an excited line in order to be introduced to the marquis, Baron de Kalb, and

[238]

the young French officers. Americans had accepted Paine's *Common Sense* and his ridicule of the divine right of kings. They had approved his protest against the heritage of nobility, and yet, here they were, flattered by the attentions of a French aristocrat—though he was no more than a thin blond boy—and bowing even to the Baron de Kalb, honored to shake his hand.

When the line dispersed, Paine approached the guests of honor. Washington stood at Lafayette's side, the hub of a little circle made up of themselves, de Kalb, President Laurens, James Lovell, John Adams, and Gouverneur Morris. Morris turned, with an arc of his peg leg, and, seeing Paine, hesitated to greet him. Paine's appearance, though not shabby, was not in keeping with the pomp of the occasion. Then, as though prompted by Laurens' welcome and Washington's warm smile, Morris introduced him to Lafayette and Baron de Kalb. His voice assumed a deprecatory inflection as though he were presenting a not-too-welcome but yet interesting exhibit of the Colonies.

The marquis had offered Paine a courteous hand and suddenly, realizing who he was, cried to de Kalb, *"C'est Monsieur Paine; c'est Monsieur Paine!"* He had flung his arms about him, his speech so fast and excited that Paine had caught no single word except the repetition of his name, which he pronounced as though it were spelled P-a-y-a-n.

When Lafayette had finally released him, James Lovell had translated for Paine, "The marquis says that he has all but memorized your *Common Sense.* He insists that his wife has had all your essays and articles translated and bound into a volume from which she gives readings at her soirees."

Paine had been startled to learn that the young marquis was married. He could understand leaving one's country for adventure, but to leave one's wife—at so tender an age!

As Muhlenberg's brigade reached the Commons now, Paine's thought came back to the parade again. One would not

[239]

take the big man on horseback for a minister. Inspired by Paine's *The Crisis,* he had resigned from the ministry and accepted a brigadier's commission. Soon Weedon's brigade came into view, the men marching twelve abreast. Riding at their head, evidently fully recovered, were Lieutenant Monroe and Captain Washington. The men were not quite in step, but they carried their arms like soldiers. There was no uniformity of dress and, to overcome the differences in their attire, they all wore a sprig of green leaves in their hats. As they reached the Statehouse, the watching crowd waved and cheered. On the Commons, across from the Statehouse steps, in the midst of the crowd, Paine thought he recognized Catherine Nicholson, waving a lace handkerchief. His heart tripped for an instant and then resumed its normal beat as he realized that it was not she.

He had met Catherine Nicholson, the daughter of a sea captain, at the formal reception for the marquis. She and her sister, Hannah, attended a school in Bordentown where the Kirkbrides and the Nicholsons had become fast friends. They were visiting, from New York, and Colonel Kirkbride had brought them to the reception.

There had been something magnetic about Catherine Nicholson. She had attached herself to Paine with childish impetuosity. "Do you really feel, sir," she had asked, "that women should have the same rights and privileges as men? There are some who say that you do not champion a cause, but that you fashion an opinion only for the sake of a controversial article."

Paine had been immediately indignant. "I have no interest in the opinions formed by what I say. I express only what I believe to be right!"

She had looked up at him and laughed. "Anger becomes you, Mr. Paine. Shall we dance?"

He had been startled. She was but a child. Why, she was no older than Mary Lambert had been. She even resembled

[240]

her, with her dark hair and the way she had of tilting her head and looking at him. But that had been so long ago. His thoughts of Mary Lambert were almost like a remembered dream.

"Well, then, come; we shall sit and talk." She had guided him across the ballroom. She had clung to his arm as though he were an intimate friend of her family and chatted gaily as she led him. "In your 'Reflections on Unhappy Marriages,' Mr. Paine, you say that it is the young who are undone. The rash and amorous, the . . . the . . ."

"The young whose hearts are ever glowing with desire, whose eyes are ever roaming after beauty; these dote on the first amiable image that chance throws in their way, and when the flame is once kindled, would risk eternity itself to appease it."

She had looked at him, excitement in her dark eyes, and he had blushed as he realized that she had tricked him into quoting from an essay that he did not wish to be a topic of conversation; When they reached a divan, he was strangely touched by the grace with which she settled herself upon it, spreading the blue satin of her skirt into uniform folds.

"We discuss your essays in school, Mr. Paine, and your pamphlets at home, when my brother and I are there for the holidays. He attends classes here, at the College of Philadelphia."

Paine had not known what to say. He had stared across the room at General Washington, who seemed to be enjoying himself dancing. An orchestra of three French horns, a bassoon, and three fiddles played spiritedly. It did not matter if it were Lady Coventry's Minuet or a Trumpet Air; Washington danced almost every dance, magnificent in his military dress. His scabbard hung elegantly at his side and his full, white wig caught a glint from his gold epaulets. Even John Adams, despite his paunch and his short legs, looked well enough as he danced a quadrille with Mrs. Lynch.

Paine had been startled when Catherine Nicholson rose, took his hand, and led him toward the dance floor. He had altered her course and guided her to a little group about the young marquis and presented her. To his relief, Lafayette had extended an arm and led her off to a dance. Later, he had caught her eye as the frail marquis turned her about with graceful elegance. It had been a reproachful look. He had turned away and caught sight of himself in a mirror—he was still slender, there was no trace of grey in his hair, he still felt vigorous, youthful—but he was forty years old! And there was talk of Catherine's father being appointed a commodore, whereas he himself was penurious. Had he been fooled? He did not know. He knew only that his heart had raced madly when he had thought he had spied her on the Commons.

While his thoughts had been on Catherine Nicholson, Stirling's Division had passed by. Now Lincoln's Division reached the Statehouse. The men wore breeches that fastened below the knee, cotton stockings, and cowhide shoes that were ornamented by large buckles. Their coats were loose and of huge dimensions. Some carried heavy muskets that had done service in the French and Indian War twenty years before.

As Paine watched the men march by, he realized how much Washington's army had grown during the summer. Congress now offered twenty dollars in cash and 100 acres of land to any who would enlist for a term of three years. Laurens had estimated that there were now 16,000 men in the Continental Army.

So far, the watchers had been spellbound. Now, as the sound of fife and drum receded, they rushed into the street with wild cheers. Children broke away from parents and raced after the fading column. It was a heartening sight. Paine wondered if the war might not soon be over. One decisive battle and then? Well, perhaps . . .

Two weeks later, he was awakened from a fitful sleep. He had been troubled by disturbing dreams ever since seeing the marquis again. This night he dreamed that he was back in London, standing in Bull Lane with John Horne, looking up at Elizabeth who was beckoning from a window. He rushed into the bedroom only to find her gone. He turned from the window and to his amazement, Catherine Nicholson was sitting on the bed. The firelight glinted on her satin gown. She must not be seen here! It was scandalous! What would Sarah Ollive say? He rushed to her and it was Mary Lambert on the bed. She was in her nightdress, weeping; she was with child. The fire flickered out and the room grew dark. He sensed his young wife shuddering in the cold. "Do not leave me, Tom. Please! You must not leave me."

As he awoke, he thought he heard footsteps in the street. The first streaks of dawn were thrusting themselves through the windows. Suddenly there was a pummeling on his door and a voice cried, "Mr. Paine! Mr. Paine!" He sprang from the bed and pulled open the door. The Statehouse caretaker stood at the threshold. He held a list of names in his hand.

"Congress is to meet at six o'clock. Mr. Laurens has got a dispatch from General Washington. Congress is to meet at once, he says."

Paine dressed hastily. Seldom giving too great an attention to his attire, now he was careless of it and did not bother to wear a stock. If there were delegates who would be affronted by his hasty dress, then let them.

It was a warm September morning as he hurried up Second Street. A drift of fog hung in the air and an easterly wind tainted it with the smell of Howell's tan yards. Above the mist, the sky was filling with pink light. On Chestnut Street, he caught up with John Adams, walking to the Statehouse with neither concern nor hurry. Despite the early hour and the uncertainty of the call to the Congress, he was meticulously dressed. He stock was neatly pleated, his stockings were pulled tightly over his short thick legs, and every button of his overcoat was in its proper buttonhole.

"Ah, Tom Paine, good morning," he greeted him, as Paine came abreast of him. "Your city sleeps. There is no doubt in my mind but that General Howe is but a few hours march from us and this Philadelphia mass of cowardice and Toryism lie in their beds." Did he expect every citizen to rush from his home with a musket in his hands?

Paine and Adams were among the latecomers. Most of the delegates were already assembled. The attire of many gave every indication of an unexpected awakening and a hasty dressing. Henry Laurens read Washington's dispatch, without gesture or emotion.

". . . The van of the British fleet has dropped anchor in the Elk River that empties into Chesapeake Bay. Two regiments of British light infantry, two of grenadiers, and Hessian and Anspach Jägers have passed Elkton, passed Wilmington, and reached Brandywine Creek. . . ."

Paine forced himself to listen to the dispatch. It spoke of desperate fighting at Chadd's Ford. Young Lafayette had received a bullet in his leg. They had retreated, crossed a bridge at Chester Creek, and were now encamped "behind Chester."

Paine shut his eyes and imagined Washington writing the dispatch upon some improvised table at midnight. He must have been fatigued in body and anguished in mind.

President Laurens offered, "I suggest, gentlemen, that we leave and reassemble at ten o'clock."

"To what purpose?" challenged John Morton.

"When we reassemble, we could call on Putnam, at Peekskill, to send down 1,500 Continentals. Or on Smallwood and Gist, in Maryland, to send their militia. Meanwhile we must consider our own situation."

Robert Morris stepped to Laurens' side and whispered a comment. Laurens nodded. "It has been suggested, gentlemen, that we donate thirty hogsheads of rum to the soldiers of the army, in compliment for their gallant behavior; each man to receive one gill per day, while it lasts."

"Are they to fight or drink, Mr. Laurens?" cried Wilson.

"We can vote upon it when we reassemble."

When Paine reached his lodging, he went to his desk to begin a new pamphlet. He would touch upon every sentiment of patriotism and courage that he could. The country must not feel that all was lost because of a single battle! The room was filled with morning light. Without taking the time to remove his coat, he wrote:

THE CRISIS IV

It is not a field of a few acres of ground, but a *cause,* that we are defending; and whether we defeat the enemy in one battle, or by degrees, the consequence will be the same. . . .

He wrote until long after noon. He was not too pleased with what he had hurriedly written. But he signed the manuscript *Common Sense,* dated it September 12, 1777, and set off to the printer's.

The next morning, he carried the finished pamphlets from the printer's. Some had been bound by candlelight while an apprentice and a carpenter boarded the windows of the printing shop. Copies of it had been tied into bundles and carried to a waiting wagon he had purchased with great difficulty to transport his books, manuscripts, pamphets, accumulated boxes of letters, and the important papers of the Continental Congress. The Congress was preparing to move to Lancaster, Sam Adams had informed him, and, fearful that its documents and diplomatic correspondence might fall into the hands of the British, they had entrusted them to Paine.

Paine had lifted the last bundle of pamphlets into the wagon when a mounted officer cantered down Second Street. Four members of a cavalry patrol rode with him and, behind them, six farm wagons rumbled over the cobblestones. Paine shielded his hand against the sun and recognized Alexander Hamilton.

"Wouldst come with me to Congress, Major," he asked. "I would see those impotent gentlemen." He held up a gloved hand to the line of wagons that had reached them and instructed the cavalrymen, "Wait here for me. I shall return shortly." Turning back to Paine, he informed, "Congress need not see my empty wagons."

"There is no Congress. The delegates have scattered like fruit from a shaken tree." Paine leaned closer to Hamilton and whispered up to him in the saddle, "They will assemble again in Lancaster."

"What?" cried Hamilton in anger. "Washington wrote to Congress but two days ago . . . begging for blankets!"

"Blankets?" asked Paine, not realizing their need in September.

"Among other things . . . blankets! In the confusion at Chadd's Ford and in the heat of the day, thousands of the damn fools shed their blanket rolls and left them on the field!"

"The days are still warm."

"Warm?" cried Hamilton. "Would you know the shelter of a blanket in a rainstorm? Do you know what Congress answered Washington?"

Paine shook his head. "I have been busied with a new *Crisis.*"

"*Crisis?* The crisis is now in Pott's Grove. Do you not know what your cowardly Congress has done? Instead of provisions they have voted Washington a special authority 'to take, wherever he may, all such provisions as may be necessary for the comfortable subsistence of the army under his command.' Comfortable subsistence! Wouldst care to see the authority, Paine? I have it here." He tapped a breast pocket beneath his coat.

"But why you?"

"I volunteered to come. Captain Alexander Hamilton, col-

[246]

lector of blankets and old shoes! Take a look in the wagons, Major Paine. I have been in the city since sunrise and I have as much in the wagons as I can carry upon my back."

Paine glanced into the wagons. Most of them were empty.

"I intend to see Congress face to face," insisted Hamilton. "There must be someone with authority left. Do you come with me, Major?"

When they reached the Statehouse, they saw a crowd in front of it. Four matched dray horses had been harnessed to a farmer's wagon. The sides of the wagon had been removed and its bottom reinforced with stout planks. A dozen laborers and draymen had hoisted the Statehouse bell upon it and were engaged in securing it. Heavy ropes still swung from the Statehouse steeple. To one side was a guard of militiamen. Their clean white breeches and their new gaiters, buttoned to above the knee, gave evidence that they had not yet served away from home.

Paine looked about and saw Sam Adams, watching from the Statehouse steps. He noticed Paine and thrust his way through the curious who had gathered about the wagon.

"There's nobody here, Tom. Except me. Hanging about like an old cat."

The smartness of Sam Adams' attire was gone. He had grown a bit seedy. "There are no other delegates?" asked Hamilton.

Adams shook his head. "The Assembly Room has been locked. Congress stands adjourned. There is no one."

"And the bell?"

"To Allentown. For safekeeping."

Paine pushed to the side of the wagon, to better observe the big bell, and noticed an inscription that ran about its circumference. Hamilton followed him and, edging carefully about it, so as not to soil his coat, read the inscription aloud, "Proclaim Liberty throughout all the land unto all the inhabitants thereof."

[247]

"Leviticus: chapter twenty-five, verse ten," said Paine.

"A proper inscription for the dead at Brandywine," said Hamilton.

Paine's eyes glowed with a defiant light. "And I say that the care taken to guard it is a most propitious omen."

Paine had congenial company on the long trip to Lancaster, for Sam Adams rode with him. They had carried Paine's battered desk from his lodging and placed it in the wagon, its drawers stuffed with manuscripts, pamphlets, and unanswered letters. Despite Adams' shaking head, Paine had also insisted on taking along a hogshead crammed with books and a pair of worn military boots. Over the chest that contained the confidential papers of the Congress, they tossed an old blanket, so arranged that the chest would look but haphazardly covered. They had shoved a peck of ripe apples and two bottles of wine beneath the wagon seat and Adams had unsaddled his horse and tethered him to the back of the wagon. Thus prepared, they set out.

They drove north on Second Street and turned west on Sassafras Street. There was not a horse or cart to be seen. But after they crossed the Schuylkill River, they found the road to Paoli choked with refugees. Not only urban Philadelphians but outlying farmers were deserting their homes. Wagons were piled high with personal possessions, furniture, and children. The ribbon of rutted hard-packed earth was jammed from ditch to fenced-in meadow by squealing pigs, milch cows that protested against the barren earth underfoot, horses that shied at yapping dogs, and at least 100 lost children who cried up into 100 shaking heads. Paine's wagon moved at a snail's pace. Its hubs creaked angrily despite the greased axles.

There was a tinge of early sunset in the sky, and Paine looked at it, critically, and turned a questioning eye on Sam Adams. Adams shrugged. "We sleep tonight in the wagon, Tom. And it does not matter, I assure you. The war will not be over when we get to Lancaster. And the farther from Philadelphia, the better. Will you have an apple and some wine now or later?"

"I shall write still another *Crisis* in Lancaster," said Paine.

"You have not yet distributed the ones in the wagon, Tom."

"I shall address the new one to General Howe," said Paine, as though he had not heard him. "The man has a philosophy that holds humanity in contempt." His lips twisted with bitterness as he looked at the tired, slow-moving mass that clogged the road. "It is the prerogative of animals to be insensible to the feelings of others. It is not possible that the man does this for money. He must do it, then, for fame; and I shall point out to him that Judas is as much known as John."

Sam Adams leaned back into the wagon and lifted a bundle of pamphlets onto his lap. He loosened the knotted twine and pulled a copy from the batch. He was surprised that it contained but a half-dozen printed sheets. They were unnumbered and he looked to see if any were missing.

"They are all there," said Paine, holding the useless reins, as the horse stood idly between the wagon shafts. "I had no time to write more. And there would have been no time to print a longer work."

Adams pushed the brim of his tricorn from his forehead so that it sat more comfortably on his head. He examined the poorly cut sheets that the printers had rushed from their press and read:

> Those who expect to reap the blessings of freedom must, like men, undergo the fatigues of supporting it. The event of yesterday was one of those kind of alarms . . .

Paine studied Adams as he sat and read *The Crisis*. One could no longer call him an impressive figure. Unlike Franklin, or his kinsman John, he did not age well. He now looked all of his fifty-four years, or more. His eyes watered and his

[249]

hands shook slightly as he held the pamphlet. His thin lips were set above a double chin and only a strong, rather large nose rescued him from possessing a soft, womanish face. Despite his polished Harvard manners, his clothes were inelegant, and it did not seem to bother him that he was not a man of property.

Adams and Paine slept in the wagon. Many of the travelers tented in the fields. The congestion eased before they reached Paoli. One or more families, with their domestic animals and heavily laden wagons, left at every crossroad.

They reached Lancaster the following night and learned that the Congress had crossed the Susquehanna River and retreated further west, to York. It was late before they found food and lodging in overcrowded Lancaster.

When they arrived in York, Paine was immediately taken to one side by President Laurens. A house had been provided for him, on the outskirts of the town. The chest of Congressional papers and the military and diplomatic correspondence would be more secure there in case of a sudden attack.

Paine studied his guide as they drove out from York. He seemed an old man, judging from his grey beard and his sunken cheeks; yet his lean raw-boned body appeared as vigorous as a youth's. He sat on the wagon seat, a rifle across his homespun-covered knees, and glanced about with squinting, restless eyes. "I is to be your hired man," he said. "Cook for ye, does ye wants me to. An' look a'ter them there things." He jerked a thumb over his shoulder to indicate the contents of the wagon.

They stopped soon before a house on a creek bank. It was obscured by a grove of chestnut trees. Paine looked up and noticed an oblong stone under its eaves. Into the stone's face had been chiseled: "J. B. Cookis, 1761." They alighted and the guide thrust open a solidly built door. So that the new tenant should not be dismayed at the sooted fireplace, the cobwebbed rafters, and the badly planed wood floor through

[250]

whose chinks a few adventurous shoots had thrust themselves, he apologized, "Ole Cookis weren't too fussy. Ah'll brush 'er down in no time."

19

PAINE WAS not happy in York, although it was a pleasant community, made up chiefly of Germans. In their schools, they taught their own language, and the services in their churches were conducted in German. Aside from their personal freedom, however, they had no interest in the country or its government. It was as though the war and independenc itself did not concern them.

When General Roberdeau arrived, he immediately bought a large house near the Congress building. He was now a delegate from Pennsylvania and had brought his family with him. He invited John and Sam Adams, Elbridge Gerry, and Tom Paine to stay with him. Laurens, however, frowned upon Paine's acceptance of the invitation. The Continental Congress had entrusted their papers to Paine's guardianship. He himself had chosen the Cookis House for the sake of the chest's seclusion and safety. Paine must not neglect its care. Nevertheless, Paine spent most of his evenings in Daniel Roberdeau's home, while his days, when not in the Congress, were confined to the Cookis House. He had spent most of his life in one-room lodgings, yet here on the Cadorus Creek, where he had a whole house to himself and a caretaker for company, he felt lonely. His very soul died without someone to talk to, and the caretaker was so taciturn that a week went by before Paine learned his name. He started a *Crisis V,* but it did not go well. Amidst the dappled sunshine of the woods, the whisper of the wind through the autumn leaves, and the sound of crickets, frogs, and birds, he could stoke no anger against General Howe and the task that Britain had set him to do.

On September 26 he learned that Cornwallis had taken possession of Philadelphia! Then, like a windfall, four days later, Paine himself received a letter from the Pennsylvania Assembly. Because of "his experience in the field with General Greene, as well as his journalistic success," they offered to engage him "to act as observer with Washington's army and to furnish regular and constant intelligence of the proceedings of the forces."

Rushing to catch up with his secretarial work—for he was now in the midst of diplomatic correspondences with the courts of France, Spain, and Holland—he entrusted the Congres chest to the caretaker at the Cookis House and set out for Wahington's camp.

He reached it on October 2, to find it stretched out on both sides of the Skippack Road, sixteen miles from Germantown. It was evening and campfires were being lighted in the fields and in clearings in the woods. He was directed to Washington's headquarters, a stone farmhouse at the edge of the road, and there, as though some premonition had urged his haste, he found the large front room of the farmhouse filled by a council of war. They were debating an attack on Germantown. Accepted as the representative of the Pennsylvania Assembly, he stood and listened.

General Wayne was speaking before a map. "This Germantown," he said, glancing at the circle of men about him, "is a village that is strung out like beads on a cord. The houses stretch for two miles along Skippack Road. Almost every home is enclosed by a stout rail fence or high hedge, which would detain not only horse and gun but infantry as well. Here, gentlemen, in the center of the village, is a crossroad called Schoolhouse Lane." He pointed to a spot a little south

[252]

of it and said, "This is the British camp. It extends from the Schuylkill River on the west to here, beyond York Road, on the east. A short distance to the rear of the camp is Howe's headquarters."

Washington straightened from above the table and looked about. "It is agreed then," he said. "We shall attack in four columns at dawn. General Sullivan will command the first." Major General Sullivan nodded. "General Greene, the second." Nathaniel Greene inclined his head. "Smallwood and Forman, the third; and Armstrong, the fourth. How many would you say are now in Germantown?"

He looked directly at Sullivan. "No more than 9,000, sir," answered Sullivan.

Washington smiled at his officers. The lamplight gave a strange emphasis to his outthrust jaw. "Good. Gentlemen, let's give them hell!"

Not until after the battle of Germantown was over, was Paine able to piece together what had happened.

He himself had sat his horse at Greene's side and watched Greene's column begin to march down the Limekiln Road that ran due south to Germantown. He had wished silently for victory. He would write to the courts of Europe: "The flame of human freedom will never expire! At Germantown, with recruits who had never fired a musket or used the bayonet, but whose spirit of liberty . . ." The four columns were to arrive within two miles of the enemy's pickets, on their respective routes, by two o'clock. They were to halt until sunrise. Then they were to make simultaneous attacks at five o'clock, with fixed bayonets and without firing a shot.

Every half hour, Greene had to hold up to wait for laggards. The men had begun to cover less ground. Officers dismounted and waited for them to close ranks, until a scout came back and reported that they were now approaching Meetinghouse Lane. Luken's Mill was less than a mile away. Paine looked up at the sky. The sun was rising, struggling to cast its light through a grey mist. Over an open field, the air was like a heavy fog at sea. Suddenly there was the sound of firing—sporadic at first, and then a volley of musketry. It came from the northwest. Paine could see Greene turn his horse and try to make an interpretation ... and suddenly there was the boom of artillery. It meant that the element of surprise was gone.

As they reached Luken's Mill, they were met by the aroused British advance guard. The Continentals swept forward and fired into the British lines. Militia and recruits alike spilled over into the bordering fields and shot into the British from left and right. A column of Hessians rushed up the road to reinforce the engaged British. At the sight of their spit-and-polish uniforms, the Continentals went wild. Deserting the fields, they charged into the column with fixed bayonets and clubbed them with their heavy muskets. Wounded men did not stop but struggled onward, into the thick of the combat. Those wounded who fell to their knees persisted in reloading their muskets and fired again and again into the British ranks. Suddenly the British and the Hessians turned and fled.

Paine's horse, unaccustomed to the tumult, reared and spun about, seeking a way to liberty, but there was no open space into which to dash. As Paine soothed his mount, he saw Muhlenberg riding across a field. He was recalling his charging men and reassembling his brigade, while Greene was directing the main column westward on Mill Street, where, according to plan, he would attack on the British right.

Behind them, like a bluish-grey cloud, battle smoke hung in the windless air. As the head of the column reached the Skippack Road crossing and waited for orders, there was no sound but that of shuffling feet and the clink of metal. In a moment, as though drifting across a marshy field, a fog settled over them and obscured them from view.

When Paine reached the crossing, his heart was beating like a broken ratchet in a clock. His keen mind remembered each rendezvous. Here, at this crossing, they were to join Washington's main column and smash into the sleeping British camp. But where was Washington? Where were Nash and Maxwell and Stirling and Conway? Where, in God's name, was Sullivan's column? Suddenly, to the north, from where they had marched, there was once again the sound of musketry and the heavy boom of artillery. And then, as though swept away by a mischievous wind, the fog lifted and, to Paine's amazement, there was a British line immediately in front of them. The regulars were standing with fixed bayonets, lifted muskets, and closed ranks. They stood in a half circle, in front of the Market House that had been lost in the fog until now.

Paine expected the Continentals to disperse. To his wonder and pride, the men charged at the British without an order. The redcoats had time to fire but a single volley when the Continentals were upon them with swinging muskets and wild fierce shouts. Not stopping to reload, the redcoats turned and fled past the Market House. A column of reinforcements came running. The retreating redcoats joined them and began to regroup. Muhlenberg and Greene gave them no time to pattern a defense but led a bayonet charge directly at them. The Continentals, goaded by the fresh faces of the British, smashed at the forming lines with uncontained fury. Wayne and his men tore into them. Some of the British fired without taking the time to aim. Most turned and fled as though before a stampede. The Continentals' charge drove clear through the fleeing redcoats. The British threw down their muskets and lifted their arms in surrender. They packed themselves into milling circles, like cattle, and stood in mute silence. For an instant, it seemed like victory. But the fog was lifting now and still there was no sign of Washington's column. Without support, it would be disastrous for Greene, Muhlenberg, and Wayne to attack the main British camp.

From a slight rise in the ground, Paine could see it now. From their tents in a meadow, the troops were fully aroused and were engaging Muhlenberg's brigade. Far beyond the camp, where the impetus of a mad charge had evidently carried them, were Wayne's men and a portion of Muhlenberg's brigade. On a rise, in front of Paine, Greene's artillery was trained on the camp. They had fired no single shot because of the Continentals already in the camp. Just when Paine thought Muhlenberg and Wayne lost, their men turned their bayonets against the encircling British lines, charged back through them, rushed up the rise of ground, and joined Greene.

Greene hesitated at first. British and Hessians were pressing upon his left and right. Then he ordered his artillery men to fall back. As they began to withdraw, he insisted that the precious fieldpieces not be left behind. His Quaker frugality would not permit him to abandon them to the enemy. To protect the fieldpieces, the Continentals engaged in a delaying action as they retreated. As they withdrew through the village, they used fences, trees, and the very houses themselves as shelters from which to fire at the advancing British.

Muhlenberg urged his men to make room for the guns. But the narrow road was now tightly packed with wagons and retreating, stumbling men. Some supported wounded comrades. Others turned to stop, load, and fire at the British.

A horse stepped into a deep rut and pitched forward. Impeded by the traces and shafts of the wagon to which it was harnessed, it struggled frantically to rise on three legs. Paine dismounted to go to its aid. To his consternation, his legs crumpled under him as he reached the ground and he tumbled over into the road. He had not known that he was so fatigued that his legs would not support him. As a retreating infantryman helped him to his feet, he saw Muhlenberg dismount, inspect the horse's broken leg, and fire point-blank into its head. The big man was too tired to regain his own saddle. One foot in the stirrup, he struggled to remount, while his uncooperative horse moved away in a pivot. He hopped on one boot, at the side of the turning mount. As Paine watched, two

Continentals grasped the horse's bit and bridle while another lifted him into the saddle.

Halfway to Mount Airy, where the road led through open fields, Greene again arranged his artillery in a wide arc. Muhlenberg's division had been holding back the British, firing into their cautious pursuit. Now Greene opened his guns upon them while the Continentals retreated further.

Suddenly, with a burst of energy that they did not know they possessed, the retreating men scattered in every direction. They had spied a party of horsemen racing down upon them with drawn sabers. Paine turned his mount to face the horsemen. It was Pulaski's cavalry contingent. They had been hovering in the rear, atacking the British dragoons. Finding themselves greatly outnumbered, they had been forced to flee and were now riding up Skippack Road and into the retreating Continentals. Paine recognized Casimir Pulaski at their head. With his fair skin, his small nose, and the finely arched eyebrows above his large grey eyes, the Polish nobleman could have been taken for a woman but for the well-trimmed mustache that lent an air of elegance to his martial bearing. Washington had appointed him chief of dragoons, with the rank of brigadier general. He lifted a slender arm and waved his cavalry to a halt.

Paine reached the edge of Sullivan's column at the foot of Chestnut Hill. The men were in full rout, pressing up the rising road that led through a grove of chestnut trees. To Paine's astonishment, Washington sat his horse in the midst of them. White-faced with anger, the sound of his voice lost in the confusion, he was swinging his crop at the routed men. As though in apology for their retreat, the men waved empty cartridge boxes at him. Paine curbed his horse and watched the confused mass rush by. Washington ended his efforts for a rally. He turned his horse and permitted himself to be swept along.

Sick at heart, Paine rode on in silence. There was a tear in his coat that a musket ball had made—he knew not where or when—but it did not trouble him half as much as the sight of the retreating Continentals. The battle had almost been won. What had gone wrong? If only Greene's flanks had been protected as they should have been, ... If Sullivan's column had reached them, as they had planned, ... There had been no sound of musketry for some time now; far to the rear, there was the sound of firing. A scout tore through a field that bordered the road, spurred his mount to hurdle a fence, urged him through a mass of straggling men, and coaxed him to Washington's side.

"Sir! Sir! Cornwallis has brought up three battalions from Philadelphia. They could close the distance between us at will."

Washington did not appear to listen. He tapped the horse with his reins and rode onward.

By four o'clock they reached last night's camping ground, sixteen miles from Germantown. Officers dismounted, sliding from their saddles as though they were wounded. The men, recognizing the fields where they had camped the day before, sank to the ground in sheer exhaustion. They had marched over thirty miles. They had had neither food nor sleep. They lay in the postures into which they first fell—upon their backs, their sides, their bellies. They scattered their muskets about them and nestled their heads in their arms. As they left the road, they stepped over comrades and dropped into the first open spot. The fields soon gave the appearance of graveyards filled with unburied dead. With effort, Paine turned in the saddle and looked back. The road was pressed with men who clutched each other as though for mutual support. He could see commissary wagons on the crest of the hill. Men swarmed about them like flies. They held on to the sides and the backs of the wagons, to the shafts and to the harness of the horses, to whatever a hand could clutch that would help to drag them forward.

Washington looked neither to the side nor back. He sat on his horse and continued up the road at his slow pace, and, as the men realized that they could not camp here, they roused themselves and followed him.

The following noon, Major Monroe filled in the missing pieces for Paine.

"I was with General Sullivan's column," said Monroe. "Just north of Meetinghouse Lane, we came across a solid stone house."

Paine nodded. "The home of Benjamin Chew. Chief Justice of the Province. His Tory family have long left it."

"Pickets had spotted us and spread the alarm to a full regiment of the British. Over 100 of them fortified themselves in that stone house. They bolted the heavy ground shutters and posted themselves at the second-story windows. The mist had thickened into a fog and we could just see the muskets jutting from the windows. General Knox rushed to Washington's side and insisted that we must not by-pass the house. It was against sound military tactics to by-pass a *fortified* position. If I may say so, Major Paine, I could see General Sullivan chafing as Washington listened to Knox. When General Washington was convinced that we must take the house, Sullivan ordered his men to surround it. They scattered over the lawns and fired ineffectually at the second-story windows. When General Sullivan felt that the British realized that they were surrounded, he ordered a cease-fire and sent a young officer to demand a surrender. Lieutenant Matthew Smith. A Virginian. Did you know him?"

Paine shook his head.

"We were friends," said Monroe, with a touch of bitterness in his voice. "Matt drew his sword, tied his stock to it as a flag of truce, and marched toward the house. Halfway up the carriage drive, he was shot at and killed. The dirty British bastards!"

Paine was surprised at Monroe's invective. It was not in

[259]

keeping with his aristocratic face and his cultured voice.
"There are some who say that the gunsmoke and the fog hid the stock on the sword. It's a lie! General Knox went wild with anger. He insisted that no one leave and ordered the artillery turned against the house. The six-pounders blew in the door and smashed the windows, but the balls rebounded from the thick stone walls. He ordered a charge through the smashed door, but the British had barricaded the hallway with furniture and thrust musket bayonets through its gaps. When the charge was repulsed, Knox shouted, 'Burn the damn house down! Burn it to the ground!' Two volunteers tried to reach the steps. One was immediately shot down, the other barely reached the safety of a tree. Two young officers decided to try again. To the one who was French, Washington cried, 'Non! Non! Do not attempt it!' The other officer was Colonel John Laurens of South Carolina. Do you know him?"

Paine nodded. So the impulsive young Laurens was a colonel now. . . .

"Colonel Laurens rushed to the stables and raced back, his arms full of straw. Wait now, here he comes." Paine looked up and saw Colonel Laurens leaving Washington's headquarters. There was a large bandage over one arm and across his chest. A young man walked with quiet dignity at his side. He was dressed in satin breeches and an expensive gold-embroidered coat.

Laurens smiled to Paine as they approached. Anticipating Paine's asking, he informed, "A flesh wound in the shoulder. The ball was not deep and it touched no bone. Would you please inform my father not to be concerned?" He introduced his companion. "Chevalier de Mauduit du Plessis."

"I was telling Paine of your daring at the Chew House," said Monroe.

"Oh, that," laughed Laurens. "I fear the glory belongs to the chevalier."

"You meant to burn down a solid stone house?" asked Paine.

[260]

Laurens shrugged. "You do not stop to think on the field. My friend here had reached an unguarded window that had been smashed by the artillery. He clambered over it and waved to me. As I reached it, I saw a British officer crossing the room, with a pistol aimed at de Mauduit's back. There I was, my arms full of straw, and too astonished to shout a single word. The British officer, not yet seeing me, and evidently perplexed by de Mauduit's civilian dress, demanded to know what he was doing there. And de Mauduit," laughed Laurens, "as though it were a most natural thing for him to be there, answered, 'I'm only taking a walk, monsieur.' In a moment the British officer caught sight of me outside the window, my arms still full of straw. Just as he cried, 'Surrender!' a redcoat rushed into the room and opened fire on de Mauduit, but the ball struck the British officer. And now my friend has become *célèbre*. He is greeted everywhere by a smile and the phrase, 'I am only taking a walk, monsieur.' If you write of it, Major Paine, would you neglect to mention that my wound was received in going away from, and not toward, the enemy?"

In the late afternoon, Paine came across de Kalb. It was the first time that he had seen him without young Lafayette at his side. He was looking out over the fields where the tentless men were bivouacked. "It was a complete fiasco!" he said in his deep-throated English when Paine questioned him. "And it was not General Washington's fault. I was at his side, while he watched General Knox direct that futile bombardment. Rank forbade me to interfere, but I could see your General Washington grit his teeth with impatience. What a bungled opportunity! *Solch eine Gelegenheit. . . .*"

De Kalb's other details were appalling. General Conway had deserted his column, on retreat, and had been found asleep in a barn. Count Pulaski, unable to push himself further, had bedded down in a farmhouse and left himself open to capture. General Stephen had disobeyed orders when he had taken his division away from Greene. He had drunk "to combat extreme fatigue" and was found lying in a fence corner, helplessly intoxicated. He had been cashiered, and the command of his division had been given to Lafayette.

Such was the unpalatable truth about Germantown. An engagement that involved 20,000 men had been lost because of a single stone house! Yet the Continental Army was a fresh one, raised within the year. The engagement, though not victorious, had not been a rout! He wrote to Franklin, now in France:

> Everyone marched his own pace. The enemy kept a civil distance behind, sending every now and then a shot after us, and receiving the same from us. The army had marched the preceding night, fourteen miles, and, having full twenty to march back, were exceedingly fatigued. They appeared to me to be more displeased at their retreating from Germantown than anxious to get to their rendezvous. . . .
> I breakfasted next morning at General Washington's quarters, who was at the same loss with every other to account for the accidents of the day. . . .

On October 19, Howe, unable to stomach another such "victory," withdrew his troops from Germantown and concentrated his entire force in Philadelphia.

A dejected Paine rode back to York. At the Cookis House, it was as though he had left but yesterday. The caretaker tucked his rifle under an arm and took the reins of Paine's tired horse without comment.

"Has anyone been here?"

"Nope."

"Has anything happened?"

"Nope."

"Any messages?"

"Nope."

20

PAINE FOUND only the remnant of a Congress when he returned to York. Georgia and Delaware were without representation; New Hampshire, Rhode Island, Pennsylvania, and Maryland had only one delegate each; and, of those delegates who were in York, many were seldom in attendance. Paine felt that Hancock would never be back. He had been affronted. When he had resigned as president of the Continental Congress, after two years' service, Henry Laurens had offered a resolution to tender him something "for the unremitted attention and steady impartiality that he had manifested in the discharge of various duties of his office." New Hampshire, Pennsylvania, and even Massachusetts had voted against thanking him.

Now, the news of Germantown had preceded Paine's return, and gloom and uncertainty once more overwhelmed the remaining delegates, as it had the year before when the Congress had abandoned Washington to his fate at the Deleware and fled to Baltimore. To add to their discomfiture, the Pennsylvania Assembly itself sent to Paine a letter addressed to the Congress, in which the Assembly stated that, having heard that Washington intended to have his army go into winter quarters at Valley Forge, the Assembly wanted the Congress to remonstrate most urgently against this. Pennsylvania and New Jersey would be ravaged by the British if the Congress allowed this to happen. The inhabitants would be obliged to flee or submit to such terms as the enemy might prescribe. If the Congress thought the Pennsylvania Assembly exaggerated, let them go and view pillaged Morrisania or what was left of Dickinson's estate, which the Hessians had recently occupied. The place was desolate. They had dug up the floor of Colonel Dickinson's greenhouse in search of money and killed his orange, lemon, and lime trees. They had pillaged his furnishings and left his home filthy and defaced!

Paine wrote to Greene, and General Greene answered. Yes, it was true that Washington had decided upon winter quarters at Valley Forge. It was unduly cold for this time of year. They had already had a second snowfall. The men were poorly fed and half naked. They could not be asked to endure the rigors of a winter campaign. Washington had held a council with his officers and they had all agreed. Even impetuous Lafayette, eager to exercise his new command, had admitted that they could not carry on a winter campaign.

Before any answer to the Assembly's protest could be devised, however, at the end of October, like a burst of cannon on a quiet day, came the news of a stupendous victory up north. Wishful but unconfirmed rumors had trickled into York for days. Some had been wildly estatic. Now a military report arrived. It advised that on the morning of October 17, at Saratoga, the British army, under General Burgoyne, had surrendered to General Gates, in command of the American forces in Canada. Paine read the detailed dispatch. The Americans had captured great stores of ammunition, food, and clothes. Five thousand British had surrendered! Two major generals, two lieutenant generals, three brigadier generals with their staffs, and 300 other officers. Paine's enthusiasm knew no bounds. For the first time, at long last, the ill-organized American "amateurs" had defeated the British and Hessian regulars in a pitched battle. Now he could write to Franklin in France, to the courts of Holland, Spain, and Prussia. If France and Spain recognized American independence, perhaps Holland would negotiate a loan. . . .

Overwhelmed by work, yet bored with his associates, he decided late in November to visit Valley Forge as the correspondent of the Pennsylvania Assembly.

He reached Valley Forge on a Saturday morning, and what he saw when he reached Washington's camp depressed him to the depths of his soul. The sentry who challenged him was standing on an old hat to keep his half-shod, bleeding feet from the snow. Mud-splattered sleeves, torn from an old coat, served him for stockings. His hands were wrapped in rags. An old muffler was tied clumsily about his head and his teeth chattered in a very lean, unshaven face. Beyond a snow-trodden path, men who looked like scarecrows were chopping at trees. Others were urging horses with sunken bellies to tug the branch-trimmed trunks into clearings, where small shelters were being made of logs notched together.

Before Washington's tent, the General himself was standing in the cold, under a linen marquee that was fastened with taut ropes. The blue cloak he had flung about him seemed to be the same one that he had worn at Trenton. Generals Greene and Muhlenberg were with him, as well as de Kalb and Lafayette. Their chins were half hidden in their coat collars.

General Greene was the first to greet Paine. "It's Tom Paine. Welcome, Tom! What news from York?"

Paine was lost for words. He dismounted and joined them in silence. Lafayette, forgetting that Paine knew no French, spoke to him with a rapid stream of phrases in his native tongue. He gesticulated with a quickly moving hand that pointed to the half-finished huts, the half-frozen men, the horses with their heaving ribs, and ended by thrusting an accusing finger at General Greene.

Sober-faced de Kalb translated for Paine: "Le marquis keeps telling his Excellency that he is horrified by our soldiers' plight. They have no coats! They have no shoes! He says, in his France, the women would bring food and clothing to these soldiers who struggle for liberty. With a few wagons and a handful of men, he could go into the provinces, the

[265]

towns, and take what we need. At gunpoint! His Excellency says, 'No!' Even General Greene says, 'No!' He asks you, patriot Paine, should he not do this thing?"

Paine looked at Lafayette. His thin face was flushed with anger despite the cold.

"If you will forgive our absence, gentlemen," said Greene, "I would like to show our friend the camp. Since he now reports for the Pennsylvania Assembly, perhaps he can more fully impress them with our needs."

He moved off with Paine and lamented, "It took us more than a week to march here from Whitemarsh. A distance of thirteen miles, Tom. Thirteen miles! We had four days and nights of snow and sleet. I know not how the poor wretches survived. I watched them, milling about like cattle, huddled around smoking campfires, trying to cook their rations over wet, smoldering wood fires. I saw them shiver in their sleep, unsheltered and in wet clothes on the snow-covered ground. I all but wept for them!"

Paine turned to watch a half-finished hut being chinked with mud. "Wait here till I get my horse," said Green. "I will ride with thee to the lookout."

Paine sat on his horse and looked about him. He shuddered as he suddenly thought of Jason Witherspoon and what the provisioner had said to him little more than a year ago: "Tom Paine. Mr. *Common Sense!* Why, your name is cursed by Whig and Tory alike. By the one for urging an impossible task . . . and by the other for destroying the peace!"

Greene was back with his mount. As he rode at Paine's side, he urged, "Thee must get us provisions, Tom. Make Congress listen to thee. Shame them! We have the full Continental Army here and for this noon's meal we have but twenty barrels of flour and no meat. Where can we get provisions but that Congress sends them from York and Lancaster? The countryside hath been stripped by the British. Only with food can we survive until spring!"

[266]

Greene nudged his half-starved horse with worn boot heels. Paine followed him up a steep hill to where a lookout tower was being built. They circled as they reached the observation post. Sentries stood with clenched teeth and flapping mufflers in a whistling wind, keeping a continuous lookout. Far below, he could see the Schuylkill River. It shimmered between its white banks. Below the wooded plateau, whose timber was being cleared for the construction of the huts, Paine could see Valley Creek. He could make out the ruins of the old forge that the Hessians had burned over a year ago. His heart was stirred by the sight of this land that spread from horizon to horizon. It was too beautiful to be enslaved!

When they returned to Washington's tent, Paine found the general engaged in writing letters. To one side of the marquee, a group of French officers sat on camp stools, about a brisk fire. Inside the tent, a brazier of glowing wood embers had been placed upon the table where Washington sat. The general looked up as Greene and Paine entered. He hunted among the letters on the table and, finding what he searched for, offered it to Paine. "For your Pennsylvania Assembly," he said, his voice touched with anger.

Paine saw no need for the possessive adjective. He was merely engaged by them as an official observer. As he was placing it into his pocket, Washington advised, "You may read it, Major Paine. I make no secret of its content."

Paine opened the unsealed letter to the Pennsylvania Assembly. It was a bitter tirade. They had given Washington assurances that they had not fulfilled. The general felt that their seeming indifference and neglect was because, despite their protest, he had led his troops into winter quarters. Greene stepped to Paine's side and Paine read aloud:

> ... and that these same gentlemen should think a winter's campaign and the covering of these States from the invasion of an enemy so easy and practicable a business. I can assure these gentlemen that it is a much easier and less distressing

thing to draw remonstrances in a comfortable room by a good fireside than to occupy a cold, bleak hill and sleep under frost and snow without cloaths or blankets. . . .

Paine would read no more. He folded the letter and placed it into his pocket. "I assure you, sir, that it will reach its destination."

Washington leaned forward and insisted, "The Virginia Assembly would not have acted in this manner!"

Paine's eyes grew wide with anger, but, before he could reply, Greene pointed out, "Tom is not an assemblyman, George. I should not need to assure thee that he does what he can."

The big man rose and placed an apologetic arm about Paine and drew him to the tent flaps. "Those officers," he said, inclining his big head toward the half-circle of Frenchmen behind him, "are accustomed to good living and the best hospitality . . . and I offer them only stinking whiskey. And not always that. They are served beef without vegetables and so much New England salt codfish that they have finally developed a plebian taste for it. The few servants I have with me wait upon them in tattered liveries. Do you forgive my anger, Major Paine!?"

When he wished to show it, Washington had the attraction of a warm sun on a cold day, and Paine's own anger was gone instantly. Yet he could hardly feel much sympathy for the plight of the French officers who missed their delicacies. His thoughts were with the common men who, but a short distance from the tent, were building their crude shelters with torn and frozen hands.

Paine left Valley Forge the next day. He ate breakfast with the enlisted men. For his benefit, they insisted on breaking into a barrel of salted herring that they had been saving. The herrings were decayed and so Paine shared their common diet —a diet of thin cakes made of flour and water that they had baked on hot stones. They called them "firecakes." They assured him that, three days ago, they had been given strips of salted beef and pork as Christmas rations. He offered them leftover copies of his *Crisis IV.* He was affronted by those who did not hold out their hands and then, as he looked into their haggard yet friendly faces, he realized that they could not read.

It was early in May, 1778, amid reports that Howe had resigned and that the British had begun to evacuate Philadelphia, that a rider brought dispatches to York from a ship just in at Boston Harbor containing the stunning news that Franklin's Treaty of Alliance with the court of France had at last been signed. The day after its receipt Paine started for Valley Forge with the news.

As he traveled eastward from York, the affluent farms gave way to neglected fences and pastures. He studied the fields that bordered the road. Only portions of them had been plowed and seeded. The rest lay fallow in the spring sunshine. There was no stock to be seen; not a single grazing cow or horse in pasture. Past Downington, the land seemed almost as though it had been ravaged by a plague.

At the Paoli crossroad, Paine let his horse climb slowly to higher ground. The dogwoods were in blossom. The branches of the diminutive trees were covered with a profusion of white and delicate pink petals. He stared about him when he reached the Valley Forge plateau. It was as though he had taken a wrong turn and had come upon some new encampment. He had seen the huts when they were being built, but they had a new appearance now. Most of them had windows cut into their sides and the clay-daubed chimneys looked like stone.

Paine let his horse pick his way across the spring grass between a long line of huts that faced each other. When he approached the ground where he remembered Washington's tent had been, he was surprised to see a vast clearing. As he drew closer, he realized that it was a drill field. The Continental Army had never had one!

Paine dismounted and led his horse closer. Only a squad of men was being drilled but, in a wide semicircle, dozens of officers and more than 100 foot soldiers were watching. The drillmaster, dressed in a military coat of some European army, marched the squad to the rear, faced them about, marched them forward, slashed at the air with a powerful arm, and bellowed, "Vun, two! Vun, two!" And then, as though forgetting himself, he cried in a guttural roar: *"Eins, zwei, drei . . . halt!"* and Paine immediately recognized von Steuben.

Fascinated, Paine continued to watch the drilling. He had thought that nothing could keep him from delivering his news to Washington and yet here he was, dallying. He spied John Laurens and Alexander Hamilton, sitting on hogsheads, at one side of the clearing. He edged toward them and they rose and offered welcoming hands. Hamilton was as smart as ever in polished boots, clean uniform, and well-tended wig.

"I do not see General Washington's headquarters," said Paine.

"At Dewee's place," explained Hamilton. "Almost a mile from here. Come, I'll walk with you. Do you stay here, John?" Laurens nodded. Hamilton led Paine from the drill ground. "How do you like the winter quarters now? Lighthorse Harry has been making forays into Delaware, bringing back British cattle. Wadsworth has applied himself to the collection of clothing and Greene to their transportation." He pointed to a long shed. Its sides were made of split rails and its roof was well tarred. "Stored with barrels of salted fish. There's a spring run of shad in the Schuylkill, and the men are netting thousands of them. Salting them down. There is now a daily ration of a pound and a half of bread to each man, a pound of beef, and a gill of whiskey. But Steube insists that we salt them down just the same. Says that they do it with herring, over there. And in the winter the men live happily on a diet of potatoes and herring."

"Do you call von Steuben 'Steube' from familiarity or disaffection?"

"Washington calls him 'Steube.' " He turned to Paine and confided, "I learned from his aide that the man has no claim to the 'von' and that he has never been a lieutenant general in Frederick's army nor his aide. His highest rank, in Germany, was that of captain! He speaks, casually, of an estate in Swabia, but there never was such an estate."

"You do not approve of him?"

Hamilton laughed. "Approve of him? I respect him." He lifted a finger and pointed out, "Not for what he is, mind you, but for what he has done. Until he came, we had almost no discipline. There was no manual of arms. I watched him at the first inspection of the troops. He marched in front of the men and, to everyone's amazement, tore rusting muskets from them and flung the neglected arms into the snow."

They had been climbing a sharp rise of ground and, as they reached its crest, an abominable stench of decay and rotting flesh assailed Paine's nostrils. He held his coat sleeve across his nose and mouth and cried, "My God! Captain Hamilton, what is that?"

"I cannot say we are accustomed to it, but we anticipate it when we come up here," said Hamilton in a muffled tone. It is only at this point that it is most perceptible, and only since the spring thaw. For lack of wagons, there was no forage, and almost 500 of our horses starved to death. We could not bury them in the frozen ground. They were dragged up here, thinking we would roll them down into Valley Creek . . . but we use the water for drinking and could not afford to pollute it."

Washington's headquarters was a two-story structure with a pitched roof and shuttered windows. A breezeway divided the main building from a storage room and cookery. There was an appetizing scent of fresh baking. They were admitted by an orderly and found the general still at lunch. It seemed as though the table could seat no more, yet Washington, an ever gracious host, insisted that they join them. Greene, Lafayette, de Kalb, and Wayne were there. As were Muhlenberg, John Marshall, and Charles Lee, who had arrived in April, after fifteen months in British hands.

Paine was introduced to Martha Washington and a Lieutenant Joel Barlow, a most handsome young man from Connecticut, who was serving as a chaplain. A young Negro servant, dressed in elegant livery, brought fresh-baked biscuits, boiled potatoes, and baked shad for Hamilton and Paine. The shad were in a butter sauce and sprinkled with freshly ground West Indies pepper. Paine lifted the glass of Mount Vernon wine that was poured for him and toasted: "To his Excellency's lady, Mrs. Washington, whose hospitality at table is outdone only by her courage and devotion in joining us here."

"Hear! Hear!"

Washington was in a gay mood. With his wife at his side and his congenial friends about him, he seemed as though at home. He stretched out his long legs and permitted himself an anecdote. "I do not know if Major Paine remembers, but I attended a meeting at Princeton with him one Sunday. I do not know if he wished to impress me with the devotions of his sect or if he were led there by his personal desire for prayer. Do you recall the incident, Tom?" Paine smiled. "Before entering the meeting house, Major Paine entrusted his overcoat to the care of an Irish servant. When we left, we discovered that the rascal had absconded with it. Tit for tat, I gave Major Paine a bit of my own common sense: 'It is necessary to watch as well as pray.' And how did you find the coat I gave you, Tom?"

"So long in the sleeves, I had no need for mittens," laughed Paine. He pushed back his chair, rose, and looked about him. "With your leave, gentlemen, I have news of the utmost importance. I was seduced by the shad and, since good news is better celebrated on a full stomach, ..." He reached into his portmanteau and extracted a letter for Washington.

When the general read it, he rose to his full height, helped Martha Washington from her chair, and put an arm about her. He looked at the members of his staff and informed them, "Gentlemen, Dr. Franklin has effected an alliance with France."

For a moment they were dumbfounded, and then they thrust back their chairs, shook each other's hands, slapped each other's backs, and, in the midst of their outburst, young Lafayette kept shouting, *"Viva la France! Vive le Docteur Franklin! Vive le bon roi Louis! C'est magnifique! Viva la France!"*

Greene wiped tears from his eyes and they all grew hushed as they noticed Muhlenberg, on his knees, in silent prayer. The big man glanced about him as he rose and asked, "Is it really true, Tom?"

Paine nodded. "When I left, the delegates were proposing a list of gifts to be sent to France, as presents to the ladies of the court. Mr. Rittenhouse's planetarium has been suggested, as have things American—Narragansett pacing mares, moose, wood-ducks, flying squirrels."

"I suggest they send me," said Hamilton with his fetching smile.

"Shall we advise the men?" suggested Paine.

They decided to walk to the drill ground and Martha Washington quickly chose Paine as her escort. She insisted on discussing his essays. He had been writing political tracts for so long, he had almost forgotten them. Mrs. Washington had put on a light shawl and a lace cap with a bow in front. Light brown hair that was greying could be seen from beneath the ribbons of her cap. Her round face was as small as a child's, but her hazel eyes contained an adult's sharpness. Though small, her mouth was as uncompromising as her husband's.

Von Steuben was drilling still another squad. To one side of the clearing, the spring sunshine glinted from a long row

[273]

of polished cannons. General Washington informed the men, and Lafayette hastened to translate the news to the baron. The men stared about them with open mouths and then, dropping their muskets, tossing their hats into the air, hugged each other and shouted themselves hoarse. Tears streamed down the cheeks of many faces. Suddenly von Steuben shouted commands that were half in English and half in his native German. The drill ground was cleared. The squad marched to their posts and formed a line of battle with rapidity and precision. As von Steuben shouted and dropped his hand, there was a fire of musketry. It started at the right of the front line and ran, shot by shot, to its left with military exactness, hesitated, and then ran back again along the second line.

Lafayette could not contain himself and cried, *"C'est le feu de joie! C'est le feu de joie! Très bien. Vive le General Washington!"*

Hamilton, not to be outdone, raced across the field. As the smoke of the gunfire drifted upward, there was suddenly a booming salute from the cannon. Echoes boomed back from the northern hillsides and the men broke into wild shouting. Their voices quieted and Paine recognized Hamilton's order, clear across the field, "FIRE!" A second salute thundered from the cannons. There was a third salute and then Hamilton returned across the drill ground. His fresh uniform was smudged by gunpowder, but there was a broad smile on his handsome face.

When they returned to Washington's headquarters, almost every officer in the camp joined them. The house could not contain them and they spilled over onto the grounds. Paine stood to one side and watched them. An exuberant Washington was threading his way among them and assigning tasks for a celebration. Tench Tilghman, a lieutenant colonel now, brought a young man to Paine and introduced him as Major Gibbs, commander of Washington's guards. Joel Barlow and Hamilton joined them. As though attracted to any circle of more than three or four, Washington approached them and

[274]

directed, "Major Gibbs, you will see to the illumination . . . and the fireworks." His glance fell upon ruddy-cheeked Joel Barlow. "Lieutenant Barlow, would you see to the ladies of the neighborhood? Provide escorts if need be."

As Washington left, Barlow complained, "I entered the service as a chaplain, not a diplomat."

"Come now, Joel," Hamilton interrupted. "What better diplomacy than that a chaplain should invite the ladies to the ball?"

Paine looked at the happy officers. Even Charles Lee, with his enormous nose and his arrogant, sarcastic disposition, seemed in a happy frame of mind. A few more months. Perhaps this time the war would be over.

21

TWO MONTHS later, while Washington's army harried the British, now under Clinton, throughout New Jersey, the Continental Congress reassembled in Philadelphia. But to Paine it did not seem the same.

John Adams had joined Franklin in France; Jefferson was still in Virginia, where there was talk of his succeeding Patrick Henry as Governor; Hancock was in Boston; Dr. Rush, although he had resigned as surgeon general, had not returned; jovial-faced Harrison and slender George Wythe were in their native state; and even Charles Carroll, who had affixed not only his signature but his address to the Declaration of Independence, had returned to his estate in Maryland. Above all, Henry Laurens had resigned as president and the Congress had elected John Jay to replace him. Jay was not unfriendly, but he was not an intimate of Paine's.

[275]

The Statehouse was in a most deplorable condition. The twin fireplaces were black with soot; the andirons and the burnished screens were gone. The flags and the drums had been torn down from where they had hung over the doorway. The floor was filthy. In the west wing, everything of value had been torn or smashed. The east sheds, in which prisoners of war had been quartered, were reservoirs of filth.

Like a homing pigeon, Paine sought his old lodging on Second Street. The room was untenanted and he rented it again. It was as though he had never been away. The pottery bowl and pitcher were on the dresser as he had left them. Batches of mail had been left to accumulate with the expectation of his return. He glanced through them hurriedly. To his wonder, there were three letters from Catherine Nicholson. He was delighted with them. She had signed them "affectionately, Kitty." He tried to evaluate the reason why she wrote to him. Was it because of the novel ideas that his essays expressed? Was it an attraction that young girls sometimes have to older men?

Paine visited the Indian Queen and found, to his regret, that he was not the welcome guest he once had been. The city had been blighted by the curse of inflation. The Congress had printed so much paper money that now a purseful could hardly buy a hogshead of ale. Everyone hoarded their silver dollars and their Spanish pieces of eight. The farmer hid his beef and the baker piddled out his bread. Somehow the revolution and the breaking of ties with England seemed a mistake . . . and Paine's incendiary pamphlets were at the root of it!

Nor could Paine find companions in other taverns. Now that they knew the city better, most delegates lodged in private homes. Even Sam Adams had established himself in new quarters on Fourth Street, near Market Street, in the home of a much-talked-about widow by the name of Cheeseman. Paine had met her. She was a stout woman, with a cheerful countenance, and much given to bright colors and frills. Gossip was dispelled by the presence of two other boarders in the Cheeseman House—Roger Sherman, the ungainly and unsmiling Puritan, and a Colonel Thornton who, although droll and congenial, was a staid man. Paine accepted the fact that he had lost the company of his friend Adams to a more lively atmosphere.

In the mornings, he began to wander along the wharves and watch for incoming ships. Somewhere along the Jersey or Delaware coasts, there was a French fleet under command of Comte d'Estaing. Oysterman and fishermen spoke of having sighted it. This should have raised the city's hopes, but instead its citizens seemed more elated to learn that England proposed to repeal the Tea Tax and the Boston Port Act, lift restraints on trade, and offer a large measure of self-government. Paine felt that the country must not welcome Britain's proposed magnanimity. Magnanimity was a poor exchange for freedom. He drafted a new *Crisis,* a *Crisis VII,* and wrote in it:

> The true interest of Britain lies in proposing and promoting the independence of America. The title that she assumed of parent country led to and pointed out the propriety, wisdom, and advantage of a separation; for, as in private life children grow into men, and by setting up for themselves, extend and secure the interest of the whole family, so in the settlement of colonies large enough to admit to maturity the same policy should be pursued, and the same consequences would follow. Nothing hurts the affections both of parents and children so much as living too closely connected and keeping up the distinction too long. . . .

Two weeks later, early in December, as Paine sat in the Congress, three men were escorted into the Assembly Room. One of them was Silas Deane, who had been recalled from France as commercial agent for the Colonies. The second man was de Francey, whom Paine had seen a number of times. The third man was Conrad Alexander Gerard de Rayneval, former secretary to Comte de Vergennes, in the French Office for Foreign Affairs. Now, with the open acknowledgment of the French alliance, he had been sent to America as a minister. He was a rather small man who carried himself with elegance in his dress and a courtly grace in his manners. He spoke a well-tutored English with drawn-out nasal accents. The delegates treated him with the greatest deference, and affluent citizens were honored to invite him into their homes.

Paine waited to hear the occasion for this little triumvirate's visit, and, when he learned that it was but another plea for a payment of the old "de Beaumarchais debt," he returned his attention to the reports on his desk. Among them was a letter from Jason Witherspoon, the provisioner from Bedford Village:

> ... many soldiers prefer death to capture and confinement on a British prison ship. The *Jersey,* rotting at anchor off Brooklyn, is filled with agony and disease. The prisoners are starved and crowded together like dogs ... without heat in the winter, without a breath of air in the summer. We have estimated that more than six thousand men have already died in that veritable hell of a British prison ship. They cast their bodies into the East River and in a few days they are washed up, like diseased animals, on the shores of Long Island. I tell you I have taken a walk along that shore and on just one morning, I have counted the bones of more than two hundred unfortunates, whitening in the sun. ...

Paine looked up from his reading. De Francey was addressing President Jay. His fluttering hands lent an ineffectual emphasis to his insistence. Paine recalled de Francey's first petition. He had made it almost a year ago, in December, 1777. He had presented himself to the Continental Congress, then in York, with a letter of introduction from Silas Deane. He had told the Congress that he was an agent of Monsieur de Beaumarchais and had submitted documents, bills of lading, and vouchers to show that the Americans owed Hortalez and Company the sum of 4,500,000 livres. He had been sent to collect the debt. Despite his credentials and his bills of lading, Paine had thought him a fool. The Congress was without the means of raising funds for its own purposes. Where would it acquire 4,500,000 livres? And under what circumstances had it received credit for so large a sum? Who had contracted it?

When de Francey seated himself, Silas Deane rose and addressed the Congress: "In deference to the cause of freedom . . . in regard to myself as an American agent . . . Hortalez and Company has been influenced to accept 1,000,000 livres as a full payment. Monsieur de Francey will be notified to accept the terms."

Paine was intrigued by Deane's plea. Why was he so insistent that the debt was a valid one? He set aside the atrocity reports and watched as Deane finished his address. President Jay rapped for attention and suggested that the debt be honored and done with. It had been kicked about for too long. He, himself, was satisfied with the vouchers, the bills of lading, etc. The delegates could vote upon its payment the next day.

Paine was amazed. As Secretary to the Committee on Foreign Affairs, he was familiar with all the transactions of the Continental Congress. This one could only stem from the subterfuge gift that the court of France had extended two years ago! The request for payment was a sham! Last year, in York, he had taken it as a gesture of diplomatic courtesy that the Congress had not given de Francey a stout *No*. And now a payment was suggested by President Jay. Paine wondered if the Congress was being influenced by Silas Deane.

The Committee of Foreign Affairs had once been the Committee of Secret Correspondence. Its less-important papers were now stored in a second-floor room that faced the courtyard. After the Congress adjourned, Paine went there, gathered all the letters and references to Hortalez and Company, and arranged them in chronological order. An old desk became cluttered with opened envelopes, unfolded sheets of script, and unfurled rolls.

Slowly, letter by letter, the references fell into their proper order. They confirmed what he had presumed. Long before he had set foot on American soil, France had had secret agents in Boston, New York, Philadelphia, and Charleston. They had reported on the possibility of a rebellion—a rebellion that could not succeed! They had advised the French throne to aid the Colonies. Although the cause was a lost one, a war would drain the coffers of England and help exhaust her. Paine imagined the court of France, still reeling from the blows that England had given her in the Seven Years' War. She had not only lost Canada, the largest of her colonial possessions, but much of her prestige. He could understand how revenge would be a cardinal principle of French policy—a revenge that must be concealed by a pleasant manner, for she was at peace with England.

As Paine studied the letters and documents that he had spread upon the desk, he learned the manner in which the court of France had consented to give subterfuge aid to the American Colonies. Comte de Vergennes, the French Minister of Foreign Affairs, with the help of de Beaumarchais, evidently a shrewd business man as well as a court favorite and playwright, had set up a plan by which France would be able to send muskets, cannon, gunpowder, and clothing to the American Colonies and, despite British spies in France, be in a position to deny it. This de Beaumarchais, of whom Paine had often heard Lafayette speak, would establish a concern to be known as Roderique Hortalez and Company. This imitation of a commercial house, which would exist only on paper, would ship guns and supplies across the Atlantic. Their ostensible destination would be San Domingo, but their real one would be an American port. On the surface, the French Government would know nothing of the private affairs of Roderique Hortalez and Company.

There was a letter from Arthur Lee: King Louis had approved the scheme and his treasury was turning over a million livres to de Beaumarchais. France's ally and confident, the King of Spain, was giving de Beaumarchais another million. De Beaumarchais, or his commercial house, would ask payment, as a matter of form, but such a request should be disregarded.

Paine tried to piece together what he had learned of this Pierre Augustin Caron de Beaumarchais. Was he a patriot or a scoundrel; this man whose *Barber of Seville* had become the talk of the courts of Europe? Lafayette had said of him, through not disparagingly, that he was the son of a watchmaker.

Paine folded the letter into its original creases and replaced it in its envelope. He came across a letter from de Beaumarchais himself. He heard the door open as he started to read it. Startled, he rose from the desk and turned about. Henry Laurens was in the doorway. He closed the door behind him and ran his eyes over the disarrayed correspondence on the desk. He glanced at the unlighted candles and at the fireplace that Paine had let stay cold. "What do you here, Tom?" he finally asked.

"Getting at the bottom of the de Beaumarchais affair."

"And having learned its truth, what will you do with it?"

"Bring it to light! Hear . . . hear . . . do you but listen to this. A letter from de Beaumarchais himself, written on August 18, 1776, and addressed to the Secret Committee." Paine stepped to a window, because of the failing light, and read with a touch of anger:

> An extensive commercial house has been formed solely for the purpose of serving you in Europe, to supply you with necessaries of every sort—clothes, linen, powder, ammunition, muskets, cannon, or even gold for the payment of your troops, and in general everything that can be useful for the honorable war in which you are engaged. . . .

[281]

"Did you hear, Henry? To supply us with gold for the payment of our troops. What commercial house would supply us with gold? And to what purpose?"

Laurens rushed to Paine and tore the letter from his hands. "Are you a fool?" he cried. "What would you do with this . . . with these?" He swept his hand to indicate the cluttered desk. "Would you read them aloud in Congress? The letters of the Secret Committee?"

Paine watched his friend gather all the letters and scrolls. "Would you place a seal upon my lips while we are defrauded of a million livres?" he demanded. "Would you have me watch . . . even write into the records that we have paid a fortune to scoundrels, for naught . . . and not protest it?"

"There is nothing you can do. It has been decided upon. Even Robert Morris and James Wilson have sanctioned the payment."

Paine's quick mind evaluated the worth of a million livres. "A million livres!" he cried. "Not Continental money but a million French livres! We could furnish new arms and clothes with such a sum . . . food for the entire army for a year . . . and the war not yet won. I shall not stand by and see it wasted on a fraud!"

"I entreat you, Tom. You must not reveal what you have seen here. Come, help me place these back. Hast not yet learned Franklin's much quoted proverb, 'He who spits against the wind . . .'"

On the following day, Paine watched de Francey present his petition that was to be voted upon for payment. Silas Deane, Livingston, and Robert Morris gathered about the French minister. Gouverneur Morris roused himself from his chair, stomped to them with his heavy-gaited peg leg, and joined their clique.

Paine could contain himself no longer. He left his desk, which was to the right and a little behind President Jay's table. He hurried to Laurens and pleaded, "There is no such debt, Henry. Please, help me refute it!"

He was angered when Laurens shook his head. "We cannot," Laurens insisted. "The Correspondence Committee was a secret one. Neither I, as a delegate, nor you as a secretary, can make its affairs public."

"And the million livres?"

"President Jay has committed himself to its payment. As have others."

Paine turned toward Jay's table. As he reached it, Silas Deane whispered to Gerard, and the French minister hurriedly addressed John Jay. *"Monsieur le President . . . Monsieur le President . . .* two years 'ave gone by since the contract for thees debt. The element of time and the alliance of France support the claim. *Certainement,* you would not permit, to our embarrassment, yet another delay."

Before Jay could reply, Paine raised his voice so that it would be heard above the chatter that filled the Assembly Room. "Minister Gerard, I have spoken no single word in protest and yet you already wish me silent. If I am at the president's side, it is only to suggest that he ask for a few more days. There has come to my attention . . ."

Jay's face was flushed with anger. "Mr. Paine! You forget yourself! Your position in Congress is as secretary and as secretary only. Confine your sentiments to your pamphlets and not to expressions in Congress."

There was a hubbub of voices in the room as Laurens stepped between Jay and Paine. Suddenly Livingston offered in a raised voice, "I do not think that the renowned and respected Monsieur de Beaumarchais would present a bill that was not due. I vote that an honorable debt should be paid."

To Paine's chagrin, William Ellery of Rhode Island rose and cried, "Of course! How then should we look to our ally if we refuse an old debt?"

Paine felt that these men knew nothing of the truth and

[283]

were influenced by sentiment and not conviction. Unable to restrain himself and without asking permission to do so, he addressed the Congress: "With apologies to Minister Gerard, perhaps even to Monsieur de Francey, may I say that they are mistaken where their friend, Mr. Deane, is concerned. A full month before the arrival of Mr. Deane in Paris, and six months before Dr. Franklin arrived there, a plan to extend a million livres in aid to America had already been approved by the French court."

"Hear! Hear!"

Oblivious to the cries, Paine continued, "The plan was·not only approved, but a good part of the money turned over to Pierre de Beaumarchais on June 10, in the year 1776."

Deane sprang to his feet and cried, "It is not true! I give my word, gentlemen. . . ."

"I have no quarrel with our friend, Mr. Deane. I say only that, if he believes it to be otherwise, then de Beaumarchais deceived him!"

The French minister sprang to his feet.

"Messieurs! Messieurs! Monsieur le President! I will not 'ave the honor of Pierre de Beaumarchais taken lightly."

"The million livres was a gift!"

"A gift? A gift? Why should my country make a gift of all thees money to . . . to a rebellion that 'ave not yet been recognize'? What would be gained by such a gift?"

"Exactly, Monsieur Gerard. Exactly. What would be gained?"

Gouverneur Morris was seeking attention by clearing his throat. He brushed imaginary bits of lint from his coat while he waited for the delegates to turn to him. Deep-throated, he spoke without rising. "I, for one, gentlemen, have no interest in a debate between Minister Gerard and our clerk, who is evidently without manners, without facts, and without authority. I came this morning to vote on the payment of an old and much-abused debt. If the entity of this day's session is to be resolved by a personal squabble, then I bid you good day. And mark me for the settlement of the debt."

Laurens hurried to Paine's side and whispered, "For your own sake, Tom, give it up. The payment has been determined upon."

"I cannot, Henry! I cannot! Would you have me stand by and see this fraud perpetrated—and by men of substance—when the money could buy raiment and food and munitions!" Rancor rising in his throat, he turned and cried, "Well then, go, Mr. Morris! And take all who will go with you. As for me, I will stay and speak my facts if but the empty chairs remain to listen! You ask what could be gained by such a gift, Minister Gerard. Then, if any do not know, I shall tell them. France had much reason to be aggrieved with England at the time of our revolt. She had suffered not only the loss of territory but had been sorely humiliated. Our revolt gave her an opportunity to avenge her wrongs. But not openly—King Louis would not abrogate France's treaty with England. So what the court of France could not openly sell . . . she secretly gave! Did you think your most Catholic Majesty interested in a financial advantage, Minister Gerard? Did you think King Louis interested in a profit in sols and tobacco? For the money came most assuredly from his own treasury."

"I protest!" cried the French minister. "I protest!"

"Your protest shall be entered in the records, Minister Gerard. I assure you, I myself shall enter it. Let me continue, gentlemen. The aid was to be sent through the camouflage of a commercial house, as though without the French Government's knowledge. A house to be known as Roderique Hortalez and Company—a mercantile name dreamed up by Pierre de Beaumarchais. Oh, I admit the aid. I am grateful for it. A half million livres in gold! A half million livres in gunpowder! But where did this gunpowder come from, gentlemen? This gunpowder for which we are now asked to pay? Did it come from clockmaker de Beaumarchais? Did it come from Rode-

[285]

rique Hortalez and Company, which is just a fictitious name on a secret ledger? No! Gentlemen, the gunpowder was taken from French magazines and with the knowledge of the King!"

There were protesting cries from Gouverneur Morris and Deane and de Francey. Sam Adams rose and insisted that Paine be permitted to speak. As though unaware of the furor he had created, Paine continued, "An investment, gentlemen, a loan for financial profit is well guarded. But a gift, especially an unacknowledged gift, is left to shift for itself. Must I remind you that this unprotected gift was sent to us in the ships *Amphitrite, Seine,* and *Mercury* . . . and that only the *Amphitrite* arrived and the unescorted *Seine* and *Mercury* fell into the hands of the enemy?"

Minister Gerard, beside himself with fury, rushed to Jay's table and, his arms gesticulating wildly, shouted: *"Monsieur le President! Monsieur le President!* My position does not permit me to stay and listen to thees . . . thees distortion of facts. I consider it an affront to the alliance that my country has offer' to yours." Turning upon his heels, he stormed out of the Assembly Room. De Francey and Deane followed him.

A hush fell upon the Congress. Gouverneur Morris stomped to Paine's side. "You will never acquire a paunch, Mr. Paine. You have the tongue of a rabble-rouser. Friends may forsake a man; but his enemies, never. They stand a constant vigil . . . hoping for the proper moment to redress a grievance."

Sam Adams joined Morris at Paine's side. "Friend Tom," he advised, "we must not jeopardize the French alliance. A million livres is a nominal sum with which to secure it."

"Do not anger me, Sam! One cannot buy an alliance. Alliances, like friendships, are made only for personal benefit or mutual affection. An old nation can endure corruption, a young one must insist upon truth!"

Delegates were leaving their chairs and forming animated groups and cliques. John Jay, his face suffused with anger,

called them to order. "Gentlemen.... Gentlemen....
We must acknowledge this debt. I move that we draw bills
on Dr. Franklin, at long sight, for one million pounds ster-
ling."

Paine looked at Laurens. His friend, reading the anger in
Paine's eyes, touched his finger to his lips.

A few days later, Paine was awakened by an insistent
knocking on his door. He was surprised to find his early
visitors the French minister and de Francey. Paine had not let
the de Beaumarchais matter rest but had commented upon it
in the *Pennsylvania Packet*. His published observations had
created a sensational interest in what he termed the "Deane
Affair."

Paine welcomed his guests with courteous politeness. De
Francey entered the lodging without hesitation, but Conrad
Alexander Gerard de Rayneval hesitated in the doorway.
Paine watched the minister's dark eyes flit about the untidy
poverty of the room. *"Bon matin,"* he finally greeted. *"Bon
matin,"* and permitted himself to step across the threshold and
onto the bare wood floor.

"You are surprised that I have no personal fortune?" asked
Paine.

Gerard's hands fluttered as though they were apologizing
for the discourtesy that his eyes had shown. "Money ees not
everything. *N'est-ce pas, Monsieur de Francey?"*

Paine offered his only chair and de Francey, in deference
to the minister, permitted Gerard to seat himself. Gerard sat
for a moment in silence and then, as Paine seated himself on
the unmade bed, he said, "Monsieur Paine, I am most ag-
greved by your indiscreet public assertions. To say that
France was generous and a friend . . . ees acceptable. But to
declare that she gave arms to America, *before* the alliance,
while my country still honored a treaty with England, . . ."

Gerard's eyes seemed veiled. There was neither question
nor threat within them. Paine looked to de Francey. The man

[287]

stood at the side of Gerard's chair and gave no indication of speaking.

"Gentlemen," said Paine. "I did not imply that the court of France has not acted honorably. And I speak for every American when I say that we are grateful for your country's alliance."

The minister's eyes brightened. He glanced at de Francey and permitted himself a fleeting smile. *"Exactement! Exactement!"* he emphasized with a waving hand. "Monsieur Paine, I recognize and respect your devotion to your cause . . . the cause of freedom. But I assure you, you are in error. The supplies sent through Monsieur de Beaumarchais were never intended as a gift. Our generosity 'as not stretched to the point of a million livres and *certainement* not while we honored a treaty with England! Monsieur de Francey, may I?" De Francey handed Gerard a portfolio. The minister leafed through some papers and extracted one. He looked up and asked, with disarming courtesy, "With your permission, Monsieur Paine?" Paine nodded and Gerard read from the paper:

> All the supplies furnished by Monsieur de Beaumarchais to the States, whether merchandise or cannons and military goods, were furnished in the way of commerce, and the articles that came from the King's magazine and arsenals were sold to Monsieur de Beaumarchais by the Department of Artillery.

Paine studied the well cared-for fingers that held the document. When the minister finished its reading, he looked him full in the face and asked, "Minister Gerard, are you implying that the court of France—that the King himself—engaged in the transfer of military goods for profit?"

A flush of anger spread slowly across the minister's face. "I did not say for profit. I said that the government of France was not involved in the sale of supplies to your States. The goods were bought and sold through a private company!"

"Then if you will permit one question? Do the duties of the minister of France include the collection of private debts?"

Gerard sprang from his chair. "I find you impossible! Impossible! If I leave here, Monsieur Paine ... if I leave here without your retraction, I go directly to your Congress and place before them a protest against your public statements. As a diplomatic *bouc émissaire,* Monsieur Paine, as a scapegoat ... you will be dismissed from office!"

Paine seemed neither intimidated nor impressed. "A pity, messieurs," he said quietly. "A pity. They will miss me more than I shall miss the $70 a month that the position pays."

De Francey looked about at the poverty of the room and spoke for the first time. "Monsieur Paine, what Minister Gerard 'ave said ... it ees true." He hunched his thin shoulders as though to imply that he was not personally involved. "But Monsieur de Beaumarchais, whom I represent, would not wish to be ...," he waved his hands as he struggled for a word, "... to be embroiled." He looked to Gerard for an endorsement of his choice of the word. The minister sat with pouting lips. "Monsieur de Beaumarchais is an admirer of yours. And so I 'ave the authority to offer you a ... a grand payment ... in return for an admission of an error in judgment." He could see anger being kindled in Paine's eyes and he hastened to add, "You 'ave been indiscreet, Monsieur Paine. You 'ave published information from private papers—from documents entrusted to your care while in public office."

"I have betrayed no trust!" cried Paine. "And I will print no retraction! Had I a desire for affluence, I could accrue it with honor and not in the manner in which you offer it. And now, good day, messieurs. Good day! I have work to do."

Paine was summoned to the Continental Congress that very afternoon. He found the delegates sitting in secret session, behind closed doors. He glanced at each one and saw no encouraging expression on any face. John Jay cleared his throat. His eyes confined themselves to a document in his hands and, addressing the Congress, he said, "We have been sent an official protest, from the French minister, against 'indiscreet assertions' by an American public official. The minister insists that Congress, and I quote, 'take measures suitable to the circumstances.' " Not raising his eyes from the paper, he asked, "Mr. Paine, do you profess to be the author of the articles that have appeared over the signature, *Common Sense?* Articles that have castigated Silas Deane?"

"The articles are true!" protested Paine. "Mr. Deane fabricates when he says that he has suffered for the American cause! As agent in France, he lived well and enjoyed himself while American soldiers were half starving and almost naked!"

Jay studied the document as though he were reading it for the first time. He asked, "You are the author of the articles in the *Pennsylvania Packet,* that refute the claims of Monsieur de Beaumarchais . . . inferring that the supplies in question were a gift from France?"

"I am."

"Then I must ask you to withdraw as Secretary."

Paine looked at Jay, but the President would not raise his head. When it seemed that his preoccupation with the papers must be known to be a pretense, he finally raised his eyes to Paine. Always ostentatiously dressed, he now assumed an air of defiant dignity.

Suddenly Sam Adams and Robert Morris, though seated apart, rose simultaneously from their chairs. Morris relinquished the floor to Adams with a gesture of his hand and Samuel Adams offered: "Mr. President, I submit that we tender Mr. Paine an opportunity to . . ."

There was a commotion on the floor in the midst of which James Wilson and Gouverneur Morris, unhindered by his peg leg, rushed to Jay's table. The president stared at Adams in anger. "This is a matter of diplomacy, Mr. Adams! You know as well as I that the matter has been decided upon. Mr. Paine is excused and we wait for his leaving in order to take up other pertinent matters."

The delegates sat in silence as Paine left the Assembly Room. He returned to his lodging with a taste of ashes in his mouth. The Congress had disowned him! They had intimated that he resign. He would not do it. He would not do it!

Two days later, Henry Laurens called on Paine. "General Roberdeau is in town," he informed him. "He has impressed President Jay, as have others. I am told Jay is considering asking Congress to hear you. He intends to reopen the discussion."

In the Statehouse an hour later, Paine could see the looks of surprise on many faces as he entered with Laurens. They walked at once to President Jay's table, where Laurens asked and received permission to plead with the delegates to allow the secretary an opportunity to defend himself. Yet even as Laurens began speaking, Paine realized that little attention was being paid to what he was saying. The Congress seemed to have turned into another House of Commons, indifferent and led by men with personal aims.

Paine strode to Laurens' side and interrupted him, challenging the complacent delegates into silence. His voice, sharpened by a touch of wrath, seemed to cut the very air. "I would not have it thought that I am not appreciative of what Mr. Laurens is asking for me," he said coldly. "But I will not let any man plead for a privilege that I consider to be a right! My friend would beg for the privilege that I be permitted to defend my conduct. I insist that it is my due! And I will not be contrite for, but yesterday, news reached me . . . authoritative news, gentlemen . . . that for the gunpowder 'sold' to us by Roderique Hortalez and Company for twenty sols a pound, our 'benefactor,' de Beaumarchais, paid only four sols a pound!"

There was a murmur among the delegates. Raising his voice

in order to be heard, Paine continued: "And the muskets sent to us . . . the muskets had been discarded by the French Army and turned over to de Beaumarchais free of cost; and he billed them to us at half the cost of new muskets!"

The murmur rose to loud, protesting voices in the midst of which Jay pounded upon the table and pleaded for silence. "Mr. Paine is out of order! He is not a delegate. The chair has not recognized his motion to speak, and this . . . this . . . what he has disclosed is in no way to be considered as a defense against his proposed dismissal."

Gouverneur Morris rose from his chair. A big man, heavily-jowled and pompous, Morris looked much older than his twenty-eight years, despite the fact that his loss of hair was beautifully concealed by an expensive wig. Meticulous in his dress, his manners, and his speech, he waited for complete attention and then said in a cultured voice that carried well: "Mr. President, members of Congress, I am certain that this was not intended to be in the order of the day. But since it is here, I say let us vote upon it and, by disposing of it, end it. Mr. Paine has raised his voice to speak of rights and privileges . . . when all that has been proposed is to turn a man out of office who ought never to have been in it." There was a murmur of protesting voices.

Morris waited until they subsided and then continued: "What would be the idea of a gentleman in Europe of this Mr. Paine? Would he not suppose him to be a man of the most affluent fortune, born in this country of a respectable family, with wide and great connections, and endowed with the nicest sense of honor? But, alas, what would he think, should he accidentally be informed that this, our Secretary of Foreign Affairs, was a mere adventurer *from England,* without fortune, without family connections, and ignorant even of grammar? And yet, sirs, this is the man whom we would remove from office, and this is the man who has just now puffed himself up to speak of rights and privileges. I say we vote now, to place

[292]

upon record, that we do not wish our ears to be irritated by pleas and unfounded grievances under the ... the cloak of defense."

Paine was dismayed as he watched them vote. The southern states resented his attitude on slavery; New York and Pennsylvania had begun to lose sympathy with the cause that his inflammatory pamphlets had urged them to support; many delegates had begun to fear his articles against profiteering. By a vote of eight to four, Rhode Island divided, the Congress decided that he should not be heard.

Paine spent a restless night. Of what had Gouverneur Morris accused him? Of being poor? Of having no family with great connections? Of being a common man? He admitted it. Did this then deny him his rights? Damn them all ... he would speak and write the truth as he saw it! And neither king nor beggar nor Congress would gag him. Nor would he give an unfriendly Congress the satisfaction of voting upon a dismissal from his official post. He arose early and wrote his resignation to the Continental Congress with great care:

> ... I have betrayed no trust because I have constantly employed that trust to the public good. I have revealed no secrets because I have told nothing that was, or I conceive ought to be, a secret. I have convicted Mr. Deane of error and, in so doing, I hope I have done my duty. ...

With the exception of Arthur Lee, the Congress thought that the matter was settled. To their consternation, they found that Paine's resignation merely released him from the tether of their censure and gave Arthur Lee fresh fuel to keep alight his original feeling that all was not right with the whole transaction. With bridled anger, they watched Paine shift the Deane controversy from behind the closed doors of the Congress to the open pages of the newspapers and call it to the attention of his beloved *common man*. In an unending stream of informative articles, Paine struck out against the Deane clique as though the payment to de Beaumarchais was to come from his own penurious pocket. Men were making profits out of the prerogatives of office! Out of the sufferings of their fellow men! Not public spirit but private greed motivated Silas Deane and Gouverneur Morris and the others! *"To what degree of corruption must we sink,"* he demanded, *"if our delegates and ambassadors are to be permitted to carry on a private partnership in trade!"*

By the end of the week, Minister Gerard called again upon Paine. This time, he brought Don Juan Mirralis, the minister from Sapin. Gerard seated himself, immediately, upon the single chair. He began to remove his gloves, glanced at the sooted fireplace in which a single piece of kindling gave the barest warmth, thought the better of it, and kept them on. Mirralis glanced uneasily at Paine, who was wrapped in an old robe. He had seen Paine often at the Statehouse, but never unshaven and unkempt. He hesitated and then, as though to end a distasteful mission, he said quickly and without courteous overture: *"Señor* Paine, le Minister Gerard, as I too, is aware of the prodigious effects of your writings among the peoples of these States. There is here, as there is not in my country, nor in France, an enthusiasm for the, shall we say, the license of the press. There is even an absence of laws to repress statements of audacity against foreign courts."

Paine did not know if the minister had dressed in order to impress him. He wore polished black boots, a silver-hilted sword that hung in a gilded scabbard, and a royal blue overcoat. *"Señor,"* he continued, "le Minister Gerard regrets the loss of your position. As a gesture of friendship, he would like to engage your pen. To impress on the peoples of your country more favorable sentiments toward France."

Gerard glanced from Mirralis to Paine, who sat on the bed and regarded them both. There was an enigmatic smile upon Paine's face, as though he were laughing at them. The French minister sprang from his chair and insisted, his voice rising with uncontrolled anger, "Monsieur Paine, I come here with the dignity of a representative of the court of France! I offer you a salary, in His Majesty's name, in the place of that which I 'ave cause' you to lose. One thousand dollar' a year!"

Paine still seemed to smile. Damn the man! If one could only guess what he was thinking!

"For thees salary," explained Gerard, "there is only one condition. That you publish nothing on political affairs without advising with me."

Paine rose from the bed. To their chagrin, he said, "The weathercock points the direction, gentlemen, but it cannot alter the wind. I have work to do. Good day, gentlemen, good day."

As though to defy the minister, Paine published his overtures that very day, stating in a gazette:

> Had I been disposed to make money, I undoubtedly had many oportunities for it. . . . Any service I can render to either the countries in alliance, or both, I shall readily do, and Mr. Gerard's *esteem* will be the only compensation I shall desire.

Not until some time later did he realize that he had been eminently successful in his exposure of Silas Deane. Unable to refute the facts that Paine had presented and having been pressed mercilessly by Arthur Lee, Deane failed to give any adequate explanation and retired in disgrace.

22

PAINE HAD not realized how much he depended upon the meagre salary that Congress had paid him as Secretary to the Committee on Foreign Affairs and found himself almost penniless by the end of February. He confined himself to his rooms, lived for days on brandy and crusts of bread, yet continued his *Crisis* writings. When the Pennsylvania Assembly appointed him its clerk, he wrote to his friend Laurens:

> The clerkship is not much, but it is something like business and has released me from that hopeless thinking that got so much the upper hand of me for three or four months past . . .

Early in November, Paine received a surprise visit from Col. Laurens. He hesitated at the door until Reed, who accompanied him, insisted, "It's all right, John. Come in. Make yourself at home."

Paine welcomed them and noticing the young colonel's reaction to the small, rather untidy, sitting room, he wondered what he would have thought of his old lodging. He had moved in September and now lived on Front Street, between Robert Bell's shop and the Sign of the Sugar Loaf. His new quarters consisted of the sitting room and a bedroom. He had acquired a set of bookcases, two spindle-back chairs, a slightly used settee, and an old but still presentable gateleg table.

Paine asked immediately if Colonel Laurens had heard from his father. Congress had sent Henry Laurens to Holland to arrange a loan and the vessel having been captured by a British frigate off the coast of France, the Colonel's father was now imprisoned in the Tower of London. John Laurens shook his head.

"I have been going over your latest *Crisis*," said Reed, "and wonder at your foundation for taxes. Congress does not question the amounts that you have estimated as necessary to continue the war . . . only the means of raising them. They would rather accept your plan for obtaining the needed aid from France."

Paine looked sharply from Reed to young Laurens. "You are going to France, Joseph?" he guessed. "With John?"

Reed hesitated. "Not I, Tom; but our young friend, yes."

He could see disapprobation on Paine's face as he glanced at young Laurens. He was quite a presentable figure in his military dress. He was as tall as his father and as handsome. And one could not say that he lacked courage. Paine recalled the Chew incident at Germantown. But where Henry approved of compromise, there was a touch of overbearing impatience about the son.

Young Laurens gave Paine an infectious smile. "I have not yet accepted the mission, Mr. Paine. There is a condition to my going—that you accompany me."

Paine was taken by surprise. "I speak no French," he pointed out as a first thought.

"John speaks it well enough for two," Reed insisted. "With you at his side, Tom, my heart will rest easy; not only on the success of the mission but on our young friend's well-being."

Paine turned to Reed and asked, "And Congress?"

"I shall be frank with you, Tom. There are many who are opposed to giving you an official standing in this mission; yet none are averse to your going in a private capacity. We have finally given credence to the rumors that the French do not want this war ended but would wish it continued for years . . . to exhaust the British. Perhaps you could achieve what the diplomatic pleas of Franklin and Lee and Adams have not yet accomplished."

A touch of bitterness tugged at the corners of Paine's lips. "Congress would eat the broth but will not recognize its cook!"

"We are to ask for ten million *livres,*" informed Laurens. "We could settle for six."

Paine's eyes were reflective. "You are not going to a market place to haggle over the price of fish, John. You are going to the court of France! To our ally, King Louis. We will petition for no more than what we need—and insist upon no less!"

[297]

"I have assured General Washington that you would accompany me," smiled Laurens.

Paine walked to the window that faced Front Street and looked out at the shops that had mushroomed along its length. War was pestilence that enriched the profiteer, imposed hardships on the poor and delayed the country's growth and prosperity. It must end. It must!

"Tell the General that I shall go to France," he said quietly. "You may make the necessary arrangements, John."

Colonel Laurens dashed about the countryside to bid goodby to friends, collect letters, and attend bon voyage parties. He was chagrined when he visited Paine and found no luggage in evidence. He thought him engaged in farewell notes to friends but when he glanced over his shoulder he saw that he was drafting a pamphlet.

"May I?" he asked.

Paine handed him a few sheets with one hand while he continued to write with the other. Laurens read:

Public Good: Being an examination into the claims of Virginia to vacant western territory . . .

The succession of the United States to the vacant western territory is a right . . .

Only the United States and not any particular state can lay off new states and the vacant territory is their property collectively . . .

Laurens had thought the pamphlet of pressing importance but it concerned itself with the boundaries of Virginia and insisted only that national sovereignty should precede states' rights. He replaced the papers and informed, "A Captain John Barry, of the frigate *Alliance*, has been recommended to me for our voyage." When Paine did not immediately look up he censured, "Do you consider a pamphlet on state boundaries of such importance that it cannot wait until our return?"

To his surprise, Paine flung down his quill and cried, "Important? Why Virginia claims land that stretches back to the Mississippi River and then runs northwestward to an indeterminate boundary. I can understand the conservatism of the old, but the young . . . ! You, John, have you no vision? In the natural course of events new states will be formed in the West. Will Virginia then claim such states as subsidiary provinces? If we permit this, then North Carolina, Georgia and even Connecticut and Massachusetts will insist upon their own claims to western territories."

"Virginia will detest you for this, Mr. Paine."

"Then must she detest truth too, for her claim to the Western Territory rests on some misty titles granted by a king of that England to whom we no longer owe allegiance . . . titles that were established, theoretically, upon a piece of parchment, long before the geography of the continent was known. Do you think I expend myself for the creation of thirteen independent Republics whose acquisition of feudal territories will make them no different than the jealous and competitive countries of Europe!" He hesitated and asked, "We sail from Boston, John? Then I should like to go there by way of New York. I have friends I would like to say good-by to." He had thought often of Kitty Nicholson in these last weeks and the trip would afford an excuse for visiting her.

"New York!" cried Laurens. "You would be informed upon by every Tory who would recognize you. I would matter little to Sir Clinton . . . but Thomas Paine! And it is you who are supposed to curb my rashness."

In the end, they went directly to Boston, where the *Alliance* rode at anchor.

23

THE *Alliance* docked at Lorient on March 9, 1781. Paine and John Laurens were met by Jonathan Williams, a commercial agent for America and a grandnephew of Dr. Franklin. He insisted that they accompany him to Nantes. Young Laurens immediately declined. "I cannot," he excused himself to the stocky Williams. "I am laden with gifts and personal letters from Lafayette, de Kalb, du Plessis, and innumerable others. I have committed myself to delivering them. I shall be here forever if I do not get to Paris immediately. But Mr. Paine can accompany you to Nantes. I surrender him into your care, and we shall meet in Paris. You are not offended, Mr. Paine?"

It was days before Paine could tear himself away from the festivities that had been prepared for him in Nantes. Once he had arrived in Paris, however, he went directly to Laurens' hotel. While Laurens' own servant watched, a French valet was helping him with some newly purchased clothes. "I thought you spoke no French, Mr. Paine," Laurens said as he studied his reflection in a wall mirror.

"Nor do I," said Paine.

"And you know no French women in Paris?"

"I have never been in Paris, John. Until now."

"Then your fame is more universal than I had imagined." He stepped to an ornately carved escritoire and took an envelope from it. He held it to his face, sniffed at it, and winked an eye. "She was quite fashionably dressed, Tom. Black hair . . . eyes as dark as a cockatoo's . . . She called you Thomas Pay-enn."

Laurens studied Paine's face, but it showed no perplexity.

To his surprise, Paine stuffed the scented letter into his pocket, with indifference.

"I have been to court," said Laurens. "I think Vergennes a fool. He insists that he is in sympathy with our cause, and yet he complained that I was overemphatic in my petition to the King."

The complaint had reached Paine in Nantes. Franklin had sent him a confidential note, urging him to hasten to Paris. Young Laurens, it seemed, had all but ruined the mission by an imprudent speech. Vergennes had diplomatically ascribed it to his inexperience, but he had confided to Franklin that the King was most unfavorably impressed. Paine recalled Franklin's advice, those many years ago in England: "A petition, no matter how fancifully camouflaged, is still a begging. It should contain no intimation of insistence."

"You attend some special affair tonight, John?"

"I go to the home of the Duc d'Orleans. The King's nephew is giving a ball in my honor." He turned to the valet and asked, *"Quelle heure est-il, Jerome?"*

The valet tugged at the back of Laurens' waistcoat. He smoothed the satin cloth across the shoulders with a graceful movement of his hands. *"Il est de bonne heure,"* he said with assured composure.

Paine accompanied Laurens to the hotel's lobby. They seemed like strangers to each other—Paine like a provincial clerk walking beside a young aristocrat.

Paine spent his second day in Paris walking its streets alone. At noon, he wandered into a cul-de-sac off one of the quays on the Seine. It was a twisting cobbled street, no wider than a carriage breadth. It was littered with debris. Four-story houses thrust themselves through grey shadows into a sunless sky, while gaunt faces watched from decaying balconies that threatened to collapse. Beggars, sitting in tattered uselessness upon the curbs of streets filled with stagnant puddles fell upon him with outstretched arms, clawing hands, and screeching pleas that needed no interpretation. Suddenly he realized that he had never seen anyone beg in the Colonies. No one starved. And no man took another's insult, let alone his threat or his lash! Even the bondsmen had their pride, their rights, and their eventual freedom. What a difference!

He hurried back to the boulevard that led to the hotel. Here the shops gave off an aura of affluence. He noticed that Dr. Franklin must have captured the hearts of the French, for his likeness was displayed in almost every shop window. Many offered little plaster busts and prints of him for sale. His features were on medallions and on the lids of snuffboxes. They were unmistakable—the short nose, the full round face, the stout chin. He noticed a Capuchin cape for sale in a window. It was made of bright red velvet. The hood was lined with gold satin. It would make a beautiful gift for Kitty Nicholson. Could he afford it? Would its giving be misunderstood? It was an opportunity to express his regard for her—a gift from France. He went into the shop. . . .

On the following day Franklin sent a carriage for Paine. Paine read the note that the *cocher* gave him:

> I do not complain; I am now, after all, seventy-five. But I have a "stone" in my bladder that is pained by the jolting of a carriage. I remain at Passy and let the world come to me. Would you be so kind as to come? You are being impatiently awaited.

Paine permitted himself to be driven to the quiet little suburb that was a half hour's ride from Paris. Franklin's house, set off by a garden, was on the grounds of the Hotel Valentinois. It had been put at the ambassador's disposal, without rent, by its owner, a prosperous merchant by the name of Ray de Chaumont. Paine was greeted on the steps by Temple Franklin, who had become Dr. Franklin's secretary and constant companion. Young Benjamin Bache was with him. Paine hardly recognized Franklin's other grandson, he had grown so tall.

In Franklin's residence, away from the sounds and sights of Paris, Paine felt almost as though he were back in the States. The dining room was attended by well-known faces, the drawing room was filled with visiting Americans, and either John Adams or Arthur Lee, both of whom were staying with Franklin, was constantly in the library. Lee was waiting to be sent as ambassador to Madrid. Adams, who had returned to Paris with his thirteen-year-old son, John Quincy, awaited final instructions as an emissary to Holland.

John Adams welcomed Paine with unexpected effusiveness. He was hampered by his unfamiliarity with the French language, bored by unassigned duties, and chagrined at his inability to make friends easily. "I wrote a long letter to Vergennes," he confided to Paine. "I urged that France increase her naval effort, in American waters, in order to prove the sincerity of her alliance. Believe me, Tom, I suggested the matter most diplomatically. And yet Vergennes has made it plain that I am not a minister to France and that he will deal with no one but Franklin!" His face was flushed with anger as he waited for Paine's comment.

The next day, Franklin informed Paine: "The Marquise de Lafayette will attend dinner tonight. She cannot wait to see you. She has bombarded me with inquiring billets since she learned that you are here."

As Franklin had predicted, the young Marquise de Lafayette sat next to him at dinner that night. Paine had expected to meet an aristocratic young woman of hauteur and disdain. To his pleasant surprise, she was warm, friendly, and gracious. Despite a delicate thinness that matched her husband's, she wore a dress that was very décolleté. When he was introduced to her, she held out her hand with a most inviting smile. *"Je suis enchanté,* Monsieur Paine." He gave her hand a fleeting kiss. As he bent over it, he could not help but see her exposed young breasts—charmingly firm for so slender a body.

[303]

At the dinner table, she talked volubly of the marquis. How was the wound that he had received at Brandywine? Was it truly healed? Did it give him no discomfort? Had he received the warm clothes she had sent? She had had a letter from Mrs. Washington. How old was Mrs. Washington? Truly! Paine could see that she asked the question with a woman's concern. "I assure you," he laughed, "the general's lady has a son the marquis' age."

She was flustered for a half moment. "You must come and dine at my father's home," she smiled. Le Duc d'Ayen. He has asked that I invite you."

Paine glanced across the table at Franklin's much-discussed friend, Madame Helvetius. She seemed merely a woman in her early fifties, with a gay, infectious laugh.

"The late Monsieur Helvetius would have taken pleasure in knowing you, Monsieur Pay-enne," she said. "You have set yourself up as a champion of the rights and privileges of man. You Americans are so full of principle. And pride. And self-righteousness. Like Mr. Adams here . . . who will not admit that God speaks French. The Abbé Raynal, though, does not think well of your desire for independence. He has suggested that even a nestling will not leave its home until it is thrust out by its parent."

Paine looked into Madame Helvetius' smiling face. He glanced at Franklin, as though for permission, and replied, "If you will forgive my disputing your friend, the Abbé may be an excellent philosopher, but a poor naturalist. It is a fledgling's only way to freedom. It would be against the instinct of nature for a mother bird to imprison her fledglings in the nest, like a government its colonies, in order to exploit them."

At the end of his first three days in Paris, Paine inquired regarding his presentation to the King. Franklin lifted a startled brow. His face was still round and full, but little wrinkles had begun to imbed themselves about his lips and eyes. He shook his head at the impatient Paine. "Your *Common Sense,* your *Crisis,* and your pamphlets have all been translated and printed here . . . and I must say, very well received. But they have been printed in carefully expurgated editions that have expunged your unfavorable references to the divine rights of kings and monarchical governments." Franklin nodded as Paine stared at him in disbelief. "Tis true. After all, though your writings may infuse a desire for freedom among most men, you could hardly expect a king to like them. His Majesty's ministers have permitted the abridged translations only for the support of France's political policy. They themselves have read your blunt words and cannot accept your statement that King Louis and King George stand upon the same pedestal."

"If I could see the King, perhaps I could persuade him differently."

"You could not persuade him if you talked with him for a fortnight. And if you did, . . . the court would destroy in a thrice what you had sweated to achieve. No! Vergennes is the man to impress. He is, after all, the foreign minister. I wrote you that our impetuous Laurens had angered him. The young fool not only insisted upon an outright gift of twenty-five million livres but threatened that, unless France takes a more active part in the war, America will make peace with England and join them in their war against France. And he made this threat not to Vergennes alone but to the Duc d'Orleans and to the King himself. As it is, we have an appointment with Vergennes for day after tomorrow. Meanwhile, we must send for a tailor, a wigmaker, and a shoemaker to equip you properly for your appearance."

Two days later, Franklin and Paine set out for Versailles. They were early for their audience with le Comte de Vergennes, and as though to instill a sense of meekness into Paine,

Franklin took him on a tour of the magnificent palace. Leaning heavily on his cane, he guided Paine through galleries, past marble statues set into oval niches, past paintings, tapestries, and frescoed walls and ceilings. It seemed as though he wished Paine to realize the luxury of Versailles so that he could form a proper sense of proportion between the petitioning States and the grandeur of France. As they walked through a corridor in which portraits of the royal family were hung between marble columns that supported a vaulted ceiling, the King and his retinue entered it, probably on their way to a council. His Majesty was rather short and stout, with a round, cheerful face that was framed by a massive curled wig that fell down to his shoulders. But for his smooth cheeks and his unperturbed eyes, one would think him older than his twenty-four years. He gave Paine a fleeting, unconcerned glance. As he walked by, he recognized Franklin and gave him a gracious smile that curled a thick, moist underlip. Paine stared after the courtiers that flanked the King, after the Swiss guards, tall in their shakos, their chins thrust tightly against the straps of their headdresses. The ceremony of marching through a corridor appeared to have a rigid formality. The life of the court, though opulent, seemed filled with the strictest of conventions.

"Would you care to see Count Maurepas, the Prime Minister?" asked Franklin. "His chambers are a short way to the right. We still have time."

"Are you offering me two counts instead of one king?" smiled Paine. He shook his head.

At the end of yet another corridor, they came to Vergennes' chambers and a secretary to the Minister of Foreign Affairs ushered them into an ornately decorated library whose windows faced a small courtyard. The room contained but a single occupant. He stood with his hands behind him and seemed to study, with indifference, the titles of the volumes in the glass-fronted bookcases. He evaluated the exact portion

[306]

of a moment that he should keep them waiting. Then he turned and bowed with courtly grace. He smiled at Franklin and, fluttering a plumpish hand, as though to indicate that an introduction was unnecessary, he extended it to Paine. "So we see each other at last," he said. "I regret that your resignation as Secretary of Foreign Affairs . . . a most unfortunate circumstance, the de Beaumarchais affair, most unfortunate . . . put an end to our correspondence."

"What I said in the Deane affair has been corroborated, sir," said Paine. "Mr. Lee has informed me . . ."

Vergennes fluttered a hand at Paine. "It is of no importance. Your Silas Deane is a scoundrel." He leaned across the table and confided, "And so is Pierre de Beaumarchais. A man of prodigious talents, mind you. And accepted as an aristocrat, even by the Queen. Though I understand you have no regard for aristocracy, Monsieur Paine?"

Paine smiled. "I have no objection to anyone's being an aristocrat, Count Vergennes. Only to their insistence that the rest of the world be their subjects."

"Touché!" said Vergennes quietly. *"Touché!"* He seemed a man who was not impulsive in speech and now, as though the courteous host had left and the diplomat remained, his face assumed a guarded expression and he said with quiet emphasis, "Monsieur Paine, if I have judged your pamphlets rightly, you object to the appointment of authority, to the inheritance of wealth, to the possession of colonies that, if I may point out, is a basis of French administration, and yet you come here for our support . . . for our support against a nation that thinks and governs as we do. It was I who favored support for your independence, but now, with that independence so nearly won, . . . I begin to wonder. I see the spread of your sentiments here, in France, Monsieur Paine. There are those, at court, who laugh at them and dismiss them with a shrug . . . as I do not. My allegiance is still to the King, Monsieur Paine, and to the King's government."

[307]

Paine glanced at Franklin. He was sitting quietly as though he had arranged for the audience but would not take part in it. "Forgive me," said Paine. "I am a guest in your country. As a representative of America, though without authority, I would not want to seem ungrateful for all that you have done for us. I have come neither to beg for the active support of France, though such an expression may sound presumptuous and proud, nor to make threats for it as our young friend, Colonel Laurens, has so foolishly done. I have come to offer France an opportunity ... an opportunity upon which its foreign minister cannot turn his back, since he has his country's welfare at heart."

Vergennes looked at Paine in silence. Not to petition as Adams and Franklin constantly did, not to threaten as young Laurens had done, ... what, then?

"Count Vergennes," said Paine, "let us accept that the universe is governed by logic. Let us then apply its principles, with reason, to the problem at hand and, having studied it, solve it. First, there can only be two possible courses for this war—for our war—for the war between the States and England. We shall lose it, or we shall win it. Do you agree?"

Vergennes nodded.

"Good. Let us then take first things, first. If we lose the war and England is victorious, I say that she will then be in a position to divert all her forces and all her efforts against France. She is already at war with you, but as yet an unengaged war. Her fleet, her armies, her energies, and her monies are being expended in the States. Should the war end in our defeat, it will begin here. I promise you! I know Great Britain well. She will do her utmost to force France to her knees. The penalties that you suffered at the end of the Seven Years' War will be as a coin in a beggar's cup to what a victorious England would demand of you."

Vergennes' dark eyes were expressionless. He sat as though

he were unaware that a muscle twitched and tugged at an eyelid.

"And now for the second course—we may win the war. And this must be divided into two forks in the road to victory. We may win the war with your actual aid, or without it. To win the war without you will take longer, the risk is greater, the hardship more extreme. But if we do and we negotiate a peace, England will turn upon France with a double hatred and vengeance, both for having given us what support you already have and to salvage from you some compensation for her losses in America."

Paine fell silent and waited for Vergennes to affirm or deny what he had expressed thus far. An enigmatic smile touched the minister's thin lips. It was impossible to guess what was being thought behind those dark, intelligent eyes. The twitching stopped and he asked, "And if, Monsieur Paine, by God's grace and the consent of His Majesty, you win the war with the . . . the actual aid of France?"

"Then we will be her ally in peace, as we were in war. One moment, Count Vergennes. I have not yet spoken a single word of the opportunity that I mentioned. There are three million people in America. Half the number that there are in England. Were it not for the war that keeps newcomers from our shores, we would grow and multiply as Europe cannot. The territory of America stretches from its northern tip, in a straight line southward, for 1,500 miles—the entire extent of Europe. She stretches westward, unexplored and unsurveyed, for a breadth that staggers the imagination.

America is a land of indescribable fertility, with a wealth of timber, furs, metals, and fisheries. She has a constant and growing need of every import that you can imagine. She has a trade in her future that will replenish the coffers of the old world and enrich their every inhabitant. And with whom will she trade, Count Vergennes, with her past enemies or her new friends?" Paine could not contain himself. He rose and strode

[309]

the room. "We already have French to the north of us, in Canada—stepchildren whom you have denied. We have French to the south of us, in Louisiana—stepchildren whom you have set adrift, to shift for themselves. And yet you hesitate!"

Vergennes lifted the decanter and filled the glasses. "My dear Monsieur Paine, your States already have France's alliance. It is no secret that a French fleet has convoyed 5,000 of our soldiers to your shores. Would you have us support both your armies and our own?"

At the White Hart Tavern, Paine had always been able to discern whether he were winning or losing a debate. At the Indian Queen, he had always known if his arguments were convincing. Here, Vergennes sat with seeming indifference. There was only his enigmatic smile and the muscle twtich beneath one eye. Paine said quietly, "Count Vergennes, my good friend, Dr. Franklin, taught me long ago that to petition is to beg and the word does not fashion itself easily upon my tongue. I know, as who does not, that an army of your regulars has come to America. Last July, they arrived at Newport, in a northern State called Rhode Island. For more than nine months they have done nothing but entertain the citizens of that State, who are free from want and deprivations as though there were no war. In return, the Rhode Islanders have given receptions, balls, and theatricals without end in your officers' honor. General Washington has been unable to persuade your Rochambeau to abandon the festivities or to send a single regiment from Newport. I do not speak for Dr. Franklin, in his capacity as American ambassador, but I petition: Would you please recall General de Rochambeau, Count Vergennes? And his troops . . . and your fleet! There was a time when their presence gave a stimulant to the hopes of Americans, but that time is past and now they foster only a complacency where there should be none. Recall them, Count Vergennes, and permit us to wage our own battles without the distraction of looking over our shoulders for your much-touted aid!"

Franklin seemed startled. Vergennes calmly offered a glass of wine to Paine. He insisted that Franklin accept one, though he pointed to his gout-inflicted foot. "To what do we drink?" asked Paine.

Vergennes permitted himself a half smile. "A toast to the independence of the Colonies?"

"To an alliance that was ratified three years ago?"

Vergennes raised an eyebrow that was strangely black against the pallor of his face and wig. "To a quick end to your war?"

"I drink to that," said Paine. "And to the minister of France who will make it possible!"

Paine spent a very pleasant spring in Paris. Though Franklin's health did not permit him to escort the inquisitive Paine everywhere, he furnished him with a copy of *Le voyage pittoresque de Paris,* and Paine did not lack guides. He visited the Hôpital des Invalides, with its grand chapel, its paintings, and its sculptures; the École Militaire, with its statues of the great French generals—Luxembourg, Turenne, Saxe, and Condé; and even spent an evening at the Palais Royal, where he was astonished by the freedom with which men of prominence paraded their mistresses, whom they introduced as *ma petite amie.*

When Paine learned that Comte de Vergennes had secured not only the sought-for aid but an active participation in the war, he could not wait to return home. The French Ministry informed Franklin that casks containing 2.5 million livres in silver were being placed in the hold of a French frigate, *La Resolute,* and that a brig crammed with military stores and clothing would accompany her to the States.

Despite Colonel Laurens' desire to prolong their stay, they sailed from Brest, on July 1, on *La Resolute.* Paine looked toward England as the frigate left the tip of Britany. He had learned that Elizabeth was living in Cranbrook, Kent, with her brother Thomas, who was now a watchmaker. He wondered about his parents in Thetford. It was seven years since he had seen them. "So near and yet so far," he said to Laurens. "Were the war over, I could go to them."

"And I to my father," said Laurens.

La Resolute reached Boston in the early morning of August 25, 1781. Paine was awakened by the fully clothed Laurens. Involuntarily, he grasped the bunk posters, to steady himself, and realized that he was in calm Boston Harbor. A glass leaded casement window had been opened to a view of windless sky. Paine glanced about the disordered cabin. Laurens was packing. He had gathered his packets of letters and his gifts and had rolled to the cabin door a small cask of French wine that he had refused to tap on the voyage home.

"Where to?" asked Paine.

"Where?" laughed Laurens. "Where but to Washington and then to Congress. Surely you would not shackle such excellent news as we have brought to the traces of a dray? Or entrust it to the miscarriage of a post? No, I go myself. Captain Barry has already arranged for horses. Have you any personal letters that you would entrust to me? From Franklin? Lee? Adams?" He hesitated and asked, "From le Comte de Vergennes?"

Paine sat with his legs dangling over his bunk. As he realized Laurens' earnest intention to leave him, he swung an arm toward an open closet that was crammed with Laurens' wardrobe and at his personal effects that were scattered over chairs and a heavy table.

"Take them with you . . . as a favor," said Laurens. "You will be conveying the silver, so a little more will not matter. Come, do not look so dour. Wish me Godspeed." He allowed himself time for a mere handclasp, hesitated at the cabin door, and called back over his shoulder, "I shall send a seaman for the cask. And I leave Caleb with you. He will help you pack my things and travel with you."

"Caleb!" thought Paine. What use did he have for Laurens' servant! It meant an extra horse and food and lodging for 300 miles! Didn't the affluent fool realize that he had returned to America almost penniless! He had explained to Laurens, only last night, that it would take at least sixteen teams of oxen to roll the silver and supplies to the Treasury at Philadelphia. Where would the expense money come from?

Harnessed to the snail's pace of a wagon train, his news was no longer a topic of conversation by the time he reached Philadelphia. The casks of silver were carried to the Bank of Pennsylvania and Robert Morris, now Superintendent of Finance, ordered the money to be piled on the counters as an exhibit. The people filed into the bank for hours on end to see the amazing spectacle of so much silver money. It seemed incredible! As Paine stood by, Morris enjoyed the scene with exuberant enthusiasm. As he watched the endless procession of viewers, he confided to Paine, "They think the silver is piled on the counters because there is no more room in the vaults!"

"I was hard pressed not to tap a cask myself," said Paine. "Wouldst believe it, Robert, I had to borrow money at Bordentown with which to cross the ferry. The draymen wait at Peg Mullen's, as yet unpaid. And with the Assembly adjourned, . . ."

"Are you serious?" cried Morris. "You bring back a mountain of silver and it seems your first concern is for a score of unpaid ox goaders!"

Three weeks after Paine's return to the city, the combined American and French armies marched through it. The Continental troops had received their back pay and fresh outfits. De Rochambeau, in obedience to orders from Paris, had moved his army away from Newport and joined Washington. Now,

[313]

with drums beating and flags flying, they were marching south to join Greene and Lafayette in Virginia, to try to trap Cornwallis.

Paine stood on a doorstep, unnoticed, and watched as crowds cheered the passing columns. There was a feeling, all about him, that the war was finally coming to a close. What would he do then? He was unemployed even now. The Assembly had appointed another clerk during his absence. Dressed in his French coat, his point-lace stock, and his satin breeches, he walked the streets seemingly well repaid for his trip to France. Yet he was penniless. Never had a man so poor exhibited so affluent a façade. What could he turn to? A clerkship in a brokerage house? No! He would not prostitute his talents once again as he had done at Owen Biddle's.

Six months ago, there had not been hours enough in his days. Now, as though the anticipated end of the war and the country's utter disregard for the part he had played in it had created a void in him, he could not interest himself in any single thing. For want of something better to do, he opened the French valise that was a gift from Franklin. The red velvet Capuchin cape was carefully folded with it. He could not give it to Kitty yet—he was penniless and without prospects. He had expected to return under far different circumstances. He had not thought that the Continental Congress would congratulate young Laurens and sweep his own efforts under a rug.

He lifted the cape from the valise and a letter fell to the floor. He wondered about it, and then remembered. Laurens had given it to him . . . in the hotel . . . in Paris. He had thrust it into a pocket, and then left it in the valise. He opened it now. As the roguish Laurens had intimated, a delicate scent still clung to it. He read the fine, careful script and looked for the signature at the bottom of the second page: *Annette Colbert*. Annette Colbert! From the little mill in Thetford!

She must see him, she had written. She had never forgotten

him. When she learned that he was in Paris, she had rushed to him immediately. She was married . . . she had two children . . . a boy and a girl—and she had named the boy Thomas. She would be in Paris for but two days and would be staying with her brother, Pierre, at number 22 Rue des Cordeliers. Surely, he remembered Pierre! Would he come? He had not forgotten them?

With mixed feelings of regret for both the old and the new, Paine replaced both the letter and the cape in the valise.

24

IT WAS the surrender of Cornwallis at Yorktown that first made Paine realize that his old friends in the Continental Congress felt he was no longer needed. To pare down expenses he had moved to a single room on Second Street, near Norris Alley, where a sense of the country's ingratitude filled him with bitterness. To petition a grant from the Congress, he felt, would be like Prometheus calling to the angry gods. His oldest friends seldom attended the sessions and Thomas McKean, with whom he had exchanged bitter words regarding the control of inflation, was now its president. Often hungry, sometimes unshaven, unkempt, and feverish, he remained in his room for days at a time.

Early on the morning of October 20, however, he was awakened by a town crier. He sat up in bed and listened. He had shut the windows against an early frost, but he could hear the words distinctly: "Past three o'clock an' Cornwallis is taken! Past three o'clock an' Cornwallis is taken!" He rushed from his room and caught up with the crier, a ludicrous figure in a cast-off coat that was much too large for his wasted frame. "When?" cried Paine. "When?"

The crier lifted his lamp, with its yellow circle of light. Unimpressed by Paine's breeches and waistcoat, which were as shabby as his own, he mumbled, "I am to say only as wot Cornwallis is taken."

As he turned to resume his shuffle across the cobblestones, Paine spun him about. "I am Tom Paine! Mister *Common Sense!* Now tell me when and where!"

Paine's name had not lost its magic. The old man raised an apologetic hand. "The news was brought by a lieutenant colonel . . . a Colonel . . . Tilghman! 'At's it. A Colonel Tilghman, sir. Covered wi' mud 'e was. An' 'is 'orse so 'eaven' an' tremblin', I thought as wot 'e would drop in the street. I took 'im straight to Mr. McKean's 'ouse." He stood as though waiting for a comment and then, as windows were raised and candles lighted in the homes along the street, he raised his lantern and cried, "Three o'clock an' Cornwallis is taken! Past three o'clock an' Cornwallis is taken!"

Paine hurried to President McKean's home. A group of hastily dressed men were already gathered in front of it. The windows were ablaze with light and voices and laughter could be heard through the front door, which someone had left ajar. He entered and found the drawing room half filled with jubilant men. They were all talking at once, insisting to be heard, yet paying no attention to a single word themselves. Decanters of wine were upon a sideboard and a sleepy servant kept filling glasses that were passed about. McKean, the hub of a circle of delegates, was toasting Washington, the victory, the end of the war.

Paine looked about and noticed an officer, fast asleep on a chair. He had unbuttoned his dust-soiled waistcoat and his boots were caked with mud. His long legs were stretched stiffly to the floor, as though his knees would not bend, and his head lolled against the back of the chair. It was Tilghman.

His young face wore the sallowness of deep exhaustion. As he opened his eyes, Paine knelt at his side and waited until he saw recognition in them.

"The news you brought. It's true?"

Tilghman permitted himself a wide smile and offered a still unwashed hand. "If you will forgive my not rising," he laughed. "General Greene said to look you up. I have letters for you." He touched the pockets of his coat and then, as though remembering, "In my saddlebags. The surrender could not be more valid, sir."

A servant reached Paine's side, hesitated at his shabbiness, and offered Colonel Tilghman a glass of wine. The colonel passed it on, but Paine refused it. Not even waiting for his mail, he left the growing celebration. Outside, men, women, and sleepy-eyed children overflowed the narrow pavement and filled the street. Here and there, lighted lanterns were held aloft. Suddenly, church bells began to peal. Their sound vibrated strangely in the cold night air. Paine turned back to his lodging. He had often thought of the war's end. He had never imagined that he would greet it in this fashion—unnoticed and far from the hub of its celebration.

Two days later, on receipt of Washington's official dispatch, the delegates went in a body to the Lutheran Church for thanksgiving services. Paine watched them file from the Statehouse steps. But the war was not over! The letters that Tilghman brought confirmed it! Only one of the three British armies, and that the weakest, had capitulated at Yorktown. The enemy still held the port of New York and they still occupied Wilmington, North Carolina; Savannah, Georgia; and Charleston, the capital of the South! Benedict Arnold had gone over to the enemy, and Washington's army was down to 8,000 men.

Paine kept to himself. Conserving not only his firewood but his candles, he often sat in the dark and remembered happier days. Burdened with overdue rent and many small debts, he decided to write to Washington. If he explained, confidentially, the distressing situation in which he now found himself, . . . He toyed with his quill. He had encountered no difficulty, five years ago, in drafting a Declaration of Independence. Ideas had rushed to his mind more quickly than he could set them on paper. He had been inspired by the ideals of tolerance and equality and motivated by his desire for the country's freedom and self-government. Now he found it difficult to pen a letter to a friend.

Paine started, finally, and wrote:

> Second Street, opposite the
> Quaker Meetinghouse, November 30, 1781

Sir:

It is *seven years* this day since I arrived in America and tho' I consider them as the most honorary time of my life, they have nevertheless been the most inconvenient, and even distressing.

I never thought (if I thought at all on the matter) but that if I dealt generously and honorably by America, she would deal the same by me.

Almost everybody knows, not only in this country but in Europe, that I have been of service to her, and yet so confined have been my private circumstances that for one summer I was obliged to hire myself as a common clerk to Owen Biddle, of this city, for my support. . . .

I am totally at a loss to what to attribute the poverty and unemployment; for wherever I go I find respect and everybody I meet treats me with friendship; all join in censuring the neglect and throwing the blame on each other, so that the civility disarms me as much as their conduct distresses me. But in this situation I cannot go on. . . .

For two months he heard nothing. Then, at the end of January, he was invited to Robert Morris' home. The note insisted that it was most urgent. Paine borrowed a horse and traveled over a road encrusted with snow. At the Morris estate, 200 acres of what had once been William Penn's Springettesbury Manor, windswept drifts lay against sheepcotes, farmhouses, and granaries. In the gardens, where urns and boxwoods were lost to sight, spruce and pine thrust themselves through the snow like gigantic tapered shafts. Morris had not shied away from profiteering. Last winter, in collusion with a Mr. Solikoff of Baltimore, he had cornered the market in flour.

Paine was ushered into a south parlor of the manor house. He was surprised to find Robert Livingston in Morris' company. He felt no animosity toward the wealthy New Yorker. They were most friendly, but he seemed to have stepped adroitly into Paine's shoes. He had served on the committee that had "drafted" the Declaration of Independence and now he was Secretary of Foreign Affairs. The two men were comfortable before a crackling fire. Above the mantel of the hearth, in a frame that was inlaid with satinwood, was a large oil portrait of Robert Morris. The dark brown eyes seemed to look out over the room with prideful possessiveness— across the deep Aubusson carpet, across French candelabra on marble-topped tables—and to be reflected in a polished mirror whose gilded frame was decorated with carved wreaths and topped by a classic urn.

When the amenities were over, the conversation touched lightly upon his need. Livingston apologized, saying that Paine could have come to him at any time. He had not known that he was in want.

"As he could well have come to me," said Morris. "And do not think that Washington has neglected your interest. Twice he suggested that we do something about your financial difficulties. You wrote to him, Tom?"

Paine nodded admission.

"How to avert your pride—that was the problem. But we

have solved it. We have agreed to offer you a salary from the Secret Service Fund. You know that, as Superintendent of Finance, I am not required to make any report on the disposal of Secret Service monies. The entire affair need not be disclosed and Washington and Robert have agreed that it would be the present best policy. If I may, Tom?"

Morris offered Paine a single sheet of paper. It was a very formal statement:

> The subscribers, taking into consideration the important situation of affairs at the present moment . . . considering also the abilities of Mr. Paine . . . and that he has been of considerable utility to the common cause by several of his publications, they are agreed that it will be much for the interest of the United States that Mr. Paine be engaged in their service. We are therefore agreed that Mr. Paine be offered a salary of $800 per annum. The salary to commence from this day, and to be paid by the Sectretary of Foreign Affairs out of monies to be allowed by the Superintendent of Finance for secret service. The subscribers being of the opinion that a salary publicly given . . . would subject him to injurious personal reflections.

> ROBT. MORRIS
> ROBT. LIVINGSTON
> GEO. WASHINGTON

Paine looked up from the document and asked, "A salary, gentlemen? For what?"

"Tis true that there are no fixed duties," said Livingston. "No office or recognition and yet, in carrying out my own official work, I have often wished for your advice. Now, I shall not hesitate to call upon it."

"Exactly, Tom. We shall expect only that you comment, from time to time, upon public affairs."

"Expressing my personal opinions or yours, Robert?"

Morris hestiated. He glanced at Livingston and promised, "Expressing your own, Tom. We have learned that you would express no other."

Paine had sat with his wineglass untouched. Now he raised it and offered, "I drink to that, my good Robert. And let it not be said that the character of Tom Paine was marred by ingratitude."

Within the month, Colonel Kirkbride wrote and urged him to buy a home in Bordentown. It was an opportunity, he advised, that might not come again. The house was next to his on Hill Top, and was now for sale. He could look after it while Paine was in Philadelphia, and Paine could take his meals with them when he was there. After all, Bordentown was only a few miles from Philadelphia!

Paine glanced about his rented rooms and admitted to himself that they were back in their old disarray. True, he had become accustomed to his pitcher and basin, his battered desk, and his narrow quarters. But he could afford a home now, a place for his papers and unanswered letters. He would be able to save a little money from his salary, and newspapers and magazines throughout the States would still accept his articles and pay well for them. Bordentown was halfway to New York! Halfway to the Nicholsons! "I'll buy the house!" he wrote Kirkbride.

It was only a small, plain cottage, on a plot of ground 40' x 100', but Bordentown welcomed him with a celebration. He wrote to the Nicholsons and, when Kitty answered that his purchase of a home next to the Kirkbrides was wonderful, that her mother could not understand why he did not visit them, he permitted himself the extravagance of purchasing a horse and set out for New York.

The Nicholsons lived in a fine brick house that suggested affluence or a middle-class success. It ws filled with curios from Commodore Nicholson's voyages, and an east wing contained additional bedrooms for guests. Beyond a landscaped garden, a field and woods ran for twenty-six acres to where they joined Morrisania, the estate of the Morrises, with whom they were friends.

The Nicholsons made Paine welcome and Kitty confided

that the Commodore was no longer antipathetic. Paine raised a quizzical eyebrow. "Your father objected to me?"

Kitty shrugged and smiled. "Parents!" she laughed. "He objected to my constant quotations from your articles."

At dinner, Paine was prodded into speaking of his visit to France. Had he actually seen the King? Had he visited the Tuileries? Was the palace at Versailles as beautiful as they claimed? If Mrs. Nicholson had ever had objections to him, she seemed not to have nay now. She was as much enraptured by his anecdotes as were Kitty and her sister.

When he left, at the end of three days, Kitty accompanied him as far as the crossroads. She rode in a chaise that was driven by one of the servants. "Have you named your horse, Tom," she asked Paine as he rode beside them.

He shook his head and ran a hand possessively down the black mane. "Name him. It will bring us luck."

"I christen him 'Button.' It's what holds things together. Let him be the button between our place and Hill Top. Do not stay away." She leaned over the side of the chaise and whispered, "Sister is being courted. I think she may be married soon. Peace will come any day. Everyone says so. Don't you think so, Tom? One gets so tired of waiting."

He meant to kiss her cheek, but she embraced him as he leaned from the saddle and kissed him on the mouth . . . moist, lingering. His face was aflame as he left her.

He turned his horse when he reached a rise. The chaise was still at the crossroads. She raised a slender hand and waved to him. He did not know if she were tired of waiting for peace or for him.

In the fall, influenced by Paine's articles and Robert Morris' advice, the Continental Congress proposed a 5 per cent duty on imports. The money thus raised would pay the interest on loans from Holland. Unanimous consent of the States was necessary to grant the Congress the power to levy such

[322]

an import duty, and Rhode Island refused her assent.

Not for the first time was Paine angered. It was import and export merchants like the wealthy Browns of Providence that influenced the two Rhode Island delegates. And it was not only the tax! As the war drew to a close, Rhode Island, the smallest state, had begun to voice objections to remaining in the union! As the Congress adjourned for the day, Paine thrust past the departing delegates until he stood before Ellery and Hopkins. "How now, gentlemen," he accused, "would you let others sow the wheat and harvest it and grind the grain and yet hold out your hand for a portion of the bread when it is baked?"

Delegates formed a circle about them, anticipating a debate. The Virginians had not yet forgiven Paine for his arguments that had defeated their claims to the western territories. They waited to watch how Rhode Island would fare. Ellery glanced about him. He straightened his thin shoulders and defended, "Rhode Island wishes to guard her sovereignty and will accept neither law nor tax not imposed by herself alone."

"Sovereignty!" cried Paine. "And how long would the sovereignty of Rhode Island last if left to contend, alone, with a foreign power!"

Stephen Hopkins, governor of his state for nine years, came to Ellery's aid. "If Rhode Island would not be governed by England, Mr. Paine," he said with quiet emphasis, "no more will she be governed by the dictates of a union of states."

Paine glanced about him. He looked to Rhode Island's neighbors—to Sherman and Huntingdon, of Connecticut; to Elbridge Gerry, of Massachusetts, who favored Rhode Island's views; to Sam Adams, who wore his roguish smile of interested spectator. It was as though they wished to see him spend himself with futile arguments. "Gentlemen," he said, addressing the circle about him, "in '76, Dr. Franklin insisted that states should be permitted to vote in proportion to their population. He suggested that, if small states were given equal votes, they should make equal contributions to the treasury. No one can refute the logic and justice of that proposal! And yet most, and even I, for the sake of a union of the states, protested it. Rhode Island, the smallest state, was granted an equal legislative power with the greatest, and yet she speaks now of being governed. And even if she were, gentlemen . . . if she were, would it not be like a child by a parent? For the general good of all the family? What would we have accomplished against England as independent States?"

"We will not relinquish our sovereignty," said Ellery stubbornly. As though to encourage him, Hopkins nodded his greying head.

Paine glanced once more about the circle. If only he had Patrick Henry's gift of oratory, Richard Lee's gestures, the commanding influence of Franklin. He raised his voice and defied, "I consider the individual sovereignty of a state, since the act of confederation, to be a second-class right. It is defective in the power necessary to support it! It answers the pride and purpose of a few men in each state, but the state, collectively, is injured by it! If I may remind those of you who were present more than five years ago, in Lancaster, there were signed Articles of Confederation and Perpetual Union Between the States! May I quote, in their order, the States that signed that article of perpetual union, in good faith? New Hampshire, Massachusetts-Bay, Rhode Island and Providence Plantations . . ." A hush fell upon the circle of delegates and Paine repeated, "Honorably signed, gentlemen, by the representatives of Rhode Island and Providence Plantations!"

There was the stamp of Morris' wooden leg upon the floor. "Enough!" he cried. "Enough! There is no need for the penurious son of a British staymaker to speak to us of honor!"

There was a hush in the room and, as though to remind the delegates that there was neither purpose nor validity to the dicsussion, McKean thrust his way through the circle and said,

"Gentlemen, the Congress is adjourned."

One by one, they turned their backs upon Paine and filed from the Assembly Room.

In reply, Paine published a series of letters addressed to the people of Rhode Island and wrote protesting articles for the *Providence Gazette* and the *Newport Mercury.* When these failed, he appointed himself a committee of one and set out for the dissenting state.

Colonel Kirkbride saw him off. He stuffed Paine's saddle-bag with fresh baked bread and slices of smoked meat. "I still say that you should wait for spring," he suggested. "There is time. We have not yet achieved our full independence."

Paine glanced at the snow-covered road that ran past their cottages. "I feel I must go now, Joseph. Our independence has waited so long, it can wait a little longer. But our union cannot. A stronger central government must be fashioned now or we shall not have one. Without one, we will be like the spokes of a wheel without a hub."

He returned from Rhode Island filled with disappointment. He had intended to stop at the Nicholsons on his way back but learned, to his dismay, that Robert Morris had resigned as Superintendent of Finance. As a result, his salary from the Secret Service Fund would come to an abrupt end and, with so gloomy a future, he did not permit himself to see Kitty.

There was no doubt, however, that the war was over. On April 18, 1783, Washington made the formal announcement of cessation of hostilities, and great festivities were held in Philadelphia, in New York, and in Princeton where the Continental Congress was now in session. A mansion for General Washington was prepared at Rocky Hill, not far from Princeton, and members of the Congress, friends, and well-wishers went in great numbers to pay their respects and to be entertained.

In Bordentown, Colonel Kirkbride raised a questioning

eyebrow. "Why do you not go too, Tom? No one should be more welcome."

"I have better work to do," said Paine, with a touch of bitterness in his voice. "Independence is like the apple blossom—welcome to the eye, but meaningless without its fruit, its very reason for being. We must not let Rhode Island's worm of disunity spoil the fruit."

He had started *Crisis XV* in Providence, but now, as soon as it was finished, he did not rush to show it to anyone, as he had done in the early days of the war. It was a brilliant and forceful insistence upon a strong central government in which States' rights should be secondary to a national allegiance and welfare, and he knew it must stand on its own feet. Late in April he published it and saw it become a great controversial success.

When the summer drew to a close, he received a letter from Washington himself. He studied it in order to determine its true motive. He read and reread:

Rocky Hill, September 10, 1783

Dear Sir:

I have learned since I have been at this place that you are at Bordentown. Whether for the sake of retirement or economy, I know not. Be it for either, for both, or whatever it may, if you will come to this place, and partake with me, I shall be exceedingly happy to see you.

Your presence may remind Congress of your past services to this country; and, if it is in my power to impress them, command my best services with freedom, as they will be rendered cheerfully by one who entertains a lively sense of the importance of your works, and who, with much pleasure, subscribes himself.

Your sincere friend,
GEO. WASHINGTON

When Paine arrived at Rocky Hill, he was impressed by the lavishness of the mansion that the Continental Congress had furnished for Washington. It seemed that no expense had been spared. On a wide expanse of lawn, though it was now too cold for outdoor dining, the British tent was still up. All of the well-wishers and most of the guests had departed, but General Lincoln and General Roberdeau and his wife and daughters still remained, as did Washington's aides-de-camp, Colonels Humphreyes and Cobb. For weeks the house had been overrun, the grounds filled with arriving and departing guests at all hours of the day and night. "Our dinners are now quiet ones," said Washington as he welcomed Paine. "Just us."

Nevertheless, the dinner was extremely solemn, as though it were attended by dignitaries of state, not just old friends and Washington's aides-de-camp. Once Washington began on his favorite nuts and honey, Colonel Cobb touched upon Paine's trip to Providence and his failure to reconcile Rhode Island.

It was the news that a final peace had been signed in Paris that ended Paine's visit to Rocky Hill and his long discussions, for Washington immediately began making preparations to go to New York, where he would bid farewell to the officers of the Continental Army.

"There will be none there you do not know," said Washington as he invited Paine. "All are your friends—Nathan Greene, Lewis Morris, Henry Knox, Tad Kosciuszko, who is having your writings translated, Muhlenberg, Tony Wayne." He swept a hand toward the growing list of invitations that his aides were addressing.

Paine shook his head. "A lone major? And that for so short a time? No, General. The farewell is for those who fought and not for those who scribbled."

He left Rocky Hill feeling like an outsider. He thought of his friends who had their homes and families. His little cottage

[327]

in Bordentown was all he had—and now he could not maintain even that. He decided to rent it and throw himself, again, upon the hospitality of the Kirkbrides.

When spring came, he was advised in a letter from Morris that the State of New York was about to present him with a farm of some 300 acres in consideration for his eminent services rendered in the progress of the late war.

The farm had been the property of Franklin De Voe, a convicted Tory, whose possessions had been confiscated. The house on it, a fine stone one, had once been a patrimonial mansion of the Jays. It faced the main road between New Rochelle and White Plains, seventeen miles from the City of New York.

When he visited it, dust had long since settled on the well-planked floor and cobwebs hung from the ceiling corners; but the house was intact . . . even most of the furniture had been left behind. Heavy short-legged andirons were in front of a wide stone fireplace. Burnished tongs and a poker stood leaning against a wrought-iron hoop, as though waiting to be used at the first chill of evening.

By fall, as though the ownership of land was the springboard of acceptability, Paine found himself invited to many New York homes. At a reception given in his honor by the Nicholsons, he was introduced as the new owner of the Jays' former manor house. Kitty Nicholson thrust her arm through his and paraded him about. The Commodore, a red-faced, heavy-gaited man, smiled and nodded his approval. In the midst of the festivity, Kitty guided him through a hallway and a kitchen that was filled with firelight, the warmth from an immense oven, the odors of baking, the sounds of servants' chatter, and the clatter of dishes. A Dutch door opened into a back garden, and in it a narrow path led to a grape arbor. Lifting her skirt to avoid the hedges, Kitty invited Paine into its seclusion. It was a bower of latticework, entwined with old vines from which bunches of purple grapes hung down in the semidarkness. Here and there, like the thrust of a silver rapier, a star shone through an aperture that was poorly guarded by twig and leaf and lattice lathe.

Once screened from the eyes of others, Kitty turned and nestled into Paine's embrace. He put his arms about her and she was all satin bodice and hooped skirt, all perfume and scented powder. "Oh, Tom ... Tom," she whispered. "Father does not now disapprove. We will live in New Rochelle and we shall not be far from home."

For a moment the blood pulsed in his temples at the touch of her in his arms. Then the mention of New Rochelle chilled it. How could he explain, in countinghouse mathematics, the deep crevice that still, despite the New Rochelle gift, yawned between want and comfort? How could he tell her that he could not afford to occupy it? Nor afford to marry her? That he had leased the house and farm to a tenant farmer?

25

IT WAS in the little cottage in Bordentown that Paine decided upon inventions as a means of making money. He was forty-seven years old. His dark blue eyes were still brilliant, his skin fair, his brown hair untouched by grey, his body lean, and his enigmatic smile as provocative as ever. He did not look his age but, for the second time in his life, he had reached an impasse. He had the cottage in Bordentown, as well as the leased farm and house in New Rochelle, and he could now live quietly, with freedom from want. But he could not yet afford to marry; and, if he could not afford Kitty Nicholson now, ... when?

During that winter he devoted himself first to designing a

planing machine. When it did not work out, he turned to a kind of heavy crane that would pull up tree stumps. Kirkbride was not impressed. He felt it would be easier to plow around big stumps. So Paine worked on a steam engine that would turn a horizontal shaft but found it unsatisfactory. By summer, however, there had begun to form in his mind a totally original project: an arched suspension bridge.

In the meantime, he had learned that the Continental Congress had passed a resolution to compensate him for his service. He received a copy of it and read:

> The early, unsolicited, and continuous labors of Mr. Thomas Paine, in explaining and enforcing the principles of the late revolution by ingenious and timely publications upon the nature of liberty and civil govenment . . . In consideration of these services, and the benefits produced thereby, Mr. Paine is entitled to a liberal gratification from the United States.

Characteristically, he was angered by the words "the early, unsolicited . . . labors" and fumed over their employment. Certainly his labors had been unsolicited at first, even unwelcomed by many. But would the country have fared as well without them? Even his mission to France, though most fruitful, had been unofficial and without recognition.

Nevertheless, on October 3, after much wrangling, the Congress instructed its treasurer to pay Paine—as a "liberal gratification from the United States"—the sum of $3,000; and he promptly put it to work by hiring a John Hall, just emigrated from Leicester and possessing mechanical ability, to help him in translating his finished design for the suspension bridge into small iron sections in the local blacksmith's shop.

It was to be a new type of bridge. Not a drawbridge, with people, carriages, and draymen waiting on either side for a barge to pass, but a bridge high enough for boats to pass under it. An arched bridge! One that would free man and beast from an upward climb and a downward rush by a gradual incline, much of it over land and the part over the water supported by a high arch that would bear the weight of the bridge upon its back, the way Harry Snook's half hoops of metal had resisted pressure in Tucker's Bell Inn in Thetford.

To make sure that his design was faultless, he spent portions of each day going over the plans, modifying them, changing them, and, at the end of January, he brought his completed plans to the Kirkbrides. He spread them upon the living room table and watched the colonel invert the main sketch. Paine turned it back to its true position.

"It is not upside down."

When Kirkbride looked at him questioningly, he explained, as though it were a perfectly natural thing, "The arch does not rest upon the river bed. No part of the bridge touches the water. The arc carries the bridge upon its back and the ribs support an almost level roadway. Boats may pass under it, floods will not wash away its foundations, ice will not form about its piers, and the damp will not rot it . . . for it will be made of iron!"

Kirkbride glanced at Paine. He seemed carried away by his own enthusiasm. As for himself, he had greater faith in Paine's political philosophies than he had in his inventions.

"One could never transport it. You would have to build it at a river's edge. And even then, how could you raise it across the river? Build one of your mammoth cranes to lift it? It would take a lifetime to do it!"

"It will be transported easily," said Paine. "And just as easily spanned across a river. I shall have it built in sections. Each section will be designed for a particular stress and cast so that it will join its matching neighbor. The entire bridge, transported piecemeal, will be assembled and arched across a river, section by section. I have watched a spider spin a cobweb in this manner, supporting himself by each thread as he worked. How now, Joseph, is this not an invention for which there is already a necessity?"

[331]

Completely convinced himself, Paine spent the rest of the winter constructing a model for the bridge. A shed was converted into a workshop and, while Hall, by now a devotee, fashioned molds for castings and the village smith began on the bolts and the forging of ribs, Paine constructed a wooden model.

It did not take long for the news of the bridge to spread through the village of Bordentown. Curious children came to the shed and lingered to watch the work. Townsmen looked in as though but passing by. The wooden model was covered with sacking. There was nothing to be seen in the shed but forged bars, metal plates, and stacks of wooden molds for castings. The village formed opposite camps as to the outcome of Paine's invention. Few were influenced by John Hall's enthusiasm.

Building the iron model itself was a slow and painful task. Castings proved to be too brittle, wrought iron was substituted, and much of the work had to be done twice. When winter came again, Paine himself helped to bolt the arcs of the arch together and set the ribs at proper distances. He filed and hammered, pushed and pulled, lifted and strained in the half-light and freezing cold of the shed. His tender hands, which had never held anything but a needle and thread, a quill, or the reins of a horse, became quickly torn and calloused. The progress was too slow for the villagers and the workshop ceased to be a place of interest.

In the meantime, Paine learned that the Assembly itself was considering the construction of a bridge across the Schuylkill River. Various designs were being submitted. He wrote to the Assembly and asked them to wait. He would not only submit a design but an actual model. He wrote to George Clymer:

> Come and see the model. The stageboat comes to Bordentown every Wednesday and Sunday from the Crooked Billet Wharf.

Colonel Kirkbride, still unenthusiastic, stared at the stretch of metal ribs that now ran the length of the shed on the sagging planks of the floor. He feared the waste of Paine's time and money. However, as the work on the bridge neared its end, Bordentown began to have an influx of distinguished visitors. Dr. Franklin, back from France, made a special trip to see Paine and his bridge model. Robert Morris, grateful for Paine's pamphlet, *Dissertations on Government, The Affairs of the Bank and Paper Money,* came and, though he doubted its structural soundness, promised his aid. Dr. Rush, Rittenhouse, Redman, and Tench Francis came in a group to see the "iron monster."

Three days before Christmas, Paine had the sections of his finished bridge model loaded upon a sled that had been constructed for the purpose and set out for Philadelphia. All Bordentown gathered in front of the shed to view the departure. They watched with bated breath as the driver slapped the team with his reins. To their surprise, the sled moved gaily forward. They wished it Godspeed, with shouts and cheers.

At Franklin's invitation, the model was set up in the garden of his home on Market Street. Townspeople were permitted to examine it, walk upon it, and test its strength. Temple Franklin, Rittenhouse, Dr. Franklin, and Paine watched from parlor windows as a steady stream of men, women, and children came to view it. One unconvinced townsman, to the delight of a gathered group, carefully led his horse across it. Rittenhouse admitted that it was sturdy enough but feared that its construction would be too expensive.

Paine shook his head. "You are thinking in terms of watch springs and clocks. The price of heavy iron does not rise in direct proportion to its weight. And an iron structure will stand long after a wooden one has rotted away."

Dr. Franklin turned from the window and regarded Paine closely. "If you will forgive what I may intimate, Tom, you

[333]

have changed. I have never seen you so interested in . . . in the making of money."

Paine was startled, as though Franklin had accused him of a wrong. "Is it then a crime to wish for affluence? Must one only inherit it?"

"But you would devote all your time in order to gain it. I object only to that change in you. Will you now offer no portion of your talent to the new nation? You know that delegates are being chosen to meet in a convention on the 14th of May."

"And they would choose me as a delegate?"

"If you wish it, and I sponsor it."

The sly old fox. He was still drafting others to present his petitions!

"Do not think me ungrateful, Dr. Franklin, but I do not wish it," said Paine. "When my *Dissertations on Government* was published, half my friends turned their backs upon me. The rest swung this way and that, like weathercocks. The Union needs men who can compromise. Were you not so long in France, to hear of me only by hearsay, you would know that there is something within my nature that insists that a matter is, like mathematics, either right or wrong. I cannot, with the butter of politics, rub the two together without friction. New York imposes a customs duty on firewood and vegetables brought across the Hudson from New Jersey as though she were some foreign country. Jerseymen, as though their own boats are not guided by it, levy a tax of thirty pounds per month on the lighthouse at Sandy Hook, which, though it is the property of New York, stands on Jersey soil. Connecticut claims a portion of Pennsylvania that was settled by her own former residents and insists that its inhabitants, though removed, should pay their taxes to collectors from Hartford. Every state has its own claim and is angered at the man who refutes it. How can I partake in compromise when I insist, whole hog, upon a central government? No, Dr.

Franklin. If this convention is to draw up a constitution, then I shall hinder it more by presenting myself than by abstaining from it. Let me but insist upon a measure and, for purely personal reasons, it will be defeated!"

"You have more friends than you think."

"Yes, but not for my opinions, Dr. Franklin. When I say that every man should have a right to vote, they think the belief prompted by my common origin. My petition that there should be free public schools offends them and my plan for old-age pensions angers them. You know, even better than I, that the prestige of the Congress of the Confederation is now so low that some states no longer bother to send representatives. Do you ask me to attend what others have deserted?"

Franklin, leaning heavily upon his grandson, shuffled to a chair. The tip of his tongue extended itself between his lips as he marshaled his thoughts. "And yet . . . and yet, Tom," he said quietly, "with all its weaknesses, Congress has managed to ratify the peace, establish executive departments, and administer the western territories."

"Do not urge me, Dr. Franklin. I have given my time, my efforts, and such fortune as I have denied myself to the country's independence. Now I seek stability, a modicum of some means . . . perhaps I would marry. . . ."

Franklin smiled in disbelief, while a blush stole into Paine's cheeks at the thought of Kitty Nicholson. To cover the necessity for elaboration he said, "Is it so wrong? Washington is back home in his beloved Mount Vernon. John Adams is in London with his Abigail. Patrick Henry and Clinton prefer to serve as governors. Robert Morris devotes his time to private business. Livingston has resigned as Secretary of Foreign Affairs. Must I enumerate more? No, Dr. Franklin. For once, I must think of myself."

On January 17, 1787, Paine was invited to attend a banquet at the Bunch of Grapes Tavern, in honor of Dr. Franklin's eighty-first birthday. The affair was given by the city's printers, but somehow the talk turned to Paine's bridge; his model had been moved to the large committee room of the Assembly. A committee had been appointed to inspect the model and to test it. Paine had watched while members had run their hands up and down the ribs, placed a foot, tentatively, upon the span, or thrust against it to test its weight. They seemed to know as little of the principles of its construction as an unlettered man the fixed position of a star.

At the banquet table, Tench Francis, a member of the committee, asked, "The Schuylkill is 400 feet wide, Tom. How many tons of iron would such a structure require in order to span it?"

Francis had shown a great interest in the bridge when he had seen the unfinished model in Bordentown. Now, as a committee member, he hesitated to endorse an experiment that might lead to failure and ridicule. Paine glanced at the men about the table. He wondered how many had any idea as to the size of a ton of iron as compared to the size of a ton of wood. He hesitated and said, "I have estimated 520 tons."

There was a look of incredulity upon all their faces. Even Franklin looked doubtful.

"Five hundred and twenty tons!" cried Francis. "Five hundred and twenty tons! And you say that this most tremendous weight will neither sag nor break without a single pier to support its middle?"

"No more than my model. The weight of the bridge is distributed and, mathematically, the burden it can support is in direct proportion to the size of its arch. There is a ratio between . . ."

"And the cost?" Tench Francis interrupted him. "Come, come, Mr. Paine," he prodded as Paine hesitated. "You must have given some thought to the cost."

The man seemed to be enjoying the approbation of those about the table. Abandoning discretion, Paine confided, "We

[336]

estimate the cost of the bridge to be a little over $33,000."

Bradford interrupted him. "$33,000 to build a single bridge? Even your good friend, Dr. Franklin, would not endorse such a folly."

"And there you are wrong!" cried Paine. He looked to Franklin, who had sat silent until now. Reading endorsement in his eyes, he said, "I shall tell you what Dr. Franklin said to me. He said, 'I hope they will not divide its benefits by its initial cost and arrive at a false sum.' "

When it became apparent that a decision concerning the bridge would not be reached for many months, Franklin advised Paine to take the model to France. "Have it examined by the French Academy of Sciences," he counseled. "It needs but their endorsement to be accepted everywhere. Jefferson will give you what aid he can."

When Paine returned to Bordentown, he found a letter from Kitty among his mail. Her parents had retracted their endorsement of him. Did he realize that she had passed her twenty-fourth birthday? It seemed that he had no intention of occuying the former Jay manor house in New Rochelle, and it was months since he had called. Her mother insisted that she extend her courtesy to a Colonel William Few, a wealthy Georgia planter with whom her father had become acquainted. He was now courting her.

There it was . . . in the very heart of the letter! Kitty had not written that she was being courted by someone younger, someone more talented, better schooled, better known, more attractive—though she had every right to berate his neglect. No, she wrote that attentions were being paid her by a wealthy planter. A *wealthy* planter! And Franklin had censured him for his sudden interest in money! Well, he would sell his bridge. He would sell it if he had to go to France for an endorsement! He wrote to Franklin for letters of introduction:

My stay in Paris, when with Colonel Laurens, was so short that I do not feel myself introduced there; for I was in no house but at Passy, and the hotel Colonel Laurens was at. . . .

I am on exceeding good terms with Mr. Jefferson, which will necessarily be the first place I go to. . . .

He engaged passage on a French ship that would sail from New York. It would give him an excuse to stop at the Nicholsons. For already, he had begun to enlarge upon his high hopes, thinking he would return from France with the probability of becoming more affluent than any planter. He bypassed his tenanted farm in New Rochelle, where the apple orchard was in blossom and April sunshine splashed the trees with green all along the road, in favor of going first to the Nicholsons. He had not written to them. He would surprise them and perhaps regain their approval.

When he reached the Nicholson house, he found himself welcomed coolly. He was introduced to a handsome young man and realized, with a pang of distress, that he was the new suitor. He had not given much thought, of late, to the gap of years between Kitty and himself. Now, seeing the young man at Kitty's side, it seemed most apparent. He had intended to expatiate to the Nicholsons on his bridge, his trip to France, and his great expectations. Instead, he remained depressed and silent.

When he left, Kitty, despite her mother's worried glance, accompanied him to the hallway. He turned to her and saw that she was weeping. The display of affection choked him with emotion. She trembled as he embraced her. "Take me with you, Tom. Please. . . ."

He shook his head. "I'll be back before the summer is gone. I'll leave Button with you. You'll take care of him and remember me." He meant to kiss her forehead. He brushed back a strand of her dark hair and she raised her face and offered her lips, moist and quivering. There was the sound of footsteps. He tore himself away and half stumbled through the doorway.

26

HE LEFT New York on April 26, 1787, and for the first time found no interest in either his fellow passengers or the voyage. When he arrived at Le Havre, thirty days later, he decided to go straight to Paris and wait there for the customs authorities to release his model, which had been carefully stowed in the ship's hold.

In Paris, he learned that Jefferson was on a trip to the south of France. Chafing with impatience, he rented two rooms in a modest hotel and waited for his friend's return. His former visit had been in the spring of 1781 and it was spring again now. Six years had raced by. Yet Paris seemed little changed, except that Jefferson was now the minister from an America that was free and, in his capacity as ambassador, had rented a pretentious mansion known as the Hotel de Langeac that far outdid Franklin's "little place" in Passy.

Here, upon Jefferson's return, Paine found him in earnest conversation with two men in a large oval room whose ceiling was richly ornamented with a painting of the rising sun, whose walls were hung with tapestries, and whose French doors opened onto a landscaped garden.

The room itself was in great disarray. Paintings leaned against the walls, statuary and *objets d'art* were on the tables and chairs, heaps of books were scattered on the floor, and even the tall, gangling Virginian himself seemed only a figure of elegance and wealth. He had on a brocade waistcoat that showed neither crease nor wrinkle, a stock of delicate lace, and a French wig that was meticulously curled at the sides. Catching sight of Paine, he removed the wig, tossed it on a chair, and embraced him warmly. Did he know William Short from William and Mary College? Did he know John Trumbull, the painter? His advice was invaluable!

Trumbull and Short excused themselves and Jefferson waved an encompassing arm at the objects that were scattered about the oval room. "I fear my stay in France will impoverish me," he laughed. "This is but an unpacked portion of what I have bought."

The scene recalled to Paine's mind the time that they had walked over High Street to his lodging. He had been impatient to show Jefferson his draft and Jefferson had insisted that they stop at the Sign of the West's Head, on Second Street, to examine the print shop's offering of glazed pictures and English paintings. Eleven years had drifted by since then. Eleven years!

Jefferson mistook Paine's silence for disapprobation. "They are not all for me, Tom. Almost 200 of these books are for Washington. He and Martha have made a purchasing agent of me. Wait, ... wait. ..." He lifted a much-folded letter from a cluttered table and insisted, "Hear now. Hear. ... For our dear George":

> As much of the best superfine blue cotton velvet as will make a coat, waistcoat, and breeches for a tall man with a fine silk button to suit it ... all other necessary trimmings and linings, together with garters for the breeches.
> A riding waistcoat of superfine scarlet cloth and gold lace. Three gold and scarlet sword knots. ...

"And look now, for Mrs. Washington:"

> A salmon-colored tabby of the enclosed pattern, with satin flowers, to be made into a sack. One cap, tucker, and ruffles to be made of Brussels lace, proper to wear with the above negligee. One pair black and one pair white satin shoes of the smallest, and one black mask.

[340]

Paine edged toward the table that was stacked with the books and read the titles: *Life of Louis XV, Life and Reign of Peter the Great,* Voltaire's *Letters,* Robertson's *Charles the Fifth,* Sully's *Memoirs* . . .

"He has requested these?"

Jefferson smiled. "He has also asked for a copy of Rousseau's *Social Compact.* I could only obtain one in French. I shall pass the request on to Adams. Come here, Tom. Let me show you a thing of beauty. I purchased it in Nantes. I fell in love with it at once." He lifted a cloth and disclosed a piece of sculpture. "It is called Sleeping Adriane. I thought it was an original, but Trumbull informs me that it is a copy of a sculpture in the Vatican."

"Does its papal origin not taint it?"

"Come now, Tom! You are not speaking to Sam Adams. If it will endear me to you, may I say that I am quite unimpressed by the King and Queen? The liberal aristocrats—the Duc de la Rochefoucauld and the Marquis de Condorcet—are of greater interest to me. You have heard of Vergennes' death?"

"A few weeks before I left New York."

"A pity. We have lost a good friend. We discussed your *Dissertations on Government* at great length. Until the publication of this work, he had accepted you with reservation. Now, he would have presented you at court."

Paine was unimpressed. "It would not have been done with ease," said Jefferson. "An intrepid young printer by the name of Bonneville has courageously published an unexpurgated translation of your *Common Sense.*"

"I have divorced myself from politics," said Paine. He held out a scale drawing of his iron bridge. "I have come for an endorsement of my bridge. And I cannot stay long in France."

"You must rush back?"

"For years I have wanted to see my parents. First the war and then my personal lack of funds prevented me. Now that

I am but across the channel, something tugs me to my father's home." He walked to the French doors and thrust them open. The garden was a pool of sunshine. Statuary lined every walk. A fountain splashed against a blue sky. He had not mentioned Kitty Nicholson and his sudden desire for affluence. "If I do not see my parents now," he confided, "I know not when." He thought for a moment and said, "My mother is now ninety years old."

"Then I suggest that you write regarding your bridge to Sir Joseph Banks, the president of the Royal Society in London. It cannot be that England, now that the war is done, will hold your writings against you. You can visit your parents and see to the bridge at one and the same time."

"And what of France? With a French endorsement, what do I need of England?"

Jefferson studied the bridge plan. "I received the copy that you sent me a month ago, Tom. I have given it much thought. I would point out that England is the chief iron-producing country in the world. English ironmasters will not be alarmed at the thought of building an iron bridge with a 400-foot span. There may come a time when things may alter, but, just now, England more than France has a need for bridges."

Paine was filled with a sense of uncertainty such as he had not known since he left New York. "Come to the point, Jeff!" he cried. "You must not parry words with me . . . nor thoughts. What is it I should know?"

Jefferson hesitated for a moment. "I have learned that the French Academy of Sciences has already considered an iron bridge."

Paine was dumbfounded . . . bewildered. It was not true! It could not be! Even as a denial shaped itself upon his lips, he realized that, if Jefferson said it, it must be so.

"Come, come, Tom. What I say may hurt your vanity, but not your bridge."

"I have no vanity! Only pride."

"Then give no second thought to it. Four years ago, a French architect by the name of Vincent de Montpetit published a proposal to construct an iron bridge of a single arch. I have seen an exhibited model. His bridge, like yours, is made of individual parts and is portable. But there the similarity ends. I have studied the drawing of the ingenious spider web that you sent me . . . the crisscross pattern of the spaced ribs that you designed. There is no comparison between Montpetit's bridge and yours. It would take ten times as much iron to construct his and there are those who have confided to me that they would not trust it against a strong wind or a constant jarring."

"Then there is no problem."

Jefferson shook his head. "No, Tom. There is an undercurrent of unrest in France that will not lend itself to any new venture. I say write to Banks."

"You misunderstand me, Jeff. I want to build my bridge in America. I want only French endorsement. The approval of the French Academy! I have brought letters of recommendation from Franklin to . . . to the Duc de la Rochefoucauld."

He looked up from his search in the portmanteau and Jefferson commented, "Excellent . . . excellent."

Paine uncovered another letter. "I have a letter for le Comte de'Estaing. I gave one to a Jean-Baptiste le Roy and have already presented some sketches to the Academy. They have set up a committee in anticipation of the model's arrival."

Jefferson shrugged his shoulders. "Who knows? They may build your bridge across the Seine. You have no idea with what esteem the people of France regard you."

Jefferson insisted that Paine stay with him at his Hotel de Langeac, but Paine declined. He had decided to publish a pamphlet discussing the *Principle of Philanthropy*, in which he would attempt to reconcile the misunderstandings between the French and English people, and he wished to begin writing it. Nevertheless, he found time to ride with Jefferson at least once or twice a week, in the Bois des Boulogne. Jefferson took him once to see the bridge at Neuilly-sur-Seine. When he pointed out its beauty, Paine said, with a touch of pride, "My bridge is just as beautiful, Jeff. More, for this one's beauty depends upon the nostalgia of its past, while mine offers a vista of the future."

From where they stood, they could see a long row of big chestnut trees on the further bank. They ran in an unbroken line of brown trunks that seemed to offer their green bouquets to a flawless early June sky. Paine looked across the Seine where the bell towers and spires of Paris were a grey silhouette against the sunshine and said, "I have been invited to attend a soiree at the salon of a Madame Roland. It is the second time that she has urged me to come. Would you suggest I go?"

Jefferson's grey eyes became reflective as though he were looking through a dossier that he had compiled on Madame Roland. "She is a strange phenomenon," he finally said. "She is like a political flame that attracts all manner of moths. Her soirees attract not only the talented and the gifted, but idealists and political dissenters. Never to have been there is a social stigma and, yet, to frequent her home is to engender the suspicion of the court." He studied Paine and evaluated to what extent conservatism had dominated the selection of his new clothes. "I would suggest that you go," he advised. And then, his eyes twinkling, he added, "Madame Roland likes to be called 'Manon' by all her intimates."

A week later, at the Hotel Brittanique, he was surprised to learn that the Rolands were on the fifth floor of an inside court, where a large salon was filled with a press of people crowded into niches and corners and overflowing into adjoining rooms. While women occupied all the chairs and settees, the men stood and gave them polite attention. It was like a

[344]

gilded and elaborate beehive, buzzing with animated talk of which Paine could interpret no single phrase. Suddenly he spied a familiar face ... the Marquise de Lafayette. She was engaged in a whispered conversation with a young friend, her smile accenting, perhaps, a bit of gossip. He brushed through the press of guests and presented himself.

She sprang to her feet and embraced him. "Shame on you!" she cried. "Here you are, at Madame Roland's and you have not yet come to us. Gilbert will be furious when he learns of it." Turning to her companion, she asked in French, "You do not know who this is? Shame on you! *C'est le célèbré* Thomas Paine. Monsieur Paine, forgive her. I assure you that, though she did not know you by sight, she is familiar with all your writings and ideals. May I present my cousin, Comtesse de Tesse."

The countess, who had sat quietly while the marquise had embraced Paine and had resented the bad manners with which a seeming stranger had had the effrontery to present himself, now grew voluble. Turning to her cousin, she burst into an endless stream of French.

The marquise smiled at Paine. "My cousin here will never forgive you until you have learned to speak French. But she wants you to know that she admires the writings of only two men—Voltaire and you."

A young woman approached them, nodding graciously to each group that she passed. She seemed too young to be the hostess—the famous Madame Roland. Her hand rested upon the arm of a young man who bowed gracefully to the Comtesse de Tesse and to the Marquise de Lafayette and kissed their hands. The young woman smiled and then, without embarrassment, said to Paine in excellent English, "I am Madame Roland. I was at the point of rebuking you for making me look for you, but since I find you in such excellent company, I forgive you." She extended a hand in welcome. Paine brought the fingers to his lips and kissed them without

[345]

hesitation. He was surprised to find that this charming young woman—no older than her early thirties—was Madame Roland.

She introduced her escort, "Constantin François Chasseboef, Comte de Volney," left the count in the company of the Marquise de Lafayette and Comtesse de Tesse, and led Paine away. "The marquise, as you may well know, Monsieur Paine, has imbibed the spirit of liberty from her husband's cup. But you must be careful of the countess. She scoffs at the bible and insists that she is a deist, yet fingers her rosary most tenderly at every mass. She refers to the court with satire and cynicism, yet remains in the household of Marie Antoinette. She talks incessantly and often with indiscretion." She caught Paine glancing at a familiar face as she led him slowly about the salon. "You know Madame Helvetius?" When Paine smiled, recalling his meeting with her at Passy, Madame Roland confided, "I assure you, it was her late husband's reputation and your Dr. Franklin's friendship that opened more doors for her than her own *savoir-faire*. Come, we shall not keep you from the proper amenities."

To Paine's surprise, the Comte de Volney was already at Madame Helvetius' chair. Madame Helvetius seemed decidedly older than when he had last seen her, but she insisted upon rising and embracing him. "Should Monsieur Paine call you Comte or Docteur, Constantin?" she asked Volney. "Le comte has spent three years in the study of medicine. Three years. And now, when he has reached the point where he can do our bodies some good, he has turned his interest to the philosophy of religion, as though our souls were sicker than our bodies." She raised a slightly arthritic hand in emphasis. "And he is right, you know. They are."

"Then he has given up the treatment of an affluent few in order to influence the faith of a penurious many," said Paine.

"Well now, Constantin. What do you say to that?" asked Madame Roland. As though she had no expectation of hear-

[346]

ing an answer, she placed her hand lightly upon Volney's arm and led him adroitly away, leaving Paine with the aging Madame Helvetius. There was no end to her questions regarding Franklin. When Paine spoke of the dinner given in honor of Franklin's eighty-first birthday ... when he informed her that he was well, active, and in excellent spirits ... she grew reminiscent.

"I should have kept him here," she said. "Surely he has no better friends in America than he had here. And France needs him. There is a witch's cauldron of anger and vengeance boiling here. Your country's liberty was gained by amputating the infected arm of tyranny, but here it is the very heart that is diseased. Can one save the body of France by cutting out its heart?"

As though Madame Roland alloted only so much time to each group of guests—so that they would meet and yet not bore each other—she now came circling back. She stopped and her new escort bowed his thin shoulders and his balding head to Madame Helvetius. Madame Roland introduced him to Paine: "Jean Marie Roland de la Platière, my husband." Paine was surprised. He seemed a man much older than Paine, and in delicate health. Paine thought immediately of the age difference between Kitty and himself, until he realized with a start that Madame Roland was speaking to him. "We are still young lovers, Monsieur Paine. We have been married but a half-dozen years. Come, there are many I would have you meet."

"You must keep your eye on young Volney," she said as she guided Paine through the salon. "He has a bent for theology that may one day shake the tree of religion. I do not intimate that he will strike it like lightning, but shall we say that he will tremble it like a storm—and that here and there, some of the dry branches may crack and fall?"

From the crowded salon, she led him to another room. There she sat down and looked up at him. "What do you see

[347]

in me, Monsieur Paine?" she asked. "There are those who say that they see only philosophy, history, theology, and foreign languages in my eyes . . . but no love. But that is only because I have confessed to them that I prefer Plutarch and Fénelon to Rousseau and Montesquieu. What do you think?"

In answer, Paine blushed. He had never met anyone like her. There was a strange fascination about her, and he felt she knew he was glancing at her full bosom whose cleft was almost entirely exposed.

"Well, Monsieur Paine?" Apparently Paine's shyness was a novelty to her. "Come!" she laughed. "We are not complete strangers. A friend has told me about you . . . when you were a boy, in England. I wrote to you, in America, but you never answered. May I express my gratitude for your essay on women's rights? I have memorized entire passages. I should have been born a Roman or a Spartan . . . at least a Frenchman." Her laughter was deep-throated. "Come." Instead of guiding him by the arm she took his hand and led him back to the salon as though they were lovers. Paine wondered who could have told her about his youth. Who in France had known him in England?

She stopped in the doorway and pointed to a group who were in earnest conversation. "Le Monsieur with his back to the fireplace—no, the one with the dignified stance of a tall spruce—he is Baron de Cloots, Jean Baptiste du Val-de-Grâce. You, Monsieur Paine, have confined yourself to the independence of the Colonies, but Baron de Cloots has set himself up as an apostle of humanitarianism for the entire continent."

"He does not look French," said Paine.

"Nor is he. He was born in the town of Cleves. Have you been to Cleves?"

Paine shook his head. He was impressed by both the quiet dignity of the Prussian baron and Madame Roland's evaluation of him. "A most beautiful town—built upon three little

[348]

hills that overlook the Rhine. The counts and dukes of Cleves have been buried there since the fourteenth century. I predict that you will be friends with Baron de Cloots. He dreams of a union of all peoples in one fraternal bond."

Paine was fascinated by Madame Roland's seeming knowledge of men and times and places. He was entranced by the subtly throaty accent of her English.

"And now, le Monsieur who is lifting his glass to Jean—the portly one, with his hair greying and the look of worry on his brow—Turgot. Do you know him?" She caught a glimpse of recognition in Paine's eyes. "Turgot, Baron de l'Aulne. Now that he is vice-president of the Académie des Inscriptions et Belles-Lettres, he is loved by everyone. When he was Controller General of Finance and insisted that the aristocracy should be taxed, he was despised by most. And deeply resented by the Queen, whose grants and favors he questioned."

"I remember him," whispered Paine. "I was presented to him when I was last in France. He gave me a copy of his *Réflexions sur la formation et al distribution des richesses.* We have corresponded and discussed his assertion that the sole source of wealth is land."

"Come . . . there are at least a dozen more to whom I must present you. And I assure you, you will be most impressed by them." She placed her hand upon his arm to guide him. "May I call you Thomas? Everyone calls me Manon." Her full mouth was smiling and her dark eyes laughed at his seeming shyness.

Paine could not remain idle while he waited for an endorsement of his bridge. England was considering waging war on little Holland. It seemed that she would not forgive her for having signed an alliance with the "rebellious American Colonies." Paine began a pamphlet that would show the error of England's motivation. He called the pamphlet *Prospects on the Rubicon* and spent his evenings on it.

Knowledge of his presence in Paris had spread and people came to his hotel in hopes of seeing him and talking with him. French political societies gave a number of receptions in his honor. After toasting him and his writings, the gatherings would drift into loud argumentative debates. He was reminded of the White Hart Club in Lewes, only here he could only sit and watch. He was angry with himself for not having mastered French. It seemed that these societies had waited for the outcome of the American struggle for independence and were now casting the seeds of new ideologies upon the continent. They were whispering of a new government for France!

In July, Paine attended a reception given by Jefferson. Knowing Jefferson's liberal opinion of religion, Paine was surprised to find that a clerical group, headed by de Brienne, the Archbishop of Toulouse, had been invited. Perhaps it was because, now that his younger daughter Polly had arrived, Jefferson would have two children in a convent school.

Jefferson took Paine on an immediate round of introductions, as though he were the guest of honor. He had already met John Trumbull and knew William Short quite well by now. He was delighted to find that the Marquis de Lafayette and his wife were present. The Comtesse de Tesse was with them. He was introduced to the Duc de la Rochefoucauld, who acknowledged Paine with an inclination of his head that seemed a mixture of dignity, disdain, and interest. He had not yet sent Paine an answer to Franklin's letter of introduction. Suddenly Paine spied John Paul Jones and, asking Jefferson's forgiveness, rushed to him. Jones swept him into his arms. "Ah 'eard tha wert 'ere, tha effeminate scroobler," he cried. "Tha ne'er didst coom' wi' me ta the Albatross Inn!"

He presented Paine to the young woman at his side— Aimée de Tellison. Paine had heard of her. She was a natural daughter of Louis XV, upon whom His Majesty had bestowed a fortune. It was whispered that she was Jones's mistress, but Jones introduced her as his intended bride. She smiled enchantingly. She seemed in her early twenties with burnished red hair, bright blue eyes, and an exposed bosom that seemed as though it were molded of rose petals. Paine was overwhelmed by her beauty.

"I go ta Roosia soon. Wouldst tha believe it—the Empress 'erself 'as a prooposition fer me." Suddenly he turned and shouted across the vast drawing room. "Littlepage! Littlepage!" It did not disturb him to halloo across a room filled with aristocrats, as though he were on the deck of a ship. When the man hurried to them, he introduced him as Lewis Littlepage, a fellow Virginian. "Actin' agent fer the King o' Polan' 'e is. We Americans 'ave begun ta scatter oorselves throo the worl' lak the damn British. Eh, Lewis?"

Paine noticed that Jefferson had adopted the French customs. The gentlemen wore their swords and stood or walked about from one part of the room to the other. Their *chapeaux de bras,* their small silk hats, were always under their arms as though they had just arrived or were about to depart. The guests scattered themselves and engaged in murmurous tête-à-têtes.

As the ladies sat and the men drifted about, Paine realized that he was being watched from a corner of the room by a slightly aloof, rather tall man in his late thirties. He had the look of an aristocrat. His wig was curled and well powdered, a double chin suggested good living, and an unhurried poise was indicative of a man not easily intimidated. If Paine remembered correctly, he had not been introduced to him.

As though having made up his mind, the man left the corner and approached Paine. He hesitated and, with a slight bow, presented himself. *"Je suis* Marie Jean Antoine Nicolas de Caritat, Marquis de Condorcet. I see that you do not speak French," he said in excellent English. "Permit me then to be your host while the busy minister neglects you. But first let us find a vantage point from which we can both observe and talk." He led Paine back to the seclusion of the corner from which he had come. "I have followed all of your works very closely, Monsieur Paine," he said. "I am fascinated by your ideas concerning the dignity and the robbed heritage of the common man."

As was Paine's habit, although listening to the marquis, he seemed inattentive. His brilliant eyes were darting from guest to guest, as though he could overhear or understand their talk. Suddenly Condorcet startled him by saying, "I am the secretary of the Academy of Sciences."

Paine turned to him and cried, "You have seen the model of my iron bridge!"

Condorcet nodded. "I am fascinated by it. The members of the Academy consider me a philosopher . . . which I may be . . . but I am also a mathematician. The geometrical structure of your bridge is a brilliant departure from the idea of Vincent de Montpetit."

"Then it will be endorsed?"

Condorcet shrugged. "You have met Monsieur Jean-Baptiste le Roy, *non?* He has told me, in confidence, the nature of the committee's deliberation. They agree that the model is strong, but they cannot agree upon the cause to which to attribute its strength. The Abbé Bosson regards an iron arch of 400 feet such an unprecedented innovation that it would attract worldwide attention. He not only advises caution in the committee's judgment, but insists that an endorsement would be ill-advised."

"But you have just said that you understand mathematics. The geometrical design of the bridge . . ."

Condorcet shrugged. "I give you my word, Monsieur Paine. I do what I can. Le Roy is a very good friend, but the Abbé Bosson—that is another matter. We are not, shall I say, hand in glove. He refuses to forgive my political ideas. Nor does he accept yours." He hesitated and confided, "It is rumored, Monsieur Paine, that you have not really come to France to sell a bridge."

[352]

Paine was startled. Unperturbed, Condorcet glanced at the aristocrats who postured and drifted about the room. "Even your good friend, le Marquis de Lafayette, doubts that it is an interest in a bridge that has brought you here."

On August 29, Paine finally received a report from the French Academy of Sciences.

He had been studying French in his spare time. So with the help of his reader, he translated it hurriedly:

It is certain that when one gives thought to such a project as an iron arch of 400 feet and when we consider the effects that would result from an arch of such vast extent, it would be strange if doubts were not raised as to the success . . .

The Academy was adroit in phrasing its rejection so that it would affront no one. The iron bridge was ingenious; it was strong. It was deserving of a trial—but not by them. Had the French no vision, Paine wondered. No courage? Or was the country filled with such unrest that it would underwrite no single venture? He had wasted three months—three months during which he had heard no word from Kitty. Well, what France had not welcomed, England would be eager to accept.

27

WHEN HE arrived in England, Paine rushed at once to Thetford. He did not remember the village as being so small, the streets so narrow, or the brick and mortar houses so crowded, elbow to elbow in a long unbroken line. When he reached his childhood home, he realized that he had always recalled the house as being taller and his father's shop as being larger. He stood for a moment and looked about him. A September drizzle fell unhurriedly from a grey sky. The street was deserted. He lifted the worn latch and found that the door would not budge. He tried again. He peered through a pane of glass and saw that the shop was deserted.

The floor was swept and the old cutting table looked scrubbed. With a sense of nostalgia, he suddenly recalled the feel of smooth whalebone and the scent that had clung to it —the scent that his father had called the scent of ambergris. The work benches had been pushed to one side, along a wall. The counter was empty. On the shelves behind it, there was not a single bolt of cloth, or spindle of lace, or spool of ribbon. He remembered the patterns, hanging from their hooks. His eyes glanced to the familiar spot. The wall was bare. He shook the door. He waited a moment and pounded on it. As he was about to leave, he saw a little woman shuffling toward him, through the shop. Despite the warmth of the day, she clutched a shawl about her thin shoulders. She struggled with a bolt and drew open the door. He stared at the wasted form. It could not be ... and yet it was. It was his mother! He had left England but thirteen years ago. Could one age so much in thirteen years? He had not realized that the gap between seventy-seven and ninety was filled with such desiccated time. He bent toward her and gathered her into his arms. She had never displayed an emotion, but now she wept.

"Tom? Tom?" she queried in a tremulous voice, as though a doubt still touched her fluttering heart.

" 'Tis I," he answered. And then, as though the roof that had sheltered him as a child still claimed a tithing of his speech, he said, "I did not write to thee and father. I wished to return, unheralded, like the prodigal son."

She lifted her gaunt face to his and studied him with moist, rheumy eyes. Moistening her lips, as though it were an aid to

[354]

her speech, she said, "Hast thee not gotten my letter, Tom? I had Mr. Falkland write to thee. Joseph is gone. Dead these many months."

When the rain ceased, Paine's mother took him to where his father was buried. He expected to find his grave in the cemetery of the Anglican church, on Bridge Street. She led him, instead, to the Meeting House. "'Twas I who finally gave up my faith for his," she explained. "His virtue was patience and, when I learned to hush the clapper of my tongue, I found peace."

When they reached a plain stone marker, she bowed her head and prayed. She looked up at him and asked, "Thee sayest no single word, Tom?"

He was remembering his father at work in the shop, his hair in unruly ringlets where their lengths were not secured by a ribbon, smoothing a pattern against a woman's back while his china-blue eyes were fixed upon a corner of the ceiling. "Forgive me," he said. "I was thinking of him in my heart, where we have no need for words."

He stared at the marker. Joseph Paine had died on November 14, 1786—just a few months before he himself had left for France.

Thetford was now, for Paine, a mixture of the strange and the familiar. The Bell Inn had a new owner, the old smith was gone, Reverend Knowles was dead; but the shops were the same, the little school still stood near the crossroad, and the prison was still at the end of Cage Lane. He was strangely drawn to the pillory and the stocks. At the crossroad, a new gaunt figure, with his wrists tied behind his back, hung from the gallows. Paine wondered what crime this man had committed. Had he poached? Cut down a young tree? Passed a counterfeit note that he thought, perhaps was genuine? What a far cry from America!

Paine spent the autumn months with his mother. He accompanied her to the old ivy-covered Meeting House on the

Sabbath. Reacting from the stern creed of the Anglican Church, she had become greatly attached to the Quaker faith. Without rituals or priests who looked down upon her near poverty and her unorthodox marriage, she found comfort in meditation.

In order to keep busy, Paine wrote a treatise on the origin of Freemasonry, an order to which many of his friends belonged. Actually, he was bored. There was nothing for him to do in Thetford. The English Government had discouraged the circulation of his pamphlets and, with the exception of the aged residents, he was unknown in the village.

He called on the septuagenary Frederick Falkland, who was still the recorder in Thetford. He arranged a trust fund from which his mother could draw nine shillings a week for the rest of her life. The Thetford house was not encumbered and the income would provide food, clothing, and firewood. He felt that he could stay no longer in Thetford.

Nostalgia drew him now to Lewes. He thought of visiting Elizabeth but decided that seeing her would be pointless. The years had severed all but the remembering. He went to the White Hart Tavern. The painting of the stag still hung behind the bar. The ceiling beams were smoke-stained, the scarred tables glistened where their porous tops had soaked in the spilled wine, and the benches were polished from the touch of sweating hands and the rubbing of breechcloth. The tavern had a new owner and a new clientele. Even old Nolan had been replaced. Paine sat in a corner and had a gill of ale. There was no song . . . no heated debate. His old friends were gone. He left and walked the streets of Lewes. Unlike the tavern, they had not changed. Brick and mortar seemed to endure forever. Flesh and blood decayed . . . were resurrected in a birth . . . but the city endured. He took the London coach, to call on the Royal Society.

In London he found that his works were widely distributed, despite the government's proscription. He had become a celebrity. To his surprise, the affluent sought him out and invited him to their homes. He spent a full week as a guest at Beaconsfield, the country estate of Edmund Burke. He dined with the Duke of Portland, Charles James Fox, Sir George Staunton, and other parliamentary leaders. It did not take Paine long to guess the reason for the dinners. The former colonies were now an independent nation. New relations were important and they knew of no one with more influence than Paine.

One day, Paine received a letter from Lafayette. The marquis wrote that there were political upheavals in France. One could not discern them upon the surface, but the pot was boiling. He wished the author of *Common Sense* would return. His country was considering a constitution! Mr. Jefferson was aiding, but he was hampered by his position as the American minister.

That same afternoon, there was a caller at Paine's hotel room. The man was portly, well dressed, and somehow familiar. Suddenly Paine realized that he was Clio Rickman. "I searched for you in Lewes," cried Paine. "I sought for old friends at the White Hart Tavern. They seemed as dispersed as seeds by a wind."

"Not dispersed, Tom. Moved to more fertile ground . . . to London. You must come and stay with me. You will find that we have not abandoned our battle for reforms. I am a publisher now," he confessed. "And I have surreptitiously reprinted thousands of your pamphlets and circulated them. John Horne teases me that you have come to London to collect your royalties."

"John Horne?" laughed Paine. "That defrocked minister? No, but I shall write a protest upon the wide practice. I shall insist upon the need for an international copyright. But as of now, I accept your hospitality in lieu of the royalties. Here —let me look at you."

Rickman seemed to have lost the softness that his earlier

[357]

plumpness had implied. But for a slight balding, he had aged little; he had merely changed.

"You have not met my wife, Tom. Please, do your utmost to impress her, for I have not only named my first born Thomas Paine Rickman but two others, Washington and Franklin."

Paine was elated when the patents for his iron bridge were finally granted, after almost a year of waiting. He felt that they would be the basis for a substantial fortune. He would return to America, marry, settle on the Devoe farm, permit Kitty to add a wing to the Jay Manor and to furnish it as she wished.

To his dismay, however, he soon found that he could persuade no ironworks to construct an iron bridge. Experts assured them that, despite Paine's enthusiasm and England's grant of patents, such a bridge, constructed entirely of iron, would collapse of its own weight. To offset the skepticism, Edmund Burke took him on a tour of the northern iron foundries and, in Rotherham, the Walker Ironworks, owned by four brothers, promised to consider the project.

Paine moved there in November, 1788, and began to supervise the construction of the first bridge segments. But, soon, the Walkers began to regret their contract. Their forges had been confined to castings of ornamental pieces and an occasional bell. Their wrought iron had been worked into gates and ship fittings. They had never undertaken so large a project and began to doubt its success.

One night when Paine returned to his lodging, he found a letter that had been forwarded from Thetford. There was no telling when it had been dispatched. It had been originally sent to France. He tore open the envelope and found that it was from Kitty Nicholson. She had married Colonel William Few, the affluent Georgia planter. He felt a rush of blood to his head. Though not given to acts of temper, he tore the letter

[358]

in half, rushed outdoors, and walked the soot-stained narrow streets of Rotherham until he could control his sense of irremediable loss. What was the point of living now?

A few days later, when he felt able to see things in a truer perspective, he went to London and wrote to the new Mrs. William Few:

> London, January 6, 1789
>
> . . . And I sincerely thank you for your very friendly and welcome letter. I very affectionately congratulate Mr. and Mrs. Few on their happy marriage, and I request my fair correspondent to present me to her partner and to say, for me, that he has obtained one of the highest prizes on the wheel.
>
> Though I appear a sort of wanderer, the married state has not a sincerer friend than I am. It is the harbor of human life. It is home; and that one word conveys more than any other word can express. For a few years we may glide along the tide of youthful single life, and be wonderfully delighted; but it is a tide that flows but once, and what is still worse, it ebbs faster than it flows, and leaves many a hapless voyager aground.
>
> I am one, you see, that hath experienced the fate I am describing. I have lost my tide; it passed by while every thought of my heart was on the wing for the salvation of my dear America.
>
> Though I am in as elegant a state of acquaintance here as any American that ever came over, my heart and myself are 3,000 miles apart; and I had rather see my horse, Button, in his own stable or eating the grass of Bordentown or Morrisania, than see all the pomp and show of Europe. . . .

This was what he wrote, but it did not keep Kitty Nicholson from his thoughts, nor did it lift him from the despondency into which the news of her marriage had plunged him. Abandoning work on his bridge, he crossed the English Channel and sought Jefferson for comfort, only to find that he had not returned from a Christmas holiday in the south of France.

To his surprise even Paris seemed gloomy and despondent.

[359]

The streets were filled with frightful men from the farms and provinces, clad in coarse woolen jupes and wide leather girdles studded with copper nailheads. Their stature was heightened by wooden clogs that they called "sabots." Their uncombed hair was long and greasy, their necks were encrusted with dirt, and their haggard faces were frightening.

Even on the main streets, such as the Rue de Rivoli and Rue Royale, Paine could see a change. The gap between the affluent and the poor had widened into a chasm. In the shops, the women of the rich were dressed in voluminous satin skirts with dusters over them. They had fur muffs and tremendous hats with ribbons and ostrich plumes. Out in the freezing cold, the women of the poor, with wide aprons over their coarse skirts, their bare feet in wooden shoes, looked in upon the shoppers with malevolently envious eyes.

On his third day in Paris, Paine received a note from Madame Roland. Would he attend a soiree at her salon on Friday evening. "I insist," she wrote. "There are many who have not met you and are most anxious to talk with you. They will come especially to see you."

To his surprise, she sent a carriage for him that conveyed him through the congested streets of Paris. When he entered the salon, he immediately sensed a new atmosphere. Suddenly he realized that there were no women. Even the men were of a different kind. Their voices were raised, their faces were flushed, and their arms and hands gesticulated in vulgar emphasis as they talked.

It was a good twenty minutes before Madame Roland noticed Paine. She rushed to him and embraced him. She kissed him upon each cheek while she thrust her ample bosom against him and imprisoned his back with her strong hands. But to Paine's surprise, she did not lead him subtly from group to group as she had done before. Stamping her foot upon the parquet floor and clapping her hands, she cried, *"Regardez! Regardez!"* When she had received a modicum of

[360]

attention, she introduced him in French: "I give you Monsieur Thomas Paine, the author of *Common Sense*. The Thomas Paine who would restore dignity to man and wrest the scepters from the hands of kings!"

Paine glanced about him. Among all the new faces, he recognized only the Marquis de Condorcet. He was standing aloof, as Paine had first seen him in Jefferson's drawing room. He was now modestly attired, yet still aristocratic in his bearing. He made his way to Paine and rescued him from the center of the floor. "I see that no place is completely strange to you, Monsieur Paine." He smiled as he noticed Paine watching a group that was in the midst of an earnest debate. "That, Monsieur Paine, is what we call the 'Rousseau group.' They argue his philosophy and his ideal state. The man in the middle is Robespierre. I do not know why Madame Roland tolerates him. He is a man sprung from no family, yet he desires to create the impression of having done so."

Paine felt the tug of Condorcet's hand upon his arm, but he lingered to study Robespierre more closely. He was somehow drawn to him. He appeared most fastidious in his dress, from the curled wig that seemed too large for his small head to the polished silver buckles on his high-heeled shoes. Paine recalled a letter that he had received from a Robespierre, regarding *Common Sense*. But that had been almost a dozen years ago . . . . this quiet young man looked no more than thirty . . . could it be the same?

"Now there is a man you must know," said Condorcet as Paine followed where he led. "He speaks English well. You will be friends with Danton at once."

Paine saw a tall man, foppishly dressed, with an intimation of boredom in his bearing. "No, not him," said Condorcet. "He is La Croix, a devoted friend. Danton, the man beside him, is who I mean. He is but an obscure *avocat* at the Chatelet, but mark my words well . . . there is history in his big fist. He has the devotion of a child, the temper

[361]

of a stallion, and the strength of an ox."

Paine looked at Danton. The man was like a bull on two legs. He had a massive chest and wide, heavy shoulders, from which there rose a thick, animal throat on which rested a pimpled and angry-looking countenance.

"Come, I will introduce you. But do not let your first impression of Georges Jacques Danton sway you."

As Condorcet presented Paine, Danton gave him but a fleeting glance and then, as though the name Thomas Paine had struck a bell, he thrust out a big hand, pumped Paine's arm with uncontained enthusiasm, and embraced him. "Thomas Paine! Thomas Paine!" he cried in a voice that sounded strangely guttural as it issued from his bullish throat.

Held close by Danton's embrace, like a terrier by a bear, Paine could see that the man's heavy face was pock-marked and his wide mouth was set in a sneer by a deep scar on his upper lip. His great bulk seemed to belie his age . . . he could be no more than thirty. Suddenly he released Paine, waved his arms, and let out a bellow that tinkled the prisms of the chandeliers. "Camille! Come see whom we have here. Thomas Paine! Camille Desmoulins is my neighbor," he explained in English. "He lives in the apartment above mine. He is like you, Monsieur Paine. He loves the common man."

Again Paine noticed a familiar face. "Isn't that Brissot? Surely that is Brissot," he asked and pointed to a slender man whose frailty was emphasized by deep-set eyes in a wan and haggard face.

"Jacques-Pierre? You know him?"

Paine nodded. "I met him in America. Over a dozen years ago . . . when he proposed the abolition of slavery. If you will forgive me, gentlemen . . ."

Danton's brute face broke into a grin that disclosed strong wide-spaced teeth. "Danton forgives no one!" He thrust his arm through Paine's and swept him forward. "Come. We shall see Jacques together. I have not yet talked to you,

[362]

Monsieur Paine. Eh, Camille! Come with us."

Brissot was no longer the young elegant Frenchman that Paine remembered. He wore neither wig nor stock, the collar of his shirt was open, and his waistcoat was unbuttoned. His dark hair was lifeless and sparse, and a vein, like a bent twig, throbbed within a pale temple. He welcomed Paine with deep affection. Danton turned and waved an arm about the salon. "I must talk with Monsieur Paine!" he bellowed. "One cannot talk here. One cannot even think here. Come, let us go to le Café de la Parnasse. It's a place where we can talk in quiet. Come, we shall walk there. What's a little walk to the Quai de l'École?"

Condorcet excused himself, saying that he must remain, but Danton, on the way to the door, his impulse to fete Paine undampened, gathered two more friends. He introduced one as Nicolas de Bonneville, a young author and publisher, and the other as simply Jean Paul Marat. Marat, a man in his early forties, held himself stiffly erect as though, despite his rather homely face, with its dark protruding eyes, he possessed something that insisted upon dignity and respect.

As they walked out into the street, Danton at Paine's side, Brissot, La Croix, and Desmoulins following, and Bonneville and Marat bringing up the rear, Paine found himself reevaluating his first impression of Danton. The man seemed to possess an animal magnetism that drew everyone to him. "Do not be taken in by Marat's dignity," he whispered to Paine. "He is a physician, and they all hold their heads in the air. But I assure you, he is one of us."

Paine wondered what Danton meant by "one of us." He was leading the little party through a narrow street that was lined with four-story houses and presently he stopped at number 8 Quai de l'École and ushered them into a modestly pretentious café.

Although there were candles at every table, the light inside was dim. The air, though heavily scented with cooking and wine, was musty, as though they were above a damp cellar. Danton was immediately surrounded by girls and students, whom he hugged or kissed and shooed back to their tables in rapid, boisterous French. An obese Frenchman, in a dark coat and a wig as round as his mustached face, hurried to welcome them. He waddled toward them as though he had swallowed a hogshead of wine. Danton clasped him in his arms and, despite the man's weight and girth, lifted him and shook him. "My father-in-law, Monsieur Charpentier," he cried to Paine in English. "Never did a decent night's work in his life— except when he created his daughter. Eh, father-in-law?"

Paine could see that the father-in-law did not understand English. Danton cried to him with his bull's voice, *"Regardes ice, beau-père.* Thomas Paine. Do you know who he is, father-in-law? Pah! You do not even know good wine." He waved to his mother-in-law, a buxom amiable-looking woman, who sat on a high stool in back of a cashier's desk. She had a broad face and a cheerful grin. She was delighted as Danton called to her, *"Bon soir, belle-mère.* Let me know when you are ready to make another Gabrielle. I will help you."

The café filled with bursts of laughter and Brissot translated the remark for Paine, explaining, "Gabrielle is Danton's young wife."

When they were finally seated, the talk turned immediately to people and governments. "Condorcet believes in human perfectability," said Danton. "But you do not, do you, Monsieur Paine? Surely you do not think that man can live like a mathematical equation? That he can govern himself without outside help?"

Paine found it difficult to talk to the group. Marat seemed to grasp what he said but neither La Croix nor Desmoulins appeared to know any English. Ignoring Paine, Marat began a dissertation in rapid French. Everyone seemed deeply interested. When he finished, Danton explained to Paine, "Dr. Marat says that he has met a certain Fourier, a young man who

[364]

insists that he is in the process of evolving a new philosophy. What makes men happy? Their passions. What makes them miserable? The inhibition of their passions. Instead of controlling passions by self-imposed restrictions, this Fourier says we must create a society in which men and women can indulge their passions to the full, yet live safely and harmoniously."

Paine studied Marat. His receding forehead, his prominent cheekbones, his thin-lipped mouth, and his emaciated throat suggested that he was repulsive to women. There must be a personal, deep-seated bitterness in him to want mankind ruled by passion. And the idea was not even new. It had been offered by the deranged Marquis de Sade. "I believe in reason," said Paine quietly. "Whether it be the science of mathematics, of astronomy, of government, or even of religion . . . if it is not based on reason, on the deductions of the mind that God has given us, then it is based on nothing. I leave passion to brutes and not to men." He turned to Brissot and asked, "Do you say nothing, Monsieur Brissot? Do you not agree with me?"

"Your friend Jacques is in poor spirits as well as poor health," laughed Danton. "He has spent four months in the Bastille and has been but lately released." He looked into Paine's eyes and informed him, "Imprisoned for having written an impetuous *brocheur* against Marie Antoinette. And, but for the intervention of the Duc d'Orleans, he would still be there. Robespierre and I wanted to help, but he insisted upon his own defense. Eh, Jacques?"

"The charge was false, but the pamphlet was not," said Brissot.

Paine glanced at Nicolas de Bonneville. He recalled being informed that he had been the first to publish an unexpurgated French translation of *Common Sense.* He looked like a young man who was waving good-by to his twenties. Danton followed his gaze and bellowed, "Nick! You have not said three words!"

Bonneville smiled. "You know I have but three words, Georges." He struck the table sharply with his glass. *"Liberté —Égalité—Fraternité!"*

Suddenly Paine was aware of a powerfully built man who sat alone in a far corner of the café. He had removed his coat and unbuttoned his peasant's goatskin vest against the warmth of the room. A shock of straight black hair, like a lion's mane, hung down each side of his broad face. His resemblance to Annette's brother Pierre in Thetford was striking. "Excuse me," said Paine. "I think I know that man. I must see."

As Paine approached his table, immediate recognition sprang into the man's dark eyes. He did not rise but thrust out a welcoming arm as thick as a sapling's trunk. "Tom Paine!" he cried. "Tom! Annette looks everywhere for you, and finds nothing. And I sit and have a drink and you walk into my arms. It is as Monsieur Charpentier says, 'Everyone comes, if only but once, to le Café de la Parnasse!' Let me look at you . . . let me look at you."

When Jefferson returned, Paine was relieved to see no preparations for a departure. Instead, Gouverneur Morris, but lately arrived in Paris, had made himself at home in the Jefferson mansion as though he were an honored guest. He informed Paine that he had come to France as a business agent for Robert Morris . . . in the export-import trade. Paine knew better. He had come to interest French aristocrats in the purchase of western lands in America. Fortunes were being made in their speculation.

At the moment, Jefferson and Morris were about to attend a soiree at the home of Madame Helvetius in the village of Auteuil, so Paine immediately excused himself. But Jefferson would have none of it. "There will be many there whom you know. Don't be unreasonable." He drew aside a drape and glanced outside where his coach-and-four were waiting. "Come, let us go!"

When they arrived at Madame Helvetius' salon, it was filled with old friends and new faces. She herself welcomed Paine by clasping him to her and kissing him. She seemed to have shed whatever restraint she had assumed at Madame Roland's and was back to the free and easy manner that she had displayed at Passy. Though she was now sixty, time had not robbed her of grace. *"Mon dieu,"* she laughed to Jefferson, "I do believe Monsieur Paine is blushing." As though Paine's blush was of greater interest than Gouverneur Morris' peg leg with its scarlet ribbon, she led him quickly away. When they reached a settee, in a far corner of the salon, she permitted herself to plop upon it with little feminine delicacy.

"You have brought me a letter from Benjamin . . . *un bon mot?* He has turned reprobate. He does not write to me anymore. When he was here, he wished to marry me. Now he neglects me completely."

Paine was surprised. Did she not realize that Franklin was now in his eighties . . . and 3,000 miles away?

"Well!" she sighed, "if you will not talk of our beloved friend, then we shall talk of my late husband and Denis Diderot, and Montesquieu and Rousseau." Her voice dropped to a lower key. "Look about you well," she confided. "I have an intuition that, even in this little village of Auteuil, something is drawing to an end. Notice well the fluffing of hair and the delicate complexions, artificially preserved. And the men with their gallant swords. I know that they are rusted, though their scabbards are still well polished. Their delicate hands, unaccustomed to even the hilt of a fencing foil, now lift only the lids of their snuffboxes."

Paine looked about. Everyone was dressed as though for a fancy ball. The women moved with a rustle of silk and satin. Their bare shoulders were like the petals of tall flowers. The candlelight glinted on their necklaces and pendants. The well-bred gentlemen wore gold trinkets at the end of chains. They clinked as they moved languidly from group to group.

[367]

Madame Helvetius watched Paine's eyes and, inclining her coiffured head so that her lips almost touched his ear, she whispered, "You are watching the little trinkets, *mais non?* Dear Benjamin called them the little golden fetters by which the aristocracy of France is chained to an unfortunate destiny. Observe them well, Thomas . . . you do not mind if I call you Thomas? They toil not, neither do they spin. All but Lafayette. And here he comes for you. I lend you for a little while, Thomas, See that you return."

Lafayette bowed to Madame Helvetius and Paine rose from the settee. The Marquis' face had filled out. The scrawny duckling had grown into an attractive man. Affectionately he took Paine under his wing and led him through a seemingly endless round of presentations. Madame de Flauhaut . . . Baron de Staël . . . his wife, Germaine . . . the Bishop of Autun, Charles Maurice de Talleyrand-Périgord. Paine looked at the bishop and noted his high cheekbones, hs uncouth mouth, and deep-set eyes beneath heavy eyebrows. Despite his ostentatious wig and dress, he was still a plain man. Could it be that Morris was not completely truthful in intimating that Madame de Staël was his mistress?

A circle of men and women were forming now in the center of the salon. A latecomer of about fifty years of age was being presented. He was slender and of medium height, with a bent-forward posture that made him seem shorter than he was. Despite a collar embroidered with gold, a lace-edged stock, and an elegant blue velvet coat, he seemed ill at ease.

Lafayette edged closer to Paine and whispered, "Joesph Ignace Guillotin." The name meant nothing to Paine. The circle broke suddenly and two servants carried an object covered with a sheet into the center of the room. "It is an invention," Lafayette informed him. "A device for capital punishment. Guillotin proposes that it be adopted to take the place of hanging."

"Here?"

Lafayette shrugged. "Dr. Guillotin has demonstrated it,

with the aid of sheep, to show that executions can be made swiftly and painlessly. Since Madame Helvetius no longer goes to Paris, she has invited him here."

The guests craned their necks as the servants uncovered the model. An awesome chill constricted Paine's chest as he saw it and yet, drawn by every new idea, he pressed forward with the rest in order to study the device. There were two upright posts, grooved on the inside and connected at the top by a crossbeam. An oblique sharp-edged heavy iron blade was within the grooves. It was supported at the top by a simple catch, to which a rope was attached. At the base, between the posts, cut out like the frame of a pillory, was a board in which the victim's neck could be secured. A tug at the rope—and gravity was the executioner!

Dr. Guillotin shed his reserve and grew voluble.

Paine turned to Lafayette and the marquis translated, "He says that he could whisk off heads, with his machine, in a twinkling and no one would have any pain. He wants everyone to endorse it. It is most humane."

Paine edged closer to the suspended ax. He urged Lafayette to question Dr. Guillotin as to what had inspired him to design it. The physician caressed his mustache, as though to assure himself that each hair was in place, before he replied.

"He says that several years ago, when he was teaching at a Jesuit college at Bordeaux, he witnessed a hanging. It was poorly executed. The victim's neck was not broken and he choked and twitched and dangled interminably."

Paine was depressed as he stepped away from the carefree circle. It was a bad omen—a physician, dedicated to the prolongation of life, devising a means for dispatching it more swiftly.

His visit over, Paine returned to Rotherham to speed up the work on his bridge. It was soon half completed and he wrote elatedly to Jefferson:

The Walkers are to fit and frame (all the materials) ready for erecting, put them on board a vessel, and send them to London. I am to complete the erection. We intend first to exhibit it. My principal object is to open the way for a bridge over the Thames. . . .

Jefferson congratulated him on the progress and informed him that he was giving a dinner party for the Americans in Paris, on July 4. Paine must return to Paris and attend it. He had news that he could not entrust to a letter.

Paine found that Jefferson's fourth of July celebration was not confined to Americans. Many Frenchmen were present. Paine was pleased to find Joel Barlow among the guests. He recognized Paine immediately. He was in France, as an American representative, to sell acreage in an Ohio Land Company. "As what American is not here to sell something?" he laughed.

Paine remembered Barlow as he had first seen him—a young officer at Valley Forge. Now he reminded him of Clio Rickman. He was handsome, well built, and tall.

To Paine's surprise, young Martha Jefferson presided at the dinner. She was but a child, but looked older. She had inherited her father's tallness and it emphasized her grace. Like her father, her hair was highlighted by a reddish glint. She had parted it in the middle and permitted it to fall about her slender neck in a profusion of thick curls. She spoke French without hesitation and had acquired a mannerism of accenting some of her phrases with gestures of her delicately slender hands.

Immediately after dinner was over, as though to shield his daughter from Morris' recitals of his intrigues with the ladies of the court, Jefferson led the guests into the oval room. Here, Jefferson uncovered an assemblage of items beneath three large sheets and presented them to le Comte de Buffon. To his amazement, Paine saw the bones and skin of a moose, the antlers of a caribou, an elk, a deer, and the spiked horns of a roebuck. The skin of the moose had been dressed with the hair on, but a great deal of it had been shed.

"These have all come from New Hampshire and Massachusetts," said Jefferson. "I do not wish to minimize le Comte's faculty as a naturalist, but I must impress upon him that America is a new and comparatively unexplored land. The new is not always a simple mutation of the old."

The disagreement between Buffon and Jefferson concerning the appearance of America's animals was well known in Paris drawing rooms. Buffon accepted the strange specimens with good grace. While he and his countrymen gathered about them, Jefferson led the Americans to a far end of the room and showed them a collection of busts. He had ordered them in preparation for his return to America. He had paid the sculptor Houdon 1,000 livres for them. They were presumably plaster models: John Paul Jones, Franklin, Voltaire, Washington, and himself.

Leaving his guests behind, he motioned to Paine to follow and led him to the library. To Paine's surprise, it was already occupied by Lafayette, Pierre Dumont, Condorcet, Emmanuel Sieyès, and le Comte de Mirabeau.

"Do you see, messieurs," said Jefferson. "I said he would come."

Paine looked about. The doors were closed, the windows shut, the men expectantly silent. He was reminded of one of Sam Adams' early caucuses.

The group turned to Mirabeau as spokesman. He seated himself with affected grace and said, his voice slightly tinged with anger, "Two and a half weeks ago, Monsieur Paine, on the seventeenth of June, we proclaimed a National Assembly."

Paine nodded. He had learned of it. He had been in Rotherham, but Rotherham was not at the end of the world.

"Three days later, Monsieur Paine, the members of the Assembly were barred from the meeting hall by a royal de-

cree. We assembled on a tennis court, at Versailles, and swore
... we swore, Monsieur Paine, that we would remain in
session until we had drafted a constitution for France!"

Mirabeau fell silent, as though waiting for a reply or a
proposal from Paine. Paine studied Mirabeau for an indelicate few minutes. Both his ill health and his eyesight, all but
destroyed by the years spent in the gloom of a cell, were
self-evident. He was the eldest son of a neurotic father who,
under the pseudonym of *"L'Ami des hommes,"* had preached
loving-kindness in his works, yet had cast his wife into a
lunatic asylum, driven his daughter to suicide, and imprisoned
his son because he had refused to marry the wealthy bride that
he had selected for him.

When Paine still remained silent, Emmanuel Sieyès said,
"We have accepted le Marquis de Lafayette's suggestion that
we solicit your aid in drafting a Declaration of the Rights of
Citizens. We would like its philosophy to be patterned after
the American Declaration of Independence. And Monsieur
Jefferson, though his position as the American minister prevents an open endorsement, has privately advised that we ask
you, Monsieur Paine, to draft the Declaration. We offer you
le Marquis de Condorcet and Monsieur Dumont as collaborators."

Paine glanced at Jefferson. Jefferson smiled and shrugged.
Paine looked at Mirabeau. His eyes were half shut, as though
the candlelight annoyed them. He glanced at Pierre Dumont
—he had heard that he had once been a priest. His face was
round and carefree. He glanced at Condorcet. Quietly aloof,
he had once confided to Paine that he desired the destruction
of prejudices and wished for a constitutional monarchy. What
could one hatch from so many strange eggs? Despite his better
judgment, Paine smiled and said, "Gentlemen, you do me an
honor. If a time comes when you need me, I shall render you
what services I can."

[372]

Back in London, to keep in touch with the work on his bridge, Paine was saddened when he learned that Jefferson had finally received his leave of absence and would depart from Paris on September 23. He had felt as though, across the channel, there was a bit of America that he could visit. Now it would be gone. He wrote to him:

> September 15, 1789
> I am looking out for a place to erect my bridge. I expect it in London by the latter end of October. Whether I shall then sell it in England or bring it over to Paris, and re-erect it there, I have not determined in my mind. . . .

Nostalgia touched him as he thought of the Nicholsons, of Kitty who was now Mrs. Few, of his leased farm in New Rochelle, and of his friends in Bordentown. He could not help but add:

> Absent from America, I feel a craving desire to return and I can scarcely forbear weeping at the thoughts of your going and my staying behind.

As autumn drew to a close, French emigrés began to drift to England. They brought eyewitness accounts of the most barbaric atrocities that had taken place in Paris. At the fall of the Bastille, its governor, the old Marquis de Launay, had been torn to pieces by a mob. His mouth had been stuffed with grass, his head hacked from his body and paraded on a pike through the streets. A half-crazed, delirious mob, drunk with wine and mad with vengeance, holding blood-smeared severed heads and limbs aloft, had dragged dead bodies through the Paris streets by torchlight!

Emmanuel Sieyès had not written of this! They had corresponded regarding the *Declaration of the Rights of Man and of Citizens,* as though he and Paine were playing a game of chess by letter, but he had written no single word of the atrocities. Nor had Dumont, nor Condorcet, nor Joel Barlow, with whom he now frequently corresponded. When Lafayette invited him for the Christmas holidays, he left for France with unwelcome forebodings.

In Paris, he found a congested city, where people swarmed the streets and parks. They seemed to mill about, aimlessly, and yet as though they contained wound springs within them that but waited to set them in violent motion. He had been told that the population of the city had swelled to almost a million people. One-third the population of America! One-sixth the population of England! All in one city! It seemed incredible. Who would find work for them? Who would feed them?

He found a new breed of men in the crowded cafés. They seemed to be watching, waiting, and gave the very air about them a sense of tenseness. They were wrapped in dark cloaks and wore shapeless slouch hats. They sat and sipped their wine in silence, but an intimation of violence clung to them.

He wanted to see what was left of the Bastille before he went to Lafayette. He had heard that it was being demolished. As he turned into the Rue St. Antoine, he could hear the sound of falling stone and saw, in front of him, a great cloud of dust suspended in the windless air. They were losing no time in razing the fortress.

At the eastern end of the Rue St. Antoine, he reached the courtyard of the Bastille and remembered the last time he had seen the prison. Jefferson had pointed it out as of historical interest. It had been spring and the Bourbon flag had flown lazily over its great mass of turreted stonework. The courtyard had been guarded by grenadiers, their long coats, tall hats, and fixed bayonets giving them the appearance of marionettes. Now it was filled with the rubble of smashed stone and crumbling mortar.

On February 4, Paine accompanied Lafayette, Condorcet, and Pierre Dumont to the French National Assembly. When they reached its doors, Paine was attracted to a strange sight.

[374]

He recognized Pierre Colbert, pushing an odd contraption in front of him. It resembled a barber's chair, on wheels, but was designed in such a manner that its occupant could propel it by means of small handles that were attached to rotating cogs. A single wheel, in back, able to turn in any direction, guided its course. The man who sat in it seemed preoccupied and withdrawn. His face was sharp and thin. There were hollows beneath his cheekbones, as though bitterness had gouged them there.

"Do you know Couthon?" asked Dumont.

Paine shook his head. "Only Colbert."

"He is a confidant of Robespierre. Discovered by a jealous husband, while engaged in an escapade, he spent an entire night in a cesspool, up to his neck in water. He escaped at dawn, cured of love but crippled for life. Waste no sympathy on him."

Inside the Assembly Hall, evidence that it had been a riding school was still apparent. The floor had been left unchanged and its rather dim interior retained a scent of oiled leather and a faint smell of horse sweat. A huge poster was nailed to a wall in back of the rostrum. It contained the daring words:

NO MORE NOBILITY EXCEPT IN THE HEART

Paine glanced about and recognized many of the deputies —Danton, with his lip-scarred sneer; Robespierre, with his bird-like watchfulness; Brissot, with the dark shadows about his eyes; Desmoulins, with his lips moving as though he were practicing the correction of his stammer; La Croix, his face a mixture of boredom and disdain; Marat, with his angry mouth and his livid pustular skin. If he were a physician, as Danton had confided, why did he not treat his scabs and his weeping sores?

Paine looked up at the rostrum. Emmanuel Sieyès was presiding over a debate, but the voluble French was too rapid for Paine to follow. At the close of the debate, a note was brought

[375]

to President Sieyès. He rose and read the terse announcement. Paine understood the short phrases. Their Majesties, the King and Queen, would step over, unceremoniously, about noon.

There was an immediate hubbub in the Assembly Hall. The desk was immediately shifted down from the rostrum. A cover of purple velvet, sprigged with gold fleurs-de-lis, was slipped over the president's chair. An unpretentious deputy rushed to the rostrum. He had a roll of red velvet carpet in his arms. Paine recognized Dr. Guillotin. He unrolled the carpet in front of the president's chair and smoothed it with trembling hands toward the rostrum's single step. The extra chairs were removed from the platform. As though upon an impulse, and with a protest from no one, a deputy rushed to the wall and tore down the poster that proclaimed: NO MORE NOBILITY EXCEPT IN THE HEART.

Either the deputies had timed their preparations poorly or the King had decided at the last moment, perhaps against his will, to attend. They barely had time to regain their seats when an usher at the door announced Their Majesties. The King and the Queen were attended by a small suite and, as they entered the hall, the deputies uncovered their heads and started to their feet. They not only rose but stood upon their toes and craned their necks to see.

Paine caught a glimpse of the round full-cheeked face of the King. His eyes showed neither interest nor disdain. His thick lips drooped downward as though he regretted having accepted the advice to present himself and acknowledge the actions of the Assembly. His powdered wig was arranged in long drooping curls. He had ornamented his big feather hat with the largest of his crown diamonds, as though to impress the third estate, the *bourgeoisie,* that his personal possessions were still his own.

Marie Antoinette was almost lost to sight on the low rostrum. Paine could just about see the wide-brimmed hat adorned with dyed ostrich feathers and the high collar of her cape, which rose to her very ears. She held a handkerchief to her face and one could not tell if she disdained to disclose her much-acclaimed beauty to the uncourtly deputies or if the effluvia of the former riding school annoyed her delicate nostrils.

The deputies remained standing. No one dared to seat himself. Paine was able to catch a phrase, here and there, from the King's evidently rehearsed speech, which he gave in a low monotone. The deputies paid no attention to the King's words but craned their necks to view him and the Queen. It was as though the myth that they ruled by "divine right" held the assemblage spellbound. The very words, "Their Majesties," conjured up among the deputies a display of fealty, adoration, homage, and obeisance. It seemed inherent in their very blood!

Paine looked about at the raised toes, the craned necks, and the wide-eyed stares of those who would shortly rush away to cry exultantly: "I have seen the King and Queen! I have seen the King and Queen!" Anger began to simmer within him and, for the first time, doubt crept into his heart.

If Frenchmen got their freedom, would they know how to use it?

28

PAINE'S BRIDGE was completed in April, but the Walkers, still skeptical, refused to risk its loss over a body of water. "Man is a most curious creature," the eldest Walker insisted. "If he will pay to see a five-legged hare, or a dancing bear, then he will gladly part with a shilling or two for the privilege of inspecting the world's first iron bridge, but it will have to be on land."

Realizing that he would not return to America as soon as he had planned, Paine wrote to President Washington:

May 1, 1790

Our very good friend, the Marquis de Lafayette, has entrusted to my care the Key of the Bastille and a drawing, representing the demolition of that detestable prison, as a present to your Excellency.

I should rejoice to be the direct bearer of the Marquis' present to your Excellency, but I doubt I shall be able to see my much loved America till next spring.

I am engaged to return to Paris when the Constitution shall be proclaimed and to carry the American flag in the procession. . . .

I have manufactured a bridge (of a single arch) of one hundred and ten feet span. It is now on board a vessel coming from Yorkshire to London, where it is to be erected. It is this only thing that keeps me in Europe. . . .

The bridge, as portable as common bars of iron, was drayed to a field at Lesson Green, near Paddington, a suburb of London. It was finished and open to the public in August. Anyone who paid a shilling might examine it, walk across it, or test it. He could drive a carriage or a wagon across it, if he wished. It was twenty-four–feet wide! Four teams and wagons could pass each other upon it without waiting! It had been constructed without a single wooden timber and its arch had no need for a stone pier to support it! A constant stream of visitors came and paid their shillings to see it. The first iron bridge in the world! It was talked about as "The Wonder of London." Members of the Royal Society, members of Parliament, industrialists, and owners of ironworks came to study it.

Paine watched the seemingly never-ending queue of humanity that was attracted to Lesson Green. His dream was finally achieved. His iron bridge was built. It was a geometrical spider web of iron ribs. Its arch was as mathematically precise as the segment of a perfect circle. He loved it best in the morning, before the first visitors arrived. At such a time, it was a thing of beauty. Beneath its arch, the crisscross pattern of iron ribs was like the latticework of destiny.

When September came, Paine left the bridge in care of his construction foreman. There was nothing more that he could do in Paddington and Clio Rickman had written, urging him to come to London.

Almost immediately on his arrival there, he was invited to an informal dinner given by the English Revolution Society. The only woman to attend the dinner was introduced to Paine as Mary Wollstonecraft. She was escorted by William Godwin and insisted that she be seated next to Paine. Just turned thirty, with inquisitive grey eyes and a tumbled mass of blond hair, a few strands of which she permitted to fall down upon her forehead as though to shorten the brow, she seemed to possess both the gentleness of femininity and the spirit of an indomitable man. "I have read your essays on women's rights," she confided to Paine in a slightly husky voice. "I am deeply gratified by both your opinions and your boldness in expressing them. I do not know how they were received in America but here, . . ." She waved a hand about the table to indicate that she was the only member of her sex present. "I am at work on a feminist document. I shall call it *Vindication of the Rights of Women*. Would you care to see the rough draft?"

The general talk at dinner began innocuously enough by a reading, by a William Blake, of his two latest poems. It drifted into a discussion of monarchy, touched upon the revolution in France, and ended in an evaluation of Burke's *Reflections on the French Revolution*, which had just been published. It was suggested that Paine write a refutation of the pamphlet. Paine glanced about and smiled. He needed little encouragement for a task to which he had already committed himself.

He found little opportunity to write at Rickman's, however, so he soon took lodgings in Islington, a sleepy suburb of London. The Old Angel Inn was remote and not easy to reach by coach, and, once Paine had impressed upon its owner that his presence was not to be disclosed, he put himself to work in the privacy of his rooms. He had leafed through Burke's pamphlet in London but had never found the time to evaluate it properly. Now he turned to its very beginning and studied it carefully.

The book's contents angered him and yet he was drawn to it as though he were obsessed by its very phrases. He read where he opened it at random:

> Believe me, sir, those who attempt to level, never equalize.
> No rotation, no appointment by lot, no mode of election . . . can be generally good in a government. The occupation of a hairdresser, or a tallow chandler, cannot be a matter of honor to any person, to say nothing of a number of other more servile employments. . . . The state suffers oppression if such as they, either individually or collectively, are permitted to rule.

In a footnote at the bottom of the page, Paine read, with mounting fury, the quotations that Burke had chosen as a precedent for the exclusion of the common man from a voice in government:

> *Ecclesiasticus, chapter xxxviii, verses 24–25*: The wisdom of a learned man cometh by opportunity of leisure; and he that hath little business shall become wise. How can he get wisdom that holdeth the plough, and that glorieth in the goad; that driveth oxen; and is occupied in their labors; and whose talk is of bullocks?

> *Verse 33*: They shall not be sought for in the public counsel, nor sit in the high congregation.

Burke had reached into the Protestant Apocrypha for his precedents, as though all the world looked to England for an example of government and to the Anglican Church as an authority on the word of God!

Paine worked on his answer to Burke for practically the rest of the year. He refused to leave a single paragraph unchallenged in Burke's defense of inherited wealth and landed property. At one point, as he read Burke's defense of the church, he was touched by nostalgia. Burke had written:

> The monks are lazy. Be it so. Suppose them no otherwise employed than by singing in the choir. They are as usefully employed as those who sing upon the stage. They are as usefully employed as if they worked from dawn to dark in the innumerable, servile, degrading, unseemly, unmanly, and often most unwholesome and pestiferous occupations, to which, by the social economy, so many wretches are inevitably doomed. If it were not generally pernicious to disturb the natural course of things, ...

"How now!" cried Paine, as though someone were in the room with him. "It is then pernicious to disturb the natural course of things! And who is to say what is a natural course and what is not?" Suddenly, in his mind's eye, he could see the Cluniac monks circling the parapet of their grey stone abbey, once again. Nothing disturbed the unhurried stride of their sandaled feet. From the embrasure of his childhood sanctuary, in the belfry of the Anglican church, he could see once again the idiot in the stocks ... dead for having trespassed in a field. The monks could see him too, would they but raise their tonsured heads ... and disturb the "natural course of things."

Paine completed his refutation of Burke's *Reflections on the French Revolution* before the Christmas holidays. He entitled it *The Rights of Man* and dedicated the book "To George

Washington, President of the United States of America."

To his dismay, however, he at first found it difficult to find a publisher. Rickman offered to do so, but Paine did not wish him involved. He had already been marked as a political offender by his reprints of Paine's writings. To Paine's surprise, a man named Johnson, a former school rector turned printer, volunteered to publish it. A mild-mannered man, given little to debate, he prided himself upon his tolerance and liberalism; so, despite a sense of misgiving, Paine entrusted the manuscript to his care, only two weeks later to find the little publisher in a state of great agitation. He had put the entire book in type and then, after having printed a few copies, his courage had suddenly failed him. "You read the manuscript," insisted Paine. "No one coerced you into this."

"I know . . . I know. . . . But I did not realize its full intent until I read it in actual print."

"What intent?"

Johnson leafed excitedly through a freshly bound copy. "Why . . . why it contains an actual *Declaration of the Rights of Man and of Citizens* by the National Assembly of France. How do I know this declaration is authentic?"

"Because I have a copy that was sent to me by the Assembly. Did you think I dreamed it up?" He was on the verge of confessing that it was the product of his pen, in collaboration with Condorcet and Dumont.

Johnson stood first on one foot and then on the other and protested, "The book is treasonous." When he saw anger touch Paine's face, he riffled through the pages, stopped, and read aloud:

> When it is laid down as a maxim, that A KING CAN DO NO WRONG, it places him in a state of similar security with that of idiots and persons insane, and responsibility is out of the question with respect to himself.

"And you do not believe this to be true?" cried Paine.

"It is not a matter of truth, Mr. Paine. It is a matter of treason."

"And I say that you do not know what the word 'treason' means!"

"And here . . . here," protested Johnson:

> When there is a part in a government that can do no wrong, it implies that it does nothing.

"And here . . . it says here:

> It is somewhat curious to observe that, although the people of England have been in the habit of talking about kings, it is always a foreign house of kings; hating foreigners, yet governed by them. It is now the House of Brunswick, one of the petty tribes of Germany . . .

Paine glared at Johnson and the publisher defended, "Oh, it is true . . . it is true. To know it is one thing. But to print it . . ."

"What did you think when you first read it? Before it was in print? Did you think it but a witch's tale to frighten idiots?" He tore the book from the printer's hands. "Have you other copies? I would have them all! And my manuscript! Five weeks lost. Five full weeks! Thank God I am not a violent man, Johnson, or I would lay hands upon you."

In England, *The Rights of Man* was a still an unspun web upon a printer's disassembled type, but the framework of those rights was being fashioned in France, and Paine's very soul urged him to help further in its construction. So, at the suggestion of Mary Wollstonecraft, he entrusted the publication of his book to William Godwin and two new friends, Thomas Holcroft and Thomas Brand Hollis. Partially relieved of its concern, he went to Paris.

He found Lafayette in a despondent mood. "I do not concern myself regarding the Constitution or the Assembly," he confided. "It is the King and the Queen. They are on my conscience. King Louis and Queen Marie Antoinette are still in the Tuileries, but they are prisoners and I their jailer. I do not like it! Each week there are letters addressed to the National Assembly, in His Majesty's hand . . . complaining of his suffering and expressing his convictions that he alone can make his people happy."

Paine studied his dejected friend. Worry had begun to crease his brow and shadow his gray eyes. He seemed to have aged. "You have a deep sense of loyalty to your King?"

Lafayette shook his head. "You know my disregard of *aristocratie*. Was not I among the first to relinquish my title? No, Thomas, it is not loyalty that troubles me. It is that I am a soldier and not a *geôlier*. But two weeks ago, King Louis gave notice that he would enjoy the warmer weather at Saint-Cloud for a few days. He has suffered much from *le catarrhe* lately." He glanced at Paine to see if he could catch an expression of sympathy for the King.

"It was immediately impressed upon me . . . oh, it does not matter by whom . . ." He waved a still-delicate hand as a gesture. "It was impressed upon me that the King may not go to Saint-Cloud. He might make off to Compiègne and then, perhaps, to the frontier. How does one tell a king what he may or may not do, eh Thomas? They do not trust him. They do not trust even me!"

The next weeks were busy ones for Paine. Godwin, Holcroft, and Hollis had not been idle. J. S. Jordan, a London printer, had agreed to publish *The Rights of Man*. A first edition had been rushed from the press, offered to the public on March 13, 1791, at a price of three shillings per copy, and immediately became a best seller. Enthusiastically, Paine turned over the distribution and sale of his new book to the Constitutional Society and advised them that they could keep all of the proceeds that would accrue.

He instructed that fifty copies be given to a Mr. Green of Portsmith, England—a friend who was about to sail for America. They were to be entrusted to Washington, to be distributed among the president's friends—and Paine's. A copy should be given to Thomas Jefferson, who was now Secretary of State, Vice-President John Adams, Secretary of the Treasury Alexander Hamilton, Senator James Monroe, Samuel Adams, Patrick Henry, John Hancock, Nathaniel Greene, Henry Laurens, Dr. Rush, David Rittenhouse, etc., etc., etc.

To the surprise of those who were not familiar with Paine's passion for getting things done, translated copies of *The Rights of Man* were offered to the Parisians in May. Paine had given François Lathenas, a deputy to the Assembly, a London copy of the pamphlet and urged him to translate it into French. He met Lathenas a few days later, in a café in the Cordeliers district. Condorcet and Nicolas de Bonneville were with him, as was a swarthy heavy-set young man who was introduced as Achille Duchatelet. The son of a French duke, he preferred posing as a commoner for the sake of "equality." He had a slow smile, a frank and open countenance, and dark eyes that seemed at peace with the world.

Lathenas informed Paine of their plans. The four, along with Jacques Brissot, who could not come this night, were about to organize a republican club that they would call *Société Républicaine*. Under Bonneville's direction, they would issue a publication in the cause of liberty—an anti-Royalist paper that they would call *Le Républicain*. They would print a portion of *The Rights of Man* in each issue.

"We have all read it," said Duchatelet, with his slow smile. "We cannot praise it enough."

Paine stared into his wineglass for a long moment before he answered them. They were friends and he must not offend them. He was in their country. They were not in his, as Lafayette had once been, standing humbly on the Statehouse steps. "I am flattered, gentlemen," he finally said. "I accept with thanks, a membership in your new club; but I cannot wait to have *The Rights of Man* piddled out to your countrymen in small weekly installments. When nature drops a child from its mother's womb, the parent's breasts are already engorged with milk. The suckling cannot wait for its sustenance to be dribbled, drop by drop, into its mouth."

With the persistence of the obsessed, Paine combed the printers of Paris. On the Rue Hautefeuille, he found a printer, Monsieur Buisson, who agreed to engage a translator for *The Rights of Man* and to publish it. The translator, a scholarly man by the name of François Soule, timidly signed his work F. S. but did not hesitate to translate the dedication to Washington or the special preface that Paine wrote for the French edition. As he had done with his *Common Sense* and his *Crisis* pamphlets, Paine hounded poor Buisson until the work was rushed from the press. It won immediate acclaim in Paris, spread to the provinces, and by June was being read in Boulogne and Lille with excitement, in Rennes and Poitiers with interest, and in Bordeaux and Toulouse with an undercurrent of antipathy.

Early in the morning, on June 21, Paine, still a guest at Lafayette's, was awakened from a sound sleep. Someone had burst into his bedchamber. As he tried to rouse himself, a hand was laid on his shoulder and shook him. It was Lafayette. He was holding a flickering candle in the semidarkness.

"Thomas! Thomas! Their Majesties have flown! The royal family have fled and no one knows where!"

Paine seemed undisturbed. He sat up and studied Lafayette's white face. "Perhaps it is as well."

"Are you mad? I am already mistrusted and accused of Loyalist sentiments. Now they will howl that it was I who arranged the flight!"

Suddenly the loud sound of bells being rung in a nearby

church tower assailed their ears. In half a moment, the clang of other bells joined them. The air in the warm room vibrated with the brazen clanging of the tocsin. Paine rushed to a window and drew aside the drapes. The first pink bands of dawn were in the sky. Below, the garden was still filled with shadows and a grey mist.

"Last night," insisted Lafayette, "on a prescribed round, I found the King and Queen at cards with the Comte and Comtesse de Provence. They even asked if I would sit and talk a while."

His fists, the only part of him that had not grown fleshy, clenched and tightened. Suddenly he burst out, "I shall go to the Tuileries and find out the worst."

"Wait!" cried Paine. "Wait! I'll go with you."

By the time they left the Lafayette garden, it was as though they had awakened at sunrise and stepped into the city at high noon. All Paris was awake! Its streets were crowded with people, its cafés bustled with excitement, carriages and coaches rushed here and there. When they reached the Hotel de Ville, they encountered a milling mob. There was an uproar of raised voices. Some shouted that the King and the Queen had abandoned Paris in order to join the Royalist garrison in Metz. Others cried that the royal family had already reached the banks of the Rhine. There were angry outcries that Marie Antoinette—that despicable *Autrichienne,* that *Madame Déficit*—was hurrying the royal family all the way to her father's court in Austria!

Suddenly Lafayette cried, "I shall go after them! I did not stop their going but, by God, I shall force their return!" Paine grasped Lafayette's arm, but he tore away.

In search of more news, Paine sought the Palais Royal. When he reached its stone arches, he found a larger gathering —a mob that was splashed with impatient violence, like a touchhole that waited for a spark. Hastily summoned guards had stationed themselves in front of every entrance. A platform was being constructed by placing boards across four empty wine barrels. An officer sprang upon it, waved his sword, and cried: "Attention! Attention! By order of the National Assembly . . . there are to be no demonstrations. No demonstrations!"

When Paine returned to Lafayette's, he began work on a manifesto to show that the King's flight would be a crisis only if the people made it one. He had but outlined its draft when he was filled with a sense of misgiving. It was as though a chill wind had swept into the room and filled the air with foreboding. The French, roused from their beds in the night, were not like Americans . . . people to be led. The mob outside the Palais Royal had been made up of men with haggard faces and empty bellies. Gentleness had been flayed, long ago, from their lean and twisted forms. Their very souls were filled with a vengeance against a lifelong oppression!

Lafayette returned by evening. His legs could hardly support his weariness. His eyes were bloodshot. He dropped into a chair and cried, when he had recovered enough breath, "The very earth has swallowed them up! Troops of horsemen on all the roads . . . nothing! I searched all the way to Montmirail. If they were on their way to Metz, I would have overtaken them!"

"You have done your duty, and more. Let the pursuit die. I assure you, by tomorrow the citizens of France will say to each other, 'We have no King, yet we have slept soundly enough.'"

"*Vous comprenez mal!* I am responsible for them. They were in my charge! I am already suspect of being in secret accord with them."

"If you will but attune your ears to sounds other than those of a fleeing carriage, you will notice that the tocsin has ceased. No single bell is being rung. I can hear neither the sound of hurrying feet nor a raised voice in the street. It is the calm after the passage of a storm. And who knows how long it may endure? Would you bring back the tumult and the violence? Perhaps bloodshed? And for what . . . to keep a throneless king and queen prisoners in a palace? To what end, Gilbert? To what end?"

Lafayette shook his head in distraction.

Late the next day, Paris was filled with the news that the royal family had been intercepted. "It is true!" cried Lafayette. "It is true! I was right all the time. They were on their way to Metz! I turned back too soon. Who would think that King Louis would have the fortitude to rock in a berline for twenty-two incessant hours? I go to escort them back!"

Paine watched as a servant helped Lafayette struggle into his boots. "I shall go with you."

"*Partez*!" cried Lafayette with a sudden burst of anger. "Were there no one else to ride with me, you are the last man I would take! Is it not disgrace enough that the King has disguised himself as a common valet, the Queen as a governess, the children with false names? Must I take you to see common hands affront the King of France? So that you may write of it in your pamphlets?" He rushed from the room and as quickly rushed back. "Forgive me, Thomas," he cried. "I am distraught. My spirit belongs to liberty, but my blood belongs to the royal house of France."

News of the apprehension of the King inundated Paris like a rising tide. Not wishing to finish the manifesto until the King's return was assured, Paine frequented the cafés near the Tuileries where many of the deputies gathered. With careful sifting, he pieced together the facts. The escape had not been attempted on the spur of the moment but had been well planned and well executed. A huge berline had been built especially for the flight. King Louis had made arrangements for a chain of military escorts from Pont de Sommeville, northwestward as far as Montmedi. It was the King's insistence upon his protection that had alarmed the countryside. At every post village and town a troop of dragoons had gathered,

[389]

for no evident purpose. They had sat on their horses, watching the road to the south. When a heavy coach had rolled by, rocking on its springs, they had galloped away in its wake.

Paine spent most of Saturday on the right bank of the Seine. People lined the Rue de Rivoli and the Rue Royale to the north in order to witness the return of the King. Some had been there since early morning. Others had gone home and returned, fortified with little paper cornucopias of lunch. It was five days since the royal family had fled. It was three days since they had been apprehended at the village of Varennes, 150 miles from Paris. It could not be much longer, for the returning berline had been sighted at Bondy.

Paine threaded his way toward the crowded gardens of the Tuileries. It was seven o'clock, but the heat of the day had not abated. Everyone waited in silence or spoke in whispers. Paine had seen a large placard in the Rue St. Antoine:

Silence! Whosoever insults King Louis shall be caned; whosoever applauds him shall be hanged!

Directly across from the Tuileries gardens, Paine noticed Robespierre and Marat. They were standing side by side. Slender Robespierre looked as though he had just left his tailor. His breeches and his coat were without a wrinkle. There was something different about him . . . and then Paine realized that he was wearing spectacles—green-tinted ones, it appeared.

Paine had not recognized Marat at first. He looked like a peasant. Instead of a stock, he had carelessly knotted a dyed kerchief under the open collar of his shirt. He had tied a soiled bandanna over his uncut black hair and wore a long cheap-looking coat and low boots. It was as though he were trying to exemplify the *egalité* that he had begun to declaim in his fast-growing revolutionary paper, *L'Ami du Peuple.*

Just as Paine crossed the Rue de Rivoli to join them, there

was the sound of horses and the first of the National Guards turned into the street from the Rue Royale. Paine could see the huge berline. Lafayette and his aide-de-camp were directly behind it. A full troop of National Guards clattered after them. The people were silent. One could not tell if they approved or were disappointed by the King's return.

Three yellow-clothed couriers had been bound atop the berline. At the sight of them, angry citizens rushed to the coach and tried to tear them to the ground. They pressed upon the coach from all sides, careless of being trodden underfoot by the rearing and plunging horses. The heavy berline rocked upon its springs. There was an order from Lafayette and the guardsmen drew their swords and dispelled the mob from the street.

The dust-covered berline was motionless. The frightened horses shivered and shook their traces. Paine could see the faces of the children within the coach. Their eyes, as dark as a squirrel's, were wide with fright. They were the royal children—the little Dauphin and the little Madame Royale. Their governess, Dame de Tourzel, was holding their hands but she, herself, was weeping. The King's round face was expressionless as he watched the rioters being driven from the coach. He waited, as though unconcerned, for the berline to move on. His eyes seemed to say, "Well, here I am. And now what would you do with me? After all, I am still the King!" In his flat hat, his inexpensive peruke, and his plain light coat, he seemed less a king than the valet he had represented himself to be. "He has spilled his royalty with his own hand," thought Paine. "Like wine from an overturned cup." At the signal from Lafayette, the coachman cracked his whip, the horses pushed against their breast collars, and the heavy berline creaked and plunged forward.

Paine felt a tug on his arm. It was Robespierre. The sunlight, filtering through his spectacles, made his eyes seem green. "And now, Monsieur Paine, you have just seen the end

[391]

of the flight to Metz. Like a serpent swallowing its own tail. What should we do with the King, Monsieur *Common Sense?* Depose him? What would you advise should be done with a king who needs to be guarded in his very bedchamber that he may stay and govern you?"

"The monarchy is lost," said Paine. "The King has deposed himself. I shall never understand for what purpose the Assembly wished him back. Unless, having him back, they intend to bray through his mouth."

"One could easily dislike you, Monsieur Paine. You seem to have a reverence for no single thing."

"For two things, Monsieur Robespierre. For truth and for God."

Robespierre's eyes clouded with anger. Marat's wide mouth was set in a sneer as he listened. A finger tortured a scab on his chin. *"Allons-nous,* Max!" he prodded Robespierre. "You waste your time with *un anglais."*

Paine hurried back to Lafayette's in order to make changes in his manifesto regarding the King's flight. Dashing after the royal family and forcing them to return had been a mistake! It was a stupid gesture of neither fealty nor rebellion. It would give birth to conditions and obligations for which compromises would be poor answers. His original draft was too mild . . . too calm. He sat up most of the night, writing a new manifesto.

When morning came, he rushed to find Lathenas in order to have it translated. Unable to find him, he sought out young Achille Duchatelet. Duchatelet, though he spoke and read English well enough, lacked the confidence to translate the manifesto. He insisted that they call upon Étienne Dumont for aid. He knew exactly where to find him. He would be having his *petit déjeuner* in a small café adjacent to the Cheval Noir, on the right bank, directly across the bridge from the Ile St. Louis. Had Monsieur Paine eaten? The café was patronized by the men of Champagne. The food was good.

They found Dumont at the café, as Duchatelet had said. He read the manifesto between sips of *café nature* and asked, "And what would you do with this . . . once it is translated, my friends?"

"We shall have it printed and plaster all of Paris with copies!" cried Paine.

"And the inside of your cell, perhaps? Have you consulted Lafayette, since he regards you, Monsieur Paine, with such esteem? President Sieyès, *non?*" And when they shook their heads, "Monsieur Paine, the law requires the signature of a citizen—a French citizen—on every paper that contains a political opinion."

"I shall sign it myself," cried Duchatelet.

Étienne Dumont pushed the written sheets across the table. "I am so much a Republican, messieurs, that I would wish what Monsieur Paine insists upon. But I am also so much a Frenchman that I consider it vulgar and undignified for even an American to refer to my King as Monsieur Louis Capet. You go too far, Monsieur Paine! And I go not with you! When it will be said that an impassioned American and a young madcap of the nobility rushed to change the government of France—perhaps the face of Europe—it will not be said that Étienne Dumont rushed blindly with them!"

In the end, Duchatelet translated the manifesto as best he could and signed his own name under the caption *Société Républicaine.* In the early morning hours of Friday, July 1, six days after the forced return of the King, the walls of Paris were plastered with printed copies of the manifesto.

At noon, Paine and Duchatelet went, arm in arm, to see how well the hired distributors had done their work. All along the Rue de Rivoli, in front of the Tuileries gardens, and as far as the Rue St. Antoine, crowds were gathered in front of the manifestoes. Those who could not read stood silent and alert, while others read aloud Paine's inflammatory phrases. Along the grey stone quays that fronted the Seine—from the

Quai de l'Hotel de Ville, across from the towers of Notre Dame, to the Quai des Tuileries—semicircles of men and women ebbed and flowed in front of freshly posted placards. Despite the heat, Paine and his friend crossed to the left bank of the Seine and strolled up Saint Michel to the Luxembourg Palace. Even here, the manifestoes had been well distributed.

The following morning, Paine and Duchatelet were summoned to the National Assembly. The manifesto had created a furor and had been angrily denounced. Upon seeing Paine, Malouet, a Royalist deputy, rose to his feet, waved a manifesto above his head, and cried, "I tore this down! This pack of lies! This incendiary flame of revolt and civil disobedience from the very doors of the Assembly! It is a disgrace to the National Assembly . . . a dishonor to Frenchmen . . . an insult to His Majesty, who has neither abdicated nor been denounced."

As he sought for additional phrases, Martineau, a deputy from the city, rose and cried in a nasal voice, "I insist upon the prosecution of Achille Duchatelet and this . . . this Monsieur Paine! A compatriot of his, a Monsieur Morris, has assured me that it was Paine's pen that drafted this . . . this diabolical manifesto. I insist upon the prosecution of the entire *Société Républicaine!*"

Paine whispered to Duchatelet and Achille rose and faced the rostrum, upon which Emmanuel Sieyès and the two secretaries were seated. "Monsieur President. Monsieur Paine would like to know—is the Assembly aware how many members there are in the *Société Républicaine*? When Deputy Martineau says that the entire society should be punished, does he wish the Assembly to prosecute ten men or 100? Or perhaps 1,000."

There was a hush in the Assembly. No one had asked how many members the Republican Society comprised. No one suspected that there were but five members. Upon Paine's insistence, Duchatelet pressed his sudden advantage. With a touch of defiance in his voice he cried, "Monsieur President. If I may be permitted to read the manifesto . . . perhaps with a second attention to its . . ."

Deputies sprang to their feet in protest. Others cried, "Let him read it! Let him read it!" It seemed that some had not yet seen an actual copy. President Sieyès lifted a quieting hand and nodded to Duchatelet. Duchatelet glanced but once at Paine and, as the hall grew hushed, he read:

Brethren and fellow citizens:

The mutual confidence that prevailed amongst us during the time of the late King's escape, the indifference with which we beheld him return, are unequivocal proofs that the absence of a King is more desirable than his presence, and that he is not only a political superfluity, but a grievous burden, pressing hard on the whole nation.

He has abdicated the throne in having fled from his post. Abdication and desertion are not characterized by the length of absence, but by the single act of flight. In the present instance, the act is everything and the time is nothing.

The nation can never give back its confidence to a man who, false to his trust, perjured to his oath, conspires a clandestine flight, obtains a fraudulent passport, conceals a King of France under the disguise of a valet, directs his course toward a frontier covered with traitors and deserters, and evidently meditates a return into our own country with a force capable of imposing his own despotic laws.

With the words "false to his trust, perjured to his oath," there was a dissenting murmur. It grew in volume. Duchatelet glanced at Paine. Paine waved him on.

Whether ought his flight to be considered as his own act, or the act of those who fled with him? Was it a spontaneous resolution of his own, or was it inspired into him by others? The alternative is immaterial; whether fool or hypocrite, idiot or traitor, he has proved himself equally unworthy of the important functions that had been delegated to him.

In every sense that the question can be considered, the

reciprocal obligation that subsisted between us is dissolved. He holds no longer any authority. We owe him no longer obedience. We see him no more than an indifferent person; we can regard him only as Louis Capet.

With the words "Louis Capet," half the deputies sprang to their feet. Whether Republican or Royalist, whether commoner or titled aristocrat, none had ever heard His Majesty, King Louis XVI, called by the undignified bourgeois name of Louis Capet. True, it was his Christian name, but he was the King of France! The direct descendant of sixty kings! All eyes looked toward Duchatelet and Paine. Duchatelet bit his underlip in hesitation. "Read on," whispered Paine. "Read on! Look about you, friend Republican. There is indignation and outrage on every face, but I see violence in no single one. One can be angered by truth, but the anger cannot destroy it. Read on!"

> The history of France presents little else than a long series of public calamities that takes its source from the vices of the Kings: we have been the wretched victims that have never ceased to suffer either for them or by them. . . .

One by one, the deputies regained their seats. A low murmur, like a sea shell held to an ear, gathered in volume and then died away.

> What kind of office must that be in a government that requires for its execution neither experience nor ability? That may be abandoned to the desperate chance of birth, that may be filled by an idiot, a madman, or a tyrant, with equal effect as by the good, the virtuous, and the wise?

Paine recalled that he had written almost the same phrases in America, against the King of England. What did it matter? It was worth the repetition as long as there were those who had not read them or refused to accept them.

An office of this nature is a place of show, not of use. The grandeur of nations consists, not as kings pretend, in the splendor of thrones, but in a just disdain of those barbarous follies and crimes, which, under the sanction of royalty, have hitherto desolated Europe. . . .

When Duchatelet finished, a hush hung over the Assembly. The deputies looked to each other as though they waited for someone to cast the first stone. No deputy realized that Thomas Paine's manifesto had planted, within sight of all, the dragon's seed of their revolution.

29

DEEPLY DEPRESSED, Paine left Paris and arrived in London on Thursday, July 13, 1791, in order to attend the celebration of the success of *The Rights of Man* by the Constitutional Society. He did not go to Rickman's but registered at the White Bear Inn in Piccadilly. The next day, when he went to the Crown and Anchor, he was astounded by the throng standing outside the tavern doors and the dozens of old friends who had gathered to welcome him back. To his surprise, however, they seemed gloomy.

"There will be no meeting, Tom," Rickman explained. "The government has taken every precaution to prevent the celebration."

Paine looked toward the doors of the Crown and Anchor, but Rickman shook his head. "We have tried pleadings and arguments, Tom. The landlord has not only been intimidated but well rehearsed. He insists that the meeting has been too much advertised. He cannot accommodate so large a gathering. He does not want the publicity. He, personally, has no interest in the fall of French prisons."

There was a protesting murmur for a moment, and then the gathering began to fall back from the doors of the inn. A gang of ruffians had turned into the street. They were eight abreast and at least four deep. Some were armed with cudgels. Some carried broken branches from which the bark had been newly stripped. To Paine's amazement, three constables were at their head. He glanced about him. Mary Wollstonecraft was urging the gathering to make a stand. "No!" cried Paine. "No! A broken head will gain us nothing! To our homes! We shall meet elsewhere!"

Back at the White Bear Inn, Paine became filled with anger at what had happened. It was a denial of assembly! It was curtailment of free speech! It seemed that England, more than France, needed a Bill of Rights and a reformed constitution. *The Rights of Man* had concerned itself with an answer to Burke ... a defense of the revolution in France. He would write a sequel to it. He would defend human rights in general —the rights of man everywhere! It was not the remembrance of the armed brutes that disturbed him. It was the thought that government constables had evidently been paid to hire them and march at their head.

By the end of the following week he was so enthused by his progress that he wrote to Washington:

London, July 21, 1791

Dear Sir:

The work (*The Rights of Man*) has a run beyond anything that has been published in this country on the subject of government, and the demand continues. The same fate follows me here as *at first* in America; strong friends, and violent enemies. But as I have got the ear of the country, I shall go on and at least show them, what is a novelty here, that there can be a person beyond the reach of corruption.

After the establishment of the American Revolution, it did not appear to me that any object could arise great enough to

[398]

engage me a second time; but I now experience that principle is not confined to time or place. I have another work on hand that I intend shall be my last, for I long much to return to America.

I do most sincerely wish that there were some person in this country that could usefully and successfully attract the public attention, and leave me with a satisfied mind to the enjoyment of quiet life, but it is painful to see errors and abuses and sit down a senseless spectator.

Paine spent the rest of July and all of August working on *The Rights of Man: Part II.* He learned that, despite John Adams' insistence upon a government by "the rich, the well-born, and the able," Jefferson, Madison, and Randolph were trying to find a place for him in the Washington Administration. He considered returning to America. He was now fifty-four. It was time to go home! He did not know that Washington, anxious to free America from the remaining British garrisons, was about to offer to England a most liberal commercial treaty to which he would strenuously object, particularly since a secret mission to achieve it had been entrusted to, of all men, Gouverneur Morris!

When the first portion of his book was finished, he read it to a circle of friends at Rickman's home. He did not like to address an audience but enjoyed the attention and adulation of a small group. He looked about and said, "In this second part of *The Rights of Man,* I am permitting myself an introduction. I hope you will forgive my linking exact geometry with indefinite politics." He held the sheets of his manuscript to the light and read:

What Archimedes said of mechanical powers may be applied to Reason and Liberty: "Had we," said he, "a place to stand upon, we might raise the world."

The Revolution of America presented in politics what was only theory in mechanics.

No sooner did the American governments display themselves to the world than despotism felt a shock, and man began to contemplate redress.

All the monarchical governments are military. War is their trade, plunder and revenue their objects. While such governments continue, peace has not the absolute security of a day. . . .

Paine was tired long before he finished reading the manuscript. He let the pages drop to his lap and suggested, "Another time, gentlemen? I fear it is too lengthy for a single night's reading."

When the guests had left, Clio joined Paine in a nightcap. "Do you know a Mr. Chalmers, Tom?"

Paine shook his head. He knew so many people who insisted that they knew him.

"He is an American, but he claims that he knew you here, in England, when you both were young."

"In Thetford? In Lewes?"

"He is not explicit. He is writing a biography of you—in the pay of the government. I have been advised that it is being monstrously overdone. Perhaps filled with lies."

Paine raised his glass.

"I am used to lies by the British Government. So are all of us in America. Ask Washington about the Bew letters, put out in New York by the British to smirch his reputation in 1778. Lies do not concern me."

Late in January, however, he began to realize that the enmity of the British Government was not something to be taken lightly. He received a letter from the prospective publisher of *The Rights of Man: Part II,* accompanied by the manuscript itself. He felt he should advise Paine, the publisher wrote, that the authorities were trying to suppress publication of the book for the following reasons:

The opinions expressed in the manuscript were dangerous and might incite riots.

[400]

Its publication might involve prosecution by the government.

There might be trials and the confiscation of property.

Paine had dedicated the book to a Frenchman for whom the British Government had little regard.

Paine unwrapped the manuscript. He had dedicated the book to Lafayette, but there was nothing in the dedication that should offend England.

Damn the British Government, he thought. Were the lives of men so expendable in England that they should be forced to labor like beasts with no thought to their ignorance, their miseries, and their spiritless existence? Even the trees of the forest were not flagrantly hewed!

He rewrapped the manuscript and rushed to Jordan, the Fleet Street publisher who had brought out his first *The Rights of Man* a year ago.

Jordan glanced at the manuscript and shoved it back across the desk.

"It has been a year of great change, Mr. Paine. When I published *The Rights of Man,* there seemed few who knew of it. Despite the outcry by the press, no government stigma was attached to it. But now ... now every publisher has been made aware of this manuscript. I have been informed not to publish it, except at great risk." Impelled by curiosity, he lifted a page and read at random—first a paragraph, then another, then a full page, until at last he looked up from his reading. He appeared fascinated.

"I have changed my mind," he said slowly. "I cannot say 'no' to such a book. I shall print it and bring it out."

The Rights of Man: Part II was brought out late in February, 1792, and, almost immediately, a biography of Paine was offered to the English public. It was entitled *The Life of Thomas Paine, Author of The Rights of Man,* by Francis Oldys, A.M., of the University of Pennsylvania.

Paine purchased a copy and read its contents avidly. He was

described in it as a monstrously vile character, but the vilification was so overdone that he felt it would not convince readers attracted only out of sheer curiosity. He did not mind a scurrilous biography calling him a congenital liar and a crook, but it hurt when it touched upon tender portions of his life. The book claimed that, when he left Sandwich, where he had failed as a staymaker, he had sold the furniture of the cottage, although it had not belonged to him. It described how he had slipped away from Sandwich with his first wife, Mary Lambert, in April, 1760, "carrying the stays of a customer and a stove belonging to the house." He was saddened with nostalgia. The years had gone by so swiftly. He was filled with bitter anger when the author blatantly hinted that Mary Lambert's death was due to her husband's "ill treatment."

It did not take Paine long to learn that the biography's author was in reality George Chalmers, a clerk in the office of Lord Hawksbury.

By the end of April, *The Rights of Man: Part II* was having an unprecedented sale. The Tory press screamed its denunciations of Paine's "ideas" so loudly that Paine's friends, fearful that he might be harmed, perhaps murdered by some hired ruffian, whisked him off to Bromley. There, one evening, Rickman and William Blake brought the news that publisher Jordan had been served with a summons. He was to appear in court and face a charge of having printed and circulated seditious literature. "He is frightened out of his wits," said Clio. "It is rumored that he has agreed to plead guilty and will make no attempt to defend himself."

Paine hurried to London only to find that no argument or promise could influence Jordan to offer a defense. He had lost his courage and had turned everything over to the prosecutor's office.

Paine returned to Rickman's and waited for the inevitable. On May 21, a royal proclamation was issued against the writing, printing, selling, and circulating of seditious publications, such as Paine's *The Rights of Man*. Paine himself was served with a summons.

From Henry Dundas, Secretary of the Home Office, Paine secured a copy of the complaint on which his indictment was based. It covered forty-one hand-written pages and he read carefully the innumerable quotations that the Crown had decided were seditious and treasonous. Treason indeed, when he no longer considered himself an English subject but an American!

Paine showed the copy of the indictment to Robert Frost and Joel Barlow. Barlow, who was engaged in translating Count de Volney's anticlerical *Ruins of Empires,* shook his head. "Leave, Tom," he advised. "Go to France. Or go back to America."

Frost agreed with him. "This can mean only imprisonment. Perhaps, even death."

Paine shook his head. "They shall not gag me! They can neither bribe me nor intimidate me and, unless they kill me, they shall not silence me! Let us have our day in court. Unless they drag me from it, I shall prove that English royalty costs too much ... that the moral obligation of providing for old age, helpless infancy, and poverty is far superior to that of supplying the invented wants of courtly extravagance, ambition, and intrigue!"

"You must not stay," advised Barlow. "I shall say it again and again. You must not stay!"

When Paine went with Frost to the court of the King's Bench, on June 8, prepared to make his defense, they were informed that the case had been postponed until December, six months away!

The English gentry were furious, for, in *The Rights of Man: Part II,* Paine had written:

The aristocracy are not the farmers who work the land and raise the produce, but are the mere consumers of the rent; and, when compared with the active world, are the drones, a seraglio of males, who neither collect the honey nor form the hive, but exist only for lazy enjoyment.

Yet the royal proclamation seemed to have no effect upon the secret distribution of *The Rights of Man: Part II.* Cheap paperback copies of the book were seen everywhere. It was rumored that they were being brought out by a Thomas "Clio" Rickman, a bookseller and bookbinder, in cooperation with a D. H. Symonds, a printer of Paternoster Row.

As a result, during the rest of the summer, a well paid-for campaign was begun against Paine and all his writings. Bonfires were made of his confiscated books. Tavern loungers and ex-jailbirds were hired to burn him in effigy on village greens and at country crossroads. Toughs and ruffians, bribed with sixpence and free mugs of ale, threatened anyone who dared to defend him in any public place, while the government instituted a prosecution against Rickman and Symonds for printing and distributing copies of the "seditious" book.

In the midst of all this, Paine was surprised by an unexpected visitor from Paris—Achille Audibet. Paine knew him slightly, having met him at Madame Roland's. Audibet was now almost effusive with his praise of *The Rights of Man.* "Come over and you will see," he promised. "In Paris, the book is like an *apéritif* at every café table." He drew an official-looking paper from his pocket and gave the document to Paine. He put his arms about him, affectionately, and kissed him first upon one cheek and then upon the other.

"He is now an honorary citizen of France," Audibet explained to the watching Rickmans' He indicated the paper in Paine's hand. "Monsieur Paine ... *Citoyen* Paine." He held up a hand with its thumb hidden against the palm. "Four departments have chosen you to represent them, as a deputy, at the newly formed National Convention." He folded the extended fingers, one by one. *"Le Pas de Calais, le Somme, le Puy de Dôme, et le Oise.* You may represent only one and so . . . you will select my *Pas de Calais, non?* You will honor us!"

Paine unfolded the document. Audibet watched him struggle with the French. "May I, Monsieur? It is signed by representatives of the nine communes and endorsed by Louvet."

> Come, friend of the people, to swell the number of patriots in an assembly that will decide the destiny of a great people, perhaps of the human race. The happy period you have predicted for the nation has arrived. Come! Do not deceive their hope!

Suddenly William Blake and Robert Frost burst into the room. Frost rushed to Paine's side and cried, "The Home Office has issued a warrant for your arrest! Officers of the Crown are on their way, here, to execute it!"

"But what of our defense, Robert?" exclaimed Rickman.

Frost glanced about him. "Believe me, Clio," he cried. "There is no defense that can save him. If our friend stays, he stays to his death!"

Audibet rushed to Paine and shook him by the arms. " *Prenez qarde!*" he cried. Do not let them do this to you. Let us leave. *Tout de suite, Monsieur Paine. Tout de suite!*"

By early morning, Robert Frost, Audibet, and Paine reached Dover, where they could board a boat for Calais. A small, crosschannel boat was bobbing at the wharf, its unfurled sails heavy with mist and a light rain that had begun to fall from a windless sky. The hawsers had been cast off, but the boat had been unable to get under way. Audibet and Paine hurried aboard just as two small rowboats began to tow the ship out into the channel. They leaned against the rail and watched as the boat slipped sluggishly from the wharf. Frost stood in the drizzle and waved to them. Suddenly two riders raced through the town and pulled up at the wharf. The flanks of their horses steamed in the rain. They were the King's constables. One waved a drawn sword, while the others stood upright in his stirrups and shook a scroll at the boat.

"*Ma foi*!" cried Audibet. "*Ma foi*! Destiny has just spared you for the sake of France!"

A whisper of wind bellowed the wet sails and the boat got under way. The tugging rowboats cast away the slack ropes and rowed off. Paine lifted his collar against the light rain. In a few moments the cliffs of Dover, where he had once worked as a staymaker, were lost in the grey sky. . . .

Paine's arrival at Calais was very different from his departure from Dover. Baron de Cloots met the channel boat as it drifted into the old harbor, a battery was fired, and the townspeople gathered on the quay. There were cheers, shouts of welcome, and waving flags—the new red, white, and blue tricolor of France. A troop of light-horsemen escorted the carriage that drove Paine, Audibet, and Baron de Cloots to la Place d'Armes. The baron now insisted upon being called Anacharsis Cloots. He had adopted the name Anacharsis from a character in a philosophical novel by Jean-Jacques Barthelemy.

At the Place d'Armes, two columns of soldiers were drawn up to welcome them. The officer in charge presented Paine with a National Cockade and the mayor's attractive young wife was given the honor of placing it on Paine's hat. She delivered a short rehearsed speech in which she thanked him for his efforts on behalf of liberty, equality, and France. She concluded it with a kiss and an affectionate embrace. The townspeople, their spirits undaunted by a light rain, shouted themselves hoarse.

In the evening, Paine attended a meeting of the Constitutional Society of Calais, where the president presented him, embraced him as the representative of *le Pas de Calais,* and took him to a theatrical performance where his box had been decorated with large letters in both French and English: The Author of *The Rights of Man.* After this there had been a hastily arranged banquet in his honor, so that when he returned to his hotel room it was very late.

Nevertheless, he had scarcely fallen asleep when he was awakened by a discreet knocking on his door. He opened it to find Cloots, with a finger to his lips. Half asleep, Paine groped in the room and lit a candle, but Cloots bent over and blew out the flame.

"I came to talk . . . not to see. I am not drunk. And what I have to say is best listened to in the dark. Go home, Tom Paine. Go home!"

Paine was startled. There was a long moment of silence and then Cloots confessed, "I would go home myself, but that I have none now. I dreamed of a universal republic. I insisted that I was a citizen of the world, and now the French have circumscribed a smaller and smaller domain for me until my world will end in a plot of earth. They will lay my severed head on my chest and stuff my throat with grass. Go home, Tom Paine! Do you have a drink?"

"It was not what you said to me this evening."

"Ah, this evening . . . today we played a game. Like actors voicing the lines of a play they did not write. But this is almost tomorrow and the play is done."

"I have been elected a delegate to the Convention and I shall attend it."

"The Convention . . . ah, yes, the National Convention. A bastard child, ripped out from the expiring womb of the Assembly! And the Assembly, Tom Paine. What of the Assembly? You do not ask why it was disbanded. Has not the news of the massacres reached you in England or do you, like myself, wear a mask?"

Paine shook his head in the dark.

It was as though Cloots, with cat's eyes, could see its motion. "What! More than a week and England has not heard? Have the ports of France, then, been so closely guarded? Or has the terror sewed our lips with cobbler's thread?"

Paine rose to get them drinks, but Cloots stretched out a

restraining hand. "I am sober, Paine. Speaking of it has sobered me and I drink no more this night. One would think Paris insane. Everyone plots to seize control of the municipal government of Paris and establish a Commune. Twenty-five million people in France and they think only of Paris! It is as though Paris is the heart of France and whoever makes it throb governs the entire nation!"

There was no silencing Cloots. It was as though what he knew must be drained from his mind and spat from his throat. "Do not think the Girondist Ministry not at fault," he insisted. "Inspired by Roland, encouraged by Manon in order to support their tottering power, they summoned to Paris such a band of cutthroats as the world has never seen. A Pole, Lazowski, was hired to bring the unemployed from Marseilles. Instead, he brought a scum of criminals that were not even French. They were homeless brigands that had been vomitted from the prisons of Greece and Genoa and Sicily and Corsica! They had no more respect for rights or life itself than aroused beasts! There were more than 300 of them and, by the time they brought with them the drunken dregs from the Faubourgs St. Antoine and St. Marceau, their number swelled to more than 500. No sooner had they arrived in Paris than Marat sought out the treacherous Lazowski and made a pact with him. A pact with him and the Paris Commune!"

"Marat?" Paine could not believe it.

"Marat. Yes, vile Marat! He appointed himself head of a Committee of Surveillance. He was determined to catch the Girondists in a net of self-proclaimed authority and have them massacred by the very beasts that they, themselves, had invited to Paris!"

"And Danton?"

"Danton! How well do you know Danton? He whispers when he speaks of his Gabrielle, but he roars when he demands the right to guide the destiny of France! He opposed

[408]

Marat's intrigue at first. That much I grant him. But in the end he consented. More than 4,000 persons were arrested in four days. The orders were stamped with but one word: 'suspect' ... 'suspect!' ... 'SUSPECT!' " He stamped his fist onto an open palm with each word's reiteration.

"Suspect? Suspect of what? Suspect by whom?"

Cloots shrugged his shoulders. It was an unseen gesture in the dark. "Marat and his Committee of Surveillance furnished the Sections with lists of 'suspects,' lists of those who opposed him. The names of citizens without political attachments were added to the lists. They were suggested by private animosities, by vindictiveness, and by jealousies. Many of the innocents were priests, some were aristocrats, most were ordinary citizens. They were herded into the prisons like cattle. Has Achille Audibet told you nothing? I cannot believe it! He was in Paris! I was with him during the terrible days of the massacres!"

Cloots sat, for a long moment, in silence. It was as though Paine were alone in the dark. Then he said, "Forgive me, Thomas. I must speak of it. I must spit out what I saw or I must choke on the very phlegm of its remembrance. Thank God that you were in England! Had you returned ten days sooner ... But five days sooner ... Once the political 'suspects' and the 'innocents' were imprisoned, there was the problem of dispatching them. This, Thomas ... this is what now motivated the secret meetings of the guiding minds of France—how to murder 4,000 citizens of the new Republic. How to massacre 4,000 members of the human race, without an accusation and without a trial, in order to strike terror into the hearts of the dissenters. You, drafter of constitutions, designer of governments, what will you dare to write in your next *Rights of Man*? How Marat proposed setting the prisons on fire? Yes, he proposed it. And, when it was feared that it might endanger the city, he cried: 'Then we shall flood them!' "

"I do not believe it!"

"Varennes proposed butchering them!"

"I do not believe it!" cried Paine. "Jean Tallien would not have permitted it!"

"Tallien!" Cloots spat out the name as though it were a taste of aloes on his tongue. "It was he who told me. He was there, at those secret meetings held in a dark cellar. He insists that he was sickened by the thought of it, yet he had not the courage to oppose it. The Commune enlisted the services of the most degraded prisoners as additional killers—murderers and felons who had been convicted of crimes of violence. They were released and taken to swell the ranks of Lazowski's horde. Threatened by directives, plied with wine until they had lost half their brutish senses, they were promised a pay of twenty-four livres each for their assassins' work and told that they could rob their victims with impunity.

Do you think they confined themselves to the prisons? Armed with pikes and sabers, axes and shovels, they tore through the streets of Paris like Huns! Guards, armed with fixed bayonets and loaded muskets, though ordered not to fire upon them, were stationed as a defense at every public place. The theaters must stay open! The cafés must serve their guests as though nothing were amiss! Slaughter without end at the Abbaye de Saint-Germain-des-Prés, butchering at the prisons of the Chatelet and the Conciergerie and La Force, but Paris must be entertained!"

"And the citizens?" cried Paine. "A million people in Paris! What of the decent and humane citizenry?"

Cloots seemed not to hear him. "I saw the victims the next day—heaped carcasses on the Pont du Change. As I walked down the Rue Saint Jacques from Montrouge, the street was filled with carts into which naked bodies had been hastily flung. They were on their way to the burying ground, the stripped bodies of men and women tossed together into the last cold intimacy of death."

As though he realized only just now what Paine had asked, he said, "Shall I tell you what Manon said? Our little innocent *chienne?* She cried, as though she, herself, were free from guilt, 'All Paris let this happen! All Paris is accursed in my eyes! I no longer hope that liberty may be established among cowards, among cold spectators of crimes that the courage of fifty might have prevented!' "

Paine realized that Cloots was weeping. "I wish I could go home," he wept. "The Assembly is dead. The Convention will never be more than a delegation held together by fear and haunted by ghosts. The three vices of social man—avarice, ambition, and power—have blinded them to liberty."

He sensed that Paine was groping in the dark. When Paine handed him the glass of wine, he accepted it gratefully.

"I have committed myself to drafting a Constitution for the people," said Paine.

"The people!" cried Cloots, his voice suddenly raised in bitter anger. "What do you know of the damned French people? The people have turned into animals. Animals!"

"And the King and Queen?"

"They are prisoners in the Temple jail, while Marat and Danton and Robespierre decide what to ask the National Convention to do with them."

30

TWO DAYS later, Paine attended the first meeting of the National Convention. The Salle de Manège had been abandoned and the Convention was being held in the Tuileries, which had been renamed the Palais-National.

Paine's curiosity led him into the ground floor of the palace from which the royal family had been evicted. The royal furniture had been removed and the entire downstairs had been converted into guardrooms. They were littered with weapons, cots, and uniforms. Debris from smashed furniture and broken bric-a-brac had accumulated in the corners. Catchwords had been scrawled on the walls. It was in odd contrast with the elegance of the untouched ceilings.

He climbed the magnificent staircase to the King's private theater, which had been converted into an assembly hall for the Convention. Led to his seat by a bailiff, he could see, hung on a wall, a gigantic copy of the *Declaration of the Rights of Man and of Citizens.* It had been painted to simulate the pages of a book and was enclosed by a nine-foot frame.

Paine looked about him. There was a multitude of strange faces from every corner of France. The deputies sat, ill at ease, worried perhaps by the recent massacres. They held their commissions—their *pouvoirs,* as they called them—in their hands, but it seemed that only Jacobins (members of the Jacobin Club) were seated on the benches that rose in tiers in the semicircle behind the rostrum. There he saw Robespierre seated beside his brother Augustin, while, to Robespierre's left, Danton and Marat sat together—almost like a giant and a dwarf.

Paine had not remembered Marat as so short but now, seated at Danton's side, he seemed almost deformed. And he did not seem well. His eyes were bloodshot. His face was still covered with livid blotches and pitted with weeping sores.

There was whispering among the new deputies. They were watching Couthon being pushed in his wheelchair by Colbert. When they reached the semicircle of Jacobin benches, Colbert lifted Couthon from the chair and carried him up into the rising tiers as though he were a child.

Paine had not expected the National Convention to be so completely and so quickly given over to public affairs. He could not follow the proceedings well in French, but it seemed as though most of the proposals had been decided upon beforehand and needed but the confirmation of a vote.

He glanced at the Jacobins and was surprised to see Bareré seated among them. He had thought that he despised Marat. A clerk was reading a decree. A delegate leaned toward Paine and whispered, "It is an official announcement of the calendar change. Our time is now to be dated from the first day of the year one, and that is today, September 22, 1792. Only it is no longer to be referred to as September. The Convention has given France not only a new government, but a new calendar. Everything that has happened before today is to be of no significance."

"It will accomplish nothing and but compound confusion," protested Paine. "If something is good, it is worth remembering. If it is evil, denying that it once existed will not efface its memory."

The man lifted a finger to his lips. "You do not understand, Monsieur Paine," he whispered. "Reforming the calendar will throw off the influence of Church and Royalty. It will do away with the observance of 'holy' days and the celebration of historical events that we have not occasioned." He ticked off the new months on his fingers as the clerk continued to read the proclamation. "From this day forth the Revolutionary calendar will be divided into four seasons. Autumn will consist of *Vendémiaire,* the vintage month; *Brumaire,* the month of mists; and *Frimaire,* the month of frosts. Winter will be *Nivôse,* the month of snow; *Pluviôse,* the month of rain; and *Ventose,* the windy month. Spring will have *Germinal,* the month of budding; *Floréal, the month of flowers; and Prairial,* the time of the hayfields. Summer will consist of *Messidor,* the month of . . ."

Paine was paying scant attention. It seemed a rebirth of mythology. He recognized the clerk on the rostrum. He was young Saint-Just. He seemed paler than when he had last seen him. There were shadows of fatigue beneath his eyes. He was

[413]

reading a decree that royalty was, from this day forth, abolished in France! The Jacobins, as though they had not been aware of the edict, were tumultuous in their applause. Paine could see Danton waving his arms. He was bellowing so that the galleries echoed with his cries. The Girondists, seated about Paine, joined only halfheartedly in the applause.

On October 11, the Convention finally selected a committee of nine to draft a Constitution for the Republic of France. Because of his unfamiliarity with the French language, Paine had been placed second—but he was not displeased. Of the other eight men, only Villeneuve and Gensonné were strangers to him. And Brissot, Condorcet, Danton, and Bareré spoke English fluently. He had collaborated with Condorcet on the *Declaration of the Rights of Man and of Citizens.* And they had not asked that he work with Robespierre or with Marat, whom he had begun to distrust.

When he returned to the Philadelphia House that night, he was surprised to find Lafayette waiting for him. A single year had changed his appearance. His face still retained the plumpness it had acquired, but it had aged. Lines of worry had settled themselves about his eyes and little muscles tugged down the corners of his mouth. He would not be seated but strode about, impatient, as though angered by the turn of events. "My dear friend," he said. "My very dear friend. But a year ago, there were those who said that I held the destiny of France in my hands. And now I am neither *poisson* nor *volaille!* The Jacobins have no regard for me because I advocate a constitutional monarchy and the court party regards me with aversion because of my zeal for the revolution. On one side, Marie Antoinette refuses me an audience and, on the other, your friend Lathenas has omitted your dedication to me in his edition of *The Rights of Man.* Even the Girondists, at Madame Roland's soirees, are turning their backs to me."

Paine studied Lafayette in silence. He felt that he had come to him for neither sympathy nor personal assistance. His pride would not permit the one, his courage and convictions would be offended by the other. After what seemed like a few moments of indecision Lafayette said, "You know that the royal family has been confined to the Temple since August. Since August! And now there is a plot afoot to execute King Louis and Queen Marie Antoinette. To guillotine them in a public place, as a spectacle and as an example to the world! To drag them through the streets, like common criminals, and behead them in front of a multitude!"

Paine's eyes widened with shock. Lafayette mistook his silence for disbelief. "You do not believe me? Well, I tell you it is true! This is not America, my friend. This is France! A nation of twenty-five millions. A country capable of raising such a tidal wave as could engulf all of Europe! You have been away. I tell you that with each day a wall rises higher and higher between the citizenry and the aristocracy of France. The country needs both but the aristocrats, the best blood of France, are leaving by the hundreds. If the King is executed, . . ."

"They would not dare!"

"Would not dare? You presume too much, Thomas. They would dare anything! When the royal family was ordered from the Tuileries, I suggested that they be taken to the Luxembourg. 'No!' cried Robespierre, as though he had been accustomed all his life to deciding what should be done with a king. 'The Luxembourg has too many cellars and issues!' he cried. 'It would take a municipality to watch it!'

"Thomas . . . Thomas . . ." Lafayette seemed tortured. "Isn't a compromise better than a civil war?"

"A constitutional kingdom? Forgive me, Gilbert, I can neither advocate it nor accept it. I have voiced too much sentiment against it. But I promise you, I shall not stand idly by and watch the needless execution of your King. The revolution does not need his blood. Nor anyone's. You may be wrong, Gilbert. This may be an old wives' tale."

[415]

"No!" cried Lafayette in anger. "No! I tell you they are like dogs, baying at a scent!"

At the end of October, a certain Lord Edward Fitzgerald arrived and immediately attached himself to Paine. He insisted upon breakfasting, dining, and supping with him. "I have come to enlist your aid in fomenting a revolution in Ireland," he explained. "I shall persist until you agree. There are now 4,000 volunteers who assemble for one-day periods. They are prepared to battle for freedom. They but wait for someone to guide them."

"I am not a military man," protested Paine.

"I am. With you to inspire them, all of Ireland will be up in arms. Take me to Madame Roland's. I have been informed that all manner of lovers of freedom congregate at her soirees."

Paine escorted Fitzgerald to the Rolands'. Jean Roland de la Platière was now the Minister of the Interior. Upon his appointment, Madame Roland had immediately forsaken the upper-floor hotel apartment on the Rue Saint Jacques and moved to the Ministry of the Interior in the Hotel de Calonne, on the Rue Neuve des Petits Champs. It was one of the most beautiful buildings in Paris—an immense establishment with stabling facilities for sixty horses. She gave her soirees in the sumptuous salon once occupied by Madame Necker. A liveried footman asked their names so that he could announce them. When he heard the name, Lord Edward Fitzgerald, he opened both halves of the gilded doors. The salon was ornamented with Venetian mirrors and bright tapestries. Vanloo portraits hung between gilded bas-reliefs. To Paine's surprise, a portrait of Louis XIV was among them. A carved buffet was crammed with delicacies and decanters of sparkling wines. Two liveried servants stood at each end. It was a far cry from the apartment on the fifth floor of the Hotel Brittanique.

As Paine looked about, he could not help but notice that

[416]

the members of Madame Roland's Girondin Club had fashioned an aristocracy of their own. Their dress was elegant, their postures haughty, and their voices self-contained. There was now no violent Danton, no shrewd Robespierre, no inflamed Marat, no festering Brissot, and no wildly enthusiastic, stammering Desmoulins. These men, who had made the former gatherings so colorful, had broken away and formed their own Jacobin Club in the tenderloin Cordeliers District. Madame Roland would have liked to retain at least Danton ... for he had been appointed Minister of Justice.

Paine did not see Madame Roland but pointed out her husband to Lord Edward. Jean Roland seemed out of place in his own salon. His clothes were somber in color and plain in cut. He still tied his shoes with ribbons instead of buckles and he moved quietly about the salon. It was said that his wife, and not he, was the real minister.

Paine noticed Anacharsis Cloots. Defiantly, he had returned to his one-time elegance of dress. As though to show the postural bourgeois imitators what a true aristocrat was like, he had dressed himself in a blue foxskin cloak and a foxskin hat that was ornamented with an ostrich feather that had been dyed the tricolor of the Republic. He wore chiné stockings with gold clocks and velvet shoes whose buckles were studded with precious stones. Diamonds sparkled brazenly on his shirt frill. He might have relinquished his title, but he had not given up his income of 100,000 livres a year. When Paine introduced Lord Edward, Cloots stared at him as though he were a specimen in a collector's cage. "An English Lord!" he cried. "Have you not heard that royalty is dead? It is the only thing that is deceased yet walks about unburied. And England ..."

Lord Edward's face reddened and his eyes glinted with anger. "I am the Duke of Leinster, sir. In Ireland."

Cloots paid no attention. "England! That pitiful, unproductive little island that the waters of destiny washed away from the coast of France a million years ago! She is like a voracious fish that feeds upon its own young!" It was evident that he had been drinking heavily.

As Paine turned away, Cloots grasped Fitzgerald by the arm. "Wait! Wait! Permit me to introduce myself properly. Thomas says that I am Anacharsis Cloots. But who is Anacharsis Cloots? Nobody! Do you want to know who I really am? I am the orator of the human race. Its orator! I have dedicated myself to the ideal of a Universal Republic. China, America, and Arabia should become districts of France. And if you wish it, . . . we shall make room for Ireland!"

At the mention of America, Paine protested, "America has its own Republic. And the Republic of France has its own natural limits, for the present. The Rhine, the Alps, the Pyrenees, and the ocean."

Cloots turned to Fitzgerald and asked, almost insultingly, "Then what do you here, Irishman? What have you come for?"

Fitzgerald drew himself erect. "I seek aid in fostering a revolution in Ireland."

Cloots raised his arms as though he were astounded. His foxskin cloak slid from his shoulders and fell to the floor. "A revolution? To what end? So that your aristocrats may be tumbled from their chairs and the proletariat scramble to seat themselves and imitate them? Look about you. What do you see? A few years ago Manon was shelling beans in a garret of the Ursulines Convent. Now she disdains to either serve them or eat them. A few years ago she welcomed everyone with open arms. Now she permits bald-pated Jean Roland to drift about as her ambassador. And among the Jacobins, Marat plots to spill her blood . . . to bore a hole through her navel and rip out her guts in a long unravelling like a twisted skein. I have seen the way he looks at her." As though he thought he had said too much, he touched a trembling finger to his lips. He bent forward and whispered, "You are as drunk as

[418]

I am. You would not dream of a revolution if you were not drunk. Come, I shall have Manon put you to bed."

"You have been directed to the wrong club," said Paine as he led Fitzgerald away. "The reins of the revolution are in the hands of Jacobins. The Girondists furnished the horses . . . but the Jacobins are driving them."

Lafayette had not exaggerated when he had confided his concern for the safety of the King and Queen of France. When November came, the month that the new calendar called *Frimaire,* all other matters in the Convention were set aside in order to determine the fate of Louis XVI. There seemed to be no proof, yet the King was accused of communicating with foreign powers, of appealing for aid, and of plotting with foreign governments to invade France. Jean Baptiste Mailhe outlined the accusations and a formal debate regarding the condemnation of the King was begun.

As Paine listened to the arguments, he understood more clearly why the Jacobins and the Girondists had drifted apart. The Jacobins advocated the nationalization of the estates of the nobility. Without estates themselves, they insisted upon a redistribution of wealth and the abolition of the Church. They seemed extremists. To condemn the King would be to condemn his property also!

The Girondists were merely liberals who desired a republican form of government. They defended private ownership of property. They were opposed to violent measures and believed that government should be limited in its authority over human affairs. Paine watched them both in the Convention. While the Jacobins, oblivious to dress or common courtesies, grasped the reins of power, the Girondists paraded about like children at play. Toga-like cloaks and large flowing bows of muslin, worn as cravats, had become the accepted uniform of their party. They had let their hair grow and had it cut in a Brutus fringe. When they spoke from the Tribune, they did so with grandiloquent gestures. Their ideals were close to his own, Paine felt, but he could see no need for their histrionics.

When it became apparent that the King would not be permitted to offer a defense against the accusations, Paine considered calling a private meeting of a number of deputies. He decided upon Marat, Robespierre, and Danton, for they seemed to have the greatest influence. He considered inviting Vergniaud, who was now the president of the Convention, but felt that he would create too much dissension. Marat hated him. And he had seen Danton mimic him, with a put-on hauteur: "We Girondists prefer to think of ourselves as having stemmed from Peloponnesus rather than Gironde."

The meeting was held in Danton's apartment. Marat had at first refused but came when he learned that it would be held without him. Danton's wife, Gabrielle, served them wine and little cakes that she, herself, had baked. She had inherited her mother's wide face, heavy chin, and dark hair, which grew too low upon her brow. Danton pulled her down upon his lap and fondled her with unabashed familiarity. He slapped her behind as she struggled free and rebuttoned her blouse. She hurried into the bedroom and busied herself in putting the children to bed.

Marat glowered at Paine and pried at a scab on his cheek. As though impatient with the amenities and Danton's display of affection, he suddenly cried, "There shall be no trial for the King of France! I insist upon a penalty for treason! Do I ask for a pound of flesh when I demand that treachery be punished?"

Paine looked into Marat's dark eyes. They were filled with malevolent anger. He glanced at Robespierre. Maximilien had dressed himself fastidiously, as though he had been invited to a large affair. He wore his green-tinted glasses, as though to shade his eyes from the candlelight. Danton seemed to be enjoying himself. A two-day stubble blackened his cheeks, his shirt was open at the throat, and his face wore his perpetual grimace.

"Kings can commit no treason," said Paine quietly. "They can be cruel, foolish, infantile . . . yes. But not treasonable, for they consider the government their own."

"Hear him!" bellowed Danton. "Hear our *Rights of Man!* Have you then fallen so much in love with Louis Capet?"

"I do not plead for the man, but for France," said Paine. "The treatment accorded the King will influence the progress of the revolution. The world is watching us and will condemn us for any inhumanity."

"Let them watch," said Robespierre suddenly. "There was a time when I admired you, Deputy Paine. That time is past. France, her revolution, and her government are her own. Not the world's. Let them watch!"

"I do not defend the innocence of the King," insisted Paine. "I only advise that he not be accused in a spirit of vengeance."

Marat slammed his fist on the table. "There shall be no trial! No trial!" he cried. "He is to be condemned, and no one shall hinder it. Your friend, Lafayette, has not raised his voice in the King's behalf. Has he come, perhaps, to you? Take care, Deputy Paine! Take care!"

"Sh . . . Sh . . ." whispered Danton with a forefinger that hid half his mouth. "You'll awaken *les petits enfants!* Gabrielle will be furious."

Danton's use of the French words reminded Paine of when he had been with him and Marat in the Café de la Parnasse. Marat had spoken only French then. Now, he spoke English fluently. Refusing to be intimidated, Paine said quietly, "The Bill of Rights insists that every man is entitled to a trial . . . and a king no less than a peasant. The execution of a king can contribute nothing to the cause of human freedom. Royalty has been abolished in France. What could be accomplished by condemning and executing helpless Louis Capet?"

Suddenly, as though he had gone mad, Marat flung an accusing finger at Paine. "I accuse you as 'suspect!'" he cried. "I accuse you as 'suspect!'" His wide frightening mouth was suddenly twisted as though his tongue were striving to stem

[421]

an overabundance of saliva from dribbling onto his chin. "I understand you damned English better than you think! I practiced medicine in Pimlico for two years. You did not know that, did you? You English speak against kings but deep in your hearts you venerate the nobility. You wish to foment a revolution with words written in a book. Erect a government with phrases! But I know better. I, Jean Paul Marat, devote only two hours out of twenty-four to sleep and only one to my meals and domestic necessities. I have not had fifteen minutes of relaxation in more than three years. Nor will I relax until there is no king in France. No king! Do you hear? No king!"

"Sh . . . Sh . . . *Diminuez votre voix,*" whispered Danton.

There was a knock on the door and it was pushed inward discreetly. Camille Desmoulins stood on the threshold.

"Entrez! Entrez!" cried Danton.

"I . . . I was upstairs with Lucille," stammered Desmoulins. "I heard the raised voices . . ."

Marat paid no attention. "Inform your Lafayette," he cried. "Your *Sieur Motier . . .* that I have not forgotten him. Two years ago he marched into the Cordeliers District, at the head of an army of 3,000 men, with orders for my arrest. And could not find me! But I shall have no difficulty in finding *him.* I swore then that I would tear out his heart in front of his battalion of lackeys and I shall do it yet. See that you are not with him when I come!"

Paine glanced at Danton, who shrugged his brutish shoulders; at Robespierre, who was silent behind his tinted glasses; and back again at incensed Marat. There was no point in staying longer. It was evident that these three had committed themselves to the King's death.

Despite Marat's threat, Paine went to the Convention on November 21 with a plea that urged a trial for the King of France. He was virtually alone in the expression of such a sentiment . . . but he had been alone before. First the King had

[422]

been shorn of his pomp and his wealth because he had inherited them and not earned them. And now he was to be condemned to death because he had accepted an inheritance that all France had thrust upon him with shouts of *"Vive le Roi!"* Somewhere there was illogic!

Paine was still fatigued from the night before. He had sat up late with the Marquis de Condorcet. As he had worked on his address in English, Condorcet had translated it into French. Now and again Condorcet had paused and advised him, "You are a fool, Thomas. I tell you there will be no single word raised in the King's defense but yours."

"Translate it!"

"And I am an imbecile. For I insist that you are a fool, and yet I admire you. Only an imbecile would admire a fool. I translate it, but I do not condone it. This entire address is *à contrecoeur.* It will gain you nothing but ill will. And there you have the crux of it."

Now he sat with the transcript of his speech in his lap and glanced about. The spectators, who came each day to watch the proceedings, had given common names to the two portions of the Convention. They called the tiers of seats on which the Jacobins sat the "mountain," and the Jacobin deputies, the "mountaineers." They nicknamed the Girondist pit in front of the rostrum the "plain." There were those who called it by the more vulgar term the "marsh."

Lifting his hand to President Vergniaud for recognition, Paine now left his seat and approached the rostrum. He sensed an ominous silence among the Jacobins as he handed the transcript of his speech to Secretary Saint-Just. Robespierre sat with seeming indifference. Paine could not tell if Marat, with his twisted mouth, smiled or leered. He had expected at least one protesting voice. It could not be that they were all uninformed of the transcript's plea. Saint-Just gave the Jacobins a fleeting glance and read in his nasal tones:

Citizen President:

Little attention was paid to the transcript's introduction, and then a hush fell over the hall and its galleries as the secretary read:

> I think that Louis XVI ought to be tried. This advice appears to me just, lawful, and conformable to sound policy. . . .
> Louis XVI, considered as an individual, is an object beneath the notice of the Republic . . .

There was a sporadic clapping of hands in the "Mountain" and a burst of cheers in the galleries. When they subsided, Saint-Just continued:

> . . . beneath the notice of the Republic; but, when he is looked upon as a criminal whose trial may lead all the nations in the world to a knowledge of the plots and intrigues of their own courts, he ought to be, and must be, tried!
> The despots of Europe dread the effect of the French Revolution in the bosom of their own countries. . . .

There was a tumultuous burst of applause in the galleries. The Jacobins sat in silence as though they but waited for the end of the transcript. Saint-Just continued its reading. As the applause died down, one could hear his voice again:

> These are my motives for demanding that Louis XVI be judged.
> Seeing no longer a Louis XVI, but a weak-minded and narrow-spirited individual . . . whom the National Assembly raised again, imprudently, on a throne . . .

There was wild cheering as Saint-Just finished reading the address. Paine saw Marat rise from his chair. Without waiting for the approbation to die away, he rushed to the rostrum with jerky convulsive strides. He had a portfolio of papers in one hand and what looked like a memorandum in the other.

There was a smile on Robespierre's pale face and a wide grin on Danton's dark countenance. The secretary raised his hand for silence and read from the memorandum:

> A few days ago, there came to certain members of the Jacobin party, a locksmith who had been employed by the royal household to do some work in the Tuileries. He informed the deputies that, on the King's order, he had built a secret safe in a wall of the King's chamber.

A hush of deep attention filled the hall. Marat waited impatiently for Saint-Just to finish.

> Yesterday, the workman was taken to the palace. He had not lied. As a citizen of France, he pointed out the safe . . . beautifully concealed in a wall. The safe was opened and a portion of its contents are here now.

Marat could not contain himself but waved the portfolio aloft and cried, "The contents, *citoyens* . . . the contents are proof, without a doubt, that the King is in secret correspondence with the enemies of his country! Deputy Paine shall have his wish . . . a trial for the King of France! A trial for the King of France!"

The Jacobins, restrained until now, rose from their benches and gave vent to a tumultuous acclaim of Marat's promise. Marat was dancing about the rostrum as though possessed.

Suddenly Paine realized that he had been tricked. They had used him! If the portfolio actually contained the proof of the King's treason . . . if he had invited Austria and Prussia to send their armies into France . . . then they had used him, as a pawn, to insist upon a trial for the King. He glanced at Marat. He had played a game of chess with the very devil himself, and now the King's life was in check!

31

ON THE tenth of December, Joel Barlow, returning from a trip to England, brought Paine news of his coming trial in London. "You are to be tried *in absentia,* by the court of the King's Bench, in Guildhall, on the eighteenth," he advised him.

Paine had been so taken up with the trial of King Louis that he had almost forgotten his own. A debate had taken place in the Convention concerning the manner in which the King's trial should be conducted. Saint-Just had read Paine's views:

> It is not only Louis XVI that we are going to judge; it is the monarchy. We have knowledge of the treaties of confederation made at Padua and at Pilnitz; it is a general conspiracy of kings against people. . . .

Marat had screamed in a torrent of French that Paine could follow only with difficulty: "The trial must not be hindered by technicalities and legal phrases! As a physician, I know that the only cure for a rotting leg is amputation and the only treatment for treason is execution! Execution! Execution!"

Paine was brought back to the present by Barlow's well-modulated voice: "I spoke with Tom Erskine. The liberals have raised quite a fund for your defense; but I do not think it is the money alone that has influenced Mr. Erskine to defend you. It is known that it will be a 'packed' jury. He cannot possibly win an acquittal. When one considers that he resigned as Attorney General for the Prince of Wales in order to act as chief counsel for a lost cause . . . that he has been told in plain terms, by the Royal Government, that he must not defend you, ..."

"He is not defending me. He is defending the liberty of the press! It is a case to determine how far the government can go in proscribing writers and publishers. I consider myself no longer English and, as a foreigner, I am not the object of the prosecution. It is the freedom of expression and of thought that is on trial!"

Barlow hesitated and confessed, "In Hertfordshire, the effigy of Dr. Priestley was burnt by a mob and he, himself, was brutally beaten. In Manchester, Thomas Walker's home was set on fire. He had to defend himself at the point of a musket. Wherever I went, bonfires were made of your confiscated books. I brought souvenirs with me. I had not meant to show them."

"Of burnt books?"

Barlow shook his head. He unwrapped a package and set its contents, one by one, on the table. Paine was surprised at the collection. He picked up a medal that closely resembled an English coin. A man dangling from a gibbet had been stamped upon it. The inscription read: THE END OF PAINE. Another medal showed a decapitated serpent and a dagger. The serpent's decapitated head had a human face ... evidently intended to be his own. Paine looked up and Barlow said, "The country is full of them. There are tokens the size of a penny, a halfpenny, and a farthing ... with all manner of inscriptions. They pass as regular copper coins and the government does not object." He untied a batch of scurrilous cartoons and handbills that lampooned Paine and spread them upon the table.

Paine lifted a beer mug that Barlow unwrapped. "This interests me most," he said. "The common man drinks more than he reads. And it will be seen where it can be debated." He examined the curious mug closely. It was made of pottery and baked into its clay were a half dozen lines:

[427]

The Convention spent the first two weeks of January in preparations for the trial of Louis XVI. To Paine, it seemed no longer a question of guilt, but an insistence upon vengeance. All of Paris was incited against the former King. Paine caught a glimpse of him once, on his way to the Convention. He was transported from the Temple, each morning, in Mayor Chambronne's green carriage. With him were two attendants and Procureur Chaumette. The citizens paid little attention, yet the carriage was proceeded by Commandant Santerre and a group of cavalry with drawn sabers, while a double row of infantry marched on each side, and a cannon with four cannoneers trundled behind. When the King alighted from the carriage, Santerre grasped him by the arm —an affront for which his hand would once have been severed at the wrist. Paine recalled how, but two years ago, Dr. Guillotin had rushed about the Assembly in order to spread a red velvet carpet for His Majesty. Now President Vergniaud would say in the Convention, *"Asseyez-vous . . .* you may be seated, Louis," and the King would seat himself. "You are invited to withdraw, Louis," and the King would leave.

On Tuesday morning, January 15, Paine took his seat in the Convention and watched as the fate of the King was gradually unraveled.

Up to now, the citizens of Paris had shown little interest in the doings of the Convention. Now, with the trial of the King, the galleries were filled. They watched the proceedings and stared discourteously at their former King. Now and then they yelled derisively at Deseze, the younger of the King's advocates.

Jean Roland was called upon to testify. With his egg-shaped

[428]

head, his somber clothes, and his scarecrow body, he seemed more a petty clerk than the Minister of the Interior. "Yes," he answered in an indistinct voice. "Yes, I accompanied Gemain, the smith, when *le armoire de fer* was disclosed and wrenched open." He testified to the authenticity of the letters . . . the handwriting . . . the seals.

There was a murmur in the galleries as King Louis was permitted to speak. He roused himself from his bored inattentiveness. His round face was flushed with suppressed spite. His dark eyes glared about him. He stared up at the galleries and cried, "I never plotted to spill my subjects' blood!"

There was a shouting of epithets in the galleries. His referring to them as *sujets* aroused them. The King reseated himself. Paine could not tell if he had nothing more to say or if he had been intimidated.

One of the King's advocates rose and read petitions from foreign courts, in a low monotone. The Court of Austria implores the National Convention of France . . . the Court of Spain . . . the Court of Prussia. Catcalls and jeers from the galleries drowned out the pleas.

The Convention ruled that any deputy who desired to do so would be granted permission to speak—but in a proper order. A list would be made. As Paine watched, the list swelled to an impossible number. It seemed that everyone wished to voice his personal conviction of the King's treason. President Vergniaud rose and motioned toward the Tribune. The denunciations must be cut short. There was not enough time to hear everyone's oration. It would serve no purpose. The Convention was ready to vote upon the question: *Is Louis Capet guilty of conspiring against the State?*

Paine lost count as the voting progressed. The great hall grew quiet. Even the galleries were hushed, until Secretary Saint-Just announced that an overwhelming majority had voted the King *guilty*! Then wild shouts of acclaim filled the galleries.

When the Convention convened the next day, the voting was immediately begun to determine the King's penalty. Shrill-sounding bailiffs echoed the secretary's call and summoned each deputy by name and department. The deputies left their seats in order to cast their votes from the Tribune. The King and his advocates were absent. Having judged the King guilty, there was no longer any need for their presence. Now and then a deputy climbed to the Tribune, looked about him, and cast his vote in but a single word. There were 749 deputies. Only some twenty were absent. From the galleries, packed with brutish faces and exhibitionist women, there was applause for the deputies who voted "death" and epithets and vulgar threats for those who voted "imprisonment."

The Girondists were called upon to cast their votes. Brissot climbed to the Tribune, stared straight before him, and voted in a single word, "Death."

Vergniaud voted from behind the President's table— "Death." He busied himself immediately with some papers.

Bareré ascended to the Tribune and cried in a loud clear voice, "The tree of liberty does not grow if it be not watered with the blood of kings!"

There was a roar of approbation from the galleries. Paine wondered if Bareré had been intimidated. Emmanuel Sieyès was called. He hesitated and turned to glance at Marat, whose eyes burned as though with a dark charcoal flame. He glanced at Robespierre, at Danton, at Couthon—at Couthon who had already voted. Unable to climb the steps to the Tribune, Couthon had been held aloft by Colbert while he had shrieked, *"Mort au traître!"*

In a voice that could hardly be heard, Sieyès too voted— "Death."

Paine's own name was now being called: "Thomas Paine, *député de Pas de Calais.*" He left his seat and climbed to the Tribune. As he stepped onto the small platform, he stared directly into Pierre Colbert's eyes. He had raised his head, with its lion's mane of black hair, so that it hovered above Couthon. Colbert shook a hand at him and then, hesitantly, he pressed it over his mouth. Was he warning him not to speak? Suddenly there was a hush in the Convention. A thousand pairs of eyes were upon him. Let them look! He was Tom Paine, the author of *The Rights of Man*. He was Tom Paine who insisted that governments should tax hereditary wealth, educate the poor, hospitalize the sick, and pension the aged. He was Tom Paine who had laid the axe to monarchies and the divine right of kings! Let them look.

Despite the advice of friends, he had carefully rehearsed a single sentence in French. He now enunciated each of its words clearly. "I vote for the detention of Louis till the end of the war, and, after that, his perpetual banishment."

A murmur of protest filled the galleries and the tiers of the Jacobins. Ignoring its buzz, Paine handed his address to Saint-Just. The secretary was startled. He looked to President Vergniaud. Vergniaud glanced at Marat. As though angered by Vergniaud's looking to Marat for approval, Danton bellowed, "Read it!"

Saint-Just cleared his throat and began to read the translation of Paine's address:

Citizen President:

My hatred and abhorrence of monarchy are sufficiently known; they originate in principles of reason and conviction, nor, except with life, can they ever be extirpated; but my compassion for the unfortunate, whether friend or enemy, is equally lively and sincere.

Saint-Just stopped his reading and glanced about. The Convention was hushed. Even the galleries were quiet. Marat alone had half-risen from his seat. As though suspended in space, he was neither seated nor standing. Turning back to the manuscript in his hand, Saint-Just continued:

[431]

I voted that Louis should be tried, because it was necessary to afford proofs to the world of the perfidy, corruption, and abomination of the monarchical system. The infinity of evidence that has been produced exposes them in the most glaring and hideous colors. . . .

Nevertheless, I am inclined to believe that if Louis Capet had been born in an amiable and respectable neighborhood, at liberty to practice the duties of domestic life; had he been thus situated, I cannot believe that he would have shown himself destitute of social virtues.

Suddenly Saint-Just was interrupted by Marat springing up and screaming at the top of his lungs. "We will not listen to any pleas in Louis' defense! The sentence of death shall be passed with or without Paine's vote! Why, then, must we listen?"

President Vergniaud stared Marat into silence. With his pockmarked face, his wide mouth, and his bristling eyebrows raised in anger he shouted at Marat, "I am still President! President! Do you hear? And while the office is mine, we shall conduct the proceedings with regulation!" He motioned for Saint-Just to continue.

I seriously confess that, when I reflect on the unaccountable folly that restored the executive power to his hands, all covered as he was with perjury and treason, I am far more ready to condemn the constitutent assembly than the unfortunate prisoner, Louis Capet!

The deputies were stunned. The spectators in the galleries murmured among themselves. Saint-Just continued:

It is to France alone, I know, that the United States of America owe that support which enabled them to shake off the unjust and tyrannical yoke of Britain. Let then these United States be the safeguard and asylum of Louis Capet. There, hereafter, far removed from the miseries and crimes of royalty, he may learn, from the constant aspect of public prosperity, that the true system of government consists not in kings, but in fair, equal, and honorable respresentation.

The galleries were becoming noisy. The spectators were growing restless. Saint-Just was no orator. The address was too long. He hurried through until the end:

I submit the following propositions:
First, the National Convention shall pronounce sentence of banishment on Louis and his family;
Second, Louis Capet shall be detained in prison till the end of the war; and at that epoch the sentence of banishment be executed.

There was no applause. The Jacobins and the Girondists sat unmoved. The galleries were silent. Marat rose and cried, "I move that the voting be resumed!"

When the last vote was cast, a dozen Jacobins rushed to the rostrum and gathered about Vergniaud and Saint-Just. They stood, shoulder to shoulder, and watched as the votes were tallied.

Vergniaud held up his arms for silence and attention. "It is apparent that a great majority have voted for the execution of the King. It remains only to be decided *when.* The Convention is adjourned until tomorrow morning, when we shall vote upon it."

The galleries were immediately filled with a wild, tumultuous applause. papers in which lunches had been wrapped fluttered down upon the deputies. A spectator dropped an empty wineskin. Thinking the act intended, others flung theirs across the hall. Some, not quite emptied, splashed a dripping stain of red, like a foreboding of blood, where they smashed against a wall. Paine sat and listened to the tumult. His throat felt dry and constricted. There was a taste of bitterness in his mouth.

That night, Paine went to see Gouverneur Morris who was now the American minister. Lafayette had fled and there was no one else whose aid he could enlist. He must save the King, he told himself. He must save him. The fools! Did they not realize that, if they executed the King, it would be a deed of vengeance and not an act of political policy! Could they not foresee that his execution would bring down on them the execration of mankind? That it would open the sluice gates through which the swollen waters of 1,000 personal vengeances would immediately rush? It was Saturday night. Could not the voting be delayed a single day?

Paine had not seen Morris for months. He had purchased a large estate in Sainport, a provincial village twenty miles outside Paris. There, to the neglect of his diplomatic duties, he entertained the hopeful and reactionary aristocrats who plotted a new flight for the royal family.

It was late by the time Paine reached Sainport. He found Morris' country villa in the midst of landscaped gardens now filled with shadows. In an oval dining room, the remains of delicacies and a disarray of cushions and settees gave every indication of the close of a gala soiree from which guests had departed, while a few left to gather in the large drawing room, where chandeliers were reflected in a polished mosaic floor.

Morris greeted him there and immediately led him into a small sitting room, as though he were a poor country cousin of whom he was ashamed. He waved a hand at Paine's excuse for the late hour, but, when Paine insisted that his visit was urgent, he cried, "Urgent? I assure you, sir, what is urgent to one is of no consequence to another."

"I have come in an effort to save the King!"

"Ah, yes. To rescue the King." Morris permitted himself a cynical smile. His eyes were clouded as though they were affected by drink. "First you incite Their Majesties' destruction and now, with the whirlwind in your own ears, you would save them from the holocaust. How, Tom Paine? How?"

[434]

"The British Ministry can save them. The Convention will grant Pitt any favor in order to keep England a neutral."

"Your head, perhaps?" And when Paine did not answer, "It is your friend, Brissot, who said, 'The grievance of the British cabinet against France is not that Louis is in judgment, but that she endorses Tom Paine's *The Rights of Man*.'"

"For expressing the truth!"

"Truth or treason, you have begun a reign of terror with your books and your pamphlets. England will have no dealings with a government that harbors you. Let me show you what I have collected . . . *objet-souvenirs* for Washington, John Adams, and Hamilton." He left the room in his heavy peg-leg gait and returned with a collection of mugs. They bore caricatures of Paine in various guises. One was molded with the lines:

> Observe the wicked and malicious man,
> Projecting all the mischief that he can.

"I have seen them," said Paine.

"Whether you have learned it or not, it is still wealth and aristocracy that govern. And it will always be so. Your writings are laughed at by the educated and not understood by the poor. Just now, for a brief moment, you have touched the heart of Parliament with a chill finger of fear; but in six months there will be no single copy of *The Rights of Man* in all of England. People who read or sell your scribblings are fined, imprisoned, or transported. Constables are directed to inspect bookshops and report street corner conversations.

"Let me give you some instances that have been brought to my attention," he continued. "Do you know a Thomas Muir?" Paine nodded. "He has been sentenced to fourteen years for sedition, banished to Botany Bay." He touched the fingers of his hand as though he were ticking off the dates on a calendar: "Symonds, of London, two years' imprisonment for publishing your *Rights of Man* and a two-year sentence and a £100 fine for distributing your *Letters to the Addressers*. The printer of the *Manchester Herald* earned seven indictments for selling but six copies of your works!"

Paine was sick at heart, but Morris seemed to be tasting a strange satisfaction in imparting the news. "Your friend, Mr. Rickman, is being prosecuted. I understand that much of your writing was done in his home."

"You are misinformed! I saw him but two weeks ago."

"Two weeks?" laughed Morris. "My news is fresher than two days."

Paine's calm was shaken. He bit at his lip. "I came only to speak of the King. I know someone who can save him. And since you love aristocracy so well . . ."

Morris lifted a questioning eyebrow. It was true—though his face was fuller and his eyes were dark, he did resemble Washington. Or was it because Paine had not seen Washington for so long? "Who?" demanded Morris with sudden interest. "Who?"

"Danton. With a million *livres* with which to buy the necessary votes . . ."

"Danton! Is that bull, then, so corrupt?"

"Not corrupt but bribed by avarice. In parting he said to me, 'I warn you. Even though I might save the King's life, I, myself, shall vote for his death. I am quite willing to save his head, but not to lose mine.' "

"And the million *livres*?"

"Pitt will raise it if you but ask him. King George will favor it for his own peace of mind."

"And I say that King George would rather spend ten times a million *livres* on a war, should Louis be executed. Which they will not dare! You . . . you have incited them to an impasse!"

"And I tell you, Gouverneur, they will execute him! I would go myself and ask it of Pitt, but . . ."

"Go yourself?" cried Morris. "Go where? Come now,

Paine. It is no secret that you have been tried *in absentia* and found guilty of high treason. You would be recognized in an hour and hanged in a day!"

Paine gathered his hat and coat from where he had dropped them on an armchair. "Then I must return to the Convention. I shall inform them that, if they execute the King, it will be a signal for my departure. I will not abide among such sanguinary men!"

Morris did not extend a farewell hand, but his usual appearance of disdain was gone. His eyes seemed subdued by respect. As he saw Paine to the door, he said, "Franklin once said of you that you are a man who spits against the wind. And so you do. I would ask you to spend the night but that a few paces from here there are guests who would run you through with their blades did they know of your presence."

When he arrived at the Convention hall the next morning, an ominous sense of fatality seemed to hover over it. The galleries of the former theater were so packed that spectators straddled the carved cornices at the risk of tumbling from them. In the additional gallery, an iron bar had been erected as a guard rail.

As the president ascended the rostrum, dozens of deputies sprang to their feet and waved their arms above their heads. They clamored to be heard. They had not been permitted to speak the day before. They wished their few inconsequential words to be added to the history of France. Vergniaud shook his head at them.

Paine looked about and wondered how many Girondist deputies had been intimidated by Marat. It was now common knowledge that Villette had been threatened with death if he did not vote for the execution of the King. He glanced up at the benches of the Jacobins that rose almost to the cornices of the galleries. Danton was looking down at him. He was watching him as though for a sign. His dark eyes were ablaze. He was seated between Robespierre and Marat. He half rose from his bench. Paine shook his head at him. Danton reseated himself. The fire in his eyes extinguished itself. For him, the proceedings of the Convention were now an anticlimax.

A massive hand bell had been brought in and placed upon the president's table. It was almost big enough for a belfry. Vergniaud raised the bell with both hands and shook it. Its brazen clapper gave forth a tremendous clang that reverberated from the walls. The deputies seated themselves. Paine remained standing. After a long moment, Vergniaud glanced up at the Jacobins. Danton nodded. One could not tell if he were granting permission or settling his bull's neck more comfortably in his stock. Vergniaud hesitated and then signaled Paine that he was permitted to mount to the Tribune. Paine urged his translator to follow him.

The tribune was reached by way of a staircase of nine steps. The risers were high and the incline steep. Fatigued, Paine found them difficult to climb. He counted them unconsciously, until they reached the top, where Bancal glanced at Vergniaud. The president nodded. There was a murmur of protest from the Jacobins. But it simmered down and Bancal read:

> I have voted for the detention of Louis and his banishment after the war.

It was apparent that Bancal was hesitatingly translating the address, phrase by phrase. Marat, livid with rage, almost stumbling in his haste, rushed to the rostrum. With wildly flailing arms, he turned first to Vergniaud and then to spectators in the galleries, who watched him in fascination. "This is not the language of Thomas Paine!" he cried. "I denounce the interpreter! This is a faithless translation!"

Bancal was stricken dumb with fear. Half the deputies rose to their feet. Saint-Just studied Paine's phrases and declared the translation accurate. Bancal was visibly shaken. He wiped his brow and waited for Marat to regain his seat. "Read on," whispered Paine. "Read on."

At a nod from Vergniaud, Bancal traced with his finger to where he had left off and read in a shaking voice:

> The United States of America had the utmost veneration for Louis, who gave them liberty. And I can pledge myself to you, that the sentence of Louis will overwhelm all the Americans with consternation.
>
> Citizens, let not a neighboring despot enjoy the satisfaction of seeing that man mount the scaffold who has helped my much-loved America to break her chains!

The great hall was hushed. When Paine and Bancal left the Tribune, there was an immediate huddle about Vergniaud's table. Desmoulins, Marat, and Danton rushed to the rostrum. Robespierre, as though deciding at the last moment, joined them. His complexion had become pasty, as though his digestion was poor. They returned to their seats and Vergniaud addressed the Convention:

> The sentence of banishment has not been considered except in the mind and voice of one deputy. I therefore instruct you that, when the roll is called, you vote only for either imprisonment or immediate death.

The voting was begun. The deputies ascended the Tribune, cast their votes, and quickly left the little platform. When it was Paine's turn to vote, Marat sprang again from his seat and shouted to Vergniaud: "I submit that Deputy Thomas Paine is incompetent to vote on this question! As a Quaker, his religious principles are opposed to the penalty of death!"

As though he had not heard Marat, Paine grasped Bancal's arm and hurried with him to the Tribune. He climbed the steep steps, once again, and whispered the opening phrase of an impromptu speech that he wished interpreted.

Marat seemed suddenly wild with anger. A hoarse cry issuing from the depths of his throat drowned out Bancal's words and he cried, "He is a Quaker! He is a Quaker! I submit that Deputy Paine is a Quaker and thus is incompetent to vote on this question! His mind is contracted by the narrow principles of his religion! He is incapable of condemning men to death! His religion has predetermined his vote!"

A thunderous roar of approval came from the galleries. Tallien rose and, without being recognized by Vergniaud, cried from where he stood, "As I said yesterday, there must be no reprieve. No imprisonment! Humanity requires that we shorten the waiting agony of even a king. It is barbarous to leave him in doubt as to his fate." The galleries took Tallien's little speech as a subtlety and gave him a thunderous ovation.

Bancal turned to go. Paine, refusing to descend from the Tribune until he had been heard, grasped Bancal's arm and detained him. When the hall was quieted, Paine faced Vergniaud and insisted, "Freedom of speech is an important principle in the Declaration of Rights. It is to be contained in the Constitution on which not only I, but Deputy Sieyès, Bareré, Danton, and even yourself now labor. If my right to speak is not acknowledged here, then I most assuredly will not find it in the rest of France . . . and I leave you."

Immediately, not only from the Girondists but from those Jacobins who understood English, there were cries of "Let him speak! Let him speak! Permit Deputy Paine to speak!"

Bancal, leaning close to Paine in order to catch every whispered word, interpreted:

> Very sincerely do I regret the Convention's vote of yesterday. It is nearly twenty years that I have been engaged in the cause of liberty. My language has always been that of liberty AND humanity.
> Could we carry our thoughts into the future, what today seems an act of justice may then appear an act of vengeance.

A dissenting murmur filled the galleries. It grew into many-tongued jeers and catcalls. Vergniaud lifted the massive bell

[440]

and quieted them with a clang of authority from its throat. Bancal continued:

My anxiety for the cause of France has become, for the moment, a concern for her honor. If, on my return to America, I should employ myself on a history of the French Revolution, I had rather record 1,000 errors dictated by humanity than one inspired by a justice too severe. . . .

Could I speak the French language . . . I would descend to your bar, and become your petitioner to respite the execution of the sentence on Louis.

The clamor of the spectators in the galleries could not be silenced. Marat was urging them on. He flung his arms above his head and cried, *"La voix du peuple! La voix du peuple!"* To which a voice answered and 100 others took up the cry: *"Je crache sur député Payan! Je crache sur député Payan!*

Paine realized that his plea had failed. A mixture of bitterness and anger filled his heart as he waited for order to be restored. Without Bancal's aid, he reiterated his rehearsed French phrase: "I vote for the detention of Louis until the end of the war, and, after that, his perpetual banishment." There were cries of *traître* and *bâtard* in the galleries as he stepped defiantly from the Tribune.

Bareré took his place, cleared his throat, and waited for the hall's full attention. "Deputy Tallien is right," he said. "It is inhuman to keep a man in an indefinite state of reprieve. And Deputy Paine is right to remind us of the Bill of Rights and the Constitution. They have been neglected since the beginning of this trial. This endless trial has consumed our time while the philanthropic aims of the Revolution lie forgotten. The reforms have been rolled from sight until the unpleasant business of Louis Capet is disposed of. I say, let us stop wasting time! The King has been tried and found guilty! Are there any here who would dispute this? Then let us end the settlement of this guilt and wash our hands of it. Treason earns an identical penalty in every nation. I vote—immediate death to Louis Capet!"

Grey shadows had began to settle on the hangings. When all the votes were finally cast, Saint-Just handed the tally sheets to Vergniaud and the president checked them against the roll call. Of the 721 deputies, 334 had voted for imprisonment, two having expressed themselves: "I vote to put the King in chains!"; while 387 had voted for an immediate execution. A majority of fifty-three votes had sentenced Louis XVI to his death!

Vergniaud rose and cleared his throat. A hush swept across the "plain," quieted the Jacobins, and muted the spectators in the galleries. Vergniaud's eyes were on the long list of votes, but he did not read the sums. "I declare," he said, "in the name of the Convention, that the punishment it pronounces on Louis Capet . . . is that of immediate death."

32

PAINE AWOKE in the morning as from a feverish dream. He remembered having gone to his room and having locked himself in. There was a taste of vinegar in his mouth. He recalled that he had been drinking. He looked out of a window. The street was deserted. The day seemed cold, with hardly enough sun to dispel the morning fog. Suddenly there was the sound of approaching feet. It was one of Santerre's patrols, marching with fixed bayonets and grim faces.

Paine dressed and left the hotel. Outdoors, Paris seemed deserted, as though it had been touched by a plague. The shops were closed, the cafés empty; no face appeard at any window. He walked southward along the Rue Royale. As he approached the Place de Louis Quinze, now called the Place de la Révolution, it seemed as though all of Paris had gathered there. The press of people was tremendous. They lined the streets and spilled over into a garden of the Tuileries, where the more adventurous ones had climbed into the bare trees. As Paine thrust his way to the square, he was suddenly aware that he had seen no single deputy's face. They had secreted themselves behind the locked doors of the Convention hall to wait in tense silence for the *fait accompli.*

The guillotine was mounted on a hastily constructed platform in the center of the square. It was near the old pedestal that had once held the equestrian statue of the King of France. Dr. Guillotin's instrument of death was tall and frightening. A shaft of winter sunlight thrust itself through the low clouds and glinted weakly on its cold blade. A ring of cannon encircled the platform as though they were trained upon the guillotine. Beyond them, in a wider circle, there were more cannons, horses, and cannoneers. The cannoneers stood at attention beside their iron monsters. Their *flambeaux* flickered yellow and red and sent spirals of grey-black smoke into the cold windless air. The snouts of their cannons, too, were fixed upon the platform. Armed guards, six deep, stood shoulder to shoulder behind the circle of cannoneers. It was a circle that was broken only where it touched la Rue de Rivoli. There the guards stretched eastward, on both sides of the wide street, as far as the Temple prison.

The vast crowd stood in patient silence. No one heeded the cold. Small children were held in arms as though it were a spectacle to be remembered. Paine looked about for a familiar face, and could find none. Suddenly there was the sound of a clapper against a bell. The hour was being struck. Every church tower hastened to measure time with its own pendulum tongue. Paine counted the reverberations of the nearest bell, knowing that it would strike ten. As the brazen ripples of sound lost their echoes, there was the sound of drums in the distance. They were muffled yet loud; muffled yet insistent; death, beating a cadence to approaching feet. The multitude listened in silence and waited expectantly.

As the sound of the drums grew louder, Paine pressed forward and edged toward the scoffold. No one barred his way. Everyone stood as though entranced. From his new vantage point, Paine could see the royal carriage now, approaching at a slow pace. It was within a square of armed soldiers. The drummers who led them had tied black cloths about their drums. General Santerre rode at the head of a company of grenadiers. A platoon of gendarmes, with drawn swords, followed them. As they passed, onlookers spilled into the street, despite the armed guards, and followed them.

The horses were reined into a slower pace. The carriage drew up at the edge of the platform and Paine could see within it. The King's head was lowered. There was a missal in his hand. He was evidently reading his prayers—the prayers of the dying. Abbé Edgeworth, his confessor, was at his side. The Abbé was telling the beads of a rosary. The minutes ticked by. They seemed interminable. The carriage door opened and a lieutenant stepped down. Suddenly an impatient spectator exclaimed, *"Hâtez-vous-en!"* A brutish hand was immediately clapped across his mouth. The King stepped from the carriage. The Abbé and Mayor Chambronne remained within its shelter.

As King Louis and the lieutenant ascended the scaffold, the drums began a muffled roll. The King turned upon the drummers and cried, *"Taisez-vous!* Silence!" Not a drumstick fell upon a drum. He was to be executed, but, until his last breath, he was the King! He mounted the last steps slowly. He was dressed in a puce coat, grey knee breeches, and white stockings. His head was bare. He stripped off his coat and disclosed a waistcoat of quilted white flannel. Paine recalled the first time he had seen him . . . in a palace corridor at Versilles. How round and cheerful his face had seemed . . . how young!

He had been twenty-four years old then. He was thirty-eight now. How quickly those fourteen years had flown!

Paine was abruptly recalled to the present. The King was resisting the executioner, who had approached him in order to bind him. To the executioner, he was no longer His Majesty but a "condemned." As he grappled with him, the Abbé left the carriage and ascended the scaffold. They pressed about the struggling King—Santerre, the Abbé, and a grenadier who had laid down his musket. Paine looked away. His eyes traveled over the hushed and expectant faces all about him. He still could see no single deputy. It was as though, having sown the seed, they would deny its fruit.

The King had struggled free but his hands were now tied behind his back. His face was very red. He turned and cried to the watching crowd, "Frenchmen—I die innocent! Innocent! I tell you so from this scaffold and near appearing before God. *Pardonne! Pardonne!* I have desired that France . . ."

The multitude surged forward so that they could hear a king plead.

Suddenly Santerre cried, *"Tambours! Tambours!"* He whipped out his sword and threatened the silent drummers. They tore away the black cloths and hurriedly sounded their drums. The reverberating rolls drowned out Louis' words. He was grasped by three grenadiers who sprang to the scaffold at an order from Santerre. With the executioner's help, they bound the King's feet and thrust him upon the guillotine's plank. His red face was a kaleidoscope of violent anger, fear, and horror. His head, now held fast in the guillotine's yoke, turned back and forth as though seeking a savior. His lips kept shouting, "No! No!" but his voice was lost in the sound of drums. The executioner lifted aside the thick ringlets of hair at the nape of his neck. He straightened, reached up, and tugged at the release. The heavy triangle of death rushed downward. There was a crunch of bone, a sickening blow, and Paine turned quickly away. He began to

[445]

elbow a path through the crowd. Behind him there was the dreadful sound of the King's legs, beating a frightful tattoo on the guillotine's plank, to which they had not been securely tied.

For an instant, there was a stunned silence all about him. A motionless sea of faces, lifted upward. And suddenly a wild tumultuous shouting broke from 1,000 throats. *"Vive la République!"* they cried. *"Vive la France!"* They surged forward like a tidal wave. He stood still and they pushed past him toward the scaffold, like beasts.

As Paine had predicted, the execution of France's King and the French declaration of war against Austria furnished all the aristocratic governments of Europe a pretext to destroy a revolutionary system of self-rule that threatened their own foundations. Three days after hearing of the execution of Louis XVI, Pitt handed the French representative his papers. By February, 1793, England and France were officially at war. In a few more months every country in Europe, excepting Switzerland, Denmark, and Sweden, was at war with France!

In Paris, Danton, Robespierre, Couthon, and even Marat, who had cried, "We must oust from the Convention all those faithless members who betrayed their duties in trying to save a tyrant's life!" now decided that the Convention had a great need of Paine's services. He was forgiven his "heresy" and appointed a member of the Committee of Surveillance. In an effort to arouse the country's patriotism, Paine wrote in the press:

> The tyrants of the earth are leagued against France; but with little effect. . . . The nation will perish to a man, or be free!

Nevertheless, Paine was not deceived by his own eloquence. France was now alone in a hostile Europe. Even her former ally, Spain, had turned her back upon her. She could look only to America for aid. Equally alarming was the fact that the religious peasants along the coast of France, as far south as the Bay of Biscay and as far north as Nantes, had already begun to flock to the aristocratic banners of a hastily formed Royal Army. A civil war! Armies at every border of France, and now a civil war within her own bowels!

Danton demanded a decree to search for arms all persons who were "suspect." All citizens were ordered to remain within doors after dark, and the streets were empty except for guards at each end.

Soon, inflated prices began to cause bread riots, and workmen gathered in angry groups. The curfew was lifted, as an appeasing measure, and a Committee of Public Safety was formed. When Paine was appointed a member, he learned that Marat himself was actually inciting the Paris mobs to pillage!

As April drew to a close, Paine realized that he was accomplishing nothing. Every day saw a greater portion of Paris fall under the spell of Marat's incendiary speeches. Once, as they passed each other in the Convention hall, Marat spat a half-dozen phrases at Paine in his rapid French. Danton, who was standing close by, laughed. "Shall I tell you what Marat said?" he chuckled as though it were some great joke. "He said, 'Frenchmen are mad to allow foreigners to live among them. They should cut off their ears, let them bleed a few days, and then cut off their heads.' "

"A rather reckless suggestion," said Paine. "Since Marat is himself a foreigner. It is no secret that he was not born here but in Neuchâtel, of a Swiss mother and a Sardinian father."

Danton winked a black-lashed eye. "Come now, Thomas. When Marat says foreigners, he means English. And when he speaks of cutting off heads, I assure you, he has you in mind. He is infuriated by your criticism."

"I shall not criticize him much longer. I am thinking of going home, Georges. But not because I am intimidated but because the adoption of the Constitution has been again postponed."

Suddenly Danton clasped a hand across Paine's mouth. The massive fingers reached almost from ear to ear. "Not here," he whispered. "Not here. Come, let us go to my home where we can talk unobserved. You will have some of my Gabrielle's roast chicken. She stuffs them with chestnuts."

"Georges . . . Georges," insisted Paine. "I must tell you what John Adams has predicted. He says that the Republic will last but six more months. Is he right, Georges? Is he right?"

The big man threw back his bull's head and laughed. "I have met your John Adams and the apron strings that lead him this way and that. Your vice-president does not know the French. And he does not know Danton. The Republic shall last as long as I, Danton, will support it. Do you come or stay? I am hungry!"

That night, Paine wrote to Jefferson:

> . . . Had this revolution been conducted consistently with its principles, there was once a good prospect of extending liberty throughout the greatest part of Europe; but I now relinquish that hope.
>
> As the prospect of a general freedom is now much shortened, I begin to contemplate returning home. I shall await the event of the proposed Constitution, and then take my final leave of Europe. I have not written to the President, as I have nothing to communicate more than in this letter. Please to present him my affection and compliments, and remember me among the circle of my friends.
>
> Your sincere and affectionate friend,
>
> THOMAS PAINE
>
> P.S. I just now received a letter from General Lewis Morris, who tells me that the house and barn on my farm at New Rochelle are burnt down. I assure you, I shall not bring enough money to build another.

[448]

He made no mention of the execution of the King. Three months had gone by, yet it was still fresh in his mind. When he had left, the crowd had fought their way to the scaffold in order to dip their handkerchiefs, their scarves, their very fingers into the warm blood! For weeks thereafter, blood-stained bits of cloth had been worn as boutonnieres. Samson, the executioner, had taken Louis' puce coat. He had cut it into ribbons and sold the strips as souvenirs. There had been an endless line of buyers!

By May, Paine saw plainly that the Revolution now was turning into a blood bath! The guillotine, which had been left standing in the Place de la Révolution, was now in constant use. There seemed to be no end to the intrigues, accusations, arrests, and executions. The condemned were placed in tumbrels—two-wheel carts with open backs and low-planked sides. There was nothing on which to sit. Their hands tied behind their backs, the prisoners stood with spread feet, precariously; while a single field horse. harnessed between the tumbrel shafts, was guided through the streets. Paine could not help but notice them. He saw them daily on his way to the Convention.

Once within the hall, he would be overwhelmed by the unending lists of accusations, denunciations, and proscriptions. The galleries were now constantly filled with libertines, with vulgar women and ferocious-looking men who permitted themselves obsenities within sight of all, sang coarse ballads, and applauded each denunciation so that a speaker on the Tribune could seldom be heard. The Convention had become a travesty!

On May 31, when he appeared in front of the doors of the Palais-National, he was stopped by ex-valet Hanriot, who was now commander of the guards. He was certain that Hanriot knew him, yet the man insisted that he produce his *pouvoir*. Paine showed him his card. Hanriot smiled, showing strong, yellowed teeth. His dark eyes laughed at Paine. "If it is not endorsed by Marat, then it is as worthless as curling paper."

Paine was about to protest when suddenly Danton, who was leaving the Convention, rushed to him and led him away. "Do not go in," he warned him in English. "If you show yourself, it will be a reminder that you have not yet been proscripted."

By evening, in his rooms at the Philadelphia House, he learned that, even while he had talked with Danton, twenty-two Girondist deputies had been "accused" in the Convention. Two days later, when he entered the vast hall, he was shocked to see what was left of the Girondists. But for the "accused" twenty-two, who had grouped themselves together, most of the benches in the "plain" were empty. He glanced up at the galleries and found, to his amazement, that there was no single spectator. He looked up at the "mountain." Many former Girondists were seated among the Jacobins. Danton glared at him. Robespierre sat with seeming indifference. Big-chested Laurent Bassé, though not a deputy, was seated beside Marat. He had been a proofreader for Marat's periodical, *L'Ami du Peuple.* He was now a bodyguard and Marat went nowhere without him.

Bareré ascended the Tribune and proposed that the twenty-two "accused" Girondists should voluntarily resign their *pouvoirs.* They rose in a body and indignantly refused. Paine was startled to see Vergniaud among them. Suddenly, as though at a given signal, a side door was flung open by Hanriot and a mob rushed into the hall. They looked as though they had been recruited from the dregs of the Paris cul-de-sacs. Suddenly Camille sprang from his bench, flung a hand at the Girondists, and cried, "Let us vomit the traitors from our midst! Vomit them!"

Hébert, as though inspired by Camille's words, raced down to the pit shrieking, "Kill the traitors! Kill them! Kill them!"

[450]

The ruffians rushed upon the Girondists. Paine was grasped by one of them. Vergniaud sprang up and cried to them, "You will be guillotined! We have the immunity of deputies. Violate it by placing a hand upon us and you will be executed! *Vous êtes trompés!* Your heads will be thrown to the dogs!"

The hirelings stopped in their tracks. Fear supplanted the look of violence upon their faces. A few turned and ran from the hall. Others followed them. A detachment of Paris National Guards marched into the hall and restored order. As Paine watched in dismay, the twenty-two "accused" Girondists were led away, at gunpoint, under house arrest.

To Paine, the incident revealed the fact that it had become vitally necessary to complete the Constitution and its Bill of Rights. If it were but adopted, some sense of law and order would result. If not, all Paris would soon be bathed in blood. But, he was now working on it almost alone. Villeneuve had fled. Gensonné and Vergniaud were under house arrest. Condorcet was in hiding. Only Bareré took time out to collaborate with him and he, himself, was constantly interrupted by callers. Many were foreigners who wanted him to intercede with the government on their behalf. Some were aristocrats who sought to bribe him for passports so that they could leave France. Others were Americans who considered them an unofficial ambassador.

Finally, on June 25, the French Constitution was voted upon. Dozens of changes had been proposed, many amendments were made, but at least it recognized the rights of the poor, guaranteed the middle class its property, and permitted political expression. Paine watched it being adopted as the basic law of the land and then, in consternation, saw it immediately suspended. Danton ascended to the Tribune, flung out his arms, and cried, "France is now at war with England, Austria, Prussia, Holland, and Spain. There is no time for internal affairs. The guarantees of private property and personal liberty must wait until we have won the war! We now have our Constitution. When we shall win the peace, we shall exercise it!"

They had known all along! thought Paine. Danton and Marat and Robespierre. Even Bareré! They had planned its suspension from the very beginning! He could accomplish almost nothing in France now; it was time for him to leave. But how? He could have gone home in May, before every border was patrolled. But now every port was watched and blockaded by the British. They boarded all American vessels at sea and searched them. If found aboard, he would no doubt be taken to England and hanged!

33

AT THE end of June Paine moved out of Paris. Clio Rickman, who had come to France to escape his own trial for sedition, had found comfortable quarters in a small mansion in Saint-Denis, then a suburb of the city. The mansion had been converted into apartments and was listed simply as number 63 Rue du Fauberg. There was one more apartment to be leased. He suggested that Paine rent it.

Paine was glad to do so. He arranged with the management of the Philadelphia House for the use of two rooms, twice a week, so that he could receive visitors and sleep over . . . and left for Saint-Denis. As he approached the mansion, he recognized it instantly. It was the Bellevue Mansion that had once been occupied by Madame de Pompadour. Its gardens were no longer well kept, its façade had become shabby, but it still retained the ornate beauty of its architecture. He recalled that Franklin had first pointed it out to him. That had been thirteen years ago, when he had come to France with young Laurens.

Paine's new apartment consisted of a small dining room that had evidently been converted from a corridor, a huge bedroom, and a more than ample sitting room. The bedroom was hung with a profusion of gilded mirrors. Shabby paintings of birds in flight decorated alcoves from which pedestals and statuary had evidently been removed. A magnificent ebony bedstead was in the cener of the room. Its high tester was supported by the beak of a gilded pelican. The tall windows were hung with dusty green silk curtains, which were trimmed with a gold fringe.

The sitting room contained a door that opened upon a landing and a flight of narrow steps that were almost hidden by an overgrowth of vines. The stairs led to the garden. It gave the apartment a bit of privacy, for one could descend into the garden without going downstairs through the house.

Here Paine felt no urge to attend the Convention, until he learned that Robespierre was calling for more drastic action against foreigners. In order to protest, he went and found himself the only deputy in the "plain." Rows of empty benches stretched all about him. The Girondists were in hiding or under "house arrest." The Convention had taken on a pall of death. When he rose to protest the decree, Robespierre looked down at him and said, without rising, "The law will not affect the two foreign deputies of the Convention: Anacharsis Cloots, who is Prussian, and Thomas Paine, who is English."

Marat immediately sprang up and cried, "But let it be a warning to them!"

Paine was now like a vessel in the doldrums. He neither wrote nor planned. When Clio would leave, he would wander about the Fauberg garden. For the first time, he felt remote from the disaster that had befallen France . . . perhaps all of Europe. The house and its garden were enclosed from the street by a wall and gateway, and the courtyard was like a farmyard—stocked, by the *hôtelier,* with fowl, ducks, and geese. There were hutches for rabbits and a sty with two pigs. There was a grove of fruit trees. The untended footpaths were covered with wild grasses, but greengage plums were ripening overhead. The summer air was filled with the scent of acacia blossoms, honeysuckle, and wisteria. It was what he would have wanted in New Rochelle. It was what he might have had with Kitty!

However, his retreat into Arcady soon ended. When his friends learned his new address, 63 Rue du Fauberg was filled with a constant flow of weekend guests—Nicolas Bonneville, Joel Barlow, Mary Wollstonecraft, the Marquise de Condorcet. Even Madame Roland, her own soirees disbanded, came upon occasion, disguised as a Breton peasant.

The privacy of the garden was also interrupted one evening, when the *hôtelier,* who went to the city each day to bring back pamphlets and the daily journals, rushed into the garden greatly excited. He waved the journals above his head and cried, "*Marat est mort! Marat est mort! Assassiné dans son maison!*"

It was true. Marat had been assassinated! It was July 13, the eve of Bastille Day!

Paine left for Paris the next morning. He felt that the slaying of Marat was a godsend. It removed an obsessed man who had caused fanaticism to triumph over reason and anarchy over order. He was the Jacobin who, as though mad, had cried to the Paris mobs, "A man who is starving has the right to cut another man's throat and devour his palpitating flesh!" With his death, perhaps the Girondists would return, the Convention be united again, and the Constitution enacted. Danton, despite his ferocity and his avarice, had a regard for the peasant from whose stock he had sprung. Robespierre, despite his evident ambition, was an idealist. The others would follow where they led. It could be a turning point for the Revolution!

Paine hurried to the Faubourg Saint Germain. He was

[454]

familiar with Marat's address though he had never been invited to his home, where he had lived in seclusion with a mistress and a sister, in a large apartment at number 30 Rue de l'École de Médecine.

Paine tried to recall Marat's mistress. He had seen her but once. She was a spindly, unattractive woman whose soft-brown intelligent eyes were her only saving grace. He remembered her name—it was Simonne Evrard. She had been employed as a laundress and then at a factory that made watch parts. She had become Marat's servant, his nurse, the editor of his newspaper, and then his "wife," married *à la Rousseau,* before an open window.

A crush of citizens and a band of students from the nearby School of Medicine kept Paine from approaching close to Marat's residence, which was now guarded by a cordon of gendarmes. The house was set back from the street and fronted by a narrow carriage entrance that ran through a small courtyard. It had a rather squalid appearance, but then Marat had been a rather squalid man.

Everyone was speaking of the assassination. Paine caught drifts of sentences. The name Charlotte . . . Charolotte Corday, the murderess, was mentioned again and again. A hand was placed upon Paine's shoulder and he turned to see Joel Barlow.

"You are not at the Tribunal? I understand that Marat's assassin is being arraigned at this very moment."

Barlow insisted that he would like to see this Charlotte Corday. He was certain that Paine could gain them an entrance. Manon had advised him, in confidence, that this young girl came from Caen, where the fled Girondist deputies had rendezvoused—Buzot, Barbaroux, Louvet, Guadet, Petion, and others.

They pressed back through the throng. When they reached the Rue Saint Germain, Barlow hailed a hackney coach and asked to be taken to the Palais de Justice. In the Rue des Vieux

Augustins, the horses could not push their way through. A tremendous crowd had filled the street in front of the Inn de la Providence and would not be dispersed. It was where Charlotte Corday had engaged a room when she had arrived from Caen.

"These French have a curiosity for everything and a respect for nothing," said Barlow. "I understand that when this Mademoiselle Corday gained an audience with Marat, he was stewing in a slipper bath. Though fresh from a convent, she did not hesitate to enter where Marat was soaking his naked body and seemed to have no compunction in driving a knife into his chest. These French intrigue me. One of our women would have fainted at the sight of the stream of blood that must have run into the tub and stained its water crimson."

Paine sat without comment until they arrived at the Palais de Justice. A great throng of people was milling about in front of it. Vendors of apples and *petits pains* thrust their way among them and cried their wares. A guard glanced at Paine's *pouvoir,* lowered his thin bayonet, and informed him, "The arraignment is over. The accused has been taken back to le Conciergerie."

On July 17, Paine and Joel Barlow attended the trial of Charlotte Corday at the Palais de Justice. Paine had attended trials before and knew his way about. He led Barlow into a long vaulted chamber where Tinville, the State Prosecutor, and his assistants were already seated behind a table upon which indictments and affidavits had been carefully spread. To the left of them sat the judges with their black plumed hats. The jurymen were opposite the prosecutor and his assistants. The steps of a wide stairway were packed with onlookers. Some had straddled the balustrade. With their feet hanging down, they were like so many birds on a slanted fence.

Paine recalled that he had at first refused to attend Marat's funeral the day before. He had changed his mind at the last moment. The services had been organized by Jacques David. Marat's ugly face had retained a look of violence that even death had not softened. His body had been placed on a couch that rested in an open carriage that was drawn by a dozen Jacobins. Young girls, dressed in white smocks, had formed a cordon about the funeral carriage. They had carried wands and branches of green cypress. The whole of the Convention, or rather what was left of it, had followed. Next had come the municipal authorities beneath the banners of their sections. The body had been carried to a temporary tomb in the garden of the Cordeliers' Club, where urns of incense had been ignited, and Danton, as though he had lost a blood brother, had led the populace in revolutionary hymns.

Now, however, a cutler, from a shop in an arcade of the Palais Royal, was being called in order to testify. He approached the witness box with lagging steps and a frightened face. Tinville lifted a large sheath knife and asked him to identify it. "Is this the knife that you sold to the defendant?"

Suddenly Charlotte Corday rose from her seat. Tall and slender, her face held an unexpected beauty and dignity . . . and a calm that was almost angelic. Her light brown hair, though long, was worn in low-cut bangs in front. Her nose was Grecian, with a straight cameo line. Her cheeks were as softly round as a cherub's and the gentleness of her chin was in contrast to her terse firm lips. It seemed incredible that she should have planned and executed the murder of Marat! She looked directly at Tinville and said in a clear voice that Paine had no difficulty in understanding: "All these details are needless. It is I who killed Jean Paul Marat. I admit it."

Her advocate stepped to her side and whispered to her admonishingly. Tinville rang a hand bell to quiet a growing murmur in the courtroom. "By whose instigation?" he demanded. "We must know who incited you to this."

A blush crept into Charlotte Corday's cheeks. "I swear it was by no one's instigation but my own."

"What tempted you, then?"

"His crimes!"

There were cries of "*Elle est aliéné!*" from the spectators on the stairway.

Charlotte Corday turned and faced them. Without a note of anger in her voice, she said, "Marat violated the sovereignty of the people by causing members of the Convention to be expelled and arrested. He has kindled a civil war that is desolating France."

Tinville paid no attention. He was busy writing a note. The spectators' cries of "*Elle est aliéné!* She is deranged!" had given him an idea. He would order Chaveau Lagarde, Charlotte's advocate, to plead insanity. It would humiliate Charlotte Corday and her idealism. The note was passed to Lagarde and he whispered earnestly to Charlotte. Paine could see her glance again and again to where Marat's common-law wife was seated. Simonne Evrard's face was tear-stained. It seemed incredible that one could weep for such a tyrant as Marat. Charlotte brushed Lagarde's hand from her shoulder and cried to the court, "There are some who weep for the death of Marat. I weep over the misfortunes of my country. While Marat lived, no one could be sure of a single day's existence. I killed a man to save 100,000 . . . a villain to save innocents . . . a savage beast in order to give repose to France! All of Caen will give testimony to what I say."

"But," cried Tinville, half rising from his seat, "who inspired you with so much hatred of Marat? Who were the others?"

"There were no others. I wanted peace for my country. Peace and liberty."

"The blow was skillfully dealt. If not thrust at the exact spot, Jean Marat might have survived. Where you instructed? You seem well practiced in this sort of crime."

Charlotte stared at Tinville with wide eyes. Her face was flushed with indignation. "Good heavens!" she cried. "Do you take me for an assassin?"

Paine touched Joel Barlow upon the arm and suggested that they leave. There was no point in staying longer in order to witness the formalities. No one could save self-confessed Charlotte Corday. There could be no other sentence but death. It was enough that he had seen this slender girl admit, with quiet dignity, that she had carried out what 100 men had not dared to attempt.

Paine had promised himself that he would witness no more executions, yet by early evening he was drawn once again to the Place de la Révolution. At seven-thirty, a half hour before sunset, a single tumbrel left the gates of le Conciergerie. It was led by Executioner Samson and followed by a bodyguard of troops. A vast crowd had lined the Rue de Rivoli in order to get a good look at Marat's assassin. They stood hushed and as though undecided. As the tumbrel approached the square, Paine saw some men remove their hats. A few women stealthily made the sign of the cross upon their breasts. The multitude pressed forward when the tumbrel was drawn up at the scaffold. There were cries of *"Elle est une fille de joie! Elle est aliéné!"* As the cries died away and the crowd grew hushed, there were insistent whispers of *"Elle est une religieuse!"*

They had dressed Charlotte in a red smock—to indicate that she was a murderess—but her face was serene. They had shorn the long locks from the back of her head and tied her hands behind her. She had refused an offered stool and stood with her bare feet half hidden in the straw. Samson helped her from the tumbrel with affected courtesy. Suddenly there was a flash of lightning overhead and then a clap of thunder. A thundershower broke and sent down a torrent of rain. The crowd did not disperse. Charlotte, who had gained the scaffold, was immediately soaked to the skin. Her body was outlined in all its slender, graceful form. She resembled one of David's statues as the wet smock clung to her. Samson's hands trembled as he began to bind her feet. She turned her head and shoulders and protested that she would not have her courage so insulted. He explained the necessity and she

[459]

apologetically submitted. The summer squall ended as abruptly as it had begun. The planks of the platform steamed in the July heat.

Paine refused to let himself see more. His mind was already filled with enough nightmares. As he shouldered his way through the crowd, there was suddenly a tremendous gasp, as though it had issued from the depths of 1,000 throats. Paine glanced back. Samson was occupied in unbinding the bleeding body from the plank, but his assistant, Legros, had lifted Charlotte's head from the basket and was showing it to the throng. Scarlet drops of blood still dripped from the severed throat, the rain-washed face was serene, the lips slightly parted. The half-closed eyes reflected the sunlight and it seemed, almost, as though two trickles of tears ran from them. . . .

Despite the proscription of his friends, Paine's hope for the liberty of France refused to expire completely. He spent long hours in the Bureau of Foreign Affairs, with Bareré, in order to expedite shipments of grain and rice from America.

One day, in the Convention, Bareré invited him to sit on the "mountain" among the Jacobins. Seated in the "plain," amidst the empty benches, he was an irritating reminder of what had happened to the Girondists . . . to the men who had been called brother and *citoyen.*

Danton did not oppose the suggestion. Even Robespierre smiled and said, "We do not see enough of Deputy Paine. It gives a wrong impression to see him still seated in the 'marsh.' "

Paine looked up at the tiers. "The seat of Marat has not yet been filled," he said. "Does Deputy Robespierre wish to seat me there? Until then I am comfortable where I am. I await the release of my friends. I would not want to be elsewhere when they return."

Robespierre sprang to his feet. His face was white with

rage. Danton grasped his arm and restrained him.

When the Convention adjourned, Danton hurried to Paine and led him aside. "Do not rely too much upon your pen," he advised. "The printed word did much good in America, but it can avail nothing in a country as highly corrupted as France. We have but one certain influence now, my friend . . . the little window of the guillotine, through which the careless thrust their heads."

On Monday, October 14, 1793, Joel Barlow called at Paine's apartment in the Rue du Fauberg. It was almost noon, but Paine was still asleep. Letters and papers were scattered across the floor and two empty bottles and a broken wineglass lay among them. Paine's clothes were heaped at the foot of the bed, where he had dropped them the night before. He had evidently been drunk. He had tossed his hat on top of the bedstead. It now sat, at a rakish angle, on top of the gilded pelican. He regarded Barlow though half-shut lids and atoned, "Forgive me, Joel. There are times when forgetfulness is more inviting than awareness. There are days when it seems that all I attempt is washed into a common sewer along with the vilest acts of these sanguinary French!"

"You do not attend the Queen's trial?"

"To listen to its mockery or to lift my voice in her defense? If I could do nothing for Louis Capet, what, then, can I accomplish for his widow? And now, with Brissot and Valazé and Gensonné and Fauchet and all the others under house arrest, who would listen to me? With Vergniaud gone, who would let me speak?"

"You will go at least to Paris? Where you will not be alone?"

"Alone? I am never alone, friend Joel. I have with me the ghosts of those who were proscribed."

Nevertheless, he returned to Paris with Barlow and secluded himself in his rooms at the Philadelphia House, where Barlow brought him the news of the Queen's trial as it progressed. Marie Antoinette was being tried by the Revolutionary Court. It was presided over by Fouquier-Tinville. On Wednesday morning at four o'clock, after two days and nights of continuous interrogations and charges, the jury, without deliberaton, found the Queen guilty of having plotted against France and having urged Louis to treachery. It was as though the jury had decided upon its verdict before it had ever entered the large chamber that was now called "Tinville's Hall of Death."

At a quarter past four the next morning, Paine was rudely awakened by drums beating "to arms." He looked out the window. The street was still dark. He could hear the sound of hurrying feet and then the trundling of a cannon, its heavy metal rims grating over the cobblestones. He poured himself a drink and suddenly Barlow rushed into the room. Paine swept a hand in the direction of a chair and pointed to another glass.

"They have judged Marie Antoinette guilty!" cried Barlow as soon as he caught his breath. "They intend to execute her immediately! Are you coming?"

Paine shook his head. "No, Joel. No! I shall sit here and contemplate the finger of God."

"You drink too much of late."

"And you do not drink enough. Have a drink with me. As a friend. If you will not drink with me, then just listen. There is no need to rush away. The French are never prompt."

Paine was right. Marie Antoinette was not led from le Conciergerie until eleven o'clock. An armed force had been gathered since sunrise. Cannons had been placed at the extremities of the bridges, in the squares, and at every cross street. Thirty thousand men and horses had been drawn up under arms. It was as though they expected the Queen's brother, Leopold of Austria, to appear at any moment in order to rescue her. Or was such a show of artillery, infantry, and cavalry needed in order to bolster the courage of the

French to execute the once envied Marie Antoinette, the Viennese Archduchess who had married their King and lived among them for almost twenty years!

Barlow returned to Paine's room at noon and found him still seated at the table where he had left him. Barlow gratefully accepted a glass of brandy, sat for a few moments in silence, and then said, "She was led to her execution like a common criminal. In a tumbrel! She looked mostly at the streamers on the housetops. The tricolor streamers. It was as though they were strange to her. On reaching the Place de la Révolution, she turned and looked toward the Tuileries. I could see her lips moving, Tom. She seemed to be whispering, 'Adieu .. adieu.' "

"She was thirty-eight," said Paine. "Thirty-eight! Why do you remain in this accursed country, Joel? Why don't you go home!"

34

WHEN BARLOW had called on Paine, urging him to come to Paris, Paine had been loath to go. Now he could not get himself to return to Saint-Denis. There was no one left at number 63 Rue du Fauberg but the *hôtelier,* a frightened old man who trembled at the approach of every strange step. And there were no visitors. Who could be there? Even Madame Roland, whose husband had fled to Rouen, had been arrested and imprisoned. Somewhere between the planting of its seed and the flowering of its blossom, the Revolution had been mutated and was now bearing the fruit of a nightmare. The Convention still recognized Paine's influence in foreign affairs and heeded his advice on inflation, but shut its ears to his insistence on personal rights. Outside its doors, he was avoided by every deputy. He had inspired the Revolution with *The Rights of Man* and now no one would speak of those rights, as though they were made silent by a sense of guilt at having permitted them to be gelded and cast aside. Even Couthon, pushed in his cripple's chair, would turn his head away; while Pierre Colbert stared at Paine with sad dark eyes.

After the execution of Marie Antoinette, the twenty-two Girondists, under house arrest, were brought to trial. They were taken from their confinement in the Luxembourg and brought before Tinville's bar in the "Hall of Death." Paine attended the trials. They were his friends, the former flower of French patriotism. They were the most educated and gifted men in France, who had given up their personal pursuits in order to dedicate themselves to the liberation of the common man!

Paine sat and watched in dismay as the Revolutionary Tribunal strove to prove the "accused" guilty of conspiring against the Republic. It was a farce! The Republic had been inspired by these men. Their only guilt was that they had dared to stand in the path of Marat's and now Robespierre's desire for personal power. There was Vergniaud, with his angry face; Brissot, with his sharp chin and his dark restless eyes. Of what could they accuse Brissot, save his hatred of the Jacobins? Untouched by ambition, he was as poor now as the day the Revolution began. There was restless Gensonné and eloquent Valazé, whose loquacity was now silenced. Fauchet sat withdrawn. His lids and lashes were so pale that he seemed not to have any. He had been a priest and constitutional bishop of Calvados. When he looked at Tinville now, it was as though his reddish eyes were cursing him and imploring the very devils of hell to rise up and sear him with their flames.

The trial wore on, day after day. Suddenly, on September 28, Hébert rose and shrieked, "This . . . this trial threatens to become eternal! The Tribunal is shackled by forms of law! A

[464]

patriotic jury ought to have the power of cutting short debates when they feel themselves convinced. Who would say that we are not convinced?"

Paine rose in defiance of Hébert's recommendation. He stood alone amidst a sea of hostile stares. He wanted to plead that, in the interest of justice, Hébert's suggestion must not become a decree! But no one offered to translate his words. Filled with bitter anger, he turned and left the vaulted room.

All night he walked the streets of Paris, from café to café. The "accused" Girondists had all been judged guilty and sentenced to death! It was rumored that Valazé had stabbed himself to death before the guards could reach him. It was said that Vergniaud had concealed a dose of poison, but had flung it from him at the last moment. Paine would hear no more. It was after midnight, but the streets of Paris were thronged with revelers. Theaters spewed forth their audiences. He followed in their wake. At every street crossing, a portion of them was swallowed by cafés and dance halls. A *procureur* tapped him on the shoulder and swung an arm to where two women, with painted faces and bared breasts, stood in the shadows of a vestibule.

"I do not dance," said Paine.

The *procureur* grimaced as though it were a poor joke. "One dances in many ways, *citoyen*. And if one does not 'dance,' one can drink and watch. *Chacun à son goût.*" He guffawed as Paine rushed away.

He was still in the streets when the shadows thinned and orange bands of dawn appeared in the sky. No one seemed to have an interest in what was happening. The King was dead and pleasure reigned. *The Rights of Man* was a myth. The Constitution was deferred. Even God was no longer needed!

In the Rue Saint Honoré, the bakers, the brewers, and the grocers were opening their shops. Now that they had wares to sell, they unlocked their doors with anticipation. Their bellies were full and they yawned at the early hour. Furtive *vendeurs,* as though they had been in the street all night, offered pornographic confessions of hack writers. Paine found himself but five minutes away from the Rue Royale and not many minutes more from the executions. The wide Rue de Rivoli had been abandoned as a route for the tumbrels. They now crossed the Seine at the Pont Neuf, continued past the Quai de la Megisserie, through the twisting Rue de la Monnaie and the Rue du Roule, and did not turn left until they reached the narrow Rue Saint Honoré. In this way they avoided passing the Tuileries. The deputies no longer heard the tramp of the heavily armed *gendarmerie* or the shouted epithets of those who cursed them.

As Paine reached the Rue Royale, he heard the sound of the tumbrels behind him. There was a clutch at his heart as he turned and caught sight of them. The sentenced Girondists —the one-time deputies—stood bareheaded in the death carts. October sunlight, the last morning sunlight of their lives, fell full upon their unshaven faces. They were in shirt-sleeves. Their hands were bound behind them. As though to save time, their coats had been flung loosely about their shoulders.

The square of the Place de la Révolution was filled with a waiting mob as though it were the middle of the day. They had learned to sense the timing of the important executions and were drawn to them, like an enormous wolf pack. Paine thrust his way through the crowd. They seemed to be mostly from the Cordeliers District. Those who were about to protest or bar his way were deterred by the sight of his clenched teeth and the wildness in his red-rimmed eyes. As the first tumbrel reached the scaffold, the mob burst into shouts of *"Vive la République! Vive la République!"* To the crowd's amazement, there were answering cries from the tumbrels. Vergniaud and Gensonné, in the first cart, raised their voices and replied to the surging crowd, *"Vive la Ré-*

[466]

publique!'' They had never wished it to be otherwise.

Paine pushed forward for a better view. Brissot, half sunk in silence, leaned against the rail of his tumbrel and stared at the stained straw at his feet. Poor Brissot! Poor Brissot! The tumbrels were circling about the scaffold and its newly erected railing. Suddenly Paine noticed Valazé's body in the last cart. He was lying on his back, in the center of the tumbrel. A large red-brown stain covered a complete side of his coat. It was true, then. He had really stabbed himself! They had not shut his lids and his eyes stared fixedly at the cloudless sky. Even in death, these sanguinary French would not deny the guillotine his head. They would carry his unprotesting body to the plank and thrust his rigid neck through its yoke!

The guards approached the tumbrels to help the bound men alight. As though attracted by a scent from the disturbed straw, 1,000 enormous flies buzzed from beneath the stained scaffold and swarmed about the horses. The animals, trapped by the shafts of the tumbrels, swished their tails and pawed their hoofs on the cobblestones. The sentenced deputies now stood in a single file. Guards were tugging Valazé's body from the last cart. It caught on a large splinter of wood beneath the straw. There was the sound of cloth being ripped and then it refused to be budged. The guards gave an angry, impatient tug and the corpse flew at them. It tumbled from the cart as they held onto its feet, and Valazé's head cracked open as it struck the cobblestones. His unseeing eyes seemed to stare at the trickle of grey matter that oozed from beneath his hair. A ragged unkempt woman pointed at Paine and cried, *"Regardez ici! Regardez ici!* A *citoyen* with breastmilk in his veins!''

He had not realized that he was weeping.

Suddenly there was the sound of the *Marseillaise* being sung. He recognized Vergniaud's deep voice. The words were loud and clear:

Allons, enfants de la patrie,
Le jour de gloire est arrivé!

A voice joined Vergniaud's. Was it Gensonné's? Paine could not tell. Another voice joined them . . . then another and another. In but a moment, almost everyone joined the singers. Those who had room swung their arms to the cadence of the chant that now filled the square with a tumultuous sound. Suddenly the singing died away. A few quavering voices persisted in a lower and lower pitch until they ceased and there was only an ominous hush. There was a crush of bone . . . a thud . . . a breath-taking silence, and then a roar as though from the throats of 1,000 wild beasts. There was another silence . . . and then another roar.

Paine was thrusting his way out of the mob. They surged back into each space that he momentarily occupied, like water in a sand hole at a beach. Suddenly there was a wild, animal scream. The scream was a mixture of protest and wild fright. It turned into a high-pitched shrieking that filled Paine with horror. It sounded as though it could be Fauchet's voice. It was cut off in the midst of a shriek and, as though its stifling created a void, a roar from the watchers trembled the air in its stead. There was another silence and then another roar.

Paine shouldered his way out of the surging mob. He had been sickened by the sight of the guillotine and its bloody blade, and yet his eyes had been magnetically drawn, as though in a nightmare, to each blood-spattered headless corpse that was flung into a tumbrel—just as he had been drawn to the naked corpse on the gibbet, in Thetford, when he was a boy. And where is God? *And where is God?* Where was He then? *Where is He now?* The question shrieked within him. But a short time ago these people, this very mob, had entered their churches with righteous steps and prayed to their God! What had they prayed? What had they solicited?

Still walking with his bitter and furious thoughts, Paine

reached le Quai des Tuileries, where coachmen had drawn up their horses in order to watch the executions. They were standing in their boxes, fascinated, pointing with their whips.

"*Cocher! Cocher!*" cried Paine in deep exhaustion. They glanced down at him and looked back at the scaffold immediately. It was ridiculous! Where would one wish to go when the spectacle was here?

Once again at the Philadelphia House Paine secluded himself and would see none but his most intimate friends. He no longer attended the sessions of the Convention and ventured into the streets of Paris only after dark. Attired in a shabby coat, a knitted wool hat, and mud-encrusted shoes, he was recognized by no one. When he had first come to France, each cafe had had its own political sentiment. Opinions had been openly expressed and debated. Though he had understood but half their untranslated arguments, he had enjoyed listening to them. The Café de Choiseul had been Jacobin, the Café Patin had been Royalist, the Café du Theatre-Français had idolized Voltaire. Now there was no spoken word in any that might be interpreted as tinged with political sentiment. Robespierre had his police and his spies everywhere. Payan spied in the Commune, Coffinhal in the Revolutionary Tribunal, artist Jacques David in the Committee of General Surety, and crippled Couthon in the Committee of Public Safety. Disguised police watched and listened in all the cafes.

Living like an owl, sleeping by day and venturing out by night, Paine was drawn to the cafes into which wisps of news still drifted. There were shocking stories of atrocities. Everywhere in France, "suspects" were being brought before revolutionary tribunals, convicted, and guillotined. It was said that, in Nantes, a tribunal headed by Jean-Baptiste Carrier was sending 1,000 "suspects" to their deaths each and every week. Four years ago, Paris had exulted in the fall of the Bastille. Now there were more than 40,000 political prisons in the country! Were there so many voices that had to be hushed? Paine felt that he was being sucked into a vortex of death and horror! If only he could leave! If only he could escape!

On November 10, he learned of still another new decree. The National Convention had ordered, officially: *The Worship of God Is Prohibited*! The worship of God—the expression of man's humility in the sight of the universe that had fashioned him, the expression of his innate aversion to the denial of spiritual existence. *The Worship of God Is Prohibited*!

Barlow brought him the news. Paine was stunned, filled with a sense of shock. To show man, with reason, the errors of a creed was one thing, but to insist, *thou shalt have no creed*! It could not be! He must hear from others what Joel told him. Unbelieving, he rushed from his rooms.

A drizzling November rain fell on him as he hurried aimlessly through the streets. He had expected to find them deserted. Instead, they still teemed with people. A huge statue of liberty had been erected in la Place de la Révolution. It towereed over the timbers of the guillotine, as if to remind him that there, but two days ago, Madame Roland had been executed. He stared at the guillotine, in the rain, and recalled how Jeanne-Marie Phlipon had welcomed him in her salon, six years ago, with her peasant's hands, her full breasts, and her husky voice. "You may call me Manon," she had said.

Was there to be no limit to the horrible executions!? But a month ago, he had protested against them to Bareré. Robespierre's latest confidant had laughed, "We are coining money in the Place de la Révolution, Deputy Paine. For always the property of the guilty is confiscated. The guillotine is like a printing press!"

Paine now, in the drizzling night, walked toward the Quai des Tuileries, crossed to the left bank, and came to the Cathedral of Notre Dame. There, students with sad lean faces milled about in the rain. They seemed lost. The University of Paris and the theological schools of Notre Dame had shut their doors. A decree had abolished all the colleges in France! The Jesuit schools of Picardy and the College of Navarre had been ransacked.

Suddenly there was a commotion in front of the cathedral. A vociferous mob of marchers burst into view from the direction of le Quai de Montebello. Their faces were lighted by reflections from a dozen *flambeaux.* The torches were held aloft and swung in large arcs. Their fires sputtered and smoked in the rain. The mob was led by a fanatic with unshorn locks. An immense mustache gave his dark face a ferocious look. He had dressed himself in a stained tricolor waistcoat and shag breeches. A red nightcap was pulled down to his brow and he brandished an enormous rusted saber. The marchers behind him howled and danced in the rain.

An ass, dressed ridiculously in a chasuble, was in their midst. The forelegs of the animal had been thrust through the sleeves of a priest's cloak and the hem of the garment buttoned over its girth. It was being led by a tether that had been fashioned from a priest's stole. A biretta had been tied to its head and a metal crucifix hung from its neck. Its tail dragged a mud-stained Bible over the wet cobblestones, and a cart was being pushed behind the ass. As a portion of the mob rushed across the court and up the wide steps of the cathedral, they thrust and tugged at the massive doors, adorned with Gothic carvings and rows of Old Testament figures, but they would not yield. They glanced up at the huge rose windows above the center door. It was too high a climb.

In the court, suddenly, a chair on wheels was pushed to the side of the cart. It was Couthon! He held a sputtering torch in an outstretched arm, and there was a touch of madness on his face. His eyes were ablaze with the reflected light from the torch. He held the *flambeau* aloft and recognized Paine. "*Regardez!*" he cried. "*Regardez*! Here is the Englishman who protests against the tyranny of man! See now, Deputy Paine, I do more than you. I protest against the tyranny of God!" He

[471]

cranked the gears of the wheelchair, as though Colbert had not pushed him close enough, and thrust his torch into the contents of the cart. The flames disclosed not only vestments and missals but crucifixes, rosaries, religious paintings, and chalices that had been looted from some desecrated church. Unable to rise, Couthon lifted both arms and screamed, "*La loi te frappe!* The law strikes thee. I, Couthon, strike thee!"

Paine looked at Colbert, but Pierre turned his head aside. At the same time there were loud exultant shouts from the shadowed cathedral steps. A portion of the mob had discovered two priests and three nuns. They were rushed into the circle that had formed about the burning cart. Their cassocks, their girdles, their crucifixes, their tunics, and even their sandals were stripped from them and quickly tossed into the flames. They stood naked in the rain, their mouths half open, their arms entwined about themselves. Paine could not interpret the vulgar threats that were flung at them, but a peasant woman burst toward them. She held a wineskin in one hand and, to Paine's consternation, she poured its contents upon them and cried, "The blood of Christ! The blood of Christ! See . . . I annoint you with the blood of Christ!" One of the priests looked up at her with supplication in his eyes, and she bent down, grasped him by the testicles, and tugged him up from his crouch. "Look now, *citoyens!*" she screamed. "We shall teach it to do something else than pee!"

A big man, dressed in a wet woolen shirt and breeches that were held up by wide bretelles, began to move in the rhythm of a dance. His sabots clacked against the cobblestones. There were immediate shouts of "*La carmagnole! La carmagnole!*" With shaking hands and stamping feet, the crowd formed a circle about the nuns and priests, whose naked backs and buttocks were now in wet shadows and now in the red glow from the rising flames of the cart. The crowd whirled about as if unheard drums were beating a frenzied staccato in their minds. Paine tore away and rushed to the steps of Notre

[472]

Dame. He watched them from the sanctuary of its shadow. It was not a dance of humans but a dance of demented devils!

Appalled by the decree that prohibited the worship of God, Paine decided to attend the National Convention again. To amend a myth-corrupted religion was commendable. But of what use would it be to free man's physical body from tyranny and want if his morality and his spirit were washed back into vestigial beastliness!

It was weeks since he had ventured into the city by day. Now, he found Paris filled with peasants who had migrated to it from all the provinces. On the Rue Saint Honoré, he stopped in front of the Church of St. Roch. In the narrow street a crowd was watching workers clamber over the gargoyles on the stone parapet of the church. They were lowering the bells of the church's carillon, leaving a single bell in the tower that it might sound a tocsin. The massive church doors stood open. One was splintered as though a battering ram had smashed it. A long line of citizens, directed by military guards, was hurrying in and out like gargantuan ants. The men carried plush dalmatics, linen albs, and burnished censers from the church. Some held glistening chalices, metal crucifixes, and figurines of saints. Paine felt a hand on his shoulder. He turned and saw Cloots. He was swaying on his feet. His eyes were red-rimmed and his face was flushed. "You . . . you do not look happy, Deputy Paine," he stammered.

"Wanton sacrilege does not please me."

"Come now, Deputy Paine! If we are to have a Universal Republic . . . then we must also have a Universal God. *Non?*"

"A God of violence or a God of reason, Anacharsis?"

"It will be a God of reason, Thomas. But first we must destroy the old myths. You were not at the Convention yesterday. Our new calendar has established a tenth day of rest. Not a seventh but a tenth! From this day on, there shall be

[473]

no Christian sabbath in France! Robespierre insists that he does not intend to adopt atheism as the religion of France. *Nous verrons,* Thomas. *Nous verrons.*"

Paine turned and left while Cloots stumbled after him. On la Rue de Rivoli, they were held up by a procession of farmers' carts, an immense train that stretched all the way to the gardens of the Tuileries. The carts were piled high with metal crucifixes, twisted candelabra, bells, ciboria, silver plates, and molded candlesticks. Asses were led by men in hairy goatskin boots. Woven baskets had been slung over the animals' sides and were filled with communion cups and censers. Women who had adorned themselves like mummers, in looted sacerdotal vestments, marched beside the small pack animals.

Paine, with Cloots tagging along, pressed his way behind the slow-moving procession until it reached the very doors of le Palais-National. Here, peasants, their arms filled with plunder, were climbing the wide staircase that led to the Convention hall, where the floor was being piled high with treasured objects that had been looted from defenseless churches. The men who led the peasants were arguing in front of the rostrum. They were not asking for thanks for their contribution to the Republic! They wanted only permission to dance *la carmagnole* in the very Assembly that had set them free!

At the rostrum, Robespierre was shouting that there must be respect and decency in the Convention. To invade it in this manner, despite their long march and their offering, to insist upon dancing in it. . . .

But Danton soon rose and shouted down Robespierre's prudishness. These uncouth rustics, these men and women of the fields, with their uncontained expressiveness, were his own people! The Convention must not deny the citizens of France their pleasure! He waved his arms and gave them permission to dance *la carmagnole.*

The peasants rushed to toss their last armfuls of plunder onto the mound, their sabots clacked across what was once the

[474]

polished parquet floor of the King's theater, and *la carmagnole* began. There was no sound of fifes, no beat of drums. The rhythm was in their minds. A rhythm that grew wilder and wilder and faster and faster as they twisted about as if possessed. The Convention's proscription against the worship of God had directed them into a bottomless pit of abandon in which they now whirled about in senseless frenzied seizures.

Watching it, Paine's throat went dry, his chest constricted. It would be useless, he realized, to voice his reason for having come to the Convention. Who would listen to his protest against its latest decree? He turned to leave as the dance ended and Procureur Chaumette rushed into the hall. He was followed by children, boys and girls, dressed alike in white tunics, bearing a palanquin upon which a much-powdered and rouged young woman reclined. She was draped in a sheer azure mantle through which her breasts and their tinted nipples could be plainly seen. A dark triangle showed where her legs were crossed beneath the folds of the transparent cloth. She wore a garland of red-brown oak leaves and held a pike of Jupiter in her right hand.

Paine recognized her—Demoiselle Candeille, of the Opera. He had seen her once at a performance, at the Palais Royal. As though it had been rehearsed, the secretaries stepped down from the rostrum and gave her a fraternal kiss upon each rouged cheek. She alighted from the lowered palanquin, climbed the steep steps, and seated herself on the president's right. The deputies in the upper tiers gaped at her. The dancers roused themselves from the floor and stood where the Girondists had once sat.

Danton raised his hands. "*Citoyens!*" he bellowed. "*Citoyens!* We gave you liberty and freedom from tyranny. Now we release you from superstition. The national representatives of the people are about to proceed to the *antérieuse* Cathedral of Notre Dame to deify our new Goddess of Reason. We invite you to attend. Do you hear?" he roared. "We invite you to

[475]

attend the first communion service of the new religion of France!"

"A harlot!" cried Paine. "An abomination of even the golden calf!" He had not meant to cry aloud.

Cloots, back at Paine's side, touched a finger to his lips. "Thou canst not halt the Juggernaut of destiny, Thomas. Nor create a vacuity of worship. Some form of homage must rush in to fill the void."

"They would destroy an inherited religion by threat and violence and offer no more than idolatry in its stead?"

The Goddess of Reason was descending now to the palanquin. "Do you go with us?" asked Cloots.

"I wash my hands of it! It is worse than idolatry! I would rather be a savage and worship a harmless stone than deify a prostitute that inflames the carnal and incestuous impulses of man!"

He intended to remain behind and yet, as the deputies filed out, Paine's curiosity impelled him to go with them. Outside, a tremendous rabble had gathered. Gobel, the new constitutional Bishop of Paris, was at their head. A few days ago, he had been ordered by Hébert to adjure the Catholic faith publicly. Hébert had threatened him with the finger of "accusation": "You shall forbid confessions and sacraments! You shall be held responsible for clandestine masses held in cellars or attics! You will be a live patriot or a dead bishop!"

Humbly, the Bishop had presented himself before the Convention and abjured his faith. He had dropped his miter to the floor. He had cast aside his crosier and his maniple. He had removed his pallium, his chasuble, his stole, and his dalmatic. Standing only in his tunicle and his alb, he had declared, "There shall be no other worship in France but that of Liberty and Equality." The Hébertists had roared their acclamation. Now Bishop Gobel was leading the march to Notre Dame . . . to the "Festival of Reason."

At the cathedral, Paine stood aghast at its desecration. The interior had been stripped of all its religious paintings. Its icons had been smashed and the statues in every niche broken. The altar and the doors of the confessionals had been removed. It had been hastily decorated as though it were a great tavern. Tables had been set up in the interior of the choir and its walls painted to resemble landscapes, with thatched cottages and green trees. A Greek temple, made of papier-mâché, had been constructed in the nave. The boys and girls carried Candeille and her palanquin into it. The deputies burst into the "*Ça Ira.*" Everyone joined in. Candeille was handed a wand of osiers, tied together with a tricolor ribbon, and enthroned as the "Goddess of Reason."

The deputies hurried to the tables that were loaded with flasks of wine, baskets of fruit, sausages, large slices of meat, roasted fowl, and pastries. The rabble, who had followed the deputies to the cathedral, drifted in through every open door and helped themselves. Children ate and drank without notice or reprimand. They grew quickly intoxicated and staggered into the confessionals and fell asleep. The gathering grew boisterous. The rabble became exhilarated. The women tore the shirts from their breasts and spun about as though in a sensual denial of the restraints that the church had exacted of them until now. The men, as though enticed and overcome by the passions of beasts in rut, rushed them into the sacristy and gratified their lust.

Sick at heart, Paine stumbled away.

35

APPALLED AT the vortex of immorality into which the populace was being driven, Paine secluded himself in his apartment on the Rue du Fauberg. The converted mansion was now deserted. Even its old *hôtelier* had abandoned it. It was early November and the paths of its garden were overgrown with browning weeds. The hutches had been broken into, the pigsty had been smashed, and the ducks and geese were gone. There was not a single fruit left on any tree. Yet it was a sanctuary where he could be alone and could think. The entire country had become a cauldron of war, fratricide, perversion, and sacrilegious atrocities.

It seemed to Paine that, if the French had had a religion based upon reason—a religion based upon morality and the love of a creator instead of a worship founded upon superstition and myth-pervaded theology—they would have defended it and not so quickly and happily abandoned it. He decided to write his concept of a true religion—a deism based upon moral principles and an understanding of the universe. After a few days of deliberation, he wrote at the head of a first sheet:

A GE O F R E A S O N
being an investigation of
TRUE and FABULOUS THEOLOGY

Once begun, he set down his thoughts at a furious pace:

I believe in the equality of man; and I believe that religious duties consist in doing justice, loving mercy, and endeavoring to make our fellow creatures happy.

All national institutions of churches, whether Jewish, Christian, or Turkish, appear to me no other than human inventions, set up to terrify and enslave mankind. . . .

I do not mean by this declaration to condemn those who believe otherwise; they have the same right to their belief as I have to mine. But it is necessary to the happiness of man, that he be mentally faithful to himself. Infidelity does not consist in believing or disbelieving; it consists in professing to believe what he does not believe!

It is impossible to calculate the moral mischief that mental lying has produced in society.

Every national church or religion has established itself by pretending some special mission from God, communicated to certain individuals.

Each of those churches show certain books, which they call *revelation,* or the word of God. Each of those churches accuses the other of unbelief; and for my own part, I disbelieve them all.

When he had finished the first two dozen pages of his manuscript, he thrust it from him. It seemed a useless task. The common man accepted his inherited faith, no matter what its origin, and defended its theology without questioning it. It could be that, unlike *Common Sense* or *The Rights of Man,* the world would read but the first few pages of his new work and, urged by prejudice, cast it aside.

When December came, with its cold winds and its biting frost, Paine was still in the Rue du Fauberg. He had begun his book again, but he was not enthsuiastic; yet he felt that it should be written. A belief in God—based upon reason and not foundationless dogma—was the world's only salvation. His nights were restless and his days interrupted by fitful naps. He no longer ventured into the city. No one came to see him. It was as though the world had forgotten him. But he urged himself on to the task.

One night, in mid-December, he was startled by the sound of footsteps. It seemed as though someone was trying the doors. He had had but a single visitor in almost a month—an Englishwoman who had obtained his Saint-Denis address from Rickman. She had introduced herself as Lady Smythe and made light of his excuses for his unkempt appearance and the untidiness of his rooms. They had discussed the Revolution, and it was not until Paine confessed that reason had given way to chaos that she had broached the real purpose for her visit. Her husband, Lord Smythe—surely Deputy Paine remembered him; Robert had spoken of him often—her husband had been arrested and she was gravely concerned. She had been advised that a letter from Deputy Paine could save him. Perhaps a sum of English pounds . . . in the right hands . . .

Paine had explained that he had little influence. He no longer attended the meetings of the Convention. He had given her a note to Barlow and a short letter to Danton.

Now, again, there was the sound of footsteps and a noise on the small landing outside the sitting room. He heard his name being whispered. He opened the door and was face to face with Pierre Colbert. With his deformed back, his big head, and his massive arms, he looked like an animal in the shadows. "You must leave," he said hurriedly as Paine let him in. "You must leave!" He went to the fireplace and warmed himself.

Paine motioned to a flask on his writing table. Colbert shook his head. "I cannot stay. I came only to warn you. You have been proscripted and may be arrested at any moment! You have been seen buying paper and ink. Robespierre insists that you are collaborating with foreign governments."

"I write a book on religion, Pierre. On theology."

"Religion is dead!" He turned his back to Paine. The firelight shone full upon his sad unshaven face. He was slowly and fearfully making the sign of the cross upon his massive chest. "If you stay, you stay to your death."

"Then I would rather die as a patriot in France than an outlaw in England, for I cannot escape. Tell Couthon that I am not engaged in any political work. And if you would do something for me, Pierre, bring me food. And would you bring me a Bible? Yes, a Bible," he insisted as Colbert stared at him in amazement. "Surely there are Bibles in France that have not yet been burned."

When Colbert left, Paine hurriedly resumed his work. He was filled with a sense of urgency. If he was about to be

[480]

arrested, then he must first finish what he had begun. If only one in 1,000 were to read it and give it thought—one in 10,000 one in 100,000 . . . He wrote:

> As to the theology that is now studied, it is the study of human opinions and of human fancies *concerning* God. It is not the study of God himself in the works that He has made, but in the works or writings that man has made; and it is not among the least of the mischiefs that the Christian system has done to the world . . . to make room for the hag of superstition.

He interrupted his writing in order to replenish the fire with a few broken branches. Curled, crisp leaves still clung to some of the twigs. He nibbled on a crust of bread. He had begun a work that seemed to have no end. He wondered which would be terminated first—the book or his life.

On the evening of December 27, 1793, he was startled again by a furtive knocking on his sitting room door. Pierre Colbert was on the landing with a flask of wine, a slender loaf of bread, four eggs, and a breast of chicken.

"It is a waste of food," Pierre insisted, "unless you eat it immediately. The Convention has decreed that no foreigner may represent the French people and the Committee of General Surety has ordered your arrest. I overheard Robespierre and Couthon discussing it. Robespierre has agreed to the order and Bourdon de l'Oise is to carry it out."

"Danton will not permit it!"

Colbert shook his head. "I have spoken with Annette. If you will go to her, in Rouen, she will take you in."

"No, Pierre. No! I will not run and hide."

Refusing Pierre's offer, Paine packed a few belongings and hurried to the Philadelphia House. It was still his official residence, and, if he was being sought, it might be the first place they would look for him. But it was where he would most likely find Joel Barlow to whom he would entrust his hurriedly finished manuscript.

[481]

Not finding him, Paine decided to sleep over. He retired to his room and locked himself in. He was awakened in an hour, by an insistent knocking on the door. Outside stood the *hôtelier,* two officers of the Committee of General Surety, and five National Guardsmen. They had come to arrest him and examine his papers. The *hôtelier,* who had long been friendly, shrugged an apologetic shoulder.

Paine dressed hurriedly and thrust the *Age of Reason* manuscript under his shirt. It was almost midnight as the guards began to search the rooms for incriminating papers. In the midst of the search, Barlow burst into the apartment. "I am a fellow American," he cried. "I insist on *Citoyen* Paine's right to an interpreter!"

"I have a manuscript that I must entrust to your care, Joel," Paine whispered. But when he slipped the manuscript from under his shirt, to give it to Barlow, an officer seized it immediately.

"It is a book on the worship of God," defended Paine.

"Boissant!" called the officer. "Would you translate this, please."

A guard came running. He glanced now and then at Paine as he translated a paragraph at random:

> The only idea man can affix to the name of God is that of a *First Cause,* the cause of all things. And incomprehensible and difficult as it is for a man to conceive what a first cause is, he arrives at the belief of it from the tenfold greater difficulty of disbelieving it. . . .

He shrugged his shoulders at the officer.

"I have nothing to hide," insisted Paine. "I ask only that my friend be permitted to take it to a printer to have it published."

The officer permitted Barlow to accompany them to the offices of the Committee of General Surety. It would be for them to decide.

It was four in the morning by the time they arrived at the offices. The Deputy-Secretaries, Martin and Lamay, had waited up all night for Paine's arrival. They knew him well. They listened apologetically while the guard, Boissant, translated another passage from the manuscript:

> It is only by the exercise of reason that man can discover God. Take away that reason, and he would be incapable of understanding anything; and, in this case, it would be just as consistent to read even the book called the Bible to a horse as to a man.

The Deputy-Secretaries looked at each other, as though for affirmation, and permitted Barlow the custody of the manuscript. Papers that Paine recognized as his lay scattered over a table. They had evidently been taken from his apartment in Saint-Denis.

"We have found nothing of suspicion in your papers," Lamay assured him. "Perhaps this is a mistake. *Non?*"

A door opened and Anacharsis Cloots, guarded by two officers, entered the room. He had evidently been roused from sleep. He had not even been permitted to dress properly. He was hatless and unshaven. "My, how the fishnet grows!" he cried as he saw Paine.

They set out in a group for the Luxembourg Prison. Cloots walked beside Paine in silence. Lamay excused himself to Barlow, by whom he seemed impressed, "You understand, Citizen Barlow, it is not our doing. We carry out an order."

As they turned into the Rue d'Assas, they could see the Luxembourg gardens in the cold morning sunlight. The trees, with their leafless branches, were disheartening. They waited in an airless office while a clerk went to fetch the concierge. He was a stooped old man with a shock of white hair, and a sad face, as though he did not enjoy his position. He accepted the official report from Lamay, adjusted his spectacles, and read the papers with great care. "I am Benoit, the concierge," he finally said. "And now if you two citizens will follow me. *S'il vous plaît,*" he said politely.

"I shall see Gouveneur Morris immediately," Barlow promised Paine. "You are an American citizen. They have no right to imprison you for no crime!"

"His crime is the same as mine," said Cloots. "He loves his fellow man."

The Luxembourg itself retained little of its former magnificence as a palace. The room to which Benoit led Paine was level with the earth and had a brick floor. A small window, shoulder high, set into a thick dampish wall, gave a narrow view of the garden. There were four truckle beds in the room, of which three were occupied. The men in them threw off their covers and sat up as Benoit and Paine entered. They had been sleeping fully clothed. Benoit introduced them: Joseph Vanhuele, of Brugge; Michael Robyns and Charles Bastini, of Louvain. They had read his *Rights of Man* and his political articles and were astounded at his arrest.

"Citizen Paine . . . Citizen Paine," Benoit apologetically interrupted. "Have you brought some money? Everyone here must pay for their board. I am pressed to keep an account of it. Also, it is encumbent upon me that I enforce certain regulations. All must do their own cleaning. Since you have no fireplace, you may enjoy the communal one at the end of the hall. Prisoners are permitted to visit with one another by day. You must return to your room by six. You are permitted candles until ten o'clock. If there is anything that I can do, within the province of my duties, of course, . . . And now I must leave you."

Robyns, a dark-haired rather young man with a thick mustache and an unshaven face, spat defiantly on the brick floor as Benoit left. "Do not be taken in by his seeming concern," he advised. "When you visit the communal room, you will find that it stinks of piss and decayed garbage. We go

[484]

there for warmth, but we do not stay long."

Paine looked to Vanhuele and Bastini. "It is true," said Vanhuele. "Benoit is effusive with his apologies but his actions belie them. He takes our good money and feeds us as though we were pigs. You will be kept alive on boiled haricots, rancid butter, and raw pickled herrings. You can buy brandy from the turnkeys. I would suggest that you purchase some and rinse your mouth with it morning and night."

The news that Paine was a prisoner spread through the Luxembourg. He was somewhat cheered by the steady stream of visitors that crowded to see him and express their regrets at his arrest. At noon, when it seemed that everyone must have paid his respects, Anacharsis brought three more visitors to see him. Two of them were English, the third, though dressed in the uniform of a British general, had a jovial Irish face. Cloots introduced the Englishmen as Mr. Bond, a surgeon, and Dr. Graham, a physician. The heavy-set Irishman introduced himself as General O'Hara.

"O'Hara, . . . O'Hara. . . ." The name was familiar. "Not the General O'Hara who surrendered at Yorktown?"

"Aye, an' I be the same."

Momentarily touched by nostalgia, Paine recalled the days he had spent at Rocky Hill.

O'Hara's red-cheeked face took on a roguish smile. "Ya 'ave come 'ere a bit late, frien' Paine. Three weeks ago, they removed all the ladies ta a separate wing. An' robbed us o' our oonly exercise." He looked about as though for confirmation. " 'Ere's nothin' lak coonfinement an' a sense o' lost time ta prune a woman o' 'er prudishness." He stepped closer and whispered, "D'ya 'ave some money wi' ya, Paine? I coul' buy ma freedom wi' two hunner' poonds."

A month later, Paine was permitted his first visitor from outside the Luxembourg. It was Joel Barlow. Barlow embraced Paine with affection. He glanced about the cold room, bare but for the truckle beds, and shivered. The grey stone walls depressed him. He had brought some money for Paine. When Paine thanked him, he handed him a thick envelope and turned away. He could not bare to look at his friend. Paine's cheeks had lost their ruddiness. His skin had taken on the pallor of the musty walls and his face had thinned. Paine stepped to the single window and removed a sheet of paper from the envelope. It was a copy of a petition to the Convention, asking for his release. It was signed by Joel Barlow and eighteen other Americans. He unfolfded a second sheet. It was a copy of a reply to the petition—a reply by Vadier, who was now the Convention's new president. He began to read it, but his eyes filled with tears.

"The Convention declared that the petition was without any authority from the American Government," said Barlow. "They could not consider a petition simply because it was endorsed by American residents in Paris."

"Then you must advise Gouverneur Morris. Believe me, Joel, every day that I remain here, . . ."

Barlow was silent and then said softly, "I have put the manuscript of your *Age of Reason* in the hands of a printer, Barrois. His shop assistants are experienced in the use of English."

"Did my sentiments offend you?" asked Paine.

Barlow shook his head. "No."

"I have written a preface for it. Do you think the printer would have time to include it?"

Barlow nodded. It could be that his friend might never see his work in print.

When, after many days, Paine finally received a communication from Gouverneur Morris, it came in the form of a bulky envelope and simply contained copies of letters. One was a letter that Morris had sent to Deforgues, the French Minister of Foreign Affairs. He read the letter avidly:

Paris, February 14, 1794

Sir:

Thomas Paine has just applied to me to claim him as a citizen of the United States. . . .

I beg you, sir, if there be reasons that prevent his liberation, and that are unknown to me, be so good as to inform me of them so that I may communicate them to the Government of the United States. . . .

"Inform me of them . . . Inform me of them . . .," as though Morris and Deforgues did not see each other almost every day! He unfolded Deforgues' reply and read:

Paris, 1st Ventôse
2d year of the Republic
One and Indivisible

The Minister of Foreign Affairs
To the Minister of the United States:

I am ignorant of the motives of his detention, but I must presume they are well founded. I shall nevertheless submit the demand you have addressed me to the Committee of Public Safety, and I shall lose no time in letting you know its decision.

DEFORGUES

There it was. Even Deforgues claimed ignorance of "the motives of his detention." And Morris was obviously only making perfunctory inquiries. Had he gotten hold of one of the early copies of *Age of Reason* and been angered by its outspokenness? Paine wrote him at once:

They have nothing against me except that they do not choose I should be in a state of freedom to write my mind freely upon things I have seen. Though you and I are not on terms of the best harmony, I apply to you as the Minister of America.

The moment he had sent the letter, despair threatened to overwhelm him. His ideals had been proscribed in June, his

French friends executed in October, and he himself imprisoned in December. Now it was nearly March and, in the weeks in between, the pace of the executions had so quickened that no one in the prison could count upon his life for more than a day. It seemed as though Robespierre and his committee feared to leave alive even a single dissenting voice. No day passed that did not see yet another deputy "accused," arrested, and brought to the Luxembourg: de Séchelles, who as president of the then National Assembly had welcomed him to France; Chaumette, who had had his moment of glory in accompanying the King back and forth from the Temple to the trial; young Camille Desmoulins, whose stammer had metamorphosed into oratory and whose impish laughter had degenerated into invective.

One morning Robyns returned to the room shortly after all but Paine had left it. He was greatly excited. "And who do you think is here, Thomas?" he cried. "I tell you it is incredible! The Revolution is like a plague! Like a fever that reaches no crisis!"

Paine refused to interrupt his work upon the second part of his *Age of Reason.* There could be no surprises left.

"Georges Jacques Danton!"

Paine dropped his quill and hurried to the communal room.

Suddenly, he was whirled about and smothered in an embrace that lifted him from his feet. It was Danton. Cloots and Desmoulins were at his side. "Needleman Paine!" cried Danton. "Do you see, now? A man's destiny is in a woman's womb. And the further he steps from it, the closer he steps to death. I should have stayed on the farm and raised pigs and children. And you ... you should have contented yourself with your staymaking. What a profession! Eh, Camille? Pushing tight the soft little rolls of fat that make a woman."

Paine looked at Danton. The big man seemed undaunted by his misfortune. "I have no regrets," said Paine. "I have spent my life in an effort to rescue the common man from tyrany. It has been my destiny and I would not have wished it otherwise." He glanced at Cloots, who no longer visited him. He was changed. He was unshaven, though barbers were regularly admitted.

But now Danton was speaking again, booming in his deep voice: "Your Revolution prospered. Ours has turned out badly. What you did for the happiness and liberty of your country, I tried to do for mine. For it, they will send me to the scaffold. But you, my friend, of what could you possibly be guilty?" He led Paine to one side and confessed, "Robespierre is mad! I recognized his ambition and his Machiavellian skill too late. He watched while the Girondists destroyed the monarchists. He waited while Marat and I destroyed the Girondists. Who would have thought that that chaste and incorruptible eunuch was plotting my ruin. I would have eaten his entrails! But his time will come. Look about you. No one is free of suspicion. The city of Paris is dying. All of France will soon expire . . . *tant de plaisir, tant de grâce, tant d'étourderie!*" His eyes clouded, like a marsh that fills with mist, and he clenched his strong uneven teeth in bitter anger.

Anacharsis Cloots was beheaded on March 24. On April 6, Benoit brought to Paine the news of Danton's execution. He had promised Danton that he would witness it and advise Paine of his death. Now he stepped close to Paine and whispered, "Danton was like a bound Jupiter with thunderbolts in his eyes. His tumbrel was surrounded by heavily armed *gendarmerie* all the way from the Cour du Mai, as though it was feared that the *citoyens* would rise up and rescue him. When the tumbrel turned into la Rue Saint Honoré, the shutters of Duplay's house were closed, but Danton, as though he were certain that Robespierre watched from behind them, shouted . . ." Benoit hesitated, looked about to assure himself that they were alone, and whispered, "Danton shouted, 'Vile Robespierre! You will follow me! Your house will be leveled and the ground where it stood will be sown with salt!' Even in death, they feared him and none would lift his head from the basket. Executioner le Bourreau finally held it aloft. It was frightening. Frightening!"

When Paine made no comment, Benoit turned to leave. He glanced at the written sheets that had accumulated on Paine's bed. "You will make a good farmer, Deputy Paine. Any man can raise a crop in a fertile field, but to insist on sowing an arid land, *àcontrecoeur. Nous verrons* . . . perhaps your words will one day bear fruit."

In mid-April, O'Hara, as a prisoner of war, bought his freedom. Paine was now visited only by the two Englishmen, Bond and Graham. He would recite entire passages from his *Age of Reason* to them from memory. Vanhuele, Robyns, and Bastini would listen without approbation. Upon one occasion, Dr. Graham asked, "Do you fear no retribution, Mr. Paine? No punishment from a deity whom you so malign?"

"Malign? I malign no deity, Dr. Graham. Only the manner of His worship. Every national church or religion has established itself by pretending some special mission from God, communicated to certain individuals. The Jews have their Moses; the Christians their Jesus Christ, their apostles and saints; and the Turks their Mohammed. I only maintain that the way to God is open to every man alike."

"I grant you the implausability of Genesis," said Mr. Bond. "But the Book of Revelations . . . Would you not think the less of a Moslem who derided his Koran, or a Jew who scoffed at the Old Testament?"

Paine looked, with tired eyes, at Mr. Bond. He glanced at quiet Dr. Graham. He welcomed their company, as a respite from his writing, but he was almost angered by the narrowness of their Anglican minds. He thrust his hands beneath his thighs on the hard bed and said, "I do not scoff at the Book of Revelations. Let us rather say that I ignore it. When Samson ran off with the gateposts of Gaza, if he ever did so (and whether he did or not is nothing to me), or when he visited

[490]

his delilah, or caught his foxes, or did anything else, what has revelation to do with these things? If they were facts, he could tell them himself; or his scribe, if he kept one, could write them. If they were fictitious, revelation could not make them true and, whether true or not, we are neither the better nor the wiser for knowing them. When we contemplate the immensity of that Being who directs and governs the incomprehensible whole, we ought to feel shame at calling such paltry stories the word of God."

"I have always enjoyed the Proverbs," said Dr. Graham. "I remember, as a child . . ."

"And I," interrupted Paine. "I had an aunt, of the Anglican faith, who had me commit to memory whole chapters of the Proverbs. But I insist that the Proverbs, which are said to be Solomon's, though most probably a collection, are no more than an instructive table of ethics. They are inferior in keenness to the proverbs of the Spaniards and not more wise and economical than those of Dr. Franklin. I have asked Benoit for a copy of the Bible. He fears to bring one lest it be found on his person. I could point out to you that the parts of the Bible, generally known . . ."

Bastini clapped his hands over his ears. "I refuse to hear your sacrilegious words!" he cried. "I will not listen to them! I shall pray for you. I shall pray for us all." He took a rosary from where he had secreted it beneath his shirt and began to tell, "Hail Mary, full of grace . . ."

When the devotions seemed endless, Paine turned to Dr. Graham and whispered, "Here you see an example of man's boldest presumption—selfish and dictatorial prayer directed to the Almighty. When the sun shines, he prays for rain. And when it rains, he prays for sunshine. He follows the same idea in everything that he prays for. And what is the amount of all his prayers but an attempt to make the Almighty change His mind and act otherwise than He does. It is as if man were to say, 'Thou knowest not so well as I.' "

[491]

When Bastini finally rose from his knees, he left the room. Young Robyns and Vanhuele went with him. Paine looked at Mr. Bond and Dr. Graham and shrugged. "I did not mean to offend them. But there you have an illustration of the deep-rootedness of Catholic indoctrination. As for myself, I insist upon exercising my God-given reason. Moses believed darkness to be a form of matter. He spoke of a darkness that could be felt. And there used to be on exhibition, in Rome, a bottle of the darkness that overspread Egypt! Would you accept it per se, Dr. Graham? Would you believe it, Mr. Bond?"

"Take the city of Toulouse, where the clergy once enjoyed absolute domination, where no Protestant could practice a profession or be engaged as a servant or a clerk by a Catholic. Shall I tell you what the city was famous for? For its holiness! And for its sacred relics. It was the only city in the world that owned a part of the dress of the Virgin Mary . . . miraculously preserved from decay. The bones of saints and pieces of the original cross could be bought there. I can understand why they were sold. But for what purpose were they bought? To be prayed to?

"Toulouse claimed, as its most sacred relic, the foreskin of Jesus Christ. It was on display, in a glass case, and carried in processions on holy days. That made Toulouse more celebrated than the town of Embrun, where the generative organ of Saint Foutin was once revered. A jar was placed beneath the penis, to catch the wine with which it was annointed. The wine was left to sour and then it was known as 'Holy Vinegar.' Women drank it in order to be blessed with children. Do not smile, Dr. Graham. But a few moments ago you offered a defense of the Revelations and the Proverbs. Your own superstition is but a matter of another time and another place. Open to the first page of your Bible and see if it does not read:

[492]

"To the most high and mighty Prince James, by the Grace of God, King of Great Britain, France, and Ireland, Defender of the Faith, etc.

"And in smaller print:

"Great and manifold were the blessings, most dread Sovereign, which Almighty God, the Father of all mercies, bestowed upon us the people of England, when first He sent Your Majesty's Royal Person to rule and reign over us.

"Do you believe this? Well, I do not!"

36

BY EARLY SUMMER, even the pathetic amenities of prison life in the Luxembourg were abolished. Benoit was removed as being too kind to "his children" and Guiard, a ferocious-looking member of the National Guard, was appointed concierge. New regulations were immediately posted and enforced. Visitors and communications of any kind were forbidden. Prisoners were not permitted to congregate in the communal rooms. The newly "accused" were brought to the Luxembourg only after dark. The nights were broken up by the sound of marching feet and the guards shouting to one another: *"Sentinelles, prenez garde à vous!"*

The new prisoners spread rumors of still more horrible atrocities. They insisted that a tannery, at Meudon, was making blond perukes from the heads of guillotined women. The shops on la Rue Royale did not hesitate to offer them for sale and the wives of deputies were setting a new fashion with them. The bodies of guillotined citizens were carted to the same tannery. The headless corpses were flayed and the skin

[493]

tanned. The human hides were made into breeches and jackets. The smaller pieces were sold as wash leather. A prisoner had brought a piece of the chamois-like skin and passed it about as evidence.

In the prison itself, things grew steadily worse. Even the lean soap, to which Paine had accustomed himself, was no longer obtainable. Washing water was curtailed. Each prisoner was allowed but a single wine bottle full of water each day. He washed himself, as best he could, with what he did not drink. Paine and his roommates became infested with lice. They shed their last semblance of dignity and undressed in front of each other in order to beat their clothes between stones that they pried from the damp walls.

Now that they had no money, they were served a watery soup with pieces of meat in it that the turnkeys called *bouillie*. Paine and Vanhuele were always sick after eating it. Vanhuele suggested that it might be made of human flesh from the guillotined. Paine probed uncertainly at the boiled pieces of half-rotted meat. Bastini and Robyns resented Vanhuele's intimation. It could not be! Did he think that the French were animals because he, himself, was Flemish? One must not judge the nation by the actions of Robespierre, the late Hébert, and the others! It was decided that the meat was horses' or asses' flesh—perhaps dead cows'. The soup was supplemented by two slices of bread each day. It was made of barley and difficult to swallow without a mouthful of water.

Paine fell sick with a fever that would not subside. Guiard sent Dr. Markoski, the prison physician, to see him. Dr. Markoski recommended that Graham and Bond be permitted to treat ex-Deputy Paine. He had developed a large abscess that would require intensive care if he were to be kept alive.

Paine was confined to his truckle bed for more than a month. Graham and Bond visited him every day. His roommates took turns in nursing him during the night. When his delirium was gone and he was well enough to ask questions, he learned that Robespierre had been executed. He was astounded.

"And what of Couthon? And Saint-Just, and Le Bas . . . ?"

"Dead," said Bastini. "Guillotined."

"Vomited forth," said Robyns. "All of France was polluted with their poison."

"It was inevitable," said Vanhuele. "You have no idea, Thomas. Your imagination cannot conceive what happened while you lay racked with fever. No . . . do not get up. You must not!"

Paine clapped a hand to his side.

"You had a large abscess there. It is still draining. You are fortunate that Bond is an excellent surgeon."

"I seem to have lived in a bedlam of sounds. In a continuous nightmare. What date is it?"

"It is the fifth day of Fructidor."

Paine stared at Vanhuele in disbelief. Bastini nodded. "It is true that you have lived through a nightmare, Thomas," he said. "A nightmare that even these walls could not keep out. The 'accused' were sent here by the hundreds. As soon as Guiard dispatched them to le Conciergerie, they were replaced by more. I have no idea how we survived." He looked to Robyns and Bastini as though for confirmation. They nodded their heads.

"There was no end to the horror," said Robyns. "The guillotine was shifted to the poor quarter of the Place de Bastille. When the residents rose in arms against its putrefaction, it was trundled to Saint-Antoine, to Saint-Marceau . . . and still the executions continued. There were rumors that catacombs were being dug for the butchering."

"What of Henriot?"

"Dead," said Bastini.

"And Augustin, the younger Robespierre?"

Bastini shrugged. "You ask after the deaths of individuals when 10,000 perhaps 12,000, have been guillotined."

[495]

"Let him sleep," said Robyns. "You must regain your health, Thomas."

As he slowly became better, he learned that the terror, like a prairie fire, had finally burned itself out. The two groups in the Convention, the docile in Paris and the firebrands from the Provinces, sickened by the endless executions, fearful for their own necks, had joined forces and destroyed the leaders of the "Republic of Virtue" on July 28.

The prison rigors were relaxed. Prisoners were permitted to correspond with the outside world, to visit each other, to congregate in the communal rooms, and to stroll in the courtyard. As though they had been given a stay of execution, there was but one phrase on every tongue: *"J'ai vécu! J'ai vécu!* I have kept alive!"

The Luxembourg itself was gradually being emptied. Not a day went by but some pardoned friend came to wish Paine well and express his *au revoirs.* Robyns left. Then Bastini. Then Dr. Graham. It seemed that every prisoner had friends who were able to appeal successfully to various committees.

One morning, Pierre Colbert stood in the doorway, apologetically, and twisted his hat in his big hands. "Forgive me," he said. "I leave Paris. I go to Normandy where *mon père* still lives. Where manure is spread upon the fields and not the blood of men upon cobblestones. I go back to the life of a miller. I should never have left it. Couthon's death has set me free. Now no one shall ask me where I go, or what I do, or what I think. If there is aught that I can do before I leave. . . ."

"Would you go to see someone in the Faubourg Saint Germain? Achille Audibet. A deputy."

"I know him."

"There would be no risk, now. I shall entrust you with an appeal to the Convention. Inform Achille that, for the sake of our friendship, I would like his presence when it is read."

Paine could scarcely hold the borrowed quill in his hand,

but he forced himself to write an impassioned plea while Colbert waited.

At the end of August, Paine heard from Achille Audibet. He had not only sent Paine's appeal to the Convention but had enclosed one of his own. No mention was made of their receipt. The appeals had been most likely put to sleep in the official *oubliettes,* where embarrassing documents were buried. Perhaps they feared what Paine, as a widely read writer, would disclose to the world.

Meanwhile, Paine succeeded in getting quills and ink and resumed his work on the *Age of Reason: Part II.* He was seldom interrupted, for he was now alone in his Luxembourg Prison room. Writing was difficult, for his nose seemed, at times, to intrude itself upon his field of vision. He would touch it now and then, in disbelief. It had swollen to more than twice its former size. A painful series of boils had afflicted it and, with both Dr. Graham and Mr. Bond gone, he had no treatment for it.

As the summer progressed, he worked on his manuscript at infrequent periods. Relapses of fever kept him in bed for days at a time. One morning, a rumor reached him that Gouverneur Morris had been recalled as the American minister. Deeply compromised by his intrigues with the Royalists, he had fled to the Swiss border, where he joined a big shipment of his wines and an entourage of his paramours. James Monroe had been sent to replace him. He was already in Paris. Paine lay in bed and wondered about James Monroe— the young lieutenant who had received a ball in his shoulder at Trenton, the young Virginian who had studied law under Jefferson. What orders concerning him had Monroe brought from Washington? From Jefferson? From Randolph, who was now the Secretary of State? He lapsed into a fitful sleep and dreamt of his American friends—of Rittenhouse and Muhlenberg, of Greene and Laurens and Washington. He awoke dazed. The small room, with its bare walls and the unoccupied truckle beds, seemed strange to him. When the realization of his circumstance returned, he hurried to write a letter to Monroe:

> September 10, 1794
> I have never abandoned America in thought, word, or deed, and I feel it incumbent upon me to give this assurance to the friends I have in that country, and with whom I have always intended, and am determined, if the possibility exists, to close the scene of my life. It is there that I have made myself a home. It is there that I have given the services of my best days. . . .

He entrusted the letter to a prison lamplighter who displayed a great regard for him. "Are you certain that you can find the American minister? If you cannot reach him, look for a Mr. Whiteside. Shall I write the name for you? He is most likely at the Philadelphia House. And be discreet!"

The lamplighter nodded, like an old rooster pecking at kernels of corn. "Trust me, Deputy Paine. Trust me."

By October, Paine knew not whom to trust. A month had gone by since he had written to Monroe, but he had heard nothing. Then, on October 18, he received an official letter from Minister Monroe. He opened it with trembling fingers. He was touched by bitter anger as he noted its date—September 18, 1794. It had taken the letter a month to reach him. It had been neglected or deliberately detained. He rushed to the window, where the light was better:

> It is unnecessary for me to tell you how much all of your countrymen, I speak of the great mass of the people, are interested in your welfare. . . . The crime of ingratitude has not yet stained and I trust never will stain our national character. You are considered by them . . . the friend of human rights and a distinguished advocate in favor of public liberty.
>
> To the welfare of Thomas Paine, the Americans are not, nor can they be, indifferent. . . . To liberate you will be an object of my endeavors, and as soon as possible.

As soon as possible. . . . As soon as possible. . . . It could not be too soon! He had learned that there were rumors, in England, that he had been executed. He had been given a copy of a rhyme that was being toasted in the taverns:

> The Fox has lost his tail,
> The Ass has done his braying,
> The Devil has got Tom Paine. . . .

On November 6, 1794, Paine was led out into the gardens of the Luxembourg. The formalities were over and he was free.

Halfway through the Luxembourg garden, Paine leaned against a tree, exhausted by the short walk. He noticed a carriage, drawn up on la Rue de Vaugirard, in front of the gardens. Its door opened and a well-dressed man stepped from it. He seemed tall and reserved. He left his hat in the carriage. His thick, dark brown hair was parted in the middle and combed straight back without affectation. As he walked toward him, Paine recognized James Monroe. He had remembered him as a gangling boy. He was now a man in his middle thirties! Monroe hastened his steps so that he was almost running when he reached Paine. He flung his arms about his wasted form and held him close. Tears rushed to his eyes as he saw that Paine's hair had turned grey, that his hollow cheeks were blotched, and that his once slender nose was bulbous with infection. He noticed that Paine could hardly stand without support and waved an arm to the coachman.

Paine saw Monroe glance at the bundle of papers that he held in both arms. "It is all of my baggage," he said quietly. "All my worldly possessions. And where do we go from here, friend Monroe?"

"To my home," said James Monroe.

Monroe's wife, Elizabeth, flung herself into the task of nursing Paine back to health. She had read Paine's social

[499]

essays, as a girl, and had been inspired by them. A native of New York, she had known the Nicholson girls and still corresponded with Kitty upon occasion. She gave up her warm sun-exposed bedroom and, with the help of a recommended physician, attended to Paine's every need.

Paine himself started a pamphlet that interested Monroe:

> The true and only basis of representative government is equality of rights. . . . Every man has a right to one vote, and no more, in the choice of representatives. The rich have no more right to exclude the poor from the right of voting, or of electing and being elected, than the poor have to exclude the rich. Wealth is no proof of moral character; nor poverty the want of it. . . .

"I agree," said Monroe. He leaned over the desk that he had ordered placed in Paine's bedroom and noticed the growing pages of the manuscript of *Age of Reason: Part II.* He lifted a few pages, as though urged by curiosity. "May I?" he asked, and, when Paine nodded, he read to himself:

> Take away from Genesis the belief that Moses was the author, on which only the strange belief that it is the word of God has stood, and there remains nothing of Genesis but an anonymous book of stories, fables, and traditionary or invented absurdities. The story of Eve and the serpent, and of Noah and his ark, drop to a level with the Arabian tales . . . and the account of men living to 800 and 900 years becomes as fabulous as the immortality of the giants of Mythology. . . .

Monroe stopped reading. He looked across the room as though deep in thought. He replaced the sheets of the manuscript. It was only after a long moment of deliberation that he was able to listen once more to Paine.

"Man can achieve little without reason, James," said Paine. "And nothing when shackled to superstition. If the God of the Bible is interested in our destiny, then He is aware of the conclusions my mind makes before I arrive at them. If man's destiny is his own, then he must not shape it in the dark of ignorance. Do I embarrass you by writing this in your home?"

Monroe shook his head unconvincingly. Yet he said nothing.

In early December, the Convention recalled Paine. The Committee of Public Safety advised him that he could not be spared and the Convention offered him a pension. He was not flattered by the former and hesitated to accept the latter. Why did they want him to return? So that they could point to him as an example of the new Convention's liberalism? The Thermidorians, the survivors of the old Convention, still met in the Tuileries. But they were dominated by a new group—men like Talleyrand-Périgord, Fouché, and Barras, who had come out of hiding after the overthrow of Robespierre. They were backed, in Paris, by the Beauharnais family and by a clique of Corsicans, enamoured of an army officer, Napoleon Bonaparte. The men who had defended the original principles of the Revolution had been carted away in the tumbrels and tumbled into unmarked graves. Paine decided not to accept the Convention's offer. Instead, he gave a portion of each day to Monroe's service, as an unofficial secretary. With his intimate knowledge of French affairs, he was of invaluable assistance. In return, Monroe supplied him with books, pocket money, and clothes.

In midsummer, Paine fell ill again. When he did not respond to the excellent care given him, no one expected him to recover. The Monroes had planned to spend the autumn at Saint Germain, but instead they provided Paine with the services of a physician and an excellent nurse—a widow who had once been a teacher of English in a private home—and refused to leave him. The nurse ordered his bed moved closer to the window so that, while he worked, he would benefit from the light and warmth of the late October sun. Seated at his bedside, she would read paragraphs from his still unfinished *Age of Reason: Part II* and make such changes as he wished.

When Paine finally recovered, he flung himself into writing new political pamphlets. It was as if he had a premonition that there was not enough time left in which to express all his opinions. Monroe said nothing at first, but, when Paine published an attack on a proposed Anglo-American treaty, he felt it incumbent upon him to have a talk with his guest.

Since his convalescence, Paine had gradually converted his bedroom into a literary workshop. Books, pamphlets, and manuscripts lay in disordered piles upon the desk, the chairs, and even the bed. Monroe seated himself on the edge of a chair that was half covered with octavo sheets and waited for Paine to be aware of his presence. He was so engrossed in his writing that he did not look up. Suddenly he heard Paine's voice.

"James . . . you have come at a most opportune time. Would you care to see a letter of mine to Sam? Sam Adams."

Monroe accepted the proffered letter and read:

My Dear Friend:
    When I came from America it was my intention to return the next year, and I have intended the same every year since. I am now almost the only survivor of those who began this Revolution, and I know not how it is that I have escaped. . . .
    The appointment of Gouverneur Morris to be Minister here was most injudicious. I wrote this opinion to Jefferson . . . and said the same to Morris. . . .

Monroe did not finish reading the letter. "You embarrass me, Tom," he said. "Shortly after I brought you here, as a guest, I asked of you to write nothing on American affairs. To which you agreed."

"And would you hold me to it, even now?"

"I am embarrassed by your renewed political activities."

"Political activities! You mean my condemnation of Jay's treaty."

Monroe knew not what to say to this man who had been mistreated and abused in America, in England, and now in France. Endowed with many talents, he had neglected his private interests for the sake of the common good. Even now, he concerned himself with matters that could gain him nothing but new enemies.

"You are making observations upon a treaty that is not yet common knowledge. I have not been advised of its official context."

"Then, if I may inform you, James, Jay was sent to negotiate this treaty, with Gouverneur Morris' help, while I was still in prison. A courteous request from Washington would have released me. None was sent. Why? Am I a stranger to him? And even if I were? Should that have stopped his reclaiming me? Or was it because he knew that, were I free, I would protest Jay's negotiations. And so I would have! The treaty shames America! It restricts American traders from entering a British West Indies port in a ship of more than seventy tons. It excludes American vessels from all the ports of Canada, Nova Scotia, and New Brunswick; while British vessels have unlimited access to all the ports and rivers of the United States! Washington knew I would protest these concessions, James. He knew it well! I was with him, at Rocky Hill, when I protested against the selfsame prohibitions. It gives England's captains free rein to board American vessels and seize cargoes! And you would have me write no single word against the Jay treaty?"

Monroe stared at Paine in silence. Finally, he said, "I share your political sentiments, Tom. But I am the American minister. I cannot countenance attacks upon official acts of the government of the United States. Especially by a guest in my home."

Paine rose from his desk and walked the few steps to

Monroe. "I think I must leave you, James," he said quietly. "No, no . . . Do not protest. And do not think me ungrateful. To ask me not to express my sentiments and my political opinions is to ask me to vegetate . . . to die. And have no concern for my health. I am more improved than I appear."

When Paine left the Monroes, he was invited by Fulwar Skipworth, the American Consul, to stay with him at his home in Versailles. A dapper young man, with a warm smile, a friendly personality, and bright eyes that refused to recognize intimidation, Skipworth was affluent and did not depend upon the consulate for an income. Nevertheless, Paine felt that he should call the consul's attention to his political efforts.

"I have left Minister Monroe's hospitality because I did not want to involve him. Nor do I wish to see you embroiled. If it has not come to your attention, my sentiments on the Jay treaty have been published in the *Aurora*. Other periodicals have reprinted them."

Skipworth gave no single glance at the American newspapers and clippings that Paine had laid upon the desk. He sat, with folded arms, and watched Paine's eyes. They had regained their former luster.

"I am presently engaged on a work entitled *A Maritime Pact*. I shall point out the necessity for maritime laws to protect the neutrality of vessels and seas and to prohibit the search and seizure of men and cargoes on vessels not engaged in war. But in the meantime, my sentiments against the Jay treaty have aroused the common man in America. They have stoned Hamilton for defending the treaty and burned Jay, in effigy, from New England to Georgia. There are rumors, malicious, of course, that both Jay and Washington have been bought by British gold. The president has even been threatened with impeachment. I am about to send an open letter to him, for publication in the *Aurora*. If you wish, I shall not use your address."

"You flatter me," laughed Skipworth. "I enjoy your company. As to my personal refutations or endorsements of what you may write, they would be like a breath of wind in a hurricane."

By the time summer came, Paine was a frequent guest at the Smythes' house. They were intimate friends of Skipworth and had a summer house in Versailles, within walking distance of his estate. They insisted that it was Paine's intervention that had gained Sir Robert his freedom in that despairing December of 1793.

On his first visit, Paine was presented by Sir Robert and Lady Smythe to their daughters and a half-dozen guests in a drawing room that was decorated with tapestries and paintings and filled with delicately carved white and gold chairs and settees. After listening to a rendition on a harpsichord, Paine expected the conversation to turn to his newest pamphlet, *The Decline and Fall of the English System of Finance,* for Sir Robert's interest was still in banking, and he was English. Instead, the talk turned to his *Age of Reason,* which had created a growing sensation since its publication.

"I believe that atheism is a temporary phase," said Lady Smythe. "Like a child's disillusionment when it learns that its parents are not possessed of all the possible virtues." She glanced at her daughters and smiled. "I was told that even Danton asked for a priest before he was executed."

"I am not an atheist," said Paine quietly. "I am a deist. I believe religion to be socially beneficial and individually satisfying. I only wish to humanize it and divest it of its superstitions."

"And it was only this that led to your acute examination of the Bible?"

"Religion and superstition are not compatible to a thinking man, Lady Smythe. He must discard theological superstitions or his religion will be suffocated by them."

A florid-faced Englishman, who had been introduced as William Torrence, broke into the conversation. "H'rrmph, h'rrmph," he said, "scholars are taking your work seriously, Mr. Paine. As, I assure you, I do not. I understand that Dr. Richard Watson, the Bishop of Llandaff, and a number of theologians are preparing a reply to your *Age of Reason.*"

"I shall welcome it. I profess a natural religion, Mr. Torrence. A religion based upon the repugnance we feel in ourselves to bad actions and the disposition to do good ones. What could they say against it? Christianity is a species of revealed religion based on supernatural communications from God to man. It imposes three modes of superstition upon us—mystery, miracle, and prophecy. I offer, in their stead, reason and scientific observation."

Lady Smythe excused herself and drew off her daughters, on a pretext. A French guest, who reminded Paine of Dr. Guillotin, with his dark mustache, his slender form, and his bent-forward posture, offered: *"Entre nous,* the people will never discard their inherited religions."

"Have they not done so?"

"À contrecoeur. I am told they are secretly reverting to the masses and the confessionals."

"Then the world has nothing to fear from my *Age of Reason.*"

"We do not fear it," said Torrence. "We resent what it says."

"Come now," laughed Paine. "You do not resent what I say, but the manner in which I say it. There is the rub. Skeptics and deists such as Shaftsbury, Bayle, Diderot, Volney, and Voltaire have spoken only partially and by innuendo. But I have dared to prove, in a language that the common man can understand, that the Bible is not the word of God. The freethinkers, Collins, Tyndale, Gibbon, and even Rousseau were scholars, speaking to the educated. But I . . . I speak to the common man, who toils for his daily bread and reads my *The Rights of Man* and my *Age of Reason* by the light of a single candle."

[506]

A young man, who had been introduced as Guadet Montpellier, sipped his wine and studied Paine with great interest. He was a portrait painter who had been engaged to do an oil of the Smythe girls. He had studied for the priesthood until a decree had terminated the theological school at Notre Dame. *"Citoyen* Paine," he said. "Have you not written that every man's religion should be a private affair between himself and his Creator? That no third party has the right to interfere? Then why do you contend against the beliefs of others?"

"I do not write against religions but against the superstitions and the untruths that they contain," said Paine. He looked about to make certain that the Smythe girls had not returned and added, "If I were to tell you that God Almighty ordered a man to make a cake and bake it with a turd and eat it, you would protest it. If I were to tell you that it was in the Bible, you would deny it. And yet, in Malachi, chapter two, verse three, the Lord says:

"Behold, I will corrupt your seed, and spread dung upon your faces. . . .

"And in Ezekiel, chapter four, verse twelve:

"And thou shalt eat it as barley cakes, and thou shalt bake it with dung that cometh out of man, in their sight."

Montpellier's face grew flushed. He glanced at Sir Robert, who knew of his ecclesiastical leanings. "If there are some who could believe that those are the words of God," said Paine, "let them. I cannot. And do not imagine an immediate revolt against the Bible. The priests have done their work well and the common man will abandon his superstitions with the same reluctance that he gave up his myths in Greece and his gods and goddesses in Rome. The hell of dead gods, if there is such a place, is more crowded than we think. Sutekh, the once high god of the entire Nile Valley, is there. And Ash-

[507]

toreth and the Isis and Baal and Osiris and Moloch. They were not myths—they were gods! They are mentioned with respect and fear in the Old Testament. There were hundreds of 'gods'—Ninazu, Mami, Odin, Vesta, Nin, Tammuz, Kuski-banda. . . . They were not the spirits of savage lands but the gods of civilized peoples. Though all are now dead, millions once believed them to be omniscient, omnipotent, merciful, vengeful, and immortal. The 'believers' defended the honor of their gods with fire, with sword, and with their very lives! And gave up their worship with great reluctance."

Torrence dabbed at an overflowing eye and called attention to himself by noisily clearing his throat. "If I may draw the conversation back to earthly things, and to England," he said. "I have news of your bridge, Mr. Paine."

"My iron bridge?"

"None other. It is being torn down and drayed from Paddington to Sunderland. The materials will be used to build a bridge across the River Wear."

"What kind of bridge? What kind?"

"An iron bridge such as yours."

"How?" cried Paine. "I hold the patents to its design. I am half owner of the one at Paddington."

"You are outlawed in England, Mr. Paine. It is common knowledge. Would you try the courts?"

Paine shook his head. "Would you know the span of the intended bridge, Mr. Torrence? Would you know its span?"

Torrence nodded and a newly formed teardrop dripped from his eye. "Two hundred and thirty-six feet."

"Two hundred and thirty-six feet," whispered Paine as though to himself. "Two hundred and thirty-six feet." He wished he were in England so that he could watch its construction. He had originally designed an arch of over 400 feet. The one at Paddington Green was only 110 feet. Now Torrence said that the new one would be over 200 feet. "May I offer a toast," he said as he rose from his chair. "To the iron bridges

[508]

of the future, gentlemen. To the advancement of engineering and the iron bridges of the future!"

When James Monroe paid him a visit soon afterward, Paine thought that he had come to protest the publication of *The Decline and Fall of the English System of Finance,* his sensational pamphlet on English finance written in the Monroe home. But Monroe shook his head at Paine. "Of course it's not your treatise, Tom. I have simply been recalled. I do not disagree with your views."

"Nor will you. The English people and most of the world consider the Bank of England as impregnable as the rock of Gibraltar. I insist otherwise. No bank can issue paper money without a reserve to support it and no country can borrow beyond its capacity to tax its people. I have pointed out that there is not enough gold in England to meet a trickle of the paper currency that they have issued. If a flood were once begun, no dam could contain it. The Bank of England would have no alternative but to suspend payments."

When Monroe made no comment, Paine asked, "Do you doubt it?"

"No," laughed Monroe. "I was merely thinking that we are both trying to sail against the wind. Have you learned that Mr. Jefferson has accepted the vice-presidency?"

Paine nodded. "I thought him a fool, at first. . . . But then I wrote and congratulated him. John Adams has such a talent for blundering and offending, it will be necessary for someone to keep an eye over him."

"I shall be glad to return home," said Monroe. "We are making preparations to sail from Le Havre in the spring. Would you come with us, Tom. It is the reason for my visit. I understand that Mr. Skipworth, too, is thinking of leaving."

Paine sat with compressed lips. Tears fashioned themselves in his eyes and blurred his vision. He was nearly sixty years old and homesick. It was almost ten years since he had been in Bordentown or New Rochelle. His hair was grey, a cheek was sunken where he had lost four teeth, and the infection in his nose had never been completely cured. "Thank you, dear friend," he finally said. "I dream of it . . . but we both know that I cannot. How would you disguise me or hide me? As a valet? British vessels patrol the channel and search every neutral ship. They spy upon me as though I were the greatest single enemy their piddling island has ever known. I would rather remain in France than be taken to England in irons. And do not worry about me. The Bonnevilles have invited me to come to live with them. You remember Nicolas de Bonneville? The editor of *La Bouche de Fer?*"

Nicolas de Bonneville occupied an apartment above his printing shop. Of the circle of friends that Paine had met at Madame Roland's, of the group with whom he had gone to le Café de la Parnasse—La Croix, Danton, Brissot, Desmoulins, Cloots—Bonneville alone had escaped the guillotine. All the vehement and revolutionary newspapers that he had once owned were now a thing of the past. He had begun the publication of a new periodical, which he called *Bien Informé*, but it was not doing well. Paine insisted that he would come only as a paying boarder. The Bonnevilles could ill afford to keep him as a guest. And he would stay only until an opportunity to return to America presented itself.

To make him comfortable, the Bonnevilles gave up two rooms of their apartment—one a bedchamber and the other a small room that Paine could use as a study. It contained a desk, two chairs, and a large bookcase. Marguerite Bonneville watched in amazement as Paine moved in. A single trunk contained all of his clothes, but there seemed no end to the bundles of pamphlets, letters, and books that were carried into the study. They were piled upon the desk, thrust into the bookcase, and lined against the walls.

To his great relief, Paine felt immediately at home with the Bonnevilles. Marguerite had married Nicolas three years ago, when she had been twenty-one. She had been with child the last time Paine had seen her. Now, with an infant in her arms and her middle still distended, she looked matronly despite her youth. Her slender arms and expressive face predicted what she would look like, once again, in a matter of weeks. Her eyes, shadowed by long lashes, were almost black. Her hair was profuse and dark. She knew no English but made Paine as welcome as she could with gestures and a wide smile.

Paine fell into an undisturbed routine of life. He would sleep late, have a *petit déjeuner* of coffee and buttered bread, and then read all the newspapers. He had learned to read and write French well but, having been told that his accent was atrocious, he still refused to converse in it. He spoke English even to Marguerite, who would shrug her shoulders and laughingly answer him in French. He contributed articles to Bonneville's *Bien Informé* and in the evenings he visited the Bonneville sitting room, where Marguerite knitted while he and Nicolas discussed the political events of the day. Occasionally the child would awaken and Marguerite would leave them. He could hear her, in the next room, rocking the cradle. At such moments, the home life of the Bonnevilles filled him with nostalgia.

37

ONE FREQUENT guest at the Bonnevilles was Abbé Fauchet, whose friendship with Nicolas dated back to the spring of 1790, when they had organized a club called *le Cercle Social.* They were now trying to revive it, using a Masonic Lodge recently established at the Palais-Égalité as a nucleus. Evenings, they would argue their viewpoints and enlarge upon their aspirations for a happy society. Nicolas wished to impose Masonic ideals upon the club. Fauchet, despite the proscriptions, insisted upon guiding its activities in a Christian direction.

At first, Paine did not join their discussions. He was giving his support to the founding of a new religion—Theophilanthropy. The members met in large rooms, whose interiors they decorated as though they were places of worship. Altars, which they used as lecterns, were decorated with flowers. Texts from philosophical works were framed and hung upon the walls and lectures or sermons upon the primary virtues were delivered.—It was actually an ethical society, its purpose to encourage the brotherhood of man.

Fauchet learned that Paine had endeavored to obtain permission for the Theophilanthropists to use some of the Catholic churches. The author of the *Age of Reason* seeking such a favor for a heretic group. It was a travesty! He turned to Paine and asked, "How goes your own social circle, Thomas? I understand that your request to use the churches has been denied. And why not? Theophilanthropy is not a religion but a fraternal organization. A religion is based upon three things —faith, piety, and fidelity. The well-being of a man does not depend upon himself but upon divine providence. And since this is so, man has only one duty—a duty to God!"

Paine glanced at the Abbé. He was a man who was approaching fifty, yet the skin of his face was a delicate pink, as though it had never been exposed to the heat of summer or a winter's frost. "My dear Abbé," said Paine quietly. "May I disagree with you? The Hebrews have a word that they call *tszduka.* The gentler portion of their religion was built around it. *Tszduka* has been loosely translated to mean charity, but scholars insist that it means 'good deeds.' I cannot conceive of 'good deeds' to God, who has no need of them, but only of 'good deeds' to my fellow man. As you no doubt know, my dear Abbé, the very name 'Theophilanthrophy' is compounded of three Greek words that signify God, love, and man. If the love of both God and man is not the basis for a religion, then there is none."

One day he borrowed from the Abbé a copy of Boulanger's *Life of Paul.* The print was fine and he found it a strain to read. In the evening he asked Nicolas if he would read it to him aloud.

"Fauchet loaned you this?" Bonneville asked in surprise.

Paine smiled. "I only ask that you read from it, Nicolas. Here comes Marguerite. You do not mind her listening?"

Bonneville shrugged. Marguerite seated herslf beside her husband and settled her knitting in her lap. Her nimble fingers guided the slender needles in their swift little spirals of motion. Nicolas rested the heavy leatherbound volume on his knees and prepared to read when the door opened and Fauchet himself stood in the doorway. As though his friendship with Nicolas and his former position in the Church gave him the authority, he had a habit of entering without knocking. Bonneville shut the book and made him welcome.

"They are discussing the life and the writings of Paul," said Marguerite.

Fauchet smiled. *"Eh, bien.* To talk is to think. To think is to conclude and to conclude is to believe. I have come at a most judicious time. I do not doubt but that our Apostle Paul needs a defender."

"Defender," laughed Paine. "My dear Abbé, the character of the person called Paul had in it a great deal of violence and fanaticism. Is that what you would defend? He persecuted with as much heat as a Jew as he afterward preached as a Christian."

"And you are not an extremist?"

"Come now, Abbé. You know otherwise. I leave each man to his own thoughts. I ask only that he think. I have no grievance against the fourteen Epistles ascribed to Paul, since the writer does not pretend to have been a witness to any of the scenes told of the resurrection and the ascension, and even declares that he had not believed them. But his doctrine of immortality . . ."

"And you do not believe in the immortality of the soul?"

"If you would follow me," said Paine, "the doctrine Paul sets out to prove by argument is the resurrection of the same body. He advances this as evidence of immortality. But it appears to me to furnish evidence against it. If I have already died in this body and am raised again in the same body in which I have lived, it is presumptive evidence that I shall die again. For my body is too full of ills. To believe in immortality, I must have a more elevated idea than is contained in the gloomy doctrine of the resurrection."

"To be dissatisfied with our bodies is to take too lightly the premise that we are fashioned in the image of God, my friend."

"The image of God!" laughed Paine. "I confess to you, Abbé, as a matter of choice, as well as of hope. I had rather have a better body and a more convenient form than the present."

"But the intellect of man, Thomas, His intellect!"

"Of course, Abbé. The intellect! But the intellect of the common man is chained. Chained by superstitions and the taboos of his religious dogmas. Would you immortalize his body and keep his mind imprisoned? I insist that the *consciousness of existence* is the only conceivable idea we can have of another life, and the continuance of that consciousness is immortality. As against Paul's doctrine of the resurrection of the body, I say that the consciousness of existence, or the knowing that we exist, is not necessarily confined to the same form, nor to the same matter, even in this life. We have not in all cases the same form, nor in any case the same matter that composed our bodies twenty or thirty years ago, and yet we are conscious of being the same persons. Even legs and arms may be lost or taken away, and the full consciousness of existence remains; and were their place supplied by wings or other appendages, we cannot conceive that it would alter our consciousness of existence."

"I have some brandy," offered Nicolas anxiously.

The Abbé shook his head. He turned to Paine and said, "I admire the brilliance of your mind, Thomas. But I also regret the absence of its faith. I shall pray for you. As I pray for all who deny the Revelations."

"I am no longer a child, Abbé. I refuse to accept a lie. There was no such book as the New Testament until more than 300 years after the time that Christ is said to have lived. And when the books ascribed to Matthew, Mark, Luke, and John began to appear is altogether a matter of uncertainty. The originals are not in the possession of any existing Christian Church any more than the two tables of stone written on, they pretend, by the finger of God and given to Moses are in the possession of the Jews."

"We have no need of physical proofs, Thomas. Faith needs no material foundation. The Revelations are of the spirit and cannot be contested."

"And I insist that the most detestable wickedness, the most horrid cruelties, and the greatest miseries that have afflicted the human race have had their origin in this thing called revelation, or revealed religion. The assassinations of whole nations of men, women, and infants, the bloody persecutions and tortures unto death, the religious wars that have laid Europe in blood and ashes—all rose from the impious belief that God had spoken to man. The lies of the Bible began them and the lies of the Testament prolonged them!"

"I have read your *Age of Reason,* Thomas," said Fauchet with a touch of anger in his voice. "You need not quote to me from it. I think I shall have a little of the brandy, Marguerite."

Paine was agitated and insisted upon expressing his views. "Some Christians pretend that Christianity, the religion of love, was not established by the sword," he said. "But of what period of time do they speak, Abbé? Naturally, it was impossible that twelve men could begin with the sword. They had not the power. But no sooner were the professors of Christianity sufficiently powerful to employ the sword than they did so. And the stake and the fagot, too. The only sect that has not persecuted others is the Quakers. They are rather deists than Christians."

Nicolas looked quietly from Paine to Fauchet and back again.

"*Vous êtes ivre,*" muttered Fauchet.

"What, on a glass of *eau rouge?* Do not be offended, Abbé. I have said no single thing that I have not expressed in my *Age of Reason.* Were man impressed as fully and as strongly as he ought to be with a belief in a God, his moral life would be regulated by the force of that belief. But when, according to the Christian Trinitarian scheme, one part of God is represented by a dying man and another part, called the Holy Ghost, by a flying pigeon, it is impossible that belief can attach itself to such wild conceits. Remember the book of Matthew, chapter three, verse sixteen? 'And he saw the Spirit of God descending like a dove, and lighting upon him.' And in chapter two of Acts, verses three and four: 'And there appeared unto them cloven tongues like as of fire, and it sat upon each of them. And they were all filled with the Holy Ghost.' Such absurd stuff is only fit for tales of witches and wizards."

"*Blasphème!*" cried Fauchet. "*Blasphème!* I was told that you and Satan are the most talked of characters in England. I begin to understand why. It is small wonder that the country, though Protestant, considers your attack on the Bible as a national insult."

"And here, in France, Abbé?"

"The tide has turned, Thomas. With Camille Jordan as our spokesman, I predict that priests will be restored to their churches and public worship will be recognized again by the

State. As it should be. What a common man thinks is of no importance. How he acts shapes his destiny and secures his happiness. Religion and not the laws of a State teach him how to act. Your criticism of the Bible has been made possible by the Revolution in France and the unrest in England. In a dozen years there will be no single copy of your *Age of Reason* to be had nor its text remembered."

"I fear you have made an enemy," said Nicolas when the Abbé left. "He will never forgive you."

"I do not wish for his forgiveness. I wish only for the enlightenment of man. The anger of a hundred Fauchets will not deter me from insisting that the study of theology, as it stands in Christian churches, is the study of nothing. It rests on no principles, it proceeds by no authorities, it can demonstrate nothing, and it admits of no conclusion. It has been the scheme of invented systems of religion to hold man in ignorance of the Creator, as it is of bad government to hold man in ignorance of his rights. The Bible makers have undertaken to give us, in the first chapter of Genesis, an account of the creation and, in doing this, they have demonstrated nothing but their ignorance. All the knowledge man has comes from the structure of the universe and the constant and unwearied observations of men. Not Moses and the prophets, nor Jesus Christ, nor his apostles provided it. The Bible and the Testament are impositions and forgeries!"

He rose and stretched. "The hour is late. Go to bed. I forgive your inattention. I prattle a twice-told tale."

In mid-September, denunciations against Paine rose to a new height in England. The Bank of England suspended payments as he had predicted it would do, and riots and the bankruptcy of small firms ensued. No one would admit that the fault lay with the British Treasury and the Bank's neglect to accumulate a reserve for the redemption of its paper money. "It is the fault of Tom Paine!" was the cry upon everyone's lips. London editorials insisted that Paine had purposely and maliciously caused the Bank of England to close its doors with his pamphlet *The Decline and Fall of the English System of Finance.*

The American newspapers and magazines that he received informed him that his popularity was no better off in the States. His open letters to George Washington had been reprinted as a pamphlet and widely circulated. As a result of his criticism of the first president and the effect on American export trade of the Bank of England's suspension of payments, the newspapers were filled with vile and caluminous editorials against him.

In Paris, a new *coup d'état* overthrew what remained of constitutional government and a proclamation declared that dissidents would be executed. Since most of Paine's political writings now put him under threat of death, to keep himself occupied, he combined the two parts of his *Age of Reason* and supervised its publication in a single volume.

Two months later, he received a surprise visit from Napoleon, himself. He had but recently arrived from his victorious campaign in Italy and had become a national hero. The November morning was fresh and bright. The people in the street gathered about the carriage that was drawn by two matched roans. Its doors had been painted with a symbolic crest that consisted of a gilded "N" that was encircled by sprigs of green laurel. An armed escort guarded the carriage while Bonaparte entered the printing shop alone.

Bonneville left the shop and guided Napoleon up the stairs to Paine's quarters. Marguerite, whose pregnancy with a second child was beginning to show, was excited and impressed by the unannounced visit. She shuttled back and forth from Paine's study to the front bedroom from whose windows she could see the carriage, the grenadiers, and the crowd that had gathered in the narrow street.

[518]

Napoleon knew little English and Nicolas acted as interpreter. The general seemed impressed by Paine's accumulated books. Nicolas and Paine had shelved three sides of the small study, from floor to ceiling, with unpainted boards. They were crammed with books, manuscripts, pamphlets, and journals.

Napoleon was most effusive. He told Nicolas to inform Paine that his military career did not preclude his reading. He had read Plutarch, Plato, Cicero, Livy, Tacitus—though not in Latin but in French. He had acquainted himself with the works of Montaigne, Montesquieu, the Abbé Raynal's *Philosophical History of the Two Indies, . . .*

Paine studied Napoleon. He was extremely short for a military man—even for an artilleryman. Paine could not tell if his skin was darkened by his Corsican heritage or jaundiced. His hair was receding and his brow was wrinkled, so that he looked older than his twenty-eight years.

Napoleon, too, watched as Paine listened. Apparently he was not aware that Paine understood his words before Nicolas translated them. His dark blue eyes looked directly at Paine and not at Nicolas as he added, "I always sleep with a copy of his *Rights of Man* under my pillow. I could not exercise his principles, away from home, but now that I am back, his ideals of democracy will be my own."

It was a strange meeting between a young general who was riding the crest of glory and a failing expatriate who could not fulfill a desire to go home. As Napoleon left, after a brief visit that seemed apropos of nothing, he insisted that Paine must dine with him soon. He would send a carriage for him.

Marguerite, who had been peeking from behind a door, much to Napoleon's discomfort, rushed to a window from which she could watch his departure. The traffic in the street had stopped. It was congested with onlookers. As Napoleon appeared, there were cries of *"Vive Bonaparte! Vive Bonaparte!"*

"Well, Nicolas," said Paine. "Shall we attempt to discover a reason for his visit?"

Bonneville smiled and lifted empty hands.

"It is not yet apparent, Nicolas, but I assure you that he did not come merely to impress me with his courteous manner or his intelligence, or to profess a belief in the ideals of a democracy that the coup has effaced. The man is an opportunist, Nicolas."

"And you think he wants . . . ?"

"I do not know. And I do not intend to ask. It is neither in the *Age of Reason* that he did not mention, nor in *The Rights of Man* that he claims to keep under his pillow. Let us wait, Nicolas. He is neither shy nor patient. I wager he will be back before the flattery of his first visit grows cold."

Napoleon visited Paine again the following week. He avoided any reference to his successful Italian campaign but spoke, instead, of sailors who had staged a brief mutiny in England. "I would do as much," he affirmed. "I understand that they issued a manifesto that proclaimed, '*The Rights of Man* has at length evolved!'"

"You flatter me," said Paine, "if you intimate that it was only I who inspired them. Actually, their mutiny was against wormy cheese, lashings, and a wage scale fixed in the time of Charles II. In England, Parliament fixed a scale of wages upon the excisemen and years ago . . ."

Napoleon was no longer listening. As though the word "England" were a cue for which he had been waiting, he rudely changed the tone of their conversation, turned to Bonneville, and said, "I understand that in your *Bien Informé, Citoyen* Paine has recently published a plan for a maritime invasion of the British Isles. The article advised that we are now admirably suited for such an invasion."

Napoleon glanced at Paine and realized that he had understood every French word.

"It would be easier to land ten thousand men in England

than to send them to India," said Paine. "That much is true. But for what purpose would they land? You were received as a liberator in Italy, but your looting and the extortions of your men soon disillusioned them."

Napoleon rose and paced the room with short rapid strides and cried, "Do you think it was my purpose or intent? The cash-starved Directory insisted that I levy twenty million gold francs in Italy. *Citoyen* Paine, I assure you, despite all the reins with which they harnessed me, the war in Italy was fought on the principles of *The Rights of Man.* I am first a soldier. True. But, in my mind, I am also a democrat. All future wars will be fought for no other purpose than the ideals of liberty. The Italian people are ill suited for freedom, but the prospect of an invasion of England fascinates me. The intention of such an expedition would be to give the people of England an opportunity of forming a new government for themselves . . . and to bring about peace."

"If you will excuse me," said Paine. He rummaged through a mass of pamphlets. When he found what he sought, he returned to his chair.

"This is a copy of my document on the invasion of England. It is complete, with a design of the boats and a map of the North Sea." Napoleon eagerly thrust out a hand, which Paine calmly ignored.

"The document is called *Observations on the Construction and Operation of Navies with a Plan for the Invasion of England and the Final Overthrow of the English Government.* You have never seen it?"

"I was informed of it but two weeks ago. But then I have been away."

"You would influence the Directory to adopt such a plan?"

"Influence them? It is only necessary to say that I will lead the expedition!"

Paine still held the papers in his hand. "I drew this up while I was living in the home of Fulwar Skipworth, the American

Consul. I showed it first to Mr. Monroe, who was then the American Minister to France. I say this to impress upon you that I intended its use, at the time, for both the American and French governments, and its purpose was not conquest and subjection, but an overthrow of monarchy and the establishment of a free republic in England. The peace of Europe can be obtained only by the establishment of a democratic England."

"I could wish for no less," said Napoleon as he eagerly held out his hand for the document.

Though still dubious of Bonaparte's sincerity, Paine threw himself, with mind and pen, into the new project—the invasion of England. With articles in Bonneville's *Bien Informé*, reminiscent of his *Crisis* days, he sought the support of the Directory and encouraged the enthusiasm of the French people. He drew up a scheme for obtaining ten million livres to pay for the construction of 1,000 gunboats. There would be no need for new taxes. The money for the gunboats would be raised by patriotic contributions. It would come to only two and a half livres per person. He offered to subscribe 100 livres himself and urged others to pledge what they could, so they might share in the honor of annihilating a government that was "the plague of the human race."

In a short while, Napoleon's visits were replaced by messengers with questionnaires. Could Paine furnish details on the topography of England? A thousand gunboats, each carrying 100 men, would mean an army of 100,000. Could they feed themselves in England or would they be dependent upon a supply line from France? And most important, would *Citoyen* Paine accompany him on the expedition? Not only for advice but for his influence. The English had always been antipathetic to the French. Paine answered: Certainly he would come. One of his dreams was to see England free and Europe at peace.

The Directors sent Napoleon to reconnoiter the coast and Paine accompanied the expedition to Belgium, from where the descent upon England was to be made. Two hundred and fifty gunboats had already been assembled. They had been constructed according to Paine's design and resembled the Durham boats in which Washington had crossed the Delaware. They were sixty feet long, sixteen feet broad, and drew about two feet of water. Each carried a thirty-six–pounder in the head and a fieldpiece in the stern. Unlike the Durham boats, which had been poled, they were propelled by twenty-five oars on each side.

The rest of the details Paine had carefully evaluated—the number of rowing hours, the advisability of setting out immediately after a storm, or in a calm, or in a fog. "It will not be easy," Paine advised. "The English will not believe that we come only to liberate them. They will defend their homes with their lives."

"Only let us land!" cried Napoleon, "and you shall see! Your pen would take a lifetime to liberate them. My cannon shall do it in weeks. A musket affects only the man it strikes, the thunder of cannon frightens an entire countryside!"

Paine looked into the face that was by turns earnest, impatient, and flushed with ambition. He recalled young Hamilton boasting of his cannon at Trenton. But he had jested. This young man did not. He was beginning to have genuine doubts about the ambitious Corsican.

"One thing more," said Napoleon. "I understand that you have submitted a plan of attack to Director La Revellier-Lepeax. I am now Commander-in-Chief of the Army of England! From now on you shall submit all your plans to me. And with my first order, I suggest that you learn more French."

Paine's eyes widened with anger. Abandoning discretion, he answered, "It is a thought, general. For there is a possibility that you may never have a need for English!"

"Impossible!" retorted Napoleon.

When Paine returned to Paris, it was with a heavy heart. "I have been disillusioned in my evaluation of Bonaparte," he confessed to Bonneville. "He cares nothing for human rights, only for his own power and glory. I envision England's green and pleasant land with its crops destroyed, its homes in flames, and its inhabitants put to the sword. All those horrors that I have seen perpetrated in your country I may see again in England. I shall not let him taint the Thames with blood as the Seine has been. I shall not let him do it!"

Nevertheless, hurried by Napoleon, the Military Council met for a consultation to which Paine was invited. Bonaparte fretted while the members of the Council examined the charts of the invasion of England. Unable to contain his impatience, he strode up and down the room with his hands clenched behind him. Paine watched and listened. Those who held the measure to be dangerous and impracticable were becoming a majority.

General d'Arcon opposed the proposed invasion. He had gained his reputation by having organized the siege of Gibraltar. He was tall and slender, with the dark eyes of a scholar rather than a soldier. He pointed to a chart of the English Channel and said, "The English control the sea. We cannot surprise them. We could land only at the cost of heavy losses. And those who achieve a landing, how are we to supply them with food and the necessities of war? I say that an invasion would be doomed unless . . . unless it were supported by an uprising among the British people."

As though General d'Arcon's reference to an uprising burst the bubble of Napoleon's impatience, he rushed to the Council table and cried, "That is exactly what is planned! There is no need for charts and columns of figures. Here is *Citoyen* Paine. Would you ask for anyone with a greater knowledge of England? He will tell you that the whole English nation is burning for fraternization. Let me but land and the exploited poor will flock to my banners by the thousands!"

Everyone turned to Paine for confirmation. He hesitated and then, trusting his own French, he said, "It is now several years since I have been in England and therefore I can only judge of it by what I knew when I was there. I think the people are very disaffected—but they are English. By that I mean that, if the expedition should escape the British fleet, I think the army would be cut to pieces. The only way to kill England is to annihilate her commerce."

There was a murmur among the members of the Council. Napoleon was pale with anger. In his left temple, where the hair had receded, a large vein distended itself in an irregular course. "You . . . you think that an army I would lead could be repulsed by a nation of shopkeepers!" he cried.

"It is not what a man is, but what he thinks he is fighting for, that matters."

Napoleon glanced at the Council members. They seemed influenced by Paine's opinion. Damn the English bastard for having turned traitor to a venture that he, himself, had proposed and until now supported! He inclined his head to the men who sat around the charts, turned smartly upon his heel, and strode from the room.

38

IN THE spring of 1798, the Bonnevilles had another son. Paine stood as godfather and the boy was christened Thomas Paine Bonneville. When the few friends left the Bonneville apartment, after a subdued celebration, Paine sat and talked with Nicolas. The conversation drifted, inevitably, to politics. Napoleon had impressed the Directory that an expedition to Egypt, through the Mediterranean, would threaten the British

Empire in India, divide the British fleet, and assure the success of a future invasion of England. Only two days ago, on May 19, he had sailed from Toulon with a treasury of four and a half million francs and the Directory's blessing. He was to be joined by three other convoys from Genoa, Ajaccio, and Civitavecchia. Together they would have an armada of almost 400 ships and 16,000 sailors and marines, along with an army of over 34,000 land troops.

"Our hero of Italy aspires to the glory of Alexander," said Paine. "This past winter, he affected a modest aversion for plaudits and honors. When I attended the celebration given by the Directory, Talleyrand praised him for his studious habits and civic devotion. He replied with a pretty little speech: 'The era of dominance by religion, feudalism, and monarchy is yielding everywhere to the era of self-government. I am but the instrument of that change.'

"Later I happened to walk into an anteroom where he was being toasted by his confidants. Flushed with the anticipation of his expedition to Egypt, he cried to them, 'Do you suppose that I gain victories to increase the reputation of the lawyers of the Directory? The nation wants a chieftain covered with glory and cares nothing for theories of government, fine words, or the dreams of idealists.'

"He happened to turn as I entered and, seeing me, he said in a loud aside to General Lannes, 'The English are alike in every country. They are all eavesdroppers.' He had spoken no single word to me since I discouraged the invasion of England. I believe the man to be a complete charlatan. Now he is off to Egypt, and it will be a campaign no different than that of Italy. He takes with him a Commission for the Research of Artistic and Scientific Objects in Conquered Countries. A hundred and sixty-seven members! The commission is a farce. It travels with him for but one purpose—to supervise the looting of cultural treasures. I shall take no part in any world-conquering program. My sympathy is for the people and not to help exchange one despot for another. If he returns with glory, and he may, then this French charlatan will not take lightly the articles I intend to write against his campaign and his ambition. Perhaps I should have them published elsewhere, Nicolas."

"*Mais non!*" cried Bonneville. "The *Bien Informé* has never hushed the truth!"

The winter of 1799 was a disheartening one for Paine. His hope for a lasting peace in Europe and worldwide liberty for man seemed farther from reality than ever. News of the Egyptian campaign cured him of any doubts he had entertained of Bonaparte's professed "ideals." Even the welfare of his own men seemed to give Napoleon little concern. He wrote to the Directory: "We lack nothing here. We are bursting with strength, good health, and high spirits." Yet Paine was informed by Barlow, who was now in Tunis, that the French troops, fighting in a strange land of deserts and sandstorms, were tormented by homesickness and despair. They were afflicted by an Egyptian eye disease, weakened by sexual infections, and ravaged by a bubonic plague. They would desert by the thousands . . . if only they could walk across the Mediterranean Sea.

By the end of summer, Paine learned that Napoleon was in France! He had left the remnants of his army in General Kleber's care and slipped out of Cairo with a handful of chosen men. He had landed at Frejus and was proceeding to Paris amidst a continuous pageant of acclaim. He insisted that he had returned in order to defend his country against the "Second Coalition." Were not Austria's armies driving the French from the Rhine? Were not the Russians and Austrians, under Field Marshal Survarov, routing the French in Italy?

His official reception was tepid. At first, the Directory considered putting the little Corsican on trial for having abandoned his army. But he was defended by Sieyès, by Barras, and by his brother, Lucien Bonaparte, and soon was left to fashion his own destiny, with the result that in November the Council of Elders, influenced by Talleyrand-Périgord and Lucien Bonaparte, declared an emergency and appointed him commander of the troops of the Paris region. Immediately, the city was flooded with proclamations that the "Revolution" was over. General Bonaparte would lead France to victory and prosperity. He would see that each citizen reaped long awaited-for benefits. The country would soon be filled with *bonhomie.* The masses welcomed the leaflets and their promises. They were weary of ten years of war, restrictions, and sacrifices. In a *coup d'état* that they hailed with joyful demonstrations, Sieyès, Ducos, and Napoleon were named provisional consuls—the chief executives of a new regime.

Paine watched as Napoleon spun a web of public virtues about himself. He was a soldier—but he was also a man of peace. He wished for the glory of France—but he would not sacrifice the public good in order to achieve it. In England, the Whig opposition predicted a demilitarized France. In Russia, Tsar Paul withdrew from the coalition. Paine remembered Napoleon's impatience and his words, "The nation wants a chieftain covered with glory!" He mistrusted the destiny of a country whose democracy would depend upon the ambition of but one man.

When Napoleon became First Consul, he ordered Bonneville imprisoned for having referred to him as a "Cromwell" in his *Bien Informé.* It came at a bad time. Nicolas was without funds and Marguerite was pregnant again. Paine exerted all his influence for Nicolas' release. One night he received a visit from Abbé Fauchet. The Abbé's skin was still a delicate pink, his eyes bright, and his body plump. He smiled as Marguerite, with a worn shawl about her thin shoulders, freshened the fire in Paine's study. She would not look at him. He had started a rumor that Paine had sired her second child.

"Do not leave," he said as she turned to go. "This concerns you, too. Nicolas is to be released." He glanced at Paine and added, "But his newspaper is to be suppressed and you, Thomas, are to guard your tongue."

"And you, Abbé—you bring me such a message? Does it not provoke you that a nation, but lately so enthusiastic for liberty, should now voluntarily rush down the path to despotism? Mesmerized by a charlatan's bauble of conquest and glory? You may tell this Corsican that I shall continue to speak my mind freely and openly on every subject. And if this includes God and religion, then it must also include the First Consul."

Fauchet inclined his head and confided, "Napoleon makes enemies as easily as friends."

"He has no friends. Only followers. I am not one of them."

The First Consul returned to the theater of war, and Paine followed his career. It was apparent that those who were close to him feared him. They knew not what to make of a man who had gratefully accepted a second lieutenant's commission at the École Militaire fifteen years ago and now dared to insist: "I will endure no negative criticism! In France, there is but a single party and a single will!"

Despite his *Age of Reason,* Paine retained his prestige with a colony of Irish revolutionists in Paris. They had settled on the left bank of the Seine, near le Quai St. Michel. With Napper-Tandy as their chief, they discussed a descent upon Ireland and hoped for France's aid. One night, at a patriotic rally, Paine suggested that they go home. "I warrant you," he said, "you will accomplish nothing in France. Would you have this fellow, Bonaparte, help you achieve more freedom than he extends to his own countrymen?"

The gathering grew hushed. They could not tell if Paine were slightly drunk or not. The infection in his nose had never completely healed. It was now inflamed and his eyes were reddened. "Take my word for it," he said. "France is victorious because she has twenty-seven million citizens. More than the combined populations of Spain, Italy, Prussia, the Confederation of the Rhine, and the Austrian Empire. But this Corsican is decimating her youth! I not only see things distinctly, but I have the courage to take them up, soft or hard, pretty or ugly, and to turn them upon their backs in spite of tooth or claw. Depend upon it. This insensate man will conquer all of Europe, only to make it more miserable than it was before." He rose unsteadily to his feet and, as though to cheer them, said, "I propose a toast. To the three guarantees of republics: that there may be freedom of opinion, that there may be equality of rights, and that the majority govern the rest as it governs itself."

Time trickled slowly by for expatriate Paine. The letters that he received from home each month were his only consolation. He corresponded regularly with Jefferson. He expanded upon conditions in France and Jefferson kept him informed of events in America. He intimated that he would like to return to America on a warship, if such a vessel should visit France. The British would hesitate to search a warship. In April, Paine received a letter that set his heart beating wildly. Jefferson had written it two weeks after he had assumed the presidency:

> March 18, 1801
>
> You expressed a wish to get passage to this country in a public vessel. Mr. Dawson is charged with orders to the captain of the *Maryland* to receive and accommodate you back, if you can be ready to depart at such short notice. Robt. R. Livingston is appointed Minister Plenipotentiary to the Republic of France. . . . I am in hopes you will find us returned generally to sentiments worthy of former times. In these it will be your glory to have steadily labored, and with as much effect as any man living. That you may live long to continue your useful labors, and to reap the reward in thankfulness of nations, is my sincere prayer. . . .

Paine's elation was short-lived. His *Age of Reason* had un-closed a landslide of abuse and slander against him in Amer-ica. His *Crisis,* his *Common Sense,* his *The Rights f Man,* and his political writings were swept into oblivion. A new genera-tion of "common man" was informed by the press only that he had written a blasphemous and sacrilegious book in which he denied the holiness of the Bible. When it was learned that the newly elected president was sending a warship for him, almost every newspaper howled objection filled with vilifica-tions and reproach. An editorial in Dennie's *Portfolio* read:

> . . . An article is current in all the newspapers that the loath-some Thomas Paine, a drunken atheist, is invited to return in a national ship to America. A measure so enormously prepos-terous we cannot yet believe has been adopted, and it would demand firmer nerves than those possessed by Mr. Jefferson to hazard such an insult to the moral sense of the nation. . . .

The abuse heaped upon Jefferson grew in violence. He was accused of every possible crime—even the paternity of all the "pickaninnies" on his plantation.

When the frigate *Maryland* reached its French port, Paine refused to board her. Unwilling to injure his friend Jefferson any further, he remained in France.

Meanwhile, he watched with contained bitterness as France's representative system of government collapsed. Na-poleon was discarding most of the civil benefits for the sake of which so many idealists had lost their lives. Pitying Paine's quiet retired life, Barlow introduced him to a young Ameri-can who was now living with him in Paris. Paine was de-lighted to find that he was Robert Fulton, a native of Lancaster County, in Pennsylvania. Fulton was interested in the build-ing of canals. He had a patent for a machine that sawed marble and had designed several types of boats. He had experimented with a steamboat on the Thames and had come to Paris in order to complete a new invention—a boat that could be propelled under water. Paine was fascinated. They met almost every evening in the Irish Coffee House, on the Rue Conde, and stayed until closing.

Nevertheless, Paine was not completely idle. In July, 1801, Bonaparte ratified a concordat with Pope Pius VII. It again established Roman Catholicism as the official and only religion in France. According to its terms, bishops were to be nominated by the First Consul and the clergy was to be paid by the government. Outraged, Paine published an open letter, entitled *On Worship.* He insisted that no religion had a right to special sanctions or privileges. The state had more important concerns—the welfare of the poor and the aged, education for the young, the propagation of a morality that was unfettered by superstition.

Barlow begged him to desist his criticism. "This is a new France, Tom. Napoleon is Emperor in all but name. Those who oppose him are jailed. Those who merely disagree with him are deported. Every Republican who is not in prison or in exile has adapted himself to the new circumstances. They accept his ribbons and occupy seats in his Senate."

"And would you suggest that I do the same? In a mock Senate, Joel? No, Joel. No! France has permitted this ambitious Corsican to lavish her with glory, land, and markets. She has not stopped to consider the loss of her own liberty and the multitudinous deaths on the battlefield. This Corsican—this butcher of liberty—is the greatest monster that nature ever spewed! He has shed so much blood, what would a few more drops of mine matter?"

When the Treaty of Amiens was signed, on March 25, 1802, Paine prepared at last to go home. Temporarily, there was peace and British frigates would no longer blockade French ports. The Bonnevilles promised to follow Paine to America as soon as it was practicable. They had formed a deep attachment for him and, besides, they would be destitute without his aid. The *Bien Informé* had remained suppressed since Nicolas' imprisonment and he was under constant surveillance. He earned a most meager living by translating English and German books into French.

Before Paine left for Le Havre, he was given a small farewell party by Ruth and Joel Barlow. It was attended by Audibet, Fulton, Volney, who was now a member of the Senate, Clio Rickman, and the Bonnevilles. Sir Robert had died, but Lady Smythe was present. Many of the guests were expatriates who could now go home. When Clio, saddened by Paine's wasted form, expressed a concern for his welfare in America, Paine laughed at his anxiety.

"Have no concern regarding my future, Clio. I intend to dispose of my property, live on the interest, and amuse myself by writing the memoirs of my life. I am taking new and improved models of my inventions along with me and may make a business of them. I understand that the iron bridge at Sunderland is a great success."

Paine insisted that the party maintain a spirit of gaiety. It was only when Volney spoke of America that he was prompted to speak of Napoleon and of France. Paine raised his glass and toasted, "To America, the only republic in the world! In a few years the citizens of France, despite all their past labors, will be worse off than the slaves of Constantinople. There they expect to be bashaws in heaven by submitting to be slaves below, but here they believe neither in heaven nor hell, and yet are slaves by choice. Shall I tell you how I see Napoleon? I do not see him as Consul—or as Tribune—I see him as Emperor! The man is wilfull, headstrong, proud, morose, and presumptuous. There is not on record one who has committed so many crimes with so little temptation to commit them. Tyrants, in general, shed blood upon plan or from passion. He seems to shed it only because he cannot be quiet!"

"It is a good thing that you are leaving," said Volney. "I would fear for your safety if you stayed."

Paine arrived in Baltimore on Thursday, October 30, 1802. He was sixty-five years old. He had been away from America for fifteen years. He disembarked with mixed emotions. His heart was quickened by the joy of being home at last, but his mind wondered how he would be received. The American press knew of his arrival, in advance, and a large crowd had gathered at the wharf. A few citizens attempted to welcome him, but they were intimidated by angry cries and epithets. The anti-Jefferson newspapers had reprinted excerpts from his *Age of Reason* and the Baltimoreans had come to see if there were horns growing from the forehead of the world's "most notorious deist, social leveler, and loathsome reptile."

He had expected antipathy because of his work on religion, but he had not anticipated the violence that seemed to simmer in the crowd. It was as though they but waited for a spark to ignite their wrath. He supervised the unloading of his models and effects. He had left almost all of his books with the Bonnevilles, but he had two trunks that were filled with letters and manuscripts. He had difficulty in engaging a drayman and the first two hotels refused to lodge him. He finally rented a room in a frame house at the edge of the city and immediately began a letter to Jefferson, to advise him that he would be in Capital City in a few days.

Paine set out for Capital City on November 9. He was confident of at least one cordial welcome—the president's. He had sent his mechanical models on ahead to the Executive Mansion and had no doubt that he would be immediately invited there, despite the animosity of both the people and the press. He would renew old friendships and discuss the possibility of an appointment—at least to an advisory post in the government. There was no one in America who knew the politics of Europe as well as he.

[534]

Capital City, which some called Federal City, was on the east bank of the Potomac River, about thirty miles southwest of Baltimore. Paine found it to be a village of about 3,200 inhabitants. He had read conflicting articles regarding it. Most of the newspapers poked fun at it. One claimed that it was:

> ... neither town nor village. It is a country seat where sportsmen can run horses and fight cocks and impress foreign representatives with our less than provincial state.

Another wrote:

> It is a scattered hamlet, crowned by three unfinished edifices upon separate hills, in one of which the President sits, during the summer recess, like a pelican in a wilderness.

Paine took a room in Lovell's Hotel and found, to his chagrin, that no one called on him. He waited for a message from Jefferson. He slept late and in the afternoons he read all the papers and journals that he could purchase. In the evenings, when he dined, he noticed that he was the center of attraction. It could not be from admiration, for no one came to his table to introduce himself or join him. As though to inform him of the reason, one newspaper wrote of him:

> He dines at the public table and, as a show, is as profitable to Lovell as an orangutan, for many strangers who come to the city feel a curiosity to see the creature. ...

Paine took long walks after it grew dark. He would walk in the direction of the Executive Mansion and then turn eastward along a wide street that had been named Pennsylvania Avenue. He noted that room had been left for ten-foot gravel walks and thirty-foot lawns, portions of which had already been planted with saplings. And they had left at least an eighty-foot width for carriages. Grass still grew along the edges of the street; at some spots clusters of forest trees were still standing, but many four-story brick homes were in the midst of construction.

At the end of ten days, he wrote caustically to President Jefferson:

> I will be obliged to you to send back the models, as I am packing up to set off for Philadelphia and New York. My intention in bringing them here, in preference to sending them from Baltimore to Philadelphia, was to have some conversation with you on those matters and others I have not informed you of.
>
> But you have not only shown no disposition toward it, but have, in some measure, by a sort of shyness, as if you stood in fear of federal observation, precluded it. . . .

To Paine's surprise, Jefferson sent an immediate reply and invited him to the Executive Mansion as a houseguest. He saw the mansion by daylight for the first time and was impressed by the simple dignity of the building. It was a pleasant contrast to the ornateness of the French palaces. Wide-spreading maples and elms had been left standing at its approach. Their fallen leaves lay where gusts of wind had swirled them into multicolored undulations. A grove of red oak trees, to one side of the mansion, was ablaze with reflected sunlight.

The years had been kind to Jefferson. There was no grey in his reddish hair, his face was unwrinkled, and his eyes were as bright as ever. He had retained his slenderness but now, with the slower movements of his form, his tallness gave an impression of loose-jointed postures.

To Paine's delight, Jefferson gave him a welcome home dinner on his first night. The president was still a widower and his daughter Martha, now Mrs. Eppes, was the hostess of the Executive Mansion. She remembered Paine and asked after friends in France with whom she still corresponded. It was strange how quickly this young nymph had turned into a mature woman! He forgot that it was a dozen years since he had last seen her.

It was an impromptu dinner and, as settings were removed,

Paine realized that a number of guests had sent their regrets at the last moment. He needed no introductions. He knew everyone: Major General Henry Dearborn, who was now Secretary of War; William Duane, the editor of the *Aurora;* James Madison, Secretary of State; Albert Gallatin, Secretary of the Treasury. Perhaps things had not really changed so much. He instantly recognized Mrs. Gallatin, the former Hannah Nicholson. The resemblance she bore to her sister Kitty was more than striking. Or was he mistaken? It was fifteen years since he had seen either. She smiled and took his hand warmly but seemed lost for words. He could see that she was slightly shocked by his wasted form.

Martha seated him between Hannah and Albert Gallatin. He could not refrain from asking after Kitty. He had not heard from her in years. Was she in Capital City?

Hannah Gallatin's face clouded over. She hesitated to reply. Her husband, having heard Paine's question, leaned toward him and said softly, "I fear my brother-in-law has a somewhat narrow view upon religious matters and permits his intolerance to dominate both his domestic as well as his political affairs. If they are absent, it is not because the president neglected to invite them."

The dinner group had expected to find Paine either unassuming and grateful to be back in America or angered by the neglect with which he had been treated. Instead, they found him quite unconcerned. He was replete with amazing anecdotes and a conversationalist of uncommon interest. If one could find fault with him, it would be with his outspokenness. When Dearborn commented that it was already three years since Washington's death and that the late president would have warmly welcomed Paine's return, Paine gave a wry smile and answered, "I do not know if your intent is to flatter me or the late Mr. Washington. I assure you that, in either case, you are in error. Mr. Washington's greatest talents were in surveying and in land. Though already exceedingly affluent, he accepted, as a present, 100,000 acres in America and left me to occupy six feet of earth in France."

Duane turned the conversation, immediately, to a less controversial subject. "And what do you think of our Federal City?" he asked. "Do you know what Governeur Morris said of it? Let me see if I can quote him correctly. He said, 'We want nothing here but houses, cellars, kitchens, well-informed men, amiable women, and other trifles of this kind to make the city perfect. It is the best city in the world for a future residence.' And when John Adams was here, Abigail confessed to Mrs. Duane that she was more a woodsman's wife than a president's. She used to hang her wash to dry in the unfinished East Room."

"You are being unfair, Mr. Duane," chided Martha. "The Executive Mansion was not completed when former President and Mrs. Adams moved into it. The city is growing beautifully, Mr. Paine. For the sake of a bit of editorial humor in his *Aurora,* Mr. Duane was used to referring to it as the Wilderness City, the City of Magnificent Distances, or the City of Streets Without Houses. But you have desisted, haven't you, Mr. Duane?"

After the last guest had departed, Jefferson led Paine to his study. The room was lined with bookcases and warmed by a deep fireplace. Paine noticed the Sleeping Adriane sculpture on a pedestal. The figurine still reclined upon a couch and her head rested as gracefully as ever upon a marble hand.

"I am attached to it," said Jefferson. "I brought it here from Monticello."

He excused himself and, when he returned, Paine was surprised to see that he had attired himself in an old red waistcoat, smallclothes, woolen hose, and slippers without heels. Paine smiled. His thoughts took him back to the young Jefferson who had brushed his gloved hand down the flanks of his horse in front of the Statehouse, to the fashionably dressed Minister to France. Jefferson slouched onto a chair and said,

"I have reached a point where I enjoy such comforts as I can. The press is most unkind to you, Tom. I urge you to disregard its slurs. Given time, either the water boils away or the fire dies out."

The conversation drifted to politics, and Paine confessed, "I have never been farther west than the Susquehanna River, Jeff. I would like to go to the Mississippi. And then down to New Orleans." When Jefferson said nothing, Paine added, "When I was a member of the French Assembly, I was consulted on the political future of the Louisiana Territory. Even then, I envisioned it as a part of America, not governed by any European power. And now Spain has ceded the territory to France."

Jefferson nodded. "The new government of France is not too friendly."

"It is not the French. It is Napoleon Bonaparte. He will settle the Louisiana Territory with the scum of Europe unless we buy it. And by the way, Jeff, when it is bought, and it should be, we must see that settlers and not Negro slaves are brought into the territory. If Liverpool has not sent them to the French, neither must she send them to us."

Jefferson shook his head. "Let us not rouse a sleeping dog. It is not a question of right but of politics. I hear you contemplate the publication of a Part III to your *Age of Reason.* I advise against it, Tom. What would it gain you?"

Paine stared quietly into the fire. Did Jefferson understand him as little as that? After all these years?

"I have no personal objections, Tom. Religion, to me, is no more than a system of morals. Let me show you my own Bible. Martha says that I have simply expurgated the Gospels. I have clipped such texts as I consider to be of moral value and collected them into a book of ethics. I have entitled it *The Philosophy of Jesus of Nazareth.*"

Paine leafed through the booklet. "You have accurately termed it a philosophy. It is no more."

[539]

"It is my personal Bible, Tom, though I admit no Christian sect would accept it. Merely to live by the doctrines of Jesus is to be a Christian."

"And my *Age of Reason?*"

Jefferson shrugged. "Have I spoken a single word against it? Years ago, I wrote to my nephew, Peter Carr . . . Do you know him?" He rose and searched in the drawer of a large desk. "Do you think that only you write letters, Tom? Would you believe that last year, when I had the curiosity to count the letters I received, they were well upwards of a thousand? It is small wonder that I drudge so long at the writing table. I do not doubt but that I have on file upwards of twenty thousand letters that I have received and copies of twelve thousand that I have written. Not counting the innumerable ones that were of no importance to keep. I kept a copy of my letter to Peter . . . ah, here we are. Peter was young then, and I felt it incumbent to advise him."

He handed Paine a letter whose creases gave evidence of many foldings and unfoldings. Paine read:

> Fix reason firmly in her seat and call to her tribunal every fact, every opinion. Question with boldness even the existence of a God; because, if there be One, He must approve of the homage of reason, rather than that of blindfold fear.
>
> Read the Bible, then, as you would read Livy or Tacitus.
>
> Your own reason is the only oracle given you by heaven.

Paine refolded the letter with care. "You always wrote better than I. We have our opinions in common, but not our expressions. You tend your garden well and water it with care. But I have no garden. Only the stony fields and the barren wastes where the common man struggles against ignorance, poverty, and superstition. Do not dissuade me from my new work. I am committed to it. When I return to New Rochelle, it is my intention to rewrite the *Age of Reason* and have it published."

Paine stayed on as a guest at the Executive Mansion. The November days were still warm and filled with sunshine. The trees were shedding their last leaves. Jefferson supplied him with a horse and Martha escorted him about the changing countryside. When alone, he would ride to the end of Pennsylvania Avenue, where it tapered off into a half-dozen brickyards. The grey smoke from the kilns would spiral into the windless air like twisted skeins of wool. Beyond a cluster of scrub oaks and a deep morass that was covered with alder brushes, he could see the tranquil Potomac River. Small vessels would be in view, running down to Alexandria. The prospect of what Federal City might one day become filled him with a realization of the rush of time from his own hourglass.

The Federalist press howled and screamed against Jefferson's friendship for Paine. They were seen taking walks together, after dark, strolling arm in arm like old cronies—the president and his atheist! The newspapers accused Paine of all the excesses and atrocities of France's Reign of Terror. Editorials insisted that Jefferson's friendship for Paine was incontestable proof that the "Republican Administration sought to turn the United States into a mob-dominated anarchy of atheism and immorality."

Paine felt that he would be remiss, as a friend, if he involved Jefferson further. His days at the Executive Mansion had been brightened with reminiscences and touched by nostalgia. He was grateful for them. There would be a time when the country would again recognize his talents and his devotion to its welfare, he predicted to Jefferson. "And until then, dear friend, *au revoir.*"

He left after dark. Jefferson had never seen him so filled with emotion.

39

WHEN PAINE returned to Lovell's Hotel, he found himself as much shunned as ever. He would confine himself to his room and read all the newspapers and magazines that he could obtain. He would fortify himself with half a tumbler of brandy and study the abuse that the press heaped upon him for having written the *Age of Reason:*

... this demi-human arch-beast. This lying, drunken, brutal infidel.

... this object of disgust, of abhorrence, of absolute loathing to every decent man except the President of the United States!

Ogre of reason! Look what a long nose he has got.

He drank all the brandy in Baltimore in nine days.

When he would go down to the dining room, for his evening meal, he would be stared at by the curious, who came to see the "monster" that the press described. He wondered if they were disappointed that they smelled no brimstone and could see no horns on his head.

After sunset, he would leave the candlelighted hotel and go for a walk. His life had been filled with innumerable activities and countless personalities. Now he walked alone. His illness had affected his posture so that he bent forward a little as he walked. He had developed a habit of holding one hand in the other—as Roger Sherman had done so many years ago. With his plain dress and his slow gait, one would think him a retired farmer, out for a bit of air.

One day William Duane called on him at Lovell's. His newspaper, the *Aurora,* was the only one that had not commented upon Paine's stay in Federal City. Duane shook his head at Paine and urged him to desist from his defense of deism. "Your stand on religion will invalidate your political writings," he predicted. "It will destroy your fame."

"You, too, Duane? In '76, I was warned that independence was a dangerous word, but I used it. And nothing will stop me from exercising the right to express my religious views. Is not John Adams now a Unitarian, holding essentially the same theological opinions as I? Would you say that the Federalists detest him for it?"

"You are a most stubborn man, Tom. It is your insistence upon the natural rights of citizens that angers those in high office. They but use your criticism of organized religion as a weapon with which to incite the public against you."

"I shall defend myself."

"Defend? How?" He glanced about the room and noticed the heap of journals and newspapers on a table. "There is no defense against the press. I tell you that, if you reopen the subject of the *Age of Reason*—if you discuss religion in any form—even the friends who respect you will desert you."

Prodded by Duane's visit, Paine began a series of letters under the general title: *Letters to the Citizens of the United States.* He wrote that he had returned to a country that had won its separation from Great Britain but not its own personal liberty! In twenty years of self-government, the new republic had not passed a national law abolishing slavery, and it permitted only a small fraction of the male population to qualify as voters. Only the affluent or the influential were elected to office. Trade unions were forbidden by law and there were no regulations for working hours or minimum wages! The sentiments of his *The Rights of Man* were as much disregarded here as in England!

The Philadelphia *Aurora* published one of the open letters. The Trenton *True American* printed another. Only the poorly circulated *National Intelligencer* published the rest.

By Christmas, Paine decided to leave Capital City. He was embittered by his neglect and decided to retire to his farm in New Rochelle. The tenant farmer had abandoned it when he had been advised of Paine's return. He had not known that he was a "disciple of the devil."

Paine left Federal City on January 3, a cold and windy day. He had entrusted his bridge models to Madison, the Secretary of State, and had sent a carefully penned letter to Congress:

> I have deposited in the office of the Secretary of State, under the care of the patent office, two models of iron bridges.
>
> My intention is to put the country in possession of the means and of the right of making use of the construction freely; as I do not intend to take any patent right for it.
>
> I request that this memoir be put on the journals of the Congress, as an evidence hereafter, that this new method of constructing bridges originated in America.
>
> THOMAS PAINE
> Federal City, January 3, 1803

Paine stopped in Philadelphia, on his way to New York. The old and familiar sights filled him with nostalgia. Shops and homes had sprung up everywhere, but Carpenters' Hall and the Statehouse were just as he remembered them. He passed Christ Church, on Second Street, and recalled the first time he had climbed the stone steps to its steeple. The city had grown, but it had not changed. When he returned to his room at the Cross Keys, which was now owned by McKinley who had renamed it the Moon and Seven Stars Inn, Paine sent a porter, with a note, to the home of Dr. Rush. There was no doubt in his mind that Rush would gather old friends to greet him. There would be faces he had not seen for sixteen years. The porter returned without a written reply. He had been asked to convey a message that he had evidently rehearsed on his way back.

"Dr. Rush says, sir . . . He say . . . your principles avowed in the *Age of Reason* are so . . . so offensive to 'im, as wot 'e do not wish to renew . . . to renew . . ."

Paine ended the message with a wave of his hand. He had intended to stay in Philadelphia at least a week, in search of old friends. He did not bother to unpack his trunk.

Paine took the coach to Bordentown. His cottage, which John Hall still occupied, seemed smaller than he had last remembered it. The wooden shed in which he had constructed his first bridge model had been razed. Tall weeds thrust their half-frozen stalks between the rotted timbers.

Colonel Kirkbride, to whom he had written of his arrival, welcomed him warmly but there was a tension in the air. Hall, whose limp was more pronounced and whose drooping mustache was now a tangle of yellow and white bristles, eyed him with suspicion through half-shut lids. Samuel Rogers, a brother-in-law of Kirkbride, who had always admired Paine, now refused to shake his hand because he had written the *Age of Reason.* No, he had not read it and he had no intention of doing so. It was a verbal snake pit of blasphemy and corruption!

When the news spread through the village that Tom Paine was at Colonel Kirkbride's, its citizens gathered at the taverns and in the marketplace. When their curiosity overcame their fear, they passed the cottage in twos and threes in hopes of catching a glimpse of the "monster." On Sunday, the preachers denounced infidel Paine in their sermons. They enlarged upon his certain punishment in hell and threatened Kirkbride for harboring the outcast who had blasphemed against Christ. John Hall, who had not attended a service for years, now sat devoutly in the back of a church. He listened in awe to a description of the brimstone and fire to which the former "saintmaker" was doomed.

Paine cut short his visit to Bordentown. Kirkbride drove him to nearby Trenton, in a chaise, so that he could board the

[545]

stagecoach for New York. The news of Paine's coming had preceded them, and a mob had gathered at the stagecoach station. Someone had brought an old drum and, as Kirkbride drove the chaise over the stone bridge to King Street, he began to pound it as an alarm. Mothers gathered their children and scattered out of sight. A half-dozen men rushed out from a tavern and unfurled an American flag as a rallying point against "monster" Paine. Kirkbride left Paine in the chaise and inquired after accommodations on the stage. When the passengers learned that Paine intended to board the stagecoach for New York, they refused to ride with the accursed man who had sold his soul to the devil.

Kirkbride returned to the chaise and urged his mare up King Street, in the direction of Pennington Road. His face was suffused with anger. His underlip trembled as though he were muttering to himself. Paine sat, unperturbed, as though nothing were amiss.

"It is sixty miles to New York, Tom. But I can drive you there, sleep over, and return tomorrow. I never imagined such ingratitude and misunderstanding."

Paine was not listening. He had bundled a blanket about his legs and sat hunched against the cold. A light snow had fallen the night before and it muffled the sound of the mare's clop, clop, clop on the road. Drifts of white shifted and glistened in the wind-swept fields. To the east, the trees stood sharp against the sunlight.

"If only you had not written the *Age of Reason,* Tom. You could have returned as an esteemed and influential American. History would have claimed you as a patriot."

Paine smiled. His face filled out and his cheeks were not as sunken when he smiled. "You are mistaken, Joseph," he said. "The bigoted resent not only my *Age of Reason* but *The Rights of Man* and all my political writings. History might have claimed me if I had been guillotined! But then, who would there be to spit against the wind? Eh, Joseph? Who?"

Gratefully, Paine found bustling New York City not as provincial as the rest of the country. Its citizens seemed to have little concern about his personal convictions. He settled himself in a boardinghouse run by a James Wilburn, at number 16 Gold Street. As he immersed himself in the flux of the expanding city and bobbed up as a new personality, he attracted fresh friends. John Fellows with whom he had once corresponded and James Cheetham, a radical journalist, became frequent visitors.

Fellows, who was a deist, was twenty years younger than Paine. He was a graduate of Yale College and had been the editor of the *New York Beacon* for a short time. One evening, Paine suggested to him, "I have a sequel to the *Age of Reason.* A part three."

Fellows shook his head. "I am now an auctioneer," he laughed. "Not a most-respected profession—but it earns me an income. My venture as a publisher was short-lived, as you may remember. But I still have contacts," he said, as though to cheer the evidently disappointed Paine. "May I offer my services as a literary agent? I would be most happy to read your manuscript. Elihu Palmer might raise the funds for its publication and help distribute it."

James Cheetham also was friendly. He had been a member of the Constitutional Society in Manchester. Now he was the editor of a daily New York newspaper, the *American Citizen.* Would Paine send him some articles? No one would have to know that he had solicited them. Paine was grateful to find an outlet for his work and Cheetham published every article that Paine sent him. He was astounded by the increased circulation of the *American Citizen.* One day Paine suggested that he print the *Age of Reason: Part III* in serial form. "Surely, you are not serious, Mr. Paine?" he said. "Your political articles are controversial, which is manna for a newspaper. But your *Age of Reason* . . . your *Age of Reason* cannot be defended."

In August, Paine received a letter from Marguerite Bonneville. She had arrived in Norfolk, Virginia, with her three sons. She had evidently delayed leaving France in hopes that Nicolas could come with her. He wrote to her:

> I this moment received your letter with great pleasure, for I was anxious for your safe passage.
>
> I have written to Colonel Kirkbride, of Bordentown, in the State of New Jersey, who will expect your coming there, and from whom you will receive every friendship.
>
> Embrace the boys for me and tell them they will soon see me at Bordentown. I shall write again to Colonel Kirkbride to inform him of your arrival. . . .

Colonel Kirkbride had advised Paine that he could find work for Mrs. Bonneville, teaching French. There were many families in Bordentown who would be happy to engage her services. The Bonnevilles could live in Paine's cottage, for John Hall had left it, and in this way they would not be a drain on Paine's finances.

When Colonel Kirkbride died in November, Paine set aside his work and rushed to Bordentown. He found an extremely unhappy Marguerite. The people in the village were not friendly. The citizens intimated that she was Paine's mistress and that Thomas, Louis, and even little Benjamin, whom she endearingly called Bebia, were his children.

"Did I look like this in France?" she cried. "Look at me! Nicholas would not know me."

It was true. Her youthful gaiety was gone. Her face had thinned, there were dark shadows under her eyes, and her lids were reddened from weeping. She was not accustomed to the confinement of four walls in an unfriendly provincial town.

Paine looked down at Louis who was now seven, at Thomas who was six, and at little Bebia who was but four. They gathered about him with affection. His was the only face that was not strange to them in this country. "I have a small farm in New Rochelle," he offered. "It is untenanted at present.

We could all move there until Nicolas arrives. I could engage someone to farm the land, perhaps a woman to help cook and clean, . . ."

Marguerite rushed to him and embraced him, *"Est-ce vrai? Est-ce vrai?* It would be wonderful!"

Paine had not been to New Rochelle since his return. He had never seen the new cottage. It had been built in 1793, after the manor house had burnt down. It was a frame house on a rise of ground that afforded a good view of the surrounding country. It had two stories and an attic, a brick chimney, a pitched roof, and shingled sides. An enclosed porch led to an unpretentious but wide doorway. It was a far cry from the stone manor house of the Jays, but its gently sloping lawn was shaded by well-spaced maples. Marguerite and the children were immediately impressed by it. Despite the squalor in which the tenant farmer had left it, they moved in with great expectations. Paine engaged a handyman farmer by the name of Dean and a mulatto cook who called herself Rachel Gidney. He anticipated a degree of comfort and wrote to Jefferson:

> It is a pleasant and healthy situation, commanding a prospect always green and peaceful, as New Rochelle produces a great deal of grass and hay. . . .

Unfortunately, the pleasant days that Paine foresaw came to naught. They had gone to the farm at a bad time. Snow fell shortly after they moved in and subsequent snowfalls soon confined them to the cottage. Marguerite could not adjust herself to a sedentary life. She was accustomed to the hustle and bustle of metropolitan Paris, to the noise of a crowded street outside her window and the clatter of a press beneath her floor. She missed the visits of Nicolas' innumerable friends. Though she had not taken part in their talks, she had been stimulated by their squabbles, protests, debates, gossips, and hates. Here, there were only the inarticulate shuffling

Rachel Gidney and busy Tom Paine. She had the greatest respect and admiration for Paine, but he was sixty-seven and she was less than half that age. And he was constantly absorbed in his books, his manuscripts, and his tremendous correspondence. Paine had stocked the farm in anticipation of spring, but she refused to stay. She was not a provincial! She had been born and bred in a city. "I will die of ennui!" she cried. "I will die of ennui!"

Paine saw the family off for New York. He heartened Marguerite with a letter of introduction to John Fellows, who had written that he had procured a position for her, as a teacher of French, in a private home. He had made all the arrangements.

Paine stayed on at the farm. He had had a falling out with Cheetham, and other publishers would not accept his controversial articles. The man who had helped shape the destiny of nations could not get a single word into print. To Cheetham's vexation, the *American Citizen* lost many of its subscribers. In an effort to bolster its circulation, he began a series of editorial tirades against Paine. He advised his readers that, unless the influence of Tom Paine's religious heresy was checked, it would undermine civilization and rush the world back to primitive savagery. Like a pack of hounds baying at a scent, other newspapers took up the hue and cry against "infidel" Paine. Calumnious and vituperative editorials reached New Rochelle. The preachers in the quiet town were suddenly aware of a fresh topic for their Sunday sermons— Tom Paine and the hellfire to which he was doomed.

Boys, as a test of courage, perpetrated acts of vandalism on the farm at night. The handyman deserted him and even Rachel slipped away without a word. Paine left the cottage only after dark. He knew the necessity for some exercise and took his walks at night. If one would but stop to look, one would see only a tired old man, out for a breath of air, but he was avoided on sight, for it was whispered that his shoes covered cloven hoofs and his baggy smallclothes hid a curved tail.

He would walk along the rutted tree-lined road that ran to White Plains and wonder at his destiny.

That Christmas Eve was a lonely night for Paine. He thought of other places and other days. He had no friends in New Rochelle. He decided to finish a letter to Jefferson that he had begun the day before. The sun had set early and he lighted the candles on a table that he had moved close to a window. From here, he could look out at the wide lawn and the newly fallen snow. His friends had not only deserted him, many of them had died.

He thought of Alexander Hamilton, who had been need-lessly killed that summer in a duel with Aaron Burr. The last years had not been kind to Alex. He had been living in semiretirement, practicing law in New York. Despite a profitable practice, he had been deeply in debt. Unfortunate land investments and the mansion he had built on Washington Heights had sapped his fortune. But to be shot in a duel! Paine recalled him as the young Captain of Artillery, with his fresh uniform and his polished boots, at Washington's headquarters, where he had protested the essay on dueling. Poor Alex! He had been heir to many faults, but at least he had been true to his convictions.

Paine reread the unfinished letter:

> I suggest a thought for your consideration. . . . If a way could be found out to bring about a peace between France and Domingo through mediation, and under the guarantee of the United States, it would give us a great commercial and political standing, not only with the present people of Domingo, but with the West Indies generally. . . .

Suddenly there was a musket report and a splintering of wood. A pane of glass was shattered in the window in front of him. A gust of wind flickered the candles on the table.

Paine rushed outside and recognized two young men who were kneeling in the snow. One held a musket, the other a jug of spirits. At sight of Paine, they rose to their feet and tried to totter away. But Derrick, the one who held the musket, stumbled. His face filled with fright. The other, a handyman by the name of Purdy, cried, "I tol' ya. I tol' ya, ya could no' kill 'im! Now d'ya believe as wot 'e's the devil's disciple like preacher Symmons claims? 'E's Lucifer. Lucifer!"

Paine thrust an arm past the shattered glass and reached a candlestick. Three inches below the window there was a hole through which he could see the flames flickering in his fireplace. The shingles about the hole were blackened with powder. A stillness hung in the crisp night air. The trees shimmered in the starlight. He went back into the cottage and hung a blanket over the broken window. He pushed the table close to the fireplace. He thought of the two fools who had tried to murder him. It could not have been religious zeal that had impelled them to it—they were irreligious. Superstition! If they thought him to be the devil, where did they find the courage with which to attempt to harm him? In the jug? Derrick owed him $48 for which he was to have built a stone fence on the farm. He had foolishly paid Derrick in advance and he had never placed a stone. Was it to free himself of the debt? Was his life worth but $48 now?

He shrugged off the speculation and returned to his letter to Jefferson. He wanted Jefferson to declare to the powers of Europe that the western world wanted nothing from Europe but freedom from its entanglements and its intrigues. That the United States of America, now secure in its own liberty, would not stand idly by and watch the exploitation of its smaller neighbors by foreign domination. But he would have to speak softly. He must not estrange yet one more friend. He wrote:

[552]

The United States is the only power that can undertake a measure of this kind. She is now the parent of the Western world. . . .

There was no point in expressing his loneliness in New Rochelle or writing of his narrow escape from death.

When summer came, Paine set out for New York despite the news that a yellow-fever epidemic had struck the city. The plague was decimating its citizens. The roads were barricaded and stagecoaches and wagons that attempted to leave the city were shot at and burned by farmers and villagers who feared a spread of the contagion.

The stage discharged Paine at Weehawken, on the west side of the North River. The coachman insisted that he could approach no closer. Paine was undismayed. It would not be the first time he had crossed this selfsame countryside on foot. He reached New York the next day and found that no one had exaggerated the disaster. Almost whole families were struck down by the epidemic. Hungry orphaned children roamed the deserted streets. Looting was widespread and every business had barricaded its doors. The wharves were deserted. Death carts were pulled through the streets by emaciated horses. They were led by drivers who had wrapped their faces with strips of muslin. They rang hand bells and called for the living to bring out their dead. The corpses were flung into the carts with as little ceremony as though they were sides of beef.

Paine was recognized by one of the drivers. He introduced himself as William Carver and said that he was a blacksmith. There were now no horses to be shod and he was doing this to earn a few coppers. Paine could not recall him, but the man insisted, through the muslin that muffled his mouth, that he had known Paine in Lewes, when a boy. He had often stabled Paine's horse—across from the White Hart Tavern. The cart, with its load of sprawled corpses, was a macabre background for their conversation. Carver boasted that he had a comfortable home at 36 Cedar Street. He was a great admirer of Paine's writings. If Paine needed lodgings, and if he was not daunted by the plague, Carver and his wife would be glad to take him in.

Paine availed himself of the Carvers' hospitality at an agreed-upon price of a dollar a day for his lodging.

The frost brought an end to the epidemic. Residents drifted back and shops were reopened. It seemed that it would take more than a pestilence to retard the bustle and growth of New York City. Paine began his political writings once again, and an anti-Federalist newspaper printed them. He even published an essay on the cause of Yellow Fever and the means of preventing its spread, insisting that a contributing factor was the filth that was created by the "raising of solid wharves of earth on the mud bottom of the shore."

When winter came, Paine suffered a slight stroke one day as he climbed the stairs to his bedroom. As the Carvers watched Paine's slow recovery, they were astonished at the numerous friends who came to see him—blind Elihu Palmer, head of the Deistical Society of New York; Quaker Willet Hicks, a cousin to the Elias Hicks who had denied the divinity of Jesus; Thomas Addis Emmet, the renowned lawyer and Irish patriot. John Fellows was a frequent visitor. Marguerite Bonneville came to see him daily. She was dressed in frills, with her black hair swept high under a plumed hat. The fact that she carried warm soup in a small kettle did not diminish her dignity. Sometimes she brought one child with her, sometimes another.

The Carvers had thought Paine an affluent man without friends or relatives, and had planned to ingratiate themselves as his heirs. They were startled by the comings and goings of these visitors who seemed, in some manner, beyond the edge of acceptability—watchmaker Hicks with his ill-fitting spectacles, expatriate Emmet, Palmer and his heretical sect of

Theophilanthropists, Madame Bonneville and her French airs. When they learned that Paine was about to sell his cottage in Bordentown, in order to pay his debts, they insisted that he leave as soon as he was able.

In April, when Paine was able to get about again, he was approached in a tavern by a young man who seemed to recognize him. He seated himself at Paine's table and asked permission to buy him a drink. He seemed in his early thirties and was rather Bohemian in his attire. He had a scarlet cravat, a collarless shirt, and a doeskin waistcoat that was stained with paint. "Am I right in assuming that you are 'infidel' Tom Paine?" he asked. "Then permit me to introduce myself. You are looking at John Wesley Jarvis. I paint the likenesses of men upon canvas and mold their images in clay. I rebel against their sentiments, yet I insist that every man has a right to express himself. Even you."

"Those were the words of David, once. Before he was corrupted by success."

"You knew Jacques Louis?"

"Well enough to criticize him." Paine could see that the young man was not befuddled, though he gave every indication that he had been drinking heavily. "I knew most of Europe's painters," said Paine. "The difference between expression by pen and brush is only in the medium. I sat for David. And for Houdon once, with Jefferson. I knew Reynolds and Ben West in England. I sat for George Romney in London."

"Then, by God, you shall sit for me! Without a charge, mind you. Without a charge. And you are not to take this as an implication that I accept your *Age of Reason.* Though I do not reproach you for having written it. It is enough that Dr. Franklin rebuked you. Must I add my own criticism?"

Paine's interest was immediately aroused. The American Tract Society had issued and circulated an "authentic" letter, supposedly written by Benjamin Franklin, rebuking Paine for having written the *Age of Reason.* Paine had heard of it during his illness, but had not as yet seen a copy.

"You have read the tract, Mr. Jarvis?"

"Of course I read it. I have a copy of it."

"May I see it?" And, when Jarvis nodded, Paine asked, "Tonight? Now?" Jarvis hesitated, rose heavily, and gave Paine a travesty of a bow. "My pleasure, Mr. Paine. If you will come with me."

Paine followed Jarvis' unsteady footsteps to 85 Church Street, where the artist had a second-floor apartment. It consisted of but a single bedroom and a large studio whose air was tainted with the smells of turpentine, linseed oil, fresh canvas, and wet clay. Suddenly Paine noticed a heavy rough-hewn table and his heart stood still with shock. A dozen severed heads lay on its wide boards! The blood froze in his veins as he recognized Cloots, Vergniaud, Danton, Brissot. They stared at each other with dreadful accusations. As his eyes grew accustomed to the dim light, he saw that they were only death masks and clay busts of people whom he had never known. Still haunted by the horror of the guillotine, his subconscious had deluded him.

Unaware of what had happened, Jarvis swung an arm as though to encompass the studio within its arc and cried, "Welcome to Bachelor's Hall, Tom Paine! Welcome to Bachelor's Hall!" He groped among scattered papers in an old desk and finally found the sought-for pamphlet. He sank into a chair and watched quietly while Paine read the tract.

I have read your manuscript with some attention. You strike at the foundations of all religions. Without the belief of a Providence that takes cognizance of, guards and guides, and may favor particular persons, there is no motive to worship a deity, to fear his displeasure, or to pray for his protection. Though your reasons are subtle and may prevail with some readers, you will not succeed so as to change the general sentiments of mankind on that subject and the consequences of printing this piece will be a great deal of odium drawn upon yourself, mischief to you, and no benefit to others. He that spits against the wind spits into his own face. . . .

Jarvis could no longer remain silent. He must speak or fall asleep. "How now, Mr. Paine!" he cried. "Would you so ignore the late Dr. Franklin's advice that you . . ."

"Exactly!" cried Paine. "You have put your finger upon it, exactly, in calling him the *late* Dr. Franklin. Franklin never saw my manuscript. Nor any portion of my *Age of Reason.* The world knows that my friend died in 1790. And I did not write the *Age of Reason* until three years later!"

"My God! Mr. Paine, is this true?"

"Of course it's true. But it's not the first lie that has been circulated about me. Nor will it be the last. I am engaged upon a third part of my *Age of Reason* . . . if I can find a lodging in which to finish it. I am, at last, not only discredited but homeless. The Carvers were eager enough to have me come and live with them last summer, when there were no horses to be shod and they thought me affluent. Now they can't wait to turn me out. They suddenly fear to harbor a man who insists that, if Adam subjected himself and all posterity to eternal damnation for having eaten of the forbidden fruit, it would have been better and simpler to have crucified him upon the forbidden tree and created a new man."

Jarvis gave Paine a twisted smile. He went into the bedroom and returned with a pillow and two blankets. "You shall come and stay with me. We will get you a bed and you will tell me if anyone posed for David's 'Assassination of Marat.' And I shall paint you . . ." He hesitated at what he saw. The shadows in the studio made Paine's cheeks seem twice as sunken. His nose looked almost bulbous.

"I shall paint you as you were once. You must bring such sketches as you say you have. By Houdin, Romney and the others. I wonder what my late uncle, John Wesley, would think of you. Eh, Tom Paine? What would Uncle John think?"

"I met him in London," said Paine. "He enumerated sins and religious duties as methodically as a broker counts his pence. I was not impressed by his assurance of salvation through faith in Christ alone."

Paine moved into Jarvis' studio and they became great friends despite the difference in their ages. Jarvis made a bust of Paine as he was—his eyebrows grown bushy, his nose distended, his face slightly wrinkled, and his lips sunken in upon seemingly toothless gums. One could see enough of the throat and exposed chest to imagine a form that was beginning to waste away. And he painted a portrait of him as he had promised—from the sketches and miniatures done by others —a young Paine with a showy cravat, his hair neatly combed, his nose slender, his eyes gleaming, his lips almost smiling.

Jarvis would spend most of his evenings at social clubs and Paine would sit up late and wait for him. They were both Bohemians and avid talkers, and they enjoyed each other's company. Jarvis would burst into the studio and cry, "What! You still scribble!"

Paine would remove the spectacles without which he could no longer read or write. "I must, when the books that are read are filled with absurdities."

"Why concern yourself? Does it irritate me that some other sculptor molds his clay poorly? Or paints his characters as they are not?"

"It is not the same thing, John. The . . ."

"I have sold the lop-eared bust," laughed Jarvis as he kicked off his shoes. "Imagine an illiterate butcher wishing to be remembered by posterity, because he has filled his purse with sovereigns. Wilt have a drink with me, or do I go to bed?"

One night, when Jarvis returned to the studio, he found Paine lying on the floor, felled by a stroke. He had lost the use of his left arm and could not support himself when Jarvis tried to help him up, nor could he make himself understood when he tried to talk.

Jarvis gave up his bedroom and Mrs. Palmer came each day and took care of Paine's needs. She lived on the same street and had been widowed by the unexpected death of Elihu. She read to Paine, took care of such of his correspondence as she could, and nursed him back to health. Marguerite would call, once or twice a week, and bring *petits pains, oeufs à la coque, potage,* and cookies that she called *gâteaux secs.* Bachelor's Hall was filled with the patter of women's steps. It was dominated by the flutter of dust cloths, the comfort of made beds, the tidiness of shoes that were arranged side by side and garments that were hung from sight. The studio was aired, and the smell of its pigments and oils dissipated. Jarvis, who was now frequently away for days at a time, insisted that Paine be moved where someone could be in attendance during the night.

In April, when Paine was well enough, Mrs. Palmer found a new lodging for him with a baker named Hill, on Broome Street. Paine was given the use of a small sitting room, into which his books and his trunk of letters and unpublished manuscripts were moved. An adjoining bedroom was just barely large enough to contain his bed. He ate his meals with the Hill family. They were at first as unconcerned by his thoughts as they were by his presence. He lived almost in solitude. Mrs. Palmer called on him three or four times a week. Marguerite's visits became infrequent. By the end of the summer, the neighborhood learned that the lodger who lived in seclusion at the Hills' was none other than the accursed and execrable blasphemer who was hand in glove with the devil. Bats were seen alighting on his bedroom window at night. Weird sounds were heard in front of the house, after dark.

The Hills finally asked him to move.

Paine began to drift from lodging to lodging. For the first

time in years, he wrote to no one and received neither visitors nor mail. He felt tired, old, unwanted, and useless. In February, he moved to 63 Partition Street, near the Bear Market. His lodging consisted of a single room above a small tavern that offered a daily six-penny show. He began to frequent the tavern. It was but a flight of steps from his room. Though he never saw a familiar face, and no one ever asked him who he was, it was more pleasant to drink in the tavern than spend the time alone in his room.

In June, Mrs. Palmer discovered where he was. She called upon him, with a group of friends that included Fellows and Thomas Emmet. They insisted that he move. Had he thought that his friends had deserted him? He had dropped from sight, and they had supposed him in Philadelphia or in Federal City.

A drayman, by the name of Ryder, was prevailed upon to board him. The Ryders had a comfortable frame house on Herring Street, in Greenwich Village, a mile and a half from the city. A price of $7 a week for his room and board was settled upon and Mrs. Ryder gave him a first-story room that faced the street. Almost unable to walk, Paine would shuffle to a small table that he had ordered placed near the window. His mind still clear, he tried to resume his writings. He would rest between each paragraph, sometimes between just one or two sentences. The effort of moving the quill across the paper would tire him. Passers-by would notice him at the window. He seemed gaunt, grey—a spectacled old man who sat and supported himself upon one elbow. He stared back at them with bright lucid eyes that contrasted oddly with his wrinkled face.

As friends learned of Paine's new address and his visitors became numerous, the Ryders raised the price of his board. When the neighborhood discovered that the seemingly inno-cent-looking old man who sat at Ryder's window was none other than the corrupt author of the blasphemous *Age of Reason,* the Ryders found it "impossible" to keep him. Groups of curious villagers began to parade in front of the house in order to catch a glimpse of the infidel. Ryder declared that he had been intimidated and insisted that Paine leave.

Marguerite, now well employed, offered to accept him in her own household. She could do no less for him than he had done for her. She was sure it was what Nicolas would want. Maria Thompson, a niece of the late Elihu Palmer, put a house at Marguerite's disposal. It was owned by her husband, who had been a law partner of Aaron Burr. He would have no objections. He had been impressed by Paine's *Prospect Papers* at the time that Elihu had published them. And he would see to it that no one was molested.

Marguerite rented the house that, though unpretentious, had a well-tended back garden. It was at 59 Grove Street, but a stone's throw from that of the Ryders. The entire rear portion of the house was turned into quarters for Paine. A door from a bedroom led directly into the garden, where beds of snowdrops and crocuses were already in bloom. Ryder, heavy-set and gruff, carted Paine's books, his few clothes, and his crammed trunk to the new quarters. He was eager to be rid of Paine, yet dismayed at the thought of losing the board money, which he had raised to $20. On the morning of May 4, Willet Hicks and Jarvis carried Paine, in an armchair, to his new home.

Marguerite engaged a trained nurse by the name of Mrs. Hedden. She was unaware that James Cheetham had recommended her services in order to spy upon Paine's last days. With an eye for publicity, Cheetham considered Paine excellent "copy."

Marguerite persuaded Dr. Romaine, a physician in the community, to attend Paine. Surely, he did not have to agree with his writings in order to treat him. There was the Hippocratic oath—was it less observed here than in France?

As Paine grew worse, he was pestered by an endless stream of visitors. Some were religious fanatics who urged him to recant. Others were only the curious, who wished to boast that they had dared to look upon Tom Paine. Benjamin, the youngest Bonneville boy, stayed at his bedside. Louis had returned to Paris to be with his father, who could not leave France; Thomas had been sent to a small boarding school in Bergen, New Jersey; but Bebia, now age nine, remained with Paine and did what he could to discourage visitors. With childish frankness, he would confess to Marguerite that Nurse Hedden accepted bribes from unwelcome visitors.

Aided by devoted Bebia, Paine struggled to put his last thoughts on paper. He would dictate in a tired and almost inaudible voice and Bebia would interrupt almost every phrase to question the spelling of words. Sometimes the dictation was broken up by periods of stillness during which Paine would sit as though in a trance. His faded blue eyes, though wide open, would stare ahead unseeingly. Occasionally, he would glance at his trunk that was crammed with manuscripts. Many of them had never been published. He had written an article against the Blue Laws of Connecticut that obliged a person to sit still on the Sabbath, from sunrise to sunset, and thus waste a seventh portion of his life!

He had written essays on dreams, his private thoughts, a future state, and his thoughts on predestination. The trunk contained letters to the Honorable T. Erskine, on the prosecution of Thomas Williams for publishing the *Age of Reason.* It contained his early poems and fables and patriotic songs, and letters . . . and letters. . . . What would become of them all? While Bebia sat and watched him, his mind drifted back to earlier days . . . to Paris, when he had sent a missal to Lady Smythe in an effort to match Sir Robert's phrases on *What Is Love.* Faultlessly, his mind recalled every word of the lines that he had composed:

> Tis that delightful transport we can feel,
> Which painters cannot paint nor words reveal,

Nor any art we know of can conceal.
Canst thou describe the sunbeams to the blind,
Or make him feel a shadow with his mind?

What are the iron chains that hands have wrought?
The hardest chains to break are those of thought.

He was weeping. Weeping inwardly. It was a lament without sound and without tears. "Call Mrs. Hedden." he said
aloud to Bebia. "I am tired. I would lie down again."

Before the end of May, with the help of Thomas Addis
Emmet, whom he appointed one of his executors, Paine
drafted a will. He learned that Elizabeth, to whom he still sent
money upon occasion, had died in Cranbrook in September.
They had not corresponded, but he had been aware of the
quiet life that she had lived in Southwark and later in Kent.
He had intended to remember her in his will. Now he directed that his land in New Rochelle be sold and one-half the
proceeds be given to Clio Rickman and the remainder to
Nicolas and Marguerite Bonneville, to be held in trust for
their children.

When it became known that Paine was dying, a pilgrimage
of sects began to call on him to urge him to recant. Catholics,
Presbyterians, Methodists, Lutherans, and even Calvinists offered him redemption and a final resting place if he would
renounce his religious opinions. He would wave them from
the room. Exhausted, he would accuse Mrs. Hedden of laxity
in her duties. He wanted no visitors. No one! When he complained to Marguerite that the religious bigots would even
deny him a piece of wormy earth, she assured him that he
would be buried on the farm.

"The farm? The farm will be sold."

He was unconvinced, though Marguerite shook her head.

"I know. I know. If not immediately, then soon. They will
dig up my bones before they are half rotten."

Knowing that Willet Hicks was a member of the committee

that supervised Quaker funerals in a nearby Quaker cemetery, he asked Willet if he could get permission to have him buried there. He joked at Hicks's solemn face.

"Why should the subject of our conversation disturb you, my friend? As I am going to leave one place, it is necessary to provide another; and the Quakers are not unused to granting such indulgences. My father belonged to that profession and I was brought up in it."

He was surprised when a downcast Hicks returned the next day with the committee's refusal. "It does not matter," said Paine. "I have informed Marguerite that I wish to be buried in a square of twelve feet. And that I would like the square to be enclosed by trees and a stone or post and rail fence. I would like a headstone with my name, my age, and *Author of Common Sense* engraved upon it. The Friends would not grant me that much space, would they? Or the ostentation of such a marker?"

Paine's last days were excruciatingly painful. His feet became swollen and even his abdomen became distended with fluid. He became incontinent. The large ulcers that formed upon his back, his fleshless shoulders, and even his heels became gangrenous. One day, as he roused himself between soporific doses of laudanum, he found himself staring at a new visitor. She was standing at Marguerite's side . . . weeping. Her dark hair was brushed back from her forehead and her face was partly hidden by a handkerchief with which she dabbed at her eyes. She was Catherine Few. Her face had filled out and her body had grown plump. It was a full moment before his eyes widened with recognition. "Kitty . . . ," he whispered. "Kitty. . . ."

"Will is in the garden," she said. "I'll call him."

He shook his head. "You have neglected me," he whispered. "You have neglected me."

Paine died at 8 A.M. on Thursday, June 8, 1809, after a tranquil night. He was seventy-two years and five months old.

Jarvis came and made a death mask, which showed tightly sealed lips, tired eyes, and a resigned face.

Friday, June 9, was a bright, sunny day. Willet Hicks and Marguerite Bonneville waited at 59 Grove Street for such friends as might wish to attend Paine's funeral. Marguerite had sent to Bergen for her son Thomas, and Hicks had hired a wagon and engaged two Negro men to carry the coffin and dig the grave. An obituary had been placed in the *New York Advertiser:*

> With heartfelt sorrow and poignant regret, we are compelled to announce to the world that Mr. Thomas Paine is no more. . . . The friends of the deceased are invited to attend his funeral by nine o'clock in the morning from his late residence at Greenwich, from whence his corpse will be conveyed to New Rochelle for interment.

When ten o'clock came, Marguerite decided to wait no longer. It was twenty-two miles to New Rochelle. Not a single friend had arrived. No one came to pay his last respects; no one came to shed a tear or utter a single word of regret that the world had banished Thomas Paine because he had found it impossible to worship a God that the religionists insisted had made only this single world that, to him, was but a speck of dust . . . a mote that danced and revolved in the immensity of the universe!

The Negroes carried the coffin to the waiting wagon. They clambered aboard in order to ride beside it. A pick and two shovels lay at their feet. Willet Hicks drove and Marguerite sat beside him. The Bonneville boys rested on boxes behind the wagon seat. Passers-by paid them scant attention.

On the farm, at New Rochelle, Hicks and the Bonnevilles waited inside the deserted cottage while the Negroes dug the grave. When they were called, they walked to the mound of earth and watched as the pinewood coffin was lowered into the freshly dug grave. Tears coursed down Marguerite's face. The boys were weeping too. She hugged them to her and looked up at the cloudless sky. "Oh, Monsieur Paine! Monsieur Paine!" she broke down and cried. "If none else are here . . . my sons are here! They stand as a testimony of the gratitude of America, and I for France!"

Postscript

SHORTLY AFTER Paine's death, James Cheetham published a scurrilous and libelous biography of him. The biography stated that Paine had seduced Madam Bonneville and had induced her to leave her husband and come to America as his mistress. Once she arrived, he treated her and the boys (especially Thomas, who was called his illegitimate son) with "meanness and tyranny."

Emmet urged Marguerite to take Cheetham to court. At the trial, her character was supported by Mrs. Palmer, by Maria Thompson, and by the mothers of her pupils. Robert Fulton, now back in America, defended the reputation of the Paine he had known in Paris and John Wesley Jarvis testified to the brilliance and gentleness of the Paine who had shared his quarters on Church Street. Judge Hoffman, who tried the case, found Cheetham guilty and ordered the libel expunged from future editions of the book, but refused to deal harshly with the author. He expressed an opinion that Cheetham:

> . . . should be favored as a man who had written a book against the Prince of Deists and for the Holy Gospel.

The notoriety of the trial immediately gained wide circulation for a biography filled with unwarranted abuse, calumny, and defamation. The book became an authoritative reference for a growing legend of a slothful, drunken, and debauched Paine.

Ten years after Paine's death, William Cobbett, influenced by the popularity of Cheetham's biography and the probability that it had received a British Treasury favor, returned to England in order to research Paine's early life and familiarize himself with his works in order to refute them. However, when he read Paine's *Agrarian Justice* for the first time, its initial words shocked him into an awareness of the late Paine's thoughts and efforts:

> To preserve the benefits of what is called civilized life, and to remedy, at the same time, the evil that it has produced, ought to be considered as one of the first objects of reformed legislation.
>
> Whether that state that is proudly, perhaps erroneously, called civilization, has promoted or most injured the general happiness of man is a question that may be strongly contested. On one side, the spectator is dazzled by splendid appearances; on the other, he is shocked by extreme wretchedness; both of which he has erected. . . .

He admitted that, although he had never met him or read his works, he had been one of Paine's "most violent assailants." Filled with remorse, he began the publication of a weekly journal known as *Cobbett's Register* and urged the publication and distribution of Paine's works. The radical *Register* attracted few readers, however, and, in 1817, Cobbett returned to America and bought a small farm on Long Island Sound, across from New Rochelle.

When Cobbett visited Paine's grave, he was dismayed by the evidence of vandalism all about him. The farm was untenanted, the windows of the cottage were broken, and its doorway was spattered with mud. Curiosity seekers had torn away the low-hanging branches of the cypresses and weeping willows that Marguerite had planted. Pieces of marble had been hacked from Paine's marker for souvenirs. He went to the farm once or twice a month and made what repairs he could. He built a post and rail fence such as Paine had wanted. Passers-by on the road that ran south to Pelham Manor would sometimes see him on a summer's day, standing at the side of the grave, bareheaded and bowed in an attitude of reverence.

In 1819, when Cobbett learned that the English Government had sentenced Richard Carlisle to three years' imprisonment in Dorchester Gaol for publishing Paine's theological writings and selling them in his Fleet Street shop, he decided to return to England. But he would not return alone. He would take Paine's body back with him! Paine's adopted country had neglected him, but in England the common man, for whose welfare he had unceasingly labored, would gladly contribute their shillings, their pence, and their farthings for a new trial for Carlisle and a shrine for Paine.

One night in October, with the help of two hired men, Cobbett dug up Paine's coffin. He had it placed in an open wagon, covered it with a tarpaulin, and rushed it from New Rochelle. He concealed

[568]

Paine's remains on his farm until the first frost and then shipped them to England in an ordinary merchandise crate. He wrote to a friend:

> I have done myself the honor to disinter his bones. I have removed them from New Rochelle and they are now on their way to England. When I myself return, I shall cause them to speak the common sense of the great man; I shall gather together the people of Liverpool and Manchester in one assembly with those of London, and those bones will effect the reformation of England in Church and State.

Cobbett's plans came to naught, The *Liverpool Journal* reported his intentions and the government refused to permit any spectacle or subscription. His project became the inspiration for grim jokes and macabre puns and rhymes. Disillusioned, Cobbett insisted on keeping Paine's remains in Liverpool, until his own death in 1835.

Rumor says that the remains passed into the hands of a furniture dealer, who utilized only the wood from the coffin. Where Paine's bones were scattered is speculation.